The Canterbury Tales

The Canterbury Tales

by

Geoffrey Chaucer

Translated into Modern English

by

Ronald L. Ecker

and

Eugene J. Crook

Hodge & Braddock, Publishers

To my parents,
Roy and Lucille Ecker,
with love
R. L. E.

To Louise
E. J. C.

Contents

Preface *ix*

Fragment I (Group A)
General Prologue *1*
The Knight's Tale *24*
The Miller's Prologue *83*
The Miller's Tale *85*
The Reeve's Prologue *103*
The Reeve's Tale *104*
The Cook's Prologue *116*
The Cook's Tale *117*

Fragment II (Group B¹)
The Lawyer's Introduction *119*
The Lawyer's Prologue *121*
The Lawyer's Tale *123*
The Lawyer's Epilogue *153*

Fragment III (Group D)
The Wife of Bath's Prologue *154*
Words between the Summoner
    and the Friar *175*
The Wife of Bath's Tale *176*
The Friar's Prologue *187*
The Friar's Tale *188*
The Summoner's Prologue *198*
The Summoner's Tale *199*

Fragment IV (Group E)
The Student's Prologue *215*
The Student's Tale *216*
Chaucer's Envoy *250*
The Merchant's Prologue *252*
The Merchant's Tale *253*
The Merchant's Epilogue *283*

Fragment V (Group F)
The Squire's Introduction *284*
The Squire's Tale *284*
Words of the Franklin to the
    Squire, and of the Host to
    the Franklin *302*

The Franklin's Prologue *303*
The Franklin's Tale *303*

Fragment VI (Group C)
The Physician's Tale *327*
The Pardoner's Introduction *335*
The Pardoner's Prologue *336*
The Pardoner's Tale *339*

Fragment VII (Group B²)
The Skipper's Tale *353*
Words of the Host to the Skipper
    and the Lady Prioress *364*
The Prioress's Prologue *365*
The Prioress's Tale *366*
The Prologue of Sir Topaz *373*
The Tale of Sir Topaz *374*
The Prologue of the Tale of
    Melibee *381*
The Tale of Melibee *382*
The Monk's Prologue *414*
The Monk's Tale *417*
The Nun's Priest's Prologue *441*
The Nun's Priest's Tale *442*
The Nun's Priest's Epilogue *458*

Fragment VIII (Group G)
The Second Nun's Prologue *460*
The Second Nun's Tale *464*
The Canon's Yeoman's Prologue *477*
The Canon's Yeoman's Tale *481*

Fragment IX (Group H)
The Manciple's Prologue *502*
The Manciple's Tale *505*

Fragment X (Group I)
The Parson's Prologue *512*
The Parson's Tale *514*
Chaucer's Retraction *573*

Glossary *574*

Preface

We present here, for both the beginning and more advanced student of Chaucer, the first complete new translation of *The Canterbury Tales* to appear in over half a century. The product of twenty years' labor, it is intended to be as faithful to the original, in both its poetical and prose portions, as a modern English rendering permits. We foresee this work as being useful in beginning courses such as surveys of British and world literature, intermediate courses of medieval literature in translation, and advanced courses in Chaucer as well. Beginning students may now gain a more balanced view of the genius of Geoffrey Chaucer by having before them in translation the complete *Tales* in all their variety. Likewise, advanced students will now be able to read and judge the *Tales* in their entirety without the necessity of reading some of the longer ones in Middle English.

The project was begun by Ron Ecker as a result of his finding, while studying Chaucer at the University of Florida, no satisfactory translation of the verse tales. Previous verse translations have been justly criticized for such shortcomings as lack of fidelity to content and what David Wright has called "bathetic rhyme carpentry." Mark Van Doren, in his preface to R. M. Lumiansky's prose translation, suggested that any translator, in seeking to capture the "absolute plainness" of Chaucer's poetry, should translate in prose, rhymed verse in modern English being an "impossible substitute," in Van Doren's view, for Chaucer's "wise, sweet verse." Wright seems of much the same mind, having chosen, in his own verse translation, to work in various forms of inexact rhyme and often no rhyme at all. The present project, while making no pretense of matching the poetical quality of the original, was initiated in the belief that a good, faithful translation in rhymed verse of Chaucer's verse tales was at least theoretically possible and a goal worth pursuing.

Gene Crook, as a teacher of Chaucer at Florida State University, was glad to join forces as he saw the desirability of having Chaucer's long-neglected prose pieces once again available in modern English form. Translators have habitually excluded *The Tale of Melibee* and *The Parson's Tale* on the assumption that these are long moral treatises that today would interest no general reader. But their exclusion short-changes the student and has thus been a major shortcoming of translations of Chaucer over the last five decades.

Accordingly, Ron Ecker translated the verse tales and Gene Crook the prose tales, with each translator reading and offering suggestions on the work of the other. The basis for our translation has been the text of the second edition of F. N. Robinson's *The Works of Geoffrey Chaucer*, with assistance from the editions of Albert C. Baugh, *Chaucer's Major Poetry*; John H. Fisher, *The Complete Poetry and Prose of Geoffrey Chaucer*; Robert A. Pratt, *The Poetry and Prose of Geoffrey Chaucer*; and Larry D. Benson, *The Riverside Chaucer*. The present work includes a glossary of terms and names for quick reference. Also, for the student's ease in locating particular lines, we have retained in our translation the use of line numbers, an aid that past translators have somehow seen fit to omit. It is an additional way in which we are pleased to facilitate the student's enjoyment of Chaucer.

R. L. E.
E. J. C.

The Canterbury Tales

General Prologue

When April's gentle rains have pierced the drought
Of March right to the root, and bathed each sprout
Through every vein with liquid of such power
It brings forth the engendering of the flower;
When Zephyrus too with his sweet breath has blown   5
Through every field and forest, urging on
The tender shoots, and there's a youthful sun,
His second half-course through the Ram now run,
And little birds are making melody
And sleep all night, eyes open as can be   10
(So Nature pricks them in each little heart),
On pilgrimage then folks desire to start.
The palmers long to travel foreign strands
To distant shrines renowned in sundry lands;
And specially, from every shire's end   15
In England, folks to Canterbury wend:
To seek the blissful martyr is their will,
The one who gave such help when they were ill.
    Now in that season it befell one day
In Southwark at the Tabard where I lay,   20
As I was all prepared for setting out
To Canterbury with a heart devout,
That there had come into that hostelry
At night some twenty-nine, a company
Of sundry folk whom chance had brought to fall   25
In fellowship, for pilgrims were they all
And onward to Canterbury would ride.
The chambers and the stables there were wide,
We had it easy, served with all the best;
And by the time the sun had gone to rest,   30
I'd spoken with each one about the trip
And was a member of the fellowship.

We made agreement, early to arise
To take our way, of which I shall advise.
　　But nonetheless, while I have time and space,　　　　35
Before proceeding further here's the place
Where I believe it reasonable to state
Something about these pilgrims—to relate
Their circumstances as they seemed to me,
Just who they were and each of what degree,　　　　40
And also what array they all were in.
And with a Knight I therefore will begin.
　　There with us was a KNIGHT, a worthy man
Who, from the very first time he began
To ride about, loved honor, chivalry,　　　　45
The spirit of giving, truth and courtesy.
He was a valiant warrior for his lord;
No man had ridden farther with the sword
Through Christendom and lands of heathen creeds,
And always he was praised for worthy deeds.　　　　50
He helped win Alexandria in the East,
And often sat at table's head to feast
With knights of all the nations when in Prussia.
In Lithuania as well as Russia
No other noble Christian fought so well.　　　　55
When Algaciras in Granada fell,
When Ayas and Attalia were won,
This Knight was there. Hard riding he had done
At Benmarin. Along the Great Sea coast
He'd made his strikes with many a noble host.　　　　60
His mortal battles numbered then fifteen,
And for our faith he'd fought at Tramissene
Three tournaments and always killed his foe.
This worthy Knight was ally, briefly so,
Of the lord of Palathia (in work　　　　65
Performed against a fellow heathen Turk).
He found the highest favor in all eyes,
A valiant warrior who was also wise
And in deportment meek as any maid.
He never spoke unkindly, never played　　　　70
The villain's part, but always did the right.

He truly was a perfect, gentle knight.
But now to tell of his array, he had
Good horses but he wasn't richly clad;
His fustian tunic was a rusty sight   75
Where he had worn his hauberk, for the Knight
Was just back from an expedition when
His pilgrimage he hastened to begin.
    There with him was his son, a youthful SQUIRE,
A lover and knight bachelor to admire.   80
His locks were curled as if set by a press.
His age was twenty years or so, I guess.
In stature he was of an average height
And blest with great agility and might.
He'd ridden for a time with cavalry   85
In Flanders and Artois and Picardy,
Performing well in such a little space
In hopes of standing in his lady's grace.
He was embroidered like a flowerbed
Or meadow, full of flowers white and red.   90
He sang or else he fluted all the day;
He was as fresh as is the month of May.
His gown was short, his sleeves were long and wide.
And well upon a horse the lad could ride;
Good verse and songs he had composed, and he   95
Could joust and dance, drew well, wrote gracefully.
At night he'd love so hotly, without fail,
He slept no more than does a nightingale.
He was a courteous, humble lad and able,
And carved meat for his father at the table.   100
    Now he had brought one servant by his side,
A YEOMAN—with no more he chose to ride.
This Yeoman wore a coat and hood of green.
He had a sheaf of arrows, bright and keen,
Beneath his belt positioned handily—   105
He tended to his gear most yeomanly,
His arrow feathers never drooped too low—
And in his hand he bore a mighty bow.
His head was closely cropped, his face was brown.
The fellow knew his woodcraft up and down.   110

He wore a bracer on his arm to wield
His bolts. By one side were his sword and shield,
And on the other, mounted at the hip,
A dagger sharply pointed at the tip.
A Christopher of silver sheen was worn   115
Upon his breast; a green strap held his horn.
He must have been a forester, I guess.
    There also was a Nun, a PRIORESS,
Her smile a very simple one and coy.
Her greatest oath was only "By Saint Loy!"   120
Called Madam Eglantine, this Nun excelled
At singing when church services were held,
Intoning through her nose melodiously.
And she could speak in French quite fluently,
After the school of Stratford-at-the-Bow   125
(The French of Paris wasn't hers to know).
Of table manners she had learnt it all,
For from her lips she'd let no morsel fall
Nor deeply in her sauce her fingers wet;
She'd lift her food so well she'd never get   130
A single drop or crumb upon her breast.
At courtesy she really did her best.
Her upper lip she wiped so very clean
That not one bit of grease was ever seen
Upon her drinking cup. She was discreet   135
And never reached unseemly for the meat.
And certainly she was good company,
So pleasant and so amiable, while she
Would in her mien take pains to imitate
The ways of court, the dignity of state,   140
That all might praise her for her worthiness.
To tell you of her moral consciousness,
Her charity was so great that to see
A little mouse caught in a trap would be
Enough to make her cry, if dead or bleeding.   145
She had some little dogs that she was feeding
With roasted meat or milk and fine white bread;
And sorely she would weep if one were dead
Or if someone should smite it with a stick.

She was all tender heart right to the quick.   150
Her pleated wimple was of seemly class,
She had a well-formed nose, eyes gray as glass,
A little mouth, one that was soft and red.
And it's for sure she had a fair forehead—
It must have been a handbreadth wide, I own,   155
For hardly was the lady undergrown.
The beauty of her cloak I hadn't missed.
She wore a rosary around her wrist
Made out of coral beads all colored green,
And from it hung a brooch of golden sheen   160
On which there was an *A* crowned with a wreath,
With *Amor vincit omnia* beneath.
    She brought along another NUN, to be
Her chaplain, and her PRIEST, who made it three.
    A MONK there was, a fine outrider of   165
Monastic lands, with venery his love;
A manly man, to be an abbot able.
He had some dainty horses in the stable,
And when he rode, his bridle might you hear
Go jingling in the whistling wind as clear   170
And loud as might you hear the chapel bell
Where this lord not too often kept his cell.
Because Saint Maurus and Saint Benedict
Had rules he thought were old and rather strict,
This mounted Monk let old things pass away   175
So that the modern world might have its day.
That text he valued less than a plucked hen
Which says that hunters are not holy men,
Or that a monk ignoring rules and order
Is like a flapping fish out of the water   180
(That is to say, a monk out of his cloister).
He held that text not worth a single oyster,
And his opinion, I declared, was good.
Why should he study till he's mad? Why should
He pore through books day after day indoors,   185
Or labor with his hands at all the chores
That Austin bids? How shall the world be served?

Let such works be to Austin then reserved!
And so he was a pricker and aright;
Greyhounds he had as swift as birds in flight,   190
For tracking and the hunting of the hare
Were all his pleasure, no cost would he spare.
His sleeves, I saw, were fur-lined at the hand
With gray fur of the finest in the land,
And fastening his hood beneath his chin   195
There was a golden, finely crafted pin,
A love-knot in the greater end for class.
His head was bald and shinier than glass.
His face was shiny, too, as if anointed.
He was a husky lord, one well appointed.   200
His eyes were bright, rolled in his head and glowed
Just like the coals beneath a pot. He rode
In supple boots, his horse in great estate.
Now certainly he was a fine prelate,
He wasn't pale like some poor wasted ghost.   205
Fat swan he loved the best of any roast.
His palfrey was as brown as is a berry.
    A FRIAR there was, a wanton one and merry,
Who begged within a certain limit. None
In all four orders was a better one   210
At idle talk, or speaking with a flair.
And many a marriage he'd arranged for fair
And youthful women, paying all he could.
He was a pillar of his brotherhood.
Well loved he was, a most familiar Friar   215
To many franklins living in his shire
And to the worthy women of the town;
For he could hear confessions and played down
The parish priest. To shrive in every quarter
He had been given license by his order.   220
He'd sweetly listen to confession, then
As pleasantly absolve one of his sin.
He easily gave penance when he knew
Some nice gift he'd receive when he was through.
For when to a poor order something's given,   225
It is a sign the man is truly shriven.

If someone gave, the Friar made it clear,
He knew the man's repentance was sincere.
For many men are so hard of the heart
They cannot weep, though grievous be the smart;   230
Instead of tears and prayers, they might therefore
Give silver to the friars who are poor.
He kept his cape all packed with pins and knives
That he would give away to pretty wives.
At merriment he surely wasn't middling;   235
He sang quite well and also did some fiddling,
And took the prize with all his balladry.
His neck was white as any fleur-de-lis,
His strength like any wrestler's of renown.
He knew the taverns well in every town,   240
Each hosteler and barmaid, moreso than
He knew the leper and the beggarman.
For anyone as worthy as the Friar
Had faculties that called for something higher
Than dealing with those sick with leprosy.   245
It wasn't dignified, nor could it be
Of profit, to be dealing with the poor,
What with the rich and merchants at the store.
Above all where some profit might arise
Was where he'd be, in courteous, humble guise.   250
No man had greater virtue than did he,
The finest beggar in the friary.
(He paid a fee for his exclusive right: 252a
No brethren might invade his begging site.)   252b
And though a widow shoeless had to go,
So pleasant was his *"In principio"*
He'd have a farthing when he went away.   255
He gained much more than what he had to pay,
And he could be as wanton as a pup.
He'd arbitrate on days to settle up
In law disputes, not like a cloisterer
Dressed in a threadbare cope as students were,   260
But rather like a master or a pope.
He wore a double-worsted semicope
As rounded as a church bell newly pressed.

He lisped somewhat when he was at his best,
To make his English sweet upon his tongue.   265
And when he fiddled and his songs were sung,
His eyes would twinkle in his head as might
The stars themselves on any frosty night
Now Hubert was this worthy Friar's name.

    A MERCHANT with a forked beard also came,   270
Dressed in a motley. Tall and proud he sat
Upon his horse. A Flemish beaver hat
He wore, and boots most elegantly wrought.
He spoke with pomp on everything he thought,
And boasted of the earnings he'd collected.   275
He felt the trade route had to be protected
Twixt Middleburgh and Orwell by the sea.
He speculated in French currency.
He used his wits so well, with such finesse,
That no one guessed the man's indebtedness,   280
So dignified he was at managing
All of his bargains and his borrowing.
He was a worthy fellow all the same;
To tell the truth, I do not know his name.

    There also was an Oxford STUDENT, one   285
Whose logic studies long since had begun.
The horse he rode was leaner than a rake,
And he was hardly fat, I undertake,
But looked quite hollow, far from debonair.
And threadbare was the cloak he had to wear;   290
He had no benefice as yet and, most
Unworldly, wouldn't take a secular post.
For he would rather have at his bed's head
Some twenty books, all bound in black or red,
Of Aristotle and his philosophy   295
Than finest robes, fiddle or psaltery.
Philosopher he was, and yet his coffer
Had little of the gold that it should offer.
But all that from his friends he could acquire
He spent on books and learning, didn't tire   300
Of praying for the souls of all those who
Would give to help him see his schooling through,

For study was the foremost thing he heeded.
He never spoke one word more than was needed,
And then he spoke with formal reverence;   305
He'd make it short but make a lot of sense.
Of highest moral virtue was his speech,
And gladly he would learn and gladly teach.
   A wise and prudent SERGEANT OF THE LAW,
One who at Saint Paul's porch one often saw,   310
Was with us too, a man of excellence.
Discreet he was, deserving reverence
(Or so it seemed, his sayings were so wise).
He often was a judge in the assize
By virtue of his patent and commission.   315
He had with his renown and erudition
Gained many fees and robes in his career.
A purchaser of land without a peer,
His holdings were fee simple in effect;
No one could prove one purchase incorrect.   320
Nowhere was there a busier man, yet he
Seemed busier than even he could be.
He knew each court decision, every crime
Adjudicated from King William's time.
He'd execute a deed with such perfection   325
No man could call its writing into question,
And every statute he could state by rote.
He sore a simple multicolored coat
Girt by a striped silk belt. Enough to tell,
On what he wore I will no longer dwell.   330
    There was a FRANKLIN in his company
Whose beard was lily white as it could be,
Though his complexion was a healthy red.
In wine he loved to sop his morning bread;
A devotee of all delights that lure us,   335
He truly was a son of Epicurus
(Who thought the life that's pleasure-filled to be
The only one of true felicity).
He was a great householder, and his bounty
Made him Saint Julian to those in his county.   340
His bread and ale were always fresh and fine,

And no one had a better stock of wine.
Baked meat was always in his house, the best
Of fish and flesh, so much that to each guest
It almost seemed to snow with meat and drink   345
And all the dainties of which one could think.
His meals would always vary, to adhere
To all the changing seasons of the year.
The coop was partridge-filled, birds fat as any,
And in the pond the breams and pikes were many.   350
Woe to the cook unless his sauce was tart
And he had all utensils set to start!
His table would stay mounted in the hall
All set and ready at a moment's call.
In county sessions he was lord and sire,   355
And often he had been Knight of the Shire.
A dagger and a purse made out of silk
Hung from his belt, as white as morning milk.
A sheriff he'd been, and county auditor.
There wasn't a more worthy vavasor.   360
    A HABERDASHER, DYER, CARPENTER,
TAPESTRY MAKER, and a WEAVER were
All there as well, clothed in the livery
Of guildsmen, of one great fraternity.
Their gear was polished up till it would pass   365
For new. Their knives were mounted not with brass
But all with silver. Finely wrought array
Their belts and pouches were in every way.
Each one looked like a burgess, one whose place
Would be before the whole guild on a dais.   370
They had the means and wits, were it their plan,
Each of them to have been an alderman;
They had enough income and property
And wives who would to such a plan agree,
Or else they'd have to blame themselves alone.   375
It's very nice as "Madam" to be known,
And lead processions on a holy day
And have one's train borne in a royal way.
    They brought along a COOK with them to fix
Their meals. He boiled their chicken in a mix   380

Of marrowbones, tart herbs and galingale.
He knew right off a draught of London ale,
Knew how to boil and roast and broil and fry,
Whip up a stew as well as bake a pie.
It seemed a shame, and caused me some chagrin,   385
To see he had an ulcer on his shin.
He made blancmange that I'd rank with the best.
    There was a SKIPPER hailing from the west,
As far away as Dartmouth, I'd allow.
He rode a nag as best as he knew how.   390
A woolen gown down to his knees he wore,
And round his neck and neath his arm he bore
A strap from which a dagger dangled down.
The summer sun had turned his color brown.
He surely was a festive sort of fellow;   395
Many a pilfered wine draught made him mellow
While sailing from Bordeaux, the merchant snoring.
He had no use for conscience, thought it boring.
In battle, when he gained the upper hand,
By plank he'd send them home to every land.   400
As for his skill in reckoning the tides
And all the dangers of the sea besides,
By zodiac and moon to navigate,
From Hull to Carthage there was none as great.
Hardy and shrewd in all he'd undertaken,   405
His beard by many tempests had been shaken;
And he knew well the havens everywhere
From Gotland to the Cape of Finisterre,
And every creek in Brittany and Spain.
The Skipper's ship was called the *Maudelayne*.   410
    There also was among us a PHYSICIAN,
None like him in this world, no competition,
To speak of medicine and surgery.
He was well grounded in astrology:
He tended patients specially in hours   415
When natural magic had its greatest powers,
For he could tell by which stars would ascend
What talisman would help his patient mend.
He knew the cause of every malady

Whether from hot, cold, wet, or dry it be,   420
And of each humor what the symptoms were.
He truly was a fine practitioner.
And once he knew a malady's root cause
He'd give the cure without a further pause,
For readily apothecaries heeded   425
When there were drugs or medicines he needed,
That profit might be shared by everyone
(Their fellowship not recently begun).
The ancient Aesculapius he knew,
And Dioscorides and Rufus too,   430
Hali and Galen, old Hippocrates,
Serapion, Avicenna, Rhazes,
Gaddesden, Damascenus, Constantine,
Bernard and Averroes and Gilbertine.
His diet was as measured as could be,   435
Being not one of superfluity
But greatly nourishing as well as prudent.
He hardly could be called a Bible student.
He decked himself in scarlet and in azure,
With taffeta and silk. Yet he'd demure   440
If something might necessitate expense;
He saved his gains from times of pestilence,
For gold's a cordial, so the doctors say.
That's why he loved gold in a special way.
    From near the town of BATH a good WIFE came;   445
She was a little deaf, which was a shame.
She was a clothier, so excellent
Her work surpassed that of Ypres and Ghent.
When parish wives their gifts would forward bring,
None dared precede her to the offering—   450
And if they did, her wrath would surely be
So mighty she'd lose all her charity.
The kerchiefs all were of the finest texture
(And must have weighed ten pounds, that's no conjecture)
That every Sunday she had on her head.   455
The fine hose that she wore were scarlet red
And tightly laced, she had a nice new pair
Of shoes. Her face was ruddy, bold and fair.

She was a worthy woman all her life:
At church door with five men she'd been a wife,　　　　　460
Not counting all the company of her youth.
(No need to treat that now, but it's the truth.)
She'd journeyed to Jerusalem three times;
Strange rivers she had crossed in foreign climes;
She'd been to Rome and also to Boulogne,　　　　　465
To Galicia for Saint James and to Cologne,
And she knew much of wandering by the way.
She had the lover's gap-teeth, I must say.
With ease upon an ambling horse she sat,
Well wimpled, while upon her head her hat　　　　　470
Was broad as any buckler to be found.
About her ample hips a mantle wound,
And on her feet the spurs she wore were sharp.
In fellowship she well could laugh and carp.
Of remedies of love she had good notions,　　　　　475
For of that art's old dance she knew the motions.
　　　There was a good man of religion, too,
A PARSON of a certain township who
Was poor, but rich in holy thought and work.
He also was a learned man, a clerk;　　　　　480
The Christian gospel he would truly preach,
Devoutly his parishioners to teach.
Benign he was, in diligence a wonder,
And patient in adversity, as under
Such he'd proven many times. And loath　　　　　485
He was to get his tithes by threatening oath;
For he would rather give, without a doubt,
To all the poor parishioners about
From his own substance and the offerings.
Sufficiency he found in little things.　　　　　490
His parish wide, with houses wide asunder,
He'd never fail in either rain or thunder,
Though sick or vexed, to make his visitations
With those remote, regardless of their stations.
On foot he traveled, in his hand a stave.　　　　　495
This fine example to his sheep he gave:
He always did good works before he taught them.

His words were from the gospel as he caught them,
And this good saying he would add thereto:
"If gold should rust, then what will iron do?"   500
For if a priest be foul in whom we trust,
No wonder that the ignorant goes to rust.
And it's a shame (as every priest should keep
In mind), a dirty shepherd and clean sheep.
For every priest should an example give,   505
By his own cleanness, how his sheep should live.
He never set his benefice for hire,
To leave his sheep encumbered in the mire
While he ran off to London and Saint Paul's
To seek a chantry, singing in the stalls,   510
Or be supported by a guild. Instead
He dwelt at home, and he securely led
His fold, so that the wolf might never harry.
He was a shepherd and no mercenary.
A holy, virtuous man he was, and right   515
In showing to the sinner no despite.
His speech was never haughty or indignant,
He was a teacher modest and benignant;
To draw folks heavenward to life forever,
By good example, was his great endeavor.   520
But if some person were too obstinate,
Whether he be of high or low estate,
He would be sharply chided on the spot.
A better priest, I wager, there is not.
He didn't look for pomp or reverence   525
Nor feign a too self-righteous moral sense;
What Christ and his apostles had to tell
He taught, and he would follow it as well.
    With him his brother came, a PLOWMAN who
Had carted many a load of dung. A true   530
And well-intentioned laborer was he,
Who lived in peace and perfect charity.
The Lord his God with whole heart he loved best,
When times were good as well as when distressed,
And loved his neighbor as himself, for which   535
He'd gladly thresh, or dig to make a ditch,

For love of Christ, to help the poor in plight
Without a wage, if it lay in his might.
He paid his proper tithes religiously,
Both of his labor and his property.   540
He wore a tunic and he rode a mare.

    A MILLER and a REEVE also were there,
A SUMMONER, also a PARDONER,
A MANCIPLE and me, no more there were.

    The MILLER was as stout as any known,   545
A fellow big in brawn as well as bone.
It served him well, for everywhere he'd go
He'd win the ram at every wrestling show.
Short-shouldered, broad he was, a husky knave;
No door could keep its hinges once he gave   550
A heave or ran and broke it with his head.
His beard like any sow or fox was red,
And broad as any spade it was, at that.
He had a wart upon his nose, right at
The tip, from which a tuft of hairs was spread   555
Like bristles on a sow's ears, just as red;
The nostrils on the man were black and wide.
He had a sword and buckler at his side.
Great as a furnace was his mouth. And he
Could tell some jokes and stories, though they'd be   560
Mostly of sin and lechery. He stole
Much corn, charged three times over for a toll;
Yet he'd a golden thumb, I do declare.
A white coat and a blue hood were his wear.
He blew the bagpipe, knew it up and down,   565
And played it as he brought us out of town.

    From an Inn of Court a gentle MANCIPLE
Was with us, one who set a fine example
In buying victuals wisely. Whether he
Would buy with credit or with currency,   570
He took such care in purchases he made
He'd come out well ahead for what he paid.
Now is that not a sign of God's fair grace,
That such a simple man's wit can displace
The wisdom of a heap of learned men?   575

His masters numbered more than three times ten,
All lawyers of a very skillful sort;
A dozen of them in that Inn of Court
Were worthy to be stewards of the treasure
Of any lord in England, that in pleasure   580
He might live, enjoying all that he had
Without a debt (unless he had gone mad),
Or live as simply as he might desire;
If need be, they could help an entire shire
Through any circumstance that might befall.   585
And yet this Manciple could shame them all.
    The REEVE was a slender, choleric man.
He shaved his beard as closely as one can;
His hair was shortly clipped around the ears
And cropped in front just like a priest's appears.   590
The fellow's legs were very long and lean,
Each like a staff, no calf was to be seen.
Well could he keep a granary and bin
(No auditor could challenge that and win),
And he could augur by the drought and rain   595
The true yield of his seed and of his grain.
His master's sheep, his cattle, milk cows, horses,
His poultry, swine, and all his stored resources
Were wholly left to this Reeve's governing,
For by contract his was the reckoning   600
Since first his lord had grown to twenty years.
No man could ever put him in arrears;
There was no bailiff, herdsman, not one servant
With sleight unknown—the Reeve was too observant,
And feared like death itself by all beneath.   605
He had a lovely dwelling on a heath
Where green trees stood to shade it from the sun.
In gaining goods his lord he had outdone,
He stored up many riches privately.
To please his lord, he'd give him subtly   610
A gift or loan out of the lord's own goods,
Receiving thanks and things like coats and hoods.
He'd learnt a good trade as a youth, for he
Was quite a gifted man at carpentry.

He rode a steed with quite a sturdy frame,   615
A dapple-gray (the horse was Scot by name).
He wore a long surcoat of bluish shade,
And at his side he had a rusty blade.
From Norfolk was this Reeve of whom I tell,
Nearby a town that's known as Bawdeswell.   620
His coat was tucked up like a friar's. He
Rode always last among our company.
   A SUMMONER was with us in the place
Who like a cherub had a fire-red face,
So pimply was the skin, eyes puffed and narrow.   625
He was as hot and lecherous as a sparrow.
With black and scabby brows and scanty beard,
He had a face that all the children feared;
There's no quicksilver, litharge or brimstone,
Borax, ceruse, no tartar oil that's known—   630
No ointment that could cleanse, to keep it simple,
And rid his face of even one white pimple
Among the whelks that sat upon his cheeks.
He loved his garlic, onions and his leeks,
And strong wine red as blood once he had eaten.   635
Then he would speak and cry out like a cretin,
And when with wine he was quite well infused,
Some Latin words were all the words he used.
He knew a few good phrases, two or three,
Which he had learnt to say from some decree.   640
(No wonder, what with hearing it all day;
And after all, as you well know, a jay
Can call out "Walt!" as well as any pope.)
But once a question came to test his scope,
He had no learning left to make reply,   645
So *"Questio quid juris!"* was his cry.
He was a gentle, kindly rascal, though;
A better fellow men may never know.
Why, he'd be willing, for a quart of wine,
To let some rascal have his concubine   650
For one whole year, excusing him completely.
He well could "pluck a bird" (always discreetly),
And if he found a fellow rogue wherever

He'd teach him that he should in his endeavor
Not be afraid of the archdeacon's curse—   655
Unless the fellow's soul was in his purse,
For that is where his punishment would be.
"The purse is the archdeacon's hell," said he.
(I know that was a lie; a guilty man
Should be in dread of Holy Church's ban,   660
It slays as absolution saves. He best
Beware also a writ for his arrest.)
The Summoner controlled, himself to please,
All of the young girls of the diocese;
He knew their secrets, counseled them and led.   665
A garland he had set upon his head
As great as any ale sign on a stake.
He'd made himself a buckler out of cake.
    With him there rode a gentle PARDONER
Of Rouncivalle (comrades and friends they were),   670
Who'd come straight from the court of Rome. And he
Would loudly sing "Come hither, love, to me!"
The Summoner bore him a stiff bass staff;
No trumpet ever sounded so by half.
The Pardoner's hair was as yellow as wax,   675
But hung as smoothly as a hank of flax;
In little strands the locks ran from his head
Till over both his shoulders they were spread
And thinly lay, one here, another there.
In jolly spirit, he chose not to wear   680
His hood but kept it packed away. He rode
(Or so he thought) all in the latest mode;
But for a cap his long loose hair was bare.
Such glaring eyes he had, just like a hare!
A veronica was sewn upon his cap.   685
He had his bag before him in his lap,
Brimming with pardons hot from Rome. He'd speak
In voice as dainty as a goat's. From cheek
To cheek he had no beard and never would,
So smooth his face you'd think he'd shaved it good.   690
I think he was a gelding or a mare.
But speaking of his craft, Berwick to Ware

There was no pardoner could take his place.
For in his bag he had a pillowcase
That used to be, he said, Our Lady's veil;   695
He claimed he had a fragment of the sail
That took Saint Peter out upon the sea
Before Christ called him to his ministry;
He had a cross of latten set with stones,
And in a glass he had some old pig's bones;   700
And with these relics, when he saw at hand
A simple parson from the hinterland,
He'd make more money in one day alone
Than would the parson two months come and gone.
So he made apes, with all the tricks he'd do,   705
Of parson and of congregation too.
And yet I should conclude, for all his tactic,
In church he was a fine ecclesiastic,
So well he read a lesson or a story,
And best of all intoned the offertory.   710
For well he knew that when the song was sung,
He then must preach, and not with awkward tongue.
He knew how one gets silver from the crowd;
That's why he sang so merrily and loud.

    As briefly as I could I've told you now   715
Degree, array, and number, and of how
This company of pilgrims came to be
In Southwark at that pleasant hostelry
Known as the Tabard, which is near the Bell.
And so with that, it's time for me to tell   720
Exactly what we did that very night
When at this inn we'd all come to alight;
And after that I'll tell you of our trip,
Of all that's left about our fellowship.
But first I pray that by your courtesy   725
You will not judge it my vulgarity
If I should plainly speak of this assortment,
To tell you all their words and their deportment,
Though not a word of theirs I modify.
For this I'm sure you know as well as I: 730
Who tells the tale of any other man

Should render it as nearly as he can,
If it be in his power, word for word,
Though from him such rude speech was never heard.
If he does not, his tale will be untrue,   735
The words will be invented, they'll be new.
One shouldn't spare the words of his own brother,
He ought to say one word just like another.
Christ spoke broad words himself in Holy Writ,
And you know well no villainy's in it.   740
And Plato says, to all those who can read
Him, that words must be cousin to the deed.
I also pray that you'll forgive the fact
That in my tale I haven't been exact
To set folks in their order of degree;   745
My wit is short, as clearly you may see.
    Our HOST made welcome each and every one,
And right away our supper was begun.
He served us with the finest in good food;
The wine was strong to fit our festive mood.   750
Our Host performed, so it seemed to us all,
As well as any marshal in a hall.
A robust man he was, and twinkle-eyed,
As fine as any burgess in Cheapside,
Bold in his speech, one wise and educated,   755
A man whose manhood could not be debated.
He also was a merry sort of bloke,
As after supper he began to joke
And spoke to us of mirth and other things
When we had finished with our reckonings.   760
"My lords," he then addressed us, "from the start
You've been most welcome here, that's from the heart.
In faith, this year I've truly yet to see
Here at this inn another company
As merry as the one that's gathered now.   765
I'd entertain you more if I knew how.
Say, here's a thought that just occurred to me,
A way to entertain you, and it's free.
    "You go to Canterbury—may God speed,
The blissful martyr bless you for the deed!   770

And well I know as you go on your way,
You plan to tell some tales, to have some play.
There won't be much amusement going on
If everybody rides dumb as a stone.
So as I said, I would propose a game   775
To give you some diversion, that's the aim.
If it's agreed, by everyone's assent,
That you'll stand by the judgment I present,
And strive to do exactly as I say
Tomorrow when you're riding on your way,   780
Then by my father's soul, who now is dead,
You'll have some fun or you can have my head!
Let's have a show of hands, no more to say."
    We let our will be known then right away;
We didn't think it worth deliberation   785
And gave him leave without a hesitation
To tell us what his verdict was to be.
"My lords," he said, "then listen well to me,
And may this not, I pray, meet your disdain.
Now here's the point, speaking short and plain: 790
Each one of you, to pass the time of day,
Shall tell two tales while you are on the way
To Canterbury; then each one of you
On the return shall tell another two,
About adventures said once to befall.   795
And he who bears himself the best of all—
That is to say, the one who's judged to tell
The tales that in both aim and wit excel—
Shall win a supper paid for by the lot,
Here in this place, right at this very spot,   800
When we return again from Canterbury.
For in my wish to make your journey merry,
I will myself most gladly with you ride—
And at my own expense—to be your guide;
And if my judgment one disputes, he'll pay   805
For all that we shall spend along the way.
If you will grant me that it's to be so,
Then tell me in a word that I may know
To make my preparations for the start."

It was so granted, each with happy heart   810
Gave him his oath. We therefore asked our Host
To vouchsafe that indeed he'd take the post
And function as our governor, to hear
Our tales and judge, and make his judgment clear,
And set the supper at a certain price;   815
Then we would all be ruled by his device,
Come high or low. And so it was agreed
By one assent, his judgment we would heed.
With that, more wine was fetched for every guest.
We drank it, then were ready for some rest   820
And went to bed with no more tarrying.
      Next morning, when the day began to spring,
Up rose our Host and roused us like a cock.
He gathered us together in a flock,
Then forth we rode at but a walking pace   825
Out to Saint Thomas's watering place.
Our Host there checked his horse and said to all:
"My lords, now listen, if you will. Recall
The pact, as I remind you, made with me.
If evensong and matins both agree,   830
Let's see now who shall tell us the first tale.
And if I've ever drunk of wine or ale,
Whoso resists the judgment I present
Shall pay along the way all that is spent.
Draw lots before we travel farther, then,   835
And he who draws the shortest shall begin.
Sir Knight," he said, "my master and my lord,
Now draw a lot, to keep with our accord.
Come here," said he, "my Lady Prioress,
And you, Sir Student—quit your bashfulness   840
And studies too. Lay hand to, everyone!"
And so the drawing was at once begun.
I'll keep it short and tell you how it went:
Whether by chance or fate or accident,
The truth is that the lot fell to the Knight—   845
A fact in which the rest all took delight.
As was required, then tell his tale he must,
By the agreement that was made in trust

As you have heard. What more is there to know?
And when this good man saw that it was so, 850
As one with wisdom and obedient
To that to which he'd given free assent,
He said, "Since I'm the one to start the game,
The lot I drew is welcome, in God's name!
Now let us ride, and hear what I've to say." 855
And with that word we rode forth on our way,
As he began at once with merry cheer
To tell his tale, and spoke as you may hear.

The Knight's Tale

PART I

Once upon a time, old stories tell us,
There was a duke whose name was Theseus.   860
Of Athens he was lord and governor,
And in his time was such a conqueror
That none was greater underneath the sun,
So many wealthy countries he had won.
What with his wisdom and his chivalry,   865
He conquered all the realm of Femeny,
Which then was known as Scythia, and married
The queen named Hippolyta, whom he carried
Back home with him amid much pageantry
And glorious ceremony. Emily,   870
Her younger sister, also went along.
And so in victory and glorious song
I leave this noble duke as he is bound
For Athens, with his warriors all around.

And if there weren't so much to hear, I now   875
Would fully have related for you how
That land was won, the realm of Femeny,
By Theseus and by his chivalry;
I'd tell you of the battle that was waged
As Athens and the Amazons engaged,   880
And of the siege in which was finally seen
Defeat for Scythia's fair and hardy queen,
And of the feast upon their wedding day
And the rousing welcome home. But as I say,
I must forbear describing all that now.   885
I have, God knows, a lot of field to plow,
The oxen in my yoke have got it rough.
And since the rest of my tale's long enough,
Not holding back the group is my concern;
Let every fellow tell his tale in turn   890

24

And let us see who shall the supper win.
Where I left off, then, I'll once more begin.
    This duke of whom I spoke, when he almost
Had reached the gates of town with all his host,
In such high spirits and so full of pride,   895
Became aware, as he looked to the side,
That kneeling by the road there was in rue
A company of ladies, two by two,
One pair behind another, in black dress.
So woeful were the cries of their distress   900
No living creature ever heard before
Such lamentation uttered. Furthermore
They did not cease until his horse was idle,
For they had grabbed the reins upon its bridle.
    "What folk are you, against our joy vying,   905
Disturbing our homecoming with your crying?"
Said Theseus. "So envious can you be
That you protest the honor given me?
Or who mistreated you, who has offended?
And tell me if the damage can be mended,   910
And why it is in black you are arrayed."
    The eldest lady answered, though she swayed
Half in a swoon of such deathlike degree
It was a pity both to hear and see.
"My lord," she said, "whom Fortune chose to give   915
The victory, as conqueror to live,
Your glory and honor are not our grief,
It's mercy that we're seeking and relief.
Have mercy on our woe and our distress!
Some drop of pity, through your gentleness,   920
Upon us wretched women please let fall.
In truth, my lord, there's none among us all
Who hasn't been a duchess or a queen;
Now we are wretches. As may well be seen,
Thanks be to Fortune's faithless wheel, there's no   925
One whose well-being is assured. And so,
My lord, that in your presence we might be,
The temple of the goddess Clemency
Is where we've waited for a whole fortnight.

Help us, my lord, if it be in your might. 930
    "The wretch I am, now weeping, wailing thus,
Was once the wife of King Capaneus,
Who died at Thebes—and cursed be that day!
And all of us you see in this array
Are crying so, our spirits beaten down, 935
Because we lost our husbands in that town
During the time that under siege it lay.
And yet this old Creon—ah, wellaway!—
Who is in Thebes, now lord of all the city,
Iniquitous and ireful, without pity, 940
Has for despite and by his tyranny
Inflicted on their bodies villainy:
The corpses of our lords, all of them slain,
He threw into a heap where they have lain,
For he gives no assent, will not allow 945
That they be burnt or buried, rather now
He makes hounds eat them, such is his despite."
    And with that word, they cried without respite
And then they groveled, weeping piteously.
"Have mercy for us wretched," was their plea, 950
"Your heart be open to our grief today."
    This gentle duke dismounted right away
With pitying heart when hearing these words spoken.
He felt as if his heart were nearly broken,
To see so pitiful, in such a strait, 955
Those who had once been of such great estate.
He took them in his arms then and consoled them;
He comforted as best he could, and told them
That by his oath, that of a faithful knight,
He would do all that lay within his might 960
Upon this tyrant vengefulness to wreak,
That afterwards all those in Greece might speak
Of how Creon by Theseus was served
His just deserts, the death he so deserved.
    Immediately, without the least delay, 965
His banner he displayed and rode away
For Thebes, with all his host on every side;
No nearer Athens did he choose to ride

Nor take his ease for even half a day,
But slept that night somewhere along the way.   970
The queen was not among his company,
But with her fair young sister Emily
Was sent forth into Athens, there to dwell
While he rode on his way. No more to tell.

    The red image of Mars with spear and targe   975
So shone upon his banner white and large
That up and down the meadows seemed to glitter;
A pennon by his banner was aflitter
In richest gold, upon it, as was meet,
The Minotaur that he had slain in Crete.   980
Thus rode this duke, this conqueror, in power,
The men with him of chivalry the flower,
Until he came to Thebes, there to alight
Upon a field where he was set to fight.
But only speaking briefly of this thing,   985
He fought and slew Creon, the Theban king,
In open battle, as befits a knight
So manly. Creon's men he put to flight.
The city by assault he won thereafter
And tore it down, each wall and beam and rafter;   990
And to the ladies he restored again
The bones of all their kinsmen who'd been slain,
For obsequies then custom of the day.
But it would take too long here to delay
By telling of the din, the lamentation   995
Made by these ladies during the cremation,
And honor paid, all that one could confer,
By Theseus, the noble conqueror,
To the ladies when on their way they went.
To speak with brevity is my intent.   1000

    This worthy Theseus, when he had slain
Creon and captured Thebes, chose to remain
Upon the field that night to take his rest,
With all that country under his behest.

    To rummage through the heap of Theban slain,   1005
The corpses' clothes and armor to retain,
The pillagers worked hard and carefully

After the battle and the victory.
It so befell that in the heap they found,
With grievous wounds there lying on the ground,   1010
Two youthful knights who side by side had fought,
Identical their arms and richly wrought.
As for their names, Arcite was that of one,
The other knight was known as Palamon;
Not yet alive nor dead did they appear,   1015
But by their coat of arms and by their gear
The heralds knew that these two specially
Were members of the royal family
Of Thebes, two sisters' sons. Their finders then
Removed them from the heap where they had been,   1020
And had them carried gently to the tent
Of Theseus, who promptly had them sent
To Athens, there to dwell perpetually
In prison—to no ransom he'd agree.
 And when this worthy duke thus held his sway,   1025
He took his host and rode home straightaway.
As conqueror with laurel he was crowned,
And lived in joy and honor, much renowned
Throughout his life. What more is there to know?
And in a tower, in anguish and woe,   1030
Are Palamon and his good friend Arcite
Forevermore. No gold could end their plight.
 So year by year it went, and day by day,
Until one morning it befell in May
That Emily, a fairer sight to see   1035
Than lilies on a stalk of green could be,
And fresher than the flowers May discloses—
Her hue strove with the color of the roses
Till I know not the fairer of the two—
Before daylight, as she was wont to do,   1040
Had roused herself and was already dressed.
For May will leave no sluggard nightly rest;
The season seems to prick each gentle heart,
It causes one out of his sleep to start
And says, "Arise, it's time to pay respect!"   1045
And this caused Emily to recollect

The honor due to May and to arise.
She brightly dressed, a pleasure to the eyes.
Her hair was braided in one yellow tress
A good yard down her back, so I would guess.   1050
And in the garden, as the sun arose,
She wandered up and down, and, as she chose,
She gathered flowers, white as well as red,
To make a dainty garland for her head;
And like that of an angel was her song.   1055
    The tower, of great size and thick and strong,
Which was the castle's major dungeon—there
The knights were held in prison and despair,
As I have said, though more will soon befall—
Was built adjacent to the garden wall   1060
Where Emily was then about her play.
The sun was bright, and clear the early day,
As Palamon, in woe with no reprieve,
As was his wont—the jailer gave him leave—
Was roaming in a chamber of great height   1065
From which all of the city was in sight,
As was the green-branched garden near the tower
Where Emily, as radiant as a flower,
Was in her walk and roaming here and there.
So Palamon, this captive in despair,   1070
Was pacing in this chamber to and fro,
And to himself complaining of his woe.
That he was born he often said "Alas!"
    And then by chance or fate it came to pass
That through the window (thick with many a bar   1075
Of iron, as great and squared as girders are)
He cast his eyes upon fair Emily.
He blanched and cried an "Ah!" of such degree
It was as if he'd been pierced through the heart.
And at this cry Arcite rose with a start   1080
And said, "My cousin, what is ailing you
That you're so pale, a deathlike thing to view?
Why did you cry? Has someone done you wrong?
For God's love, it's the patient gets along
In prison, that's the way it has to be.   1085

We owe to Fortune this adversity.
Some wicked aspect or configuration
Of Saturn with some certain constellation
Gave this to us, for all we might have sworn.
So stood the heavens when we two were born;   1090
We must endure it, to be short and plain."
    But Palamon replied, "You have a vain
Imagination, cousin, truthfully,
To be expressing such a thought to me.
It wasn't prison that caused me to cry.   1095
I just received a shot, struck through my eye
Right to my heart, and it will finish me.
The fairness of that lady that I see
In yonder garden, roaming to and fro,
Is cause of all my crying and my woe.   1100
I don't know if she's woman or a goddess,
But truly it is Venus, I would guess."
Then Palamon fell down upon his knees
And said this prayer: "Dear Venus, if you please
To be transfigured so, to be seen by   1105
A woeful, wretched creature such as I,
Out of this prison help us to escape.
But if it is my fate, one taken shape
By eternal word, to die in this fashion,
Upon our royal house have some compassion,   1110
For we are brought so low by tyranny."
    And with that word, Arcite then chanced to see
This lady who was roaming to and fro;
And at the sight, her beauty hurt him so
That if the wound to Palamon was sore,   1115
Arcite himself was hurt as much or more.
And with a sigh he then said piteously,
"By such fresh beauty I'm slain suddenly,
The beauty of her roaming in that place!
Unless I have her mercy by her grace   1120
That I at least may see her in some way,
I am but dead, there is no more to say."
    When Palamon heard this, with angry eye
He turned to look at Arcite and reply,

"You speak such words in earnest or in play?"   1125
    "In earnest," Arcite said, "is what I say!
God help me, I've no mind for joking now."
    And Palamon at this then knit his brow.
"It does you little honor," he replied,
"To be a traitor to me, to have lied   1130
To me, as I'm your cousin and your brother;
For we have sworn, each of us to the other,
That never we, on pain of death—until
Death do us part—would do each other ill,
In love one to be hindrance to the other   1135
Or in whatever case, beloved brother;
That you would further me in what I do
In every case, and I would further you;
This was your oath, as well as mine. I know
That you would never dare deny it's so.   1140
You then are in my counsel, there's no doubt,
And yet now falsely you would go about
To love my lady, whom I love and serve
And always will until I die. What nerve!
False Arcite, you would surely not do so;   1145
I loved her first, and told you of my woe
As to my counsel, to the one who swore
To further me, as I have said before.
And so, my cousin, you're bound as a knight
To help me, if it lies within your might,   1150
Or else be false, and such I dare to say."
    But Arcite proudly answered in this way:
"It's you instead who would be false to me,
And false you are, I tell you utterly.
For *par amour*, I loved her first, not you.   1155
What can you say? You don't know which is true,
She's 'woman or a goddess'! You profess
Affection felt in terms of holiness,
But I feel love that's for a creature, such
That I've already said to you as much,   1160
As to my brother, one who to me swore.
But let's suppose you did love her before:
Have you not heard the learned man's old saw

That 'Who shall give a lover any law'?
Love, by my crown, is law that's greater than   1165
All law that Nature gives to earthly man;
That's why, for love, decrees or laws men pass
Are broken every day in every class.
A man must love despite himself; albeit
His death may be the cost, he cannot flee it,   1170
Be she a maiden, widow, or a wife.
But it's not likely that in all your life
You'll stand once in her grace, nor myself either;
You know as well as I it shall be neither,
For you and I have been forever damned   1175
To prison without ransom. We have shammed,
We strive just as the hounds did for the bone:
They fought all day to find the prize was gone,
For while they fought a kite came winging through
And bore away the bone from twixt the two.   1180
And therefore at the royal court, my brother,
It's each man for himself and not another.
Love if you like, I love and always will,
And truly, brother, that is that. Be still;
Here in this prison we must not succumb   1185
But each take his own chances as they come."
     The strife between the two was long and great;
Had I the time, more of it I'd relate.
But to the point. It happened that one day
(To tell it all as briefly as I may)   1190
Perotheus, a worthy duke who'd been
A friend of Theseus since way back when
The two of them were children, came to pay
His friend a visit and to have some play
In Athens, as he'd often done before.   1195
In all this world he loved no fellow more
Than Theseus, who cherished him the same;
They loved so greatly, so the old books claim,
That when one died, as truthfully they tell,
The other went to look for him in hell—   1200
But that's a tale I don't wish to recite.
Duke Perotheus also loved Arcite,

Whom he'd known in Thebes for many a year.
At last, when Perotheus had bent his ear
With the request, Duke Theseus agreed   1205
To free Arcite from prison; he was freed
Without a ransom and allowed to go
Where he desired—on one condition, though.
    The understanding, plainly to relate,
With Theseus regarding Arcite's fate   1210
Was that if Arcite ever should be found,
By day or night or any time, on ground
Of any country ruled by Theseus,
And he were caught, it was accorded thus:
He was to lose his head then by the sword.   1215
There was no action Arcite could afford
Except to make for home a speedy trek;
One must beware when he must pledge his neck.
    How great a sorrow Arcite had to bear!
His heart was smitten with deathlike despair;   1220
He wept and wailed, and pitifully he cried,
And even contemplated suicide.
He said, "Alas, the day that I was born!
Worse than before in prison I'm forlorn.
It's now my fate eternally to dwell   1225
Not as in purgatory but in hell.
I wish I'd never known Perotheus!
I'd still be dwelling with Duke Theseus,
Be fettered in his prison—not like this,
Not in this woe. Then I would be in bliss;   1230
The sight of her, the lady whom I serve,
Although her grace I never may deserve,
Would have sufficed and been enough for me.
O my dear cousin Palamon," said he,
"You've won in this adventure, that's for sure.   1235
In prison blissfully you may endure—
In prison? Surely not! In paradise!
Fate's passed to you the dice to seek the prize,
You have her sight, which I no more shall see.
Since you're so near her presence, it may be,   1240
As you're a knight, a worthy one and able,

That by some chance——as Fortune's so unstable——
You may attain your great desire in time.
But I, who am exiled to other clime
And barren of all grace, in such despair   1245
That neither earth nor water, fire nor air,
Nor any creature that is made of these,
Can ever give me any help or ease——
Well should I die without a hope, in sadness.
Farewell my life, my pleasure, and my gladness!   1250
    "Alas, why do folks so complain about
The providence of God or feel put out
By Fortune, when they're often given more
In many ways than they could bargain for
Themselves? A man's desire for wealth may well   1255
Leave that man sick or murdered. From his cell
A prisoner may long for freedom, then
At home have his own servants do him in.
So many ills befall us in this way,
We don't know really that for which we pray.   1260
We fare as one who's drunken as a mouse:
Although a drunkard knows he has a house,
He doesn't know the right way there. The road
Is slippery for a man who drinks his load.
So fare we in this world, most certainly;   1265
We search with vigor for felicity,
But it's so true we often go awry.
We all can vouch for that, and namely I,
Who had this great opinion overall
That if I could escape that prison wall   1270
I then could live in perfect health and bliss——
From which I have been exiled now for this.
Since I may never see you, Emily,
I'm good as dead, there is no remedy."
    Now Palamon, meanwhile, was still confined,   1275
And when he learnt Arcite was gone, he whined
And wailed with so much sorrow it resounded
Throughout the tower. Utterly confounded,
He wet the mighty fetters round each shin
With bitter, salty tears in his chagrin.   1280

"Alas," said he, "my cousin, dear Arcite,
The fruit is yours, God knows, you've won the fight!
To walk at large in Thebes now you may go
And give but little thought to all my woe;
And you may, in your wise and knightly manner,   1285
Assemble all your kinsmen to your banner
And on this city make a sharp attack,
By treaty or by Fortune to go back
To Thebes with her, your lady and your wife,
For whom I now must forfeit here my life.   1290
When one weighs every possibility—
Since you are now at large, from prison free,
And are a lord—you have a great advantage.
I'm dying in a cage, what can I manage?
Here I must weep and wail long as I live   1295
With all the woe that prison has to give,
And with the heartache love has given me
That doubles my torment and misery."
The fire of jealousy with sudden start
Was raging in his breast, and caught his heart   1300
So madly he was whiter to behold
Than box-tree or the ashes dead and cold.
    He said then, "O cruel gods, eternal tribe
Who rule us by your word, and who inscribe
Upon a tablet made of adamant   1305
Your every judgment and eternal grant!
Why is it mankind in esteem you hold
More than the sheep that cowers in the fold?
For man is slain like any other beast,
Or dwells in prison, not to be released,   1310
Confronted with adversity and illness—
And often, by my faith, when he is guiltless.
    "What is the reason in your prescience
That torment's the reward for innocence?
And only adding more to all my strife   1315
Is that a man must live a moral life
In God's name, and keep rein upon his will,
While every beast may all his lust fulfill.
And when a beast is dead, he has no pain,

While man in death must still weep and complain   1320
Though in this world he had his share of woe.
Without a doubt that's how it stands, although
I'll leave it to the clergy to explain.
How well I know this world is full of pain.
Alas, I see a serpent or a thief,   1325
From whose deceit the righteous seek relief,
Go freely as he pleases on his way;
Yet I'm a captive, under Saturn's sway
And that of Juno, who in jealousy
And wrath has well nigh cut off totally   1330
The blood of Thebes, laid waste the walls once grand.
And Venus slays me, on the other hand,
With jealousy and fear of this Arcite."
    On Palamon I'll cease now if I might
And leave him in his prison still to dwell,   1335
That further word on Arcite I may tell.
    The summer passed. The winter nights so long
Increased twofold the pains that were so strong
In both lover and prisoner. I know
Not which one had to bear the greater woe: 1340
For Palamon, with brevity to tell,
Was damned to life inside a prison cell,
In iron fetters until he be dead;
Yet banishment had fallen on the head
Of Arcite, from that land he had to flee   1345
And nevermore might he his lady see.
    I now will ask you lovers, who's the one
Who has it worse, Arcite or Palamon?
For one may see his lady day by day
But must in prison waste his life away;   1350
The other may go riding where he please,
But now his lady nevermore he sees.
Make your own judgment on it, if you can.
I will go on, meanwhile, as I began.

PART II

    When back to Thebes Arcite had made his way,   1355
With many an "Alas!" he pined each day,

For nevermore his lady might he see.
To summarize his woe with brevity,
No creature's had such sorrow, to be sure,
Nor will as long as this world may endure.   1360
Of sleep and meat and drink he had so little
That lean and dry he grew, shaftlike and brittle;
His eyes were hollow, ghastly to behold,
His sallow skin like ashes pale and cold.
And he kept to himself, always alone,   1365
And all through every night he'd wail and moan.
And when he heard a song or instrument,
He wept, shed tears that nothing could prevent.
So feeble were his spirits and so low
That, if he spoke, no man would ever know   1370
Him by his speech or voice, he had so changed.
He moodily behaved, as if deranged
Not only by lovesickness (*hereos*
Is what it's called) but mania that grows
From melancholic humor that arises   1375
From that front brain cell where one fantasizes.
In short, all was in overturned position
In both the habit and the disposition
Of this despairing lover, Sir Arcite.
    Should I go on all day about his plight?   1380
Now when he had endured a year or so
This cruel torment, all this pain and woe
At home in Thebes (as you have heard me say),
One night he dreamt while in the bed he lay
That winged Mercury came to appear   1385
Before him, bidding him to be of cheer.
His sleep-inducing wand he held upright,
A hat was on his head, his hair was bright;
As Arcite noticed, Mercury was dressed
Just as when Argus he induced to rest.   1390
The god said this: "To Athens you shall go,
Where destined is an end to all your woe."
With that, Arcite woke with a start and said,
"No matter what sore pain may lie ahead,
Right now to Athens truly I must fare;   1395

Though death be dreaded, I'll be seeing there
My lady whom I love and serve, and I
Shall not, in her dear presence, fear to die."
    He picked up a large mirror then to see
The great change in his color, the degree   1400
To which his face looked like another kind.
Immediately the thought ran through his mind
That since his face had been disfigured so
By all that he had suffered, he could go
And live in Athens, in some lowly guise,   1405
And who he was no one would realize;
Then he could see his lady every day.
    And so at once he changed his knight's array
For that of a poor laborer for hire;
Then all alone (save only for a squire   1410
Who knew his secret, all there was to know,
And was disguised in poverty also),
He went to Athens by the shortest way.
Then to the royal court he went one day
And offered at the gate his worker's hands,   1415
To drag and draw, to follow all commands.
    To tell you what occurred without ado,
He got a job with an attendant who
Was dwelling in the house of Emily;
For he was shrewd and very quick to see   1420
Which of them served his lady there. Well could
He bear the water and he hewed as well the wood,
For he was young and equal to the task,
Big-boned and strong. What any man might ask,
Whatever one devised, Arcite could do.   1425
    He served in this way for a year or two,
The chamber-page of lovely Emily,
And said his name was Philostrate. And he
Was twice as loved as any other man
Of equal rank at court, for in this span   1430
His character was of such noble sort
That he won quite a name throughout the court.
As charity, they said, it would be noted
If Theseus would have the man promoted

To higher station, so that servicewise   1435
His virtue he might fully exercise.
And so it was in time his fame had sprung
Out of his gentle deeds and pleasant tongue
Until the duke took him and set him higher,
To serve him in his chamber as a squire,   1440
And gave him gold to keep himself in style.
From his own country, too, from while to while
Men brought to him a secret increment
That honestly and slyly would be spent,
That none might wonder how he had so much.   1445
He lived this way three years, his bearing such,
In time of peace as well as time of war,
That there was none whom Theseus loved more.
I now leave Arcite in this blissful state
That more on Palamon I may relate.   1450
    In dark and solid prison, horrid, drear,
Now Palamon endures a seventh year
And pines away in sorrow and distress.
Who feels such double wounds, such heaviness,
As Palamon whom love destroys so,   1455
Almost out of his wits through all his woe?
And Palamon's a captive, be it clear,
Perpetually, not only for a year.
    O who could rhyme in English properly
His martyrdom? It's not I truthfully,   1460
So I'll pass on as briefly as I may.
    Now in the seventh year (the old books say,
With more detail, it was the third night in
The month of May), the time came finally when,
Whether it was by chance or destiny—   1465
As when a thing's determined, it shall be—
With a friend's help, soon after midnight fell,
Palamon escaped from his prison cell
And fled the town as fast as he could go.
He'd given his jailer drink, and it was so   1470
Well mixed—a honeyed wine, along with some
Narcotics, like fine Theban opium—
That all that night, as hard as men could shake him,

The jailer slept and no one could awake him,
While Palamon fled swiftly as he may.   1475
The night was short, and fast would come the day,
When at all costs he knew he'd have to hide.
And so a grove that stood off to the side
He fearfully approached. It was his plan,
Which I will tell as briefly as I can,   1480
Inside that grove to hide himself all day,
Then at the fall of night to make his way
To Thebes. There all his friends he would implore
To help him march on Theseus in war,
And, to be brief, unless he lose his life,   1485
To win the lovely Emily as wife.
That was his whole intention, short and plain.
    And now to Arcite I'll return again,
Who little knew how nigh had grown his care
Till Fortune was to catch him in her snare.   1490
    The busy lark, the messenger of day,
Salutes now with her song the morning gray,
And fiery Phoebus rises up so bright
Till all the east is laughing in his light,
The beams of which dry every bush where cleaves   1495
The silver droplets, hanging on the leaves.
And Arcite, who is in the royal court
As Theseus's squire of good report,
Has risen and looks on the merry day.
To give the honor that was due to May   1500
(Recalling, too, his object of desire),
He set out on a courser quick as fire
Into the fields to have a little play.
A mile or two from court he rode his way
Till he came to the grove of which I spoke.   1505
By chance along that grove his course he broke
To make himself a garland from the growth,
With woodbine or with hawthorn leaf or both,
While in the sunshine singing heartily:
"O May, with flowers and with greenery,   1510
You are so welcome, fresh and fairest May!
I hope that I may get some green today!"

Down from his courser, with a lusty heart
Into the grove he promptly made his start
And roamed a path wherever it would chance.   1515
Now Palamon, as was the happenstance,
Was hidden in a bush where none could see,
As fearful for his life as he could be.
He'd no idea that this could be Arcite;
God knows, he had no cause to think it might,   1520
But it's been truly said down through the years,
"The field is blest with eyes, the wood has ears."
It's best a fellow always be discreet,
For when they least expect men often meet.
Little did Arcite know that near him there   1525
Was his old friend to hear him sing his air,
For he sat in the bush completely still.
    When of his roaming Arcite had his fill
And he had sung his rondel lustily,
Into a muse he fell then suddenly   1530
As lovers do, so variable their mood—
First treetop high, then in the briers they brood,
Now up, now down, like buckets in a well;
Like on a Friday, truly I can tell,
At first it shines, then rains start coming fast.   1535
Just so can fickle Venus overcast
The hearts of lovers; Friday is her day,
And just as she keeps changing her array
Few Fridays are like other days, for sure.
    When he had sung, Arcite became demure,   1540
He sighed and sat down without further song.
"Alas," said he, "the day I came along!
O Juno, how much longer will it be
That you wage war on Thebes with cruelty?
Alas! so much confusion is brought on   1545
The royal blood of Cadmus, Amphion—
Of Cadmus, who's the one who first began
To build the town of Thebes, and he's the man
Who was the first the city crowned as king;
I'm one of his descendants, his offspring,   1550
By true descent I'm of the royal stock;

Yet I'm just like a slave sold on the block,
For he who is my mortal enemy
Is whom I serve as squire so wretchedly.
And evermore does Juno cause me shame,   1555
For I dare not to tell them my own name;
For whereas I was once known as Arcite,
I now am Philostrate, not worth a mite.
Alas, you evil Mars! Juno, alas!
Your wrath has caused our house to all but pass,   1560
There's left but me and Palamon (in woe,
As in the dungeon he's still martyred so).
And more than that, to slay me utterly,
Love with his fiery dart so burningly
Has struck my loving heart with such a hurt,   1565
My death was knit before this very shirt.
You've slain me with your eyes, fair Emily,
You are the cause I die, that's all there be.
And for the rest of all my earthly care
I wouldn't give one weed the field may bear   1570
If but to please you I could have a chance."
And with that word he fell down in a trance
Where long he lay, till rising with a start.
    This Palamon, who felt that through his heart
A cold sword suddenly had glided, shook   1575
With anger, not much time at all he took,
For when he finished hearing Arcite's tale,
He leapt as if gone mad, face deathly pale,
Out of the thicket not one second later,
And said, "Arcite, you false and wicked traitor!   1580
Now you are caught who loves my lady so,
She for whom I have had such pain and woe;
You're of my blood, and to my counsel swore,
As I have often said to you before.
So you have fooled Duke Theseus, you claim,   1585
And also you have falsely changed your name,
But you shall die, or else it shall be me:
You shall not love my lady Emily.
For I and I alone shall love her so;
I'm Palamon himself, your mortal foe.   1590

And though I have no weapon in this place
(I just escaped from prison, by God's grace),
You'll either die—of that there's no mistake—
Or else not love my Emily. So make
The choice you will, you'll not escape from me."   1595
  Now when Arcite had heard and turned to see
That it was Palamon, as spite coursed through
His heart he fiercely as a lion drew
His sword and said, "By God who sits above,
If you were not so sick and crazed with love   1600
And if you had a weapon at your side
You'd not walk from this grove a single stride,
For by my hand you would be lying dead.
The pledge, the guarantee that you have said
I gave you, I renounce. Why, you must be   1605
A perfect fool, I tell you love is free,
And I will love her, try all that you might!
But inasmuch as you're a worthy knight
Who'd wager her to see who should prevail,
Here is my oath: tomorrow without fail,   1610
In secret, known to no one else around,
It's right here as a knight that I'll be found,
With arms for you as well—and you be first
To choose the best ones, leave for me the worst.
Some meat and drink tonight I'll bring to you,   1615
All that you need; I'll bring some bedding too.
And if it be my lady you shall win
And slay me in this wood that we are in,
You well may have her, nothing more from me."
  And Palamon then answered, "I agree."   1620
And so till then they parted, when they both
Had pledged in all good faith with solemn oath.
  O Cupid, so devoid of charity!
O rule where no compeer's allowed to be!
It truly has been said that love or power   1625
Won't willingly give fellowship an hour;
So Palamon has found, as has Arcite.
The latter rode at once to town that night,
Then in the morning, just before the sun,

Sneaked out the armor he and Palamon   1630
Would need; he brought enough to more than do
For battle in the field between the two.
So as alone as he was born he rode
His horse, with all this armor as his load,
And at the time and place that had seen set,   1635
There in the grove, the two of them were met.
The hue began to change in each's face,
Like in the hunter's who in distant Thrace
Stands in the gap with spear in hand, as there
He's hunting for the lion and the bear;   1640
He hears it coming, rushing through the branches
And breaking boughs asunder; then he blanches:
"Here comes," he thinks, "my mortal enemy!
Without fail one must die, it's him or me,
For either I will slay him at the gap   1645
Or he slay me, if that be my mishap."
That's how they were in changing of their hue
As soon as each one had his foe in view.
      There was no "Good day," not one salutation.
Without a word before the confrontation   1650
Each of the two first helped to arm the other
As courteously as if he were his brother.
And then, with sharpened spears of sturdy strength,
They plunged into a fight of wondrous length.
To watch this Palamon you might have thought   1655
He was a maddened lion, the way he fought,
And like a cruel tiger was Arcite.
They smote each other as wild boars would fight
When frothing white with foam, so mad each one.
They fought till ankle-deep the blood had run.   1660
I'll leave them, on their fight no more to dwell,
Now something more of Theseus to tell.
      That minister general, Destiny,
Who executes all that must come to be
(The providence foreseen by God on high),   1665
Is so strong that although the world deny
A thing shall be, by vow, by "yea" or "nay,"
It still will come to pass upon its day,

Though not again till pass a thousand years;
Each appetite that in this world appears, 1670
Be it for war or peace or hate or love,
Is governed by this providence above.
    Of mighty Theseus I say the same,
For he had such desire for hunting game,
Especially the great hart, all that May 1675
There didn't dawn on him a single day
That didn't find him clad and set to ride
With hunters, horns, hounds running at his side;
For in his hunting he took such delight
That it was all his joy and appetite 1680
To be the great hart's mighty bane and dread;
He served Diana after Mars the Red.
    Clear was the day, as I've said prior to this,
As Theseus—all joyful, full of bliss,
Along with Hippolyta, his fair queen, 1685
And Emily, clothed all in lovely green—
Was out upon a royal hunting ride;
And to the grove that stood so near beside,
In which there was a hart (so men had said),
Duke Theseus directly turned and sped. 1690
He rode straight for the glade, which was the place
To which the hart was wont to go, to race
Across the brook and flee as harts will do;
The duke would have a run at him or two
With hounds such as it pleased him to command. 1695
    But when the duke had reached this open land,
There in the glaring sun he caught the sight
At once of Palamon and of Arcite,
Still fighting like two boars. It seemed as though
The two bright swords, there flashing to and fro 1700
So hideously, could with the lightest stroke
Be either one enough to fell an oak.
Now who these people were he didn't know;
The duke at once then spurred his courser, though,
And in a trice he was between the two, 1705
Pulled out his sword, and said, "Halt! That will do!
No more, on pain of parting with your head!

By mighty Mars, he'll be as good as dead
Who strikes another blow that I may see.
Tell me what sort of men you two must be,   1710
In such a hardy fight here as you were
Without a judge or other officer
Though as if in a tournament today."
   Then Palamon responded right away:
"Sire, there are no more words that need be said,   1715
We both are quite deserving to be dead.
Two woeful wretches, prisoners are we,
Both weary of our lives, that's him and me.
And as you are a righteous judge and lord,
No mercy nor refuge for us afford,   1720
But slay me first, in saintly charity.
But slay this fellow here as well as me—
Or slay him first, when you have seen him right:
This is your mortal foe, this is Arcite,
Whom you have banished or would have his head,   1725
For which he's now deserving to be dead.
This is the one who came up to your gate
And told them that his name was Philostrate,
The one who's made a fool of you for years—
You made him your chief squire, from all his peers.   1730
And he's in love with Emily. And I,
Since now has come the day that I shall die,
Shall plainly here confess and have it done
That I am that same woeful Palamon
Who broke out of your prison wickedly;   1735
I am your mortal foe, and I am he
Who loves so hotly Emily the Bright
I'd die for it here in my lady's sight.
I therefore ask for death, for it is just.
But you will slay this fellow too, I trust,   1740
For both of us deserve to die, not one."
   This worthy duke then answered Palamon
At once. He said, "Then here's the long and short:
The confession from your mouth, your own report
Has damned you, so I'll thereby note the fact   1745
That there's no need to flog or have you racked.

By mighty Mars the Red, you'll die and should!"
    But then the queen, in all her womanhood,
Began to weep, and so did Emily
And all the ladies in their company.   1750
They thought it such a pity, one and all,
That ever such misfortune should befall;
For gentlemen these were, of great estate,
And nothing but of love was their debate.
To see the two men's bloody wounds so wide,   1755
Both young and old among the women cried,
"Have mercy, lord, upon us women all!"
And on their bare knees they began to fall,
And would have kissed his feet there as he stood.
At last, as pity rises in a good   1760
And gentle heart, his anger finally slaked;
For though the duke at first with ire quaked,
He gave consideration with a pause
To what had been their trespass and the cause.
Though, to his mind, of guilt they stood accused,   1765
His reason said that they should be excused;
He settled on the thought that every man
Will help himself in love all that he can,
And free himself from jail in any fashion.
And also in his heart he had compassion   1770
For all these women who were still in tears.
He gently took to heart the women's fears,
Then softly told himself, "Fie on a lord
Who has no whit of mercy to afford,
Who's lionlike in all that's done and said   1775
To those who are repentant and in dread,
As well as to a proud, defiant man
Who aims to finish that which he began.
That lord has no discriminating vision
Who can't in such a case make some division   1780
But weighs pride and humility as one."
So when its course his wrath had shortly run,
Duke Theseus looked up toward the skies
And spoke aloud, a sparkling in his eyes:
    "The god of love! Ah, *benedicite!*   1785

How great a lord, how mighty is his sway!
Against his might there are no obstacles;
Call him a god for all his miracles.
For he can mold according to his muse
All of our hearts however he may choose.   1790
This Palamon, this Arcite whom you see,
Were from my prison both completely free;
They might have lived in Thebes and royally so,
For they both know I am their mortal foe
And death for both within my power lies;   1795
Yet love, in spite of all before their eyes,
Brought them back here to die, back to the brink.
Now this is some high folly, don't you think?
Who else may be a fool but one in love!
Look, for the sake of God who sits above,   1800
See how they bleed! Are they not well arrayed?
Thus by their lord, the god of love, they're paid
For serving him, they have their fee and wage.
Yet they think they are wise who so engage
In serving love, whatever may befall.   1805
But this is yet the biggest joke of all,
That she for whom they passionately vie
Can give them thanks about as much as I—
She knew no more about this whole affair
Than knew, by God, a cuckoo or a hare!   1810
But all must be assayed, both hot and cold,
A man must be a fool, though young or old.
From long ago I know myself it's true,
For in my time I was love's servant too.
And therefore, since I recognize love's pain   1815
And know full well love's power to constrain
(As one so often captured in his net),
This trespass I'll forgive and I'll forget,
As my queen has requested, kneeling here
Along with Emily, my sister dear.   1820
But both of you shall swear to me: my land
Shall nevermore be threatened by your hand,
You shan't make war against me day or night;
You'll be my friends in every way you might,

Then I'll forgive this trespass as I may." 1825
And they swore as he asked in every way,
And for his lordship's mercy then they prayed.
He granted grace, and then this speech he made:
  "Regarding royal blood and riches too,
Were she a queen or princess, each of you, 1830
I have no doubt at all, has worthiness
To marry her in time; but nonetheless
I speak now for my sister Emily
For whom you've had this strife and jealousy.
You know that two at once she cannot marry 1835
No matter how this fight you choose to carry.
No, one of you, no matter what the grief,
Must go and 'whistle with an ivy leaf';
She cannot have you both, that is to say,
Be you as mad and jealous as you may. 1840
This proposition, then, I put to you:
Each one shall have his destiny, his due,
However it's been shaped—and listen how,
For here's your end as I devise it now.
  "My will is this (this matter to conclude 1845
Once and for all, no protest to intrude,
So if you like it, make of it the best):
Where you may wish to go, by me you're blest,
Go freely, there's no danger in your way;
But after fifty weeks right to the day, 1850
Each of you shall bring back one hundred knights,
Armed for the lists to represent your rights,
All set to fight for her. For here's an oath
That this is what shall be, I tell you both
Upon my word and as I am a knight: 1855
When we have seen which has the greater might—
That is to say, whichever of the two
With his one hundred (as I've said to you)
Shall slay or from the lists the other drive—
To him I shall give Emily to wive, 1860
To him who Fortune gives so fair a grace.
I'll have the lists built in this very place,
And—God bestow my soul with wisdom's order—

I'll be a true judge on the battle's border.
With me you have no other way to go,   1865
One of you shall be killed or taken. So
If you believe this judgment is well said,
Advise me now and count yourselves ahead.
That is your end, that's how it shall be done."
  Who looks as happy now as Palamon?   1870
And who but Arcite springs with such delight?
Who could explain, who has the skill to write
About the joy witnessed in the place
That Theseus has granted such a grace?
Then everyone went down on bended knee   1875
And gave him thanks in most heartfelt degree—
Especially the Thebans, more than once.
And so, with high hopes and ebullience,
The two then took their leave, they were to ride
Back home to Thebes, to walls so old and wide.   1880

PART III

  I know that men would deem it negligence
If I forgot to tell of the expense
To which Duke Theseus went busily
To build the lists. He built them royally,
A theatre so noble standing there   1885
I daresay none was finer anywhere.
Its circuit measured one full mile about,
Its wall of stone, a circling moat without.
As surely as a compass it was round,
And sixty rows it stood above the ground,   1890
So that a man on one row wouldn't be
The reason that another couldn't see.
  On the east stood a great, white marble gate,
Another on the west. I'll briefly state,
Concluding, there was no such other place   1895
In all the earth that took so little space.
For there was not one craftsman in the land
With math and his geometry in hand,

No single sculptor or one painter, who
Duke Theseus did not hire for the crew   1900
That worked on this theatre. So that he
Might sacrifice, do all rites properly,
At the eastern gate he had built above,
In honor of Venus, goddess of love,
An altar and an oratory. Then,   1905
Above the west gate, he constructed in
The memory of Mars the very same;
A cart of gold was spent in Mars's name.
In a turret, built on the northern wall
In coral and white alabaster all,   1910
The duke had nobly wrought an oratory
Magnificent to see, built for the glory
Of Diana, most chaste of deities.
    Yet I've forgotten to describe with these
The sculptures, paintings, noble works of art,   1915
The shapes and figures that were all a part
Of the work in these oratories three.
    In the temple of Venus you could see
(Wrought on the wall, and piteous to behold)
The broken sleep, the lonely sighs, the cold   1920
And sacred tears, the sad laments; the burning,
The fiery strokes of all desire and yearning
That servants of love in this life endure;
The oaths by which covenants they assure;
Pleasure and Hope, Desire, Foolhardiness,   1925
Beauty and Youth and Riches, Bawdiness,
Seduction, Force, Falsehood and Flattery,
Extravagance, Ado and Jealousy
(Who wears a garland, yellow marigolds,
And in her hand a bird, the cuckoo, holds);   1930
The banquets, instruments, the carols, dances,
Lust and array. All of the circumstances
Of love that I'm recounting here were all
In proper order painted on the wall—
And more than I'd be able to recount,   1935
For truly all the Cytherean mount,
The place where Venus has her major dwelling,

Was in the scenes on that wall for the telling
With all its gardens and its lustfulness.
Nor was forgotten the porter Idleness,   1940
Nor Narcissus, that ancient, fairest one,
Nor all the folly of King Solomon,
Nor yet the mighty strength of Hercules,
Medea's enchanting power nor Circe's,
Nor Turnus with a heart so fierce and bold,   1945
Nor Croesus, rich but captive with his gold.
So you can see that neither wisdom, wealth,
Nor beauty, sleight, nor strength nor hardy health
Can hold with Venus an equality,
For as she wills she guides the world to be.   1950
Look how these people, caught up in her snare,
So often cried "Alas!" in their despair.
Suffice here these examples one or two,
Though I could tell a thousand more to you.
    Venus's statue, glorious to behold,   1955
Was naked, and the sea about her rolled,
As from her navel down were shown to pass
Green waves that were as bright as any glass.
She had a harp in her right hand, and she
Had on her head, a seemly sight to see,   1960
A fresh rose garland, fragrant as the spring.
Above her head her doves were flickering.
Before her Cupid stood, who is her son;
He had two wings and was superbly done,
And blind he was, as is so often seen.   1965
He held a bow, and arrows bright and keen.
    Why should I not as well tell you of all
The paintings that appeared upon the wall
In the temple of mighty Mars the Red?
From roof to floor the wall was overspread   1970
With painted scenes like in that grisly place
That's known as his great temple back in Thrace—
That cold and frosty region where, I'm told,
He has his sovereign mansion from of old.
    A forest, first, was painted on the wall   1975
In which there dwelt no man nor beast at all.

Its knotty, knarled trees were bare and old,
The stubs were sharp and hideous to behold;
And through it ran a rumble and a sough
As if a storm would break off every bough.   1980
And downward from a hill, below the bent,
Stood the temple of Mars of Armament,
Made all of burnished steel. The entrance there
Was long and straight, indeed a sight to scare,
And out of it came such a raging wind   1985
The very gate was made to shake and bend.
    In through the doors there shone the northern light
(No window being in that temple's height
Through which to see a single light). Each door
Was of eternal adamant and, more,   1990
Was reinforced as wide as well as long
With toughest iron. To make the temple strong,
Each pillar had the girth of any cask,
Each of bright shiny iron fit for the task.
    There I first saw the dark imagination   1995
Of Felony, the scheme of its creation;
Cruel Ire that burns till like a coal it's red;
The pickpurse and the pallidness of Dread;
The smiler with the knife beneath his cloak;
The stable burning up with blackest smoke;   2000
The treachery of murder in the bed;
The wounds of open Warfare as they bled;
Strife with its threats and with its bloody knife.
With frightful sounds that sorry place was rife.
The suicide I saw, too, lying there,   2005
The blood of his own heart had bathed his hair;
The driven nail in someone's head by night;
Cold Death laid out, his mouth a gaping sight;
Right in the temple's center sat Mischance,
Uncomforted, and sad his countenance;   2010
There I saw Madness laughing in his rage,
And armed Complaint, Outcry and fierce Outrage;
The carrion found in the bush (throat slit),
A thousand slain, no plague the cause of it;
The tyrant with his booty, battle's gains;   2015

The town laid waste till nothing now remains.
I saw the burning ships dance on the tide;
The hunter strangled by wild bears; I spied
The sow devour the child right in the cradle;
The scalded cook despite his lengthy ladle.   2020
Not one misfortune that Mars could impart
Was overlooked; the carter by his cart
Run over, underneath the wheel laid low.
Of those who follow Mars, there were also
The barber and the butcher, and the smith   2025
Who forges at the anvil, busy with
Sharp swords. Above, where seated in his tower,
I saw Conquest depicted in his power;
There was a sharpened sword above his head
That hung there by the thinnest simple thread.   2030
The killing, too, was shown of Julius,
Of mighty Nero, of Antonius—
Though at that time they all were still unborn,
Their deaths appeared upon that wall forlorn
By threat of Mars and by prefiguration.   2035
So it was shown in that wall's illustration
As is depicted in the stars above:
Who shall be slain and who shall die for love.
(Old stories tell it; one example's good,
I can't recount them all, although I would.)   2040
    His statue on its chariot, lifelike
In arms and grim, looked mad enough to strike.
Two starry figures shone above his head,
Puella one (as in the old books read),
The other one as Rubeus was known.   2045
That's how this god of armament was shown.
There was a wolf before him at his feet
With red eyes, as a man he set to eat.
With subtle brush depicted was the story
Of Mars, redoubtable in all his glory.   2050
    Now to the temple of Diana chaste
As briefly as I can I'll turn with haste
To give you a description that's complete.
The walls all up and down were made replete

With scenes of hunting and of chastity.   2055
I saw how sad Callisto came to be
(When she had caused Diana some despair)
Changed from a woman first into a bear
And then into the lodestar. (That's the way
That it was painted, what more can I say?)   2060
Her son's also a star, as men may see.
There I saw Daphne turned into a tree.
(Diana I don't mean, she's not the same;
Peneus's daughter, Daphne her name.)
I saw Actaeon turned into a hart   2065
(He saw Diana nude, which wasn't smart),
And then I saw his hounds run and surprise him
And eat him up (they didn't recognize him).
And painted on the wall was furthermore
How Atalanta hunted after boar,   2070
As did Meleager and some others (though
For this Diana brought Meleager woe).
I also saw there many a wondrous tale
On which I'd rather let my memory fail.
    This goddess on a hart had taken seat,   2075
And there were slender hounds about her feet,
And underneath her feet there was a moon
(One that was waxing, to be waning soon).
Her statue was arrayed in green; she wore
A quiver filled, her bow in hand she bore.   2080
Her eyes were looking down, extremely so,
Toward Pluto's dark region far below.
Before her was a woman in travail,
Trying to have her child to no avail
As to Lucina she began to call,   2085
"Please help me, for your help's the best of all!"
How lifelike were these scenes the artist wrought!
The paint cost many a florin that he bought.
    Now when these lists were finished, Theseus,
Who'd gone to great expense in building thus   2090
The theatre and temples, was elated
With all of it as finally consummated.
On Theseus I'll cease now if I might,

Of Palamon to speak and of Arcite.
    The day of their return was drawing nigh, 2095
When each should bring one hundred knights to vie
For Emily in battle, as I've told.
To Athens, their covenants to uphold,
Each one of them thus brought one hundred knights,
Well armed and set for battle by all rights. 2100
And certainly, as thought then many a man,
Not once before since this world first began
(Regarding knighthood, deeds of gallant hand),
As surely as God made the sea and land,
Had there been such a noble company. 2105
For every man with love of chivalry
And who desired to make himself a name
Had prayed that he might take part in the game.
The chosen surely had no cause for sorrow;
If such a thing were taking place tomorrow, 2110
You know right well that every lusty knight
Who loves his paramours and has some might,
Whether it were in England or elsewhere,
Would thankfully and willingly be there.
To fight for a lady, *benedicite!* 2115
It was a lusty sight, this whole array.
    The many knights who rode with Palamon
Were of that lusty spirit, every one.
Now some of these had chosen to be dressed
In hauberk, breastplate, and a simple vest; 2120
Some wore two plates (both front and black, and large),
While some preferred a Prussian shield or targe;
Some liked to arm their legs against attacks
And have a mace of steel or else an ax.
There's no new armored style that isn't old, 2125
They all were armed, as I have briefly told,
According to the liking of each one.
    There you may see approach with Palamon
Lycurgus, who's the mighty king of Thrace.
His beard was black, and manly was his face. 2130
The fellow's eyes were glowing in his head
With light that was half yellow and half red,

And like a griffin he would look about
From neath two shaggy brows. The man was stout;
He had great limbs, with muscles hard and strong,   2135
His shoulders broad, arms barrel-like and long.
As was the custom in his land, he rolled
Along upon a chariot of gold,
Four white bulls in the traces at the fore.
Instead of coat of arms Lycurgus wore   2140
A bearskin that was coal black, very old,
Its yellow claws as bright as any gold.
His hair shone, long and combed behind his back,
Bright as a raven's feather, and as black.
His strong and shaggy head was underneath   2145
A mighty weight, an arm-sized golden wreath,
Inlaid with bright and precious stones in plenty.
White wolfhounds were around him, more than twenty,
Each one of them as big as any steer,
That he would use to hunt for lion or deer.   2150
They followed him with muzzles tightly bound,
Their collars gold with collar rings filed round.
He had a hundred lords there in his rout,
All fully armed. Their hearts were stern and stout.
    With Arcite, as we find old tales relate,   2155
The Indian king, Emetrius the Great—
His bay steed with steel trappings, covered by
A motley cloth of gold—came riding. Why,
The god of arms, new Mars he looked to be.
His surcoat was of cloth from Tartary,   2160
With all the large white pearls that it could hold.
His saddle, newly forged, was burnished gold.
A mantle from his shoulders hung, attire
Brimful of rubies sparkling red as fire.
His crisp hair into ringlets seemed to run,   2165
So yellow it would glitter like the sun.
His nose was high, his eyes bright and citrine;
He had full lips, and skin that had a fine
Sanguinity, with freckles on his face
From black to yellow and from place to place.   2170
And like that of a lion was his gaze.

His age was twenty-five, I would appraise.
His beard had very well begun to grow;
His voice thundered like a trumpet's blow.
He wore a garland made of laurel, green   2175
And freshly picked and pleasant to be seen.
Upon his hand he bore, to his delight,
An eagle that was tame and lily white.
He had a hundred nobles with him there,
Armed to the teeth with all a warrior's wear,   2180
Fully equipped with all that battle brings.
For take my word that earls, dukes, and kings
Were gathered in this noble company
For love of and the growth of chivalry.
Around this king, among this noble tide,   2185
Tame lions and leopards ran on every side.
And in this manner nobles all and some
Had on that Sunday to the city come,
There in the early morning to alight.
   Now Theseus, this duke and worthy knight,   2190
When he had brought them all into the town
To inns where they would all be bedded down
According to their rank, gave them a feast.
He honored all, ignoring not the least.
It still is said that none, however great,   2195
Could have done better. Here I could relate
The music and the service at the feast,
The gifts both to the highest and the least;
The rich array with which he decked the place,
And who sat first and last upon the dais;   2200
Which ladies were the fairest, danced the best,
Or which of them sang better than the rest;
Or who could speak most feelingly of love;
What hawks were sitting on the perch above,
What hounds were lying on the floor below—   2205
Of all this I will make no mention, though.
To tell what followed seems the best to me,
So let's get to the point, if you agree.
   That Sunday night, before day came along,
When Palamon had heard the lark in song—   2210

It was two hours till day would begin,
And yet the lark sang—Palamon right then
In hopeful spirit and with holy heart
Arose, then as a pilgrim to depart
To Cytherea, blissful and benign   2215
(That is, to Venus, honored and divine);
For in her hour he walked out to where
Her temple stood in the theatre. There
He knelt down with a humble, aching heart
And prayed, as you shall hear me now impart.   2220
    "O lady Venus, fairest of the fair,
Jove's daughter, wife of Vulcan, hear my prayer!
O gladness of the Cytherean mount!
By your love for Adonis—such amount!—
Have pity on my tears, their bitter smart,   2225
And take my humble prayer into your heart.
Alas! I have no language that can tell
The ravages and torments of my hell,
The many ills my heart cannot convey;
I'm so confused there's nothing I can say   2230
But 'Mercy, lady bright, who, as I kneel,
Knows all my thought and sees what woe I feel!'
Consider all and rue me, I implore,
As surely as I shall forevermore
(Give me the might!) your truest servant be   2235
And always be at war with chastity.
I give to you my vow, give me your aid.
For I don't care to boast of arms displayed
Nor ask that mine shall be the victory
And fame; I do not seek the vanity   2240
Of warriors' glory, praised both far and wide;
I wish but full possession as my bride
Of Emily, and death in serving you.
Determine now the way, what's best to do.
I do not care, whichever's best to be—   2245
To vanquish them or have them vanquish me—
That I might hold my lady safe from harms.
For though it's true that Mars is god of arms,
Your virtue, Venus, is so great above,

If you but will it I shall have my love.   2250
I'll worship at your temple ever biding;
At every altar where I may go riding
My sacrifice will be with fiery heat.
But if you will it not, my lady sweet,
I pray tomorrow, when we're fighting here,   2255
Arcite will run my heart through with a spear;
Then I won't care, when I have lost my life,
Though he indeed should win her as his wife.
This is my prayer, it all concludes in this:
Give me my love, dear lady of all bliss."   2260
    When the prayer of Palamon was done,
He gave a sacrifice, and it was one
Of all good form and fullest piety.
(I won't go into all the liturgy.)
Then at the last the Venus statue shook   2265
And made a sign to him, which he then took
To mean acceptance of his prayer that day;
For though the sign had come with some delay,
He well knew she had granted his request.
He hurried home with gladness in his breast.   2270
    Three hours after he had made his way
Out to the temple of Venus to pray,
The sun arose and so did Emily.
She started for Diana's temple, she
And all the maidens in her following   2275
Who brought the fire to burn the offering,
The incense, clothes, all the accoutrements
Required for sacrificial sacraments;
As was the custom, horns were full of mead;
They brought all things that sacrificers need.   2280
The temple smoked, the vestments all were fair,
As Emily, with heart so debonair,
Her body washed with water from a well.
How she performed the rite I dare not tell
Unless it's in a very general way.   2285
(A pleasure it would be were I to say,
And, meaning well, there's nothing I could lose,
But it's good for a man to pick and choose.)

She combed her loose bright hair, smooth to the stroke.
A crown of green leaves taken from the oak   2290
Was on her head, the arrangement meet and fair.
Two fires she kindled at the altar there
And then performed the rites (as men may note
In old books like the Theban Statius wrote).
The fire once lit, she in a piteous way   2295
Addressed Diana, as you'll hear me say.
   "O most chaste goddess of the woods so green,
By whom all heaven, earth, and sea are seen!
Queen of the realm of Pluto dark below!
Goddess of maidens! My heart you well know   2300
And have for years, you've known what I desire.
O keep me from your vengeance and your ire,
For which Actaeon paid so brutally!
You've seen, chaste goddess, one desire in me:
I long to be a maiden all my life,   2305
Not ever to be lover or a wife.
You know that I'm yet of your company,
A maiden who's in love with venery,
One who desires to walk the woods so wild
And not be someone's wife and be with child   2310
Or have to know the company of man.
Now help me, lady, since you may and can,
By these three forms that you possess. I see
That Palamon has such a love for me,
And Arcite too, and for them I implore,   2315
One grace I ask, and pray for nothing more:
That love and peace between the two you'll send
And turn their hearts from me, to such an end
That all their burning love and their desire,
That all their busy torment and their fire   2320
Be quenched, or else turned to another place.
But if you will not grant me such a grace,
Or destiny is shaped in such a way
That I must have one of the two, I pray
You'll send me him with most desire for me.   2325
Behold, O goddess of pure chastity,
Upon my cheeks the bitter tears that fall.

You are a maiden, keeper of us all;
My maidenhood now keep and well conserve,
And you, while I'm a maiden, I will serve."   2330
 The fires burnt clearly on the altar there
While Emily was kneeling in her prayer.
Then suddenly so strange a sight she flinched,
For all at once one of the fires was quenched,
Then lit again; and after that the other   2335
Was gone as quickly, as if in a smother—
And as it went, it made a whistling noise
Like firebrands when they're wet. She lost all poise
When from the firebrand's end began to run
What looked like drops of blood, and many a one.   2340
Poor Emily, aghast at such a sight,
Began to cry, half-maddened in her fright,
Not knowing what this all might signify;
It was pure fear alone that made her cry,
And cry she did, a woeful sound to hear.   2345
Just then Diana seemed there to appear,
Like any huntress, in her hand a bow.
"Daughter," she said, "put off your heavy woe.
Among the gods on high it is affirmed
By word eternal, written and confirmed: 2350
You shall be wedded to one of the two
Who have endured such care and woe for you.
But as to which of them, I may not tell.
No longer may I tarry, so farewell.
The fires that here upon my altar burn   2355
Shall say to you, before away you turn,
What in this case shall be your fate in love."
With that, the arrows in the quiver of
The goddess rang with noisy clattering,
Then she was gone. Upon this vanishing,   2360
Astonished by the things that she had seen,
Emily said, "Alas, what can it mean?
I put myself now under your protection,
Diana, I shall follow your direction."
She then at once went home the nearest way,   2365
And that was that, there is no more to say.

The next hour of Mars to follow this,
Arcite went to the temple in the lists
To offer fiery Mars his sacrifice
With all the rites that such a god suffice.   2370
With piteous heart and very high devotion
He said to Mars the following orison.
    "O god of strength, who in cold Thracian regions
Is honored as a lord by all your legions;
Who has in every realm and every land   2375
All arms as but a bridle in your hand,
Whose fortunes are your pleasure, your device;
Accept, I pray, my humble sacrifice.
If it be by my youth I might deserve,
And by my strength have worthiness, to serve   2380
Your godhead and to be among your train,
I pray that you'll have pity on my pain.
By that same pain, that same hot, blazing fire
In which you too were burning with desire,
When you once had the fair, the fresh young beauty   2385
Of Venus—when you had her in your duty,
When in your arms you had her at your will
(Although there was a time it brought you ill,
The time when Vulcan caught you in his net
And found you with his wife, to your regret)—   2390
By that same sorrow that was in your heart,
Now rue my pains as well, for how they smart!
I'm young, unknowing, as you are aware;
By love I'm hurt, and have much more despair
Than any creature ever drawing breath.   2395
For she, for whom I must endure to death
This woe, cares not if I should sink or swim—
No mercy from her, not a trace or whim,
Unless by strength I win her in this place.
And well I know, without your help or grace,   2400
My strength will not avail me in my plight.
So help me, lord, tomorrow in my fight.
By that same fire that once caused you to burn
(Those flames that now cause me as well to yearn),
Let victory tomorrow be my story;   2405

Let mine be all the trial, yours the glory.
Your temple I will honor without measure,
Above all places; always at your leisure
And in your crafts I'll work in mighty manner.
And in your temple I will hang my banner,   2410
And all the arms of all my company,
And henceforth, till the day I die, I'll see
That there's eternal fire before you found.
And also to this oath I will be bound:
My beard and hair, that now hang down so long   2415
And never yet have suffered any wrong
From razor or from shear, I'll give to you,
And be long as I live your servant true.
Now, lord, look on my sorrow ruefully;
I ask for nothing more than victory."   2420
   Now when this prayer of strong Arcite was ended,
The rings that on the doors had hung suspended,
And then the doors themselves, began to clatter
(With Arcite somewhat frightened by the matter).
The altar fires began to burn so bright   2425
That Mars's temple soon was all alight.
The floor gave up an odor sweet and grand.
Immediately Arcite raised up his hand,
As more incense into the fire he cast,
With other rites as well, when at the last   2430
The statue's hauberk then began to ring,
And with the sound was heard a murmuring:
Though low and dim, and word was "Victory!"
Then Mars he praised and honored joyfully;
His hopes were high as to how well he'd fare   2435
As to his inn he then went to repair,
As happy as a bird to see the sun.
   And right away such strife was then begun,
By these accords, in the heavens above
Between fair Venus, goddess of all love,   2440
And Mars, stern god of every sword and plate,
That Jupiter could hardly arbitrate—
Until his father Saturn, pale and cold,
Well taught by many fortunes from of old,

Recalled from his experience an art   2445
By which they were appeased for each's part.
It's truly said the elder has advantage,
On wisdom and on life he has the vantage;
Men may outrun but not outsmart the old.
At once to end this strife he'd seen unfold,   2450
Old Saturn (though it wasn't like himself)
Sought ways to put this quarrel on the shelf.
   "Dear daughter Venus," Saturn said, "my course
Must take a lengthy turn, yet it's a force
And power like no man can bring to be.   2455
Mine is the drowning in the pallid sea;
Mine is the prison cell where shines no speck
Of light; the strangling, hanging by the neck,
The murmur and rebellion of the throng,
The secret poison, and complaints of wrong;   2460
I take revenge, complete correction's mine,
While I am dwelling in the Lion's sign.
Mine's the ruin of many high-built halls,
The falling of the towers and the walls
On carpenter and miner. I'm the killer   2465
Of Samson as he shook the mighty pillar;
And mine are all the maladies so cold,
The plans of all dark treasons from of old;
My glance is father of all pestilence.
Now weep no more, for by my diligence   2470
This Palamon, who is your worthy knight,
Shall have her as you promised him tonight.
Though Mars shall help his knight, this has to cease,
Between you once again must be some peace,
Although you're not the same in temperament   2475
(Which causes all the day such argument).
I'm your grandfather, ready at your will;
No longer weep, your wish I shall fulfill."
   Now I will cease to speak of gods above,
Of Mars and Venus, gods of war and love,   2480
And tell you now, as plainly as I can,
The end result for which I first began.

PART IV

Great was the feast in Athens on that day,
And such a lusty season was that May
That everyone took pleasure at the chance   2485
To joust all of that Monday and to dance
And serve fair Venus as he might devise.
But by the fact that they would have to rise
Up early if they were to see the fight,
They finally went to bed that Monday night.   2490
    Next morning, when the day began to spring,
Of horse and harness, noise and clattering,
The sounds were heard in all the inns about.
Then to the palace rode a mighty rout
Of lords upon their steeds and palfreys. There   2495
One might see many styles of knightly wear,
Exotic, rich, all wrought with great appeal,
Combining gold, embroidery, and steel;
Bright shields, headpieces, gear for all alarms,
Gold-tinted helmets, hauberks, coats of arms;   2500
Lords robed on mounts, with knights in retinue
Attending to their needs; and squires too
Were in attendance, buckling up headgear
And strapping shields and nailing every spear
(The needs were such these squires were never idle).   2505
The foaming steeds gnawed at the golden bridle,
While through the throng ran armorers also,
With file and hammer, pricking to and fro;
Yeomen on foot, and many commoners too,
With short staves, were as thick as could get through;   2510
The pipe, the trumpet, clarion, kettledrum,
From which in battle bloody sounds would come;
The palace full of people wall-to-wall,
Three here, ten there, discussing one and all
The question of these two young Theban knights,   2515
Some saying this, some that; as for the fights,
Some favored yon black-headed, some the bald,
While triumph for that thick-haired others called;

Some said, "He has a grim look, he can fight;
His ax weighs twenty pounds, that isn't light." 2520
And so the hall was filled with such divining,
The sun long since arisen, brightly shining.
    Great Theseus, now from his sleep awaking
To minstrelsy and noise they were making,
Within his splendid palace chamber stayed 2525
Until the Theban knights, who both were paid
The honor due, were fetched. The duke with that
Made his appearance, at a window sat,
And like a god enthroned the duke was dressed.
At once all of the people forward pressed 2530
To see him and to pay high reverence
And hear what judgments he might then dispense.
    A herald on a scaffold bellowed "Hear ye!"
Until the noise quieted down; then he,
On seeing that the crowd below was still, 2535
Disclosed to them Duke Theseus's will:
    "Our lord discreet, upon deliberation,
Considers it would be a desolation
Of gentle blood here in this enterprise
To fight a mortal battle for the prize. 2540
Wherefore, to see that no one here should die,
His former purpose he will modify.
No man, on pain of forfeiture of life,
Shall send a missile, poleax, or a knife
Into the lists, nor bring such weapons there; 2545
No short, well-sharpened sword shall anywhere
Be drawn, nor shall one bear it by his side;
And no man shall against his fellow ride
With finely sharpened spear more than a course
(But may defend with it if off his horse). 2550
And anyone in trouble they shall take—
That there should be no slaying—to a stake
That shall be ordered, one on either side,
Where he'll be put by force and there abide.
And if one of the chieftains, once we start, 2555
Is taken, or has slain his counterpart,
The tournament is over, come and gone.

And so Godspeed! Go forward and lay on!
With long sword and with maces fight your fill.
Go on your way now, this is our lord's will."   2560
   High as the heavens rose the people's voice,
So merrily and loud did they rejoice.
"God save a lord so noble!" was the cry.
"He wills no blood be shed, that none should die!"
The trumpets blew, then with much melody   2565
Toward the lists rode all this company
In order down the city's thoroughfare,
Where cloth of gold, no serge, hung everywhere.
This noble duke was lordlike on the ride,
With these two Theban knights on either side;   2570
And after rode the queen and Emily,
And after that a mighty company
In groups that were arranged by social order.
They passed through all the city to its border,
Out to the lists, with none arriving late.   2575
The hour of day was sometime after eight
When Theseus sat high and regally,
And Hippolyta and fair Emily,
With other ladies of degree about.
Then to the seats went pressing all the rout.   2580
Then through the west gates under Mars the Red
Arcite immediately his hundred led,
His banner bright and red beneath the sun.
In that same moment entered Palamon
Under Venus on the east. His banner   2585
Was white, and there was boldness in his manner.
In all the world, were you to seek throughout,
You'd find no other two such groups without
A difference, well matched in every way
Till there was no one wise enough to say   2590
If either of the two had any edge
In worthiness or age or heritage,
So evenly, it seemed, the Thebans chose.
They lined up fairly, two opposing rows.
And when the name of everyone was read,   2595
That in their numbers no one be misled,

The gates were shut, and this cry rang aloud:
"Now do your duty, knights so young and proud!"
  The heralds cease their pricking to and fro;
Now trumpets and the clarion loudly blow;   2600
There is no more to say but east and west
The spear now steady goes into its rest,
And sharpened spur into the courser's side.
They see now who can joust and who can ride:
Shafts splinter on the stout shields tough and thick;   2605
Right through the breastbone one now feels the prick;
Up spring the spears some twenty feet in height,
Out come the swords all sharp and silver bright;
The helmets they begin to hew and shred,
Out bursts the blood in sternest streams of red;   2610
With mighty maces bones they break and bust;
Right through the thickest throng one rides to thrust;
Strong steeds begin to stumble, there's a fall,
The rider underfoot rolls like a ball;
He parries with his shaft against a thrust,   2615
Another with his horse now hits the dust—
He's wounded, so here's one whom they must take,
Despite his protests, over to the stake
Where by the ruling he will have to stay;
Another knight is led across the way.   2620
  At times Duke Theseus will have them rest,
Refresh themselves, and drink if they request.
And these two Theban knights time and again
Have clashed together, brought each other pain,
Each twice unhorsed now in their rivalry.   2625
No tiger in the vale of Gargaphy
Whose young whelp has been stolen in the night
Is so cruel to the hunter as Arcite,
So jealous, is to Palamon; and there
Is not a hunted lion anywhere   2630
In Benmarin, though crazed with hunger, so
Intent to slay, to spill blood of its foe,
As is fierce Palamon against Arcite.
The jealous strokes into their helmets bite,
Out runs the blood, down both their sides they bleed.   2635

In time there comes an end to every deed,
As when that day, before the sun had set,
Strong King Emetrius charged forth to get
At Palamon as he fought with Arcite;
His sword out of his flesh took quite a bite,   2640
Then twenty men grabbed Palamon, to take
Him, though he struggled, over to the stake.
Strong King Lycurgus moved with the intent
To rescue him, but down Lycurgus went,
While King Emetrius, for all his strength,   2645
Got knocked from his saddle by a sword's length,
From Palamon receiving such a blow.
But to the stake now Palamon must go;
His hardiness of heart went all for naught,
He had to stay right there once he was caught,   2650
By force and rules by which the jousts were run.
    Who sorrows now but woeful Palamon,
Unable to return again to fight?
When Theseus had witnessed such a sight,
To those who fought, to each and every one,   2655
He cried, "Hear ye! No more, for it is done!
As true impartial judge I now decree
Arcite the Theban shall have Emily,
For by his fortune he has fairly won."
Such noise by the crowd was then begun   2660
In joy at this, so loud and high the sound,
It seemed the lists would fall right to the ground.
    And what now can fair Venus do above?
What can she say or do, this queen of love?
She weeps at this denial of her will   2665
Till with her tears the lists begin to fill.
"Without a doubt I'm put to shame," she cried.
    "Be still, my daughter!" Saturn then replied.
"Mars has his will, his knight has all his boon,
But, by my head, you'll have your pleasure soon."   2670
    The trumpeteers, musicians playing loud,
And heralds loudly crying to the crowd
Were all in utter joy for Sir Arcite.
But stop and hear me now as I recite

A miracle that suddenly took place.   2675
    Fierce Arcite, to reveal his joyous face,
Had taken off his helmet. On his horse
He then set out across the lengthy course
While gazing up at Emily on high;
And she in turn cast him a friendly eye—   2680
For womenfolk in general, I must say,
Will follow Fortune's favor all the way—
And she was all his joy, his heart's delight.
    A Fury sent from Pluto bounded right
Out of the ground (sent by request, of course,   2685
Of Saturn), which so frightened Arcite's horse
It turned and reared, and foundered in the act,
So quickly that before he could react
Arcite was thrown and landed on his head,
And lay there as if likely he were dead;   2690
His breast was shattered by his saddlebow.
He lay as black as any coal or crow,
The blood rushed so profusely to his face.
Arcite at once was borne out of the place,
With aching heart, back to the palace. There   2695
They cut him out of all his armored wear,
Then quickly but with care put him to bed;
For he was still alive and in his head
And crying evermore for Emily.
    Duke Theseus, with all his company,   2700
As he returned to Athens, made his way
With all the usual pageant and display;
For though mischance had surely cast a pall,
He didn't want to disconcert them all.
And men were saying, "Arcite shall not die,   2705
His wounds shall all be healed." And they could sigh
As well in the relief that, though it thrilled,
The tourney ended up with no one killed—
Though some were badly hurt, and namely one
Who'd caught a spear, which through his heart had run.   2710
For other wounds and for the broken arms,
Some had some salves and some had magic charms;
They drank of sage, all herbal remedies

Designed to save them their extremities.
This noble duke, as such a noble can,   2715
Both comforted and honored every man,
And gave a revel lasting all the night
For all these foreign nobles, as was right.
For there was held to have been no defeat
Save what in jousts and tourneys one may meet;   2720
Defeat was truly no one's circumstance.
To take a fall is nothing more than chance,
As to be led by force out to the stake,
With protest it takes twenty knights to break—
One man all by himself with twenty foes   2725
And carried by his arms and feet and toes,
His courser being driven forth with staves
By footmen (some were yeomen, some were knaves).
No man could be maligned because of this;
There is no man could call it cowardice.   2730
    So Theseus at once gave the decree,
To stop all rancor and all enmity,
That one side's strength did not exceed the other's,
That both sides were alike, as if all brothers.
By rank he gave them gifts as well as praise,   2735
Gave them a feast that lasted three whole days;
Then all the kings who had been at the tourney
He rode with from his town a lengthy journey,
And every man went home his proper way,
And that was that, with "Farewell!" and "Good day!"   2740
So of this battle no more I'll recite,
But speak of Palamon and of Arcite.
    The breast of Arcite swelled, the pain and sore
About his heart increasing more and more.
The clotting blood, despite physicians' art,   2745
Corrupted as it spread out from his heart,
So that no bleedings nor the cuppings made,
Nor drinking herbal mixtures, were of aid.
The expulsive power (being the "animal")
From that one that is known as "natural"   2750
Could not void all the venom nor expel.
The pipes within his lungs began to swell,

And every muscle that was in his chest
With venom and corruption filled his breast.
And there was nothing gained, that he might live, 2755
By upward vomit, downward laxative,
For all had been so shattered in his breast
That Nature had no power to arrest.
And certainly if Nature won't work, tote
The man to church, farewell to antidote. 2760
Arcite would die and that's the summary.
And so he sent for lovely Emily
And Palamon, his cousin once so dear,
And then he spoke as you will promptly hear.
 "The woeful spirit that is in my heart 2765
Cannot describe my sorrows, all the smart,
O lady whom I love, that you might hear it.
But I bequeath the service of my spirit
To you above all creatures on the earth,
Since now my life must end, for what it's worth. 2770
Alas, the woe, alas, the pain so strong
That for you I have suffered for so long!
Alas, now death! Alas, my Emily,
Alas, bereft of your sweet company!
Alas, queen of my heart! Alas, my wife, 2775
My heart's own lady, ender of my life!
What is this world? What is it men so crave?
Now with his love, now in his frigid grave
Where he's alone with none for company.
Farewell, my sweetest foe, my Emily! 2780
Now softly take me in your arms, I pray,
For love of God, and hear what I must say.
 "I have here with my cousin Palamon
Had strife and rancor many days, not one,
For love of you and in my jealousy. 2785
O Jupiter so wise, be guide to me
To speak now of a servant as I should—
That is to say, of virtues like knighthood,
Like wisdom, honor, truth, humility,
High birth and rank, like generosity, 2790
And all the things that are to these akin.

As Jupiter may take my spirit in,
In all this world right now I know of none
So worthy to be loved as Palamon,
Who serves you and will do so all his life.   2795
And if you ever would become a wife,
Forget not Palamon, this gentle man."
And with those words, failing of speech began,
As from his feet up to his breast had come
The cold of death, which had him overcome;   2800
In his once mighty arms the vital strength
Began to wane, till finally lost at length;
And then the intellect, all that remained
And dwelt within his heart so sick and pained,
Began to fail. The heart was feeling death;   2805
His eyes were glazed, and failing was his breath.
His lady was the last thing he could see,
And his last words were, "Mercy, Emily!"
His spirit left its house and went to where
I cannot say, I've never journeyed there—   2810
I'll stop, for I'm no good at divination;
This tale is not of souls for registration
Nor do I wish opinions here to tell
Of those who write of where a soul may dwell.
Arcite is cold, Mars guide his spirit free!   2815
Now I will speak again of Emily.
    She shrieked; Palamon howled, such was his plaint;
So Theseus then took his sister, faint,
And from the corpse at once bore her away.
But would it help were I to take all day   2820
To tell how she wept day and night? For in
Such cases women have such sorrow (when,
That is to say, their husbands from them go)
They usually will grieve exactly so,
Or else fall sick with such a malady   2825
That death comes to them too with certainty.
    Unending were the sorrow and the tears
Of elders and of those of tender years
In all the town because of his demise;
For him both child and man had tearful eyes.   2830

So great a weeping surely wasn't heard
When they brought Hector, slain, to be interred
At Troy. Alas, the mourning that was there,
Gashing of cheeks and pulling out of hair.
"Why dead?" the women cry. "Why should you be,   2835
Who had both gold enough and Emily?"
No man could bring some cheer to Theseus
Except for his old father Aegeus,
Who knew this world with all its transmutation
As he had seen it change with alternation,   2840
Joy after woe, and more woe after joy.
Then cases and examples he'd employ:
     "Just as there's never died a man," said he,
"Who didn't live on earth to some degree,
So there's no man who's ever drawn a breath   2845
In all this world whose time won't come for death.
This world is but a thoroughfare of woe
And we are pilgrims passing to and fro.
Death is an end to every worldly care."
And he had many other words to share   2850
In this regard, that people might be taught
To take more comfort, not be so distraught.
     Duke Theseus then took the greatest care
In looking for a proper setting where
They'd build for good Arcite a sepulchre   2855
That most deserving honor would confer.
At last the duke decided on the one
Where at the first Arcite and Palamon
For love in battle with each other strove;
There in that very same green, fragrant grove   2860
Where Arcite spoke his amorous desires,
Where he complained of love's hot burning fires,
For services a fire the duke would light
And at the pyre perform the funeral rite.
He gave command at once for them to mow   2865
The ancient oaks and lay them in a row
Of fagots set for burning. Rapidly
His officers would run, immediately
To mount and ride away at his command.

And after this, the duke dispatched a band   2870
To go and bring a bier, one fully clad
With cloth of gold, the richest that he had,
And with a matching suit he clad Arcite.
On Arcite's hands were fitted gloves of white,
Upon his head a laurel crown of green,   2875
And in his hand a sword both bright and keen.
The duke then laid him barefaced on the bier
And wept till it was pitiful to hear;
And so that Arcite might be seen by all,
When it was day he brought him to the hall,   2880
Which roared with all the crying and the din.
   The woeful Theban Palamon came in
With frowsy beard and rough ash-covered hair,
His clothing black and stained with tears. And there,
Surpassing all who wept, came Emily,   2885
The one most grieved of all the company.
Because he thought the services should be
Noble and rich for one of such degree,
Three steeds Duke Theseus then had them bring,
With trappings made of steel, all glittering,   2890
And covered with the arms of Sir Arcite.
Upon these steeds, which all were large and white,
Were mounted men—one Arcite's shield to bear,
Another with his spear high in the air,
His Turkish bow the third one proud to hold,   2895
With quiver and with trim of burnished gold.
And forth they sadly rode at mourners' gait
Toward the grove as you'll hear me relate.
The noblest of the Greeks from far and near
Upon their shoulders carried Arcite's bier   2900
At slackened pace, their eyes a tearful red,
Along the city's main street. They had spread
Black cloth along the street, and from great height
The same hung on each side. Upon the right
Hand there came next the old man Aegeus   2905
And on the other side Duke Theseus,
In hand fine golden vessels, which had in
Them milk and honey, blood and wine; and then

Came Palamon with a great company,
And after that came woeful Emily   2910
With fire in hand (the custom of the day,
That all the rites be done the proper way).
　　Much labor and the greatest preparation
Were spent upon the pyre and ministration—
A pyre so high its top the heavens fetched,   2915
And in its breadth some twenty fathoms stretched
(So broad were all the boughs, that is to say).
First there was many a load of straw to lay.
But how the pyre was made so high to reach,
And names of trees like alder, maple, beech,   2920
Fir, laurel, plane, birch, poplar, aspen too,
Elm, willow, hazel, chestnut, aspen, yew,
Box, dogwood, ash, and oak, as well as how
They felled them all, I won't go telling now;
Nor how the deities ran to and fro   2925
(The dryads, nymphs, and fauns), all forced to go,
Abandoning the habitations where
They'd known such rest and peace without a care;
Nor how the beasts and birds in those woods all
Began to flee as trees began to fall;   2930
Nor how the ground was fearful of the light,
Not ever having seen the sun so bright;
Nor how with straw they first began the fire,
Then dry sticks split in threes to build it higher;
Then spices, then wood hewn from greenest limbs,   2935
Then cloth of gold, along with precious gems
And many-flowered garlands, myrrh, incense,
With odor great and pleasant to the sense;
Nor how among all this Arcite lay there
With riches all about him; nor how fair   2940
And mournful Emily went to the pyre,
As was the custom, with the funeral fire;
Nor how she swooned as flames began to start,
Nor what she spoke, nor what was in her heart;
Nor what jewels into the fire were cast   2945
When it was leaping high and burning fast;
Nor how one cast a shield, and one a spear,

And some parts of their clothes, about the bier;
Nor how the wine and milk and blood were poured
Into the fire, nor how it wildly soared;   2950
Nor how the Greeks in one huge mounted rout
Three times from left to right then rode about
The fire with mighty shouts, and three times more
Gave out a clatter with their lances; nor
How thrice the ladies cried out piteously,   2955
Nor how led home at last was Emily;
Nor how to ashes cold had burnt Arcite,
Nor how for him a wake was held that night,
Nor how the Greeks performed each funeral game—
To speak of such as that is not my aim   2960
(Who wrestled best while nude and well anointed
And never got in trouble or disjointed);
I also shall not tell how everyone
Went home to Athens when the games were done.
To get right to the point I intend,   2965
To bring my lengthy story to an end.
    In course of time, the length of certain years,
There ended all the mourning and the tears
Among the Greeks by popular assent.
I think that there was then a parliament   2970
In Athens to discuss affairs of state.
Among the things decided in debate
Was to ally themselves with certain lands
And also govern Thebes with firmer hands.
And so this noble Theseus decreed   2975
That Palamon appear, as was agreed—
The reason why unknown to Palamon,
Who still in black, still as a mourning one,
Came at the duke's commandment hastily.
And Theseus then sent for Emily.   2980
When they had sat, and hushed was all the place,
Duke Theseus was silent for a space;
Before a word came from the wise duke's breast,
He looked about, then his eyes came to rest.
His face was sad, he sighed as all was still,   2985
Then he began to speak to them his will:

"When the Prime Mover, that First Cause above,
First made the chain so fair that's known as love,
The effect was great, and high was his intent—
He knew the why's and wherefore's, what he meant.   2990
For with that chain of love the Mover bound
The fire, the air, the water, and the ground
To certain bounds from which they may not flee.
And that same Prince and Mover," then said he,
"Established in this wretched world below   2995
The days of the duration they may know,
All those who are engendered in this place,
Beyond which days they cannot take a pace
But which may well be shortened. Here we see
There is no need for an authority,   3000
For it is proven by experience.
I want you to be clear as to my sense:
By this Prime Mover's order men are able
To see that he's eternal, always stable;
For every man should know, unless a fool,   3005
Each part comes from the whole (a simple rule),
For Nature has not taken its beginning
From any part or portion of a thing
But from a thing that's perfect, without change,
Corrupted only in this lower range.   3010
And so he has, in his wise providence,
Established without flaw his ordinance
That kinds of things in all of their progressions
Shall have endurance only by successions
And shall not be eternal. This is seen   3015
With but a glance, you follow what I mean.
    "Look at the oak, how long its flourishing
Since way back when it first began to spring;
It has so long a life, as men may see,
Yet wasted at the last is every tree.   3020
    "Consider, too, the hardness of each stone
Beneath our feet: each one we're treading on
Will finally waste away where it may lie.
The broadest river someday will be dry,
We see great cities wane till they have passed.   3025

And so we see that nothing's born to last.
　"Of men and women, we can also see
That in whichever term of life we be
(That is to say, in youth or else in age),
We all must die, the king just like the page,　　　　3030
Some in the sea, some in the bed serene,
Some on the battlefield, as men have seen.
There is no help, we all wind up one way.
So everything must die, well I can say.
　"And who does this but Jupiter the king　　　　3035
Who is the prince and cause of everything,
Converting all that is back to the well
From which it sprung, as truly we can tell?
And here again no creature that's alive
Will find avail, however one may strive.　　　　3040
　"Then it is wisdom, it appears to me,
To make a virtue of necessity
And take well that which we cannot eschew,
Especially that which is all our due.
Complaint is folly, whoso has decried　　　　3045
Resists the very one who is our guide.
And surely one's most honored if his time
Has come while in his excellence and prime,
When he can die still sure of his good name.
He's done to friend and to himself no shame;　　　　3050
Then should his friend be gladder at his death,
When it's with honor he yields up his breath,
Than when his name is faded later on
And he's forgotten, youth and glory gone.
So it is best, in terms of lasting fame,　　　　3055
To die while at the height of one's acclaim.
　"To be opposed to this is willfulness.
Why do we groan, or let it so depress,
That Arcite in the flower of chivalry
Has passed away, with honor, dutifully,　　　　3060
Departing the foul prison of this life?
Why grieving are his cousin and his wife—
Whom Arcite loved so much—for his well-being?
Can Arcite thank them? No, God knows, when seeing

How they offend themselves, not just his soul. 3065
Yet these are feelings they cannot control.
   "How shall I end this lengthy argument
Save after woe let there be merriment,
With thanks to Jupiter for all his grace?
And I advise before we leave this place 3070
We take two sorrows and with them endeavor
To make one perfect joy to last forever.
Let's look to where most sorrow lies herein,
Where we can help amend and so begin."
   He said, "My sister, this is my intent, 3075
With the advice here of my parliament:
This gentle Palamon who is your knight,
Who serves you with his will and heart and might
(And always has since you first saw his face),
You shall have pity on, and by your grace 3080
Shall take him as your husband and your lord.
Lend me your hand, for this is our accord,
And, as a woman should, show sympathy.
He's nephew of a king, and yet if he
Were nothing but a poor knight bachelor, 3085
So many years he's served you, as it were,
And has for you known such adversity,
I'd still consider him most favorably,
For mercy should transcend one's social station."
   To Palamon he said then in summation: 3090
"I don't think there's a sermon I need bring
To get you to assent to such a thing;
Come here and take your lady by the hand."
   The two at once were joined in the grand
And holy union that is known as marriage 3095
Before the council and the baronage.
And so amid much bliss and melody
Has Palamon been wed to Emily;
So God on high, who all this world has wrought,
Has sent to him his love so dearly bought. 3100
Now Palamon had all that's known as wealth,
To live in bliss, in richness and in health;
And Emily loved him so tenderly,

And he served her with such nobility,
That not one word between this man and wife   3105
Would ever be of jealousy or strife.
So ended Palamon and Emily,
And God save all this lovely company! Amen.

The Miller's Tale

PROLOGUE

Words between the Host and the Miller

Now when the worthy Knight his tale had told,
In all the group there wasn't young or old   3110
Who didn't say it was a noble story,
One well to be remembered for its glory
(The gentlefolk believed this all the more).
"As I may walk," our Host then laughed and swore,
"This goes all right, the bag's been opened well.   3115
Let's see who's next now with a tale to tell,
For truly has the game been well begun.
So tell us now, Sir Monk, if you know one
Of any kind to match the Knight's good tale."
The Miller, so completely drunk and pale   3120
That on his horse he insecurely sat,
Unwilling to remove his hood or hat,
Would not await his turn with courtesy
But in a voice like Pilate's bellowed he
And swore, "By arms and blood and every bone,   3125
I have a noble story! I'll go on
With it and match the good Knight with his tale."
Our Host could see that he was drunk with ale,
And said, "Now, Robin, wait, beloved brother,
Some better man shall tell us first another.   3130
Let's work this thriftily, await your spot."
    "By God's soul," said the Miller, "I will not.
I'll either speak or else be on my way."
Our Host said, "What the devil, have your say!
You are a fool, your wit is overcome."   3135
    "Now listen," said the Miller, "all and some!
I want to make a statement first: I know
That I am drunk by how I'm sounding, so

83

If I should be remiss in what I say,
Attribute it to Southwark ale, I pray.   3140
For I will tell a legend and a life
Both of a carpenter and of his wife,
And how a student made him look the sap."
      The Reeve here interjected, "Shut your trap!
Let's have no lewd and drunken ribaldry.   3145
It's sinful folly to cause injury
To any man, to be defaming him,
To bring up wives and start defaming them.
You have enough of other things to say."
      This drunken Miller answered right away,   3150
Saying, "Dear brother Oswald, he who's got
No wife is not a cuckold. I do not
Mean to suggest by that that you are one.
Although there's many a good wife, far from none,
For every thousand good ones there's a bad.   3155
You know that well unless you're raving mad.
Why, then, are you so angry with my story?
I have a wife as well as you, by glory,
Yet I'd not, for the oxen in my plow,
Take more upon myself by thinking now   3160
That I'm also a cuckold. In my mind
I'm certain that I'm nothing of the kind.
One shouldn't be inquiring anyway
Into God's privities or his wife's. May
He find God's plenty in her, that's enough,   3165
He shouldn't pry into that other stuff."
      What more should I say of this Miller than
He would not hold his tongue for any man
But told his churlish tale as he saw fit?
Here I regret to be retelling it.   3170
And therefore all your gentlefolk, I pray,
For love of God, don't think what I must say
Is with an ill intent; I must recount
The bad tales with the good or else discount
Material and thereby falsify.   3175
Those wishing not to hear it, pass it by,
Just turn the page and choose another sort;

You'll find all kinds of tales, both long and short,
That touch on genteel things, on history,
On holiness, and on morality.   3180
Don't blame me if you choose the wrong one, though;
The Miller is a churl as you well know,
As was the Reeve (and others were as well),
And both of them had lusty tales to tell.
So be advised and don't hold me to blame;   3185
Men shouldn't take too seriously a game.

THE MILLER'S TALE

In Oxford there once lived a rich old lout
Who had some guest rooms that he rented out,
And carpentry was this old fellow's trade.
A poor young scholar boarded who had made   3190
His studies in the liberal arts, but he
Had turned his fancy to astrology
And knew the way, by certain propositions,
To answer well when asked about conditions,
Such as when men would ask in certain hours   3195
If they should be expecting drought or showers,
Or if they asked him what was to befall
Concerning such I can't recount it all.
     This student's name was Nicholas the Handy.
He led a secret love life fine and dandy,   3200
In private always, ever on the sly,
Though meek as any maiden to the eye.
With Nicholas there were no other boarders,
He lived alone, and had there in his quarters
Some fragrant herbs, arranged as best to suit,   3205
And he himself was sweeter than the root
Of licorice or any herb at all.
His *Almagest* and books both great and small,
An astrolabe for plotting outer space,
And counters used in math were all in place   3210
On shelves between the headposts of his bed.
His storage chest was draped with cloth of red,

And on its top there lay a psaltery
On which at night he'd play a melody,
So sweet a sound that all the chamber rang;   3215
And *Angelus ad virginem* he sang,
And after that would follow "The King's Note."
Folks often praised him for his merry throat.
And this was how this sweet clerk's time was spent,
While friends provided money for his rent.   3220
    The carpenter had newly wed a wife,
One whom he loved more than his very life;
Her age was eighteen years. He jealously
Kept her as if inside a cage, for she
Was one both young and wild, and he had fears   3225
Of being a cuckold, so advanced in years.
Not educated, he had never read
Cato: one like himself a man should wed,
He ought to marry mindful of his state,
For youth and age are often at debate.   3230
But since he had been captured in the snare,
Like others folks he had his cross to bear.
    And fair this young wife was! She had withal
A body like a weasel, slim and small.
She wore a belt with little stripes of silk;   3235
An apron was as white as morning milk
Upon her loins, pleated daintily.
Her white smock, too, had fine embroidery;
The collar was embellished round about
With lovely coal-black silk inside and out,   3240
And ribbons on the snowy cap she wore
Were of the same silk that her collar bore.
She wore a silken headband, broad and high.
And certainly she had a wanton eye;
Her brows were thinly plucked, and like a bow   3245
Each one was arched, and black as any sloe.
Indeed she was a blissful sight to see,
Moreso than any pear tree that could be
And softer than the wool upon a wether.
Upon her belt was hung a purse of leather,   3250
Silk-tasseled and with brassy spangles pearled.

And there's no man so wise in all this world,
Though you may go and search it every inch,
Could dream a doll so lovely, such a wench.
And brighter far did shine her lovely hue   3255
Than gold coins in the Tower when they're new.
Her song was loud and lively as the call
Of any swallow perching on the wall.
She'd skip about and play some game or other
As any kid or calf behind its mother.   3260
Her mouth was sweet as any mead whatever
Or as a hoard of apples on the heather.
Skittish she was, just like a jolly colt,
Tall as a mast, straight as an archer's bolt.
The brooch on her low collar was as large   3265
As is the boss upon a shield or targe.
Her shoes, well laced, high up her legs would reach.
She really was a primrose, quite a peach,
One fit for any lord to lay in bed
Or any worthy working man to wed.   3270
    Now sir, and sir again, it came to pass
That one fine day this Handy Nicholas
With this young wife began to flirt and play,
Her husband off at Osney (anyway
These clerks are cunning when it comes to what   3275
They want), and slyly caught her by the twat;
"Surely," he said, "if I don't have my will,
For secret love, dear, I'll have quite a spill."
He held her hips as he went on to say,
"My darling, you must love me right away   3280
Or I will die, God save me!" Like a colt
Inside a shoeing frame she tried to bolt,
She turned her face away defiantly.
"Upon my faith, you'll get no kiss from me!
Why, let me go," she said, "stop, Nicholas,   3285
Or I will cry 'Out!', 'Help me!' and 'Alas!'
Unhand my body, show some courtesy!"
    But then for mercy he made such a plea
And spoke so fairly, offering so fast
His all to her, that she agreed at last   3290

To grant to him her love: she made her promise
To be at his commandment, by Saint Thomas
Of Kent, when she saw opportunity.
"My husband is so full of jealousy,
If you don't wait and privy be," she said,   3295
"I know right well that I'm as good as dead.
You must be secret, keep this matter quiet."
   "Nay," Handy said, "don't you be worried by it.
A clerk has for his time not much to show
If he can't fool a carpenter." And so   3300
The two were in accord and gave their word
To wait awhile as you've already heard.
When Nicholas got through with all of this
And felt her good below the waist, a kiss
He gave her sweetly, took his psaltery,   3305
And played it hard, a lively melody.
   Now to the parish church it came to pass
That in her Christian works and for the mass
This good wife went upon one holy day.
Her forehead shone as bright as day, the way   3310
She'd scrubbed it so when washing after work.
Now in that church there was a parish clerk
Whose name was Absalon. His curly hair
Was shiny, bright as gold found anywhere,
And spread out like a broad fan on his head   3315
With straight and even part. A healthy red
Was his complexion, eyes gray as a gander.
The tracery of Saint Paul's was no grander
Than his shoes' openwork, with fine red hose.
The lad was trimly dressed from head to toes;   3320
He wore a sky-blue tunic that in places
Was tricked out with the loveliest of laces,
And over it his surplice was as bright
As any blossom seen, a purest white.
A merry child he was, as God may save.   3325
He well could let your blood, and clip and shave,
And draw you up a deed and quittance too.
Some twenty different ways the fellow knew
To demonstrate the latest Oxford dance;

He'd kick his heels about and blithely prance   3330
And play some merry tunes upon the fiddle.
Loud treble he was known to sing a little
And he could play as well on the guitar.
In Oxford there was not a single bar
That he did not go visit with his act   3335
If there was any barmaid to attract.
To tell the truth, a fart would make him squeamish,
And he was always proper in his English.
　　This Absalon so jolly, fond of play,
Went with a censer on that holy day   3340
To cense the parish wives. And as he passed,
Many a longing look on them he cast—
Especially on this carpenter's wife.
Just looking at her made a merry life.
She was so neat and sweet, this wanton spouse,   3345
That if he'd been a cat and she a mouse
At once he would have caught her. Absalon,
This parish clerk so jolly, full of fun,
Could not, for the love-longing in his heart,
Take offerings from wives, he'd take no part,   3350
For courtesy, he said, and never might.
　　The moon, when night had come, was full and bright
As Absalon took guitar under arm,
His thoughts upon whom he might wake and charm;
Thus amorous and jolly, off he strode   3355
Until he reached the carpenter's abode
Soon after cockcrow. He then took his station
Beside a casement window, its location
Right in the old man's bedroom wall. And there
He daintily began to sing his air: 3360
"Now, dearest lady, if your will it be,
It is my prayer that you will pity me."
He sang and played the guitar right in tune.
The carpenter awoke and heard him croon
And said then to his wife, "Why, Alison,   3365
What's going on? Is that not Absalon
Who's chanting there below our bedroom wall?"
And she replied, "Yes, John, no doubt at all,

As God knows, I can hear him tone for tone."
    Now shouldn't one leave well enough alone?   3370
From day to day this jolly parish clerk
Wooed her till he was woebegone. He'd work
Upon it night and day and never rest;
He'd comb his spreading locks, he smartly dressed;
By go-betweens and proxies he would woo   3375
And swore he'd be her servant ever true;
He warbled to her like a nightingale;
He sent her honeyed wine, some mead, spiced ale,
And cakes still piping hot. And since she knew
Of city ways, he offered money too;   3380
For some folks can be won by such largess,
And some by blows, and some by kindliness.
    To show her his abilities so varied,
He even went on stage, portraying Herod.
But what would this avail him with the lass?   3385
For she so loved this Handy Nicholas
That Absalon could elsewhere toot his horn;
He had for all his labor only scorn.
And so she made poor Absalon an ape,
Made all his earnest efforts but a jape.   3390
The proverb tells the truth, it's not a lie,
Here's how it goes: "The one nearby and sly
Will always make the distant dear one hated."
Though Absalon go mad, wrath unabated
Because he was so far out of her sight,   3395
Nigh Nicholas was standing in his light.
    Well may you fare, O Handy Nicholas,
For Absalon must wail and sing "Alas"!
And so it was that on one Saturday
The carpenter to Osney made his way,   3400
And Handy Nicholas and Alison
Were in accord on what was to be done,
That Nicholas should now devise a wile,
This simple jealous husband to beguile;
And if their little game turned out all right,   3405
She then could sleep in Handy's arms all night,
As this was his desire and hers as well.

So right away—no further words to tell,
For Nicholas no longer meant to tarry—
He slyly to his room began to carry   3410
Both food and drink to last a day or two.
He told her what to lead her husband through
If he should ask for Nicholas: she'd say
She didn't know his whereabouts, all day
Upon the lad she had not laid an eye;   3415
She thought some malady he had was why,
For though her maid cried out, the lad to call,
He wouldn't answer any way at all.
    So this went on for all that Saturday;
This Nicholas up in his chamber lay,   3420
And ate and slept, or did what he thought best,
Till Sunday when the sun went to its rest.
This simple carpenter began to wonder
About him, if some ailment had him under.
"By dear Saint Thomas, I'm now full of dread   3425
That things aren't right with Nicholas," he said.
"O God forbid that suddenly he's died!
For sure a ticklish world's where we abide;
Today I saw 'em tote a corpse to kirk
Though Monday last I saw the man at work.   3430
    "Go up," he told his knave at once. "Go on,
Call at his door, knock on it with a stone,
See how it is, and tell me truthfully."
    The knave went up the stairway sturdily
And cried out at the chamber door; he stood   3435
There pounding like a madman on the wood.
"What are you at, O Master Nicholay?
How can you sleep for all the livelong day?"
    All was for naught, for he heard not a sound.
But then a hole low in the door he found   3440
(The one through which the cat was wont to creep),
And through this hole he took a thorough peep
Until at last he had the lad in sight.
This clerk sat gaping upward as he might
If he were staring off at the new moon.   3445
He went back down the stairs, and none too soon,

To tell his master how he'd seen the man.
   To cross himself the carpenter began,
And said, "Help us, I pray, Saint Frideswide!
A man knows little or what shall betide.   3450
This man has fallen with his astromy
Into some madness or some malady.
I always figured it would end just so!
God's privacy's a thing men shouldn't know.
Yea, blessed always is the simple man   3455
Who knows his creed and that is all he can!
So fared another clerk with astromy:
He walked out through the fields to try to see
The future in the stars, and got for it
A fall into a fertilizer pit,   3460
One he had not foreseen. Yet by Saint Thomas,
I pity Handy Nicholas. I promise,
He shall be scolded for such studying,
If that I may, by Jesus, heaven's King!
Get me a staff, and neath the door I'll pry   3465
While you heave on it, Robin. By and by
He'll come out of his studying, I'll bet."
Then at the chamber door he got all set.
His knave was very strong in any case
And by the hasp he heaved it from its place,   3470
The door went falling in right to the floor.
Nicholas sat as stonily as before,
Continuing to gape into the air.
The carpenter assumed it was despair;
He took him by the shoulders mightily   3475
And shook him hard, and cried reproachingly,
"What is it, Nicholay? Look down! Awake,
Think on Christ's passion! Here the sign I make
Now of the cross, from elf and evil sprite
To keep you." He began then to recite   3480
At once a night-spell on the walls about
As well as on the threshold leading out:
"O Jesus and Saint Benedict, we pray
You'll bless this house from every demon's sway.
Night falls—White Paternoster, help defeat her! 3485

Where have you gone, O sister of Saint Peter?"
    And then at last this Handy Nicholas
Began to sorely sigh, and said, "Alas!
Shall all the world so soon be swept away?"
    The carpenter replied, "What's that you say?   3490
On God, like we hard workers do, now think."
    And Nicholas then said, "I need a drink,
And afterwards we'll speak in privacy
Of certain things concerning you and me.
I'll surely tell no other what I've learned."   3495
    The carpenter went down, then soon returned,
With a full quart of strong ale, up the stairs;
And when they both had finished up their shares,
Nick tightly shut the door. As to confide,
This carpenter he set down by his side.   3500
    He said, "Now, John, my host both kind and dear,
Your word of honor you must give me here
That to no man this secret you'll disclose;
For it is Christ's own secret that I pose,
And if you tell it, sad will be your fate.   3505
There's such a vengeance if you should relate
What I'm to say, you'll reap insanity."
"By Christ's own holy blood, it shall not be,"
Old John replied, "for I am not a blabber,
No, I must say, I'm not an idle gabber.   3510
Say what you will, which I will never tell
To child nor wife, by him who harrowed hell!"
    "Now, John," said Nicholas, "believe you me,
I found this out through my astrology
As I looked on the moon when it was bright.   3515
This Monday at a quarter of the night
There shall come down so furious a rain
Not half its force did Noah's flood contain.
This world," he said, "in less than one small hour
Shall all be drowned, so hideous the shower.   3520
Mankind shall thus be drowned and lose all life."
    The carpenter replied, "Alas, my wife!
My Alison, alas! She too will drown?"
And in his sorrow nearly falling down,

He said, "No remedy will make it pass?"   3525
   "Why, yes, by God," said Handy Nicholas,
"If you'll work by sound learning and advice.
Don't work from your own head, that won't suffice.
As Solomon once said (and it is true),
'Work all by counsel and you'll never rue.'   3530
If you'll work by good counsel, I've no doubt
That mast and sail we then can do without,
For I will save your wife and you and me.
Have you not heard how Noah came to be
Saved by our Lord, who warned him beforehand   3535
That water was to devastate the land?"
   "Yes," said the carpenter, "quite long ago."
   "Have you not heard," said Nicholas, "also
Of Noah's troubles with his fellowship
Until he finally got his wife to ship?   3540
There is no doubt, I daresay, as to whether
He would have given up his last black wether
That she might have a vessel to herself.
Do you know, then, what's best to do yourself?
Haste is required, and for a hasty thing   3545
No time for preaching nor for tarrying.
   "Be off at once and fetch into this inn
Three kneading troughs or tubs—we'll have one then
For each of us; but see that each is large,
So each of us may float as on a barge.   3550
And have therein some victuals too, at best
Enough to last a day—fie on the rest!
The waters will subside and go away
At nine or so on the following day.
But Robin must not know of this, your knave,   3555
And Jill your maid I also cannot save;
Don't ask me why, for though you ask of me
I will not tell a soul God's privity.
Suffice it, John, lest you go raving mad,
To have the same good grace that Noah had;   3560
Your wife I'll surely save without a doubt.
Be on your way, get busy hereabout.
   "But when you have, for her and you and me,

Secured these kneading tubs, then hang the three
Up in the roof—and hang them very high,   3565
That our provision no man may espy.
And when you have accomplished what I've said,
And stored enough good fare to keep us fed,
An ax besides to whack the cord in two
When comes the rain, so we can ride it through;   3570
And when you've knocked a hole up in the gable,
Toward the garden and above the stable,
That we may freely pass upon our way
Until the mighty shower's gone away,
Then merrily we'll float, I undertake,   3575
Just as the white duck floats behind the drake.
'How, Alison! How, John!' I'll call to you.
'Be merry, for the flood will soon be through!'
And you will say, 'Hail, Master Nicholay!
Good morning, I can see you, it is day!'   3580
And then we shall be lords, throughout this life,
Of all the world, like Noah and his wife.
    "But of one thing you must be warned about:
Be well advised, on that night never doubt
That when each one of us has gone on board,   3585
We must not speak a word. We can't afford
One call or cry but only silent prayer,
For it's God's own dear will that I declare.
    "Your wife and you, therefore, hang far apart;
That twixt you two no sinful play may start   3590
(And I refer to sight as well as deed)
This ordinance is said. God give you speed!
Tomorrow night when everyone's asleep,
Into our kneading tubs we then shall creep
And there we'll sit awaiting God's good grace.   3595
Be on your way, I have no longer space
To sermonize on this, and so I'll cease.
It's said, 'But send the wise and hold your peace.'
Well, you are wise, so you I needn't teach.
Get going now and save us, I beseech."   3600
    This simple carpenter went on his way
With many an "Alas" and "Wellaway,"

And to his wife he told his privity.
Now she was well aware, much more than he,
Of what this cunning plan was to imply.   3605
She acted, though, as if about to die;
"Alas! go now immediately," she said,
"Help us escape or all of us are dead!
I am the truest of devoted wives,
So go, dear spouse, and help to save our lives."   3610
    See what a great thing is emotion! Why,
Of what one may imagine one can die,
So deep is the impression it can make.
This silly carpenter began to shake;
He feared he was to witness verily   3615
Old Noah's flood come rolling like the sea
To drown young Alison, his honey dear.
He weeps and wails, he looks so sad and drear
As many a sigh he heaves, a mournful sough.
He goes and gets a kneading trough somehow,   3620
One tub and then another, which he then
Has privately transported to the inn;
In privacy he hangs them as instructed.
Three ladders with his own hands he constructed
By which they would go climbing rung by rung   3625
Up to the rafters where the tubs were hung.
He put in each of them some cheese and bread
And good ale in a jug, to keep them fed
Sufficiently for what would be a day.
Before beginning, though, all this array   3630
He had his knave and maid as well to go
Upon an errand to London. And so
Upon that Monday, as it drew to night,
He shut the door, lit not one candlelight,
Arranged all things to look as they should be,   3635
And up into their tubs then climbed the three.
They sat the time a furlong takes to walk.
    Said Nick, "Now Paternoster, then no talk!"
And "Mum," said John, and "Mum," said Alison.
The carpenter's devotions were begun,   3640
He stilly sat, prayed to the Holy Spirit,

And waited for the rain, intent to hear it.
　　But dead asleep from all his weariness
The carpenter soon fell—it was, I guess,
Around the curfew time. Yet even then　　　　　　　　3645
He sorely groaned, such pain his soul was in.
(He also snored, the way his noggin lay.)
Then down his ladder crept young Nicholay,
And Alison down hers as softly sped;
Without a single word they went to bed　　　　　　　3650
Right where the carpenter was wont to be.
And there the revel and the melody!
For there lay Alison and Nicholas—
What mirth and pleasant business came to pass!—
Until the bell of Lauds began to ring　　　　　　　　3655
And friars in the chancel were to sing.
　　Now Absalon, the amorous parish clerk
(Still woebegone from being so lovestruck),
Upon that Monday was down Osney way
To join companions for some sport and play.　　　　　3660
While there he chanced to ask a cloisterer
In private about John the carpenter.
They went outside the church, and to this clerk
The monk said, "I've not seen him here at work
Since Saturday. I'd say, as best I have it,　　　　　　3665
He's been sent out for timber by the abbot.
For timber he will very often go
And stay out at the grange a day or so.
If not, he's surely at his house today.
Which place he's at I can't for certain say."　　　　　3670
　　This Absalon was thrilled, his heart was light.
"It's time," he thought, "to stay awake all night,
For I saw not one stirring of the man
About his door, not once since day began.
　　"As I may thrive, at crowing of the cock　　　　　3675
Privately at his window I will knock,
The one so low there in his bedroom wall.
To Alison I'll speak and tell her all
About my longing. This time I won't miss
But at the least will get from her a kiss.　　　　　　3680

That will be, by my faith, some consolation;
My mouth has itched all day, a situation
That is a sign of kissing at the least.
And, too, last night I dreamt about a feast.
Therefore I'll go and sleep an hour or two,   3685
Then I will stay up all the night and woo."
    At first cockcrow, at once from his repose
This jolly lover Absalon arose
And donned attire as smart as any viewed.
Some cardamon and licorice he chewed,   3690
To scent his breath, before he combed his hair.
A true-love herb as well he chose to bear
Beneath his tongue, thereby to be exquisite.
Then to the old man's house he made his visit.
There quietly he stood beneath the casement   3695
(It reached down to his breast, so low its placement);
He cleared his throat and spoke in softest voice:
"What are you doing, honeycomb, my choice
And fairest bird, my sweetest cinnamon?
Awake and speak to me, sweet Alison.   3700
How little do you think upon my woe;
I sweat for your love everywhere I go.
No wonder that I sweat and slave for it:
I'm longing as the lamb longs for the tit.
Yes, darling, I have for you such a love   3705
You've got me mourning like a turtledove,
My appetite's that of a maid," he cried.
    "Get from the window, jackass," she replied.
"So help me God, there'll be no 'come-and-kiss-me.'
I love another and, by Jesus, he   3710
Is better far than you or I'm to blame.
Unless you want a stoning, in the name
Of twenty devils, let me sleep. Away!"
    "Alas," said Absalon, "and welladay,
That my true love is ever so beset!   3715
At least then kiss me, if that's all I get,
For Jesus' love and for the love of me."
    "Will you then go," she said, "and let me be?"
"Yes, darling, surely," he was quick to say.

"Get ready, then," she said, "I'm on my way." 3720
To Nicholas she whispered, "Shh, be still;
Of laughter you're about to get your fill."
   Now Absalon got down upon his knees
And said, "I am a lord by all degrees,
For after this I hope there's more to follow. 3725
Come, grace me, darling, my sweet little swallow!"
   She opened up the window then with haste.
"Come on," she said, "be quick, no time to waste,
We don't want neighbors seeing you've come by."
   Absalon wiped his mouth till it was dry. 3730
The night was dark as pitch, as black as coal,
And from the window she stuck out her hole;
And Absalon, not knowing north from south,
Then kissed her naked ass with eager mouth
Before he was aware of all of this. 3735
Then back he started, something seemed amiss:
A woman has no beard, he knew as much,
Yet this was rough and hairy to the touch.
"O fie!" he said. "Alas! what did I do?"
   "Tee hee," said she, and clapt the window to. 3740
Poor Absalon had reached a sorry pass.
   "A beard, a beard!" laughed Handy Nicholas.
"God's body, this is really going swell."
   Poor Absalon heard all this very well,
In anger had to give his lip a bite, 3745
And to himself he said, "I'll set you right."
   Who's rubbing now, who's scrubbing now his lips
With dust, with sand, with straw, with cloth, with chips,
But Absalon, who's crying out "Alas!
May Satan take my soul if I'd not pass 3750
Up owning this whole town that I might be
Avenged for this despite they've done to me.
Alas," he cried, "I didn't turn aside!"
His hot love then was cold, indeed had died;
For from the time he kissed her naked ass 3755
He didn't give one cress for any lass,
For he'd been cured of all his malady;
All lovers he denounced repeatedly

And wept just like a child who has been whipped.
Across the street a little ways he slipped   3760
To see a blacksmith, Master Gervase, who
Was known for plow parts, shares and coulters too,
And at his forge was busy making more.
This Absalon knocked softly at his door
And said, "Quick, Gervase, get this door undone."   3765
    "Who's there?" he asked. "It's me, it's Absalon."
"Why, Absalon! By Christ's sweet tree, I say,
Why up so early? *Benedicite!*
What's ailing you? God knows, some merry girl
Is what brings you out prowling in a whirl,   3770
And by Saint Neot you follow what I mean."
    But Absalon was caring not a bean
For all his play, he didn't speak or laugh,
For he had much more tow on his distaff
Than Gervase knew. He said, "My friend so dear,   3775
This red-hot coulter in the chimney here—
Lend it to me. There's something I must do
And then right soon I'll bring it back to you."
    "Why, surely," Gervase said, "if it were gold
Or a poke of nobles in a sum untold,   3780
As I'm a smith, 'twould be yours every bit.
But what the devil will you do with it?"
    "Let that," said Absalon, "be as it may.
I'll tell you all about it when it's day."
He grabbed it by the handle, which was cool,   3785
And quietly went out, and with the tool
He went again to the carpenter's wall.
He cleared his throat to give a little call
And knocked upon the window as before.
    "Who's there?" he heard young Alison once more.   3790
"Who's knocking there? It is a thief, I'll bet."
    "Why, no," he said, "God knows, my little pet,
It's Absalon. My darling little thing,
I've brought for you," said he, "a golden ring.
So help me God, my mother gave it to me.   3795
It's well engraved, it is a fine thing truly.
I'll let you have it for another kiss."

Now Nicholas was up to take a piss,
And thought he would improve upon the jape
And have him kiss his ass ere he escape.   3800
He hastened to the window, turned around,
And stuck his bottom out without a sound,
Both buttocks and beyond, right to the thighs.
Then Absalon, who had to strain his eyes,
Said, "Speak, sweet bird, I know not where thou art."   3805
And Nicholas at this let fly a fart
So great it sounded like a thunderclap—
It nearly blinded Absalon, poor chap.
But he was set with his hot iron to move,
And Nicholas was smote right in the groove.   3810
    Off came the skin a handbreadth wide and some,
The hot iron had so burnt him in his bum,
And from the smart he thought that he would die.
Just like a madman he began to cry,
"Help! Water, water! Help me, for God's sake!"   3815
    The carpenter by then had stirred awake;
He heard mad cries of "Water!" loud and clear,
And thought, "Alas, the Flood of Noel's here!"
He sat right up without the least ado
And grabbed his ax and whacked the cord in two,   3820
Then down went everything—no time for sale
Of any of his bread or any ale:
He hit the floor, and there unconscious lay.
    Then Alison and Handy right away
Cried out "Help!" and "Disaster!" in the street.   3825
The neighbors, high and low, ran there to meet,
They stood and stared at poor unconscious John
Who lay there on the floor so pale and wan,
For from the fall he had a broken arm.
But he himself was blamed for all his harm;   3830
For when he spoke, each word was then denied
By Nicholas and Alison his bride.
They made the claim to all that he was mad:
Some ghastly fear of "Noel's flood" he had,
A fantasy that had him so deranged   3835
Three kneading tubs the old man had arranged

To buy and hang there in the roof above;
And then he had implored them, for God's love,
To sit up there and keep him company.

    The people laughed at such a fantasy;   3840
Up at the roof they all began to gape,
And turned the old man's harm into a jape.
No matter what the carpenter insisted,
It was for naught, his reasons were resisted.
With such great oaths the fellow was put down,   3845
He was considered mad throughout the town;
Each learned man agreed with every other,
Saying, "The man is mad, beloved brother,"
And everyone just laughed at all his strife.
So she was screwed, the carpenter's young wife,   3850
Despite all jealous safeguards he could try;
And Absalon has kissed her nether eye,
And Nicholas is scalded in the rear.
This tale is done, God save all who are here!

The Reeve's Tale

PROLOGUE

When folks had laughed at what had come to pass   3855
For Absalon and Handy Nicholas,
Different ones had different things to say
But for the most part took it all in play.
I didn't see the tale one man aggrieve,
Except, that is, for old Oswald the Reeve.   3860
Since carpentry had been the fellow's craft,
The tale left him with ire while others laughed.
He started grumbling, carping right away.
     "As I may thrive," he said, "you I'd repay
With blearing of a haughty miller's eye   3865
If I chose to give ribaldry a try.
But I'm too old for playing anyhow;
Grass-time is gone, my hay's cold fodder now.
This white top all my lengthy years declares,
And my heart, too, is moldy like my hairs.   3870
It's as if I were like the medlar tree,
The fruit of which will worsen gradually
Till rotten in the refuse or the straw.
We old men live, I fear, by that same law,
Until we rot we never can be ripe.   3875
We jig as long as this old world will pipe;
It ever pricks our will just like a nail
To have a hoary head and a green tail,
As does a leek. Although our might is gone,
Our will is that the folly carry on.   3880
What we can't do we still can well expound;
In our old ashes fire can still be found.
     "Four burning coals, I'll tell you, we possess:
Boasting, lying, wrath, and covetousness.
The elderly are keepers of these embers,   3885
And although weak may be our aged members
Desire will never fail us, that's the truth.

Yet I have always had a coltish tooth,
Though many a year has gone by since the one
When first my tap of life began to run. 3890
Yes, surely at my birth, without delay,
Death drew the tap that life might run away,
And ever since the tap of life has run
Till almost empty has become the tun;
The stream of life is dripping all the time. 3895
The simple tongue may well ring out and chime
Of wretched woes that passed so long before;
The old are left with dotage, nothing more."

On hearing such a preachy sort of thing,
Our Host spoke up as lordly as a king: 3900
"Now all this wisdom, what's the use of it?
Are we to speak all day of Holy Writ?
The devil's turned a reeve to preacher's mission,
A cobbler's now a skipper or physician.
Now tell your tale at once, don't be so wordy. 3905
Here's Deptford, it's already seven-thirty.
There's Greenwich, where there's many a rascal found,
And of your tale we've yet to hear a sound."

"Now, sirs," responded then Oswald the Reeve,
"I pray that none among you I'll aggrieve 3910
Though I shall make this Miller look the fool.
Meet force with force and that's a proper rule.

"We now have heard here from this drunken Miller
Of the beguiling of a carpenter,
Which may have been in scorn, for I am one. 3915
And, by your leave, now justice shall be done.
In his own churlish terms shall be my speech.
God, may his neck be broken, I beseech;
He well can see a speck that's in my eye,
But in his own a beam he can't espy." 3920

THE REEVE'S TALE

Near Cambridge there's a brook, at Trumpington,
And there's a bridge that stands above the run,

And by that brook there stands a water mill.
Now it's the truth I'd tell you and I will.
A miller there had dwelt for many a day;   3925
As proud as any peacock, he could play
The pipes, knew how to fish, mend nets to boot,
Turned many a cup, could wrestle well and shoot.
A long knife by his belt was always seen,
Also a sword, no other blade as keen;   3930
His pouch contained a dagger. He was such
That none, for fear of death, would dare to touch
Him. He'd a Sheffield knife inside his hose.
Round was his face, and snub-like was his nose,
His head as bald as any ape's. He fully   3935
Was a swaggerer, a market-bully,
And on him none a finger dared to lay
Or one would pay, he promised, right away.
He also was a thief of corn and meal,
A sly one, too, his habit was to steal.   3940
Now he was known by name as Haughty Simkin.
He had a wife who was of noble kin;
Her father, who was parson of the town,
As dowry many a brass pan handed down
To get this Simkin in the family.   3945
She had been brought up in the nunnery;
Simkin would take no wife, he used to say,
Except a virgin raised the proper way,
So that his yeoman status not be hurt.
She was proud as a magpie and as pert.   3950
A fair sight were these two on which to gaze:
He'd walk before her on the holy days
Wearing his hood all wrapped about his head,
And she'd come after in a cloak of red
(His hose were of the same). And not a one   3955
Called her a thing but "Madam"; there was none
So hardy, as they went along their way,
Who dared to flirt, to have the slightest play,
Lest Haughty Simkin take the fellow's life
With bodkin or with dagger, sword or knife.   3960
For jealous folks are dangerous (or so

They want their wives to think). This woman, though,
Was somewhat smirched and talked about, for which
She'd stand aloof like water in a ditch,
And she was full of scorn and great disdain;   3965
That she deserved respect she thought it plain,
What with her kin and all the wisdom she
Had learnt while she was in the nunnery.

    These two had raised a daughter who was then
Aged twenty; there was no one else, save in   3970
The cradle lying, one-half year of age,
A child who looked a proper future page.
The daughter was a well-developed lass;
She had a snub nose, eyes as gray as glass,
Her buttocks broad, her breasts were round and high;   3975
Her hair was very fair, I wouldn't lie.

    The parson of the town, as she was fair,
Had in his mind to make this girl his heir,
Both of his chattels and his house, so he
Made sure she'd not be wed too easily.   3980
His hope was to bestow this little bud
Upon a house of fine ancestral blood;
For Holy Church's goods must be intended
For Holy Church's blood that's well descended.
His holy blood he'd honor and empower   3985
Though Holy Church he thereby might devour.

    This miller made great profit without doubt
From tolls on wheat and malt from all about—
Especially the wheat and malt they'd haul
From that great Cambridge college Solar Hall;   3990
His mill was where they had to have it ground.
Now it so happened that one day they found
The college manciple sick in his bed;
They thought in fact he was as good as dead.
With that the miller's theft of grain was more   3995
(A hundredfold) than he had dared before;
Where once he stole as if with courtesy,
He now performed his theft outrageously.
The college warden fussed about the deed
Although the miller didn't give a weed,   4000

He'd only bluster and deny his crime.
    Two students, young and poor, were at the time
Residing in this hall of which I spoke.
Headstrong and lusty, both were playful folk,
And simply for their mirth and jollity   4005
They pleaded that the warden let them be
The next to have a turn at going round
To take corn to the mill and have it ground;
Each hardily proposed to risk his neck
To see the man did not steal half a peck   4010
By sleight or use of force. To their intent
The warden finally granted his assent.
Now one was John and Alan was the other;
They had both been born in a town called Strother
Far in the north, I do not know just where.   4015
    This Alan now was quickly to prepare,
The sack was on a horse without delay
And students John and Alan rode away,
Each with a sword and buckler by his side.
John knew the way, they didn't need a guide,   4020
Soon at the mill the sack was on the ground.
Spoke Alan first: "Hail, Simon, faith abound!
How fares thy lovely daughter and thy wife?"
    Said Simkin, "Welcome, Alan, by my life,
And John as well! How now, what brings you here?"   4025
    "Need," John replied, "by God, hath not a peer.
Who hath no knave must serve himself someway
Or else he be a fool, as clerics say.
Our manciple, I think, will soon be dead,
So aching aye the molars in his head;   4030
And therefore here now I and Alan be
To grind our corn and take it back. And thee,
I pray, will speed us quickly on our way."
    Said Simkin, "By my faith, I shall! I say,
What would you do while I take this in hand?"   4035
    "By God, right by the hopper I will stand,"
Said John, "to see how 'tis corn goeth in.
Yet saw I never by my father's kin
How that the hopper waggeth to and fro."

Then Alan answered with "John, wilt thee so?   4040
Then I will go beneath it, by my crown,
To see how that the cornmeal falleth down
Into the trough; that shall be my disport.
John, by my faith, we two be of a sort,
I be as ill a miller as art thee."   4045
　　This miller smiled at all their foolery;
He told himself, "All this is but a wile;
To trick them they think no one has the guile.
But by my thrift, hoodwinked they both shall be
For all the craft in their philosophy.   4050
For every trick, each clever move they make,
The more that I can steal the more I'll take;
Instead of flour I will give them bran.
'The greatest scholar's not the wisest man,'
As to the wolf, they say, once spoke the mare.   4055
For all their learning I don't give a tare."
　　Then out the door he hurried secretly,
When he had seen his time, and stealthily
He looked both left and right until he spied
The horse the clerks had ridden, standing tied   4060
Behind the mill beneath a shady limb.
The miller then went softly up to him
And stripped him of his bridle on the spot;
When he was loose, the horse began to trot
Toward the fen, where with wild mares he then   4065
Let out a whinny, ran through thick and thin.
　　The miller went back in, no word he spoke;
He set to work, and shared with them a joke
Or two, until their corn was fully ground.
But once the meal had all been sacked and bound,   4070
John went to find their horse had run away,
And started crying, "Harrow! Welladay!
Our horse is lost! Come, Alan, by God's bones,
Get on your feet, man, come! The horse," he groans,
"Our warden's palfrey now, alas, he's lost!"   4075
Both meal and corn from Alan's mind were tossed,
Precautions no more had him occupied.
"What sayest thee? Which way's he gone?" he cried.

The wife came running over to them then
And said, "Alas! he headed for the fen,   4080
Where mares are wild, as fast as he could go—
Thanks to the careless hand that tied him so,
For someone should have better tied the rein."

   "Alas!" said John. "Alan, by Christ's sweet pain,
Lay down thy sword, I'll lay down mine also.   4085
I be as swift, God knows, as is a roe,
And, by God's heart, he won't escape us both.
But why did thee not barn him? By my oath!
Alan, by God, thee art a fool!" he cried.

   These hapless clerks immediately hied   4090
Toward the fen, Alan as well as John.

   And when the miller saw that they were gone,
One half a bushel he was quick to take
And bade his wife go knead it for a cake.
He said, "It goes, I think, as both clerks feared.   4095
Yet can a miller tweak a student's beard
For all his learning. Let them go their way!
Look how they run! Yea, let the children play.
Their catch is not so easy, by my crown."

   These hapless students trotted up and down   4100
With "Whoa now! Whoa!" and "Stay there! Stay!
       Stand clear!
Go whistle thee, I'll try to keep him here!"
To keep it short, right up to fall of night
They still had failed to catch, try as they might,
This horse, for he would run away too fast,   4105
Till in a ditch they captured him at last.

   Then wet and weary, like beasts in the rain,
Came John and Alan trudging back again.
"Alas," said John, "the day that I was born!
We'll be derided now with shame and scorn.   4110
Our corn is swiped, we'll each be called a fool
Both by the warden and our friends at school,
And mainly by this miller. Curse the day!"

   Thus John complained as they were on their way,
Bayard in hand, back to the mill with ire.   4115
They found the miller sitting by the fire,

For it was night, no farther might they fare.
They begged, for love of God, that he might spare
Some lodging, for which they'd pay rent to him.
  "If there be any," he replied to them,   4120
"Such as it is you're welcome to your parts.
My house is small, but you have learnt the arts
And by your arguments can make a place
A mile in width from twenty feet of space.
Let's see if there is room, or else you may   4125
Make room by using words as is your way."
  "Now, Simon, by Saint Cuthbert, I can tell
That thee art bright," John said, "and answer well.
'Tis said, 'A man takes one of these two things:
That which he finds or else that which he brings.'   4130
But specially I pray, our host so dear,
Get us some meat and drink for our good cheer.
We'll pay ye for it fully, that's for sure.
There's nary hawk an empty hand can lure;
Look, here's our silver, ready to be spent."   4135
  This miller into town his daughter sent
For ale and bread, and roasted them a goose.
Their horse he tethered, no more getting loose.
In his own chamber he made them a bed
With sheets and blankets that were finely spread,   4140
Not more than ten or twelve feet from himself.
His daughter had a bed all by herself
That in that very chamber stood nearby—
The best that they could do, the reason why
Being the lack of room within the place.   4145
They supped and talked at ease, and all the space
They drank strong ale, and drank it like the best.
About midnight they finally went to rest.
  The miller was shellacked out of his head,
So drunk that he was pale instead of red.   4150
He hiccuped and was talking through his snout
As if with head cold or asthmatic bout;
To bed he went, and with him went his wife,
Feeling as free as any jay with life,
Her jolly whistle she so well had wet.   4155

At their bed's foot the cradle had been set,
To rock the child and let it suck the dug.
And after all had been drunk from the jug,
The daughter off to bed was quick to go;
And then to bed went Alan, John also,   4160
And that was that, no sleeping draught they need.
The miller had imbibed till like a steed
He snorted in his sleep, and paid no mind
At all to what his tail might do behind.
His wife provided bass both loud and clear,   4165
Their snoring for a furlong one could hear.
The wench was snoring too for company.
    The student Alan heard this melody,
Gave John a poke, and said, "Thee sleepest? How?
Hast ever thee heard such a song till now?   4170
Hear what a compline by them one and all.
The fire of hell upon their bodies fall!
Is there a stranger sound that so offends?
Yea, theirs shall be the flower of evil ends.
This whole night I'll get nary bit of rest.   4175
But wait—No matter, 'tis all for the best.
For, John," he said, "if ever it be true
That I may thrive, yon wench now I will screw.
Some recompense by law is given us,
For, John, the law so reckoneth and thus: 4180
If at one point a man should be aggrieved,
At yet another he shall be relieved.
Our corn is stolen, that is safe to say,
And he hath given us a fit all day;
I can't amend the loss, but there's an action   4185
By which at least I'll get some satisfaction.
By God's soul, it shall not be otherwise."
    "Now, Alan," John replied, "let me advise,
The miller is a dangerous man," he said.
"If from his sleep he hap to rear his head,   4190
He might do both of us some villainy."
    But Alan said, "He's less than is a flea."
Then up he rose and to the wench he crept.
She was supine as peacefully she slept,

Until, when she awoke, he was so nigh   4195
It would have been too late to give a cry,
And so, I'll briefly say, she took him on.
Play, Alan! Meanwhile I will speak of John.
　　John lay the time a furlong takes to walk
And gave himself a rueful little talk.   4200
"Alas," he thought, "this is a wicked jape!
Now may I say that I be but an ape.
My friend's appeased somewhat now for his harms,
He hath the miller's daughter in his arms.
He took a chance and now his needs be fed;   4205
I lie here like an old bran sack in bed.
And when this jape be told another day,
I'll be a fool, a 'cockney' they will say.
I'll rise and risk it, by my faith, instead!
'The cowardly's unlucky,' so it's said."   4210
So up he rose and softly headed for
The cradle, which he picked up from the floor;
To his bed's foot he softly carried it.
　　Soon after this, the wife her snoring quit
As she awoke and went outside to piss.   4215
She came back in, the cradle then to miss;
She couldn't find it as she groped along.
"Alas," she thought, "I almost headed wrong!
I almost got into the students' bed.
Ah, bless me, to what ill I would have sped!"   4220
She kept on till she found the cradle and,
By groping ever forward with her hand,
Then found the bed. She thought this well and good,
Being the bed whereby the cradle stood;
It was so dark she didn't know that she   4225
Crept in right by the clerk. There quietly
She lay, all set to sleep again, until
John soon leapt up and with a hearty will
Was lying on her. Hardly had this wife
Had such a merry fit in all her life,   4230
So hard and deep he thrust as if gone mad.
A jolly life that night these students had
Until the cock a third time was to sing.

Alan grew weary, day about to spring,
For he had labored all the livelong night.   4235
He said, "Farewell, my Molly sweet! The light
Of day is come, I may no longer bide.
But evermore, where I may go or ride,
I be thy clerk, as I may thrive 'tis so!"

　　She said, "Dear lover, fare-thee-well, then, go.   4240
There's one thing I should tell you, though, and will:
When you are heading homeward by the mill,
Right by the entrance of the door behind,
A loaf of half a bushel you will find,
And it was made out of the very meal   4245
That's yours, that which I helped my father steal.
God help you, lover, may he save and keep!"
And she, with that, almost began to weep.

　　Alan arose and thought, "Before 'tis day
I'll creep back in with John." Then right away   4250
His groping hand the baby's cradle found.
"By God," he thought, "I've turned the wrong way round.
My head is dizzy from my work tonight,
It hath me straying. This is not the right
Direction, by the cradle I can tell;   4255
The miller lieth here, his wife as well."
Then he, by twenty devils, took his way
To that bed where in fact the miller lay.
Thinking to find his comrade John, he crept
Right in beside the miller where he slept.   4260
He grabbed him by the neck and softly said,
"Hey, John, wake up, for Christ's soul, ye swinehead,
And listen. Wouldst thee hear of noble games?
I tell ye by that lord they call Saint James,
In this short night three times, without a slack,   4265
I screwed his daughter, flat upon her back,
While like a coward thee hast been in dread."

　　"You rascal, so you did?" the miller said.
"You false, you traitorous clerk," continued he,
"You shall be dead, then, by God's dignity!   4270
Who dares to be so bold as to disgrace
My daughter, come from such a worthy race?"

Then he grabbed Alan by the Adam's apple,
And Alan then with him began to grapple,
And with his fist he smashed the miller's nose, 4275
And blood streamed down upon the miller's clothes.
Bleeding from nose and mouth, upon the ground
Like two pigs in a poke they roll around;
They both get up, then down again they've gone—
Until the miller, tripping on a stone, 4280
Goes falling backwards, landing on his wife
(Who nothing knew of all this silly strife,
As she, contented, had been sleeping tight
With John the student, who'd been up all night).
She started from her slumber when he fell. 4285
"Help! Holy cross of Bromholm," was her yell,
"*In manus tuas!* Lord, I call to thee!
Wake up, Simon! The fiend's on top of me!
My heart is broken! Help, I'm nearly dead,
One's on my belly, one is on my head! 4290
Help, Simkin, these false clerks are in a fight!"
    John jumped right up as quickly as he might
And groped along the walls both to and fro
To seek a staff. She jumped right up also
And, more familiar with the place than he, 4295
Found by the wall a staff immediately.
She saw a little shimmer then of light
(For through a hole the moon was shining bright),
And by that light she caught sight of the two
But couldn't tell for sure just who was who. 4300
But something white then caught her eye; when she
Gazed at this white thing, she thought it must be
A nightcap that the student wore; she then
Drew nearer with her staff, went closing in,
And, thinking to give Alan quite a whop, 4305
She hit the miller on his barren top,
And down he went, and cried, "Help, or I die!"
The clerks then beat him up and let him lie,
Made ready, took their horse without delay
(Also their meal), and rode off on their way. 4310
And at the mill they also took the cake

From the half-bushel flour he had her bake.
   And so the haughty miller took a beating,
And lost the grinding fee for all his cheating;
He bought and paid for all they had to sup,   4315
Both John and Alan, those who beat him up;
His wife was screwed, his daughter too. That's how
It is for millers who are false! And now
This proverb's truly said and understood:
"Who evil does should not expect some good";   4320
One who beguiles, beguiled himself shall be.
And God, who sits above in majesty,
Save all this group, both high and low, for glory!
I've thus repaid the Miller with my story.

The Cook's Tale

PROLOGUE

The Reeve's tale pleased the London Cook as much   4325
As a back-scratching, his delight was such.
"Ha! ha!" said he, "this miller, by Christ's passion,
Got his comeuppance in the sharpest fashion
For all that talk of lodging-space with clerks.
As Solomon well stated in his works,   4330
'Into your house not every man invite.'
It's perilous to let one lodge at night,
And well advised should every fellow be
On whom he brings to share his privacy.
I pray to God to give me woe and care   4335
If ever, since they named me Hodge of Ware,
Have I heard of a miller better duped!
To mean tricks in the dark they really stooped.
But God forbid that here's where we conclude;
And so, if here you'll grant that I include   4340
A tale, then I, who am a humble man,
Will tell to you the best way that I can
A funny thing that happened in our city."
    Our Host said, "Granted, Roger, but be witty
In what you tell, see that it's of some use;   4345
From many a pastry you have drained the juice,
And you have peddled many a Jack of Dover
When twice already you had warmed it over.
There's many a pilgrim wishes you Christ's curse;
Your parsley has them feeling all the worse   4350
(They ate it with your stubble-nourished goose),
For in your shop so many flies are loose.
Now tell on, gentle Roger, by your name.
And don't get mad, I pray, about a game;
A man may speak the truth in fun or play."   4355
    "You speak the truth," said Roger, "I must say.

116

But 'true jest, bad jest'—Flemings say it daily;
And therefore by your faith now, Harry Bailey,
Do not get mad before we've parted, sir,
Although my tale be of a hosteler.   4360
I will not tell it yet, but when I do
(Before we part) you'll have what's owed to you."
And so with that he laughed with merry cheer
And told his tale, as you're about to hear.

THE COOK'S TALE

Once an apprentice dwelt within our town,   4365
Learning the victuals trade. He was as brown
As any berry. Blithely he'd cavort
Like a finch in the wood. Well-built and short,
With locks coal-black and very neatly kept,
At dancing he so well, so blithely leapt,   4370
That he was known as Perkin Reveler.
He was as full of love, this victualer,
As is the beehive full of honey sweet,
And lucky were the wenches he would meet.
At every wedding he would sing and hop;   4375
He loved the tavern better than the shop.
When there was a procession in Cheapside,
Out of the shop immediately he hied,
And till he'd seen it all, and took a turn
At dancing, he would not again return;   4380
And there would gather many of his sort
To dance and sing and otherwise disport;
And they would make appointments too to meet
And play at dice at such-and-such a street,
For there was no apprentice in the town   4385
Who better rattled dice and threw them down
Than Perkin Reveler. And he was free
In what he spent—his master easily
Had learnt this in the shop, for that is where
He often found his box completely bare.   4390
For surely when a prentice takes to vice

Like parties, paramours, and games of dice,
His master in the shop shall be the one
Who pays though having no part in the fun.
Although a prentice play guitar or fiddle, 4395
Theft and riotous living differ little;
Truth and revel, in one of low degree,
Will always be at odds, as men may see.
  Now with his master this blithe lad remained
Until in victuals nearly fully trained, 4400
Though often chided—more than once he made
The trip to Newgate while musicians played.
Then finally one day his master thought,
When Perkin his indenture paper sought,
About an old proverb, the words that say: 4405
"A rotten apple's better thrown away
Before it spoils the barrel." That is true
When dealing with a bad apprentice too;
Less harm is done to let him go apace
Before he ruins all others in the place. 4410
And so his master gave him his acquittance,
And bade him go with sorry luck: "Good riddance!"
And so this jolly prentice left. Let him
Now revel all the night if that's his whim.
And as there is no thief without ally 4415
To help embezzle, squander, or come by
All he can steal or borrow in some way,
He sent his bed and clothes without delay
To a compeer, a chap of his own sort
Who loved to dice, to revel and disport, 4420
And had a wife who kept, for public view,
A shop, but for her livelihood would screw.

(Unfinished by Chaucer)

The Lawyer's Tale

INTRODUCTION

Words of the Host to the Company

Our Host saw that the brightly shining sun
Through artificial day's arc then had run
One-fourth the way plus half an hour or more;
And though he wasn't deeply into lore,
He knew quite well it was the eighteenth day   5
Of April, which is messenger of May.
He saw too that the shadow of each tree
Was in its length of the same quantity
As was the tree that stood producing it;
And by that shadow he judged by his wit   10
That Phoebus, who was shining clear and bright,
Had climbed then forty-five degrees in height;
The hour for that day and latitude
Was ten o'clock, our Host had to conclude.
He stopped and quickly reined his horse about.   15
    "My lords," said he, "I warn you all the rout,
A fourth part of the day's already gone.
Now for the love of God and of Saint John,
Let's lose as little time now as we may.
My lords, it's time that wastes both night and day,   20
That robs us while we sleep without defense,
And while awake, through our own negligence.
It's like a stream returning not again,
Descending from the mountain to the plain.
Well Seneca, like others of his measure,   25
Bewails the loss of time more than of treasure:
'Of chattels there may be recovery,

But we are ruined by loss of time,' said he.
It will not come again, that's safely said,
No more than may come Malkin's maidenhead   30
Once she has lost it in her wantonness.
Let's not grow moldy, then, through idleness.
    "Sir Lawyer," said our Host, "God grant you bliss,
Tell us a tale now; you've agreed to this.
You've been committed by your free assent,   35
As I may judge the case, without dissent.
Acquit your promise, then you'll be released;
You will have done your duty at the least."
    "Host," he replied, "*depardieux*, I assent,
To break agreements is not my intent.   40
A promise is a debt, and I will pay
What I have promised—what more can I say?
Laws he would give another man one should
Obey himself, it's only right, our good
Text so requires. But I know very well   45
There's not one worthy tale that I could tell
That Chaucer (though he's not too good at meter,
And not too skillful in his rhyming either)
Has not been telling folks as best he can
For quite a while, as known to any man.   50
And if he hasn't told them, my dear brother,
In one book then he's told them in another.
He's told of lovers, paid them much attention,
Much more than Ovid ever made a mention
In his *Epistles* that are very old.   55
Why should I tell what's been already told?
    "In youth, of Ceyx and Alcyone he wrote,
And since then has of everyone made note
Among the noblest wives, their lovers too.
Whoever reads his lengthy volume through,   60
The one called The Legend of Cupid's Saints,
Will find therein the great wounds and complaints:
Lucretia's; those of Babylonian Thisbe,
The sword of Dido (false Aeneas!); tree
Of Phyllis, who for Demophon would die;   65
Hermione's and Dejanira's cry,

Hypsipyle's, and that of Ariadne
(Left on that barren island in the sea);
Leander drowning for his love of Hero;
The tears of Helen, and also the woe   70
Of you, Briseis, and you, Laodamia;
The cruelty of you, O Queen Medea,
To hang your children, all for hatred of
Your Jason who was faithless in his love;
Alcestis, Hypermnestra, Penelope,   75
Your wifehood with the best commended he.
   "But certainly no word he ever wrote
Of Canace, that wicked case of note
In which she loved her brother sinfully—
Fie on such cursed stories, I agree!   80
Or of the case of Apollonius,
In which the cursed king Antiochus
Bereft his daughter of her maidenhead—
So horrible a story to be read—
When he had thrown her upon the pavement.   85
He's never written (and for good intent),
Not in a single one of his narrations,
Of such unnatural abominations.
I won't relate them now for all I may.
   "But for a tale what shall I do today?   90
I'd surely not be likened to the Muses
(Or the Pierides if one so chooses,
The *Metamorphoses* tells what I mean).
But nonetheless why should I care a bean
Though after him I've only haw to bake?   95
I'll speak in prose, his rhymes he's free to make."
And with that word, he with a sober cheer
Began his tale, as you're about to hear.

PROLOGUE

  O hateful harm, you state of poverty,
Where thirst and cold and hunger so confound!   100
You feel ashamed to ask for charity,

But, asking not, your need will be profound,
Unwrapping every hidden wound you've bound;
Your head will bow as in your indigence
You steal or beg or borrow for expense.   105

You blame Lord Jesus, saying bitterly
His temporal blessings aren't proportional;
You also blame your neighbor wrongfully,
You say that you have little, he has all.
You say, "He'll pay, by faith, it shall befall   110
That his tail will be burning in the coals
Because he doesn't help us needy souls."

And listen to the sayings of the wise:
"Better to die than live in indigence";
"Your very neighbor soon will you despise."   115
If you are poor, farewell to reverence!
And from the wise man too this sapience:
"All poor men's days are evil." So beware
Lest you should sink to such point of despair!

If you are poor, you'll have your brother's spite,   120
And all your friends, alas, will flee from you.
O merchants rich, well-being's your delight,
O noble, prudent folk, we see it's true!
Your bags have not been filled with aces two,
You're running six-and-five with every chance.   125
How merrily at Christmas you may dance!

You earn by land and sea, your wealth accrues,
While also you gain knowledge of the state
Of kingdoms; you've been bearers, too, of news,
Of tales of peace and war. And desolate   130
I'd be right now for stories to relate
Had not a merchant taught me, many a year
Ago, a tale, and one that you shall hear.

THE LAWYER'S TALE

PART I

In Syria once dwelt a company
Of wealthy merchants, dignified and true;   135
And everywhere they sent their spicery
And cloth of gold and satins rich in hue.
Their wares were all so popular and new
That everyone was pleased at bargains made
With them, and sold to them his stock in trade.   140

The leaders of this company one day
Decided that to Rome they were to wend.
Be it for business or for pleasure, they
Did not desire a messenger to send
But went in person, for whatever end.   145
As for a place to lodge, they chose to rent
One that they thought the best for their intent.

And so these merchants sojourned in that town
A certain time, as it was to their pleasure;
And it befell that of the great renown   150
Of Constance, daughter of the Emperor,
They had report. All things concerning her
These Syrian merchants heard from day to day.
I'll tell you what they heard the people say.

This was the voiced opinion to a man: 155
"Our Emperor of Rome—blest may he be!—
A daughter has, and since the world began
(To rank her worth and beauty equally)
There's never been another such as she.
Sustain her, Lord, I pray with humble mien,   160
And would that of all Europe she were queen.

"In her there is high beauty without pride,
Youth not with folly but maturity;
In all her works her virtue is her guide,
Her humbleness supplanting tyranny.   165
She is the mirror of all courtesy,
Her heart a chamber of true holiness,
Her hand a ministration of largess."

This common voice was right, as God is true.
Let's go back to our tale. These merchants, when   170
Their ships had been reloaded, and a view
They'd had of this so blissful maiden, then
Went home to Syria as happy men.
They plied their trade as they had done before
And prospered there. I cannot tell you more.   175

These merchants, it befell, stood in the grace
Of him who held the sultanate; and he,
When they returned from any foreign place,
Invited them in kindest courtesy
To entertainment, asking busily   180
For news of sundry realms, for any word
Of wonders seen or of which they had heard.

Of things they told about, especially
They told of Lady Constance, in great measure
Spoke earnestly of her nobility,   185
Till for the Sultan it was such a pleasure,
The very thought of having such a treasure,
That his desire, each effort he expended,
Was for her love until his life be ended.

It's possible that in that same large book   190
That men call heaven what would come to pass
With stars was written when first breath he took:
That love would be the death of him, alas!
For in the stars is written, clear as glass,
There to be read, God knows, by all who can,   195
Without a doubt the death of every man.

In stars, for many a winter here on earth,
Was written death for Hector, Achilles,
Pompey, and Caesar, before each's birth;
The strife of Thebes; as well of Hercules   200
And Samson, of Turnus and Socrates,
The deaths. But so dull are the wits of men,
Not one can read the full of what's therein.

This Sultan for his privy council sent
And, that the matter be dealt with apace,   205
Declared to them that which was his intent.
He told them, "Surely now, without the grace
Of having Constance, in but little space
I'm good as dead." He charged them hastily,
For his life's sake, to plan some remedy.   210

Now different men had different things to say;
They argued, casting round for a solution,
And many a subtle plan proposed to lay;
They spoke of magic arts and of delusion,
But at the last, by way of a conclusion,   215
They found no one best plan that might be carried
Forth, except that he and she be married.

But therein lay the problem, they could see,
To speak quite plainly and with level head,
Because there was so much diversity   220
Between their two religions. As they said,
"We don't believe a Christian prince would wed
His daughter under the law of Mahomet,
Which is the law taught to us by our prophet."

But he replied, "Rather than have to lose   225
My Constance, I'll be Christianized, don't doubt it.
I must be hers, no other way to choose.
In peace, I pray, deliberate about it;
Take care to save my life ere I'm without it,
And bring her. My life's in her custody,   230
And in this woe I can no longer be."

What need is there to treat in greater scope?
By pacts, I'll say, and by diplomacy
And by the mediation of the Pope,
Of all the church and of all chivalry,   235
For the destruction of idolatry
And the increase of Christian law so dear,
At last they reached accord as you shall hear:

The Sultan would with all his baronage
And lieges embrace Christianity,   240
And Lady Constance he would have in marriage,
And gold (I know not what the quantity);
Therein was found sufficient surety.
And this accord was sworn on either side.
May mighty God, fair Constance, be your guide!   245

Now some men will be waiting, as I guess,
For me to tell of all that then was planned
By the Emperor in his great nobleness
For his daughter Constance; one can understand,
However, that provisions all so grand   250
No man can tell, in but a little pause,
As was arranged then for so high a cause.

It was arranged that bishops with her wend
Along with ladies, lords, knights of renown,
And other folks; in brief that was the end.   255
And notice was given throughout the town
That everyone devoutly, kneeling down,
Pray Christ receive this marriage on its day
In his good grace and speed them on their way.

The day arrived when they were to depart;   260
That woeful, fateful day, I say, had come,
And there was nothing could delay the start
But forward they must journey, all and some.
So Constance, by great sorrow overcome,
With patience rose, preparing then to wend,   265
For well she saw there was no other end.

Alas! is it a wonder that she wept,
One being sent now to a foreign nation,
Away from friends who tenderly had kept
And cared for her, bound now for subjugation   270
To one about whom she'd no information?
But husbands all are good; from times of yore
This wives have known, and I'll dare say no more.

"Father, your Constance, wretched child," said she,
"Your daughter, young and gently reared, and you,   275
My mother—of my pleasure you would be
The best except for Christ on high—in rue
Constance your child, always commended to
Your grace, shall for the Syrian domain
Depart, and not set eyes on you again.   280

"Alas! for it is to the Barbary nation
That I must go at once, as is your will;
I pray that Christ, who died for our salvation,
Gives me the grace his precepts to fulfill.
Though I'm a wretched woman, come to ill,   285
Women are born to thralldom and to penance,
And to be under manhood's governance."

At Troy, I think, when Pyrrhus broke the wall
And Ilium burnt; at Thebes, and equally
At Rome for all the harm through Hannibal   290
Who smote the Romans not one time but three,
Such weeping wasn't heard as came to be
Inside that place when time for her to leave;
She had to go although she sing or grieve.

O primum mobile! Cruel firmament   295
That always crowds with your diurnal sway,
Hurling all from the East to Occident
That naturally would go the other way;
In crowding so, you set in such array
The heavens, when began this fateful train,   300
By cruel Mars the marriage would be slain.

O tortuous ascendancy, by force
Of which now Mars the lord falls helplessly
Into the darkest house out of his course!
O atazir of Mars's cruelty!   305
O feeble moon who moves unhappily!
You're in conjunction where not kindly taken,
Your new position leaves you now forsaken.

Alas, imprudent Emperor of Rome!
In all your town not one philosopher?   310
There's no propitious time to leave one's home?
Of times to journey, none you might prefer
For people who of high position were
And all with times of birth exactly known?
Alas, too slow or ignorant you've grown!   315

To ship was brought this fair and woeful maid
With ceremony, every circumstance.
"Now Jesus Christ be with you all," she prayed.
They said but "Farewell, lovely Lady Constance!"
She tried to show a cheerful countenance;   320
Forth in this manner I will let her sail,
As I shall now again resume my tale.

The Sultan's mother (evil well of vices)
Had seen that which was her son's full intent,
To leave his old religion's sacrifices.   325
So for her council right away she sent;
They came to find out what this summons meant,
And when there was assembled all this folk,
She sat down and, as you shall hear, she spoke.

"As you are well aware, lords," she began,   330
"My son is at the point he would forget
The holy laws contained in our Koran
As given by God's messenger Mahomet.
But to great God I make this promise yet:
The very life shall from my body start   335
Before Mahomet's law shall leave my heart!

"What should betide us with this brand-new law
But thralldom for our bodies, penance, grief?
And afterwards to hell we would withdraw,
Having denied Mahomet our belief.   340
Will you assure me, lords, for our relief,
Of your assent to what I'll say before
You here, to make us safe forevermore?"

Each one assented, each swore that he would
Both live and die for her, and by her stand,   345
That each would try the best way that he could
To get his friends' support for what she planned.
And she then took this enterprise in hand
As you shall hear, for I shall now explain;
Just in this way she spoke to them again: 350

"Christianity we'll first feign to embrace;
Cold water's all it is, we'll suffer light.
I'll have a feast and revel then take place,
And you've my word the Sultan I'll requite.
For though his wife be baptized purest white,   355
A fountain full of water will not do
To wash away the red when I am through."

O Sultaness, root of iniquity!
Virago, second Semiramis found!
Serpent disguised in femininity,   360
You're like the one that deep in hell is bound;
False woman, of all things that may confound
Virtue and innocence, all that suffice
Are bred in you, the nest of every vice!

O Satan, full of envy since the day   365
They chased you from your heritage, pursued!
To women you know well the ancient way,
As you made Eve bring us to servitude;
This Christian marriage you would now preclude.
Your instrument—and wellaway the while!—   370
You make of women when you would beguile.

This sinful Sultaness at whom I rail
Then let her secret council go their way.
Why should I tarry longer with my tale?
She went to see the Sultan then one day   375
To say that she'd renounce their law, to say
From priestly hands she'd welcome Christendom,
Repenting all her time in heathendom.

She asked if, as an honor, she could hold
A feast, with every Christian as a guest;   380
"I'll labor much to please them," he was told.
The Sultan answered, "I'm at your behest."
He knelt and thanked her then for the request,
So happy that he knew not what to say.
She kissed her son and homeward took her way.   385

PART II

    Now when this Christian folk had come to land
In Syria—a great distinguished train—
A herald rushed, at the Sultan's command,
First to his mother, then through the domain,
To say his wife had come, and, to sustain   390
The honor of his realm, pray all convene,
That everyone might ride to meet the queen.

Great was the throng and rich was the array
Of Syrians and Romans come to meet;
The Sultan's mother, richly clad, that day   395
Met Constance with good cheer, both glad and sweet,
As any mother might her daughter greet.
Then to the nearest city to the side
At slow and stately pace they turned to ride.

Not Julius Caesar's triumph, I would say,   400
Of which the author Lucan makes such boast,
Had so much royalty or rich display
As the assembly of this blissful host.

But this scorpion like some wicked ghost,
The Sultaness, for all her flattering,   405
Was then contriving mortally to sting.

The Sultan came himself soon after this
(So royally a wonder it's to tell),
To welcome her with joy, in total bliss.
And so in mirth and joy I let them dwell;   410
The fruit of this is what I have to tell.
For when the time had come, men thought it best
That revel cease and men go to their rest.

Then came the time when this old Sultaness
Ordered the feast be held of which I've told.   415
Then to this feast the Christians all progress,
They come in general, young as well as old.
Here one may feast and royalty behold,
And dainties more than my words may devise—
But all too dearly bought, none were to rise.   420

O sudden woe that ever is successor
To worldly bliss, so sprayed with bitterness!
Of all our labors' joy, the end, oppressor!
Woe occupies the end of happiness.
Hark to this counsel with assuredness: 425
Upon your day of gladness, keep in mind
The unseen woe or harm that comes behind.

To tell you in a word (if one is able),
The Sultan and each Christian who had gone
Were stabbed and cut to pieces at the table—   430
Each one, that is, but Constance, she alone.
This Sultaness, that old and cursed crone,
Had with her friends performed this cursed deed,
That she herself might all the country lead.

Not one converted Syrian in the scrape,   435
Not one who held the Sultan's counsel true,
Was not dismembered ere he could escape.

And Constance then they put without ado
Aboard a ship—God knows, without a crew—
And bade her learn to sail upon the sea   440
From Syria back home to Italy.

Some treasure that she'd taken with her there,
And, be it said, food in great quantity,
Were given her, and also clothes to wear;
Then forth she sailed upon the salty sea.   445
O Constance, young, full of benignity,
Dear daughter of the Emperor of the realm,
The Lord of Fortune steer you at the helm!

She crossed herself, and with a piteous voice
Prayed to the cross of Christ and made this plea: 450
"O holy cross, altar where we rejoice,
Red from the Lamb's blood, shed so pityingly,
That cleansed the world of old iniquity;
I pray, from the fiend and his claws please keep
Me, on that day when I drown in the deep.   455

"Victorious tree, protection of the true,
The only tree so worthy that you held
The King of heaven with his wounds anew,
The white Lamb who was speared; you have expelled
Demons from man and woman, all those who   460
Above them see your faithful limbs extend;
Now keep me that my life I might amend."

For days and years afloat she had to go,
Throughout the Sea of Greece and to the Strait
Of Morocco, as fate would have it so.   465
And many a sorry meal the lady ate,
And frequently her death she would await
Before the waves so wild would ever drive
Her to the place where she longed to arrive.

Now men may ask why Constance wasn't slain,   470
Or who was at the feast, her life to save;

I'll answer that by asking them again:
Who saved young Daniel in that horrid cave,
That all but he—the master, every knave—
Be eaten by the lion, torn apart?   475
No one but God, whom he bore in his heart.

God wished to show his wondrous sovereignty
In her, that we should see his mighty work;
For Christ, of every harm the remedy,
Will often by some means (ask any clerk)   480
Do things for certain ends, though it seem murk
Surrounds it in man's mind, which cannot sense
The prudence that is in his providence.

Now since she wasn't murdered, as we saw,
Who kept the maid from drowning in the sea?   485
Well, who kept Jonah in the fish's maw
Till spouted up at Nineveh? You see,
Men well may know it was no one but he
Who saved the Hebrews from a drowning too
When with dry feet they passed the Red Sea through.   490

Who bade the four spirits of the tempest
(With power to annoy land and sea
Both north and south, as well as east and west)
To bother neither sea nor land nor tree?
In truth, the one commanding this was he,   495
Who from the tempest too this woman kept
When she awoke as well as when she slept.

Where might she get her meat and drink? How save
The food she had, three years and more to sail?
Who fed Saint Mary of Egypt in the cave   500
Or desert? None but Christ, and without fail.
Five thousand people—marvelous the tale!—
With five loaves and two fishes he would feed;
God sent his plenty in their greatest need.

She drove forth in our ocean without aim,   505

Throughout our wild sea, till by waves at last
Beneath a castle that I cannot name,
Far in Northumberland, she had been cast;
And in the sand her vessel struck so fast,
From there it wouldn't budge against the tide;   510
The will of Christ was that she should abide.

The castle's constable had hurried there
To see the wreck. Survivors then he sought,
And found this weary woman full of care;
He also found the treasure she had brought.   515
In her own language mercy she besought,
That life out of her weary body go
And thereby bring deliverance from her woe.

A corrupted form of Latin was her speech,
But still a kind that one could understand.   520
The constable, his search done, to the beach
This woeful woman took. When on the land,
She knelt and thanked God for his guiding hand;
But who she was to no man she would say,
For foul or fair, though death she have to pay.   525

She claimed that she had lost her memory
While on the sea with such a muddled mind.
Both constable and wife had sympathy
For her to such degree they wept. So kind
She was as well, so diligent to find   530
Ways she might serve and please all in the place,
That she was loved by all who saw her face.

This constable and Hermengild, his wife,
Were pagan, like that country everywhere.
But Hermengild loved her as much as life,   535
And Constance was so long sojourning there,
With orisons and tears of such despair,
That Jesus Christ converted, through his grace,
Dame Hermengild, governess of the place.

No Christian in that land dared move about;   540
The Christian folk had all been forced to flee
Because of pagans, conquering with a rout
The regions of the North by land and sea.
To Wales had fled the Christianity
Among old Britons dwelling in the isle;   545
That was their refuge for a goodly while.

But Christian Britons were not so exiled
That there were not a few who privately
Would honor Christ (the heathen folk beguiled),
And near the castle there were dwelling three.   550
Now one of them was blind—he couldn't see,
That is, except for eyes within the mind
With which men see when otherwise they're blind.

Bright was the sun when on one summer's day
The constable and his wife chose to go,   555
Along with Constance, down the quickest way
Toward the sea, a furlong-way or so,
To frolic on the seashore to and fro.
They chanced to meet this blind man as they strolled;
His eyes were shut, hunchbacked he was and old.   560

"In Christ's sweet name," this sightless Briton cried,
"Dame Hermengild, give me my sight again!"
The woman feared, when so identified,
That by her husband (briefly to explain)
For loving Jesus she would there be slain—   565
Till Constance gave her strength, to work in search
Of Christ's own will as daughter of his church.

The constable, abashed at such a sight,
Said, "What's the meaning of this whole affair?"
And Constance answered, "Sir, it is the might   570
Of Christ, that helps folks out of Satan's snare."
And she began our law then to declare
Until she had the constable by eve
Converted, and on Christ made him believe.

This constable was not lord of the place   575
Of which I speak (where Constance chanced to land),
But strongly kept it many a winter's space
For Alla, king of all Northumberland—
A wise king, one who held a worthy hand
Against the Scots, as men may hear and learn.   580
But to my story I'll again return.

Now Satan, ever watching to beguile,
At once (on seeing Constance's perfection)
Looked for a way to foil her with his wile;
He made a young knight dwelling in that section   585
Love her so hotly, with such foul affection,
The knight thought that by passion he'd be killed
If with her once he had not what he willed.

He wooed her but his efforts were for naught,
She would commit no sin in any way.   590
Then for despite he entertained the thought
That shameful death would be the price she'd pay.
He waited; with the constable away,
One evening late, with stealthiness he crept
Into the room where Hermengild then slept.   595

There weary from their prayerful wakefulness,
Both Hermengild and Constance were asleep.
This knight whom Satan tempted to transgress
Then softly managed to the bed to creep.
He cut the throat of Hermengild, and deep;   600
He left by Constance then the bloody knife
And went his way. God's vengeance on his life!

The constable had soon come home again,
With Alla, king of all the land around,
To see his wife had been so cruelly slain;   605
He wrung his hands and wept, by sorrow bound,
Then in the bed the bloody knife he found
By Constance. O alas! what could she say,
In woe her very senses gone away?

To Alla then was told all this mischance—   610
The time, the place as well, how it occurred
Constance was shipwrecked there by happenstance
As I've explained. And when the king had heard,
His heart quaked, so much pity in him stirred,
To see a creature so benign to be
In this distress, in such adversity.   615

For as the lamb is to the slaughter brought,
So stood this innocent before the king.
The lying knight who had this treason wrought
Bore witness that indeed she'd done the thing.   620
But mighty grief all this then came to bring
Among the people, saying, "How can they
Suppose she'd act in such an evil way?"

They'd always found her virtuous; what's more,
She had loved Hermengild as much as life,   625
As everyone there in the household swore,
Except the one who'd killed her with his knife.
Suspicion in this gentle king grew rife
About the knight; King Alla thought to sleuth
More deeply into this, to learn the truth.   630

Constance, alas! no champion, it's seemed,
Wills to defend, you cannot fight your way.
But he who died that we might be redeemed,
Who Satan bound (who lies still where he lay),
May he be your strong champion today!   635
Unless Christ brings miraculous event,
You quickly shall be slain though innocent.

She got down on her knees then and she prayed:
"Immortal God, the one who saved Susanna
From false complaint; and thou, merciful maid   640
(Mary I mean, the daughter of Saint Anna)
Before whose child the angels sing 'Hosanna'—
If I am guiltless of this felony,
Lest I shall perish, my salvation be!"

Before have you not seen the pallid face,   645
Among a crowd, of someone who was led
Toward his death (one who was shown no grace),
And in his face the color had so fled
That men might know his face was one of dread
Among all of the faces in the rout?   650
So Constance stood and palely looked about.

O queens, living in your prosperity,
O duchesses, you ladies so well known,
Please have some ruth for her adversity!
The daughter of an emperor stands alone,   655
She has no one now who would hear her moan.
O royal blood, standing in dread today,
In your great need your friends are far away!

So much compassion had Alla the king
(As pity-filled a gentle heart will be)   660
That tears were running down his cheeks. "Now bring
Without delay a book to us," said he,
"And if this knight will swear to us how she
This woman slew, we after will decide
Whom we shall choose as judge when she is tried."   665

A British book was fetched, one that contained
The Gospels; on this book at once he swore
Her guilt. In that same instant that obtained,
A hand did smite his neck, the wound so sore
He fell down like a boulder to the floor,   670
And both his eyes burst right out of his face
In sight of everybody in the place.

A voice was heard by all the audience:
"You've spoken slander of the innocent,
This Holy Church's child, and in high presence;   675
So you have done, yet wrath I do not vent."
Bewildered by this marvelous event,
Each person stood aghast and like a stone,
In fear of vengeance—save Constance alone.

Great was the fear and also the repentance   680
Of those who had suspected, in delusion,
This holy innocent Lady Constance;
This miracle brought many, in conclusion
(With Constance mediating), absolution,
The king and many others in the place   685
Being converted, thanks to our Lord's grace.

This lying knight was slain for his untruth,
By judgment of King Alla, hastily;
Yet Constance had upon his death great ruth.
And after this Christ Jesus graciously   690
Had Alla wed with full solemnity
This holy maid who was so bright and sheen;
And thus had Jesus made Constance a queen.

But who had woe, if truth I shall impart,
To see them wed? None but Donegild who   695
Was Alla's mother, she with tyrant's heart.
She thought her cursed heart would break in two;
She wouldn't have him wed as he would do—
She thought it a disgrace that he arrange
To marry such a creature, one so strange.   700

I do not wish with either chaff or straw
To stretch the tale, I'll get right to the wheat.
What should I tell of royalty one saw
There at the rites, what course came first to eat,
Who blew a trumpet or a horn? The meat   705
Or fruit of every tale is what to say:
They eat and drink, they dance and sing and play.

To bed they went, by reason and by right;
For although wives be truly holy things,
They have to take with patience in the night   710
What's necessary for the pleasurings
Of those folks who have wedded them with rings,
And lay some of their holiness aside
At such a time. No better may betide.

The king begat a manchild right away;   715
He took his wife and left her in the care
Of constable and bishop on the day
He left for Scotland, hunting foemen there.
Now Constance, she so humble, meek, and fair,
So long had been with child, she stayed inside   720
Her chamber, ever Christ's will to abide.

The time then came, the child was borne by her,
Beside the font Maurice his christened name;
The constable then called a messenger,
As he wrote to King Alla to proclaim   725
The blissful tidings, how the manchild came
(And other tidings briefly to relay);
He sped him with this letter on his way.

This messenger, to suit his own advantage,
To the king's mother first was swift to ride,   730
Saluting her in best words he could manage.
"You may," said he, "be glad and full of pride!
Thank God one hundred thousand times! His bride,
My lady queen, has borne a child. No doubt
Both joy and bliss will sweep the realm throughout.   735

"Here are the letters, sealed, about the thing,
Which I must bear with all the haste I may.
If you'd send others to your son the king,
I am your humble servant night and day."
"I've nothing," answered Donegild, "to say   740
Right now. Here you will take your rest tonight,
Tomorrow I'll instruct you as I might."

This messenger consumed much ale and wine,
And stolen were his letters stealthily
Out of his box, while he slept like a swine.   745
And then was forged (and with great subtlety)
Another letter, written evilly,
Directed to the king as to appear
From his own constable, as you shall hear.

The queen had borne, so this forged letter said,   750
So horrible a creature, to be plain,
That none within the castle, out of dread,
Dared with this fiendish creature to remain.
The mother was an elf, an evil bane
Who'd come by charms or by some sorcery,   755
And everyone now loathed her company.

How grieved the king when he this letter read!
Yet he disclosed to none this wound so sore,
As in his own hand he replied instead:
"What Christ ordains is welcome evermore   760
To me, as one who's learned in his lore.
Lord, welcome is thy will and all thy pleasance,
My will I yield to thine in goverance.

"Care for this child, though it be foul or fair,
My wife as well, until I'm home again.   765
Christ, when he wills, will send to me an heir
More to my liking, heir to my domain."
He sealed the letter, weeping in his pain;
The messenger received it, no delay
As forth he went. There is no more to say.   770

O messenger, so full of drunkenness!
Strong-breathed, with limbs that falter, you betray
All that is told to you in secretness;
Your mind is lost, you chatter like a jay,
Your face begins to look a whole new way.   775
Wherever drunkenness reigns in a rout
There is no hidden counsel, do not doubt.

O Donegild, my English can't begin
To treat your malice and your tyranny!
I'll leave you to the devil—let him then   780
Become the judge of all your treachery.
Fie, manlike—no, by God, I lie, let's see—
Fie on your fiendish spirit! I dare tell,
Though here you walk, your spirit is in hell.

The messenger came from the king once more,   785
At court of the king's mother to alight.
She entertained him as she'd done before,
She pleased him in each manner that she might;
He drank until his belt was good and tight,
And then he slept (and snored in usual wise)   790
All night until the sun was to arise.

Then stolen were his letters once again,
Replaced with further forgeries that went:
"The king commands his constable, on pain
Of being hanged, strict justice the intent,   795
That he should suffer now in no event
That Constance for one quarter-hour remain
Beyond three days within King Alla's reign;

"Rather, in that same ship where she was found
Let her and her young son with all their gear   800
Be placed and then be pushed away from ground
And ordered not to be returning here."
O Constance, there's no wonder at the fear
Of woeful spirit as you sleep and dream,
With Donegild concocting such a scheme!   805

This messenger at morning did awake
And to the castle went by shortest way,
The letter to the constable to take.
When he saw what the letter had to say,
The constable cried "Woe!" and "Wellaway!   810
Lord Christ," said he, "how may this world endure,
So full of sin, of creatures so impure?

"O mighty God, if it should be thy will,
As thou art rightful judge, how may it be
That thou shouldst let the guiltless die and still   815
Let wicked folk reign in prosperity?
O good Constance! Alas, so woe is me,
I'm to be your tormenter—else I die
A shameful death! No other way I spy."

Both young and old wept all throughout the place,   820
This cursed letter Alla having sent,
As Constance with a deathly pallid face
Upon the fourth day to the vessel went.
But nonetheless she took for good intent
The will of Christ and, kneeling on the strand,   825
Said, "Welcome, Lord, all that is thy command.

"The one who has sustained me in false blame
While here on land among you won't allow
That I should suffer harm or come to shame
Upon the sea, though I may see not how.   830
As strong as he has been he still is now;
In him I trust, and in his mother dear,
And this will be my sail and help me steer."

Her little child lay weeping in her arms
As, kneeling, piteously to him she said,   835
"Peace, little son, I'll do to you no harms."
Then over the eyes of her child she spread
A kerchief she had taken from her head,
And lulled him gently in her arms. At last
Her eyes toward the heavens Constance cast.   840

"O mother Mary, maiden bright," said she,
"It's true that through woman's encouragement
Mankind was lost, with death the penalty,
For which thy child was crucified and rent.
Thy blessed eyes saw all of his torment,   845
So there is no comparing, to be sure,
Thy woe with any woe man may endure.

"Thou sawest thy child slain before thine eyes,
Yet, by my faith, my child still lives somehow!
O lady bright, who hears our woeful cries,   850
Glory of woman, maiden fair, O thou
Bright star of day, haven of refuge, now
Rue on my child as in thy gentleness
Thou rueth on all rueful in distress.

"O little child, alas! what is your guilt,   855
You who have yet to sin? What could you do
That your hard father wills your life be spilt?
Mercy, dear constable," she said in rue,
"And let my little child dwell here with you.
But if you dare not save him, risking blame,   860
Give him a last kiss in his father's name."

She took a backward look then to the land,
And said, "O ruthless husband, farewell, sir!"
Then she arose and walked down on the strand
Toward the ship (the crowd all followed her),   865
Praying her child would not cry out or stir.
Taking her leave, and with holy intent
Crossing herself, into the ship she went.

The ship was victualed, no need there for dread,
Abundant stores filled each and every space;   870
Of all necessities, so be it said,
She had enough, praise be to God's good grace.
Almighty God, give wind and weather place
And bring her home! There's no more I can say
Except that on the sea she sailed away.   875

PART III

   King Alla came, soon after this was done,
Home to his castle of which I have told,
And asked then where had gone his wife and son.
The constable then felt his blood run cold,
And plainly to the king the tale he told   880
As you have heard (I cannot tell it better),
And showed the king his seal, also his letter;

He said, "My lord, as you commanded me,
On pain of death, is what I've done, no less."
The messenger was tortured then till he   885
Had but one choice, openly to confess

Where he had slept each night. So one could guess,
When wits were used and subtle questioning,
From where this evil work had come to spring.

They recognized which hand the letter wrote,   890
Exposed the venom of this cursed deed;
I don't know how, so more I cannot note
Except to say that Alla then indeed
His mother slew (as men may plainly read)
For being a traitor. In great dishonor
Thus ends old Donegild. A curse upon her!   895

What sorrow this King Alla night and day
Felt for his wife, and for his child also,
There is no tongue so eloquent to say.
So now again to Constance I will go,   900
Who floats out on the sea in pain and woe,
As Jesus wills, forlorn five years or more
Until her ship at last approaches shore.

Beneath a heathen castle finally
(Its name within my text I fail to find)   905
She and her child were cast up by the sea.
Almighty God, who rescues all mankind,
Have Constance and her little child in mind
Who in a heathen land now fall again,
Near point of death as I shall soon explain.   910

Down from the castle many to the site
Had come, to gaze upon the ship and Constance;
Then shortly from the castle, late one night,
The lord's own steward—God give him mischance,
A thief who spurned our faith!—made an advance   915
Alone onto the ship, and said he ought
To have her love no matter what she thought.

This woman—woebegone, in wretched way,
With crying child—then cried out piteously.
But blessed Mary helped her right away: 920

As Constance struggled well and mightily,
The thief fell overboard quite suddenly
And in the sea as he deserved was finished.
So by our Lord is Constance left unblemished.

Such is your end, O foul lust, lechery!   925
For you not only weaken a man's mind
But you will ruin his body certainly;
The end of all your work, your lust so blind,
Is grief. How many times that men may find
That not just sinful work but the intent   930
Can lead to shame or death as punishment.

And how could this weak woman have the strength
For such defense against this renegade?
O Goliath, immeasurable in length,
By David how could you so low be laid,   935
By one so young, no armor and no blade?
How dared he look upon your dreadful face?
Well men may see that it was by God's grace.

Who gave to Judith such brave hardiness
That she slew Holofernes in his tent,   940
That she delivered out of wretchedness
God's people? This I say as my intent,
That just as God a vigorous spirit sent
To them, thereby to save them from their plight,
He sent to Constance too the will and might.   945

Her ship went forth into the narrow mouth
Of Ceuta and Gibraltar, making way
First to the west, then sometimes north and south
And sometimes east, for many a weary day,
Until Christ's mother—bless her, as we pray!—   950
Prepared through her eternal graciousness
A plan to end poor Constance's distress.

Of the Roman Emperor now a word,
And then right back to Constance where we've brought her.

Through letters brought from Syria he heard   955
About the Christian folks who'd gone to slaughter,
The traitorous dishonor done his daughter
By that most wicked, cursed Sultaness
Who at the feast had slain with thoroughness.

The Emperor of Rome at once sent out   960
A senator, armed with a royal order,
And other lords—God knows, a mighty rout—
To seek revenge across the Syrian border.
They burnt and slew and razed, giving no quarter
As they spread havoc there for many a day;   965
Then, briefly, home to Rome they took their way.

This senator, thus heading in his glory
For Rome, while sailing royally
Soon chanced upon the ship (so says the story)
In which was seated Constance piteously.   970
He had no inkling of whom she might be,
And she refused to speak a single breath
About herself, were it on pain of death.

He brought her then to Rome, and to his wife
He gave her and her little manchild too;   975
So with this senator she led her life.
(And thus from woe Our Lady can rescue,
Besides poor Constance, many more in rue.)
A lengthy time she dwelt there in that place,
Always in holy works as was her grace.   980

The senator's wife was in fact her aunt,
But Constance still she didn't recognize.
To tarry longer at this point I shan't,
But of King Alla I'll again advise,
Still weeping for his wife with mournful sighs;   985
To him I shall return now, leaving Constance
There under the senator's governance.

King Alla, who had had his mother slain,

Came one day to be filled with such repentance
That, if I might relate it short and plain,   990
He went to Rome, that he might have his penance
Completely under papal governance
From high to low. From Jesus Christ he sought
Forgiveness for the wicked works he wrought.

The word in Rome at once went door to door   995
("King Alla comes, a pilgrim in contrition")
By harbingers whom he sent out before.
And so the senator, as was tradition,
Rode out to meet him (kinsmen in addition
Rode out), displaying high magnificence   1000
As well as showing royal reverence.

This senator gave Alla gracious greeting,
And he in turn then greeted him as well,
Each honoring the other at their meeting.
A day or two thereafter it befell   1005
That to King Alla's inn, I'll briefly tell,
This senator went for a feast, and he
Took Constance's young son in company.

Now to the feast some men would doubtless say
He took her son at Constance's request;   1010
I cannot tell it all in every way,
Be as it may he took him as a guest.
It was indeed, though, Constance's behest
That this young fellow, while the meal took place,
Be standing, looking Alla in the face.   1015

The king was filled with wonder. Curiously
The senator he questioned, promptly so:
"That fair child over there—who might he be?"
"By God and by Saint John, I do not know.
He has a mother but no father, though,   1020
Of whom I know." Then he set to expound
To Alla briefly how the child was found.

"But God knows," said the senator when done,
"Not one as virtuous in all my life
I've ever seen as she, nor heard of one,   1025
Count every worldly woman, maid or wife.
I daresay she would rather have a knife
Plunge through her heart than have a wicked name.
There is no man could bring her to that shame."

In looks the child was as alike to Constance   1030
As any creature possibly could be.
Alla recalled to mind her countenance
And he began to wonder musingly
If this child's mother could be none but she
Who was his wife. Then inwardly he sighed,   1035
And quickly from the table Alla hied.

"By faith," he thought, "a phantom's in my head!
I have to think, if logic's any judgment,
That in the salty sea my wife is dead."
But then he gave himself this argument: 1040
"How do I know Christ Jesus hasn't sent
Her here by sea, just as she came before
To my own land before she left its shore?"

That afternoon, home with the senator
King Alla went to see if it was true.   1045
His host great honor to him did confer,
Then sent for Constance with no more ado.
She didn't feel like dancing once she knew
The reason he had issued such a call—
In fact she scarcely could stand up at all.   1050

When Alla saw her, greeting her with honor,
He wept, a truly ruthful sight to see;
For just as soon as he laid eyes upon her
He knew without a doubt that it was she.
In sorrow Constance stood dumb as a tree,   1055
Her heart so shut because of her distress
When she remembered his unkindliness.

Then twice she swooned right there in Alla's sight;
He wept, in self-defense said piteously,
"As God and all his saints and angels bright   1060
May surely on my soul have lenity,
Of your harm I'm as guiltless as would be
Maurice my son—so like you in the face—
Or may the devil haul me from this place!"

Long was the sobbing and the bitter pain   1065
Before the woe within their hearts had ceased;
Great was the pity, hearing them complain
With plaints by which their woe was just increased.
I pray that from my labor I'm released,
No more about their woe, until tomorrow;   1070
I am so weary speaking of such sorrow.

But when the truth then finally was known
(Of what she suffered through, his guiltlessness),
They kissed at least a hundred times, I own,
And twixt the two there was such happiness   1075
That, save the joy of everlastingness,
No creature's ever seen the like, for sure,
Nor ever shall while this world may endure.

She asked her husband with humility
If for relief—so long she'd had to pine—   1080
He would request her father specially
To be, for all his majesty, benign
Enough that someday he might with him dine.
She also prayed that of her in no way
One word would Alla to her father say.   1085

It was the child Maurice, some men believe,
Who to the Emperor took the request;
But I would not think Alla so naive
That to so great a sovereign—one blest
As being of all Christian folk the best—   1090
He'd send a child. It's better then to deem
That Alla went himself, as it would seem.

The Emperor accepted graciously
The dinner invitation Alla brought;
And I can say he looked distractedly   1095
At Alla's child and of his daughter thought.
Alla went to his inn and, as he ought,
Prepared for this great feast in every wise
As far as royal cunning could devise.

The next day came and Alla rose to dress,   1100
As did his wife, this Emperor to meet;
And forth they rode in joy and blissfulness.
And when she saw her father in the street,
Constance, alighting, fell down at his feet.
"Father, your young child Constance," then she cried,   1105
"From your remembrance has been swept aside.

"I am your daughter Constance," stated she,
"Whom you once sent to Syria. It's I,
Dear Father, I who on the salty sea
Was put alone and left, condemned to die.   1110
For mercy now, good Father, is my cry!
Send me not out again among the Godless,
But thank my lord here for his kindliness."

Who could describe the sweet joy that arose
Among those three when they had come to meet?   1115
But I shall bring my story to a close,
No longer I'll delay, the day is fleet.
These happy people all sat down to eat;
I leave them at their feast—their joy, I hold,
Beyond my words at least a thousandfold.   1120

This child Maurice was later by the Pope
Made Emperor, and he lived righteously;
The respect he paid the Church was great in scope.
I'll let his story pass if you agree,
For my tale is of Constance specially.   1125
In histories of Rome is where you'll find
Maurice's life, I'll pay it here no mind.

King Alla, when there came the proper day,
Then went with Constance, his sweet, holy wife,
Back home to England by the shortest way;   1130
There they enjoyed a blissful, quiet life.
But I can well assure you, woe or strife
Soon follows worldly joy; time won't abide,
From day to night it changes like the tide.

Who's ever lived one day of full delight   1135
Who has not still been moved by conscience, ire,
By envy, pride, by tragedy or fright,
By some effrontery or by desire?
I say this only as it would transpire
That joy and bliss for Alla on this isle   1140
With Constance was to last but little while.

For death, which takes its toll from high to low,
After about a year, as I would guess,
Had taken Alla from this world. Such woe
Did Constance feel, she grieved with heaviness.   1145
Now let us pray that God his soul will bless!
Dame Constance, in conclusion I will say,
Toward the town of Rome then made her way.

In Rome this holy creature has arrived
To find that all her friends are whole and sound.   1150
All her adventure Constance has survived;
And when her father she at last has found,
She falls down to her knees upon the ground
And there she weeps, so tender in her ways,
A hundred thousand times our Lord to praise.   1155

In virtue and in holy Christian deed
They live, and never from each other wend;
Till death should part, such is the life they lead.
And so farewell! my tale is at an end.
Now Jesus Christ, who in his might may send   1160
Joy after woe, govern us by his grace
And keep each one of us who's in this place! Amen.

EPILOGUE

Our Host stood in his stirrups right away
And said, "Good men, give ear to what I say!
That was a worthy tale for our intent!   1165
Sir Parish Priest, by God's bones," on he went,
"Tell us a tale as you agreed before.
Well I can see you learned men in lore
Know, by God's dignity, much good to say!"
   The Parson answered, *"Benedicite!*   1170
What ails the man, so sinfully to swear?"
Our Host replied, "O Johnny, are you there?
I smell a Lollard in the wind," said he.
"Now, good men," said our Host, "attend to me;
Abide awhile, by our Lord's worthy passion,   1175
For we shall have a sermon—in his fashion
This Lollard here will preach to us somewhat."
   "Nay, by my father's soul, that he shall not!"
The Skipper said. "Here shall he never preach,
Not here shall he the gospel gloss or teach.   1180
We all believe in one great God," he said.
"Some difficulty he would sow, he'd spread
Some cockles, sow some weed, in our clean corn.
And therefore, Host, you fairly I will warn,
A tale my jolly body now shall tell   1185
And clang for you so merrily a bell
That I shall wake up all this company!
And it shall not be of philosophy
Or medicine or of quaint terms of law;
There is but little Latin in my maw."   1190

The Wife of Bath's Tale

PROLOGUE

"Experience, though no authority
Were in this world, would be enough for me
To speak of woe that married life affords;
For since I was twelve years of age, my lords,
Thanks be to God eternally alive, 5
Of husbands at the church door I've had five
(If I have wed that often legally),
And all were worthy men in their degree.
But I was told not very long ago
That as but once did Jesus ever go 10
To a wedding (in Cana, Galilee),
By that example he was teaching me
That only once in life should I be wed.
And listen what a sharp word, too, was said
Beside a well by Jesus, God and man, 15
In a reproof of the Samaritan:
'Now you have had five husbands,' Jesus said,
'But he who has you now, I say instead,
Is not your husband.' That he said, no doubt,
But what he meant I haven't figured out; 20
For I must ask, why is it the fifth man
Wasn't husband to the Samaritan?
How many men was she allowed to wed?
In all my years I've never heard it said
Exactly how this number is defined; 25
Men may surmise and gloss how it's divined,
But I expressly know it's not a lie
God bade us to increase and multiply—
That noble text I well appreciate.
I also know the Lord said that my mate 30

154

Should leave for me his father and his mother,
But mentioned not one number or another,
Not bigamy nor yet octogamy.
Why should men speak, then, disapprovingly?
    "Look, here's the wise king, lordly Solomon: 35
I do believe his wives were more than one.
Would that the Lord permitted me to be
Refreshed as half as often as was he.
A gift from God he had for all his wives,
No man will ever have such in our lives.   40
God knows, this noble king, if I am right,
Had many a merry bout on that first night
With each of them, he was so much alive.
And God be blest that I have married five,
Of which I have picked out the very best,   44a
Both for their hanging purse and for their chest.
As many different schools make perfect clerks,
So practice that's diverse in sundry works
Will make a perfect workman certainly;
Five-husband schooling's done the same for me.   44f
The sixth is welcome when he comes along;   45
I won't be keeping myself chaste for long,
For when one husband from this world is gone
Some Christian man will wed me early on—
For as the Apostle says, then I am free
To wed in God's name when it pleases me.   50
It's no sin to be married, he has said,
For if you're burning, better to be wed.
What do I care if folks speak evilly
Of cursed Lamech and his bigamy?
A holy man was Abraham, I know,   55
And Jacob, too, as far as that may go,
Yet each with more than two wives came to dwell,
Like many other holy men as well.
And where in any age can it be said
That God on high forebade that we be wed   60
By any word express? Please answer me.
Or when did he command virginity?
I know as well as you, for there's no doubt,

When maidenhood the Apostle spoke about
He said he had no precept. To be sure,   65
A woman may be counseled to be pure,
But counsel and commandment aren't the same.
To leave it to our judgment was his aim.
For if God did command virginity,
Then marriage he condemned concurrently;   70
And surely if no seed were ever sown,
From where then would virginity be grown?
Paul wouldn't dare command, would least invoke
A thing on which his Master never spoke.
A prize is set up for virginity: 75
Who runs the best may have it, let us see.
      "But not for all is this word seen as right,
It's only as God wills it in his might.
The Apostle was a virgin, well I note;
But nonetheless, although he said and wrote   80
That he wished everyone would be as he,
It was but to advise virginity.
He allows I be a wife, if that's my place,
In his indulgence, so it's no disgrace
To marry if my latest mate should die—   85
Without the 'bigamy' that some would cry.
'It's best a man should not a woman touch';
He meant in bed or on the couch or such.
In mixing fire and tinder danger lies;
What this example means you realize.   90
And that's the sum: he held virginity
Was better than to wed in frailty.
(I call it 'frailty' unless the two
Would chaste remain till both their lives were through.)
      "I grant it well, but envy I do not,   95
That maidenhood may be the better lot.
In soul and body some like being clean,
And I can make no boasts. But have you seen
Among possessions that the nobles hold
If each and every vessel is of gold?   100
Some are of service though they be of wood.
In sundry ways God calls us to his good,

Each by his own God-given gift sustained,
Some this, some that, as heaven has ordained.
   "A great perfection is virginity,   105
And continence maintained devotedly;
But Christ, who of perfection is the well,
Did not bid everyone to go and sell
All that he had and give it to the poor
And thereby follow him; no, this was for   110
The ones desiring to live perfectly—
And by your leave, my lords, that isn't me.
For I'll bestow the flower of my life
In all the acts and fruits of being wife.
   "And tell me for what reason, if you can,   115
Were organs made for reproducing man
Who's made in such a wise and perfect way?
They were not made for nothing, safe to say.
Gloss over whoso will, tell all creation
Our little things both are for urination,   120
And that they're made so different in detail
So we can know the female from the male
And for no other reason—you say 'No'?
Experience knows well it isn't so.
That learned men I not provoke to oath,   125
I mean to say that they were made for both—
That is, both for relief and for our ease
To procreate, so God we not displease.
Why else should men into their ledgers set
That every man yield to his wife her debt?   130
And how can he pay this emolument
Unless he use his simple instrument?
That's why upon all creatures these are set,
To urinate and also to beget.
   "But I don't say that everyone possessing   135
Equipment such as this as I was stressing
Must go and use it for engendering,
Lest chastity be held a worthless thing.
Christ was a virgin though shaped as a man,
And many a saint since this world first began   140
Has also lived in perfect chastity.

I don't begrudge them their virginity;
They're bread from finest wheat, so be it said,
And let us wives be known as barley bread.
And yet with barley bread, as Mark can tell,   145
Was many a man by Jesus nourished well.
In such estate as God calls each of us
I'll persevere. I'm not fastidious,
In wifehood I will use my instrument
As freely as my Maker has it sent.   150
If I hold back, God bring me misery!
My spouse shall have it day and night, when he
Desires he may come forth and pay his debt.
I'll have a husband—I'm not quitting yet—
And he will be my debtor and my slave,   155
And in the flesh his troubles will be grave
As long as I continue as his wife;
For I will have the power all my life
Over his body, I and never he.
It's just as the Apostle said to me   160
And bade them love us well, which I must say
Are teachings to my liking all the way."
    The Pardoner spoke up immediately.
"Now dame, by God and by Saint John," said he,
"As a noble preacher on the case you'll pass.   165
I almost wed a wife, but then, alas,
Why buy it with my flesh, a price so dear?
I'd rather not get married, not this year."
    "Abide," she said, "my tale is not begun!
No, you'll be drinking from another tun,   170
Before I'm through, that tastes much worse than ale.
And when I'm finished telling you my tale
Of tribulation known to man and wife—
Of which I've been an expert all my life
(That is to say, of which I've been the whip)—   175
Then make your choice whether you would sip
From this same tun that I'm about to broach.
Be wary lest too near it you approach.
I'll tell you good examples, more than ten.
'Whoso would not be warned by other men,   180

By him shall other men corrected be.'
These words were written by Ptolemy,
You'll find it if you read his *Almagest*."
  "Dame, if you will, I prayerfully request,"
The Pardoner said, "that just as you began   185
Tell us your tale and do not spare a man
And of your practice teach us younger men."
  "If you desire, I'll do so gladly, then,"
She said. "But first I pray this company,
If I should speak as it may fancy me,   190
Will not be too upset by what I say,
For my intent is nothing but to play.
  "My lords, I now will offer you my tale.
If ever I may drink of wine or ale,
I'll tell the truth on husbands that I've had,   195
As three of them were good and two were bad.
The three men who were good were rich and old,
Indeed were scarcely able to uphold
The contract binding them. By God above,
You know exactly what I'm speaking of.   200
So help me God, I laugh to think, all right,
How pitifully I made them work all night,
Though, by my faith, it meant not much to me;
They gave me so much of their treasury
I didn't need to practice diligence   205
To win their love or show them reverence.
For they loved me so well, by God above,
That I put little value in their love.
The woman's wise who's busy till she's won
The love she wants, or she'll be left with none.   210
But since I had them wholly in my hand
And they had given to me all their land,
Why should I pay them heed and try to please,
Unless it were for profit and for ease?
But by my faith, I worked them for so long   215
That many a night they sang a plaintive song.
The bacon wasn't fetched for them, I know,
Like for some men in Essex at Dunmow.
I governed them so strictly by my law

That each of them was happy to a flaw   220
To bring me back some nice things from the fair,
And glad when I would speak with pleasant air,
For God knows I would chide them spitefully.
    "Now hear how well I bore myself, and see,
The wise among you wives who understand,   225
How you should speak: accuse them out of hand.
There's no man who can falsely swear and lie
As half as boldly as a woman. I
Don't say this to those wives already wise,
Save when they've made mistake—then I advise   230
That she who knows what's good for her and bad
Must prove the chough has gone stark raving mad
And call as witness her assenting maid.
Now listen to my typical tirade:
    " 'Old sluggard, you would have me dress this way?   235
Why does my neighbor's wife have fine array?
She is so honored everywhere she goes;
I sit at home, I have no nifty clothes.
What are you up to at my neighbor's house?
Is she so fair? So amorous are you, spouse?   240
What do you whisper with our maid? Ah, bless me!
Sir Lecher, will you stop your treachery!
Yet if I have a confidant or friend
In innocence, you chide me to no end
If I so much as walk into his house.   245
You come home just as drunken as a mouse
And preach upon your bench. Bad luck to you!
You say to me that it's a mighty rue
To marry one who's poor, for the expense;
And if she's rich and highborn, you commence   250
To talk about the torment and the folly
Of suffering all her pride and melancholy.
And if she's fair, you thorough knave, you say
That every lecher wants her right away,
That she'll not long in chastity abide   255
When she's assailed on each and every side.
    " 'You say that some desire us for our fortunes,
Some for our looks, some for our good proportions,

And some because she either sings or dances,
Some for her noble blood and flirty glances,   260
Her hands and arms so graceful—without fail
All go right to the devil by your tale.
You say that men can't keep a castle wall
That's swarmed upon as long, that it will fall.
    " 'If she looks foul, then you declare that she   265
Will lust for every fellow she may see,
Leap on him like a spaniel in a trice
Until she finds the man who'll pay her price.
In all the lake there's not one goose so gray
That it will be without a mate, you say.   270
Yet it's a hard thing, you would have it known,
To have what no man willingly would own
(You say it, loafer, when you go to bed),
And that a wise man has no need to wed
Nor any man whose aim is heaven's wonder.   275
May lightning and a bolt of wildest thunder
Come break your withered neck with fiery stroke!
    " 'You say a house that leaks, and also smoke,
And wives who scold, cause men to run away
From their own homes. Ah, *benedicite!*   280
What ails such an old fellow so to chide?
    " 'You say we wives all of our vices hide
Until we wed, and then we let them show.
The proverb of a rascal whom I know!
    " 'You say the ox, the ass, the hound, the horse   285
At various times are tested, as, of course,
Are bowls and basins ere a buy is made,
And spoons and stools, and other household trade
Like pots and clothes, and other such array;
But menfolk never test their wives, you say,   290
Till they are wed—old dotard, ne'er-do-well!—
And then we show our vices, so you tell.
    " 'And it displeases me, you also say,
If you don't praise my beauty all the day
And aren't forever poring on my face   295
And calling me "fair dame" in every place;
If you don't hold a feast upon the day

When I was born, dress me in rich array;
If you don't honor with all due respect
My nurse and chambermaid, nor deem select   300
All of my father's kinfolk and allies—
You say it, you old barrel full of lies!

  " 'And our apprentice Jenkin, by his hair—
Those curly, golden, shining locks so fair—
And by the fact he squires me where I go,   305
Gives you a false suspicion. Kindly know
I wouldn't want him if you died tomorrow.

  " 'But tell me this, why hide (be it your sorrow!)
The keys from me that lock your chest? I'll tell
You this, your property is mine as well.   310
Am I an idiot like some other dames?
I tell you by that lord they call Saint James,
You won't be—you can rave mad in the woods!—
Master of both my body and my goods;
You'll forgo one, I tell you to your eye.   315
What help is it to ask around and spy?
I think that you would lock me in your chest.
To say, "Go where you please, wife," would be best,
"Have fun, I won't believe tales told in malice,
For I know you to be a good wife, Alice."   320
We love no man who keeps such watchful eyes
On where we go, our liberty we prize.

  " 'Above all men may he most blessed be,
That wise astronomer Ptolemy,
Who wrote this proverb in his *Almagest:*   325
"He has much higher wisdom than the rest
Who doesn't care who has the world in hand."
And by this proverb you should understand
That if you have enough, why should you care
How merrily some other people fare?   330
For by your leave, old dotard, of my stuff
Tonight you surely will have quite enough.
How great a niggard is he who refuses
A candlelight from the lantern that he uses;
He'd have no less light than he did before.   335
You have enough, so don't complain for more.

" 'And if in finest clothes, you also say,
In jewelry and other fine display,
We dress ourselves, we risk our chastity;
To back up what you say, you quote to me   340
The following in the Apostle's name:
"Clothes chastely made with proper sense of shame
Is what your women's dress should always be—
No fancy hairdos, no bright jewelry
Like pearls and gold, nor other rich array."   345
About your text and rubric, let me say
I'd follow them as much as would a gnat.
   " 'You also say that I am like a cat,
For if somebody singes a cat's fur
She'll be content to stay inside and purr,   350
But if her fur is sleek and fine she'll stay
Inside the house not more than half a day;
Before the dawn can break she's to her calling,
She's showing off her fur and caterwauling—
In other words, Sir Rascal, if well dressed   355
I run out to be sure I'm well assessed.
   " 'Old fool, what help to you are all your spies?
If you asked Argus with his hundred eyes
To be my bodyguard—what better measure?—
He'd guard me only if it were my pleasure;   360
As I may thrive, I'd really tweak his beard!
   " 'You also speak of three things to be feared
For troubling all the earth, and that for sure
The fourth one there's no man could long endure.
Sir Rascal dear, may Christ cut short your life,   365
For still you preach and say a hateful wife
Is one of these misfortunes. Sir, are there
No other things to speak of and compare
In telling all your parables? Must you
Always include a poor wife ere you're through?   370
   " 'You also liken woman's love to hell,
To barren land without a stream or well,
And also to a wildly raging fire—
The more it burns, the stronger its desire
To consume all that will burn. You say to me   375

That just as little worms destroy a tree
A wife destroys her husband. "They have found
This to be true, those who to wives are bound." '
   "My lords, just so, as you now understand,
I accused all my old husbands out of hand   380
Of saying such while they were drunk. And all
Was false, but as my witnesses I'd call
On Jenkin and my niece to say, 'It's so.'
O Lord, the pain I gave them and the woe!
Their guilt? By God's sweet grief, they hadn't any;   385
And yet just like a horse I'd bite and whinny,
Complaining well when I myself had guilt,
For they'd have killed me had the beans been spilt.
Who comes first to the mill is first to grind;
I'd be first to complain, and always find   390
Our war was quickly over—gladly they
Repented things they didn't do or say.
On wenches I would give them reprimand
When they were so sick they could hardly stand.
   "Yet each was tickled in his heart to see   395
What he thought was such love for him in me.
I swore that all my walking out by night
Was just to keep his wenches in my sight.
With that excuse I had me lots of mirth.
For we are given such keen wits at birth   400
To cheat and weep and spin; these God will give
To women naturally long as they live.
So one thing I can speak of boastfully,
The one who came out best was always me,
By sleight or force, or by some other thing   405
Like long complaint and constant bickering.
Especially in bed were they undone,
For there I'd scold them and deny them fun;
I would no longer in the bed abide,
Once I could feel his arm upon my side,   410
Until he paid his ransom as he must—
Then I would suffer him to do his lust.
And so to every man I tell this tale:
Gain what you can, for everything's for sale,

And no hawk by an empty hand is lured.   415
For profit all his lust I so endured
And feigned for him a lusty appetite;
In bacon, though, I never took delight,
And that is why I would forever chide.
For even had the pope sat down beside   420
Them there, I wouldn't spare them at the table,
To pay back word for word I was so able.
So help me God who is omnipotent,
Were I to make right now my testament
I'd owe them not a word that's not repaid.   425
I did this by the wits that I displayed
So that they had to give up and be bested
Or else we never would have finally rested.
Though like a raging lion he would look,
Yet he would fail at every tack he took.   430
    "Then I would say, 'Good dear, just take a peep
At how meek-looking Wilkin is, our sheep;
Come here, my spouse, and let me kiss your cheek;
You should always be patient, always meek,
And have a good man's conscience, as so much   435
You like to preach of patient Job and such.
Be always patient, since so well you preach—
If not, a lesson we will have to teach,
How fair it is to have a wife in peace,
For there's no doubt that one of us must cease;   440
Since woman's less reasonable than the male,
You must therefore be patient. What can ail
You, husband, that so much you gripe and groan?
Is it my thing? You'd have it yours alone?
Why, take it all, here, take it every bit.   445
By Peter, curse you! such a love for it.
If I were selling some of my *belle chose*
I then could walk fresh-looking as a rose,
But I will keep it for your own sweet tooth.
You are to blame, by God, and that's the truth.'   450
    "The words we'd have were always of that sort.
And now on my fourth husband I'll report.
    "A reveler was husband number four,

That is to say, he had a paramour.
And I was young and wanton, passionate,   455
As jolly as a magpie, obstinate
And strong. How I could dance to a small harp, too,
And sing like any nightingale can do
When I had drunk a draught of good sweet wine!
Metellius, that dirty churl, the swine,   460
Picked up a staff and took his spouse's life
For drinking wine. If I had been his wife,
He never would have daunted me from drinking!
And after wine, on Venus I'd be thinking,
For as surely as cold engenders hail   465
A lustful mouth will have a lustful tail.
A tipsy woman is without defense,
As lechers know by their experience.
   "But Lord Christ! when it all comes back to me,
Remembrance of my youth and jollity,   470
It warms the cockles of my heart. Today
It still does my heart good that I can say
I've had the world, what time's been mine to pass.
But age that poisons everything, alas,
Bereft me of my beauty and my pith.   475
Well, let it go, the devil go therewith!
The flour is gone, there is no more to tell;
The bran as best I can I now must sell
And strive to be as merry as before.
And now I'll tell of husband number four.   480
   "I had within my heart a great despite
That he in any other took delight.
I paid him back, by God and by Saint Joyce,
With a hard staff from wood of his own choice;
Not with my body, not by sinful means,   485
But entertaining folks in merry scenes,
I made him fry in his own grease till he
Was quite consumed with angry jealousy.
By God, on earth I was his purgatory,
For which I hope his soul is now in glory.   490
God knows how often he would sit and sing
While his shoe pinched him, such a painful thing;

For there was none save God and me who knew
The many torments that I put him through.
He died when I came from Jerusalem;   495
Beneath the rood-beam where we buried him,
His tomb was surely not as finely done
As was great King Darius's, the one
Built by Apelles with such skill and taste.
A costly burial would have been a waste.   500
May he fare well and God give his soul rest,
For he's now in his grave, his wooden chest.
    "Of husband number five I now will tell.
God grant his soul may never go to hell!
And yet he was to me the very worst;   505
I feel it in my ribs from last to first
And always will until the day I die.
But in our bed he was so fresh and spry,
To gloss away so able, heaven knows,
Whenever he was wanting my *belle chose,*   510
That though each bone he'd beaten was in pain,
At once he'd win back all my love again.
I swear I loved him best of all, for he
Was always playing hard-to-get with me.
We women have—the truth, so help me God—   515
In this regard a fancy that is odd;
That which we can't get in an easy way
Is what we'll crave and cry for all the day.
Forbid us something and then we'll desire it,
But press it on us and we'll not require it.   520
With coyness we trade in our affairs;
Great market crowds make more expensive wares
And what's too cheap will not be held a prize.
This every woman knows if she is wise.
    "My husband number five, God bless his soul,   525
I took for love, no riches were my goal.
He once had been an Oxford clerk, but then
Had left school and gone home, and boarded in
Our town with a good friend of mine, the one,
God bless her soul, whose name was Alison.   530
She knew my heart, each of my secrets well,

Much better than the parish priest. I'd tell
Her everything, disclosing to her all;
For had my husband pissed upon a wall
Or done something that could have cost his life,   535
To her and to another worthy wife—
And also to my niece, whom I loved well—
His every secret I would fully tell.
God knows, I did this so much, to his dread,
It often made his face get hot and red.   540
He felt ashamed, but blamed himself that he
Had told to me so great a privity.
    "It so befell that one time during Lent,
As often to this close friend's house I went
(And I so loved to dress up anyway   545
And take my walks in March, April, and May
From house to house, to hear what tales were spun),
This clerk named Jenkin, my friend Alison,
And I myself into the meadows went.
My husband was in London all that Lent,   550
So I had much more leisure time to play,
To see and to be seen along the way
By lusty folks. How could I know when there
Would come good fortune meant for me, or where?
And so I made my visits, I'd attend   555
Religious vigils and processions, wend
With pilgrims, hear the sermons preached; also
To miracle plays and weddings I would go.
The clothes that I would wear were scarlet bright;
There never was a worm or moth or mite,   560
As I may live, could bring to them abuse.
Do you know why? They always were in use.
    "I'll tell you now what happened next to me.
I've said we walked into the fields, we three;
And there we really had a chance to flirt,   565
This clerk and I. My foresight to assert,
While we were talking I suggested he,
If I wound up a widow, marry me.
For certainly—I say it not to boast—
Of good purveyance I have made the most   570

In marriages and other things as well.
A mouse's heart's not worth a leek in hell
If he has just one hole for which to run,
For if that one hole fails then all is done.

"I made pretense that he enchanted me   575
(My mother taught to me this subtlety);
I dreamt of him all night, I also said,
And dreamt he slew me as I lay in bed,
My bed as full of blood as it could be.
'But still I hope that you'll bring good to me,   580
For blood betokens gold, or so I'm taught.'
And all was false, for I'd been dreaming naught,
I only followed all my mother's lore
(On that as well as on a few things more).

"And now, sirs—let me see, what was I saying?   585
Aha! by God, I have it, no more straying.

"When my fourth husband lay upon the bier,
I wept, of course, grief-stricken to appear,
As wives must do (the custom of the land),
And hid my face with the kerchief in my hand.   590
But as I'd be provided with a mate,
I wept but little, I can truly state.

"Now as my husband to the church was borne
That morning, neighbors went along to mourn,
With our clerk Jenkin being one. As God   595
May help me, when I saw him as he trod
Behind the bier, I thought that he had feet
And legs as fair as ever I could meet,
And all my heart was then in his dear hold.
He was, I think, then twenty winters old,   600
And I was forty, telling you the truth;
But I have always had a coltish tooth.
Gap-toothed I was, and that was for the best;
The birthmark of Saint Venus I possessed.
So help me God, I was a lusty one   605
And fair and rich and young and full of fun;
And truly, as my husbands said to me,
I had the finest what's-it there could be.
My feelings come from Venus and my heart

Is full of Mars; for Venus did impart   610
To me all of my lecherousness and lust,
And Mars gave me a hard and sturdy crust.
My ascendant sign was Taurus, Mars therein.
Alas, alas, that ever love was sin!
For I have always followed inclination   615
By virtue of my taurine constellation;
That made me so that I could not deny
A good fellow my Venus chamber. I
Still have the mark of Mars upon my face
(And also in another, private place).   620
As truly as the Lord is my salvation,
My love was never by discrimination;
I always catered to my appetite,
Though he be short or long or black or white.
I didn't care, just so he pleasured me,   625
How poor he was or what was his degree.
   "What shall I say except, when that month ended,
This jolly Jenkin whom I thought so splendid
Had married me midst great solemnity.
I gave him all the land and property   630
That ever had been given me. And yet
It was thereafter much to my regret;
Of nothing that I wanted he would hear.
By God, he struck me so once on the ear
(Because I tore a page out of his book)   635
That it went deaf from that one blow it took.
But I was stubborn like a lioness
And lashed him with my tongue without redress.
And I'd go walking as I'd done before
From house to house (though I would not, he swore),   640
For which he oftentimes would start to preach
To me. Old Roman stories he would teach,
Like how Simplicius Gallus left his wife,
Forsaking her the remainder of his life,
Because he caught her looking out the door   645
One day bareheaded—that and nothing more.
   "A Roman, too, he told me of by name
Whose wife had gone out to a summer's game

Without his knowledge; he forsook her too.
And then he'd go and search his Bible through   650
For a proverb of Ecclesiasticus
Wherein he gives a firm command to us:
No man should let his wife go roam about.
And after that he'd quote without a doubt:
'Whoever builds his house by using sallows   655
And goes and pricks his blind horse over fallows
And lets his wife seek any shrine one hallows
Is worthy to be hung upon the gallows!'
But all for naught, for I cared not a straw
For all his proverbs or for his old saw.   660
I'd not correct myself by his advices.
I hate a man who tells me of my vices,
And so do more of us, God knows, than I.
So mad with me this made him he could die,
But I would not forbear in any case.   665
    "I'll tell you, by Saint Thomas, face-to-face
The reason I tore from his book a page,
Why he gave me a deaf ear in his rage.
    "He had a book that he read night and day
For his amusement. He would laugh away   670
At this book, which he called 'Valerius
And Theophrastus,' with its various
Selections: there was once a clerk in Rome,
A cardinal whose name was Saint Jerome,
Who wrote a book against Jovinian;   675
This book also contained Tertullian,
Chrysippus, Trotula, and Heloise,
An abbess who once lived near Paris; these
Along with parables of Solomon
And Ovid's *Art*—the books were many a one,   680
And all of them in this one volume bound.
And day and night he always could be found,
When he had leisure or was on vacation
From any sort of worldly occupation,
Reading some passage about wicked wives.   685
Of them he knew more legends and more lives
Than of the best of wives in Holy Writ.

It is impossible, no doubting it,
For any clerk to speak some good of wives
Unless it deals with saints, their holy lives;   690
No woman not a saint he's kindly to.
Who painted, though, the lion, tell me who?
By God, if women ever wrote some stories
As clerks have done in all their oratories,
They would have told of men more wickedness   695
Than all the sons of Adam could redress.
Children of Venus and of Mercury
Have always worked in great polarity;
For Mercury loves wisdom, science pure,
While Venus loves good times, expenditure.   700
Because their dispositions are divergent,
One's descendant, the other one emergent;
So Mercury, God knows, has desolation
When Venus has in Pisces exaltation,
And Venus falls when Mercury is raised.   705
So by no clerk is woman ever praised.
The clerk, when he is old and cannot do
For Venus any work worth his old shoe,
Will in his dotage sit and write of how
A woman cannot keep her marriage vow!   710
    "Now let me tell the reason why I say
That I was beaten for a book, I pray.
One night this Jenkin, who was my fifth sire,
Was reading in his book beside the fire.
He read of Eve, who by her wickedness   715
Had brought all of mankind to wretchedness,
The reason Jesus Christ himself was slain
To bring us back with his heart's blood again.
'Of women here expressly you may find
That woman was the ruin of all mankind.'   720
    "He read to me how Samson lost his hair,
Sheared by his mistress, sleeping unaware,
And how by this he lost both of his eyes.
    "He read then to me—I will tell no lies—
Of Dejanira, she who was to blame   725
That Hercules had set himself aflame.

"He left out not a whit about the woe
That Socrates' two wives caused him to know;
When Xantippe poured piss upon his head,
The hapless man sat there as still as dead,   730
Then wiped his head and dared not to complain,
But said, 'Ere thunder stops, there comes a rain.'
        "The tale of Pasiphaë, the queen of Crete,
For cursedness he thought was really sweet.
Fie on it! I'll not speak in any measure   735
About her horrid lust, her grisly pleasure.
        "Of Clytemnestra, who for lechery
Brought to her husband death by treachery,
With greatest fervor then to me he read.
        "He told me, too, the circumstance that led   740
Amphiaraus at Thebes to lose his life;
My husband had a legend of his wife
Eriphyle, who for a brooch of gold
Had gone in secret to the Greeks and told
Of where her husband had his hiding place,   745
For which he met at Thebes with sorry grace.
        "He told of Livia, Lucilia too,
Who made their husbands die, albeit true
One was for love, the other was for hate.
For Livia, one evening very late,   750
Gave poison to her husband as a foe;
But lecherous Lucilia loved hers so
That, so he might forever of her think,
She gave him such a love potion to drink
That he was dead before the morning sun.   755
And therefore husbands always are undone.
        "He told me then how one Latumius
Complained one day to his friend Arrius
That growing in his garden was a tree
On which, he said, his wives (who numbered three)   760
Had hung themselves out of their hearts' despite.
Said Arrius, 'Dear brother, if you might,
Give me a cutting from that blessed tree,
And in my garden planted shall it be.'
        "Of later date, of wives to me he read   765

Who sometimes slew their husbands while in bed,
Then with their lechers screwed the night away
While flat upon the floor the bodies lay.
Some others would drive nails into the brain
While they were sleeping, that's how they were slain.   770
Still others gave them poison in their drink.
Of evil more than any heart can think
About he read, and he knew more proverbs
Than in this world there's growth of grass or herbs.
'It's better that your dwelling place,' said he,   775
'With a foul dragon or a lion be
Than with a woman who is wont to chide.
High on the roof it's better to abide
Than with an angry wife down in the house.
Each wicked and contrary to her spouse,   780
They hate all that their husbands love.' He'd say,
'A woman casts all of her shame away
When she casts off her smock.' He'd further tell,
'A woman fair, if she's not chaste as well,
Is like a golden ring in a sow's nose.'   785
Who could have thought, whoever would suppose
The woe and torment that was in my heart?
    "And when I saw that he would never part
With reading in this cursed book all night,
Three leaves all of a sudden I tore right   790
Out of his book while he was reading it,
Then with my fist I gave his cheek a hit
And he fell backwards right into the fire.
He jumped up like a lion full of ire
And with his fist he hit me in the head,   795
And I lay on the floor then as if dead.
And when he saw how stilly there I lay,
He was aghast and would have run away,
But then at last out of my swoon I woke.
'O false thief, have you slain me?' then I spoke.   800
'You've murdered me for all my land, that's why,
Yet let me kiss you now before I die.'
    "Then near he came and knelt down by my side,
And said, 'Dear sister Alison, my bride,

So help me God, I'd never hit my dame;   805
For what I've done you are yourself to blame.
Forgive me, I beseech you and implore.'
And then I hit him on the cheek once more.
'This much I am avenged, O thief,' I said.
'I can no longer speak, I'm nearly dead.'   810
    "But in the end, for all we suffered through,
We finally reached accord between us two.
The bridle he put wholly in my hand
To have complete control of house and land,
And of his tongue and hands as well—and when   815
He did, I made him burn his book right then.
And when I had by all my mastery
Thus gained for myself all the sovereignty—
When he had said to me, 'My own true wife,
Do as you please the balance of your life;   820
Keep your honor as well as my estate'—
From that day on we never had debate.
I was as true as any wife you'd find
From India to Denmark, and as kind,
So help me God, and he was so to me.   825
I pray that God who sits in majesty
Will bless his soul for all his mercy dear.
Now I will tell my tale if you will hear."

Words between the Summoner and the Friar

    The Friar laughed when he had heard all this.
He said, "If ever I have joy or bliss,   830
Your tale has quite a long preamble, dame!"
And when the Summoner heard the Friar exclaim,
The Summoner said, "Behold, by God's two arms!
See how a meddling friar ever swarms.
A fly and friar, good men, will fall into   835
Each dish, into all kinds of matter. You
Speak of preambulation? Amble or
Go trot, shut up, or go sit down! No more,
You're spoiling all our fun, the way you act."

The Friar said, "Summoner, is that a fact?   840
Now by my faith, I will, before I'm through,
Tell of a summoner such a tale or two
That everyone will laugh throughout the place."
 "Now, Friar, damn your bloody eyes and face!"
The Summoner said. "And damn myself as well 845
If two tales, or if three, I do not tell
Of friars ere I come to Sittingbourne.
And with them I will cause your heart to mourn,
For I can see your patience now is gone."
 Our Host said, "Peace! No more such goings-on!" 850
He said, "Now let this woman tell her tale.
You act like people who are drunk with ale.
Now, madam, tell your tale, for that is best."
 "I'm ready, sir," she said, "as you request,
With license from this worthy Friar here." 855
 "Yes, dame," said he, "speak on, you'll have my ear."

THE WIFE OF BATH'S TALE

 In the old days of King Arthur, today
Still praised by Britons in a special way,
This land was filled with fairies all about.
The elf-queen with her jolly little rout   860
In many a green field often danced. Indeed
This was the old belief of which I read;
I speak of many hundred years ago.
But now such elves no one is seeing. No,
For now the prayers and charitable desires 865
Of limiters and other holy friars
Who wander all the land, by every stream,
As thick as specks of dust in a sunbeam,
To bless our halls, chambers, kitchens, bowers,
Boroughs, cities, castles, lofty towers,   870
Villages, granaries, stables, dairies,
Have made sure that no longer are there fairies.
For where there once was wont to walk an elf
There's walking now the limiter himself,

Early and late, to give his auspices,   875
Say matins and his other offices,
Go all about the limit where he's found.
Now women may go safely all around;
In every bush and under every tree
He is the only incubus, and he   880
Won't do a thing except dishonor them.
    It happened that King Arthur had with him
A bachelor in his house; this lusty liver,
While riding from his hawking by the river,
Once chanced upon, alone as she was born,   885
A maiden who was walking—soon forlorn,
For he, despite all that she did or said,
By force deprived her of her maidenhead.
Because of this, there was such clamoring
And such demand for justice to the king,   890
This knight was all but numbered with the dead
By course of law, and should have lost his head
(Which may have been the law in that milieu).
But then the queen and other ladies too
Prayed so long that the king might grant him grace,   895
King Arthur spared him for at least a space;
He left him to the queen to do her will,
To choose to save or order them to kill.
    The queen then thanked the king with all her might,
And after this the queen spoke with the knight   900
When she saw opportunity one day.
"For you," she said, "things stand in such a way
You can't be sure if you're to live or not.
I'll grant you life if you can tell me what
It is that women most desire. Beware   905
The iron ax, your neckbone now to spare!
And if you cannot tell me right away,
I'll give you leave, a twelvemonth and a day,
That you may go to seek, that you might find
An answer that is of sufficient kind.   910
I want your word before you take a pace:
You'll bring yourself back to this very place."
    This knight with sorrow sighed, was full of woe.

What could he do? Not as he pleased, and so
To go away was what he finally chose,   915
To come back when his year was at its close
With such an answer as God might provide.
He took his leave and forth he went to ride.

 He sought in every house and every place
In hopes he could secure the promised grace   920
By learning that which women love the most.
But he did not arrive at any coast
Where he could find two people on the matter
Who might agree, if judging by their chatter.
Some said that women all love riches best,   925
While some said honor, others jolly zest,
Some rich array; some said delights in bed,
And many said to be a widow wed;
Some others said that our hearts are most eased
When we are flattered and when we are pleased—   930
And he was nigh the truth, if you ask me.
A man shall win us best with flattery;
With much attendance, charm, and application
Can we be caught, whatever be our station.

 Some said our love to which we all aspire   935
Is to be free to do as we desire,
With no reproof of vice but with the rule
That men should say we're wise, not one a fool.
For truly there is none among us all
Who, if a man should claw us on the gall,   940
Won't kick for being told the truth; he who
Does an assay will find out that it's true.
But though we may have vices kept within,
We like to be called wise and clean of sin.

 And some say that we take the most delight   945
In keeping secrets, keeping our lips tight,
To just one purpose striving to adhere:
Not to betray one thing that we may hear.
That tale's not worth the handle of a rake.
We women can't keep secrets, heaven's sake!   950
Just look at Midas—would you hear the tale?
 Ovid, among the trifles he'd detail,

Said Midas had long hair, for it appears
That on his head had grown two ass's ears.
This defect he had tried as best he might   955
To keep well as he could from others' sight,
And save his wife there was none who could tell.
He loved her much and trusted her as well
And prayed that not one living creature she
Would ever tell of his deformity.   960
    She swore she'd not, though all the world to win,
Be guilty of such villainy and sin
And make her husband have so foul a name.
To tell it would as well bring her to shame.
But nonetheless she all but nearly died,   965
So long to have a secret she must hide.
She thought it swelled so sorely in her heart
Some word from out of her was bound to start;
And since she dared to tell it to no man,
Down close beside a marsh the lady ran—   970
She had to rush, her heart was so afire.
Then like a bittern booming in the mire,
She put her mouth down to the water, saying,
"Water, make no sound, don't be betraying,
For I will tell this to no one but you.   975
My husband has long ass's ears—it's true!"
She thought, "My heart is cured now, it is out;
I couldn't keep it longer, there's no doubt."
So as you see, we may awhile abide
But it must out, no secret we can hide.   980
(As for the tale, if you would hear the rest,
Read Ovid, for that's where you'll learn it best.)
    This knight of whom my tale is all about,
When seeing that he couldn't find it out—
That is to say, what women love the most—   985
Felt in his breast already like a ghost;
For home he headed, he could not sojourn,
The day had come when homeward he must turn.
And in this woeful state he chanced to ride
While on his way along a forest side,   990
And there he saw upon the forest floor

Some ladies dancing, twenty-four or more.
Toward these dancers he was quick to turn
In hope that of some wisdom he might learn;
But all at once, before he'd gotten there,   995
The dancers disappeared, he knew not where.
He didn't see one creature bearing life,
Save sitting on the green one single wife.
An uglier creature no mind could devise.
To meet him this old wife was to arise,   1000
And said, "You can't get there from here, Sir Knight.
What are you seeking, by your faith? It might
Well be to your advantage, sir, to tell;
Old folks like me know many things, and well."

 "Dear mother," said the knight, "it is for sure   1005
That I am dead if I cannot secure
What thing it is that women most desire.
If you could teach me, gladly I would hire."

 "Give me your word here in my hand," said she,
"The next thing I request you'll do for me   1010
If it's a thing that lies within your might,
And I will tell you then before it's night."
The knight said, "Here's my oath, I guarantee."

 "Then certainly I dare to boast," said she,
"Your life is safe, for I'll be standing by;   1015
Upon my life, the queen will say as I.
Let's see who is the proudest of them all,
With kerchief or with headdress standing tall,
Who shall deny that which I have to teach.
Now let us go, no need to make a speech."   1020
She whispered then a message in his ear
And bade him to be glad and have no fear.

 When they had come to court, the knight declared,
"I've come back to the day, and to be spared,
For I am now prepared to give reply."   1025
The noble wives and maidens stood nearby,
And widows too (who were considered wise);
The queen sat like a justice in her guise.
All these had been assembled there to hear,
And then the knight was summoned to appear.   1030

Full silence was commanded in the court
So that the knight might openly report
The thing that worldly women love the best.
He stood not like a beast at one's behest
But quickly gave his answer loud and clear,   1035
With manly voice that all the court might hear.
    "My liege and lady, generally," said he,
"What women most desire is sovereignty
Over their husbands or the ones they love,
To have the mastery, to be above.   1040
This is your most desire, though you may kill
Me if you wish. I'm here, do as you will."
No wife or maid or widow in the court
Saw fit to contradict the knight's report;
They all agreed, "He's worthy of his life."   1045
And with that word up started the old wife,
The one the knight had seen upon the green.
"Mercy," she said, "my sovereign lady queen!
Before your court departs, grant me my right.
It's I who taught this answer to the knight,   1050
For which he gave a solemn oath to me:
The first thing I request he'd do for me
If it's a thing that lies within his might.
Before the court I therefore pray, Sir Knight,"
She said, "that you will take me as your wife;   1055
For well you know that I have saved your life.
If I speak falsely, by your faith accuse me."
    The knight replied, "Alas, how woes abuse me!
I know I made the promise you've expressed.
For love of God, please choose a new request.   1060
Take all my goods and let my body go."
    "No, damn us both then!" she replied. "For though
I may be ugly, elderly, and poor,
I'd give all of the metal and the ore
That lies beneath the earth and lies above   1065
If only I could be your wife and love."
    "My love?" he said. "No, rather my damnation!
Alas! that there is any of my nation
Who ever could so foully be disgraced."

But all for naught, the end was that he faced   1070
Constrainment, for he now would have to wed
And take his gray old wife with him to bed.
   Now there are some men who might say perhaps
That it's my negligence or else a lapse
That I don't tell you of the joyous way   1075
In which the feast took place that very day.
I'll answer briefly should the question fall:
There wasn't any joy or feast at all,
Just lots of sorrow, things went grievously.
He married her that morning privately,   1080
Then all that day he hid just like an owl,
So woeful, for his wife looked really foul.
   Great was the woe the knight had in his head
When with his wife he'd been brought to the bed;
He tossed and then he turned both to and fro.   1085
His old wife lay there smiling at him, though,
And said, "Dear husband, *benedicite!*
Acts every knight toward his wife this way?
Is this the law of great King Arthur's house?
Is every knight of his so distant? Spouse,   1090
I am your own true love and I'm your wife
And I'm the one as well who saved your life,
And I have never done you wrong or spite.
Why do you treat me so on our first night?
You act just like a man who's lost his wit.   1095
What is my guilt? For God's love, tell me it,
And it shall be amended if I may."
   "Amended?" asked the knight. "Whatever way?
There's no way it could ever be amended.
You are so old and loathsome—and descended,   1100
To add to that, from such a lowly kind—
No wonder that I toss and turn and wind.
I wish to God my heart would burst, no less!"
   "Is this," she said, "the cause of your distress?"
   "Why, yes," said he, "and is there any wonder?"   1105
   She said, "I could amend the stress you're under,
If you desire, within the next three days,
If you'll treat me more kindly in your ways.

"But when you talk about gentility
Like old wealth handed down a family tree,   1110
That this is what makes of you gentlemen,
Such arrogance I judge not worth a hen.
Take him who's always virtuous in his acts
In public and in private, who exacts
Of himself all the noble deeds he can,   1115
And there you'll find the greatest gentleman.
Christ wills we claim nobility from him,
Not from our elders or the wealth of them;
For though they give us all their heritage
And we claim noble birth by parentage,   1120
They can't bequeath—all else theirs for the giving—
To one of us the virtuous way of living
That made the nobles they were known to be,
The way they bade us live in like degree.
        "How well the poet wise, the Florentine   1125
Named Dante, speaks about just what I mean,
And this is how he rhymes it in his story:
'Of men who climb their family trees for glory,
Few will excel, for it is by God's grace
We gain nobility and not by race.'   1130
No, from our elders all that we can claim
Are temporal things such as may hurt and maim.
        "All know as I, that if gentility
Were something that was planted naturally
Through all a certain lineage down the line,   1135
In private and in public they'd be fine
And noble people doing what is nice,
Completely free of villainy and vice.
        "Take fire into the darkest house or hut
Between here and Mount Caucasus, then shut   1140
The doors, and all men leave and not return;
That fire will still remain as if the burn
Were being watched by twenty thousand souls.
Its function will not cease, its nature holds,
On peril of my life, until it dies.   1145
        "Gentility, you then should realize,
Is not akin to things like property;

For people act with much variety,
Not like the fire that always is the same.
God knows that men may often find, for shame,   1150
A lord's son who's involved in villainy.
Who prides himself to have gentility
Because it happens he's of noble birth,
With elders virtuous, of noble worth,
But never tries to do a noble deed   1155
Nor follow in his dead ancestors' lead,
Is not a noble, be he duke or earl;
For bad and sinful deeds just make a churl.
Sir, your gentility is but the fame
Of your ancestors, who earned their good name   1160
With qualities quite foreign to your own.
Gentility can come from God alone,
So true gentility's a thing of grace,
Not something that's bequeathed by rank or place.
    "For nobleness, as says Valerius,   1165
Consider Tullius Hostilius:
Though poor, he rose to noble heights. Look in
Boethius or Seneca, and when
You do, don't doubt the truth of what you read:
The noble is the man of noble deed.   1170
And so, dear husband, thus I will conclude:
If it's true my ancestors were so rude,
Yet may the Lord, as I do hope, grant me
The grace to live my life most virtuously;
For I'm a noble when I so begin   1175
To live in virtue and avoid sin.
    "For poverty you scold me. By your leave,
The God on high, in whom we both believe,
Chose willfully to live a poor man's life;
And surely every man, maiden, or wife   1180
Can understand that Jesus, heaven's King,
Would not choose sinful living. It's a thing
Of honor to be poor without despair,
As Seneca and other clerks declare.
To be poor yet contented, I assert,   1185
Is to be rich, though having not a shirt.

The one who covets is the poorer man,
For he would have that which he never can;
But he who doesn't have and doesn't crave
Is rich, though you may hold him but a knave.   1190
True poverty's been sung of properly;
As Juvenal said of it, 'Merrily
The poor man, as he goes upon his way,
In front of every thief can sing and play.'
It is a hateful good and, as I guess,   1195
A great promoter of industriousness.
A source of greater wisdom it can be
For one who learns to bear it patiently.
Though it seem wearisome, poverty is
Possession none will take from you as his.   1200
Poverty often makes a fellow know
Himself as well as God when he is low.
Poverty is an eyeglass, I contend,
Through which a man can see a truthful friend.
I bring no harm at all to you, therefore   1205
Do not reprove me, sire, for being poor.
    "For being old you've also fussed at me;
Yet surely, sire, though no authority
Were in a book, you gentlemen select
Say men should treat an elder with respect   1210
And call him father, by your courtesy.
I think I could find authors who agree.
    "If I am old and ugly, as you've said,
Of cuckoldry you needn't have a dread;
For filthiness and age, as I may thrive,   1215
Are guards that keep one's chastity alive.
But nonetheless, since I know your delight,
I shall fulfill your worldly appetite.
    "Choose now," she said, "one of these two: that I
Be old and ugly till the day I die,   1220
And be to you a true and humble wife,
One never to displease you all your life;
Or if you'd rather, have me young and fair,
And take your chance on those who will repair
To your house now and then because of me   1225

(Or to some other place, it may well be).
Choose for yourself the one you'd rather try."
    The knight gave it some thought, then gave a sigh,
And finally answered as you are to hear:
"My lady and my love and wife so dear,   1230
I leave to your wise governance the measure;
You choose which one would give the fullest pleasure
And honor to you, and to me as well.
I don't care which you do, you best can tell.
What you desire is good enough for me."   1235
    "You've given me," she said, "the mastery?
The choice is mine and all's at my behest?"
    "Yes, surely, wife," said he, "I think it best."
    "Then kiss me, we'll no longer fight," she said,
"For you've my oath that I'll be both instead—   1240
That is to say, I'll be both good and fair.
I pray to God I die in mad despair
Unless I am to you as good and true
As any wife since this old world was new.
Come dawn, if I'm not as fair to be seen   1245
As any lady, empress, any queen
Who ever lived between the east and west,
Then take my life or do whatever's best.
Lift up the curtains now, see how it is."
    And when the knight had truly seen all this,   1250
How she was young and fair in all her charms,
In utter joy he took her in his arms;
His heart was bathing in a bath of bliss,
A thousand kisses he began to kiss,
And she obeyed in each and every way,   1255
Whatever was his pleasure or his play.
    And so they lived, till their lives' very end,
In perfect joy. And may Christ Jesus send
Us husbands meek and young and fresh abed,
And then the grace to outlive those we wed;   1260
I also pray that Jesus shorten lives
Of those who won't be governed by their wives;
As for old niggards angered by expense,
God send them soon a mighty pestilence!

The Friar's Tale

PROLOGUE

Although this worthy limiter, the Friar,   1265
Had all the while been glowering with ire
At the Summoner, to this juncture he
Had said naught to him for propriety.
But finally the Friar said to the Wife,
"My lady, God give you a right good life!   1270
For I must tell you, here you've come to touch
On weighty questions scholars argue much.
You've said a lot and very well, I say.
But as we're riding here, dame, on our way,
We need to speak of nothing but in game;   1275
Let's leave the authorities, in God's name,
To preaching clerics and their studies too.
Now if this group would like, what I shall do
Is tell you of a summoner for game;
You know, pardie, that by the very name   1280
About a summoner there's no good to say.
(May none among you take offense, I pray.)
A summoner is one who runs around
With writs for fornication where it's found,
And gets a beating at each village side."   1285
  "Ah, sir, you should be kind," our Host replied,
"And courteous, considering your station.
Here in this group we'll have no altercation;
Tell your tale and let the Summoner be."
  "No," said the Summoner, "let him say to me   1290
What he may please. When it's my turn I'll note
And pay him back, by God, for every groat.
I'll tell him how so great an honor, sir,
It is to be a flattering limiter;
I'll also tell of many another crime   1295
That needn't be recounted at this time.

About his job for sure I'll tell him much."
    Our Host said, "Hold your peace! No more of such!"
And to the Friar after that he said,
"Now with your tale, dear master, go ahead."   1300

THE FRIAR'S TALE

    In my part of the land there used to be
An archdeacon, a man of high degree,
Who'd execute with bold determination
The punishment for acts of fornication,
Of pandering, also of sorcery,   1305
Of defamation and adultery,
Of errant churchmen, of false testaments
And contracts and of lack of sacraments,
Of usury and simony also.
To lechers, though, for sure the greatest woe   1310
He dealt, they'd have to sing when they were caught.
Small tithers, too, to foulest shame he brought
If any parson made complaint of them.
No sort of fine was overlooked by him.
For meager tithe, for too small offering,   1315
He made the people piteously to sing.
Before the bishop caught them with his hook,
Their names were down in this archdeacon's book.
So he possessed by way of jurisdiction
The power to correct them with affliction.   1320
He had a summoner ready at hand,
No slyer boy in England, for a band
Of spies the fellow craftily maintained
To let him know where something might be gained.
One lecher he'd abide, or two or more,   1325
If they could lead the way to twenty-four.
This summoner was as mad as a hare,
Yet none of his rascality I'll spare,
For we're beyond the reach of his correction.
They've no rule over friars, no direction,   1330
Nor will they ever have their whole lives through—"

"By Peter! so are women of a stew,"
The Summoner exclaimed, "beyond our care!"
    "Peace now! Misfortune to you, I declare!"
Then said our Host. "Now let him tell his tale.   1335
I pray, continue, though the Summoner rail,
And, my dear master, leave out nothing, sir."
    This false thief (said the Friar), this summoner,
Always had bawds at hand to do his stalking;
Like to the lure in England used in hawking,   1340
To him they brought all secrets they'd accrue;
The relationship they had was nothing new.
They were his agents, working on the sly,
And he was greatly profiting thereby
(His master didn't always know the take).   1345
Without a legal summons many a rake
He'd summon, and, when threatened with Christ's curse,
Each would be more than glad to fill his purse
And hold a feast, with lots of ale to swill.
As Judas had a little purse to fill   1350
And was a thief, that's just what he was too;
His master got but half what he was due.
He was, if in my praise I'm not to skimp,
A thief, also a summoner and pimp.
And he had wenches in his retinue   1355
By whom—be it Sir Robert or Sir Hugh
Or any Jack or Ralph they lured to bed—
Into his ear all dutifully was said.
Each wench and he were of a single mind:
He'd fetch a summons (counterfeit in kind)   1360
To summon both offenders to the bench,
Then fleece the man while setting free the wench.
"My friend, I shall, for your sake," he would say,
"Strike her out of the record all the way;
In this case there's no need to be dismayed.   1365
I am your friend and I can be of aid."
He knew for certain more on being bribed
Than in two years could ever be described.
No archer's hound in all this world can tell
An injured from a healthy deer as well   1370

As knew this summoner a crafty lecher,
A paramour, or an adulterer;
For therein lay the bulk of what he earned,
And that's where his intent was fully turned.

    It so befell that on a certain day   1375
This summoner, forever after prey,
Rode out to summon some old widowed hag
Whom he could rob, false summons in his bag.
It happened that he saw before him ride
A carefree yeoman by a forest side.   1380
Bearing a bow, with arrows bright and keen,
This yeoman wore a short coat, colored green,
And had a black-fringed hat upon his head.

    "Hail and well met, sir!" the summoner said.

    "Welcome to you and every man who's good!   1385
Where are you riding under this green wood?"
The yeoman asked. "Do you have far to go?"

    The summoner replied by saying, "No,
Right here close by. The reason I have come
Is that I might collect a certain sum   1390
That's overdue and to my lord is pledged."

    "You are a bailiff, then?" "Yes," he alleged.
He didn't dare to put himself to shame
With "I'm a summoner," by the very name.

    "*Depardieux*," said the yeoman, "my dear brother,   1395
You are a bailiff and I am another.
As I'm a stranger in this region, pray
Let us become acquainted if we may
And be sworn brothers too if you agree.
My chest holds gold and silver; if it be   1400
That you should ever come into our shire,
All shall be yours, as much as you desire."

    "In faith," the summoner said, "my thanks to you!"
At once their hands were joined, as the two
Swore to be brothers till their dying day.   1405
Then sociably they rode upon their way.

    This summoner, as full of idle words
As full of venom are the butcher-birds,
And always asking this and that, said, "Tell

Me now, dear brother, where it is you dwell,   1410
If looking for you I should ever ride."
To which the yeoman quietly replied:
    "In the north country, brother, far away,
And I shall hope to see you there someday.
Before we part, I'll tell you in detail   1415
About my house, you'll know it without fail."
    "Now, brother," said the summoner, "I pray,
Teach to me, as we're riding on our way
(Since you're a bailiff just the same as me),
Some craftiness, instruct me faithfully   1420
How in my office I the most may win;
And do not spare for conscience or for sin,
But as a brother tell me what you do."
    "Dear brother," he replied, "I swear to you
That I shall tell a truthful tale. Too small   1425
Have been my wages, not enough at all;
My lord is hard, he's difficult to please,
My office is but labor without ease,
And so it's by extortion that I live.
It's true, for I take all that men will give.   1430
Each year by sleight if not by violence
I take in all I need for my expense,
And that's the truth as best I know to tell."
    The summoner said, "That's what I do as well.
God knows, I won't spare anything they've got   1435
Unless it be too heavy or too hot.
What I can get, however stealthily,
On that no bit of conscience bothers me;
But for extortion I'd not be alive,
And for such ruses never will I shrive,   1440
No bleeding heart or conscience have I got.
As for father-confessors, curse the lot.
How good, by God and by Saint James, that we
Have met! Dear brother, tell your name to me,"
The summoner said. This yeoman all the while   1445
Had growing on his face a little smile.
    "Brother," he said, "your wish is that I tell?
I am a fiend, my dwelling is in hell.

And here I ride about soliciting
To see if men will give me anything. 1450
What I pick up is what I earn, the sum.
And see how for the same intent you've come:
To profit well, not ever caring how.
I do the same, for I would ride right now
To this world's end if there I'd find some prey." 1455
    "Ah, *benedicite!* what's that you say?"
The summoner said. "I truly figured you
A yeoman. You've a man's shape as I do.
Do you have a definite form as well
When you are back in Hades where you dwell?" 1460
    "No, surely not," said he, "there we have none.
But when it pleases us, we take us one
(Or make it seem to you we have a shape),
Sometimes one like a man, sometimes an ape,
Or like an angel I can walk or ride. 1465
It is no wonder, this which I confide;
A lousy juggler fools you, and, pardie,
My craft is more than his will ever be."
    The summoner asked, "Why is your wandering done
In many shapes and not always in one?" 1470
    He answered, "We take on such shapes as may
Allow us best to capture all our prey."
    "What makes you go to all this labor, though?"
    "Dear summoner, the reasons why it's so
Are many," said the fiend. "But all in time; 1475
The day is short, it's after nine, and I'm
Still looking for my first gain of the day.
My aim's to get some earnings, if I may,
And not to give away all that's at hand.
You wouldn't have the wits to understand, 1480
Brother of mine, were I to let you know.
But as you ask me why we labor so,
We sometimes serve as God's own instruments,
The means by which his will he implements
When he desires, in dealing with his creatures, 1485
In diverse ways with divers forms and features.
Without him we've no might, of that no doubt,

When he opposes what we'd bring about.
At our request we sometimes have a leave
Only the body, not the soul, to grieve,   1490
As witness Job, how we tormented him.
Sometimes we've power over both of them
(That is to say, body and soul as well),
And sometimes we have leave to come from hell
To bring to someone's soul alone unrest,   1495
Not to the body. All is for the best.
Whenever one withstands all our temptation,
That stand becomes a cause for his salvation,
Although it isn't our intent or thought
That he be saved—we'd rather he be caught.   1500
We're servants, too, of man; as an example
The archbishop Saint Dunstan should be ample.
To the apostles I was servant too."
    "Yet tell me," said the summoner, "if true:
Do you make your new bodies always so,   1505
Out of the elements?" The fiend said, "No,
Sometimes it's only some form of disguise;
Dead bodies we may enter that arise
To speak with all the reason and as well
As to the Endor witch spoke Samuel.   1510
(And yet some men will say it wasn't he;
I have no use for your theology.)
But I'll warn you of this, I do not jape:
You'll know in any case our form and shape,
For later, my dear brother, you will be   1515
Where you will have no need to learn from me;
Experience shall give you your own chair
To lecture better on this whole affair
Than Virgil did right up until he died,
Or Dante too. Now quickly let us ride,   1520
For gladly I will keep you company
Until the time you'd be forsaking me."
    "No, that won't be!" the summoner replied.
"I am a yeoman, known both far and wide;
I'll always keep my word, as I do now.   1525
Were you the devil Satan, yet my vow

I'd keep that I have made to you my brother;
For we have sworn, each of us to the other,
To be true brothers, that's the sworn condition
As we both go about our acquisition.   1530
So take your part of what to you they give
And I'll take mine, that both of us may live;
And if one of us has more than the other,
Let him be true and share it with his brother."

    "I grant it, by my faith," the devil said.   1535
And with that word upon their way they sped.
Just as they reached the town that on his ride
Had been the summoner's object, they espied
A cart on which there was a load of hay.
The carter strove to drive it on its way   1540
But it was bogged too deeply in the mire;
He lashed, cried like a madman in his ire,
"Hie, Brock! Hie, Scot! You're stymied by the stones?
The fiend fetch you," he said, "body and bones,
As certainly as ever you were foaled,   1545
For all you've made me suffer, woe untold!
The devil take all—horses, cart, and hay!"

    The summoner said, "Here we'll have some play."
He neared the fiend, casual to appear,
And privately he whispered in his ear: 1550
"My brother, listen, by your faith! Hear what
The carter has to say? Take what he's got,
Seize it at once, he's given it to you—
Both cart and hay, and his three horses too."

    "No," said the fiend, "God knows, in no event.   1555
For trust me well, that wasn't his intent.
Ask him yourself, if you are doubting me,
Or wait but for a while and you will see."

    The carter whacked his horses' rumps, and all
Forward began, with that, to lean and haul.   1560
"Hie now!" said he. "By Jesus be you blest,
You and his handiwork, from least to best!
That was a hardy pull, my dappled boy!
I pray you're saved by God and by Saint Loy!
Out of the slough, pardie, my cart's been led!"   1565

"See, brother," said the devil, "what I said?
You are a witness to the fact, dear brother,
The fellow said one thing but thought another.
Let's carry on our journey as we rode,
For there is nothing here that I am owed."   1570
    When they had gone a short way out of town,
The summoner informed him, voice down,
"Here, brother, dwells a crone, a whining fiddle,
Who'd rather lose her neck than give a little,
A single penny, of her goods. I'll gain   1575
Twelve pence at least, although she go insane,
Or have her summoned—though, God knows, admitted,
I don't know of one wrong that she's committed.
But since here in this land you fail to earn
Enough for your expense, watch me and learn."   1580
    The summoner knocked at the widow's gate.
"Come out, old hag," he said, "don't make me wait!
Some friar or priest is with you, I would say."
    "Who knocks?" the wife asked. *Benedicite!*
God save you, dear sir, what is your kind will?"   1585
    The summoner replied, "I've here a bill
Of summons. See tomorrow that you be,
On pain of curse, at the archdeacon's knee
To answer to the court for certain things."
    "Now, Lord," said she, "Christ Jesus, King of kings,   1590
In wisdom help me, I'm in such a way.
For I've been sick, and that for many a day;
I cannot go so far," she said, "or ride
Or I'll be dead, such pain is in my side.
May I not ask a copy, sir, that I   1595
Might send someone in my name to reply
To what it is they bring accusing me?"
    "Yes," said the summoner, "pay now—let's see—
Twelve pence to me, and you I shall acquit.
My profit from it's just a little bit;   1600
My master gets the most, it isn't me.
Come bring it now, let me ride hastily.
Give me twelve pence, I may no longer tarry."
    "Twelve pence!" she said. "Dear Lady now, Saint Mary,

In wisdom lead me out of care and sin!   1605
Although this whole wide world were I to win,
I'd not have twelve pence in my whole household.
You're well aware that I am poor and old;
For this poor wretch please show some charity."
    "No, may the fiend come fetch me," answered he,   1610
"If I'll excuse you, though you up and die!"
    "Alas!" she said, "no guilt, God knows, have I."
    "Pay me," said he, "or by the sweet Saint Anne,
I'll take away with me your brand-new pan
For debt you've owed me for so long a time.   1615
When you made your husband a cuckold, I'm
The one who paid the fine, your penalty."
    "You lie, by my salvation!" then said she.
"For never I as widow or as wife
Was summoned to your court in all my life,   1620
And never with my body was untrue.
Now may the devil, black, rough-hided too,
Take both your body and that pan from me!"
    And when the devil heard her curse as she
Was kneeling there, he spoke as you shall hear: 1625
"Now tell me, Mabel, my own mother dear,
Is this your real desire, what you have said?"
    She said, "The devil fetch him ere he's dead,
And pan and all, if he does not repent!"
    "No, you old cow, it isn't my intent,"   1630
The summoner said, "to have regret or rue
About whatever I may get from you.
Would that your old chemise, each thread, I had!"
    "Now, brother," said the devil, "don't be mad;
Your body and this pan are mine by right.   1635
To hell is where you'll go with me tonight,
Where you'll be more into our privity
Than any master of divinity."
This foul fiend grabbed him, no more words were spent;
Body and soul he with the devil went   1640
To where their due these summoners all find.
May God, who in his image made mankind,
Now be our guide and save us, all and some,

And grant these summoners good men become!
    My lords, I could have told you (said the Friar),   1645
Had I the leisure now, about the fire
As spoken of by Christ, by Paul and John
And other holy doctors, many a one;
About such pains your hearts would really shudder,
Though they are worse than any tongue may utter,   1650
Were I to have a thousand years to tell
The pains down in that cursed house of hell.
But to protect us from that cursed place,
Be watchful, and pray Jesus by his grace
Keep us from Satan, from temptation's snare.   1655
Heed this word and example, and beware:
"The lion ever sits in wait, to slay
The innocent by any means he may."
Have your hearts ever ready to elude
The devil, lest he bind in servitude.   1660
He may not tempt you, lords, beyond your might,
For Christ will be your champion and knight.
And pray these summoners of all they've wrought
Repent, ere by the devil they are caught!

The Summoner's Tale

The Summoner rose in his stirrups. He   1665
Was mad at the Friar to such degree
That like an aspen leaf he shook with ire.
   "My lords," he said, "but one thing I desire:
I ask that you will, by your courtesy,
Since you've heard this false Friar lie, agree   1670
That I now be allowed my tale to tell.
This Friar's boasted that he knows of hell;
God knows, that's little wonder to impart,
As friars and fiends are seldom far apart.
And, by my faith, how frequently they tell   1675
About the friar carried off to hell
In spirit once while dreaming. As it's told,
An angel took him touring, to behold
The pains of hell; yet in that place entire
He didn't catch sight of a single friar,   1680
Though many folks he saw there in their pain.
This friar asked the angel to explain:
'Now, sir,' said he, 'have friars such a grace
That none of them shall come down to this place?'
   " 'Yes,' said the angel, 'millions come!' He led   1685
The friar down to Satan then, and said,
'Now Satan has a tail that you will note
Is broader than the sail upon a boat.
Hold up your tail, O Satan,' then said he,
'Expose your ass and let this friar see   1690
Where friars here all have their nesting place!'
And quicker then than half-a-furlong race,
And just as bees come swarming from a hive,
Out of the devil's ass there shot a drive
Of twenty thousand friars in a rout   1695
Who throughout hell went swarming all about,

Until, as fast as they'd come to appear,
Each one crept back into the devil's rear.
The devil clapt his tail down, then lay still.
And when this friar thus had had his fill 1700
Of seeing the torment of that sorry place,
The friar's spirit God out of his grace
Restored back to his body. Once awake,
He nonetheless in fear was all ashake,
The devil's ass, so vivid in his mind, 1705
His heritage and that of all his kind.
God save you all except this cursed Friar!
My prologue I will end with that desire."

THE SUMMONER'S TALE

My lords, there is in Yorkshire, as I guess,
A marshy district known as Holderness, 1710
In which a licensed friar went about
To preach—also to beg, no need to doubt.
Now it so happened that this friar one day
Preached at a church in his accustomed way,
Especially, above all other teaching, 1715
Exhorting all the people with his preaching
To purchase trentals, giving, for God's sake,
That holy houses men might undertake
To build for services, excluding where
A gift would just be squandered or where there 1720
Is no necessity of having people give—
Where clergy is endowed, that is, and live,
Thank God, in wealth and plenty. "Trentals," he
Declared, "from penance bring delivery
For dead friends' souls, the old as well as young, 1725
All thirty masses being quickly sung—
Not meaning in a frivolous kind of way,
Although a priest would sing but one a day.
Get out their souls, deliver them," he'd call,
"For hard it is by meathook and by awl 1730
To get a clawing, or to burn and bake.

Make haste, get going at it, for Christ's sake!"
And when this friar finished with his say,
With *qui cum patre* he'd be on his way.
    When folks in church had given to him what   1735
They pleased, he moved on, no more rest he got.
With scrip and his tipped staff, all cinctured high,
In every house he'd pore about and pry
While begging meal and cheese or else some corn.
His comrade had a long staff tipped with horn,   1740
A pair of tablets made of ivory,
And a stylus that was finely polished. He
Would always write the names down, as he stood,
Of all the folks who gave him something good,
As if he meant to pray for them thereby.   1745
"Give us a bushel, wheat or malt or rye,
A bit of cheese or, by your grace, a cake,
Or what you will—we can't choose what we take;
A penny for a mass, or half-a-penny,
Or give a slice of pork if you have any;   1750
A smidgen of your woolen cloth, dear dame,
Beloved sister—see, I write your name!—
Bacon or beef, whatever you may find."
    A sturdy fellow always walked behind
Them as their servant, and he bore a sack   1755
To tote all they were given on his back.
No sooner was this friar out the door
Than he'd erase each name that just before
He'd written on his tablets. All he'd do
Is serve the folks with trifles, fables too.   1760
    "No, Summoner, you lie!" the Friar cried.
    "Peace, for Christ's mother dear!" our Host replied.
"Spare nothing, with your tale go right ahead."
    "As I may live, I shall," the Summoner said.
    So house by house this friar went, till he   1765
Came to one house where he was wont to be
Better refreshed than at a hundred more.
The owner there lay sick; low off the floor
Upon a couch the man bedridden lay.
    "*Deus hic!* O my dear Thomas, friend, good day!"   1770

The friar softly said with courtesy.
"May God reward you, Thomas! Frequently
I've fared well on your bench. With merry cheer
Many a fine meal I have eaten here."
Then from the bench he shooed away the cat,   1775
And after laying down his staff and hat
And scrip, upon the bench sat quietly down.
His comrade had gone walking into town,
He and the servant, to the hostelry
Where he intended for that night to be.   1780
    "O my dear master," said the ailing man,
"Tell me how you have been since March began.
I haven't seen you this fortnight or more."
    "God knows," he said, "I've labored till I'm sore,
Especially for sake of your salvation,   1785
So many prayers beyond all valuation—
For others too, God bless them all!—I pray.
I was at mass at your church just today
And gave a sermon by my humble wit
Instead of all by text of Holy Writ;   1790
Because it's hard for you, as I suppose,
I'll give the gloss of how my teaching goes.
A glorious thing it is to gloss away;
'The letter slays,' that's what we clerics say.
There I have taught them charity. They should   1795
Spend what they have where reasonable and good.
And there I saw our dame—ah, where is she?"
    "Out yonder in the yard I think she'd be,"
The fellow said, "and she'll come right away."
    "Aye, master, welcome, by Saint John! I say,   1800
How are you?" said this woman earnestly.
    The friar then rose up with courtesy,
And in his arms embraced her tight and narrow
And kissed her sweetly, chirping like a sparrow
With his lips. "Madam, I've done all right,"   1805
He said, "as I'm your servant day and night,
Thanks be to God who gave you soul and life!
I didn't see today so fair a wife
In all the church, may God in heaven save me!"

"May God indeed amend all faults," said she.   1810
"You're welcome, by my faith, in any case."
   "Thanks, madam," said the friar, "in this place
I've always found it so. But by your leave
And goodness—and I pray not to aggrieve—
With Thomas I would speak in confidence.   1815
These curates show both sloth and negligence
In searching for true conscience in one's shrift.
In preaching is my diligence, my gift,
I study Peter's words and those of Paul.
I walk and fish for Christian souls, that all   1820
To Christ be yielded as his due. To spread
His word is that one aim to which I'm led."
   "Now, by your leave, dear sir," responded she,
"Chide him well, by the holy Trinity!
For he is like a pismire in his ire,   1825
Although he has all that he may desire.
I cover him at night and make him warm,
Lay over him a leg or else an arm,
Yet he groans like our boar out in the sty.
No other bit of sport with him have I,   1830
For I can't please him in a single way."
   "O Thomas, *je vous dis!* Thomas, I say,
This is the devil's work, to be amended!
Ire is a thing that God commands be ended,
And therefore I would have a word or two."   1835
   "Before I go," the wife said, "what would you
Like for your dinner, sir? I'll get it spread."
   "Madam, now *je vous dis sans doute*," he said,
"If I had of a capon but the liver,
And of your soft bread but a single sliver,   1840
And then a roasted pig's head—though for me
No animal I wish killed—I would be
Then having with you only homey fare.
I am a man whose appetite is spare;
The Bible is my spirit's food, my flesh   1845
So on the move, always so set for fresh
New vigils, that my appetite's destroyed.
Madam, I pray that you'll not be annoyed

By what I'm telling as a friend to you.
By God, I only tell it to a few."   1850
   "Now, sir," she said, "one word before I go.
My child is dead, it's been ten days or so;
Soon after you left town the lad was dead."
   "His death I saw by revelation," said
The friar, "at home in our dormitory.   1855
But I daresay I saw him borne to glory,
Not half an hour after he had died,
In that same vision—God so be my guide!
So did our sacristan, our medic too,
True friars fifty years, which makes them due   1860
To celebrate—thank God for all his grace!—
Their jubilee, walk singly any place.
Then I arose, our whole convent as well,
With tear-stained cheeks; no clattering of bell
Nor other clamor, all that came from us   1865
Was but our song *Te Deum laudamus,*
Save for a prayer I said in dedication
To thank Christ Jesus for his revelation.
For, sir and madam, you can trust my word,
With more effect in praying we are heard   1870
(As we see more into Christ's secret things)
Than folks not of the cloth, though they be kings;
We live in poverty and abstinence,
They live for riches, saving no expense
For meat and drink and all their foul delight.   1875
All worldly lust we hold up to despite.
Dives and Lazarus lived differently,
And their rewards would thereby different be.
Whoso would pray must also fast, be clean,
Fatten his soul, and keep his body lean.   1880
As Saint Paul says, our food and clothes shall be
Enough though not the best. The purity
And fasting of us friars are the way
That we gain Christ's acceptance when we pray.
   "Look, Moses fasted forty days and nights   1885
Before God in his might came from the heights
To speak with him upon Mount Sinai;

He fasted many a day, his stomach dry
And empty, and received the law inscribed
By God's own finger. You've heard, too, described   1890
Just how Elijah, before he could speak
With God, our lives' physician, on the peak
Of Horeb fasted long and contemplated.
    "Aaron, who the temple administrated,
And all the other priests who took their way   1895
Into the holy temple, there to pray
For all the people, service to perform,
Were not allowed to drink in any form
That might result in drunkenness, but there
They were to watch in abstinence and prayer,   1900
Or else they'd surely die. Heed what I say.
If they're not sober who for people pray,
I warn you—but enough, no more of it.
Lord Jesus, as it says in Holy Writ,
Gave us examples, how to fast and pray.   1905
That's why we mendicants, we friars, I say,
Are humble and so wed to continence,
To poverty, good works, and abstinence,
To persecution for all righteousness,
To mercy, suffering, and holiness.   1910
So all the prayers we say, as you can see—
I mean we beggars in the friary—
Are more acceptable to God on high
Than yours at your feast tables. I'll not lie
To you, from Paradise it was to be   1915
That man was first chased out for gluttony,
And man was chaste, for sure, in Paradise.
    "But listen, Thomas, to what I advise.
I have no text upon it, as I guess,
But I can gloss it for you nonetheless;   1920
Sweet Jesus had especially in mind
Us friars when he spoke words of this kind:
'Blest be the poor in spirit.' You can see
Throughout the gospel if such words agree
More with us friars in what we profess   1925
Than those who wallow in what they possess.

Fie on their pomp, fie on their gluttony!
Their ignorance too I scorn defiantly.
   "They seem to me just like Jovinian,
Fat as a whale and walking like a swan,   1930
As wine-filled as a bottle in the spence.
Their prayer is of the greatest reverence
When they for souls recite the psalm of David;
Then 'Burp!' they say, *'cor meum eructavit!'*
Who follows Christ, his gospel, and his way,   1935
But we the humble, chaste, and poor today
Who work for God's word, not who simply hear?
And so just as a hawk will up and rear
Into the air, the prayer soars ever higher
Of every kind and chaste and busy friar   1940
Up to the ears of God. O Thomas, friend,
O Thomas! as I hope to ride or wend,
And by that lord they call Saint Ive, if you
Were not a brother your life would be through.
For in our chapel we pray day and night   1945
To Christ that he will send you health and might,
Your use of limbs again to quickly bring."
   "God knows," said he, "I still can't feel a thing!
So help me Jesus, in the last few years
I've spent on every friar who appears   1950
A load of pounds, yet I'm still in this way.
My goods are all but used up, safe to say.
Farewell, my gold, for all of it has fled!"
   "O Thomas, you'd do that?" the friar said.
"What need have you of any other friar?   1955
Who has the perfect doctor need inquire
About what other doctors are in town?
Your lack of faith is what has brought you down.
Do you hold me or our convent as aid
That's not enough for you, for all we've prayed?   1960
That's silly, Thomas, and not worth a bean;
You're ill because in giving you're so mean.
'Ah, give that convent half-a-quarter oats!
Ah, give that convent four-and-twenty groats!
Ah, give that friar a penny, let him go!'   1965

That's not the way it is, no, Thomas, no!
What is a farthing worth, by twelve divided?
Look, everything that in itself's united
Is worth more than when all its parts are scattered.
No, by me, Thomas, you shall not be flattered;   1970
You'd like to have our labor all for naught,
Yet God on high who all this world has wrought
Says that the workman's worthy of his hire.
None of your treasure, Thomas, I desire
As mine; no, it's because our whole convent   1975
To pray for you is always diligent,
And builds for Christ a church. O Thomas, friend,
If you would be of use as you intend,
On building churches you'll find, if you would,
How India's Saint Thomas did much good.   1980
You lie here full of anger, full of ire,
With which the devil sets your heart afire,
And chide this humble innocent your wife,
Who's been so meek and patient in her strife.
And therefore, Thomas, promise, as you should,   1985
You won't fight with your wife, for your own good;
And, by my faith, now bear this word in mind,
On which concern the wise man says in kind:
'Don't make of your own house a lion's lair,
Do not oppress the ones within your care,   1990
Or cause a friend to up and flee.' And, too,
Thomas, this charge again I give to you:
Beware of ire that in your bosom sleeps;
Beware the serpent that so slyly creeps
Beneath the grass to sting with subtlety.   1995
Beware, my son, and listen patiently,
For twenty thousand men have lost their lives
Through striving with their lovers and their wives.
Now since you've such a meek and holy wife,
Thomas, what need have you for causing strife?   2000
Surely no snake as cruel has yet been seen
(When man treads on his tail), none half as mean
As woman is when given cause for ire,
As vengeance then is all that they desire.

Ire is a sin among the greater seven,   2005
Abominable to God who is in heaven,
And leads a fellow to his own destruction.
The simplest parson here needs no instruction,
He's seen how ire engenders homicide.
Ire is the executioner of pride.   2010
I could, regarding ire, tell of such sorrow
My tale of it would last until tomorrow.
That's why I pray to God both day and night
That he'll send to the ireful little might.
How great a harm and pity, certainly,   2015
To set a man of ire in high degree.
    "One time there was an ireful potentate,
Says Seneca, and, while he ruled the state,
Two knights went out to ride about one day.
As Fortune in the case would have her way,   2020
Only one of the knights came home, and he
Was brought before the judge summarily.
'You've surely slain your fellow knight, and I
Condemn you now,' the judge declared, 'to die.'
Then to another knight commanded he,   2025
'Go lead him to his death, I so decree.'
It happened, though, that as they headed right
Toward the place where he should die, the knight
Appeared again who they had thought was dead.
When all their best advice had then been said,   2030
They took them both before the judge again.
They told the judge, 'My lord, he hasn't slain
His fellow knight, he's standing here alive.'
'You shall be dead,' the judge said, 'as I thrive,
And that means all of you—one, two, and three!'   2035
And to the first knight he said, 'My decree
Condemned you, you'll in any case be dead.
And as for you, you too shall lose your head,
For you have caused your fellow's death.' And he
Then to the third knight spoke immediately: 2040
'You haven't done what I commanded you.'
And so it was all three of them he slew.
    "Cambyses, ireful, drank beyond his might,

To be a scoundrel always his delight.
A lord, it happened, in his company   2045
Was virtuous, loved true morality,
And one day gave Cambyses this advice:
   " 'A lord is lost if he is prone to vice,
And shameful is a drunkard's reputation,
Especially if lordship is his station.   2050
Many an eye and ear are set to spy
Upon a lord, he knows not where they'll pry.
And so, for God's love, drink more moderately!
For wine will make a man lose wretchedly
His mind and the control of every limb.'   2055
   " 'No, the reverse you'll see,' he said to him,
'And promptly so, your own experience
Will prove wine does to no one such offense.
There's no wine can deprive me of my might
In hand or foot, or take from me my sight.'   2060
And for despite Cambyses drank much more,
A hundredfold, than he had done before.
And then at once this ireful, cursed wretch
Commanded that this knight's son they should fetch,
And ordered that before him he should stand;   2065
And suddenly he took his bow in hand,
Then back toward his ear the string he drew,
And there the child he with an arrow slew.
'Now, do I have a steady hand or not?'
He asked. 'Have might and mind both gone to rot?   2070
Has wine bereft my two eyes of their sight?'
What can I say, what answer from the knight?
His son was slain, there is no more to say.
Beware, therefore, with lords how you may play.
Placebo sing, and 'I shall if I can,'   2075
Unless it's to a poor and humble man.
To one who's poor should men his vices tell,
Not to a lord, although he go to hell.
   "Or look at Cyrus, Persia's king, in wrath
Destroying the River Gyndes. On the path   2080
To his conquest of Babylon, a horse
Of his had drowned within that river's course.

For that, he made it so the river shrank
Till women might wade through it bank to bank.
What said he who so well can teach? 'Don't be   2085
An ireful man's companion, nor agree
To walk with any madman by the way,
Or you'll be sorry.' I've no more to say.
     "Dear brother Thomas, leave your ire behind.
I'm as just as a wright's square, as you'll find.   2090
Don't keep the devil's knife held at your heart—
Your anger makes you all the more to smart—
But all of your confession to me show."
     The ailing man said, "By Saint Simon, no!
Today my priest has shriven me for sin,   2095
I told him wholly of the shape I'm in.
There's no more need to speak of it," said he,
"Unless I wish in my humility."
     "Give me some of your gold, then, for our cloister,"
The friar said, "for mussel after oyster—   2100
While other men have been at ease and filled—
Has been our food, that cloister we might build;
And yet, God knows, we show for all the while
Scarce pavement or foundation. Not one tile
Is yet within our habitation found.   2105
For stones, by God, we now owe forty pound.
     "Help us, Thomas, for him who harrowed hell!
For if you don't, our books we'll have to sell.
And if you lack our preaching, our instruction,
This world will then be headed for destruction;   2110
For whoso from this world would us bereave,
As God may save me, Thomas, by your leave,
Would from this world remove the very sun.
For who can teach and work as we have done?
It's not been briefly," he went on to tell,   2115
"But since Elijah, Elisha as well,
Has much, I find, been written to record
The charity of friars, thank the Lord!
Now, Thomas, help, for holy charity!"
And down he went at once on bended knee.   2120
     This ailing man went nearly mad with ire;

He would have liked to see the friar on fire
For his dissembling and hypocrisy.
"Whatever thing that I possess," said he,
"Is that which I may give, there's nothing other.   2125
Have you not told me that I am your brother?"
     "Why, sure," the friar said, "trust in the same.
The letter with our seal I gave our dame."
     "Well then," said he, "there's something I shall give
Your holy convent while I yet may live.   2130
And in your hand you'll have it right away,
But only on condition that you say
That you'll divide it up so that, dear brother,
Each friar gets as much as every other.
Upon your faith you'll swear this now to me,   2135
No bickering and no dishonesty."
     "Upon my faith," the friar said, "I swear!"
He shook the fellow's hand then to declare,
"See, here's my vow, in me there'll be no lack."
     "Then put your hand down underneath my back,"   2140
The fellow told him, "feel around behind,
For underneath my rump a thing you'll find
That I have hidden, kept in privity."
     "Ah," thought the friar, "that shall go with me!"
And then he launched his hand right down the rift   2145
In hope that at the end he'd find a gift.
And when this sick man felt the friar begin
To grope around his orifice, right in
The friar's hand the fellow let a fart.
No single horse that's ever drawn a cart   2150
Has ever let a fart with such a sound.
     The friar, lion-mad, rose with a bound.
"Ay, by God's bones! You lying churl," said he,
"You've done this for despite! Just wait and see,
That fart you'll pay for if I have my way!"   2155
     The fellow's household, when they heard the fray,
Came rushing in and chased away the friar.
He went forth on his way consumed with ire
And fetched his fellow, keeper of his goods.
He looked just like a wild boar in the woods   2160

And gnashed his teeth, so mad the friar felt.
He hurried to the manor where there dwelt
An honored man for whom he'd come to be
The sole confessor. Of that village he
Was lord, this worthy man. In came the friar,   2165
The anger in him raging like a fire,
Just as the lord sat eating at the table.
To speak a word the friar was scarcely able;
"God save you!" was at last all he could say.
    The lord looked up. "Why, *benedicite!*   2170
Friar John," he said, "what kind of world is this?
For well I see there's something that's amiss,
You look as if the woods were full of thieves.
Sit down at once and tell me what aggrieves
And it shall be amended if I may."   2175
    "I've had," said he, "such an insult today—
May God reward you—here within your town,
There's in this world no page so poor and down
That something so abominable should be
Done to him like in town's been done to me.   2180
But nothing brings for me more grief to bear
Than that this old man with his hoary hair
Has so blasphemed our holy convent too."
    "Now, master," said this lord, "I beg of you—"
    "Not master, no, but servant," said the friar,   2185
"Though I have had in school that honor, sire.
God doesn't like men calling us 'Rabbi,'
Not in the market nor your hall so high."
    "No matter," said the lord, "your grief be stated."
    "Today an odious wrong was perpetrated   2190
Against my order," said the friar, "and me,
And so *per consequens* in like degree
Against the Church. God soon avenge it yet!"
    "You know what's best to do, don't get upset,
You're my confessor," said this man of worth,   2195
"You've been the salt, the savor of the earth.
Your temper, sir, for God's love, try to hold
And state your grief!" And so at once he told
What you have heard—you know enough of that.

The lady of the house had quietly sat   2200
Until she heard all of the friar's story.
"Mother of God," she cried, "O maid of glory!
Is there more to it? Tell me faithfully."
     "Madam, what do you think of it?" said he.
     "What do I think?" she said. "God give me speed   2205
To say, a churl has done a churlish deed!
What should I say? God grant not that he thrive!
His sick head's full of nonsense. I derive
From this he's in some frenzied malady."
     "Madam, by God, I shall not lie," said he,   2210
"If I am not avenged, in every place
Where I may speak or preach I'll call disgrace
Upon this false blasphemer who's decided
That I divide what cannot be divided
And share with all. A curse on him! Mischance!"   2215
     The lord sat stilly, as if in a trance,
As in his mind he had this rumination:
"How could this churl have such imagination
And to the friar such a problem bring?
I've never heard before of such a thing,   2220
The devil must have put it in his mind.
In all our fundamentals could we find
A question of this sort before today?
Could any person demonstrate someway
That every man might have an equal part,   2225
Whether in sound or savor, of a fart?
That proud and madcap churl, damned be his face!
Look, sirs," the lord said, "God bring him disgrace!
Who's ever heard of such a thing till now?
To every man alike? Then tell me how!   2230
It can't be done, no possibility.
God grant that foolish churl ill-fated be!
The rumbling of a fart, like every sound,
Is only air reverberating round
And bit by bit it wastes itself away;   2235
And, by my faith, there is no man can say
If it has been divided equally.
And yet that churl, look how so cleverly

He spoke of such today to my confessor!
I'd say for sure a demon's his possessor!   2240
Now eat your meat and let the churl go play
Or hang himself and go the devil's way!"

Words of the lord's squire, his carver, on
dividing the fart among twelve

Now this lord's squire was standing at the table
To carve his meat for him, and so was able
To hear each word of all that I've related.   2245
    "My lord, don't be displeased," the squire stated.
"For cloth to make a gown, I'll tell, Sir Friar,
So that you need not be so full of ire,
How this fart could be shared in equal measure
By each one of your convent, at my pleasure."   2250
    "Tell," said the lord, "and you shall soon have on
Your gown of cloth, by God and by Saint John!"
    "My lord," he said then, "when the weather's fair
And there's no wind, no turbulence of air,
Let's bring a cartwheel here into the hall.   2255
But count the spokes, be sure it has them all—
They number twelve by common rule. Then bring
Twelve friars to me. You know my reasoning?
Thirteen are in a convent, as I guess,
And this confessor, by his worthiness,   2260
Completes the sum. So twelve of them shall kneel,
As it shall be agreed, right by the wheel,
For every friar a spoke, to which he goes
And firmly at the spoke-end lays his nose.
Your noble confessor shall arch his snub—   2265
And may God save him!—right up by the hub.
And then this churl, his belly stiff and taut
As any tabor, hither shall be brought
And set upon this wheel right off a cart,
Up on the hub, then have him let a fart.   2270
And you shall see, as surely as I live,
By way of proof that is demonstrative,

In equal share the sound will have its stroke,
The stink of it as well, right down each spoke;
Save that this worthy man who's your confessor,   2275
So honorable, should not be like those lesser
But rather have first fruit, and so he will.
The friars have a noble custom still
That says the worthiest shall first be served,
And certainly this he has well deserved.   2280
Why, just today he taught us so much good,
While preaching in the pulpit where he stood,
That I for one would like to guarantee
He had first smell of not one fart but three.
Deserving, too, should be his whole convent,   2285
So well he bears himself with holy bent."
　　The lord, the lady, all except the friar
Thought Jenkin spoke so well as to inspire
As much as Euclid or Ptolemy.
As for the churl, he spoke with subtlety   2290
And wit, they said, he'd pulled a clever trick,
He wasn't any fool or lunatic.
And Jenkin's won himself a brand-new gown.
My tale is done, we're almost into town.

The Student's Tale

PROLOGUE

"Sir Oxford Student," said our Host, "you ride
As still and quiet as a brand-new bride
Who's sitting at the table. I have heard
Throughout this day from your tongue not a word.
Some sophism, I think, you're pondering;   5
But Solomon said, 'A time for everything.'
    "For God's sake, can't you be of better cheer?
Now's not the time to do your studies here.
Tell us a story, by your faith, that's merry!
When one joins in a game, he mustn't vary   10
From that game's rules, to which he gave assent.
But don't preach like the friars during Lent
Who over our old sins would make us weep,
Nor tell a tale that puts us all to sleep.
    "Tell of adventures, have a merry say;   15
Your colors, terms, and figures store away
Until you need them for composing things
In lofty style, as when men write to kings.
For now use only your plain words, we pray,
That we may understand all that you say."   20
    This worthy Student answered courteously:
"I am under your rule, Sir Host," said he,
"You have us all under your governance,
And therefore I will show obedience,
Within the bounds of reason, certainly.   25
I'll tell a story that was taught to me
By a scholar of Padua rightly known
As worthy, as his words and works have shown.
He's dead now, nailed inside his coffin. May
The Lord grant that his soul's at rest, I pray!   30

215

"Named Francis Petrarch, poet laureate,
This scholar's sweetest rhetoric has set
All Italy alight by poetry,
As did Legnano with philosophy
And law and certain other arts as well.   35
But death, that won't allow us here to dwell
For longer than the twinkling of an eye,
Has slain them both, and all of us must die.

"But telling further of this worthy man
Who taught to me this tale, as I began: 40
He first composed in high style, I should note,
Before the body of his tale he wrote,
An introduction in which Petrarch speaks
Of Piedmont, of Saluzzo, and those peaks
The Appenines, which so majestically   45
Comprise the border of West Lombardy;
Especially he speaks of Mount Viso,
The place at which the river known as Po
Originates, a little spring its source,
And keeps on going on its eastward course: 50
Emilia, Ferrera, Venice too—
It would take too long to describe to you.
And truthfully to speak, I do not sense
That it's a matter that's of relevance
Save that he had to preface things somehow.   55
But here's his tale and you may hear it now."

THE STUDENT'S TALE

PART I

There's found along the west of Italy,
Below Mount Viso with its summit cold,
A pleasant plain of great fertility
With many towns and towers to behold   60
That forebears founded in the days of old,
And other sights as grand to see are legion.

Saluzzo it is called, this noble region.

A marquis once was lord of all the land
As all his worthy forebears were before;   65
Obedient to all that he'd command
Were all his subjects, both the rich and poor.
So he lived well, much happiness in store,
Both loved and feared by lord and commoner
Through all the favor Fortune may confer.   70

As for the lineage from which he sprung,
It was the noblest in all Lombardy.
He was a handsome fellow, strong and young,
One full of honor and of courtesy
And quite discreet as such a lord should be,   75
Save for some things for which he was to blame;
And Walter was this youthful ruler's name.

I blame him in that he would give no thought
To what the future held, what may betide;
His pleasure was in what the present brought,   80
Like hawking and the hunt, on every side.
He'd tend to let all other matters slide;
And he refused—and this was worst of all—
To take a wife, whatever may befall.

That one thing caused his people such despair   85
That one day as a flock to him they went,
And one of them, the one most learned there—
Or else who best could gain this lord's consent
To speak for all, conveying their intent,
Or else who best could make such matters clear—   90
Spoke to the marquis as you're now to hear:

"O noble marquis, your benignity
Assures us, it allows our forwardness,
As often as it's of necessity,
To come to you to tell you our distress.   95
Now grant, lord, through your gentle nobleness,

That we with piteous heart tell our dismay.
Let not your ears disdain what we've to say.

"I am not more involved in this affair
Than any other person in the place;   100
But seeing, my dear lord, how you've been fair
With me before and favored me with grace,
I've dared to ask that I might have this space
Of audience, to tell you our request;
Then you, my lord, do what you think is best.   105

"For certainly, my lord, you please us now—
You and your works—and always have, till we
Cannot in any way imagine how
We might could live in more felicity,
Except, my lord, that you might will to be   110
A wedded man. If marriage might you please,
Then would your people's hearts be set at ease.

"So bow your neck beneath this yoke of bliss,
Of sovereignty (not servitude), that's known
As marriage or wedlock. Consider this,   115
My lord, in your wise thoughts: our days pass on,
In many ways we spend them and they're gone;
For though we sleep or wake or walk or ride,
Time's fleeting, for no man it will abide.

"And though you're young, still in life's greenest flower, 120
Age stilly as a stone creeps day to day;
Death threatens every age and wields its power
In each estate and no one gets away;
And just as we are certain when we say
That we must die, uncertain are we all   125
About the day when death will come to call.

"Accept, then, what we say with true intent
Who never have refused what you command,
And we will, lord, if you will give assent,
Choose you a wife, she'll quickly be at hand,   130

Born of the noblest family in the land,
That it may be, as we would so apprize,
An honor both to you and in God's eyes.

"From all this fear now save us one and all
And take yourself a wife, for heaven's sake!   135
For, God forbid, if it should so befall
That through your death—your lineage at stake—
A stranger should succeed you, free to take
Your heritage, woe to us left alive!
Therefore we pray that quickly you will wive."   140

Their meek prayer and the sadness in each look
Filled the marquis's heart with sympathy.
He said, "Dear people, that of which I took
No thought at all you now require of me.
I always have enjoyed my liberty;   145
That's hard to find once marriage shall intrude.
Where I was free I'll be in servitude.

"Yet I see how sincere is your intent,
And will as always trust in what you say;
Of my free will I therefore will assent   150
To take a wife as quickly as I may.
But though you've made the offer here today
To choose her for me, I'll not hold you to it
And ask that you no further will pursue it.

"For God knows, children often aren't the same   155
As all their worthy forebears were before;
Good comes from God, not from the family name,
Not from whatever lineage that bore.
My trust is in God's goodness, and therefore
My marriage and my office and my ease   160
I leave to him; may he do as he please.

"So let me be the one to choose my wife,
That burden I will shoulder. But I pray
And give to you this charge upon your life:

Assure me, when I've chosen as I may,   165
In word and deed until her dying day,
Both here and everywhere you'll honor her
As if the daughter of an emperor.

"And furthermore, this you will swear to me:
Against my choice you'll not complain or strive;   170
For since I'm to forgo my liberty
At your request, if ever I may thrive,
How my heart may be set is how I'll wive;
And if you don't agree it's to be so,
I pray you speak no further, let it go."   175

With hardy will they swore, gave their assent
To all of this, not one of them said "Nay";
They asked the marquis then, before they went,
If in his grace he'd set a certain day
To marry, one as early as he may;   180
For still the people were somewhat in dread,
Still fearing that the marquis wouldn't wed.

He set a day—one suiting him the best—
When he would marry, gave them surety,
And said that this was all at their request.   185
With humbleness they all obediently
Then knelt before him, and respectfully
They thanked him. In pursuing their intent
They had what they desired, and home they went.

And thereupon he calls his officers,   190
Gives orders how the feast they're to purvey;
He with each squire and trusty knight confers,
Such charges as he will on them to lay;
And all that he commands them they obey,
Each one intent to do all that he can   195
To see the feast so forth with proper plan.

PART II

Not very far from that fine palace where
This marquis was arranging how he'd wed,
A village stood, the region truly fair;
There villagers, as humble lives they led,   200
Had homes and beasts, and all these folks were fed
By their own labor spent upon the land,
Work that the earth repaid with open hand.

Among the poor folks there did dwell a man
Who was considered poorest of them all;   205
But God will often send, as well he can,
His grace into an ox's little stall.
Janicula's the name that folks would call
Him by. He had a daughter, fair the same,
Griselda was this youthful maiden's name.   210

To speak of virtuous beauty, clearly she
Was of the fairest underneath the sun;
For she had been brought up in poverty,
No ill desire in her heart's blood would run.
She drank more from the well than from the tun;   215
And inasmuch as virtue was her pleasure,
She knew about hard work, not idle leisure.

For though this maiden was so young and pure,
Inside her virgin breast was found to be
A heart that was both sober and mature.   220
She cared, with great respect and charity,
For her poor aged father, and while she
Was spinning, their few sheep in field she kept;
She never quit her labor till she slept.

When she came home she'd often bring along   225
Some roots or herbs, which shredded with a knife
She boiled to make their meal. She labored long,
Hard was the bed she made. But through her strife

She ever would preserve her father's life,
With all the diligent obedience   230
That any child can give in reverence.

Upon this poor Griselda frequently
The marquis would in passing cast his eye
As he was riding to his venery;
And when this maiden he would so espy,   235
No wanton look of folly he thereby
Would give her, but a look of grave respect;
On her behavior often he'd reflect,

Commending in his heart her womanhood
And virtue, like no other one possessed   240
So young, in thought and deed so full of good.
Though virtue is not readily assessed
By common people, he was so impressed
By her that he decided that he would
Wed only her, if wed he ever should.   245

The wedding day arrived, yet none could say
Which of the district's women it would be;
This started many wondering that day,
And saying, when they were in privacy,
"Will our lord yet not quit his vanity?   250
Will he not wed? Alas, if it be thus!
Why should he so deceive himself and us?"

This marquis, though, had had his craftsmen make
Of gems, in gold and azure set, a treasure
Of rings and brooches for Griselda's sake;   255
To fit her for new clothes, he had them measure
A maiden of like build; they had no leisure,
That his bride be adorned in such a way
As would befit so grand a wedding day.

By nine upon that morn anticipated,   260
The day on which the wedding would take place,
The palace had been finely decorated,

Each hall or room according to its space,
The kitchen storerooms stuffed in every case
With luscious food, as much as one might see   265
Throughout the length and breadth of Italy.

This marquis—royally dressed, with every lord
And every lady in his company
Whom he had asked to come and share the board,
And with his retinue, his chivalry,   270
While music played, such sounds of melody—
Toward the village that I've told about
Now takes the nearest way with all the rout.

Griselda—who had no idea, God knows,
That for her sake was meant all this array—   275
Out to a well to fetch some water goes,
Then hurries home as quickly as she may;
For she had heard that on that very day
The marquis would be wed, and if she might
She'd love to catch a glimpse of such a sight.   280

She thought, "With other maidens I will stand,
Who are my friends, and from the door I'll see
The marchioness. So I'll go take in hand
The work at home as soon as it may be,
The labor always waiting there for me;   285
Then I'll be free to watch if she today
Toward her castle passes by this way."

And as she was about to step inside,
The marquis came. Her name she heard him call;
Her water pot at once she set aside   290
(Beside the threshold in an ox's stall),
And down upon her knees was quick to fall;
There soberly she knelt, completely still,
Till she had heard her lord express his will.

This thoughtful marquis spoke then quietly,   295
Addressing her as gently as he may:

"Griselda, where's your father?" Reverently,
With humble mien, the girl was quick to say,
"My lord, he's here right now." Without delay
Griselda went inside the house and sought   300
Her father, whom she to the marquis brought.

Then by the hand he took this aged man,
And said, when he had taken him aside,
"Janicula, I neither may nor can
For any longer my heart's pleasure hide.   305
If you consent, whatever may betide,
Your daughter I will take to be my wife
Before I go, and she'll be so for life.

"You love me, that I surely know, and you
Were born my faithful liege. And furthermore,   310
What pleases me—I daresay that it's true—
Is that which pleases you. Tell me therefore
Upon this special matter raised before,
If from you your agreement I may draw,
If you will take me as your son-in-law."   315

This was so sudden and astonishing
The man stood shaking, turned completely red,
Abashed till he could scarcely say a thing
Except for this: "My lord, my will," he said,
"Is as you will, and I'd will naught instead   320
Against your liking; so, my lord so dear,
As you may please, rule in this matter here."

To this the marquis gently said, "Yet I
Desire that in your dwelling you and she
And I should meet and talk. Do you know why?   325
I want to ask her if her will it be
To be my wife, obedient to me.
And in your presence all this shall be done,
No words out of your hearing, not a one."

While in the dwelling they negotiated   330

To such an end as after you will hear,
Outside the house the people congregated,
Amazed by her virtue, for it was clear
How well she cared there for her father dear.
And she should be amazed if any might,   335
For never had she witnessed such a sight.

No wonder she was so surprised to see
So great a guest come in that humble place;
She wasn't used to such grand company,
And, watching, she became quite pale of face.   340
But to the matter's heart let's go apace;
These are the words the marquis chose to speak
To this kind maiden, faithful, true, and meek:

"Griselda, you can surely understand
The wish now that your father shares with me   345
That we should wed, and also may it stand,
As I suppose, that it's your will it be.
But I must ask some questions first," said he.
"Since with the utmost haste it should be wrought,
Do you assent, or wish some time for thought?   350

"Would you agree to all by me desired,
And that, when I think best, I freely may
Cause pain or pleasure as may be required
And you would not begrudge it night or day?
When I say 'yea,' you will not answer 'nay'   355
By word or frown? Swear this, and you've my oath
That we shall be allied, here I'll betroth."

Marveling at his words and trembling so
From fear, she said, "My lord, I shouldn't be
Held worthy of this honor you'd bestow,   360
But that which you may will is right with me.
And here I swear that never willingly,
In thought or action, you I shall defy,
On pain of death, though I were loath to die."

"That's good enough, Griselda," answered he.   365
At once he went outside with sober cheer,
And out the door behind him followed she,
And to the gathered folks he made it clear:
"This is my wife," said he, "who's standing here.
So honor her, give her your love, I pray,   370
All those with love for me; no more to say."

That none of the old clothes she had to wear
Be brought into his house, the marquis had
Some women come to strip her then and there.
These ladies, be it said, were less than glad   375
To touch the garments in which she was clad,
But nonetheless they clothed from head to toes
This maiden of bright hue in brand-new clothes.

They combed her hair that, worn without a braid,
Had been unkempt; with dainty hands they set   380
A garland on her head; she was arrayed
With jewels of every size. Why should I let
Her clothing grow into a tale? And yet
The people hardly knew who she might be,
So fairly changed in such rich finery.   385

The marquis married her then with a ring
That he had brought, then placed her on that day
Upon an ambling, snow-white horse, to bring
Her to his palace—no more he'd delay—
With joyful people out to lead the way.   390
That's how the day in revelry was spent
Until the sun was low in its descent.

To chase this tale and move it forth apace,
I'll say that to this brand-new marchioness
God granted so much favor, by his grace,   395
That by appearance one would never guess
That she'd been born and bred with so much less
(Indeed inside a cot or ox's stall)
Rather than nurtured in an emperor's hall.

To everyone she grew to be so dear   400
And reverenced that folks who'd known her for
The length of her whole life, from year to year,
Could scarcely now believe—if any swore—
That of Janicula (of whom before
I spoke) she was indeed the daughter, seeing   405
How she appeared to be another being.

Though virtuous she'd been for all her days,
She showed such increase in her excellence
Of mind and habits, held in highest praise,
Was so discreet, so fair in eloquence,   410
So kind and deserving of reverence,
And won the people's hearts with so much grace,
That she was loved by all who saw her face.

Not only in Saluzzo could be found
The highest public praise for her good name,   415
But also in the regions all around;
If one spoke well, another said the same.
Of her high excellence so spread the fame
That men and women, young as well as old,
Went to that town, this lady to behold.   420

Thus Walter humbly—royally, I should say—
Was wed with fortunate honor, and he
In God's peace lived then in an easy way
At home, he seemed as blest as one could be.
And as he saw that under low degree   425
Is virtue often hidden, folks opined
He was a prudent man of rarest kind.

Not only did Griselda through her wit
Know how to do the things a housewife should,
But when the situation called for it   430
She could as well tend to the common good.
No angry strife or disagreement stood
In all that land that she could not resolve,
Restoring peace to those it might involve.

Though her husband be absent, rapidly   435
When nobles or when others in the land
Were feuding, she would bring them to agree.
Such eloquence she had at her command
And rendered judgment with such even hand,
She was heaven-sent in the people's sight,   440
To save them and to turn each wrong to right.

Now not too long after Griselda wed,
The day arrived when she a daughter bore.
Although they would have liked a son instead,
Glad were the marquis and the people, for   445
Although a little girl had come before,
Griselda wasn't barren, so she could
Still bear a manchild in all likelihood.

PART III

It happened, as so often will transpire,
That while this child still sucked the mother's breast,   450
The marquis in his heart had the desire
To put his wife's steadfastness to the test.
Out of his heart this marquis couldn't wrest
This urge to see how constant she would be;
God knows, he thought to scare her needlessly.   455

He'd put her to the test enough before
And always found her true; what was the need
To test her now, to do so more and more,
Though some men praise it as a clever deed?
As for myself, I say it's cruel indeed   460
To test a wife when there's no reason clear,
To put her through such anguish and such fear.

The marquis now proceeded in this wise:
He came alone at night to where she lay,
And with stern eye, with very troubled guise,   465
Said this to her: "Griselda, on that day

When from your poor life I took you away
For this high, noble state to which you rose—
You haven't now forgotten, I suppose?

"I say, Griselda, this new dignity   470
In which I've put you has (I trust it's so)
Not left you now forgetting the degree
In which I found you, poverty so low,
For all the comfort you have come to know.
Now listen to each word I say to you;   475
There is no one to hear it but we two.

"You know full well yourself how you came here
Into this house not very long ago;
And though to me you are belov'd and dear,
To all my gentlefolk you are not so.   480
They say that it's to their great shame and woe
To have to serve you, to be subject to
One from a little village as are you.

"Especially since you your daughter bore
There is no doubt about their grumbling.   485
Now I desire as I have done before
To live in peace with those I'm governing.
I can't be careless in this sort of thing;
I must do with your daughter what is best,
Not as I will but as they may request.   490

"God knows, this is a loathsome thing to me,
And yet without your knowledge and consent
It won't be done. But it's my will," said he,
"That in this case you give me your assent.
Now show your patience, act with the intent   495
That on that day you pledged and so have sworn,
When in that village wed where you were born."

When she had heard all this, no change it brought
In her in either word or look; thereby
It seemed that she was not at all distraught.   500

She said, "Lord, in your pleasure's where we lie.
Truly obedient, my child and I
Are yours to save or to destroy, each one
Belongs to you; and so your will be done.

"There's not a thing, as God my soul may save,   505
That pleases you that would displeasure me.
There's nothing in this whole world that I crave,
Or fear to lose, but you. This will shall be
Here in my heart, as now, eternally;
Nor death nor length of time shall it deface   510
Or turn my heart toward another place."

Glad was the marquis, hearing her reply,
Yet he pretended that he wasn't so;
A sad and dreary look was in his eye
As he then from the chamber turned to go.   515
Soon after this, he let a fellow know
In privacy about his whole intent,
Then to his wife this man the marquis sent.

This fellow was a kind of sergeant, one
His lord would often trust and send to do   520
Important things; such people, too, get done
Things that are shady, and without ado.
The marquis knew he loved and feared him too;
And when this sergeant knew his master's need,
He crept into the bedroom to proceed.   525

"Madam," he said, "you must forgive me though
I now do something that I can't evade.
As you're so very wise, you surely know
That lords' commands cannot be disobeyed;
They well may be bewailed, and plaint be made,   530
But that which lords desire must men obey,
And so shall I; there is no more to say.

"That child I am commanded now to take"—
He spoke no more, as if with worst intent

He grabbed the child, such gestures then to make   535
As though he'd slay it there before he went.
Griselda had to suffer this, consent;
Just like a lamb she sat there meek and still
And let this cruel sergeant do his will.

Of evil reputation was this man,   540
Suspicious, too, in look, in what he'd say,
And in that it was night when he began.
The child she loved—alas and wellaway!—
She thought he'd slay right there without delay.
But nonetheless she neither sighed nor wept,   545
Consenting that her lord's command be kept.

But then to speak she finally began:
She meekly asked, appealing to his pride,
As he was such a worthy gentleman,
If she might kiss her child before it died.   550
This little child Griselda laid beside
Her breast; with sorrow in her face she blest it,
And then gave it a kiss as she caressed it.

Here's what she uttered in her voice benign:
"Farewell, my child, whom nevermore I'll see!   555
Since of his cross I've marked you with the sign,
That of the Father who—blest may he be!—
Died for us on a cross made from a tree,
Your soul to him, my child, I now commit;
Tonight you die, and I'm the cause of it."   560

I think that any nurse, such come to pass,
Would find it hard, a painful thing to see;
Then well might any mother cry "Alas!"
But nonetheless Griselda quietly,
With steadfastness, endured adversity,   565
And told the sergeant, meekly as before,
"Here, you may have your little girl once more.

"Go now," she said, "and do my lord's behest;

There's just one thing I pray: that in your grace,
Unless my lord forbid, you'll lay to rest 570
My little daughter's body in some place
Where beasts or birds can't tear it or deface."
But not a word in that regard he'd say,
He took the child and went upon his way.

This sergeant came then to his lord again, 575
And of her words and how she did appear
He told him point by point, short and plain,
Presenting him then with his daughter dear.
The marquis seemed a little rueful here,
But nonetheless held to his purpose still, 580
As such lords do when they would have their will.

He told the sergeant then to go in stealth
And wind the child in nursery clothes with care,
To carry it, while mindful of its health,
Inside a chest or wrap; and to beware, 585
If from the block his head he wished to spare,
That his intent not one man come to know,
Not whence he came nor whither he may go.

To his dear sister in Bologna, who
Was Countess of Panik, he was to take 590
The child, and give her all the details too,
And ask that she herself might undertake
To raise the child, and nobly, for his sake;
And also that whose child it was she hide
From everyone, no matter what betide. 595

The sergeant did his duty. Let's return
Now to this marquis, as he busily
Involved himself in what he wished to learn:
If by Griselda's manner he might see,
Or by her words determine, whether she 600
Had changed at all; and yet he'd ever find
That she was still the same, steadfast and kind.

As glad, as meek, as anxious to display
Her love and service as she'd shown to be,
So was she now, he saw, in every way;   605
Not one word of her daughter uttered she.
No sign of change or of adversity
Was ever seen in her; her daughter's name
She never spoke in earnest or in game.

PART IV

Now in this way four years had passed before   610
She was again with child; God willed it, though,
That now a manchild she by Walter bore,
One fair and gracious to behold. And so,
When people came to let the father know,
Not only he but all the land rejoiced,   615
They thanked God for the child, his praises voiced.

When it was two years old and was removed
Then from its nurse's breast, there came a day
When by another urge this lord was moved
To test his wife again if that he may.   620
How needless he should test her anyway!
But married men like this one know no bound
When such a patient creature they have found.

"Wife," said the marquis, "you have heard before,
My people bear it ill that we were married;   625
Especially now that my son you bore,
It's grown much worse than ever. It's so carried,
The murmur wounds my heart, my soul is harried;
The voice assails my ears with such a smart
That it's well-nigh destroyed me in heart.   630

"For they're now saying this: 'When Walter's gone,
The blood of Janicula will succeed
And be our lord, we've none but him alone.'
Such words my people utter, and indeed

A murmur such as this I ought to heed;   635
For surely such opinion I am fearing,
Though they don't plainly speak within my hearing.

"I want to live in peace if that I might,
And therefore I've decided what's to be:
Just as I with his sister dealt by night,   640
So with him now I'll deal in secrecy.
I warn you so you won't be suddenly
Beside yourself, for that you shouldn't do;
Be patient, that is what I ask of you."

"I've said this and I ever shall again,"   645
She answered, "I wish nothing, in no way,
But what you will. It causes me no pain,
Although my son and daughter they may slay—
If it's at your commandment, that's to say.
For from the two all that I've come to know   650
Was illness first, and after, pain and woe.

"You are my lord; with that which you possess
Do as you will, ask no advice of me.
For as I left at home my former dress
When I first came to you, just so," said she,   655
"I left my will and all my liberty
And took your clothing. Therefore now I pray,
Do as you please, your wish I shall obey.

"And certainly if I had prescience,
Your will to know before you've ever told,   660
I'd go and do it without negligence;
But now I know your wish, what shall unfold,
And firmly to your pleasure I will hold.
If I knew that my death would bring you ease,
Then gladly I would die, my lord to please.   665

"With your love there's no way death can compare."
And when this lord had heard what she'd to say
And of her constancy was made aware,

He dropped his eyes and wondered how she may
In patience suffer such. He went away 670
With dreary-looking face, although his heart
With pleasure was about to burst apart.

This ugly sergeant, in that very wise
In which he'd grabbed her daughter formerly
(Or worse, if any worse men could devise), 675
Now grabbed her son, this child so fair to see.
Such patience still Griselda had that she
Showed no sign of the burden of distress,
But kissed her son and then began to bless;

Save only this: she prayed that, if he could, 680
He'd see that her small son be so interred
That his slender, delicate body should
Be safe from ravage by some beast or bird;
He gave her for his answer not a word.
He left as if not caring for one limb, 685
But to Bologna gently carried him.

The marquis could but wonder all the more
About her patience, thinking that if he
Had not had certain knowledge long before
That she her children loved so perfectly, 690
He would have thought it was some subtlety,
Some malice or cruel-heartedness deep down,
By which she suffered this without a frown.

But well he knew that, next to him, no doubt
She loved her children best in every way. 695
From women now I'd like to find this out:
Are not these tests enough for an assay?
What more could one hard man bring into play
To test his wife's wifehood, her steadfastness,
As he persists with his hard-heartedness? 700

But there are folks who are of such a bent
That once a certain cause they undertake,

From that intention they cannot relent;
They're bound to it as if it were a stake,
From that first purpose they will never slake.   705
Just so this marquis fully now proposed
To test his wife as he was first disposed.

He waits to see if, by her countenance
Or words, toward him changed she now appears;
But never may he find a variance.   710
Her heart and looks were one, for all his fears;
The further that she grew along in years,
The truer—if such things one ever sees—
Her love would grow, more pains she took to please.

It was as though from two you might could tell   715
One will; as Walter wished, the lord's behest,
So it appeared her pleasure was as well.
And, God be thanked, all happened for the best.
She showed well that a wife, for all unrest
Or worry, should will nothing but in fact   720
That which her husband would himself enact.

Now far and wide the Walter scandal spread,
How with a cruel heart he wickedly—
Because such a poor woman he had wed—
Had murdered both his children secretly.   725
Such murmuring was now heard commonly.
No wonder, since out to the common ear
Came not a word, so murdered they'd appear.

Because of this, where all the folks before
Had loved him well, his scandalous ill fame   730
Was something they began to hate him for.
A "murderer" bears quite a hated name;
But still in earnest, surely not for game,
From his cruel purpose he would not relent;
To test his wife remained his whole intent.   735

Now when his daughter fair was twelve years old,

He sent a legate to the court of Rome
(Which of his will already had been told)
Commanding them such bulls to send him home
As would befit his cause; read like a tome,   740
They'd say the pope, so that the land be stilled,
Bade him to wed another if he willed.

I say, he bade them counterfeit, of course,
These papal bulls, therein the declaration
That he might leave his first wife by divorce   745
As if it were by papal dispensation,
To still the rancor and the disputation
Between him and his people. That's the bull
That then was published everywhere in full.

No wonder that the ignorant in their way   750
Believed just what it said, that it was so;
But when Griselda heard the news, I'd say
The tidings surely filled her heart with woe.
But being ever steadfast as we know,
This humble creature thereby was disposed   755
To take what hardship Fortune had imposed,

Abiding ever by what he desired,
The one to whom she'd given all her heart
As to that which her very life required.
But briefly if this tale I'm to impart,   760
This marquis wrote a letter that from start
To finish covered all of his intent,
And slyly to Bologna had it sent.

The Earl of Panik (who was married then
To his dear sister) he asked specially   765
To bring home his two children—bring them in
A way befitting nobles, openly.
But this one thing he prayed most stringently:
The earl, though men should ask, must not infer
Their lineage, of whom these children were,   770

But only say the girl was to be wed
To the Marquis of Saluzzo right away.
And as beseeched, this earl then went ahead:
He started on his way at break of day
Toward Saluzzo, lords in rich array   775
Along in company, this girl to guide,
Her younger brother riding by her side.

This lovely girl, arrayed to set the stage
For marriage, had on many a sparkling gem.
Her brother, who was seven years of age,   780
Was dressed, too, in a way befitting him.
And so this great nobility, abrim
With cheer, toward Saluzzo made their way,
Riding upon their trip from day to day.

PART V

Now during all of this, the marquis who   785
(As was his wicked wont) would test some more
Her constancy, for all he'd put her through,
That he might have full knowledge, might explore
If she was still as steadfast as before—
Upon a certain day, for all to hear,   790
The marquis made this statement loud and clear:

"Griselda, it has pleased me certainly
To have you as my wife, for worthiness,
For your obedience and honesty,
Not for your name or wealth. But nonetheless   795
I now have come to see in truthfulness
That with great lordship, if I well appraise,
Great obligation comes in many ways.

"I may not do as every plowman might.
My people are constraining me to take   800
Another wife, they cry it day and night;
The pope himself, the people's wrath to slake,

Consents to it, and so I undertake.
And truly this much to you I will say:
My new wife is already on her way.   805

"Be strong of heart and vacate now her place;
As for the dowry that you brought to me,
Now take it back, I grant it by my grace.
Now to your father's house return," said he.
"No one may always have prosperity,   810
So I advise that you with even heart
Accept whatever Fortune may impart."

And once again she answered patiently:
"My lord, I've known through each and every day
That no one could compare my poverty   815
With your magnificence; no need to say
It can't be done, for no man ever may.
I never felt that I was of the grade
To be your wife, nor yet your chambermaid.

"And in this house, as lady, as your wife—   820
God be my witness, and as well may he
Gladden my soul with his eternal life—
I held myself no lady, I could be
But humble servant to your majesty,
And such I'll be as long as I'm alive,   825
To you above all creatures who may thrive.

"Since you so long a time, through kindliness,
Held me in honor, in a noble way,
When I did not possess the worthiness,
I thank both you and God, to whom I pray   830
That he'll requite you; there's no more to say.
Now to my father gladly I will wend
And with him dwell until my life should end.

"There I was fostered as a child and small,
And there I'll lead my life until I'm dead,   835
A widow pure in body, heart and all.

For as I gave to you my maidenhead
And am your faithful wife (it's safely said),
May God forbid that such a lord's wife may
Again espouse, or mate some other way.   840

"And as for your new wife, God in his grace
Grant joy to you and, too, prosperity!
For I will gladly yield to her my place
In which so blissful I was wont to be.
For since it pleases you, my lord," said she,   845
"In whom my heart awhile enjoyed its rest,
That I should go, I'll go when you request.

"As for the dowry that you'd offer me
Such as I brought, it clearly comes to mind
It was my wretched clothes, no finery,   850
And which would now be hard for me to find.
O gracious God! how gentle and how kind
You seemed to be in speech and in your look
When on that day our marriage vows we took!

"It's truly said—I find, at least, it's true,   855
For in effect it's proven here to me—
Love's not the same when old as when it's new.
But truly, lord, by no adversity,
On pain of death itself, could it so be
That in one word or deed I might repent   860
For giving you my heart with whole intent.

"My lord, you know that in my father's place
You had them strip me of my ragged dress
And clad me in rich clothing by your grace.
But surely all I brought you more or less   865
Were maidenhead and faith and nakedness;
And here again your clothing I restore,
Also your wedding ring, forevermore.

"Your other jewels you can now reclaim
Inside your bedroom as I'm sure you'll see.   870

Naked out of my father's house I came,
And naked I must now return," said she.
"I'll gladly do all you may ask of me;
I hope that it's not your intention, though,
That I be smockless when from here I go.   875

"A thing so shameful you would never do,
That this same body that your children bore,
Since I must walk out in the people's view,
Be seen all bare; and therefore I implore,
Don't make me go out like a worm, no more.   880
Remember, my own lord and dearest sir,
I was your wife, though I unworthy were.

"So in return for my virginity,
Which I brought here and can't now with me bear,
As my reward grant there be given me   885
A smock such as the kind I used to wear,
My body to be covered when they stare
Upon your former wife. I take my leave
Of you, my lord, before I may aggrieve."

"The smock that you have on your back," said he,   890
"May be retained and taken home with you."
The lord could scarcely speak; immediately
He turned and left in pity and in rue.
She stripped herself then in the people's view
Down to her smock; in bare feet, with head bared,   895
Toward her father's house Griselda fared.

The people followed, weeping as they went,
And there was many a curse of Fortune heard.
Griselda's eyes showed not one teary glint,
And during this she didn't speak a word.   900
Her father, learning soon what had occurred,
Then curst the day and time when Nature's plan
Had molded him into a living man.

This poor old man had doubted from the start,

Suspecting that the two were ill-allied;   905
For from the first he felt within his heart
That when his lord's desire was satisfied,
He'd then believe it was undignified
For his estate so lowly to descend,
He'd quickly bring their marriage to an end.   910

To meet his daughter now he went with haste,
The people's cries had told him she was near.
With her old coat, now all but gone to waste,
He covered her, with many a piteous tear.
He couldn't wrap it round her, so severe   915
Had time been on the cloth, much older now
Than on the day she'd made her marriage vow.

So for a time in her old father's place
This flower of wifely patience came to dwell,
And neither by her words nor by her face,   920
In public or in private, one could tell
That she'd been treated any way but well;
And of her high estate no memory
She seemed to have, as far as one could see.

No wonder, for when in her high estate   925
Her spirit was filled with humility;
No tender mouth, delicate heart, no great
And pompous show, no air of royalty,
But full of patience and benignity,
Discreet, always with honor, without pride,   930
And meek and steadfast at her husband's side.

Men speak of Job and praise his humbleness;
So scholars, when they wish, can well indite,
Especially of men; in truthfulness,
Though scholars' praise of women is so light,   935
There's no man who in humbleness can quite
Compare to woman, or be half as true
As woman can, unless it's something new.

PART VI

Bologna's Earl of Panik has come,
The news of which went spreading, and no less   940
There soon had reached the people, all and some,
The tidings, too, that a new marchioness
He'd brought, and in such pomp and regalness
That none in West Lombardy till that day
Had laid eyes on so noble an array.   945

The marquis, who'd arranged this from the start,
Before the earl came, a fellow sent
For poor Griselda; she with humble heart
And cheerful countenance, without a hint
Of any wound in mind or spirit, went   950
At his behest and knelt upon their meeting,
And reverently, politely gave him greeting.

He said, "Griselda, my firm will today
Is that this maiden who's to marry me
Be met tomorrow with such grand array   955
As in my house there possibly could be;
And also that according to degree
Each shall be served and seated at the table
And entertained, as best as I am able.

"I do not have sufficient women for   960
Arranging all the rooms as would befit
My liking; it is my desire therefore
That you should be in charge of all of it.
You know from old my pleasure every bit.
Although your clothing is a ragged sight,   965
Perform your duty still as best you might."

"Not only, lord, will I be glad," said she,
"To do your will, but I desire also
To serve you and to please in my degree
Forevermore; I'll never tire or slow,   970

Not ever, whether in good health or woe,
Nor shall my spirit ever take a rest
From my heart's true intent: to love you best."

With that, she worked to get the house prepared,
Set tables, made the beds, such pains to take   975
That she did all she could, no effort spared,
While begging all the chambermaids to make
More haste, to sweep and clean, for heaven's sake;
And she, the hardest working of them all,
Had every bedroom ready and the hall.   980

The next day the earl around nine o'clock
Arrived, these noble children at his side;
And all the people ran there in a flock,
And when such rich array they had espied,
Among themselves they quickly would decide   985
That Walter was no fool to have expressed
The will to change his wives, for it was best.

For she was fairer, so thought one and all,
Than was Griselda, and much younger too,
And from between them fairer fruit would fall   990
(More pleasing too), from noble tree she grew.
Her brother also was so fair to view
That when the people saw him they took pleasure,
Commending now their lord, his every measure.

"O stormy people! fickle, never true!   995
As changeable as is a weather vane!
In rumors you delight, whatever's new,
Just like the moon you ever wax and wane!
You're full of chatter, never worth a jane!
Your judgment's false, your constancy will cool,   1000
Whoever trusts you is an utter fool."

Thus said more sober-minded folks, to see
All of the people gaping up and down,
So very glad just for the novelty

Of having a new lady for their town.   1005
I'll speak no more right now of her renown,
But to Griselda I'll return, the one
So constant, with her duties to be done.

Griselda was still hard at work at all
That to the feast was to be pertinent;   1010
Nor did her clothes abash her, though withal
They certainly were crude and rather rent;
Out to the gate with cheerfulness she went
With other folks to greet the marchioness,
And after that, back to her busyness.   1015

So cheerfully her lord's guests she received,
And wisely, each according to degree,
That not one fault in her the guests perceived,
But all kept wondering who she might be;
For though she wore such ragged clothing, she   1020
Was so refined and worthy that in fact
They praised her, as deserved, for all her tact.

In all this time Griselda never ceased
This maiden and her brother to commend
With all her heart, so well that at the feast   1025
No one had cause her praises to amend.
At last, when all the lords there to attend
Were set to eat, the marquis chose to call
Griselda, who was busy in the hall.

"Griselda, what do you think of my wife   1030
And her good looks?" he asked her jokingly.
And she replied, "My lord, upon my life,
I've never seen one who's as fair as she.
I pray that God gives her prosperity;
To you I also hope that he will send   1035
All happiness till your life's very end.

"One thing I beg and warn you of as well:
That you'll not torment this young girl the way

That you have done to others; I can tell
That she was nurtured, reared from day to day   1040
More tenderly, and I would dare to say
She could not well endure adversity
As could a creature raised in poverty."

When Walter saw her patience still so strong,
Her cheerfulness, no malice shown at all,   1045
And even though he'd often done her wrong
She ever was as constant as a wall,
Continuing so blameless overall,
This marquis in his heart felt the distress
Of pity for her wifely steadfastness.   1050

"This is enough, Griselda mine," said he,
"Now be no more displeased, no more afraid.
For of your faith and your benignity,
In high estate and low, the test I've made,
As ever any woman's been assayed.   1055
I know, dear wife, your steadfastness." With this,
He took her in his arms and gave a kiss.

In wonderment, she didn't hear a word,
Of what he said no heed she seemed to take,
Until from her amazement, as if stirred   1060
Out of a sleep, she was once more awake.
He said, "By God who perished for our sake,
You are and you'll remain my only wife,
As God may grant me the eternal life!

"This is your daughter, whom you thought so fair   1065
To be my wife; the other truthfully,
As always I have planned, shall be my heir;
It's you who gave him birth, that's certainty.
Bologna's where I kept them secretly;
Now take them back, for now you see your son   1070
And daughter, you have lost them neither one.

"And folks that otherwise have said of me

I now warn well that I did what I did
Not out of malice nor for cruelty
But to assay and of all doubt be rid,   1075
And not to slay my children—God forbid!—
But to preserve them secretly until
I knew your every purpose, all your will."

When she had heard all this, she fainted then
For piteous joy, then, rising, to her side   1080
She called her son and daughter, took them in
Her loving arms while piteously she cried,
Embracing them with kisses and the pride
Of any mother, salty tears she shed
Bathing each face, the hair on each's head.   1085

O what a piteous thing it was to see
Her fainting, and her humble voice to hear!
"O thank you, lord, and God reward," said she,
"That you have saved my children young and dear!
I wouldn't care were I to die right here;   1090
As I stand in your love and grace, believe,
Death matters not, nor when my soul may leave.

"O dear, young, tender children, how in woe
Your mother always thought undoubtedly
Cruel hounds or some foul vermin long ago   1095
Had eaten you! But God so mercifully
And your kind, loving father tenderly
Have kept you safe"—that very moment found
Her swooning of a sudden to the ground.

And in her swoon so tightly she held on   1100
To her two children, still in her embrace,
It took more than a little force alone
To pry the children loose. And in the place
Were many tears on many a piteous face,
As folks stood by where she lay on the ground;   1105
Some couldn't even bear to be around.

But Walter cheered her, made her sorrow slake;
Then she arose, embarrassed, from her trance,
And cheerful comments all began to make,
And she regained her former countenance.   1110
Her pleasure Walter tried so to enhance
That it was truly a delight to view
The happiness restored between the two.

The ladies, when the proper time they chose,
Then took her, to the bedroom they were gone;   1115
They stripped her of her torn and tattered clothes,
And in a cloth of gold that brightly shone,
And with a crown of many a richest stone
Upon her head, they brought her to the hall,
Where she was honored rightfully by all.   1120

This piteous day thus had a blissful end,
As men and women both did all they might
This day in mirth and revelry to spend
Till in the sky there shone the starry light.
Indeed the feast in every fellow's sight   1125
Was far more splendorous in every way
Than was the feast upon their wedding day.

For many years in high prosperity
He and Griselda lived, at peace and blest;
He had his daughter married regally   1130
To a fine lord, one of the worthiest
In Italy; and, too, in peace and rest
His wife's old father in his court he kept
Until his soul out of his body crept.

His son succeeded to his heritage   1135
In rest and peace after his father's day,
And fortunate as well he was in marriage,
Although his wife not greatly to assay.
This world is not so tough, it's safe to say,
As it was known to be in days of yore;   1140
Pay heed to what this author says therefore:

This story's told not so that women should
Be like Griselda in humility—
It couldn't be endured although they would;
It's so that everyone in his degree   1145
Should be steadfast when in adversity
As was Griselda; therefore Petrarch writes
This story, which in high style he endites.

So patient was a woman to the end
Toward a mortal man, the more we ought   1150
To take without complaint what God may send;
It's reasonable that he test what he wrought,
Though he will tempt no man his blood has bought,
As Saint James says if you will read him out.
He tests folks every day, there's not a doubt,   1155

And so that discipline in us arise
He with sharp scourges of adversity
Lets us be often whipped in sundry wise;
It's not to know our will, for surely he
Before our birth knew all our frailty.   1160
For our own good is all his governance,
So let us live in worthy sufferance.

One word, my lords, now hear before I'm through:
It would be hard to locate nowadays
In any town Griseldas three or two;   1165
For if they all were put to such assays,
Their gold is so diluted by their ways
With brass that though the coin look good, my friend,
It's likely it will break instead of bend.

Now for the Wife of Bath and in her name—   1170
Her life and all her sex may God preserve
In mastery, or it would be a shame—
With young and lusty heart I now will serve
You with a song to gladden you, with verve,
And let's leave off this heavy stuff I chose.   1175
Now listen to my song, here's how it goes:

Chaucer's Envoy

Griselda's dead, her patience, too, long since
Both buried in some far Italian vale.
And so I cry in open audience:
No husband should so hardily assail   1180
His spouse's patience, trusting he will find
Griselda's, for he certainly will fail.

O noble wives, in all your sapience,
Don't meekly hold your tongue as with a nail,
Nor give a scholar reason to commence   1185
To write of you as marvelous a tale
As that about Griselda, patient, kind—
Lest Chichevache's innards be your bale!

Like Echo be, who from no word relents,
Who answers back as if to countervail.   1190
Do not be hoodwinked in your innocence,
Take matters in your hands and do not pale.
Engrave this lesson well within your mind,
That for the common good it may avail.

Archwives, stand up and be your own defense,   1195
You're strong as are big camels and as hale,
Don't suffer that to you men do offense.
You slender wives who are in battle frail,
Be fierce as India's tiger. Ever grind
And clatter like a mill and you'll prevail.   1200

Don't fear them, show for men no reverence,
For though your husband arm himself in mail,
The arrows of your crabbed eloquence
Will go right through his breastplate and ventail.
With jealousy keep him all in a bind   1205
And you will make him cower like a quail.

If you are fair, show folks as evidence

Your face and dress; if ugly, leave a trail
Of generosity, don't spare expense;
Let winning friends be always your travail.   1210
Like a linden leaf be sprightly, unconfined,
And let him worry, wring his hands and wail!

The Merchant's Tale

PROLOGUE

"Of weeping, wailing, care and other plight
I know enough each morning, noon, and night,"
The Merchant said, "and so do others, too,   1215
Who have been married. I believe it's true,
For well I know that's how it is with me.
I have a wife, the worst that there could be;
For if she and the devil were a pair,
She'd be more than his match, I dare to swear.   1220
What specially should I relate to you
About her malice? She's a total shrew.
There is a mighty difference between
Griselda's patience—great, as we have seen—
And my own wife's surpassing cruelty.   1225
How I could thrive if only I were free!
I'd nevermore be captured in the snare.
We married men live sorrowfully, in care.
Let whoso will assay and he will find,
By India's Saint Thomas, I've opined   1230
The truth (for most part, I won't claim it all).
And God forbid that it should so befall!
    "Ah, me! I have been married, good Sir Host,
So far, pardie, for two months at the most.
But I believe that he who's yet to wive   1235
In all his life—even though men may rive
Him to the heart—could not in any way
Tell you as much of woe as I could say
Right here and now of my wife's cursedness!"
    "Now, Merchant," said our Host, "as God may bless   1240
You, since you know so much about that art,
I heartily do pray you'll tell us part."
    "Gladly," said he, "but no more I'll relate,
For aching heart, of my own sorry state."

THE MERCHANT'S TALE

Some time ago there dwelt in Lombardy   1245
A worthy knight; born in Pavia, he
Resided there with great success in life.
For sixty years he'd lived without a wife,
Pursuing every bodily delight
With women, being all his appetite,   1250
For which these worldly fools so well are known.
But when his sixtieth year had come and gone,
Whether it was for sake of holiness
Or caused by dotage (I won't try to guess),
To take a wife he had such great desire   1255
That day and night he never seemed to tire
Of looking for a chance to tie the knot.
He prayed that God would grant it be his lot
To know at last the blissful way of life
That is between a husband and his wife,   1260
That he beneath that holy bond be found
As man and woman first by God were bound.
"No other life," said he, "is worth a bean,
For wedlock is so pleasurable and clean
That in this world it is a paradise."   1265
So said this old knight who was very wise.
    And certainly, as true as God is King,
To take a wife is a glorious thing,
Especially for someone old and hoar,
For then a wife's his treasure all the more.   1270
Then he should take a wife who's young and fair
With whom he might engender him an heir
And lead a life of solace and of joy.
The cry "Alas!" these bachelors employ
Whenever they find some adversity   1275
In "love," which is but childish vanity.
And truly it's befitting that it's so
These bachelors have often pain and woe;
On sandy ground they build, and they will find
No sure foundation like they had in mind.   1280

As bird or beast is how they live at best,
At liberty and under no arrest,
Whereas a wedded man enjoys a state
Of blissfulness, one not inordinate
But underneath the yoke of marriage bound.   1285
Well may his heart in joy and bliss abound.
For who's more than a wife obedient?
Who is as true as she, or as intent
To keep him well, or well again to make him?
Through good and bad she never will forsake him;   1290
Of serving him with love she'll never tire,
Though he bedridden be till he expire.
And yet some learneds say it isn't so,
Like Theophrastus. Should we worry, though,
If Theophrastus likes to tell his lies?   1295
"Don't take a wife," said he, "economize,
For you can save your house from the expense.
A faithful servant shows more diligence
In guarding all your wealth than will a wife,
For she'll lay claim to half of it for life.   1300
And if you're sick, so help me God, those who
Are faithful friends, or any knave who's true,
Will give you better care than she in wait
Day after day to get all your estate.
And once you have a wife, how easily   1305
And quickly then a cuckold you may be."
That's his opinion, like a hundred worse
The man has written. On his bones a curse!
Don't listen to such foolishness, away
With Theophrastus, hear what I've to say.   1310
     A wife is truly God's gift; certainly
All other kinds of gifts that there may be—
Like lands or pasture, rights or revenue
Or personal goods—are gifts of Fortune, due
To pass as does a shadow on a wall.   1315
A wife will last, of that no doubt at all,
For, plainly speaking, with you she'll abide
Longer perhaps than you may wish she tried.
     Marriage is a great sacrament, and he

Is lost, I hold, who's wifeless; helplessly   1320
He lives and all alone. (Here I refer,
Of course, to those among the secular.)
And listen why—I say this not for naught—
To be a help to man was woman wrought.
When God, once he made Adam, looked and saw   1325
The man all by himself and in the raw,
God in his goodness, for his mercy's sake,
Said, "For this man a helper let us make,
One like himself." Then God created Eve.
Here you may see, and hereby men believe,   1330
That woman is man's helper, his respite,
His paradise on earth and his delight.
So obedient and virtuous is she,
By nature they must live in unity.
One flesh they are, and one flesh, as I guess,   1335
Has but one heart in health and in distress.
     Saint Mary, *benedicite!* a wife!
How might a man have hardship in his life
Who has a spouse? I surely cannot say.
The bliss between the two is more than may   1340
The tongue express or heart invent. If poor
He be, she helps him work. She looks out for
His worldly goods, lets nothing go to waste.
In all he may desire she'll share his taste.
She will not once say "Nay" when he says "Yea."   1345
"Do this," says he; "All ready, sire," she'll say.
O blissful state of wedlock without price!
You are so pleasant, worthy, free of vice,
You're so commended as a thing to seek,
That every man who thinks he's worth a leek   1350
On his bare knees should either all his life
Thank God that he has sent to him a wife,
Or ask the Lord in prayer that he will send
Him one, to last him till his life should end.
His life will then be settled and secure;   1355
He may not be deceived, I'm fairly sure,
If by his wife's good counsel he is led.
Then boldly may the man hold up his head,

So true they are, and wisely they advise.
And so, if you would labor like the wise,   1360
What women counsel you should always heed.
　　Behold how Jacob, as these students read,
By his mother Rebecca's good advice
Tied round his neck the sheepskin, which device
Won the blessing his father would bestow.   1365
　　See Judith, by her story too we know
How by wise counsel she God's people kept,
How she slew Holofernes while he slept.
　　See Abigail, how by good counsel she
Her husband Nabal saved, the time when he   1370
Would have been slain. And Esther see also,
By sound advice delivering from woe
God's people, and who then for Mordecai
Ahasuerus' favor won thereby.
　　There's nothing in high favor in this life,   1375
Says Seneca, above a humble wife.
　　So suffer your wife's tongue, that's Cato's writ;
She shall command and you shall suffer it,
Then she'll obey you out of courtesy.
A wife is keeper of your property;   1380
Well may the man who's sick bewail and weep
If there is not a wife, the house to keep.
I warn you: wisely work, not in the lurch,
Love well your wife as Christ so loved his church.
For if you love yourself you love your wife;   1385
No man hates his own flesh but in his life
Will foster it. I tell you, then, care for
Your wife or you will never prosper more.
Husband and wife (let men jest as they may)
Among the secular hold to the way   1390
That's safe, so knit that no harm may betide,
Especially none from the woman's side.
So January, this knight of whom I've told,
Considered in the days when he was old
The life of joy, the virtuous repose   1395
In marriage honey-sweet. And so arose
The day when for some friends of his he sent

To talk about effecting his intent.
    With solemn face his tale to them he told.
He said, "My friends, I'm hoary now and old,   1400
Almost, God knows, on my grave's very brink.
Upon my soul a little I must think,
My body I have wantonly expended.
But, God be blest, that shall be soon amended!
For I will surely be a wedded man,   1405
And that at once, as quickly as I can.
To some fair girl of tender age, I pray,
Make plans now for my marriage, right away,
For I can't wait around. Now I will start
To look around for one—I'll do my part—   1410
Whom I may quickly wed. But inasmuch
As you outnumber me, you sooner such
A creature should be able to espy
And where it would be best that I ally.
    "One warning, though, dear friends, and that's to say   1415
I will not have a wife who's old, no way.
She won't be over twenty certainly;
To have old fish and young flesh, that's for me.
A pike beats any pickerel for a meal,
And better than old beef is tender veal.   1420
I'll have no wife who's over thirty, that's no more
Than bean-straw, lots of fodder. Furthermore,
Old widows have the wile to rock a boat
Till even Wade's, God knows, would hardly float.
They cause such trouble when they get the whim   1425
That I could never live in peace with them.
As many schools make students hard to collar,
A woman many-schooled is half a scholar.
But certainly a young thing men can guide,
Like warm wax to be molded, hands applied.   1430
So I'll say plainly, briefly as I can,
I'll have no wife who's old, that's not the plan.
If I had such misfortune to the measure
That in her I could not take any pleasure,
I'd live on so adulterous a level   1435
That when I die I'd go straight to the devil.

Upon her I'd beget no progeny;
I'd rather hounds would eat me, though, than see
My heritage to hands of strangers fall,
And this is what I tell you one and all.   1440
I do not dote, I know the reason why
Men should be wed. And furthermore, say I,
Some who in talk of married life engage
Know nothing more about it than my page.
It's for these reasons men should take a wife: 1445
If he cannot live chastely all his life,
Let him with great devotion take a mate
With whom he legally can procreate,
Beget to the honor of God above,
Not just because of passion or of love;   1450
That each of them should lechery eschew
And yield their debt whenever it is due;
Or else that each of them should help the other
When troubled, as a sister helps her brother,
And live a holy life in chastity.   1455
But by your leave, kind sirs, that isn't me.
For, God be thanked, I feel and dare to boast
My limbs are strong, as adequate as most
To do all that a man's expected to.
Who better knows than I what I can do?   1460
Though hoary I'm just like a tree, the type
That blossoms though the fruit is still unripe.
A blossomed tree is neither dry nor dead.
I feel I'm hoary only on my head,
My heart and all my limbs are yet as green   1465
As through the year the laurel may be seen.
And now that you have heard all my intent,
I pray to my desire you will assent."
      Of marriage different men then to him told
Examples that were both diverse and old.   1470
Some blamed it, others praised it certainly,
Until at last (to speak with brevity),
As always there befalls some altercation
Among friends who engage in disputation,
Between his own two brothers had begun   1475

A rift. Placebo was the name of one,
Justinus what they truly called the other.
  Placebo said, "O January, brother,
You had such little need, my lord so dear,
To ask advice of any who are here,   1480
Save that you're so endowed with sapience
And of such prudence in the highest sense,
You didn't wish to stray from Solomon.
This word he spoke to us, to everyone:
'Do all things by good counsel,' so he went,   1485
'Then you will have no reason to repent.'
But though Solomon spoke such words, my own
Dear brother and my lord, as God alone
May in his wisdom bring my soul to rest,
I hold your own good counsel is the best.   1490
My brother, take from me this proposition:
I've always had a courtier's position,
And, God knows, though I may unworthy be,
Yet I have stood with those of high degree,
With lords among the highest in estate;   1495
With none of them I'd ever have debate.
To contradict them I would never try,
For I know that my lord knows more than I.
With what he says I hold firm and concur,
I say the same or something similar.   1500
How great a fool is any man if he
Serves to advise a lord of high degree
And dares presume, or gives one thought to it,
His counsel rates above his master's wit.
No, by my faith, lords are no fools! To us   1505
Today have you yourself so virtuous
And high a judgment shown that I consent,
Hereby concur with all of your intent,
Each word, all your opinion, utterly.
By God, in all this town or Italy   1510
Words better spoken no man could provide!
Such counsel pleases Christ, he's satisfied.
And truly what high spirit at this stage
That any man who's so advanced in age

Should take a young wife. By my father's kin,   1515
Your heart is pricked by quite a jolly pin!
Do as you please in this, for it's the way
That I hold best, and that's my final say."
    Justinus stilly listened, sitting by,
Then promptly gave Placebo this reply: 1520
"And now, my brother, patience show, I pray;
Since you have spoken, hear what I've to say.
Among his other sayings that are wise,
Seneca says a man should scrutinize
On whom to give his land or what he's got.   1525
And therefore, since I ought to think a lot
About who is to have my property,
How much more well advised I ought to be
About my body that I give away.
For let me warn you well, it's no child's play   1530
To take a wife without deliberation.
Men must inquire, it is my estimation,
Whether she's wise, sober or fond of ale,
Or rich or poor, or mad for every male,
Or proud, or else a shrew who scolds or prattles,   1535
Or one who'd be a waster of your chattels.
In this whole world no one will ever find
A creature that is of a perfect kind,
For all one may imagine, man or beast;
It ought to be sufficient, though, at least   1540
Where there's a wife concerned to see she had
Good qualities outnumbering the bad,
And one needs time if properly to tell.
For I've wept many a private tear (so well
God is aware) since I have had a wife.   1545
Let whosoever will praise married life,
I surely find in it but cost and care
And duties, of all bliss I find it bare.
And yet, God knows, my neighbors all about
(Especially the women, all the rout)   1550
Have said that I have the most steadfast wife,
The meekest one they've ever seen bear life.
But I know best where I'm pinched by my shoe.

You may, for your part, do as you would do.
Consider well—you're elderly—before   1555
You marry, and consider all the more
If you would have a wife who's young and fair.
By him who made the water, earth, and air,
The youngest man in all this company
Has quite enough to busy him that he   1560
Might have his wife alone. You mark my word,
One year or two you'll please her, not a third;
That is, you'll never give her fullest pleasure,
A wife demands so much to fullest measure.
May you not be displeased by this, I pray."   1565
　　"Well," January said, "you've had your say?
Straw for your Seneca and your proverbs,
School talk not worth a basketful of herbs!
As you have heard, men of a wiser bent
Than you now to my purpose give assent.   1570
Placebo, what have you to say to me?"
　　"I say it is a cursed man," said he,
"Who hinders matrimony." With that word,
They all arose at once, and there was heard
A full assent among them that he should   1575
Be married when he wished and where he would.
　　High fantasies began to crowd their way
Into his busy soul as day to day
This January on his marriage thought.
Many a shapely visage to be sought   1580
Paraded through his mind night after night,
As if one took a mirror polished bright
And set it in a common marketplace
That he might then see many a figure pace
By in his glass. In this way January   1585
Reviewed in thought the maidens, which to marry,
Who dwelt nearby, which one might be his bride.
He didn't know on which one to decide;
For if one had great beauty in her face,
Another stood so in the people's grace,   1590
For her steadfastness and benignity,
That she had greatest popularity;

And some were rich and had an evil name.
But nonetheless, twixt seriousness and game,
On one of them he finally set his heart,   1595
The others from his mind then set apart.
He chose her by his own authority,
For love is always blind and cannot see.
And when this January went to bed,
He pictured in his heart and in his head   1600
Her beauty fresh, her years of age so tender,
Her tiny waist, her arms so long and slender,
Her wise demeanor, her gentility,
Her womanly bearing, her constancy.
And he thought, when his mind was set on her,   1605
He'd made the finest choice that could occur;
For once he had concluded as he had,
He judged all others' judgment as so bad
That none could match, no possibility,
The choice he made. Such was his fantasy.   1610
Then he sent word, as if an urgent measure,
To all his friends, that they do him the pleasure
Of coming right away into his hall;
He'd cut the labor short of one and all,
No longer need they run about or ride,   1615
He'd made the choice by which he would abide.
      Placebo and his friends came very soon,
And first of all he asked them as a boon
Not to dispute, no arguments to make
Against his plan, the course he chose to take—   1620
A pleasing plan to God on high, said he,
A true foundation for prosperity.
      He said there was a maiden in the town
Who had for all her beauty great renown
Although she was of humble station. He   1625
Found in her youth and looks sufficiency.
He said this maiden he'd have for his wife,
In ease and virtue then to lead his life.
And he thanked God that she'd be his alone,
No man to share the bliss he'd call his own.   1630
He prayed that they might labor in this cause

For his success, make plans without a pause,
So that his spirit might then be at leisure.
"Nothing," he said, "could then bring me displeasure,
Except one thing that pricks my conscience. Here   1635
I'll tell it, that to all of you it's clear.
    "I once was told," said he, "and long ago,
Two perfect blisses man may never know;
That is to say, on earth and then in heaven.
Though sins he shun—each of the deadly seven   1640
And every branch that grows upon that tree—
There is so perfect a felicity,
Such great delight in marriage, I have fears,
Now that I'm living in my latter years,
That I shall lead now such a merry life,   1645
One so delightful without woe or strife,
I'll have my heaven here on earth. My thought
Is that true heaven is so dearly bought
With tribulation and great penance, how
Should I, by living in such pleasure now   1650
As men do with their wives, go on to see
That bliss where Christ lives for eternity?
This is my fear. I pray, my brothers two,
Resolve for me this question put to you."
    Justinus, hating such absurdity,   1655
In mocking way replied immediately.
That he might keep it short, he didn't quote
What this or that authority once wrote,
But said, "Sire, so there be no obstacles,
God in his power of working miracles   1660
And in his mercy may bring it to pass,
Before you die and have your final mass,
That you'll repent of such a wedded life
In which you say there is no woe or strife.
For God forbid that he would not have sent   1665
To one who's married more grace to repent
(And frequently) than to a single man.
I'll give you, then, the best advice I can.
Remember this: do not despair of glory,
Perhaps she is to be your purgatory;   1670

She may be but God's instrument, his whip,
So that your soul may up to heaven skip
More swiftly than an arrow leaves a bow.
As I may hope in God, you'll come to know
There's no such thing as great felicity   1675
In married life, nor will there ever be.
Don't fear that such will hinder your salvation,
Provided you perform in moderation
Your wife's desire. Let reason be the measure,
That not too amorously you give her pleasure,   1680
And keep yourself from other sin as well.
My wit is thin, that's all I have to tell."
Of such, dear brother, do not be afraid;
From out of this whole matter let us wade.
The Wife of Bath, if you could understand,   1685
On marriage, which is what is now at hand,
Spoke to us very well in little space.
I wish you luck, God keep you in his grace.
    And with that word, Justinus and his brother
Departed, took their leave of one another;   1690
For when they saw there was no use in waiting,
They skillfully began negotiating
To have this maiden, who was known as May,
As hastily as she could see her way
Become the wife of this knight January.   1695
I think you'd find it here too long to tarry
If I each deed and bond were to relate
By which she was enfoeffed to his estate,
Or if I told you in how grand a way
She was attired. But finally came the day   1700
When to the church they went, there to be bound
By holy sacrament. With stole around
His neck, the priest came forth and bade her be
In wisdom and in wifely loyalty
Like Sarah and Rebecca. Then he prayed   1705
As customary, made the sign, and bade
The Lord to bless the two in matrimony,
Concluding with all proper ceremony.
    So they are wed with ritual and grace,

And at the marriage feast sit on the dais   1710
Where they are joined by many a worthy guest.
The palace hall was filled with blissful zest,
With instruments, with victuals, judged to be
The most delicious found in Italy.
The music played was so melodious   1715
That there was never played by Orpheus
Nor Amphion of Thebes such melody.
With every course there came loud minstrelsy
Like nothing out of Joab's trumpet known,
Sound clearer than Thiodamus had blown   1720
At Thebes when that town's fate was still in doubt.
By Bacchus was the wine poured all about.
Fair Venus laughed, with all shared her delight
That January had become her knight,
That he'd assay his heart now with a wife   1725
The same as he had done in single life.
Before the bride and all the company
She danced, her torch in hand. And certainly
(For I daresay what no one can disparage)
Not even Hymen who's the god of marriage   1730
Saw any bridegroom filled with more delight.
Peace, poet Martianus, you who write
Of nuptials that took place so merrily
Between Philology and Mercury,
Of songs that by the Muses there were sung!   1735
Too small would be your pen as well as tongue
This marriage to describe on any page.
When tender youth has wedded stooping age,
The joy is such no pen can tell or show.
Consider it yourself and you will know   1740
If I speak truth or lie concerning this.
    And May, as she sat gracefully in bliss,
Was like some fair illusion to espy;
Queen Esther never once cast such an eye
On Ahasuerus, so meek was her look.   1745
I can't tell all the forms her beauty took,
But this much on it I can safely say:
She was just like a morning bright in May,

Her beauty other pleasures to enhance.
    How ravished January, in a trance   1750
Each time he looked upon her, giving start
To passion's threat against her in his heart:
That night to give her tighter a caress
Than Paris did his Helen. Nonetheless,
This January greatly pitied her   1755
For such pain as that night he must confer.
He thought, "Alas! O creature tender, pure,
May God now grant that you might well endure
All my desire! It's sharp, keen as a blade;
You may not well sustain it, I'm afraid.   1760
But God forbid that I use all my might!
Would God that it were now already night,
And that this night would last eternally.
I wish these folks were gone." Then finally
He put forth subtle efforts, did his best,   1765
Within the bounds of honor, to suggest
That they all leave the board as soon as able.
    When came the proper time to leave the table,
The folks began to dance, imbibing fast,
As spices all about the house were cast,   1770
And full of bliss was each and every man—
All but a squire whose name was Damian,
Who'd carved meat for the knight for many a day.
He had such longing for his lady May
That by the pain this squire was nearly crazed.   1775
He all but swooned and perished, standing dazed,
So sorely Venus, dancing with her brand,
Had burnt him as she bore it in her hand.
He hastily departed to his bed.
No more of him at this time will be said,   1780
I'll leave him there to weep and to complain
Until fresh May shall rue him for his pain.
    O perilous fire that in bedstraw breeds!
Unfaithful servant, traitor to the needs
Of those you falsely serve as foes would do!   1785
You adder in the bosom, sly, untrue,
God shield us all from your acquaintance! See,

O January, drunk with ecstasy
In marriage, how your Damian—your man
Who's like a son, your very squire—shall plan   1790
Against you, has intent to do you wrong!
God grant you find this foe before too long,
For in this world there's no worse pestilence
Than a foe daily in your residence.

    The sun's diurnal arc had been completed,   1795
No longer might the sun now linger, seated
On the horizon, in that latitude.
Night with his mantle that is dark and rude
Began to overspread the hemisphere.
The company took leave, all in good cheer,   1800
Of January, with thanks on every side.
Back to their homes with joy they were to ride,
Where they would do all that they might desire
Till time when it would please them to retire.
Soon after, this impatient January   1805
Was hot for bed, he didn't wish to tarry.
He drank some wines like claret, which require
Hot spices and would heighten his desire,
And also ate some aphrodisiacs—
Don Constantine, curst monk, relates the facts   1810
About them in his book *De Coitu;*
To eat them all he nothing would eschew.
And to his closest friends he turned to say,
"For love of God, as soon as there's a way,
One that's discreet, get all this house cleared out."   1815
    To do as he desired they went about;
The toast was drunk, the curtains soon were drawn.
To bed was brought the bride, still as a stone;
And when the bed had by the priest been blest,
Out of the chamber hastened every guest.   1820
Then January held, no more to wait,
His freshest May, his paradise, his mate.
He soothed her, couldn't kiss his May enough;
With bristles of his beard as thick and rough
As dog-fish skin, brier-sharp (for in this fashion   1825
He'd freshly shaved), he nuzzled in his passion

Her tender face. And then he said to May,
"Alas! I must trespass, go all the way,
My spouse, you I must mightily offend
Before the time I'm finished and descend."   1830
And then he said, "Consider this, however:
There's not a workman, be his trade whatever,
Who can perform both well and hastily.
This will be done with leisure, perfectly.
It doesn't matter how long we may play,   1835
We two were paired in true wedlock today.
And blessed be the yoke that we are in,
For by our actions we may do no sin.
A man cannot commit sin with his wife
Nor hurt himself by using his own knife,   1840
For by the law we now have leave to play."
And so he labored till the break of day.
He took a sop of spiced wine after that,
And then upright upon the bed he sat
And kissed his wife. He sang out clear and loud   1845
And amorously behaved. He was as proud
And wanton as a colt about the matter
And like a spotted magpie in his chatter.
And as he sang and croaked, the sagging skin
Upon his neck would shake. Whatever in   1850
Her heart May thought God only is aware
As she saw January sit up there,
In shirt and nightcap, with his neck so lean.
His play she didn't value worth a bean.
And then he said, "A rest now I will take;   1855
The day is come, I cannot stay awake."
So down he lay his head and and slept till nine,
And afterwards, when he was feeling fine,
This January arose. But freshest May
Four days within her chamber was to stay   1860
As custom for new wives and for the best.
From every labor one must have some rest
Or he won't manage long to stay alive;
No creature, that's to say, could so survive,
Be it a fish, a bird, a beast, or man.   1865

Now I will speak of woeful Damian
Who as you'll hear for her love pines away.
Here is the way I'd speak to him: I'd say,
"Poor Damian, alas! now answer me,
In such a case as this how can it be   1870
That you might tell your lady of your woe?
For all that she will ever say is 'No'—
And if you speak, your woe she will betray.
God help you, that's the best thing I can say."

    This lovesick Damian so burned in fire   1875
Of Venus he was dying of desire.
His very life was put in jeopardy,
For how long might he bear it? Secretly
A pen-box he decided then to borrow;
He wrote a letter telling of his sorrow,   1880
The letter's form that of a plaintive lay
About his lady, fresh and fairest May.
He placed it in a silk purse that was strung
Upon his shirt. Above his heart it hung.

    The moon, which had at noontime of the day   1885
When January married freshest May
Still been in Taurus, into Cancer glided
While May within her bedroom still abided.
As is the custom of these nobles all,
A bride shall not go eat inside the hall   1890
Until four days (or three days at the least)
Have passed, then she is free to go and feast.
So on the fourth day, when high mass was through,
From noon till three together sat the two
Inside the hall, this January and May,   1895
Who looked as fresh as bright the summer day.
That's when it happened that this worthy man
At last again took thought of Damian.
"Saint Mary!" he exclaimed, "how may this be
That Damian is not attending me?   1900
Is he forever ill? What's occupied him?"
His squires who were standing there beside him
Excused him for an ailment that perforce
Was keeping him from duty's normal course,

For surely nothing else could make him tarry.   1905
   "I'm sad to hear it," said this January,
"He is a worthy squire and that's the truth.
His death would be a blow and time for ruth.
He is as wise, as trusty and discreet
As any of his rank I'd hope to meet.   1910
He's manly, of good service, never shifty,
And one who has a knack for being thrifty.
I'll visit him as soon as I am able,
And so will May when we have left the table.
I'll give him all the comfort that I can."   1915
Then he was blest by each and every man
That in his goodness and gentility
He'd offer in his squire's infirmity
Such comfort, for it was a noble deed.
"Now listen, dear," he said, "here's what we need: 1920
When after dinner you have left the hall
And spent some time in chamber, go with all
Your women, pay respects to Damian.
Go cheer him up, for he's a worthy man.
And tell him, too, I'll come and be his guest   1925
As soon as I've had just a little rest.
And see that you make haste, for I'll abide
Until you're sleeping snugly at my side."
And with that word, he turned aside to call
The squire who served as marshal of the hall,   1930
To tell him this-and-that, things he required.
   Fresh May went straightaway as he desired
To Damian with all her company.
She sat down by the fellow's bed, where she
Tried then to comfort him as best she might.   1935
This Damian, just when the time was right,
In secret put his purse with billet-doux
(In which he'd written his desire) into
The lady's hand. That's all that happened, save
The deeply felt and wondrous sigh he gave,   1940
And these few words he softly spoke: "I pray
For mercy, don't go giving me away,
For if this thing be known I'm dead or worse."

Inside her bosom then she hid the purse
And went her way. No more I'll add to that.   1945
To January she returned and sat
Down softly on his bed. He took her in
His arms and gave her several kisses, then
He lay back down to sleep and promptly so.
She made pretense that she then had to go   1950
To you-know-where, as everyone must do;
She took the letter, when she'd read it through,
And tore it up, known to no other soul,
And threw the pieces down the privy hole.

    And now who studies more than fairest May?   1955
Beside old January again she lay.
He slept until awakened by his cough,
Then asked that she strip all her clothing off;
He said that he desired with her some play
And all her clothes were only in the way,   1960
And she obeyed, like it or not. Lest I
Get prudish folk upset with me thereby,
How he performed I do not dare to tell,
Nor if she thought it paradise or hell.
I'll leave them there, they labored as they chose   1965
Till at the bell for evensong they rose.

    Whether it was by destiny or chance,
By some influence, natural circumstance
Or constellation, that in such a way
The heavens stood that time brought into play   1970
Such Venus-work (these students hold the view
That "all things come in time")—a billet-doux
To any woman, hoping for her love—
I cannot say. And may great God above,
Who knows there must be cause for every act,   1975
Be judge of all, I'll hold my peace. The fact
About the matter is that freshest May
Began to feel such sympathy that day
For ailing Damian she couldn't purge
This feeling from her heart—this thoughtful urge   1980
To do his pleasure, putting him at ease.
"I'll reckon not whom all it may displease,"

She thought, "for he shall have my guarantee
To love him best of all on earth though he
Had no more than his shirt." How soon will start   1985
The flow of pity in a gentle heart!
   Here you may see the generosity
In woman when she's thinking carefully.
Some lady tyrants—many a one is known
To have a heart as hard as any stone—   1990
Would simply let him die there in the place
Before they'd ever grant him such a grace.
They'd take delight in having such cruel pride
And none of them be deemed a homicide.
    This gentle May so full of pity wrote   1995
By her own hand to Damian a note
In which she made true promise of her grace.
There but remained to set the day and place,
His will by her there to be satisfied,
Which he must then arrange. When she espied   2000
Her chance one day, this squire she went to see,
And underneath his pillow cunningly
She slipped this note she'd written, that the squire
Might later read it if he so desire.
She took his hand and squeezed it tightly (though   2005
In secret, so that no one else might know),
Bade him be well, then left. She didn't tarry,
For she'd been called again by January.
   On that next morning Damian arose;
No longer sick, delivered from his throes,   2010
He combed his hair and preened, he neatly dressed,
And did all that his lady would request.
He went to fetch as well for January
As ever any dog has fetched the quarry.
Such graciousness to all he seemed to show   2015
(Skill's all it is, as those who practice know),
That all who spoke of him spoke only good,
And fully in his lady's grace he stood.
And so I leave him to pursue his need
As forward with my tale I will proceed.   2020
   Some clerks believe that pleasure is the way

To happiness. And one can truly say
This January, noble in his might,
Through proper means, befitting such a knight,
Pursued a sumptuous life while here on earth.   2025
His home, his clothes, all that his rank and worth
Had brought to him, were fashioned like a king's.
He had, among some other noble things,
A garden built, walled all about with stone.
Now there's to me no fairer garden known;   2030
I wouldn't doubt, indeed I would suppose
That he who wrote *The Romance of the Rose*
Could not with words do justice to its beauty.
Nor could Priapus, given such a duty,
Himself the god of gardens, fully tell   2035
The beauty of that garden and its well
That stood beneath a laurel evergreen.
On many occasions Pluto and his queen,
Fair Proserpina, and their company
Of nymphs, would sport while making melody   2040
About that well, and danced, as men have told.
    This noble knight, this January the Old,
So loved to walk and frolic there that he
Would let no other person bear the key
That locked the garden wicket. January   2045
That little silver key would always carry,
That when he so desired he might go through.
And when he wished to pay his wife her due
In summer season, that's where he would be
With May his wife, none else in company;   2050
And things that he had not performed in bed
He'd promptly in the garden do instead.
And in this manner many a merry day
This January lived with freshest May.
But worldly joy has no lasting feature   2055
For this knight or for any other creature.
    O sudden chance! O Fortune so unstable!
Deceptive like the scorpion, you're able
To flatter with your head when you're to sting;
Your tail is death through all your poisoning.   2060

O brittle joy! O venom cunning, sweet!
O monster, with such subtlety to treat
Your gifts in hues of faithfulness, just so
You may deceive us all from high to low!
Why have you January so deceived   2065
Whom as a friend in full you had received?
And now you have deprived him of his sight,
He grieves and wants to die, as well he might.
   Alas! this noble knight, with hand so free,
In all his pleasure and prosperity,   2070
With suddenness has now been stricken blind.
His tears and wails were of a piteous kind.
And thereupon the fire of jealousy,
Lest May fall into infidelity,
So burnt his heart that if he had his way   2075
Someone would slay them both, him and his May.
For after he should die, as in his life,
He'd have her be no other's love or wife
But live in widow's black and never marry,
Like the turtledove that lives so solitary   2080
When it has lost its mate. But then at last,
Within two months, his grief had nearly passed,
When he had learnt, since it would have to be,
To take with patience his adversity—
Except, of course, he never was to cease   2085
His jealousy. Indeed it would increase,
Grow so outrageous till not in the hall,
Some other room, or any place at all
Would January let his lady May
Go walk or ride about in any way   2090
Unless his hand was ever at her side.
So freshest May had often sat and cried,
Her gentle love for Damian so great
That either sudden death must be her fate
Or she must have him, as she longed to do.   2095
She waited for her heart to break in two.
   For his side of the matter, Damian
Became then the most sorrow-stricken man
Who's ever drawn a breath. For night and day

He couldn't speak one word to freshest May   2100
About his aim or any subject near it
Unless he'd have this January hear it
Whose hand was always on her. Even so,
By little notes that they wrote to and fro
And secret signs, he caught all that she meant   2105
And she was finely tuned to his intent.
  O January, what might it avail
Though you could see as far as ships can sail?
Deceived when blind is no worse than to be
A man who's been deceived when he can see.   2110
  Consider Argus with his hundred eyes:
For all he pored and pried, it's no surprise
That he was still deceived—like others, too,
So confident, God knows, such wasn't true.
Who feels at ease has blinked, I say no more.   2115
  Fresh May, this wife of whom I spoke before,
In warm wax made an imprint of the key
That January bore as often he
Unlocked the gate and in this garden went;
And Damian, well knowing her intent,   2120
In secret had this key then duplicated.
Of this key there's no more to be related
But for a wonder that would soon ensue
That, if you will abide, I'll tell to you.
  How true, O noble Ovid, what you say!   2125
God knows, is there one trick that in some way
Love hasn't found, as hard as it may be?
By Pyramus and Thisbe men may see:
Kept under strictest guard, in spite of all,
They made their plans by whispering through a wall.   2130
No one could figure out their tricky ways.
  But now back to our aim. Some seven days
Into the month of June, this January
(With egging by his wife) for making merry
Inside the garden—none but he and May—   2135
Had such a great desire, one early day
He said to her, "Arise, my wife, my love,
My gracious lady! Gone, my sweetest dove,

Is winter, gone with all his soaking rain;
The voice of the turtle is heard again.   2140
Come forth now, with your eyes dovelike and fine!
How fairer are your breasts than any wine!
The garden has enclosed us all about.
Come forth, my snowy spouse! Without a doubt
You've wounded me right in the heart, O wife!   2145
I've known in you no blemish all my life.
Come forth, let's have our sport, for it is you
I've chosen as my wife and comfort too."

    Such were the lewd old words he used. And she
Then made a sign to Damian, that he   2150
Precede them with his key. The little gate
This Damian unlocked, then he went straight
Inside, all this in such a way that he
Was neither seen nor heard. Immediately
Beneath a bush the fellow stilly sat.   2155

    This stone-blind January, May right at
His hand and not another with him then,
Came to his lovely garden. Going in,
He shut the gate as quickly as could be.

    "My wife," said he, "there's none but you and me.   2160
It's you whom of all creatures best I love.
By heaven's Lord who sits so high above,
How much I'd rather die upon a knife
Than give to you offense, dear faithful wife!
Think how I chose you, for God's precious sake: 2165
Not out of covetousness, make no mistake,
But only for the love I had for you.
And though I'm old and may not see, be true
To me no less, and I will tell you why—
Three things that you will surely gain thereby: 2170
First, love of Christ, and honor, number two;
And all this heritage I give to you
From town to tower, deeds as you desire.
This shall be done, before the sun retire
Tomorrow, may God bring my soul to bliss.   2175
But first, I pray, a covenant by a kiss.
Don't blame me though I be the jealous kind:

So deeply you're imprinted in my mind,
When in thought of your beauty I engage
(And with it think of my unlikely age),   2180
I can't bear for the very life of me
A moment's time out of your company,
So great my love for you beyond a doubt.
Now kiss me, wife, and let us roam about."
    When she had heard these words, this freshest May   2185
Responded to him in a gracious way
But not till she at first began to weep.
"I have as well as you a soul to keep,"
She said, "and honor, too, the tender flower
Of my wifehood, entrusted to your power,   2190
Given into your hand, as you have found
Since first the priest to you my body bound.
So here's the answer that I'd have you hear,
If I may have your leave, my lord so dear:
I pray to God that early dawns the day   2195
I die as foully as a woman may
If ever to my kind I bring such shame
Or ever do such damage to my name,
If ever I be false. If I'm so found,
Then strip me, sack me up, and have me drowned   2200
In the nearest river. Sire, I'm every inch
A worthy woman, I am not a wench.
Why do you speak that way? But men untrue
Always reprove us women. All of you,
I think, are constant in this one approach,   2205
To speak to us in distrust and reproach."
    And with that word, she saw where Damian
Sat in the bush. She coughed and then began
To make signs with her finger, by which she
Meant Damian should climb up in a tree   2210
That had a load of fruit. And up he went,
For he was truly wise to her intent,
Knew all the signs and signals she could vary,
Much more than did her own mate January;
For in a letter she had told him how   2215
To work this whole thing out. And sitting now

In the pear tree is where I leave him be,
As January and May roam merrily.
   Bright was the day and blue the firmament;
His golden streams of light had Phoebus sent   2220
Down with his warmth, to gladden every flower.
In Gemini, I guess, upon that hour
Was Phoebus found, but near his declination
In Cancer, being Jupiter's exaltation.
On that bright morning, as it would betide,   2225
Into that garden (on its farther side)
Came Pluto, who was king of Fairyland,
With many a lady in his jolly band
Behind Queen Proserpina, she whom he
Had ravished in Etna of Sicily   2230
As she was gathering flowers on the mead.
(In Claudian the stories you may read,
How in his terrible chariot she
Was fetched.) When came this king of fairies, he
Sat on a bench of turf all fresh and green,   2235
Whereon at once he said this to his queen:
   "None can deny it, wife, each passing day
Experience shows the deceitful way
You women deal with men. I could relate
Ten hundred thousand tales to illustrate   2240
Your weakness, your unfaithfulness and stealth.
Wise Solomon, unrivaled in your wealth,
So filled with sapience, so world-renowned,
How worthy are the words that you expound
To be remembered by all men who can.   2245
He said this of the virtuous kind of man:
'Among a thousand men I found but one;
Among all women I discovered none.'
   "So speaks the king, who knows your wickedness.
And Jesus son of Sirach, as I guess,   2250
Of women seldom speaks with reverence.
A raging fire and rotting pestilence
Come falling on your bodies yet tonight!
And now do you not see this noble knight
Who has become, alas, so blind and old   2255

That his own man would cuckold him? Behold,
See where he sits, the lecher, in the tree!
Now I will grant out of my majesty
To this so aged, blind, and worthy knight
That all at once he shall regain his sight   2260
Just when his wife shall do her treachery.
Then he shall know of all her harlotry;
Thus she shall be reproved and others too."

    "Is that," said Proserpina, "what you'll do?
By the soul of my mother's lord, I vow   2265
I'll grant her what to answer, she'll know how,
And for her sake all women after her;
When caught, from any guilt they might incur
With boldest face they shall themselves excuse
And argue down all those might accuse.   2270
Not one shall die for lack of good replies.
Though a man may see a thing with both his eyes,
Yet shall we women face it hardily;
We'll cry and swear and chide so cleverly
You men shall look as foolish as a goose.   2275

    "For your authorities I have no use.
I'm well aware this Jew, this Solomon,
Found many women fools. But though not one
Good woman he himself could ever find,
There's many another man who's found the kind   2280
Of woman who is worthy, good, and true.
Consider those who dwelt in Christ's house, who
As martyrs were to prove their constancy.
Remember, too, in Roman history
Is many a true and faithful wife. But, sire,   2285
Though it be true, don't let it cause you ire;
For as he says he found no woman good,
I pray that what he meant be understood.
He meant that good in absolute degree
Is God's alone, there's neither he nor she.   2290

    "Ay! by that God, the true and only one,
Why do you make so much of Solomon?
What though he built God's house, the temple? What
Though he had wealth and glory? Did he not

Have built as well a temple for false gods?   2295
What thing could he have done that's more at odds
With good? Replaster him as you prefer,
He was a lecher and idolater
And in old age the one true God forsook.
But for the fact that God, as says the book,   2300
Would spare him for his father's sake, he should
Have lost his kingdom sooner than he would.
I hold what you men write, to vilify
Us women, as not worth a butterfly!
I am a woman, I speak as I do   2305
Or else I'd swell till my heart broke in two.
For if we are such talkers (as he stresses),
As ever whole I hope to keep my tresses
I never shall—be it discourteous—
Quit speaking ill of those maligning us."   2310
    "Madam," said Pluto, "please be mad no more,
For I give up! But since my oath I swore,
To grant to him his sight again this morning,
My word shall stand, you have my certain warning.
I am a king, it suits me not to lie."   2315
    "And queen," she said, "of Fairyland am I!
Her answer she will have, I undertake.
Now let's have no more words, no fuss to make,
And truly I'll no longer be contrary."
    So let us now return to January,   2320
Who in the garden with his lovely May
More merrily sings than the popinjay,
"I love you best, and shall, and you alone."
So long about the garden paths he'd gone,
That same pear tree he soon was passing by   2325
Where Damian sat merrily up high
Among the many tree leaves fresh and green.
    This freshest May, this wife so bright and sheen,
Began to sigh, and said, "My aching side!
Now sir," she said, "betide what may betide,   2330
I've got to have some of those pears I see
Or I will die, such longing I've in me
To have some pears to eat, those small and green.

Now help me, for the love of heaven's queen.
Well I can say a woman in my plight   2335
May have for fruit so great an appetite
That if she cannot have it she may die."
    "Alas," said he, "that here no knave have I
To make the climb! Alas, alas," said he,
"For I am blind!" "Yes, sir," responded she,   2340
"But that's no matter. Would you, for God's sake,
Within your own two arms the pear tree take?
For well I know you put no trust in me,
But I could then climb well enough," said she,
"If I might set my foot upon your back."   2345
    "For sure," said he, "there's nothing, then, we lack
If my heart's blood can help you, as it should."
So he stooped down, and on his back she stood
And caught hold of a branch, and up she went—
I pray, miladies, wrath you will not vent,   2350
I can't mince words, I am an ignorant man—
And in one sudden motion Damian
Then yanked up her chemise, and in he thrust.
    When Pluto saw this sinful act of lust,
To January he gave again his sight   2355
To see as well as ever. Such delight
In anything no man has known before
As January's joy to see once more,
Although his thoughts were still upon his love.
He cast his eyes up to the tree above,   2360
Beheld the way that Damian had addressed
Her—such a way it cannot be expressed
Unless I be too vulgar in my speech—
And gave a grievous cry, one like the screech
A mother makes to see her dying child.   2365
"Out! Harrow, help, alas!" he cried. "O wild
And brazen woman, what is this you do?"
    And she then answered, "Sir, what's ailing you?
Be reasonable, have patience! Bear in mind
How I have helped your eyes that both were blind.   2370
On peril of my soul, I speak no lies;
For I was taught, for healing of your eyes,

There was no better thing to make you see
Than struggling with a man up in a tree.
God knows, I did it with the best intent."   2375
    "Struggle?" he said. "And still right in it went!
A shameful death God grant you die, the two!
With my own eyes I saw him screwing you
Or hang me by the neck till I am dead!"
    "My medicine's a failure, then," she said.   2380
"For certainly if you could really see,
Such words as those you wouldn't say to me.
You only have some glimmer, not true sight."
    "I see as well," he said, "as e'er I might,
Thank God! With my two eyes—I swear it's true—   2385
That's what I thought I saw him do to you."
    "A daze, you're in a daze, good sir," said she.
"What thanks I have for having made you see.
Alas that I should ever be so kind!"
    "Madam," said he, "let all pass out of mind.   2390
Come down, my dear; if wrongly I've declared,
God help me, I am sorry that I erred.
But by my father's soul, I thought it plain
To see that Damian with you had lain,
That on his breast was lying your chemise."   2395
    "Sir, you may think," she said, "what you may please.
But when a man first wakes when he has slept,
His eyes aren't right away fit to be kept
On anything, to see with no mistake,
Until at last he truly is awake.   2400
Just so, when blind for any lengthy spell,
A man won't of a sudden see as well,
When first to him his sight has come anew,
As one who's had his sight a day or two.
Until your sight has settled for a while,   2405
There's many a thing you'll see that may beguile.
Take warning, then, I pray: by heaven's King,
There's many a man who thinks he sees a thing
That's not at all as it appears. He who
Has misconceived will be misjudging too."   2410
And with that word, she leapt down from the tree.

This January, who is glad but he?
He kisses her, he gives her hugs, and then
He gently strokes her on the abdomen
And leads her homeward to his palace. Now,   2415
Good men, I pray that you be glad. That's how
I shall conclude my tale of January.
God bless us, and his holy mother Mary!

EPILOGUE

"Ay! by God's mercy," our Host then declared,
"From such a wife I pray to God I'm spared!   2420
See all the subtle tricks abounding in
These women! To deceive us simple men
They're always busy as bees, and never fail
To get around the truth. This Merchant's tale
Has proved it well enough. I have a wife   2425
Who's true as any steel, although in life
She has no plenty—not referring to
That tongue of hers, for she's a blabbing shrew,
And has a heap of faults, not only chatter.
But we should let that go, it doesn't matter.   2430
And yet, do you know what? I shall confide,
I sorely rue that to her I am tied.
But if all of her vices I'd recite
I'd be a fool for sure, for then it might
Get back to her. Why, she could easily   2435
Be told by some here in this company.
Which ones would tell her there's no need to say;
Such wares all women know how to display.
What wit I have would not suffice, moreover,
To tell it all, and so my tale is over."   2440

The Squire's Tale

INTRODUCTION

"Squire, come nearer, if your will it be,
Say something about love, for certainly
You know as much of that as any man."
　　"No, sir," said he, "but I'll speak as I can,
As I've a willing heart. I'll not rebel　　　　　　　　　5
Against your wish, a tale for you I'll tell.
Excuse me if I chance to speak amiss;
I mean well, and my story goes like this."

THE SQUIRE'S TALE

PART I

　　At Sarai in the land of Tartary,
A king dwelt who made war on Moscovy,　　　　　　10
In which there perished many a valiant man.
This noble king was known as Cambuscan,
And in his time so greatly was renowned
That in no other land was to be found
So excellent a lord in everything;　　　　　　　　　15
He lacked for nothing that befits a king.
And of the faith to which he had been born
He kept the holy laws as he was sworn;
And he was wise and rich, lived hardily,
Was merciful and just impartially,　　　　　　　　20
True to his word, honorable and kind,
As steady-hearted as you'll ever find,
Young, eager, strong, as set for battle's call

As any young knight bachelor in his hall.
And he was handsome, blest by Fortune's smile,　　25
And always kept so royally in style
That nowhere else on earth lived such a man.
　　This noble king, this Tartar Cambuscan,
Was father of two sons, borne by his wife
Elpheta; the elder son was Algarsyf,　　30
The younger son by name was Cambalo.
This king also begat a daughter, though,
The youngest child, whose name was Canace.
Now to relate how fair she was to see
I've not the skill, for such my tongue is lame;　　35
I dare not undertake so high an aim.
My English, too, for such is insufficient;
One needs a rhetorician, excellent,
Well versed in all the colors of his art,
Her beauty to describe in whole or part;　　40
I'm none such, I can give but what I bring.
　　It came to pass that when this Tartar king
Had twenty winters worn his diadem,
And as each year, I guess, it suited him,
He had the feast of his nativity　　45
Proclaimed throughout Sarai as by decree,
The Ides of March being the time of year.
Phoebus the sun was jolly, shining clear,
For he was near his exaltation in
The face of Mars and in his house within　　50
Aries, being the hot and choleric sign.
The weather then was pleasant and benign,
For which the fowls, what with the sun's bright sheen,
The season and its plants so young and green,
Were loudly chirping, singing songs of cheer,　　55
As they had kept themselves another year
Against the sword of winter, keen and cold.
　　Now Cambuscan, this king of whom I've told,
In royal vestment sits upon his dais
High in his palace, diadem in place,　　60
And holds a feast so rich and sumptuous
There's never been one like it. To discuss

It for you here, detailing its array,
Would occupy at least a summer's day;
And there's no need to have it here observed 65
What courses in which order there were served.
On their exotic broths I will not dwell,
Nor on their swans and herons. Old knights tell
Us, too, that in that land there is some meat
That one considers there a dainty treat, 70
But which here in this land men hardly relish.
No man can tell it all; I'll not embellish,
It's nine o'clock and so I shall refrain,
It's fruitless, waste of time, without a gain;
Here my first subject now shall be resumed. 75
  It came to pass that when they had consumed
Three courses, and this king sat in his splendor
And listened to his palace minstrels render
Their songs before the dais melodiously,
In through the door of the hall suddenly 80
There came a knight upon a steed of brass,
In hand a mirror broad and made of glass,
A gold ring on his thumb; upon his side
A naked sword was hung. He dared to ride
His steed right up to the king's high table. 85
To speak one word none in the hall was able,
This knight each one so marveled to behold;
They all intently watched him, young and old.
  This strange knight who had come so suddenly,
Armored (save his head) magnificently, 90
Gave greetings to the king and queen and all
The lords in order sitting in the hall,
With such a fine display of reverence
Both in his speech and in his countenance
That Gawain with his courtesy of yore, 95
Were he to come from Fairyland once more,
To improve upon a word would not be able.
And after this, before the king's high table,
He spoke his piece, his manly voice rung,
And this knight's usage of his mother tongue 100
Was without fault in syllable or letter.

Indeed to make his tale seem all the better,
He spoke with feeling, spirit matching word,
As those who teach the art of speech are heard.
Although his style I cannot imitate   105
(I can't climb over any stile so great),
Yet I can tell in general his intent,
That is, the gist and sum of what he meant,
If I've got such together in my head.

 "Arabia's king and India's," he said,   110
"Who's my liege lord, upon this festive day
Salutes you, sire, as best he can and may,
And sends to you by me (here for the least
You may command), in honor of your feast,
This steed made of brass, which easily may   115
Within the course, sire, of one natural day
(That is to say, in four and twenty hours
Whether it be in time of drought or showers)
Convey you bodily to every place
Where it may be your heart's desire to pace,   120
Without a harm to you through foul or fair;
Or if you wish to fly high in the air
As does an eagle soaring, harmlessly
This steed shall take you where you wish to be,
Though you may sleep upon his back throughout   125
And take your rest. And he will turn about
And bring you back at the twist of a knob.
For many a craft was known to him whose job
It was to make it; many a constellation
He watched ere he began his operation,   130
With many a seal and bond at his command.

 "This mirror, too, that I hold in my hand
Such power has that in it one may see
Whenever there's to come adversity
Upon your realm, upon yourself also,   135
And openly who is your friend or foe.

 "And most of all, if any lady bright
Has set her heart on any man who might
Then be untrue, she shall his treason see,
His newfound love and all his subtlety,   140

Not one thing left concealed about his crime.
So as we look to merry summertime,
This mirror and this ring that here you see
My lord has sent to Lady Canace,
Your excellent daughter who's here with you.   145
   "This ring, if you will hear, has power too,
Which is to say, if she be pleased to wear it
Upon her thumb, or in her purse to bear it,
Beneath the heavens there is not a bird
Whose language she won't understand when heard,   150
His meaning clear and plain, as she will learn,
And in his language answer him in turn.
And every herb borne of a root will she
Know also, and to whom it's remedy,
Though his wounds be ever so deep and wide.   155
   "This naked sword that's hanging at my side
Such power has that, smite what man you may,
Right through his armor it will carve its way,
Be it as thick as any branchy oak;
And that man who is wounded by the stroke   160
Shall never heal unless you out of grace
Then stroke him with the flat upon the place
Where he is hurt. That is to say, my lord,
That you may stroke him with the flattened sword
Upon the wound and it will close. And I   165
Know this to be the truth, it's not a lie;
While you possess it, it will never fail."
   And when this knight had finished with his tale,
He rode out of the hall, then to alight.
His steed, as shiny as the sun was bright,   170
Stood in the court as still as stone. Then led
At once to chamber was the knight; he shed
His armor, then was seated at the board.
   And then the gifts were fetched—that is, the sword
And mirror, presents royal with their power—   175
And borne at once into the lofty tower
By officers appointed specially;
And then this ring they gave to Canace
With pomp, as she was seated at the table.

But certainly—and this is not a fable—   180
The horse of brass could not be led around,
It stood there as if glued right to the ground.
Out of its place no man could even nudge it
Nor with a windlass or a pulley budge it.
And why? Because they didn't know the trick.   185
And so there in its place they let it stick
Until this knight should teach to them the way
To move it, as you'll later hear me say.
    Great was the crowd that pressed about in force
To look upon this stationary horse.   190
It was so tall and of such breadth and length,
So well proportioned to be one of strength,
That it was like a steed of Lombardy,
So quick of eye, so as a horse should be,
So like one of fine Apulian breed;   195
For from his tail right to his ears, indeed
He couldn't be improved, not one degree,
By nature or by art, as all could see.
The greatest wonder, though, to those who'd pass
Was how this horse could go when made of brass.   200
It was from Fairyland, or so it seemed.
As folks will differ they diversely deemed,
For every head an independent mind;
They murmured like a swarm of bees, opined
Their judgments, which were based on fantasy.   205
They quoted lines of ancient poetry
And said it was like Pegasus, the horse
That had two wings to fly. And some, of course,
Said it was the horse of the Greek Sinon
That brought Troy to destruction as was known   210
From all the ancient stories they had read.
"My heart," one fellow said, "is full of dread;
I think there are some men inside the horse
Whose plan it is to take this town by force
Of arms. We ought to make this matter known."   215
Another whispered to his friend alone,
"He lies. This rather is an apparition,
It's something that's produced by some magician,

As jugglers do at these great feasts." And such
Is how the people jangled, worried much,   220
As people without learning commonly
Will look at things made with more subtlety
Than they can comprehend; they're always first
To judge by this or that the very worst.
    Some of them wondered, too, about the power   225
Of the mirror borne up into the tower,
How men might such things in this mirror see.
    One of them said it very well could be
Done naturally if held in right directions,
Combining certain angles, sly reflections,   230
And that in Rome was such a mirror. Then
They talked about Witelo, Alhazen,
And Aristotle, writers in their day
On strange mirrors and optics, just as they
Well know who've heard their writings read at length.   235
    Others wondered about this sword whose strength
Was such that it could pierce through anything;
They fell to talk of Telephus the king,
And of Achilles' spear that strangely he
Could use to heal or injure equally,   240
In just the way that men this sword may use
As you've already heard. They gave their views
On various ways to harden metal, with
Discussion, too, of mixtures by the smith,
And how and when the hardening should be;   245
Such things are all unknown, at least to me.
    They also spoke of Canace's new ring,
Agreeing that of such a wondrous thing
In rings they'd never heard before, not one
(Except that Moses and King Solomon   250
Are said to have been skillful in such art).
So spoke the people, drawn in groups apart.
But people once had wonder, too, to learn
Glass can be made from ashes of a fern,
Though glass is not like fern ash in the least;   255
This knowledge furnished long ago, they ceased
Eventually to jangle and to wonder.

Some rack their brains about the cause of thunder,
The ebbtide, flood, cobweb, and mist, and on
And on, until the cause is finally known. 260
And so they jangled, no idea ignored,
Until the king got up to leave the board.
    Phoebus had moved, proceeding from the east,
Past the meridian, the royal beast
(The noble lion with his Aldiran) 265
Ascending, when this Tartar Cambuscan
Rose from the board where he'd sat loftily.
Before him loudly went the minstrelsy
Till he came to his presence chamber. There
The sound of all their music filled the air, 270
As heavenly to hear as one could wish.
Now lusty lovers danced, for in the Fish
Their lady Venus then was sitting high
And looked upon them with a friendly eye.
    This noble king sat on his throne, and right 275
Away was fetched the mysterious knight,
Who then began to dance with Canace.
There was such revel and such jollity
It's more than any dull man could recite;
He must know love and how to serve it right, 280
And be a festive man as fresh as May,
Who'd give you an account of such array.
    Who could describe for you the forms of dance
So unfamiliar, or each subtle glance,
Flirtations in disguise, all the pretension 285
For fear of drawing jealous men's attention?
None could but Lancelot and he is dead;
I leave this merriment and forge ahead,
I'll say no more but in this jolly air
I leave them till for supper they prepare. 290
    The steward called for spices right away,
And wine as well, while music was to play.
The ushers and the squires went in a trice
To bring at once the wine and all the spice.
They ate and drank and, following that event, 295
As was the custom, to the temple went;

The service done, they supped throughout the day.
What do you need to hear that I should say?
For every man knows well at a king's feast
There's plenty for the greatest and the least,   300
And dainties more than I can comprehend.
This noble king arose at supper's end
To see this horse made out of brass. A rout
Of lords and ladies gathered round about.
      There was such wonder at this brazen steed   305
That since the siege of Troy (where indeed
A horse caused men to wonder) there had passed
No wonderment as great as this. At last
The king inquired about this courser's might,
About its power's source, and asked the knight   310
To tell him how to move it from its stance.
      The horse at once began to trip and dance
When the knight placed a hand upon its rein.
"Sire," said the knight, "there's no more to explain,
Except that when you'd ride somewhere from here   315
You have to turn a knob that's in his ear.
(I shall confide this to no one but you.)
Which place you have to mention to him, too,
Or to what country you desire to ride;
And when you've come to where you would abide,   320
Bid him descend—another knob you'll twist,
Of this contraption therein lies the gist—
Then down he will descend and do your will,
And in that place he'll stay, completely still.
Let the whole world swear differently, I say   325
He shall not then be drawn or borne away.
Or if to bid him go is your desire,
Then turn the knob, that's all it shall require;
Before men's eyes he'll vanish out of sight,
And then return, be it by day or night,   330
When you may wish to call him back again,
In such a manner as I shall explain
And very soon, between just me and you.
Ride when you wish, there's nothing more to do."
      When the king was informed thus by the knight,   335

So that in his own mind he had it right
(That is, all the procedure of the thing),
Content and glad, this noble, doughty king
Returned then to his revel as before.
The bridle they into the tower bore,   340
To keep with his fine jewelry like a prize,
And vanished then the horse before their eyes—
I don't know how, you'll get no more from me.
But now I leave them in their jollity,
This Cambuscan and his lords, reveling   345
Until the day was just about to spring.

PART II

The nurse to our digestion known as sleep
Began to wink at them, and bade them keep
In mind that drink and labor call for rest;
With yawning mouth he kissed them, every guest,   350
And said that it was time for relaxation,
The humor blood then being in domination.
"Take care of Nature's friend, the blood," said he.
They thanked him yawning, two of them, then three,
And finally each man went to his rest;   355
What sleep had bidden they considered best.
    Their dreams shan't be described by words of mine;
Their heads were full of fumes from all the wine,
That causes dreams in which to take no stock.
They slept till it was almost nine o'clock—   360
That is, most of them but not Canace;
For she, as women will, lived moderately,
And of her father she had taken leave
To go to rest soon after it was eve.
She didn't wish to pale, be tired and worn,   365
Nor to appear unfestive with the morn.
She slept awhile; when once again awake,
Within her heart such pleasure she would take
Both in her mirror and her curious ring
That twenty times she changed in coloring.   370

The impression of the mirror that she kept
Had made her have a vision while she slept;
And so, before the sun began to climb,
She called her governess, said it was time
That she arise, for such was her desire. 375
The old woman, who'd know or else inquire,
Being her governess, at once replied,
"But madam, where is it you'd walk or ride
So early, for the folks are all at rest?"
 "I shall arise," she said, "I'm getting dressed, 380
No longer will I sleep but walk about."
 Of women the governess called a rout,
Some ten or twelve, to rise without ado;
And Canace herself had risen too,
As bright and ruddy as the youthful sun 385
That in the Ram but four degrees had run
(No higher was he when she started out).
And at an easy pace she strolled about
On foot and frolicked, lightly dressed by reason
Of that time of year, the love-sweet season; 390
Some women, five or six, were with her sent.
Along a path into the park she went.
 The vapor that was rising from the earth
Had made the sun seem red and broad in girth,
But nonetheless it was so fair a sight 395
It made them all in heart feel very light,
What with the season and the new day springing
And all the fowls that Canace heard singing;
Immediately she knew just what they meant
By what they sang, knew all of their intent. 400
 But if the point of each tale that's told
Is long delayed—their interest getting cold
When people have to listen for a while—
The savor passes more with every mile,
Thanks to the teller's own prolixity; 405
By that same token, so it seems to me,
I should get down to business, I intend
To bring her walk now promptly to an end.
 Amid a tree, as dry and white as chalk,

As Canace was playing in her walk,   410
There sat above her head a falcon who
In such a piteous voice began to rue
That all the wood resounded with her cry.
So terribly had she been beaten by
Her own two wings, the blood along the tree   415
On which she sat ran crimson. Constantly
The falcon cried and gave out with a shriek;
And she had pricked herself so with her beak
There's not a tiger, not one beast so mean
That lives in darkest wood or forest green,   420
That wouldn't weep, if able, in compassion,
As she kept shrieking in so loud a fashion.
And there has never been a man around—
If on a falcon I could well expound—
Who's heard of such another for its fairness,   425
As well in plumage as in gracefulness
Of shape, in all that's worthy of esteem.
She was a peregrine, so it would seem,
From foreign parts. And as she stood above,
She now and then would swoon for losing of   430
Such blood till nearly falling from the tree.
    Now this king's lovely daughter Canace,
Who on her finger bore the curious ring
Through which she understood well everything
That any fowl might in his language say   435
And in that tongue could answer straightaway,
Had understood all that the falcon spoke;
She almost died, for her heart nearly broke.
And then with haste she went beneath the tree,
And looked up at this falcon piteously   440
And held her apron out, well knowing how
This falcon must come falling from the bough
When next it swooned, its loss of blood so great.
There for a lengthy while she stood to wait,
Till Canace at last spoke to the bird   445
In such a way as shortly you'll have heard.
    "What is the reason, if you're free to tell,
That you are in this furious pain of hell?"

She asked the falcon sitting there above.
"It's sorrow over death or loss of love?   450
For those are the two things that I believe
Above all else cause gentle hearts to grieve,
Of other woes there's no such need to speak.
Such vengeance on yourself you've come to wreak
It proves that either anger or dismay   455
Is why you've acted in so cruel a way;
You chase no other creature I can see.
Have mercy on yourself, show clemency,
For love of God, or what can help? For east
Or west I've never seen a bird or beast   460
So frightful with itself, and truthfully
Your piteous sorrow's all but slaying me,
I've for you such compassion. For God's love,
Come down from this tree where you sit above.
As I'm true daughter of a king, if I   465
Were certainly to know the reason why
You're so distressed, if it lay in my might
I would amend it ere the fall of night,
So help me Nature's God so great and kind!
And herbs this very instant I will find   470
That quickly heal, to make you whole once more."
    The falcon shrieked more pitifully than before,
And swooned and fell down right away, and on
The ground she lay as if dead as a stone,
Till Canace into her lap would take   475
The bird, and she began then to awake.
And after she had come out of her swoon,
In falcon tongue she said, "That pity soon
Will surge and flow inside a gentle heart,
Which sees in other's pain its counterpart,   480
Is every day displayed, as men may see.
Experience proves, as does authority,
A noble heart will show its nobleness.
I well can see that you for my distress
Show your compassion, my fair Canace,   485
By the true, ladylike benignity
That in you Nature has instilled. It's not

Now in the hope that better be my lot,
It's to obey your generous heart and, where
I may, make others by my case beware   490
(As when a lion is chastened when he's shown
The beating of a whelp—the lion is gone),
That I shall, while I have the time to spend,
Confide my woe ere going to my end."
    And while the one began then to confide   495
Her woe, as if turned into water cried
The other, till this falcon bade her cease,
And with a sigh here's how she spoke her piece:
    "Where I was born—alas, alack the day!—
And fostered in a rock of marble gray   500
So tenderly that nothing threatened me,
I never knew what's called adversity
Till high up in the heavens I could fly.
A male falcon then came to dwell nearby
Who seemed a spring of all nobility;   505
Though he was full of lying treachery,
It was so wrapped within a humble mien,
So truthful in the way that it was seen,
Disguised as pleasant manner, good intent,
None could have thought that he could so invent,   510
So deeply were his outward colors dyed.
As under flowers will a serpent hide
Till seeing his time to bite, the manner of
This false disciple of the god of love
Was to perform each duty (so it seemed),   515
Each courtesy and ceremony deemed
Appropriate to what is noble love.
Just as a tomb appears so fair above,
And under is the corpse as you'll admit,
At every turn so was this hypocrite.   520
So he pursued his goal, that's how he went,
None save the devil knowing his intent,
Till for so long he'd shed tears and complained,
And many a year his service to me feigned,
That my poor heart, too foolish, too consoling,   525
So ignorant of his malice all-controlling,

For fear he'd die (as it appeared to me),
Upon the oaths he gave as surety,
Granted him love with but one stipulation:
That always my honor and reputation   530
In public and in private be preserved;
That is to say, as I thought he deserved,
I gave him all my heart and mind—and there
Was only one condition, God's aware,
As he was too—and took his heart as well.   535
But there's a truth from days of old they tell:
'A thief and honest man don't think the same.'
And when he saw so far had gone his game
That I had fully granted him my love
In such a way as I have said above,   540
And given him my heart as generously
As he had sworn to give his heart to me,
This two-faced tiger went right into motion,
Fell humbly on his knees with such devotion,
With so much high reverence to display,   545
Behaving in a noble lover's way,
So overcome, as it appeared, with joy,
That neither Jason nor Paris of Troy—
Jason? No other man, it's surely true,
Since Lamech (who first started loving two,   550
As it is written) has been born on earth,
There hasn't been a one since Adam's birth,
Who by one twenty-thousandth of a part
Could imitate the cunning of his art,
Or who'd be worthy to untie his shoe   555
When there is some deceitful thing to do,
Or who could thank someone as he did me!
He had a manner heavenly to see
For any woman, wise be as she may,
For he was groomed in such a careful way   560
In words as well as looks. And all the more
I loved him for his great respect and for
The truthfulness I thought his heart contained,
Till if he might by anything be pained,
However light or tiny be the smart,   565

It felt like death was wrenching my own heart.
Before too long, so far the whole thing went,
My very will was his will's instrument—
That is to say, my will obeyed his will
In all that reason would permit, though still   570
To honor's bounds forever to adhere.
I'd never had a thing, God knows, as dear
As him, nor shall again this whole life through.
    "This lasted longer than a year or two,
My thinking of him nothing else but good.   575
But Fortune then, the way things finally stood,
Desired that he should have to go away
From where we were and I would have to stay.
That this brought me to woe you needn't doubt,
Words proper to describe it I'm without;   580
There's one thing I can boldly tell you, though:
The pain of death I've come by it to know,
The hurt of parting caused me so to grieve.
And so it was one day he took his leave,
With so much sorrow that I thought it plain   585
That just as much as I he felt the pain,
To hear him speak and see his pallid hue.
But nonetheless I thought that he'd be true,
That it was safe to say he would at last
Return to me when not much time had passed;   590
And as it was with reason he must go,
For sake of honor, as is often so,
I made a virtue of necessity
And took it well since it would have to be.
From him my grief as best I could I hid   595
And took him by the hand, and as I did
I told him by Saint John, 'I'll always be
Your own. As I'm to you, be you to me.'
What he replied, no need to say—for who
Can talk as well, then act worse when he's through?   600
Once he had spoken well, then he was done.
'When eating with a fiend or devil, one
Should have a lengthy spoon,' I've heard them say.
And so at last he had to go his way,

And off he went until he'd come to where   605
He so desired. And as he rested there,
I think he had in mind the text that went,
'All things are glad when to their natural bent
They have returned.' It's plain, I guess, to see,
Men have a natural love for novelty,   610
As do the birds that people cage and feed;
Though night and day you give them what they need
And line the cage as fair and soft as silk
And give them sugar, honey, bread, and milk,
As soon as opened is his cage's door   615
He'll kick his cup right over on the floor
And take off to the woods for worms to eat.
So they would have newfangled kinds of meat,
They love by nature new things to be found;
No nobleness of blood may keep them bound.   620
     "So ventured this male falcon, woe is me!
Though young and blithe, born of nobility,
Generous, humble, pleasing to the eye,
He saw a hawk one day go flying by
And with her fell in love so suddenly   625
That all his love was swept away from me.
His pledge to me was broken in this way;
In this hawk's service is my love today,
And lost without a remedy am I!"
This bird then, after she began to cry,   630
Again swooned in the lap of Canace.
     Great was the sorrow for this falcon she
And all her women bore. They didn't know
How they might bring this falcon out of woe.
Canace took her home, and in her lap   635
With plasters gently she began to wrap
The self-inflicted wounds caused by her beak.
Then Canace could only go and seek
Herbs growing from the ground, new salves to make
From precious, fine-hued herbs that she could take   640
To heal this wounded bird. From day to night
With industry she did all that she might,
And placed a cage beside her bed's head, too,

And covered it with velvets all of blue,
Sign of the faithfulness in women seen.   645
The cage was on the outside painted green,
Depicted on it all these faithless fowls,
Such birds as these male falcons and the owls;
Depicted, too, were magpies at their side,
That they in spite might cry at them and chide.   650

    I leave her caring for her bird. No more
I'll speak about the curious ring she wore,
Until my purpose shall be to explain
How the falcon would win her love again,
Repentant (the old stories tell us so),   655
By the mediation of Cambalo,
The king's son of whom I've already told.
But henceforth I shall to my subject hold,
Such battles and adventures to discuss
As never heard of, great and marvelous.   660

    Some things of Cambuscan first I will say,
Who conquered many a city in his day;
And after I will speak of Algarsyf,
How he won Theodora as his wife,
For whom he was in many a great morass   665
But for assistance from the steed of brass;
Of Cambalo I'll speak thereafter, who
Fought in the lists against the brothers two
For Canace, she whom he sought to win.
Where I left off I shall once more begin.   670

PART III

    Apollo whirled his chariot up high
Till in the house of Mercury the sly—

        (Unfinished by Chaucer)

Words of the Franklin to the Squire, and of the Host to the Franklin

"Squire, by my faith, you surely well acquit
Yourself, and nobly. Praises for your wit,"
The Franklin said. "Considering your youth,   675
You speak with feeling, sir, and that's the truth!
My judgment is, there's not another here
Who shall be called for eloquence your peer
If you live long enough. Good luck to you,
God grant your powers keep on growing, too!   680
I've listened to your speech delightedly.
I have a son, and, by the Trinity,
Could I have land worth twenty pounds a year,
Were it to fall into my hands right here,
I'd rather have him a man of discretion   685
As much as you have been! Fie on possession
Unless a man is virtuous too! My son
I have reproved and shall again; he's one
Who's not inclined to virtue but to vice.
To spend, to lose all that he has at dice,   690
In such it is his custom to engage.
And he would rather talk with any page
Than with a noble man from whom he might
Learn of gentility and learn it right."
    "Straw," said our Host, "for your gentility!   695
What, Franklin! As it's plain for all to see,
Each one must tell at least a tale or two
Or break his pledge, and that's including you."
    "I know that, sir," the Franklin said. "I pray
You will not take offense that I should say   700
A word or two to this man whom we've heard."
    "Now tell your tale without another word."
    "Gladly, Sir Host," said he. "I shall obey
Your will, so listen now to what I say.
I don't wish to object the slightest bit,   705
I'll go as far as my wits may permit.
I pray to God you'll find in it some pleasure,
Then I will know at least it's up to measure."

The Franklin's Tale

PROLOGUE

These old and noble Bretons in their days
Would turn diverse adventures into lays 710
That, rhymed in the original Breton tongue,
Accompanied by instruments were sung
Or else they would be read at people's leisure.
There's one I still remember, and with pleasure
I'll tell it for you now as best I can. 715
But, sirs, because I am a simple man,
Right at the very start I would beseech
That you excuse my ignorant form of speech.
I've never studied rhetoric, no way,
So plain and bare must be what I've to say. 720
I've never slept on Mount Parnassus, no,
Nor studied Marcus Tullius Cicero.
I don't know any colors, none indeed,
Except the colors growing on the mead
Or used by men to dye or paint; to me 725
Colors of rhetoric are a mystery,
My spirit simply has no feel for such.
But if you'd hear my tale, you'll hear as much.

THE FRANKLIN'S TALE

In Armorica, now called Brittany,
A knight once lived and served laboriously 730
A lady in the best way that he could.
At many undertakings great and good
He for his lady worked ere she was won;
As lovely as any under the sun
This lady was, and of high birth as well, 735
So that for fear this knight scarce dared to tell

303

His woe to her, his pain and his distress.
But she at last, seeing his worthiness,
Especially the reverence he'd shown,
Such pity felt at all he'd undergone   740
That privately she made with him accord
To take him as her husband and her lord,
To grant lordship as men have over wives.
That they the more in bliss might lead their lives,
He freely gave his promise as a knight   745
That never in his life by day or night
He'd take upon himself the mastery
Against her will nor show her jealousy;
He'd be obedient, will what she would,
As every lover to his lady should,   750
Save that he'd keep in name the sovereignty
Lest he be shamed in light of his degree.
　　She thanked him, and with utmost humbleness
She told him, "Sire, since in your nobleness
So free a rein you offer, may God grant   755
That twixt us two through guilt of mine there shan't
Be ever once a case of war or strife.
Sir, I will be your true and humble wife;
Till my heart break, here is my pledge to you."
Relieved and put at ease then were the two.   760
　　For one thing, sires, I safely dare to say,
And that is, friends each other must obey
If long they wish their friendship be sustained.
Love will not be by mastership constrained;
When mastery comes, the God of Love will on   765
The instant beat his wings—farewell, he's gone!
Love is a thing like any spirit free,
And women want by nature liberty,
Not hindrance like a thrall. If I shall tell
The total truth, that's what men want as well.   770
He who in love maintains his patience best
Has the advantage over all the rest;
For patience is a virtue, to be sure,
And vanquishes—these students will assure—
More than do rigorous ways. At every word   775

Men shouldn't chide, complaint should not be heard;
Learn sufferance or, as surely as I
May walk, you'll learn whether or not you try.
There's no man in this world, I'm sure of this,
Who doesn't sometimes err or speak amiss;   780
For anger, woe, some starry constellation,
Wine, sickness, or a humor alteration
Can often cause wrong word or deed. But still
A man can't be avenged for every ill,
So moderation has to be the goal   785
Of each who knows the art of self-control.
This wise and worthy knight, that they therefore
Might live in ease, his sufferance to her swore,
And she then surely swore to him in kind
That in her not one fault he'd ever find.   790
    Here may men see a humble, wise accord,
She takes him as her servant and her lord
(Servant in love, in marriage lord). So viewed,
He was in both lordship and servitude.
In servitude? No, he was lord above,   795
As he had both his lady and his love—
His lady, surely, and his wife as well,
Consenting under law of love to dwell.
And when he had this happiness in hand,
He took his wife home to his native land,   800
Not far from Penmarch, that is where he'd live,
In all the bliss that life had come to give.
    Who could relate, unless he wedded be,
The joy, the comfort, and prosperity
That is between a husband and his wife?   805
A year and more would last this blissful life,
Until this knight—Arveragus by name,
His home Kayrrud—in hope of gaining fame
Left on a trip, a year or two to dwell
In England (known as Britain then as well),   810
In arms renown and honor to acquire,
The labor in which lay his heart's desire.
He dwelt two years, the book says, on that isle.
    Arveragus I now will leave awhile

And speak instead of Dorigen his wife,   815
Who loved him in her heart as much as life.
His absence made her weep, she sighed and pined,
As do these noble wives when so inclined.
She mourned and wailed, she fasted, lost her rest,
By longing for his presence so distressed   820
That all this world she looked upon as naught.
Her friends, who knew the burden of her thought,
Would comfort her in every way they might.
They preached to her, they told her day and night
She'd grieve herself to death, no cause, alas!   825
Each comfort they could hope to bring to pass
They offered her in all their busyness
To make her leave her burden of distress.
      In time, as by each one of you is known,
Men may engrave so long upon a stone   830
Some form's imprint at last will be perceived.
So long they had consoled her, she received
Both by their hope and reasoning's dictation
At last the imprint of their consolation
And her great sorrow started to subside;   835
Such pain much longer she could not abide.
      Also Arveragus, in all this care,
Sent letters home to tell of his welfare
And that he'd soon be coming back again;
If not, by grieving heart she'd have been slain.   840
      Her friends observed her sorrow start to ease
And begged her for God's sake, upon their knees,
To take a walk with them, to drive away
The last of heavy thoughts, her dark dismay.
And she at last then granted their request,   845
For well she saw that it was for the best.
      Their castle where it stood was by the sea,
And often with her friends she playfully
Would walk upon the bank. It was so high
That many a vessel she saw sailing by,   850
Their courses set for where they wished to go.
Yet this was part and parcel of her woe,
For to herself she often said, "Alas!

Is there no ship, of all that I see pass,
That will bring home my lord? Then would my heart   855
Be cured of bitter pain, of all its smart."
    At other times there too she'd sit and think,
And cast her eyes far downward from the brink;
She'd see the black and grisly rocks below,
Her heart for fear then quaking in her so   860
She couldn't stand up on her feet. Then she
Would sit down on the green, and piteously
Toward the waters she would cast her eyes
And speak this way with cold and mournful sighs:
    "Eternal God who through thy providence   865
Doth lead the world and govern its events,
Thou shan't create in vain, as men well know.
But, Lord, these black and grisly rocks below,
So fiendish, seem to me foul aberration
Of labor and not any fair creation   870
Of such a perfect, wise, and stable Lord.
Why hast thou wrought this work that's so untoward?
For by these rocks not south, north, west nor east
Has help been given man nor bird nor beast;
I know no good they do, they but annoy.   875
Dost thou not see how mankind they destroy?
By rocks a hundred thousand have been slain,
Though of it men no thought might entertain,
While of thy labor man's so fair a part,
Created in thy image. At the start   880
It seemed therefore thou hadst great charity
Toward mankind, and how then can it be
That mankind thou wouldst by such means destroy
That mean no good but ever shall annoy?
I'm well aware that students will contest   885
By arguments that all is for the best,
Although the causes I can never know.
May that same God who causes wind to blow
Protect my lord! And that is my summation,
To students I will leave all disputation.   890
But these black rocks if only God would make
Sink into hell, for his own mercy's sake!

They're slaying me, my heart so full of fear."
    Her friends saw that it soothed her not a bit   895
To roam the bank, the effect was opposite;
And so they made arrangements that instead
By rivers and by streams she then be led
To many another place of pleasantness;
They danced, they played backgammon, too, and chess.   900
    Now one fine day, not too long after dawn,
Into a nearby garden they had gone,
In which they had arranged to be provided
With victuals and such else as they'd decided,
And there they frolicked all the livelong day.   905
This happened on the sixth morning of May,
May having painted with its tender showers
This garden full of many leaves and flowers;
And man's hand with its craft so skillfully
This garden had arranged that truthfully   910
There'd never grown one like it, such a prize,
Unless you count the one of Paradise;
So fresh the smell of flowers and the sight,
There's not a heart that wouldn't there be light
Unless some illness had it in distress   915
Or some great sorrow held it in duress.
Amid this pleasant beauty they had soon
Begun to dance (the time was nearly noon)
And sang as well—save Dorigen alone,
Who'd still speak of her woe and ever moan,   920
Not there among the dancers in her view
The one who was her love and husband too.
For longer time she nonetheless must wait
In all good hope, and let her grief abate.
    During this dance, there was among the men   925
A squire before the eyes of Dorigen,
One livelier and brighter in array,
If I can judge, than is the month of May.
He better sang and danced than any man
Who is or was since this whole world began.   930
If one were to describe him, he'd belong
Among the fairest men alive; a strong

Young man, right virtuous, one rich and wise,
One loved and well esteemed in others' eyes.
And shortly, if the truth I shall declare   935
(Though Dorigen of this was unaware),
This lusty squire, this servitor of Venus—
Who, by the way, was named Aurelius—
Loved her above all others, such his fate
For longer than two years, while all the wait   940
He never dared his longing to confess.
Without a cup he drank of deep distress;
Despairing, not a thing he dared to say,
Save that he in a very general way
Would sing about the woe that made him yearn,   945
To love and not to be loved in return.
Upon the subject he wrote many lays,
Sad songs of love, roundels and virelays,
On how his sorrow he dared not to tell
But languished like a Fury does in hell;   950
And die he must, he said, as did Echo
For Narcissus (she couldn't tell her woe).
But in no other manner, as I say,
He'd ever dare his woe to her betray,
Except perhaps that sometimes at a dance   955
Where folks observe the rituals of romance
It may well be he looked upon her face
In such a way as one might ask for grace;
But still she'd no idea of his intent.
It happened, though, as from this place they went,   960
By reason of the fact he was her neighbor—
One folks respected, looked upon with favor—
And as she'd known this squire since long before,
The two began conversing; and the more
They talked the closer would Aurelius draw   965
Toward his aim, until his time he saw:
    "Madam, by God who made this world," said he,
"If I knew that your heart would brighter be,
I wish that day when your Arveragus
Went overseas that I, Aurelius,   970
Had gone somewhere whence I'd not come again.

For well I know my service is in vain,
My love's reward a broken heart. Have rue,
My lady, on my smarting pain, for you
Have with a word the power to slay or save.   975
Would God that at your feet might be my grave!
I've no time now to spare that more be said;
Have mercy, sweet, unless you'd have me dead!"
    Then at Aurelius the lady stared.
"Is this your will," she said, "what you've declared?   980
I never knew before just what you meant.
Now that I know, Aurelie, your intent,
By that same God who gave me soul and life,
I never shall be so untrue a wife
In word or deed, as long as I've the wit.   985
I always will be his to whom I'm knit,
And you can take that as my final say."
But after that she spoke to him in play:
    "Aurelius," said she, "by God above,
Yet I would grant you that I'd be your love,   990
Since I see you complain so piteously.
That day when from the coast of Brittany
You've taken all the rocks, stone after stone,
Till ship and boat have freely come and gone—
I say, when you have made the coast so clean,   995
So clear of rocks, that not a stone is seen,
I'll love you more than any other man,
You have my oath, as fully as I can."
    "No other way to win your grace?" asked he.
    "No, by that Lord who made me," answered she.   1000
"I know it can't be done, so from the start
Dismiss such foolish notions from your heart.
What man should have such pleasure in his life
As to go love another fellow's wife
Who has her body anytime he please?"   1005
    Many a sigh the squire now sadly breathes,
So filled with woe when she had had her say.
With saddened heart he answered in this way:
    "Madam, the task is one impossible!
Quick death be mine, however horrible."   1010

With that he turned away. There followed then
Her many other friends, together in
A group as they were strolling here and there,
Of this discussion wholly unaware;
The revel then at once began anew   1015
And lasted till the bright sun lost its hue,
Till the horizon robbed the sun of light—
Which is the same as saying it was night—
And home they went, the night in joy to pass,
Except for poor Aurelius, alas!   1020
For he went home with sorrow in his breast,
Saw no escape from his eternal rest,
So cold, he felt, his heart already grown.
He raised his hands toward the heavens, on
His two bare knees got down and said a prayer   1025
As if gone raving mad from pure despair,
So urgent in the way he started praying
He didn't even know what he was saying.
With piteous heart this plaint he had begun
To all the gods, and first of all the sun: 1030
    He said, "Apollo, god and source of power
Of every plant and herb, each tree and flower,
Who gives to each its season of the year
Depending on how distant you appear,
Your house forever moving, low and high—   1035
Lord Phoebus, cast your sympathetic eye
On poor Aurelius who's simply lost.
See how my lady's sworn, my death the cost
Though I am guiltless. Lord, benignity!
My heart is all but dead inside of me.   1040
If you but will, I know without a doubt,
Save only her you best can help me out.
Allow me to describe for you the way
In which you might assist me, if I may.
    "Your blissful sister, Lucina the Sheen,   1045
Is of the sea chief goddess and the queen
(Though Neptune is the deity of the sea,
As empress she is higher ranked than he);
And well you know that just as her desire

Is to be lit and quickened by your fire, 1050
For which she follows you so busily,
To follow her as well is naturally
The sea's desire—she's goddess, after all,
Of both the sea and rivers big and small.
This miracle, Lord Phoebus, I request 1055
(Or else my heart now burst within my breast):
When next in Leo's sign is your position,
You and Lucina then in opposition,
I pray she'll bring so great a flood to sweep
This Breton coast, at least five fathoms deep 1060
Shall lie the highest rock that now appears;
And let that flood endure for two whole years.
Then surely to my lady I can say,
'Now keep your word, the rocks have gone away.'
"This miracle, Lord Phoebus, do for me. 1065
And pray the course she runs no faster be
Than yours; I say, pray that your sister run
No faster course than yours, till two years done.
Then always at the fullest she will stay,
The flood of spring will last both night and day. 1070
If she will thus consent and grant to me
My lady sovereign and dear, may she
Sink every rock, each one that's to be found,
Into her own dark region underground
Where Pluto dwells, or nevermore shall I 1075
My lady win. Your temple in Delphi
Both humbly and barefooted I will seek.
Lord Phoebus, see the tears upon my cheek,
Have for me some compassion." And as soon
As he was through he fell down in a swoon, 1080
Lay in a trance wherein he'd long remain.
    His brother, who was privy to his pain,
Then picked him up and carried him to bed.
In this despair, with his tormented head,
I'll leave this woeful creature, let him lie, 1085
The choice be his to live or else to die.
    Arveragus in honor, health, and power,
As one who is of chivalry the flower,

Came home again with other worthy men.
O blissful may you be now, Dorigen, 1090
To hold your lusty husband in your arms,
This worthy knight, returned from war's alarms,
Who loves you as his own heart's blood. No word
Of love did he suspect she might have heard
From someone else while he was gone, no fear 1095
He had of that. To share with her good cheer,
To dance and joust, was all he had in mind,
He entertained no doubts of any kind.
And so in bliss I leave these two to dwell,
And of the sick Aurelius I'll tell. 1100
    The wretch in languor, torment, awful anguish,
For more than two years lay in bed to languish
Before again he set foot on the ground.
And in this time no comforter he found
Save for his brother, who was then a student 1105
And knew his woe and work; for he was prudent
And to no other soul, no need to doubt,
He dared to let one word of it get out.
His secret in his breast he better hid
Than Pamphilus for Galatea did; 1110
Though in his breast no wound was to be seen,
The arrow in his heart was ever keen.
As you well know, a wound healed outwardly
Is hardly cured unless the surgery
Includes the arrow having been withdrawn. 1115
In private would his brother weep and moan,
Until the thought occurred to him by chance
That while he'd been at Orleans in France
(As all young students read so eagerly
Of the occult, and search incessantly, 1120
Turn every nook and cranny inside out,
For esoteric arts to learn about)—
At Orleans, he happened to recall,
One day he'd seen a book in study hall
On natural magic, one which, as he saw, 1125
A friend of his, a student of the law
(Though learning craft of quite another kind),

Had hidden at his desk and left behind.
This book had much to say on operations
Touching on the eight-and-twenty stations   1130
Or mansions of the moon—which is to say
It dealt with stuff not worth a fly today;
For Holy Church's faith, as we believe,
Guards us from all that's practiced to deceive.
And when this book had come again to mind,   1135
His heart began to dance, such joy to find.
"My brother right away shall have his cure,"
He thought, "for there are sciences, I'm sure,
By which men may deceive with apparitions,
Diverse illusions, much as these magicians   1140
So subtly perform though all in play.
Magicians, I have often heard them say
At feasts, can in a large hall make appear
Both water and a boat in which to steer,
And in the hall go rowing all about.   1145
Sometimes a lion comes, or flowers sprout,
It seems, as in a mead; sometimes instead
They make appear a vine, grapes white and red,
Sometimes a castle made of lime and stone;
And then at once, when they so please, it's gone.   1150
So it would seem to every fellow's sight.
    "Now here's what I conclude: if but I might
At Orleans in France some old friend find
Who has these lunar mansions well in mind,
Or natural magic even higher, then   1155
His lady he should make my brother win.
Illusion such a man can so devise
That here in Brittany, before one's eyes,
All black rocks he can make to disappear,
And to and from the shore have vessels steer,   1160
And make such ruse endure a week or so.
And that would cure my brother of his woe;
She'd have to keep her promise as she swore,
Or else he'd have her shamed if nothing more."
    Why should I make a longer tale of this?   1165
He goes back to his brother's bed, such bliss

To give him by the notion they depart
For Orleans, he jumped up with a start;
Now forward with his brother he would fare
In hope of finding easement from his care.   1170
    When to that city they had nearly come
(They lacked a furlong, two or three or some),
They met a strolling scholar who was young;
He gave them greeting in the Latin tongue
With all respect, then said a wondrous thing: 1175
"I know," said he, "why you've come journeying."
And then before another foot they went,
He told them what in fact was their intent.
    This Breton student asked what he might know
About some friends he'd had there long ago,   1180
And he replied that all of them were dead;
Then many a tear the Breton student shed.
    Aurelius dismounted, no delay,
And went with this magician straightaway
Home to his house, and there they took their leisure;   1185
There was no lack of victuals for their pleasure.
No other house like this, so well supplied,
In all his life Aurelie ever spied.
    Before they supped this fellow showed to him
Some forests, parks, with wild deer to the brim;   1190
There he saw harts, their antlers standing high,
The greatest ever seen by human eye;
He saw a hundred slain with hounds, and more
That bled with bitter wounds as arrows bore.
He saw, when these wild deer no more were there,   1195
Some falconers along a river fair,
As with their hawks the herons they had slain.
    Then he saw knights out jousting on a plain;
And after this, he gave him such delight,
Showed him his lady dancing; at the sight,   1200
He danced right there beside her, so he thought.
And when this master who this magic wrought
Saw it was time, he clapt his hands—farewell!
The revelry was gone, no more to tell.
And yet out of the house they never went   1205

While seeing all these sights of wonderment,
But in his study, by his books and shelves,
The three of them still sat all by themselves.
    This master called his squire then to inquire
About their supper. "Is it ready, squire?   1210
It's been almost an hour, I declare,
Since I bid you our supper to prepare,
Back when these worthy fellows came to me
Here to my study where my volumes be."
    "Sir," said the squire, "when it so pleases you,   1215
It's ready, you can eat without ado."
    "Then let us sup," said he, "it's for the best,
For folks in love must sometimes have their rest."
    When they had supped, they then negotiated
About what sum he should be compensated,   1220
From Brittany all rocks should he dispel
From the Gironde up to the Seine as well.
    He made it hard: God save him, so he swore,
A thousand pounds he'd want, if not some more,
And even then not gladly he would start.   1225
    Aurelius at once, with blissful heart,
Replied, "Fie on it to the thousandth pound!
This whole wide world, which men have said is round,
I'd gladly give if of it I were lord.
The bargain's made, for we are in accord.   1230
You truly shall be paid, I swear it! See
That by no sloth or negligence, though, we
Shall have to wait here longer than tomorrow."
    "You won't," said he, "you have my word to borrow."
    Aurelius to bed went when he pleased,   1235
And well nigh all that night he rested, eased;
What with his toil and hope of bliss, that night
His woeful heart at last had some respite.
    When morning came, as soon as it was day,
For Brittany Aurelie right away   1240
Departed, this magician by his side,
And on arrival they would there abide.
And this was, in the books as I remember,
The cold and frosty season of December.

Now Phoebus waned, like latten was his hue,   1245
For his hot declination now was through.
Like burnished gold he'd shone, his beaming bright;
In Capricorn now faded was his light
And palely did he shine, I dare to tell.
From bitter frosts, from sleet and rain as well,   1250
The green from every yard has disappeared;
Sits Janus by the fire with double beard
And drinks out of his bugle horn the wine;
Before him stands the meat of tusky swine,
"Noel" is every lusty fellow's cry.   1255
    Aurelius did all that he could try
To show this master cheer and reverence,
And prayed that he perform with diligence
To bring him out of his pain's bitter smart,
Or with a sword he then would split his heart.   1260
    This scholar felt such pity for the man
That day and night he worked upon his plan,
To spot the time propitious for conclusion—
That is, when best to create the illusion,
By some appearance or by jugglery   1265
(I don't know terms used in astrology),
Till she and every man would have to say
That all the Breton rocks were gone away
Or at the least were sunken underground.
And so at last the proper time he found   1270
To perpetrate his tricks, the wickedness
Of all such superstitious cursedness.
He had Toledo tables, well corrected,
And brought them out, and tables he'd collected
To calculate each planetary year;   1275
He had his list of roots and other gear
Such as his centers and his arguments,
His tables on proportions, elements,
On everything of use for his equations.
And in the eighth sphere, by his calculations,   1280
He knew where Alnath moved, how far away
From that fixed head of Aries, which they say
Can always in the ninth sphere be located.

With shrewdness all of this he calculated.
    On finding his first lunar mansion, he   1285
Could figure out the rest proportionally;
He knew the rising of his moon, where at
And in whose face, which term, and all of that;
And he knew well which mansion would be best
For putting his proposal to the test,   1290
And knew as well his other calculations
For such illusions and abominations
As heathen folk were using in that day.
No longer this magician would delay,
But through his magic for a week or more   1295
It seemed like all the rocks had left the shore.
    Aurelius, still wondering in despair
If he would have his love or badly fare,
Awaited day and night this miracle;
And when he knew there was no obstacle,   1300
That every rock was gone, without delay
He fell down at his master's feet to say,
"I, woeful wretch Aurelius, to you
Give all my thanks, to Lady Venus too,
For helping me out of my cold dismay."   1305
He went then to the temple right away
Where he knew that his lady he would see;
And when he saw his time, immediately,
With fearful heart and full of humble cheer,
He greeted there his sovereign lady dear.   1310
    "My righteous lady," said this woeful man,
"Whom I must fear and love as best I can,
For all this world I'd bring you no dismay;
And were I not for you in such a way
That I may die right here before I'm through,   1315
Of all my woe I'd not be telling you.
But either I must die or else complain;
You're killing me, though guiltless, by the pain.
Though you'll not mourn my death, think carefully
Before you break the promise made to me;   1320
You should repent, by that same God above,
Before you kill me. For it's you I love,

And, madam, you well know your promise, too,
Though nothing may I claim by right from you
Except, my sovereign lady, by your grace. 1325
Out yonder in a garden—blessed place—
You know right well that you made me a vow:
You put your hand in mine and promised how
You'd love me best. God knows, you told me so,
Though I may be unworthy, well I know. 1330
I say this, madam, for your honor's sake
More than to save my life, right here at stake.
For I have done as you commanded me;
If you desire, then go yourself and see.
Do as you like, remember what you said, 1335
Right there's where I'll be found, alive or dead.
My life or death, on that you have the say,
But well I know the rocks have gone away."
    She stood astounded as he took his leave;
Her face was bloodless, she could not believe 1340
She'd fallen into such a trap. "Alas,"
She said, "that this could ever come to pass!
I never saw the possibility
That such a monstrous thing could ever be!
It's something that's against all natural law." 1345
The saddest creature that you ever saw,
She scarcely made it home, so great her woe.
She wept and wailed then for a day or so,
With fainting spells heartrending to behold.
To no one, though, the cause she ever told, 1350
For out of town Arveragus had gone.
She spoke to no one but herself alone,
With pallid face and total lack of cheer,
And in her plaint she spoke as you shall hear:
    "Alas! to you, O Fortune, I complain, 1355
For by surprise you've wrapped me in your chain;
I've no escape, no help to bring me through
But death or else dishonor. Of the two,
I must decide which one is best to choose.
But nonetheless my life I'd rather lose 1360
Than bring upon my body such a shame,

To know I am untrue, lose my good name;
I know I'll be at peace when gone is life.
Have many a maiden, many a noble wife,
Before not slain themselves—ah welladay!—   1365
Rather than with their bodies go astray?
  "Indeed these stories illustrate the facts:
When thirty tyrants, full of wicked acts,
Slew Phidon the Athenian while he dined,
They ordered that his daughters be confined,   1370
Then had them all paraded, for despite,
Before them naked, for their foul delight,
And on the pavement made them dance about
In their own father's blood. God curse the rout!
And then these woeful maidens, full of dread,   1375
Rather than lose each one her maidenhead,
Went secretly and jumped into a well
And drowned themselves, as these old stories tell.
  "The Messenians, too, a favor sought
From Sparta: fifty virgins to be brought,   1380
On whom they might perform their lechery.
There wasn't one in all that company
Who didn't kill herself, with good intent:
Each chose to die before she'd give assent
To be defiled and lose her maidenhead.   1385
And so to die why should I be in dread?
Behold the tyrant Aristoclides
Who loved a maiden named Stymphalides;
Upon her father's murder late one night,
Straight to Diana's temple she took flight;   1390
She grabbed hold of the image where it stood
And wouldn't leave, indeed she never would:
No one could pry her loose from it again
Till in that very temple she was slain.
  "Now as these maidens had such great despite   1395
For men who would befoul them for delight,
So should a wife choose rather suicide
Than be defiled, of that I'm satisfied.
What shall I tell you of Hasdrubal's wife,
Who at the fall of Carthage took her life?   1400

For when she saw that Rome had won the town,
She took all of her children and leapt down
Into the fire, for dead she'd rather be
Than suffer any Roman's villainy.
Did not Lucretia kill herself? Alas,   1405
When ravishment by Tarquin came to pass
At Rome, did she not think it then a shame
To go on living, perished her good name?
The seven maidens of Miletus, too,
Destroyed themselves, their dread and anguish through,   1410
Before the Gauls could do them wickedness.
More than a thousand stories, I would guess,
Upon this matter I could now relate.
When slain was Abradates, his dear mate
Took her own life, mixed her own blood inside   1415
Of Abradates' wounds so deep and wide;
'At least,' she said, 'I've done all that I can
To see my body's ravished by no man.'
    "Why should I more examples here provide,
So many by their own hands having died   1420
Rather than be defiled? And so I say
That suicide's for me the better way,
To kill myself before I'm ravished too.
For I will to Arveragus be true
Or somehow slay myself. So, too, in strife   1425
Demotion's daughter took her own dear life
Rather than have to face such ravishing.
O Scedasus, how pitiful a thing
To read of how your daughters died, alas!
They slew themselves in similar morass.   1430
I judge as great a pity, if not more,
The Theban maiden, fearing Nicanor,
Who took her life, so similar her woe.
Another Theban maiden did just so;
Raped by a Macedonian, for dread   1435
She with her death avenged her maidenhead.
Shall I speak of Niceratus's wife,
Who for such woe bereft herself of life?
To Alcibiades how faithful, too,

His lover was: she chose, though death her due,   1440
Not to allow his corpse to go unburied.
How great Alcestis was among all married.
And what says Homer of Penelope?
All Greece knew of her blessed chastity.
And of Laodamia old books tell   1445
That when at Troy Protesilaus fell,
She'd live no longer than his dying day.
The same of noble Portia I can say;
She couldn't live when Brutus lost his life,
Her heart his so completely. As a wife   1450
Artemisia was beyond compare,
She's honored by the heathen everywhere.
O Tauta, queen! your wifely chastity
May to all other wives a mirror be.
The same thing I can say of Bilia,   1455
Of Rhodogune, and of Valeria."
    A day or two thus Dorigen would cry,
Proposing all the while that she must die.
However, on the third night of her plight
Arveragus came home, this worthy knight,   1460
And asked her what she wept so strongly for,
And she began to weep then all the more.
"Alas," she said, "that ever I was born!
For here's what I have said, here's what I've sworn"—
She told him all that you've already heard,   1465
There's no need to repeat a single word.
Her husband like a friend and in good cheer
Then answered her as you're about to hear:
"Now, Dorigen, there's nothing else but this?"
    "No," she replied, "may God bring me to bliss!   1470
And this is too much, even if God's will."
    "Ah, wife," said he, "leave sleeping what is still.
Perhaps things soon will all be well. But now,
Upon my faith, you'll be true to your vow!
As surely as may God be kind to me,   1475
Dead from a stabbing I would rather be,
Because of this deep love I have for you,
Than see you to your promise be untrue.

A vow's the highest thing that one may keep"—
Then he broke down at once, began to weep,   1480
And said, "I now forbid on pain of death
That you should ever while you've life or breath
Tell anyone of this in any way—
My woe I'll have to bear as best I may—
Or in your countenance show a distress   1485
By which folks might divine the harm or guess."
    He called a squire and maiden to him then
And said, "Now go at once with Dorigen,
Escort her to a place without delay."
They took their leave and went upon their way   1490
But didn't know why to this place she went.
He didn't tell a soul of the intent.
    Now there may be a heap of you, I know,
Who think this man a fool for doing so,
That willingly his wife he'd jeopardize.   1495
But hear the tale before you criticize;
She may have better fortune than you've guessed,
And you may judge when you have heard the rest.
    It happened that Aurelius, the squire
Who for her was so amorously afire,   1500
Right in the heart of town she chanced to meet;
For she along the town's most crowded street
Was headed straight toward the garden where
She'd keep the promise she had made. And there
Aurelius was on his way as well;   1505
For he had watched her house so he could tell
When she might leave to head for any place.
And so they met, by accident or grace,
And cheerfully he gave her salutation
And asked her what might be her destination.   1510
She answered as if half out of her head:
"Out to the garden, as my husband said,
To keep my vow. Alas, I'm so distraught!"
    Aurelius then gave this matter thought,
As in his heart he had such great compassion   1515
For Dorigen, lamenting in this fashion,
And for Arveragus, this worthy knight

Who bade that she be faithful to her plight,
So loath to see his wife break any vow.
And in his heart he had great pity now;   1520
Looking for what was best from every side,
He'd rather leave his lust unsatisfied
Than do this churlish deed, so wretchedly
To act against such fine nobility;
These were the few words of Aurelius: 1525
   "Now, Madam, tell your lord Arveragus
That since I see this man's great nobleness
Toward you, and I see, too, your distress,
That rather he'd have shame—sad that would be—
Than have you break the vow you made to me,   1530
I'd rather suffer woe my whole life through
Than to divide the love between you two.
So, madam, I release you here and now,
Returning to your hand each oath and vow
That you have ever made to me or sworn   1535
Back to the very day that you were born.
I pledge my word, you I will never grieve
For any promise. Here I take my leave,
And of the truest and most perfect wife
That I have ever met in all my life."   1540
In what you promise, every wife, take care!
At least remember Dorigen, beware.
So can a squire perform a noble act
As well as can a knight, and that's a fact.
   On her bare knees she thanked Aurelius,   1545
Then went home to her mate Arveragus
And told him all as you've already heard.
He was so satisfied, upon my word,
It's more than I could possibly relate.
Why should I more upon this matter state?   1550
   Arveragus and Dorigen his wife
In sovereign bliss were then to share their life,
Not once did any anger come between.
He cherished her as if she were a queen,
And she was true to him eternally.   1555
On these two folks you'll get no more from me.

Aurelius, by his expense forlorn,
Now curst the time that ever he was born.
"Alas," said he, "I pledged, I can't withhold,
A thousand pounds by weight of finest gold   1560
To this philosopher! What shall I do?
There's nothing I can say but that I'm through.
My heritage I now will have to sell
And be a beggar; here I cannot dwell
And shame all of my kindred in this place,   1565
Unless from him I get some better grace.
But still I'll try to set with him a way
Whereby on certain days I yearly pay,
And thank him, too, for his great courtesy.
I'll keep my word, I'll speak no falsity."   1570
     With heavy heart he goes into his coffer
And brings to this magician gold to offer,
Five hundred pounds (so I guess it would be),
And asked if out of generosity
He'd grant him time, the rest of it to pay;   1575
He told him, "Master, I am proud to say
I've never failed to keep a promise yet.
For certainly I'll satisfy the debt
I owe to you, however I may fare,
Though I go begging in my girdle bare.   1580
But if you'll grant me, on this surety,
Extended time, two years or maybe three,
Then I'll be well; if not, I'll have to sell
My heritage; there is no more to tell."
     Then this magician answered in this way,   1585
On hearing what the fellow had to say:
"Have I not kept my covenant with you?"
     "Yes, certainly," he answered, "well and true."
     "Have you not had your lady, your desire?"
     "No, no," with woeful sigh replied the squire.   1590
     "What was the reason? Tell me if you can."
     Aurelius his tale at once began
And told him all as you have heard before;
There is no need to tell you any more.
     He said, "Arveragus, through nobleness,   1595

Would rather be in sorrow and distress
Than have his wife be to her vow untrue."
Of Dorigen's great woe he told him, too,
How loath she was to be a wicked wife
And that she'd rather lose that day her life,   1600
And that her vow through innocence she swore,
For of such magic she'd not heard before.
"I had such pity on her then," said he,
"As freely as he had her sent to me
I freely sent her back to him again.   1605
And that's the whole, there's no more to explain."
 Then this magician answered, "My dear brother,
Each of you acted nobly to the other.
You are a squire, Arveragus a knight;
But God forbid, in all his blissful might,   1610
That any scholar could not bring about
A deed that's just as noble. Never doubt!
 "Sir, I release you from the thousand pound
As if right now you'd crept out of the ground
And never once till now of me you knew.   1615
For not a penny will I take from you
For all my craft or for my labor. Sire,
You've paid me well, I've all that I require.
And that's enough, so farewell and good day!"
And on his horse he went forth on his way.   1620
 To you this question, lords, I now address:
Which one of them showed greatest nobleness?
Give me your thoughts before we further wend.
That's all I have, my tale is at an end.

The Physician's Tale

There was, as we're told by Titus Livius,
A knight once who was called Virginius,
A man of worth and honor through and through,
One strong in friends and with great riches too.
 This knight begat a daughter by his wife   5
And had no other children all his life.
This maiden had such loveliness that she
Was fairer than all creatures men may see;
For Nature in her sovereign diligence
Had molded her with such great excellence   10
It was as if "Look here!" she would proclaim,
"I, Nature, form and paint just so, the same,
When I may choose. Who with me can compete?
Pygmalion? No, let him forge and beat,
Engrave or paint, for I will dare to say   15
Both Zeuxis and Apelles work away
In vain to sculpt and paint, to forge, create,
If me they would presume to imitate.
For He who's the Creator principal
Has made of me His vicar-general,   20
To form and paint all creatures everywhere
As I desire, and all are in my care
Beneath the changing moon. And for my task
There's nothing as I work I need to ask,
My Lord and I are fully in accord.   25
I fashioned her in worship of my Lord,
And so I do with all my other creatures,
Whatever be their hue or other features."
So Nature would have spoken, I would gauge.
 Now she was only fourteen years of age,   30
This maiden in whom Nature took delight;
For just as she can paint a lily white

327

And red a rose, so in each colored feature
Had Nature come to paint this noble creature
Before her birth. And as she painted, she   35
Was free in what she thought each tint should be.
She had great lovely tresses that were done
In dye by Phoebus like his burnished sun.
Though excellent her beauty to behold,
Her virtue was to that a thousandfold;   40
In her there was no lack of things to praise,
For she was one discerning in her ways,
One chaste in soul as well as body. She
Had therefore flowered in virginity
With all humility and abstinence,   45
As one of patience, one with temperance,
With measure, too, in bearing and array.
To answer with discretion was her way;
Were she wise as Minerva, if I dare
To say, her speech was womanly and spare,   50
Without pretentious terms as counterfeit
Of wisdom. She spoke always as befit
Her station, and her words from first to last
In virtue and gentility were cast.
And shy she was, a maiden's modesty,   55
Steadfast in heart and working constantly
To keep from sloth. And Bacchus was in truth
No master of her mouth at all; for youth
And wine cause works of Venus to increase,
As men will build a fire with oil or grease.   60
And in her virtue, being unconstrained,
How frequently some sickness she had feigned
That she might thereby flee the company
Wherever folly likely was to be,
Such as is found at revel, feast, or dance,   65
Occasions not unknown for dalliance.
Such things as that make children come to be
Too early ripe and bold, as men may see,
Wherein lies peril since the days of yore.
Of boldness soon enough she'll learn the lore   70
When she's a woman, ready to be wife.

You governesses in your later life
Who have lords' daughters given to your care,
Don't be displeased by what I say, but bear
In mind that you've been put in governance   75
Because of one of two things, not by chance:
It's that you've kept your virtue, or that you,
Once fallen into sin (in which you knew
The old dance well enough), have fully spurned
All such misconduct, from it having turned   80
Away forever. For Christ's sake, therefore,
To teach them virtue strive you all the more.

    Look at the poacher: when that craft he's left,
When he gives up his appetite for theft,
To keep a forest there's no better man.   85
Now keep them well, for if you will you can.
Be certain that to no vice you assent
(Lest you be damned for having bad intent);
Who does is traitorous, don't doubt it's true,
For keep in mind that which I say to you: 90
Of treasons all, the one most pestilent
Is when someone betrays the innocent.

    You fathers too, and mothers, you with any
Children, be it one or be it many,
The charge is yours to keep them in surveillance   95
While they remain within your governance.
Beware lest by example, how you live,
Or by neglect to chasten them, to give
Them guidance, they may perish. I daresay
That if they do so, dearly you will pay.   100
When there's a shepherd soft and negligent,
Many a sheep and lamb by wolf are rent.
Let that suffice, the example here is plain,
For to my subject I must turn again.

    This maiden in this tale that I express   105
Had kept herself without a governess;
For in the way she lived might maidens read
As in a book every good word or deed
That in a gracious maid one looks to find,
She was so prudent, virtuous, and kind.   110

So sprung the fame, which spread by all the ways,
Both of her beauty and goodness, that praise
Was hers throughout the land from all who knew
And loved virtue—save only Envy who,
So sorry to see others have success,   115
Delights in others' sorrow and distress.
(The Doctor has described it in this way.)
　　This maiden went into the town one day
For temple rites, and she took with her too
Her mother dear, as all young maidens do.   120
Now there was then a justice in the town
Who governed all that region. Up and down
Her form this judge was quick to cast his eye,
Appraising her as she went walking by
The place he stood. Immediately this brought   125
A change within his heart and mind, so caught
He was by beauty of this maiden; he
Spoke these words to himself in secrecy:
"She shall be mine, in spite of any man!"
　　At once into his heart the devil ran   130
And taught him right away just how he might
This maiden to his purpose win by sleight.
For surely not by bribery nor force,
He thought, could he pursue a speedy course,
For she was strong in friends and given to   135
Such virtue that the judge for certain knew
She was a maiden he might never win
In terms of tempting her to carnal sin.
So after he had thought about it much,
With a churl in that town he got in touch,   140
One whom he knew to be both slick and bold.
The judge his story to this fellow told
In secrecy, and made the fellow swear
He'd tell it to no creature anywhere
(Or if he did, his head lose for the deed).   145
When to this cursed plan they had agreed,
This judge was glad and entertained the knave
And gifts of precious nature to him gave.
　　So they conspired, plotting the shape and thrust

Of each point in the scheme, of how his lust   150
Might be performed with fullest subtlety,
As later you shall hear it openly.
Then homeward went this churl named Claudius.
Now this deceitful judge called Apius
(Such was his name, no fable that I tell   155
But something out of history known well,
It's truthful in its substance, there's no doubt)—
This judge so false went busily about
To hasten his delight all that he may.
Soon after, it befell one certain day   160
(The story goes) this judge of lying sort
As was his wont was seated in his court
Adjudging sundry cases. Rushing in
There came this lying churl, who stated then,
"My lord, I pray, if it should be your will,   165
Do right by me upon this piteous bill
In which I've plaint against Virginius;
And if he'd say the matter isn't thus,
I'll prove, and find good witness as I do,
That what's expressed here in my bill is true."   170
    "On this, as he's not here," the judge replied,
"There's nothing definite I may decide.
Let him be summoned and I'll gladly hear;
You'll have here all your rights, no wrong to fear."
    Virginius, to learn the judge's will,   175
Then came. At once was read this cursed bill.
The substance of it was as you shall hear:
    "My lord, to you now, Apius so dear,
Shows here your humble servant Claudius
How this knight whom they call Virginius   180
Against the law, against all equity,
Against my will express, withholds from me
My servant, one who is my thrall by right,
One who was stolen from my house by night
When she was very young. This I will prove   185
With witnesses, that justly you may move.
She's not his daughter, say what he may say.
Wherefore to you, my lord the judge, I pray,

Yield me my slave, if that should be your will."
And that was all the substance of his bill.   190
  Virginius stared at the churl. But then,
Before his own remarks he could begin
And tell his tale to prove, as should a knight,
With many a witness how such wasn't right,
That all was false said by his adversary,   195
This cursed judge would not a moment tarry,
Would not hear from Virginius one word,
But gave his judgment, here's how it was heard:
  "I rule at once this man shall have his thrall,
You'll keep her in your house no more at all,   200
Go bring her forth and place her in our care.
This man shall have his slave, I so declare."
  And when this worthy knight Virginius,
Through sentence of this justice Apius,
Must to the judge his dear young daughter give   205
By way of force, in lechery to live,
Home he returned and sat within his hall
And hastily had them his daughter call.
With face as deathlike as the ashes cold,
Her humble face he started to behold;   210
A father's pity struck him in his heart,
Yet from his purpose he would not depart.
  "Daughter," said he, "Virginia by your name,
There are two ways, it's either death or shame
That you must suffer now. Alas, that I   215
Was ever born! You don't deserve to die,
Nor ever have, by sword or by a knife.
O my dear daughter, ender of my life,
Whom I have raised with pleasure of such kind
That you were never once out of my mind!   220
O daughter who's become my final woe,
And in my life my final joy also,
In patience now, O gem of chastity,
Accept your death, for this is my decree.
For love, and not for hate, you must be dead,   225
My ruthful hand must now smite off your head.
Alas, that Apius should ever lay

Eyes on you! He has falsely judged today"—
He told her of it all, as you before
Have heard, so there's no need to tell it more.   230
   "O mercy, my dear father!" said this maid,
And as she spoke both of her arms she laid
About his neck as she was wont to do.
The tears burst from her eyes as in her rue
She said to him, "Good father, shall I die?   235
Is there no grace, no remedy to try?"
   "No, surely not, my daughter dear," said he.
   "Then give me time, father of mine," said she,
"That death I might bewail a little space;
For surely Jephthah gave his daughter grace,   240
Before he slew her, to lament, alas!
And but one thing, God knows, was her trespass:
She ran that she might be the first to see
And welcome him with reverence." When she
Had spoken this, she fell down in a swoon;   245
And after, when her faint was over soon,
She rose again, and to her father said,
"Bless God that as a virgin I'll be dead!
Give me my death before I'm given shame;
Do with your child your will in our Lord's name!"   250
   And with that word she several times implored
That he might smite her gently with his sword;
With that she fell down swooning, lying still.
Her father, with a heavy heart and will,
Cut off her head. He grabbed it by the hair   255
And took it to the judge, still seated where
He held his court. When he'd come to behold
The sight, this judge bade (so the story's told)
That he be taken out and hung. But then
A thousand folks at once came rushing in   260
To save the knight in rue and sympathy,
For known was all the false iniquity.
For they had all suspected from the start,
The way the churl had challenged for his part,
That it was by assent of Apius   265
Whom they knew well as being lecherous.

And so they went to Apius that day
And threw him into prison right away,
And there he slew himself. When Claudius,
Who'd been the servant of this Apius,   270
Was then condemned to hang upon a tree,
Virginius in pity prayed that he
Be spared; and so they exiled him instead,
For certainly the man had been misled.
The others then were hung without redress,   275
All those involved in this great cursedness.

   Here men may see what sin's reward is like.
Beware, for no man knows when God will strike,
Not in the least, nor in what kind of way
The worm of conscience, quaking, may betray   280
One's wicked life, so private though it be
None knows of it but him and God. Be he
An ignorant man or learned, he knows not
How soon he may be fearing for his lot.
I warn you, then, let this advice be taken: 285
Forsake sin or for sin you'll be forsaken.

The Pardoner's Tale

INTRODUCTION

Words of the Host to the Physician and the Pardoner

Our Host began to swear as if gone mad.
"Harrow," said he, "by nails and blood! How bad,
How false a judge, how false a churl! Demise
As shameful as the heart may so devise   290
Come to these judges and their advocates!
This simple maiden's slain, as he relates,
She for her beauty paid, alas, too dearly!
I've always said what men may see so clearly,
That gifts of Fortune and of Nature bring   295
About the death of many a living thing.
Her beauty was her death, I dare to say.
She's slain, alas, in such a piteous way!
Both gifts of which I speak, as I maintain,
Have often brought men more to harm than gain.   300
But truthfully, my only master dear,
This is a tale that's pitiful to hear.
It can't be helped, let's move along our way.
God save your noble body, that I pray,
Your urinals and every chamber pot,   305
Each galen and hippocrates you've got,
Each flask full of the medicine you carry–
God bless them, and Our Lady, too, Saint Mary!
    "As I may thrive, you are a proper man
And, by Saint Ronyan, like a prelate! Can   310
I say it right? I can't speak learnedly
But well I know you've caused this heart in me
To grieve till I am near a cardiac.
By *corpus* bones! if remedy I lack,
If there's no musty draught of corny ale   315

Or I don't hear at once a merry tale,
My heart is lost in sympathy for her.
Bel ami, you," he said, "you Pardoner,
Tell jokes, some funny story, go ahead."

"It shall be done now, by Saint Ronyan!" said   320
The Pardoner. "But first, at this ale stake,
I'll have a drink and also eat a cake."

The gentlefolk cried out immediately:
"Don't let him tell us any ribaldry!
Tell us some moral thing, that we may learn   325
Some wisdom, and we'll gladly hear your turn."

"Granted, for sure," said he, "but I must think
Of something, then, that's fitting while I drink."

THE PARDONER'S PROLOGUE

"My lords," said he, "in churches when I preach
I take great pains to have a haughty speech   330
And ring it out as roundly as a bell;
I know it all by heart, what I've to tell.
My theme's always the same and ever was:
Radix malorum est Cupiditas.

"First I announce from where it is I come   335
And then show all my bulls, not only some.
My patent with the bishop's seal I show
To help safeguard my person as I go,
That no man be so bold, though priest or clerk,
As to obstruct me in Christ's holy work.   340
And after that my tales I start to tell,
And bulls of popes, of cardinals as well,
Of patriarchs and bishops, I display.
A few words in the Latin tongue I say
To add a little spice to what I preach   345
And stir men to devotion as I teach.

"And then I show to them like precious stones
My long glass cases crammed with rags and bones,
For these are relics (so they think). And set
In metal I've a shoulderbone I let   350

Them see, from the sheep of a holy Jew.
'Good men,' say I, 'pay heed to me. When you
Shall take this bone and wash it in a well,
If cow or calf or sheep or ox should swell
Because it ate a worm or it's been stung,   355
Take water from that well and wash its tongue
And right away it's whole. And furthermore,
From pox and scab and every other sore
Shall every sheep be whole that of this well
Drinks but a draught. Pay heed to what I tell.   360
If every farmer owning stock will go
Each week before the cock's had time to crow
And, fasting, from this well will take a drink
(This Jew once taught our elders so to think),
His beasts will be assured of progeny.   365
And, sirs, it also heals of jealousy;
For though a man by jealousy be wroth,
Use water from this well to make his broth
And nevermore shall he mistrust his wife,
Despite the truth about her sinful life,   370
With even priests as lovers, two or three.
    " 'Here also is a mitten you may see.
Whose hand goes in this mitten will thereby
Find that his grain will greatly multiply
When he has sown, whether it's wheat or oats   375
(Provided he has offered pence or groats).
    " 'Good men and women, of one thing I warn:
If in this church there's any fellow born
Who's done some horrid sin and who for shame
Does not dare to be shriven for the same,   380
Or any woman young or elderly
Who's done her husband wrong by cuckoldry,
Such folk shall have no power and no grace
To offer to my relics in this place.
But whoso finds himself without such blame,   385
Let him come forth and offer in God's name
And I'll absolve him by authority
That has by papal bull been granted me.'
    "And with this trick I've won each year about

A hundred marks since first I started out.   390
I stand there in my pulpit like a clerk,
These ignorants sit down, and right to work
I go, I preach as you have heard before
And tell a hundred silly stories more.
And I take pains to get my neck to stretch,   395
To nod both east and west to every wretch
Just like a dove that's sitting on the barn.
My tongue and hands go spinning such a yarn
That it's a joy to see my craftiness.
Of avarice and all such cursedness   400
I always preach, to make them ever free
To give their pence (and give only to me);
For my concern is only with collection
And not with any sin that needs correction.
Once buried, they don't mean a thing to me   405
Though their souls pick blackberries. Certainly
Many a sermon seemingly well meant
Has often come from less than good intent:
To please the folks, to offer flattery,
To get promoted by hypocrisy,   410
Some for vainglory, some for simple hate.
For if I dare not otherwise debate,
My tongue in preaching will a sting impart
That no man can escape, he'll feel the smart
And falsely be defamed if ever he   415
Has done wrong to my brethren or to me;
For though I may not call him by his name,
All men shall be aware that he's the same
By signs or by what chances may permit.
Thus folks who wrong us I repay, I spit   420
My venom under holiness's hue,
That truthful I may seem and holy too.
    "But briefly my intent I'll summarize:
It's greed alone that makes me sermonize.
And so my theme is yet and ever was: 425
Radix malorum est Cupiditas.
Yes, I myself can preach against the vice
Of avarice that is my own device;

For though I'm guilty of that very sin,
These other folks I'm able still to win   430
From avarice and sorely they'll repent.
But that is not my principal intent,
I only preach to satisfy my greed.
Enough of that, for more there's not a need.
     "I tell them many moral tales I know,   435
Old stories set in times of long ago;
The ignorant find in these tales much pleasure,
Such things as they can well repeat and treasure.
Do you believe, as long as I can preach,
Acquiring gold and silver while I teach,   440
That willfully I'd live in poverty?
It's never crossed my mind, quite truthfully!
No, I will preach and beg in sundry lands
And never will I labor with my hands
Or take up basketweaving for a living.   445
I won't be begging idly, they'll be giving.
Apostles I'll not try to counterfeit;
I'll have my money, wool, and food, though it
Be from some page whose poverty is dire
Or from the poorest widow in the shire;   450
Although her kids be starving, I'll be fine,
For I will drink the liquor of the vine
And have a jolly wench in every town.
But listen, lords, we'll set that matter down,
Your pleasure is that I should tell a tale.   455
Now that I've had my draught of corny ale,
By God, I hope to tell you something striking
That with good reason will be to your liking.
Though I'm a man of vices through and through,
I still can tell a moral tale to you,   460
One that I preach to bring the money in.
Now hold your peace, my tale I will begin."

THE PARDONER'S TALE

     In Flanders some time back there was a troop
Of youths who were a folly-loving group,

What with their parties, gambling, brothels, bars,   465
Where with their harps and lutes and their guitars
They'd dance and play at dice both day and night.
They also ate and drank beyond their might,
So that they gave the devil sacrifice
Within the devil's temple by the vice   470
Of gluttony, which is abomination.
Their oaths were great, so worthy of damnation
It was a grisly thing to hear them swear;
The body of our blessed Lord they'd tear
As if the Jews had not torn him enough.   475
Each laughed at every other's sinful stuff
And right away came dancing girls to boot,
All neat and trim, and young girls selling fruit,
Singers with harps, then bawds, girls selling cake—
All agents of the devil, no mistake,   480
All kindlers of the fire of lechery
That goes so hand in hand with gluttony.
My witness is God's Holy Writ, no less,
That lechery's in wine and drunkenness.

    Behold how drunken Lot unnaturally   485
Lay with his daughters both, unwittingly,
So drunk he was unconscious of the deed.

    King Herod, about whom one well should read,
When at a feast much wine he had been swilling,
Gave orders at the table for the killing   490
Of John the Baptist, guiltless as could be.

    Seneca says good things undoubtedly;
He said that not one difference could he find
Between a man who's gone out of his mind
And one who's drunk (except that madness will,   495
In one whose nature is already ill,
Be longer lasting than will drunkenness).
O gluttony, so full of cursedness!
O first cause of our trial and tribulation,
O origin of all our souls' damnation   500
Till we were purchased back by blood of Christ!
How dearly, I'll say briefly, it was priced,
How much was paid for this depravity!

Corrupt was all the world with gluttony.
    Our father Adam and his wife also 505
From Paradise to labor and to woe
Were driven by that vice, and do not doubt it.
While Adam fasted, as I read about it,
He was in Paradise, but then when he
Ate of the fruit forbidden on the tree 510
He was at once cast out to woe and pain.
O gluttony, with reason we complain!
O if one knew how many a malady
Must follow such excess and gluttony,
To eat with moderation he'd be able 515
Whenever he is sitting at his table.
Alas! the short throat and so tender mouth
Make men both east and west, both north and south,
In water, earth, and air, work to produce
Fine meat and beverage for a glutton's use! 520
How well this matter, O Saint Paul, you treat:
"Meat's for the belly, belly's for the meat,
God shall destroy both"—so Paul is heard.
Alas! for by my faith it is a word
So foul to have to say (but foul's the deed) 525
That so much white and red a man should need
He makes his throat his privy hole, no less,
Because of such accurst excessiveness.
    The Apostle has with so much pity mourned:
"So many walk that way whom I have warned— 530
I say this weeping, with piteous voice—
Foes of the cross of Christ, if that's their choice,
For which the end is death. Their god's the belly."
O gut, O bag, O belly foul and smelly,
So full of dung and of corruption found! 535
From either end of you foul is the sound.
By what great cost and labor you have dined!
These cooks, how they must pound and strain and grind,
And transform substance into accident,
Until your glutton's appetite is spent! 540
From hard bones they knock marrow for one's taste,
For there is nothing they let go to waste

That's soft and sweet and might the gullet suit.
With spices of the leaf, the bark and root,
His sauces will be made for such delight   545
He'll wind up with a whole new appetite.
But he who lets such pleasures so entice
Is dead while he is living in such vice.
   A lecherous thing is wine, and drunkenness
Is full of striving and of wretchedness.   550
O drunken man, disfigured is your face,
Sour your breath, you're foul to the embrace!
And through your drunken nose it seems the sound
Is "Samson, Samson" that you would expound,
Though, God knows, Samson never drank of wine.   555
You fall as if you were a stricken swine;
Your tongue is lost, your self-respect you gave
To drunkenness, which is the very grave
Of man's discretion and intelligence.
When drink in him has taken dominance   560
One cannot keep a secret, truly said.
So keep yourself away from white and red,
Especially from Lepe white wine bought
In Cheapside or Fish Street. This wine that's brought
From Spain is known to creep up subtly   565
In other wines grown in proximity,
From which there then arise such heady fumes
That when a man three draughts of it consumes,
Though he thinks he's in Cheapside at his home,
He'll find to Lepe, Spain, he's come to roam   570
And not off to Bordeaux or La Rochelle—
And "Samson, Samson" he'll be saying well.
   But listen, lords, to this one word, I pray:
All of the sovereign actions, I daresay,
All victories in God's Old Testament,   575
Through grace of him who is omnipotent,
Were all achieved in abstinence and prayer.
Look in the Bible and you'll learn it there.
   Behold Attila: that great warrior died
While in a shameful sleep, unglorified,   580
His nostrils pouring blood, a drunken sot.

A captain's life should be a sober lot.
You should above all else consider well
The wise commandment given Lemuel
(Not Samuel but Lemuel I said),   585
Expressly in the Bible to be read,
On serving wine to justices at court.
That should suffice, no more need I report.
    On gluttony I've said a thing or two,
And now from gambling I'd prohibit you.   590
For gambling is the source of every lie,
Of all deceit that curses men to die.
It's blasphemy of Christ, manslaughter, waste
Of time and property. To be disgraced,
That's what it is, dishonorable, defaming,   595
To be held one who takes to common gaming.
The higher one might be in social station
The more he'll be accused of depravation;
If there's a prince who gambles constantly,
On all his governance and policy   600
The judgment of opinion will be such
His reputation's bound to suffer much.
    A wise ambassador named Stillbon, sent
From Sparta, in great pomp to Corinth went
To arrange for an alliance. When he came,   605
It happened that by chance he found, for shame,
That all the greatest who were of that land
Were at the game of hazard, dice in hand.
With that, as soon as Stillbon could get started,
Back home to his own country he departed,   610
And said, "In Corinth I'll not lose my name
Nor take upon myself so great a shame,
I'll not ally you with such hazarders.
Send to them other wise ambassadors,
For on my oath I'd perish in defiance   615
Before I'd make for you such an alliance.
For you, with honors that have been so glorious,
Shall not ally with gamblers so notorious—
Not by my will or treaty anyway."
That's what this wise philosopher had to say.   620

At King Demetrius now take a look:
Parthia's king, so we're told in the book,
Sent him in scorn a pair of golden dice;
For playing hazard long had been his vice,
For which Demetrius's fame and glory   625
To Parthia's king were a worthless story.
Cannot lords find some other forms of play
Honest enough to pass the time of day?
   And now on oaths, when false or indiscreet,
A word or two, such as the old books treat.   630
Strong swearing is an awful thing to do
And worse yet when you swear what isn't true.
The Lord on high forbade we swear at all,
As Matthew tells. Especially recall
What holy Jeremiah says about it: 635
"Speak truth, not lies, in oaths, that none should doubt it;
Swear but for justice and for righteousness."
But idle swearing is a cursedness.
Behold and see in that first table of
The worthy laws God gave us from above: 640
The second of these laws is very plain
To say, "Thou shalt not take my name in vain."
The Lord forbids such swearing sooner, then,
Than homicide and many a cursed sin.
I tell it in the order that it stands—   645
As he who God's commandments understands
Is well aware, the second one is that.
And furthermore I now will tell you flat
That vengeance on his house will be unsparing
When one engages in such awful swearing   650
As "By God's precious heart," and "By his nails,"
And "By the blood of Christ that is in Hales,
My chance is seven, yours is five-and-three!"
"By God's arms, if you play deceitfully
You'll see how well your heart this dagger hones!"   655
This is the fruit of those two cursed bones:
Forswearing, ire, deceit, and homicide.
So for the love of Christ who for us died,
Leave off your oaths, the small ones and the great.

Now, sirs, my tale I further will relate.   660
    These three young revelers of whom I tell
Much earlier than nine by any bell
Were sitting in a tavern and were drinking.
And as they sat, they heard a bell go clinking:
A corpse was being carried to its grave.   665
Then one of them called over to his knave
And said, "Go quickly, ask without delay
What corpse that is that's passing by the way,
And see that you report his name correctly."
    "No need for that," the boy replied directly,   670
"Two hours before you came here, sir, they told
Me who he was. The fellow was an old
Comrade of yours, one who was slain at night
With suddenness. While he sat drunk, upright,
There came a stealthy thief that's known as Death,   675
Throughout this country robbing folks of breath;
And with his spear he smote his heart in two,
Then went his way without a word. And through
This plague he's slain a thousand. Master, ere
You come into his presence anywhere,   680
I think that it is very necessary
That you beware of such an adversary.
To meet him, sire, be ready evermore.
My mother taught me this. I say no more."
    "By Saint Mary," the tavern keeper said,   685
"The child is right! This year he's left for dead
In just one town (a mile from here, I'd gauge)
Both man and woman, child and knave and page—
I think his habitation must be there.
It would be very wise, then, to beware   690
Lest he should do a fellow a dishonor."
    "Yea, by God's arms!" declared this rioter,
"Is he so very perilous to meet?
I'll seek him in the by-ways and the street,
I vow it by the worthy bones of God!   695
My friends, are we not three peas in a pod?
Let's each hold up a hand to one another,
Each of us will become the others' brother.

With this false traitor Death we'll do away;
The slayer of so many we shall slay   700
Before it's night, by God's sweet dignity!"
    Together then they made their pledge, the three,
To live and die each of them for the others
As if they'd been born naturally as brothers.
Then up they jumped in drunken agitation   705
And headed down the road, their destination
The village they had just been told about.
And many a grisly oath they shouted out
And tore Christ's blessed body limb from limb—
Death shall be dead if they get hold of him!   710
    When they had gone not fully half a mile,
And were about to step across a stile,
They met a poor old man. Upon their meeting,
The old man very meekly gave them greeting:
"My lords," he said, "may God watch over you."   715
    To which the proudest of this rowdy crew
Replied, "What's that, you churl of sorry grace?
Why are you all wrapped up except your face?
Why live to be so ancient? Tell us why!"
    The old man looked the fellow in the eye   720
And said, "Because I'd never find a man,
Were I to walk as far as Hindustan,
In any town or village, who would give
His youth for my old age. So I must live,
I'm destined to remain an old man still,   725
As long a time as it may be God's will.
And Death, alas! won't take my life, and so
I walk, a restless wretch, and as I go
I knock with this my staff early and late
Upon the ground, which is my mother's gate,   730
And say, 'Beloved Mother, let me in!
Look how I vanish, flesh and blood and skin!
Alas! when will these old bones be at rest?
How gladly, Mother, I'd exchange my chest,
Which has so long a time been on my shelf,   735
For haircloth in which I could wrap myself!'
And yet she won't allow me such a grace,

That's why so pale and withered is my face.
    "But, sirs, you show a lack of courtesy
To speak to an old man so brutishly,   740
Unless he has trespassed in word or deed.
In Holy Writ you may yourself well read:
'Before an old man with a hoary head
You should arise.' I counsel as it's said,
No harm to an old fellow you should do,   745
No more than you would have men do to you
When in old age, should you so long abide.
Now God be with you where you go or ride,
I must go on to where I have to go."
    "No, you old churl, by God, that isn't so!"   750
The gambler said at once. "You won't be gone
So lightly on your way, no, by Saint John!
What of that traitor Death were you just saying?
Our friends in all this country he is slaying.
I promise you—since you're a spy of his—   755
You'll pay if you don't tell us where he is,
By God and by the holy sacrament!
For truly you and he have one intent,
To kill us who are young, you thief and liar!"
    "Now, sirs," said he, "if you have such desire   760
To find Death, then turn up this crooked way—
I left him in that grove. I truly say,
Beneath a tree he was; there he'll abide,
Your boasting will not make him run and hide.
See yonder oak? He's there, as you will find.   765
God save you, as he ransomed all mankind,
And mend you!" So replied this aged man.
And each of these three revelers then ran
Until he reached the tree, and there they found
Some florins, coined of gold and fine and round—   770
Well nigh eight bushels, that was their impression.
To seek Death was no longer their obsession,
As each of them, so gladdened by the sight
Of golden florins, all so fair and bright,
Sat down beside the hoard that they had found.   775
The worst of them was first to speak a sound.

He said, "My brothers, heed what I've to say,
My wits are keen although I joke and play.
It's Fortune that has given us this treasure
That we may live our lives in mirth and pleasure.   780
As easy as it comes we'll spend it. Aye!
Who would have thought this very morning, by
God's dignity, we'd have so fair a grace?
And if this gold be carried from this place
Home to my house, or else to yours—be it   785
Well understood, it's our gold every bit—
Then we'll be in a high and happy way.
But truly it cannot be done by day,
We'd be accused of brazen thievery
And for our gold they'd hang us from a tree.   790
This treasure we must carry home by night,
As cleverly and slyly as we might.
So I advise that lots among us all
Be drawn, and let's see where the lot will fall;
And he who draws the lot then cheerfully   795
Shall run to town, and do that speedily,
To bring some bread and wine back on the sly,
While two of us shall carefully stand by
To guard this treasure. If he doesn't tarry,
When it is night this treasure we will carry   800
To where we all agree it would be best."
In that one's fist were lots held for the rest,
He bade them draw to see where it would fall.
It fell upon the youngest of them all,
Who started off to town immediately.   805
No sooner had he left their company
When that one of those staying told the other,
"Now you know well that you are my sworn brother;
Here's something that will profit you to know.
Our friend back into town has had to go,   810
And here is gold in plentiful degree
That is to be divided by us three.
But nonetheless, if I could work it so
Between us two we split it when we go,
Would I have not done you a friendly turn?"   815

"But how?" the other answered with concern.
"For he will know the gold is with us two.
What shall we say to him? What shall we do?"
    "Shall it be kept our secret?" said the first.
"Then in a few short words you shall be versed   820
In what we'll do to bring it all about."
    "I grant it," said the other, "do not doubt,
You have my oath, I'll not be false to you."
    "Now," said the first, "you know that we are two,
And two of us are stronger than is one.   825
As soon as he sits down, as if for fun
Arise as though you'd have with him some play,
Then in both sides I'll stab him right away
While you and he are struggling as in game.
And with your dagger see you do the same.   830
Then all this gold, dear friend, when we are through
Shall be divided up twixt me and you;
The two of us can then our lusts fulfill
And play at dice as often as we will."
So these two rogues agreed they would betray   835
And slay the third, as you have heard me say.
    Meanwhile the youngest, who had gone to town,
In his mind's eye saw rolling up and down
The beauty of those florins new and bright.
"O Lord," said he, "if only that I might   840
Have all this treasure for myself alone!
There is no man who lives beneath God's throne
Who could then live as I, so merrily!"
And then at last hell's fiend, our enemy,
Put in his mind that poison he should buy   845
And give to his two mates and let them die.
The fiend had found this man's life so profane
He used his leave to bring the man to pain,
For it was plainly this man's full intent
To slay them both and never to repent.   850
So forth he went—no longer would he tarry—
Into the town to an apothecary,
Whom he asked that he sell to him if willing
Some poison: he had rats that needed killing,

And in his yard a polecat, so he said,   855
Was reason why his capons now were dead,
And he'd wreak eager vengeance if he might
On vermin that were ruining him by night.
      The apothecary answered, "Let me tell you,
So help me God, here's something I will sell you,   860
And there is not a creature anywhere
That eats or drinks this mixture I prepare,
Though in amount as little as a kernel,
That will not go at once to the eternal—
Yea, he will die, and in a shorter while   865
Than it would take you, sir, to walk a mile,
This poison is so strong and virulent."
      With this in hand, this cursed fellow went
(He took it in a box), and then he ran
Up the adjoining street to see a man   870
Who loaned him three large bottles. Of the three,
He poured his poison into two, for he
Would keep the third one clean for his own drinking.
"I'll be at work all night," so he was thinking,
"To carry all the gold out from that place."   875
And when this ne'er-do-well of such disgrace
Had filled with wine three bottles to the brim,
He went back to his mates awaiting him.
      What need is there to preach about it more?
For just as they had planned his death before,   880
So by them he was slain right on the spot.
Then that one, when they'd carried out the plot,
Said, "Let us sit and drink and make us merry,
And afterwards his body we will bury."
It happened then by chance that with that word   885
He took the bottle poisoned by the third
And drank from it, then gave some to his mate,
And both of them met promptly with their fate.
      But surely Avicenna, I suppose,
Did not include in all his canon's prose   890
More wondrous symptoms of a poisoned state
Than these two wretches suffered in their fate.
So these two killers met with homicide,

And also their false poisoner has died.
O cursed sin, so full of wretchedness!   895
O homicidal traitors! Wickedness!
O gluttony! O gambling! Lechery!
You blasphemers of Christ with villainy,
With mighty oaths from habit and from pride!
Alas, mankind, how can it so betide   900
That to the Lord who made you, your Creator,
Who with his dear heart's blood redeemed you later,
You are so false and so unkind? Alas!
Now, good men, God forgive you your trespass
And guard you from the sin of avarice.   905
My holy pardon saves you from all this;
If you will offer nobles, sterlings, rings,
Some brooches, spoons or other silver things,
Just bow your head beneath this holy bull.
Come up, you wives, and offer of your wool;   910
Your name I'll here enroll, then you may know
Into the bliss of heaven you will go.
My high power will absolve you, to be sure,
If you will give. You'll be as clean and pure
As when first born.—And, sirs, that's how I preach.   915
Now Christ, physician to the soul of each
Of us, grant you his pardon to receive,
For that is best, and you I'll not deceive.
But, sirs, one thing that slipped my memory when
I spoke my tale: I've relics, pardons in   920
My pouch, in England none could finer be,
The pope's own hand entrusted them to me.
If anyone devoutly has resolved
To make a gift and by me be absolved,
Come forth at once and meekly on your knees   925
Receive my pardon. Or, if you so please,
Take for yourself a pardon as you go—
One fresh and new at every town—just so
You offer to me, all the while we ride,
Some pence and nobles that are bonafide.   930
It is an honor for each one who's here
To have a competent pardoner near

To absolve you in the country as you ride,
In view of all the things that may betide.
There may be one (if not two) on the trek   935
Who falls down off his horse and breaks his neck;
Look what security it is for all
That in your fellowship I chanced to fall,
Who can absolve you all from first to last
Before your soul has from your body passed.   940
Let me advise our Host here to begin,
For he's the one enveloped most in sin.
Come forth, Sir Host, and offer first right now,
And kiss then each and every relic. How?
For just a groat! Unbuckle now your purse."   945
    "Nay, nay," said he, "then I would have Christ's curse!
It shall not be, if I should live in bliss!
Your breeches, I am sure, you'd have me kiss
And swear they were the relic of a saint,
Though of your foul behind they bear the taint.   950
But by the cross that Saint Helena found,
Your balls I'd like to have my hand around
Instead of relics or a reliquary!
Let's cut them off, I'll even help to carry,
We'll find a hog, enshrine them in his turd."   955
    The Pardoner then answered not a word,
He was too mad to have a thing to say.
    "Now," said our Host, "I will no longer play
This game with you, or any angry man."
And right away the worthy Knight began,   960
When he saw all were laughing at the spat:
"Now quite enough, let's have no more of that!
Sir Pardoner, be merry, of good cheer.
And you, Sir Host, who are to me so dear,
I pray that you will kiss the Pardoner;   965
And, Pardoner, I pray, draw near him, sir,
And as we did now let us laugh and play."
They kissed at once and rode along their way.

The Skipper's Tale

One time in Saint Denis a merchant dwelled
And he was well-to-do, for which men held
Him wise. He had a beauteous wife, and she
Was sociable and fond of revelry—
The kind of thing that creates more expense   5
Than justified by all the reverence
That men show women at their feasts and dances;
Their courtly gestures in such circumstances
Pass like a shadow on the wall. And woe
To him who has to finance all the show!   10
The simple husband, always he must pay;
He has to clothe us, keep us in array
(His honor served, although expensively),
In which array we dance with jollity;
And if he can't, by some course of events,   15
Or doesn't wish to go to such expense
Because he thinks it's money wasted, lost,
Then must another take care of our cost
Or lend us gold, and that's a dangerous road.
    This noble merchant had a fine abode,   20
To which some folks so often would repair
(Because of his largess and wife so fair)
It was a wonder. Listen to my tale.
Among his guests, who ranged the social scale,
There was a monk, a fair man and a bold—   25
He was, I think, then thirty winters old—
Who was forever visiting the place.
This youthful monk who was so fair of face
Had grown so well acquainted with the man
That since the day their friendship first began   30
He was as much a frequent sight to see
In this man's house as any friend could be.

And inasmuch as both this worthy man
And this young monk of whom I've told began
Their lives in the same village, cause therein   35
The monk had found to claim that they were kin;
This made the merchant, far from saying "Nay,"
As glad as any fowl is come the day;
For it gave to his heart great pleasure, pride,
To be so knit, eternally allied,   40
And each one strove the other to assure
Of brotherhood while their lives may endure.
    Don John the monk was free about expense
There in that house, for with all diligence
He sought to please, whatever cost begotten.   45
Whenever he would visit, not forgotten
Would be the lowest page, by their degree
He'd give the lord and all his company,
When he would come, some proper gift. For this,
His visits made them all as full of bliss   50
As is the fowl to see the rising sun.
No more of this, enough is said and done.
    This merchant, it befell, one certain day
Made plans to travel, readied his array;
Toward the town of Bruges he was to fare   55
Where he would buy a portion of his ware.
And so he sent to Paris right away
A servant to Don John the monk, to pray
He come to Saint Denis, a day or more
To sport there with him and his wife before   60
The merchant would to Bruges be starting out.
    This noble monk whom I have told about
Got from his abbot the desired permission
In view of his discretion and position
(An officer whose job it was to ride   65
About the barns and granges far and wide),
And so he came at once to Saint Denis.
A kinder welcome there could never be
Than that for our Don John, dear kinsman! Wine
The monk had brought—Italian sweet and fine,   70
Also a jug of malmsey—on his jaunt,

And fowls he brought as well, as was his wont.
To food and drink and play I let them go,
This merchant and this monk, a day or so.

    This merchant on the third day then arose;   75
Reflecting on finances, up he goes
Into his counting-house, where all alone
He calculates how well the year has gone—
Where at the time stood his financial health,
How he had spent what portion of his wealth,   80
If his accounts showed some increase or none.
His books and bags (and he had many a one)
He laid before him on his counting-board,
So rich the treasure he had there to hoard
That he securely shut the chamber door,   85
That not one man might interrupt his chore
While he was counting there behind the lock.
That's how he sat till after nine o'clock.

    Don John, that morning up early as well,
Was in the garden, strolling there a spell   90
And saying his devotions decorously.

    Now this good wife came walking quietly
Into the garden; there upon their meeting,
As she had often done, she gave him greeting.
There was a maiden walking by her side   95
Of whom she was the governess and guide;
She was a child still subject to the rod.
"Dear cousin John," this good wife said, "my God,
What's ailing you, so early to arise?"

    "Niece, it's enough," said he, "to realize   100
A good five hours' sleep on any night—
Unless a person's old with little might,
Like many a cowering husband lying there
As in a burrow sits a weary hare,
Distraught, hounds big and little on his tail.   105
But why, dear niece, have you become so pale?
I would believe for sure that our good man
So labored with you since the night began
You'd need to have a rest, and hastily!"
And with those words the monk laughed merrily,   110

His own thoughts having left him blushing red.
    But this fair wife began to shake her head
And gave a sigh. "Aye, God knows all," said she.
"My cousin, no, it stands not so with me;
For by that God who gave me soul and life, 115
In all the realm of France there is no wife
Who gets less pleasure from that sorry play.
Though I may sing 'Alas, alack the day
That I was born,' there is no one," said she,
"To whom I dare tell how it stands with me. 120
That's why I think at times to leave this land
Or else to end it all by my own hand,
So filled I am with dread, so full of care."
    The monk then gave this wife a startled stare.
"Alas, my niece, now God forbid," he said, 125
"That you should for some sorrow or for dread
Destroy yourself! Explain to me your grief;
Perhaps I may suggest then some relief,
Give help or counsel. Therefore let me know,
I won't repeat a thing about your woe; 130
Upon this breviary I now swear
That never in my life for foul or fair
Shall any of your secrets I betray."
    "The same to you," she answered, "shall I say.
By God and by that breviary I swear 135
That though to bits my body men may tear
I never shall, though I may go to hell,
Betray a word of anything you tell—
Not just because we're allied or related,
But truly in good faith and love," she stated. 140
And so the two had sworn, and kissed each other,
And told just what they pleased to one another.
    She said, "My cousin, if I had the space
(Which time I do not have, not in this place),
I'd tell you the sad story of my life, 145
What I have suffered since I've been a wife
Here with my spouse, although he's kin to you."
    "By God and by Saint Martin, that's not true,"
The monk replied, "he's no more kin to me

Than is a leaf that hangs here on the tree!   150
I've called him that, by Saint Denis of France,
That I might thereby have a better chance
To know you, whom I've loved especially
Above all other women, truthfully.
To that I swear upon my sacred vow.   155
Before he comes, tell me your grievance now,
Then be off on your way immediately."
    "O my Don John, my dear love," answered she,
"How willingly this counsel I would hide,
But it must out, I can no more abide.   160
My husband has been to me the worst man
That ever was since first the world began.
But since I am a wife, I shouldn't be
Telling a soul about our privacy,
Not that in bed nor in whatever place.   165
The Lord forbid I tell it, for his grace!
A wife should always say about her mate
Nothing but good, as I appreciate—
Except to you this much I dare to say:
God help me, he's not worth in any way   170
The value of a fly, not one degree.
And yet what grieves me most? He's niggardly.
For women, as you know, by natural bent
Desire six things and I'm no different;
We'd all have every husband be for us   175
Hardy and wise and rich and generous
And pliant to his wife and good in bed.
But by that very Lord who for us bled,
To honor him and purchase my array
This coming Sunday I will have to pay   180
A hundred francs or else I am forlorn.
Yet I would rather never have been born
Than be involved in scandal or disgrace,
And if my husband saw such taking place
I'd be but lost. And so to you I pray,   185
Lend me this sum, or else I die today.
Don John, I beg, lend me these hundred francs;
I will not fail to render you my thanks

If you will do for me that which I ask.
I'll pay you back someday—whatever task   190
You may require, whatever service, pleasure
That I may do, I'll let you set the measure.
If I do not, God's vengeance on me, John,
As foul as that of France's Ganelon."
    This gentle monk then answered in this fashion: 195
"Now truly, my dear lady, such compassion
I feel for you," he said, "so great a ruth,
That I now swear, I promise you in truth,
That when your spouse to Flanders starts to fare,
That's when I shall deliver you from care,   200
For I will bring to you the hundred francs."
And with that word he caught her by the flanks,
Embraced her hard, and kisses on her rained.
"Now go your way," he said, "but be restrained,
Don't make a sound. And see that soon we dine;   205
The sundial says that it's already nine.
Go now, and be as true as I shall be."
    "Naught else or God forbid, sir," answered she.
As jolly as a magpie, off she bustled
To bid the cooks make haste, to see they hustled,   210
So that the folks might dine without delay.
Up to her husband then she made her way,
She knocked upon the locked door hardily.
    "Qui là?" he asked. "By Peter! it is me,"
She answered. "What, sir! How long will you fast?   215
How long must all your calculations last,
Such tallying of sums and books and things?
The devil take," she said, "such reckonings!
For sure you have enough gifts from the Lord;
Come down today, let be the bags you hoard.   220
Do you not feel ashamed that dear Don John,
From fasting all the day, grows weak and wan?
Now let's go hear a mass and then we dine."
    "Wife," said the man, "you little can divine
The care and trouble of this occupation.   225
Among us merchants—God be my salvation,
As I swear by the lord they call Saint Ive—

Of any twelve there's scarcely two who thrive
Into their latter years. We should with grace
Then look our best, put on a happy face,   230
Pass through this world however rough it be,
And manage our affairs in privacy
Until we're dead—or else as pilgrims go
Somewhere to get away from folks we owe.
To keep right up-to-date, then, is for me,   235
In this strange world, a great necessity;
We merchants have to keep a cautious eye
On chance and fortune as we sell and buy.
      "At dawn I head for Flanders, and I plan
To come back home as quickly as I can.   240
And therefore, my dear wife, I pray that you
Will gracious be to all, show meekness, too,
And take good care of all our property,
And govern well our house and honorably.
In every shape and form you'll have the stuff   245
That for a thrifty household is enough;
You'll lack no clothes or food of any sort,
The silver in your purse will not run short."
With that he shut the counting-house's door
And went downstairs, he didn't linger more.   250
A mass was said, a hasty celebration,
Then tables set without procrastination,
And they sat down at once to break the bread.
This monk was by this merchant richly fed.
      After dinner, Don John with gravity   255
This merchant took aside, and privately
He said to him, "My cousin, well I know,
The way things stand, to Bruges you have to go.
God and Saint Austin speed you there and guide!
I pray that wisely, cousin, you will ride;   260
Watch carefully your diet, when you eat
Be temperate, especially in this heat—
No need that we be formal, as if strangers.
Farewell, my cousin, God shield you from dangers!
And if there's anything by day or night,   265
If it lies in my power and my might,

That you would have me do in any way,
It shall be done exactly as you say.
   "One thing before you go, if it may be,
I'd ask of you: that you might lend to me 270
A hundred francs for just a week or so,
For certain beasts I have to buy, to go
And stock a place that's one we now possess.
So help me God, would it were yours, no less!
I will not fail when time comes to repay, 275
Not for a thousand francs would I delay.
But let's keep this a secret if we might,
For I must buy these beasts this very night.
Farewell, my cousin, one to me so dear,
And thanks for all the entertainment here." 280
   This noble merchant then with courtesy
Replied at once: "My cousin, truthfully
It is a small request, Don John, you make.
My gold is yours; when you desire to, take
Not just my gold but any merchandise 285
You wish, and God forbid you minimize.
   "One thing, though, you know well enough by now
About us merchants: money is our plow.
We may have credit while we have good names,
But being goldless is no fun-and-games. 290
Repayment of the loan is at your leisure;
Within my means I'm gladly at your pleasure."
   He fetched the hundred francs immediately
And took them to Don John in secrecy;
No one in all the world knew of the loan 295
Except this merchant and Don John alone.
They drank and talked, they roamed awhile, disported,
Till to his abbey John again reported.
   The next day dawned, the merchant left to ride
For Flanders. Well his prentice served as guide 300
And into Bruges he brought him merrily.
This merchant now went fast and busily
About his needs, he borrowed and he bought.
To dancing, playing dice, he gave no thought,
For like a merchant, briefly I will say, 305

Is how he lives, and there I'll let him stay.
   On that next Sunday, with the merchant gone,
To Saint Denis has come again Don John,
With cleancut crown, his beard fresh from a shave.
In all the house there was no boy or knave   310
Or anyone who wasn't glad to see
Don John had come again. But now that we
Might to the point go quickly pressing on,
This fair wife made agreement with Don John
That for the hundred francs he have the right   315
To take her in his arms for all the night,
Which deed was then performed for all its worth.
That night they led a merry life, in mirth,
Till it was light, when Don John went his way
And bade the household "Farewell" and "Good day."   320
None there and none in town had any call
To be suspicious of Don John at all.
So forth he rode home to his abbey, or
To where he wished, of him I'll say no more.
   After the fair, back home to Saint Denis   325
The merchant went, and there his wife and he
Made merry with a feast. He told her, since
He'd bought his merchandise at such expense,
He had to get a loan and right away,
For he was bound in writing to repay   330
Some twenty thousand ecus that he owed.
And so this merchant off to Paris rode
To borrow francs from certain friends he had;
He brought some francs along but hoped to add.
When he arrived in town, he first of all,   335
Because of great affection, went to call
Upon Don John, to have a little sport;
It wasn't for a loan of any sort
But just to find out how his friend was doing
And tell him of the deals he'd been pursuing,   340
As friends will do when they are met. With zest
A merry time Don John showed to his guest,
Who told him once again especially
How well he'd purchased and how favorably,

Thanks be to God, all of his merchandise— 345
Except that he must, in whatever wise,
Arrange a loan the best way that he could,
In joy then to relax the way he should.
  Don John replied, "I'm glad, most certainly,
That you've come home as whole as you can be. 350
If I were rich, as I may hope for bliss,
Those twenty thousand you would never miss;
For you so kindly, just the other day,
Lent gold to me—and as I can and may,
I thank you, by Saint James and in God's name. 355
But I've already paid back to our dame,
Your wife at home, that same gold, every bit
Upon your bench. She's well aware of it,
By certain tokens of which I can tell.
Now, by your leave, on this I cannot dwell; 360
Our abbot's leaving town right presently
And I must go along in company.
Greet well our dame, that niece of mine so sweet,
And farewell, my dear cousin, till we meet."
  This merchant, who was wise and wary, when 365
He had obtained his credit, handed then
To certain Lombards there the quantity
Of gold required to pay his debt. Then he
Went home as merry as a popinjay,
For well he knew things stood in such a way 370
That gain would be his journey's consequence,
A thousand francs above all his expense.
  His wife was ready, met him at the gate
Where always she would go to greet her mate;
All night they spent in mirth, without a fret, 375
For he was rich and clearly out of debt.
When it was day he started to embrace
His wife again, he kissed her on the face,
Then up he went and really showed his stuff.
  "No more," she said, "by God, you've had enough!" 380
Then wantonly again with him she played,
Till he at last these comments to her made:
"By God, I must say I'm a bit upset

With you, my wife, although to my regret.
Do you know why? By God, it's that I guess   385
You have created something of a mess
Between me and my relative Don John.
You should have cautioned me before I'd gone
That he had paid, with ready evidence,
A hundred francs; the fellow took offense   390
When I spoke of my need to borrow money—
Or so it seemed, he looked a little funny.
But nonetheless, by God, high heaven's King,
My thought was not to ask him for a thing.
No more of such from now on, wife, I pray;   395
Always tell me before I go away
If any debtor has in my absence
Paid you, lest I should through your negligence
Request of him a thing that he has paid."

    This wife was neither fretful nor afraid   400
But right away replied to him with spunk:
"Sweet Mary, I defy Don John, false monk!
For all his proofs I do not care a whit.
He brought some gold, I'm well aware of it.
May bad luck hit that monk right in the snout!   405
For, as God knows, I thought without a doubt
You were the reason he gave it to me,
That it was for my use, my dignity,
Because of kinship and the friendly cheer
That he so often has enjoyed here.   410
But as I see I got things out of joint,
I'll answer you in short, right to the point:
You have much slacker debtors, sir, than me!
For I will pay you well and readily
Each day. And if I fail or dilly-dally,   415
I am your wife: score it upon my tally
And I shall pay as quickly as I may.
For by my oath, it was for my array,
And not for waste, that I spent every bit;
So you can see I made good use of it,   420
All for your honor. For God's sake, I say,
Do not be angry, let us laugh and play.

You've got my jolly body pledged instead;
By God, the way I'll pay you is in bed.
So let me be forgiven, husband dear;   425
Turn here to me and show some better cheer."
   This merchant saw there was no remedy
And that to chide would only folly be,
There was no way the deed they might undo.
"Wife, I'll forgive," he said, "I'll pardon you;   430
But, on your life, no more so free a hand,
Take more care of my goods, that's my command."
And so my tale is ended. May God send
Tallies enough to our lives' very end. Amen.

Merry words of the Host to the Skipper and the Lady Prioress

   "Well said, by *corpus dominus!*" said our Host.   435
"Now long may you sail up and down the coast,
My good sir, gentle mariner and master!
God give the monk a thousand years' disaster!
Ha, ha! My friends, beware of such a jape!
The monk put in the fellow's hood an ape,   440
And, by Saint Austin, in his wife's as well.
   "But now pass over, let us look about
And see who shall be first of all the rout
To tell another tale." Then he displayed   445
Such courtesy it would become a maid,
As he said, "Lady Prioress, by your leave,
Provided that I not cause you to grieve,
I'd make the judgment that it's you who should
Be next to tell a tale, if that you would.   450
Would you so grace us now, my lady dear?"
   "Gladly," said she, and spoke as you will hear.

The Prioress's Tale

PROLOGUE

Domine dominus noster

"O Lord our Lord, how marvelous thy name,
Spread so afar through this wide world," said she.
"Thy precious praise not only they proclaim   455
Who are among good men of dignity,
But from the mouths of babes thy charity
Is praised as well. Babes sucking at the breast
May often show their praises like the rest.

"Wherefore as best I can or may, in praise   460
Of thee and of that whitest lily flower
Who gave thee birth and is a maiden always,
To tell a tale I'll labor in this hour—
Increasing not her honor by my power,
For she herself is honor, root and palm   465
Of bounty (next to Christ), and our souls' balm.

"O mother Maiden, maiden Mother free!
O bush unburnt, burning in Moses' sight,
Thou who drew down, through thy humility,
The Spirit from the Godhead, to alight   470
In thee, conceiving, as thy heart grew bright,
The Wisdom of the Father—now this story
Help me to tell, related for thy glory!

"Lady, thy goodness, thy magnificence,
Thy power, and thy great humility   475
No tongue may yet express with competence;
For sometimes, Lady, ere men pray to thee,
Thou goest before in thy benignity,
Securing for us through thy orison

The light to guide us to thy precious Son. 480

"O blissful Queen, my learning is too weak
To be declaring thy great worthiness;
I cannot bear such burden, I would speak
As does a child who's twelve months old or less,
One who can scarcely any word express. 485
That's how I fare, and therefore hear my plea
To guide my song that I shall sing of thee."

THE PRIORESS'S TALE

A great city of Asia once contained,
Amid the Christians in majority,
A Jewry that a local lord maintained 490
For venal lucre, foulest usury,
Hateful to Christ and to his company;
And through its street all men might ride or wend,
For open was this Jewry's either end.

A little Christian school stood by this place 495
Down at the farther end, to which would go
Many a child of Christian blood and grace.
There they would learn, as yearly they would grow,
Such things as in that land were good to know—
That is, they learnt to sing and read, as all 500
Such children learn to do when they are small.

Among these children was a widow's son,
A little scholar seven years of age,
Whose daily wont was to this school to run;
And if he chanced to see at any stage 505
An image of Christ's mother, he'd engage
In that which he was taught: he'd kneel and say
His *Ave Maria* ere he went his way.

Thus was the youngster by this widow taught
Our dear and blissful Lady to revere; 510

And so he kept her near to him in thought—
A guiltless child learns quickly, seeing clear.
(Always when I recall this matter, dear
Saint Nicholas stands ever in my presence,
So young he was to do Christ reverence.)   515

And while his book this child was studying
As he sat with his primer in the hall,
Alma redemptoris he heard them sing,
As children learn from the antiphonal;
Nearer and nearer he would draw, that all   520
The words he might then hear, and every note,
Until the first verse he had learnt by rote.

He didn't know what all this Latin meant,
For in his tender years he was too young;
One day he begged a friend there to consent   525
To tell to him this song in his own tongue,
Or tell him why this song so much was sung;
That he might so instruct him was his plea
Many a time on bare and bended knee.

His friend (older than he) said to him thus: 530
"This song was written, so I've heard them say,
For our dear Lady, blissful, generous,
To praise her, and that she be (as we pray)
Our help and succor when we pass away.
I can no more expound, I'd only stammer;   535
I've learnt the song but still know little grammar."

"Then is this song composed in reverence
For our Lord's mother?" asked this innocent.
"Now certainly I'll learn with diligence
The entirety ere Christmastide is spent.   540
Though from my primer I shall thus relent
And get three beatings in one hour, I
Shall learn it all, to honor her on high!"

His friend taught him in secret after school

From day to day till he knew it by rote;   545
He boldly sang, and well by any rule,
He knew it word for word and note for note;
And twice a day it wafted from his throat
When off to school and homeward he would start.
On Christ's dear mother he had set his heart.   550

This little child, as you have heard me say,
As through the Jewry he went to and fro,
Would merrily be singing every day
O Alma redemptoris as he'd go,
The sweetness of Christ's mother piercing so   555
His heart that, praying to her his intent,
He couldn't keep from singing as he went.

That serpent known as Satan, our first foe,
Who has his wasp's nest in the Jewish heart,
Swelled up and said, "O Hebrew people! Woe!   560
Is this a thing of honor for your part,
That such a boy should walk at will, and start
To sing out as he's walking such offense
To spite you, for your laws no reverence?"

Thenceforth the Jews proceeded to conspire,   565
Out of this world this innocent to chase;
They found themselves a murderer for hire,
Who in an alley took his hidden place;
And as the child passed at his daily pace,
This cursed Jew grabbed hold of him and slit   570
His throat, and cast him down into a pit.

Into a privy place, I say, they threw
Him, where these Jews would purge their bowels. Wail,
O cursed Herod's followers anew!
Your ill intent shall be of what avail?   575
Murder will out, for sure, it will not fail;
That God's honor increase, and men may heed,
The blood cries out upon your cursed deed.

"O martyr, ever in virginity,
Now may you sing and follow ever on   580
The Lamb white and celestial," said she,
"Of whom the great evangelist Saint John
In Patmos wrote. He said that those who've gone
Before this Lamb and sing a song that's new
Are those who never carnally women knew."   585

This poor widow awaited all that night
Her little child, but waited all for naught;
When morning came, as soon as it was light,
Her face grown pale with dread and worried thought,
At school and elsewhere then her child she sought;   590
She'd finally learn, when she'd gone far and wide,
That in the Jewry he'd last been espied.

With mother's pity in her breast enclosed,
She went as if halfway out of her mind
To every single place where she supposed   595
It likely that her child there she might find;
And ever to Christ's mother meek and kind
She cried. At last, completely overwrought,
Among the cursed Jews her child she sought.

She piteously inquired, she prayerfully   600
Asked every Jew who dwelt within the place
To tell her if her child they'd chanced to see.
They answered, "Nay." But Jesus by his grace
Put in her mind, after a little space,
To cry out for her son, and where she cried   605
The pit wherein he lay was near beside.

O God so great, so praised in many a hymn
By mouths of innocents, behold thy might!
This emerald, of chastity the gem,
Of martyrdom as well the ruby bright,   610
With throat cut, facing up toward the light,
The *Alma redemptoris* began to sing
So loudly that the place began to ring.

The Christian folk who through that Jewry went
Came by and stopped to wonder at this thing,   615
And for the provost hastily they sent.
He came without the slightest tarrying,
With praise for Christ who is of heaven King,
And for his mother, honor of mankind;
And after that the Jews he had them bind.   620

This little child with piteous lamentation
Was taken up while still he sang. They had
A great procession then, its destination
The nearest abbey. By his bier his sad
And swooning mother lay to mourn the lad,   625
And scarcely when they had to interfere
Could they move this new Rachel from his bier.

To pain and shameful death this provost sent
Each of the Jews known to participate
In knowledge of the crime. They early went,   630
For no such cursedness he'd tolerate;
What evil shall deserve is evil's fate.
He had them drawn by horses, then he saw
That they be hanged according to the law.

Upon his bier still lay this innocent   635
Before the altar while the mass progressed.
After that, the abbot with his convent
Made haste that they might lay the child to rest;
With holy water by them he was blest—
Yet spoke the child, when sprayed with holy water,   640
And sang *O Alma redemptoris mater.*

This abbot, who was such a holy man
As all monks are (or so they ought to be),
To conjure this young innocent began:
"Dear child, I'm now entreating you," said he,   645
"By power of the holy Trinity,
To tell me by what cause you sing, for it
Would surely seem to me your throat is slit."

"My throat's cut to my neckbone," then replied
The child, "a wound that is of such a kind   650
That long ago indeed I should have died.
But Jesus Christ, as in books you will find,
Wills that his glory last and be in mind;
And for the worship of his mother dear,
Yet may I sing *O Alma* loud and clear.   655

"This well of mercy, Christ's sweet mother, I
Have always loved as best as I know how;
And when I was to forfeit life and die,
She came to me and bade me give a vow
To sing this anthem when I die (as now   660
You have already heard). When I had sung,
I thought she laid a grain upon my tongue.

"Wherefore I sing, and sing I shall again,
In honor of that blissful maiden free,
Till from my tongue they take away the grain.   665
For afterwards here's what she said to me:
'My little child, I'll fetch you, as you'll see,
When that same grain has from your tongue been taken.
Be not afraid, you will not be forsaken.' "

This holy monk (the abbot's whom I mean)   670
Pulled out the tongue and took away the grain:
The child gave up the ghost, soft and serene.
And when he saw this wonder so obtain,
With salty tears that trickled down like rain
He, groveling, fell flat upon the ground   675
And stilly lay there, as if he were bound.

Upon the pavement, too, the whole convent
Lay weeping, and they praised Christ's mother dear;
And afterwards they rose and forth they went
And took away this martyr from his bier;   680
Inside a tomb of stone, of marble clear,
They put away his body small and sweet.
There he remains. God grant we all shall meet!

O youthful Hugh of Lincoln, slain also
By cursed Jews, as is so widely known   685
(As it was but a little while ago),
Pray for us too (in sin we've wayward grown),
That gracious God, in mercy from his throne,
Increase his grace upon us as we tarry,
For reverence of his sweet mother Mary. Amen.   690

Sir Topaz

PROLOGUE

Merry Words of the Host to Chaucer

This miracle, when told, made every man
So sober that it was a sight to see—
Until our Host to joke with us began,
Then for the first time took a look at me.
"And may I ask, what man are you?" said he.   695
"You look as if you think to find a hare,
For always at the ground I see you stare.

"Come closer now, and look up merrily—
Attention, sirs, and let this man have place!
About the waist he's shaped as well as me.   700
Now he'd be quite a doll for the embrace
Of any woman small and fair of face.
He seems so baffling by his countenance,
Disporting with no one in any sense.

"Say something now, as other folks have done;   705
Tell us a mirthful tale, and promptly so."
"Sir Host," said I, "don't let me spoil your fun,
For now of other tales naught do I know
But for a rhyme that I learnt long ago."
"That's good enough," said he, "now shall we glean   710
Some worthy thing, if I judge by his mien."

SIR TOPAZ

THE FIRST FIT

Listen, lords, with good intent,
I'll truly tell of merriment,
   A pleasant story, as
It's of a knight, a worthy gent   715
In battle and in tournament,
   His name was Sir Topaz.

Where he was born lies distantly
In Flanders far beyond the sea,
   Poperinghe was the place;   720
So noble was his father, free,
And lord of all that land was he,
   As it was God's good grace.

Sir Topaz grew, a doughty swain;
His face was bread-white, yet again   725
   His lips red as a rose;
His hue was scarlet dyed in grain,
And I can say as sure as rain
   He had a seemly nose.

Like saffron were his beard and crown   730
With hair that to his belt hung down,
   His shoes were hide of Spain;
His hose of Bruges were colored brown,
He wore a thinnish silken gown
   That cost him many a jane.   735

He'd hunt wild game such as the deer,
Along the river he'd appear
   With gray goshawk for hawking;
A perfect archer (pretty near),

At wrestling he had not a peer, 740
 Each ram he took a-walking.

And many a maiden, bright in bower,
Desired him—each impassioned hour
 She'd best have slept instead;
For he was chaste, for all his power, 745
And sweet as is the bramble flower
 That bears the hip so red.

It so befell upon a day,
To tell you truly as I may, 750
 Sir Topaz wished to ride;
He got upon his steed of gray
With lance in hand and rode away,
 A long sword by his side.

He'd pricked his way before he ceased 755
Into a forest—many a beast
 Was there, both buck and hare;
And as he pricked both north and east,
He almost had, to say the least,
 A sorry bit of care.

There herbs of various sizes grew, 760
It had setwall and licorice too,
 And many a clove to offer,
And nutmeg like we put into
Our ale (whether it's old or new)
 Or lay up in the coffer. 765

The birds sang, I can truly say,
The sparrow-hawk and popinjay,
 A joy it was to hear;
The thrush as well sang out his lay,
The wood-pigeon upon the spray 770
 Was singing loud and clear.

Such lust in Sir Topaz had sprung

When he heard how the thrush had sung,
   He pricked as if insane;
His fair steed sweat, so sharply stung,   775
Till like a wet rag to be wrung,
   His sides one bloody stain.

Sir Topaz, too, tired from the chase,
From pricking round at such a pace
   With fierce heart so amazing;   780
So in the soft grass of the place
He lay, and gave his steed a space
   To rest and do his grazing.

"Saint Mary, bless me!" then said he.
"What ails this love that's binding me   785
   With head and heart so sore?
I dreamt through all the night, pardie,
An elf-queen would my lover be
   And sleep beneath my gore.

"An elf-queen surely I will love,   790
For in this world none's worthy of
   My love—no woman will I take
               In town;
All other women I forsake,
For to an elf-queen I'll betake,   795
   In dale and over down!"

His saddle he was quickly on,
Went pricking over stile and stone,
   An elf-queen for to see,
Till so far riding had he gone   800
That he found, in a land alone,
   The Fairyland, country
             So wild;
For in that land none of their own
Dared to go near this knight unknown,   805
   Neither wife nor child.

But then a giant came to vaunt,
One who was named Sir Elephant,
   A perilous man indeed;
He told him, "Child, by Termagaunt,   810
If you don't prick out of my haunt,
   At once I'll slay your steed
               With mace.
For here the queen of Fairyland,
With harp and pipe and all her band,   815
   Is dwelling in this place."

The child replied, "As I may thrive,
Tomorrow with you I will strive
   When I have all my gear,
And I am hoping, *par ma fay*,   820
That by this lance that I display
   You'll sorely suffer here;
             Your maw
I'll pierce in two, if that I may,
Before it's fully prime of day,   825
   You shall not win or draw."

Sir Topaz drew back quick and fast
As stones at him this giant cast
   With slingshot worth bewaring;
The child Sir Topaz from the scrape   830
Through grace of God made his escape,
   And through his own good bearing.

Now listen, lords, yet to my tale
That's merrier than a nightingale,
   I'll whisper up and down   835
How Sir Topaz, so trim and hale,
Now pricking over hill and dale
   Has come again to town.

His merry men commanded he
To make both game and melody,   840
   For he would have to fight

A giant whose heads numbered three,
All for the love and jollity
   Of one who shone so bright.

"Have come," he said, "the minstrelsy,   845
And jesters telling tales for me,
   While I arm as I must;
Romances that are royal,
Of pope as well as cardinal,
   Of love as well as lust."   850

They fetched him sweet fruit of the vine,
A bowl of mead came with the wine,
   And spicery for zest
Like gingerbread and cumin fine
And licorice, all to combine   855
   With sugar of the best.

He dressed as white as any seen
In linen that was fine and clean,
   Then breeches and a shirt;
A tunic next was his avail,   860
And over that a coat of mail
   To shield himself from hurt;

And over that a fine hauberk
That was all wrought of Jewish work,
   Strong-plated, too, at that;   865
And over that his coat of arms
So lily white, against the harms
   That he must then combat.

The shield he bore was gold and red,
Emblazoned on it a boar's head,   870
   A carbuncle beside;
And then he swore on ale and bread
How "that great giant shall be dead,
   Betide what shall betide!"

His jambeaux tough and leathery, 875
His sword's sheath was of ivory,
  His helmet brassy bright;
His saddle was made of whalebone,
His bridle like the sun that shone
  Or moon at brightest light. 880

Of finest cypress was his spear
(That bode of war, no peace was here),
  The head was sharply ground;
The steed he rode was dappled gray,
And it would amble on its way 885
  So gently all around
          The land.
Listen, my lords, for here's a fit,
And if you would have more of it
  I'll take it right in hand. 890

THE SECOND FIT

Now shut your mouth, for charity,
Sir knight as well as lady free,
  And listen to my spell;
Of battle and of chivalry
And lady's love, as you will see, 895
  At once to you I'll tell.

Men tell romances, strong and mild,
Both of Ypotis and Horn Child,
  Of Bevis and Sir Guy,
Of Lybeaus and Playndamour, 900
But Sir Topaz the flower wore
  Of royal chivalry.

His valiant steed he was astride,
Upon his way he seemed to glide
  Like sparks out of the flame; 905
As for his crest, it was a tower

In which was stuck a lily flower—
   God shield him, none to maim!

And so adventurous in his powers,
He slept in no house after hours   910
   But slept out in his hood;
His pillow was his helmet bright,
And his horse fed nearby at night
   On herbs both fine and good.

He drank spring water as withal   915
That knight did named Sir Perceval,
   So worthy in his wear,
Till on a day—

The Tale of Melibee

PROLOGUE

The Host stops Chaucer's Tale of Sir Topaz

"No more of this, for our Lord's dignity,"
Then said our Host, "for you are making me   920
So weary with your utter foolishness
That, as all-knowing God my soul may bless,
My ears are aching from your cruddy speech.
The devil take such rhyming, I beseech!
At best this is rhymed doggerel," said he.   925
    "Why so?" said I. "Why do you hinder me
More than you do another man although
I'm telling you the best rhyme that I know?"
    "By God," he said, "I'll tell you in a word:
Your wretched rhyming isn't worth a turd!   930
The only thing you're doing's wasting time.
Sir, in a word, no longer shall you rhyme;
Let's hear you tell us in another style
Of verse, or else in prose, something worthwhile,
In which there's mirth or doctrine anyhow."   935
    "Gladly," said I, "by God's sweet pain! I now
Will tell to you a little thing in prose—
One that you ought to like, as I suppose
(Or else you're very hard to please for sure),
A moral tale of virtue, one that's pure.   940
As it's been told at times in sundry wise
By sundry folks, allow me to advise
You first. You know that each Evangelist,
For all Christ's pains that for us he may list,
Won't tell each thing the way his fellow might;   945
But nonetheless their meaning's true and right
And all agree as to their stories' sense
Though in their telling there is difference;

Like some of them say more and some say less
When Jesus's sad passion they express   950
(I speak of Mark and Matthew, Luke and John),
Yet there's no doubt of what they're preaching on.
Therefore, my lords, you all I do beseech:
If you think that I vary in my speech
That way, and tell you proverbs that are more   955
Than any others you have heard before
(Compressed in this small treatise I select,
To give my subject matter more effect),
And find the same exact words I don't say
That you have heard some other time, I pray   960
Don't blame me. For in meaning you will find
That there's no difference of any kind
Between this merry tale I write and this
Small treatise on which it is based. Don't miss
One part, therefore, of what I have to say,   965
And let me tell you my whole tale, I pray."

THE TALE OF MELIBEE

A powerful and rich young man called Melibeus fathered by his wife
Prudence a daughter called Sophia.

One day it happened that he went into the fields for his amusement.
He left his wife and daughter at home where the doors were locked tight.
On seeing this, three of his old enemies set ladders to the walls of his
house and entered by the windows. **970** After beating his wife, they
injured his daughter with five deadly wounds (namely, in her feet, hands,
ears, nose, and mouth), and left her there for dead.

When Melibeus returned and saw all his misfortune, he began to
weep and cry, tearing his clothes like a madman.

His wife Prudence begged him as much as she dared to cease
weeping, but he began to cry and weep all the more. **975**

This noble wife Prudence remembered where Ovid, in his book *The
Remedy of Love*, says, "Only a fool would hinder a mother from weeping
over the death of her child until she has wept her fill; then a man should
do his best to comfort her with loving words and to pray her to cease
her weeping." So noble Prudence let her husband weep for a time, then

she took the opportunity to say, "Alas, my lord, why do you behave like a fool? **980** For truly it does not befit a wise man to show such sorrow. Your daughter, by the grace of God, shall recover. And even if she now were dead, you ought not to destroy yourself over her death. Seneca says, 'The wise man should not suffer too greatly over the death of his children, but certainly should endure it in patience as well as he awaits his own death.' " **985**

"What man should stop his weeping," Melibeus replied at once, "who has so great a cause to weep? Jesus Christ, our Lord himself, wept for the death of his friend Lazarus."

"Certainly I know," Prudence answered, "that moderate weeping is not forbidden to him who sorrows among friends in sorrow, rather he is permitted to weep. As the Apostle Paul writes to the Romans, 'A man shall rejoice with those who rejoice, and weep with those who weep.' But though moderate weeping is permitted, excessive weeping is not. **990** Moderation in weeping should be considered as we are taught by the doctrine of Seneca: 'When your friend is dead, let your eyes be neither too moist nor overly dry; though tears come to your eyes, don't let them fall. And when you have lost your friend, make an effort to get another; there is more wisdom in this than in weeping for your friend whom you've lost, for there's no use in that.' So if you would govern yourself wisely, put away sorrow from your heart. Remember what Jesus son of Sirach says: 'A man who is joyful and glad in heart flourishes with age, but truly a sorrowful heart dries his bones.' **995** He also says that sorrow in the heart slays many a man. Solomon says that just as moths harm woolen clothing and small worms harm the tree, so sorrow harms the heart. So it would become us to have patience as well in the death of our children as in the loss of our temporal goods. Remember patient Job. When he had lost his children and his temporal goods, and endured many a grave bodily affliction, he said, 'Our Lord has given it to me, our Lord has taken it from me; as our Lord has willed, so is it done; blessed be the name of the Lord!' " **1000**

"All your words," said Melibeus to Prudence, "are true and profitable. But truly this sorrow so painfully troubles my heart that I don't know what to do."

"Summon all your true friends and wise kinsmen," Prudence said. "Present to them your case, hear their counsel, and govern yourself according to their opinion. Solomon says, 'Work all things by counsel and you shall never repent.' "

So by Prudence's counsel Melibeus summoned a crowd of people including surgeons, physicians, old people and young, even some of his old enemies, apparently reconciled to his love and into his grace; **1005** there came also some of his neighbors who showed him respect more out of fear than of love (as it often happens), as well as a great many subtle flatterers and wise advocates learned in the law.

When these people were assembled, Melibeus sorrowfully revealed to them his case. He spoke as if bearing in his heart a cruel anger, as if ready for vengeance, wanting war to begin right away. He nevertheless asked for their counsel. **1010** A surgeon, by assent of those who were wise, arose and spoke accordingly.

"Sir," said he, "to surgeons belongs the duty to do our best for every person where we are retained, and to do no damage to our patients; so very often it happens that when two men have wounded each other, the same surgeon heals them both. So fomenting war and taking sides doesn't pertain to our art. But as for your daughter, though she is perilously wounded, we certainly shall devote ourselves so attentively day and night to her healing that with the grace of God she shall be whole and sound as soon as possible." **1015**

The physicians answered in almost the same way (but with a few more words), saying that "just as maladies are cured by their opposites, so shall men cure war by vengeance."

His neighbors full of enmity, his feigned friends who seemed reconciled, and his flatterers pretended to weep, and made this matter worse and more difficult by greatly praising Melibeus for his might, power, riches, and friends, disparaging the power of his enemies. They said straight out that he should immediately take vengeance on his foes and start the war. **1020**

Then a wise advocate arose by leave and counsel of others who were wise, and said, "Lords, it is a serious and solemn business for which we are here assembled, for the wrong and the wickedness that has been done, the great damage that could yet occur, and the great riches and power of both parties. It would be very dangerous, then, to make a mistake in this matter. **1025** So our advice, Melibeus, is this: above all take pains in so guarding yourself that you lack neither spy nor watchman to save you. After that we counsel you to set in your house a garrison sufficient to defend you and your house. But we certainly may not decide profitably in so short a time either to begin war or take vengeance. To decide this case we need leisure and time for deliberation. As the common proverb says, 'He who soon decides shall soon repent.' **1030** Men also say that that judge is wise who quickly understands a matter but judges with full deliberation; although all tarrying is annoying, when reasonable it is not to be reproved in judging or in taking vengeance. Our Lord Jesus Christ showed that by example: when the woman taken in adultery was brought into his presence to determine what should be done with her, he did not answer quickly, though he knew well himself what he would say, but deliberated and wrote twice on the ground. So we ask for deliberation, and by the grace of God we shall then counsel you what shall be profitable."

The young people were at once aroused, and the majority of that company noisily scorned this wise old man and said that **1035** just as men should strike while the iron is hot, so men should avenge their wrongs while they're fresh and new. They loudly cried, "War! war!"

Then one of the wise old men arose and raised his hand for quiet. "Lords," he said, "many a man cries 'War, war!' who knows very little what war amounts to. War at its beginning has so great, so large an entrance that anyone may enter when he likes and find war easily; the end, though, is certainly not easy to know. **1040** For truly once war has begun, many a child yet unborn shall die young because of that war, or in sorrow live and in wretchedness die. Before they start a war men must therefore have great counsel and deliberation." When this old man thought to support his discourse with reasons, most of the people began rising to interrupt and kept telling him to cut his words short. For truly he who preaches to those who don't wish to hear annoys them with his sermon. "Music at a time of mourning is disturbing," says Jesus son of Sirach, meaning that it does as much good to speak before people whom the speech disturbs as it does to sing before him who weeps. **1045** And when this wise man saw that he lacked an audience, ashamedly he sat down again. For Solomon says, "Where you have no audience, don't endeavor to speak." "I see well," said this wise man, "that the common proverb is true: 'You can't get good counsel when you need it.' "

Among his advisors Melibeus also had many people who counseled him one thing privately and the opposite in the hearing of all.

On hearing that the majority of his advisors agreed he should make war, Melibeus fully accepted their counsel. **1050** Then dame Prudence, seeing that her husband was preparing to avenge himself and make war, said humbly when she saw opportunity, "My lord, I beseech you as earnestly as I dare and can, do not be in too much of a hurry, and for goodness' sake listen to me. For Petrus Alphonsus says, 'Whoever does you right or wrong, do not hasten to repay it; then your friend will be patient and your enemy shall live in dread the longer.' 'He hastens well,' says the proverb, 'who wisely can wait.' There's no profit in wicked haste."

"I don't propose," said Melibeus to Prudence, "to work by your counsel for many reasons. Every man would certainly consider me a fool **1055** if because of your counseling I changed what has been arranged and confirmed by so many wise men. Secondly, I say that all women are wicked, there are none good among them. For 'out of a thousand men,' says Solomon, 'I found one good man, but certainly out of all women I've never found a good woman.' Also, if I governed myself by your counsel it would seem that I had given you the mastery over myself, and God forbid that it were so! For Jesus son of Sirach says that 'if the wife has mastery, she is contrary to her husband.' And Solomon says, 'Never in your life give any power over yourself to your wife, nor to your child, nor to your friend; for it is better that your children ask you for things that they need than that you see yourself in the hands of your children.' **1060** Also my counsel must sometimes be secret for a while; if I worked by your counsel that certainly wouldn't be possible. For it's written: 'The babbling of women can hide nothing except what they do not know.' And 'in bad advice,' the philosopher says, 'women outdo men.' For these reasons I must not follow your advice."

Dame Prudence with all grace and patience listened to this, then asked his permission to speak. "My lord," she said, "as for your first reason, it may easily be answered. For I say it's no folly to change plans when the affair is changed or seems different from what it was before. **1065** I say moreover that when you refrain for just cause from an undertaking you've sworn to carry out, men shouldn't therefore say that you've lied or forsworn. For the book says that 'the wise man does not lie when he changes his mind for the better.' Though your undertaking be set up and arranged by a great multitude of people, you need not accomplish that plan unless you like it. For the truth about things and the profit are found in a few people who are wise and full of reason, rather than in a great multitude where everyone cries and clatters what he likes. Truly such a multitude isn't dependable. As for the second reason, your saying that all women are wicked, you disparage, by your leave, all women that way, and 'he who disparages all,' says the book, 'displeases all.' **1070** And Seneca says that 'whoever would have wisdom shall disparage no man but shall willingly teach what he knows without presumption or pride; and he shouldn't be ashamed to learn things that he doesn't know and to inquire of folks lesser than himself.' And, sir, that there has been many a good woman may be easily proved. For certainly, sir, our Lord Jesus Christ would never have descended to be born of a woman if all women were wicked. And afterwards, for the great goodness in women, our Lord Jesus Christ, when he was risen from death to life, appeared to a woman sooner than to his apostles. **1075** Though Solomon said that he never found a good woman, it doesn't follow that all women are wicked. For though he didn't find a good woman, many another man has found many a woman good and true. Or perhaps Solomon meant that he found no woman in supreme goodness, only God alone, as he himself records in his gospel. For there is no creature so good that he doesn't lack something of the perfection of God his creator. **1080**

"You say as your third reason that if you govern yourself by my counsel, it would seem that you'd given me the mastery and the lordship over yourself. Sir, by your leave, it isn't so. If a man were to be counseled only by those who had lordship and mastery over him, men wouldn't be counseled very often. For truly a man who asks counsel about a proposal still has free choice whether to work by that counsel or not. And as for your fourth reason, your saying that the gossip of women can't hide things they know, who says that a woman cannot hide what she knows? Sir, these words are understood regarding women who are talkative and wicked. **1085** Men say of such women that three things drive a man out of his house—that's to say, smoke, dripping rain, and wicked wives—and of such women Solomon says that 'it is better to dwell in the desert than with a woman who is wanton.' And, sir, by your leave, that isn't me; for you have tested very often my great silence and patience and how well I hide and conceal things that men ought secretly to hide. And God knows that your fifth reason, where you say that women surpass men in wicked counsel, is of no avail here. **1090** For understand now, you ask counsel to do wickedness; if you would work that wickedness, and your wife restrains that wicked purpose and dissuades you by reason and good counsel, your wife certainly ought to be praised rather than blamed. That's how you should understand the philosopher who says, 'In wicked counsel women surpass their husbands.' Whereas you blame all women and their reasons, I'll show you by many examples that many a woman has been quite good and many still are, their counsels very beneficial and profitable. **1095** Some men also have said that women's counsel is either too dear or of too little value. But though many a woman is bad and her counsel vile and worthless, men have found many a good woman, both discreet and wise in counsel. Consider Jacob, who by the good counsel of his mother Rebecca won his father Isaac's blessing, and lordship over all his brothers. Judith by her good counsel delivered the city of Bethulia, where she dwelt, from the hands of Holofernes, who had besieged it and would have destroyed it. Abigail delivered her husband Nabal from King David who would have slain him, and appeased the king's wrath by her intelligence and good counsel. **1100** Esther by her good counsel greatly enhanced the fortune of God's people in the reign of King Ahasureus. Men may tell of the excellence of many a good woman in good counseling. Moreover our Lord, when he had created our first father Adam, said, 'It is not good for man to be alone; let us make for him a helper similar to himself.' Here you may see that if women were not good and their counsels not good and profitable, **1105** our Lord God of heaven would never have made them nor called them man's helper but rather man's ruin. And a clerk once said in two verses, 'What is better than gold? Jasper. What is better than jasper? Wisdom. What is better than wisdom? Woman. And what is better than a good woman? Nothing.' And, sir, by many other reasons you may see that many women are good and their counsels good and profitable. So if you'll trust in my counsel, sir, I'll restore your daughter to you safe and sound, **1100** and do so much good for you that you shall have honor in this case."

When Melibeus had heard Prudence's words, he said, "I see well that the word of Solomon is true, that 'well ordered words spoken discreetly are like honeycombs, giving sweetness to the soul and health to the body.' And, wife, because of your sweet words, and because I have tried and tested your great wisdom and loyalty, I will govern myself by your counsel in all my affairs."

"Now, sir," said Prudence, "since you agree to be governed by my counsel, I'll inform you how you shall govern yourself in choosing your counselors. **1115** First, in all your actions you should meekly ask God on high to be your counselor, and dispose yourself to the end that he give you counsel and comfort, as Tobias taught his son: 'Bless God at all times, desire that he direct your ways, and make sure all your counsels remain true to him forever.' Saint James also says, 'If any of you want wisdom, ask of God.' Afterward you shall deliberate within yourself, examining well your thoughts concerning such things as you think best for your profit. **1120** And you shall drive from your heart three things that are contrary to good counsel: anger, covetousness, and undue haste.

"He who asks counsel of himself must be without anger for many reasons. First, he with great wrath inside always thinks that he can do something that he can't. Secondly, he who is angry may not judge well, **1125** and he who may not judge well may not counsel well. Thirdly, he who is wrathful, as Seneca says, may speak only reprehensible things, and with his vicious words stirs other people to wrath. Also, sir, you must drive covetousness out of your heart. For the Apostle says that covetousness is the root of all evils. **1130** And trust well that a covetous man cannot judge or think but only fulfill the end of his covetousness; and surely that can never be accomplished, for the more abundant his riches the more he desires. And, sir, you must also drive out of your heart undue haste; for certainly you may not judge for the best by sudden problems of the heart but must often think about them. As you've heard the common proverb, 'He who soon judges soon repents.' **1135** You aren't always, sir, in the same frame of mind: to be sure, something that sometimes seems good to do may at another time seem to you just the opposite.

"When you've taken counsel within yourself and decided by good deliberation what seems the best, I advise you to keep it a secret. Don't reveal your decision to anyone unless you feel assured that by confiding you'll profit more from your plan. **1140** For Jesus son of Sirach says, 'Neither to friend nor foe reveal your secret or wrongdoing, for they will listen and support you in your presence and scorn you in your absence.' 'You can scarcely find any person,' another clerk says, 'who can keep a secret counsel.' 'When you keep your counsel in your heart,' says the book, 'you keep it in your prison; when you divulge your counsel to anyone, he holds you in his snare.' **1145** So it's better to hide your counsel in your heart than to beseech him to whom you've divulged it to keep it secret. 'If you cannot keep your own counsel,' says Seneca, 'how dare you ask any other to keep it?' If you nevertheless feel assured that confiding your counsel to some person will improve your affairs, here's how you should tell him your counsel. First, have no expression suggesting whether you prefer peace or war or this or that; do not show him your will or intention. For trust well, these counselors are commonly flatterers, **1150** especially the counselors of great lords; they endeavor always to speak pleasant words, inclining to the lord's desire, rather than words that are true or profitable. Therefore men say that the rich man seldom has good counsel unless it's from himself.

"After that you shall consider your friends and enemies. Regarding your friends, you shall consider which of them are the most faithful, the wisest, the oldest, and the most approved in counseling, and you shall ask counsel of them as the case requires. **1155** I say that first you should summon to your counsel friends who are true. For Solomon says that 'just as a man's heart delights in sweet tastes, so the counsel of true friends gives sweetness to the soul.' He also says, 'Nothing may be compared to a true friend; neither gold nor silver is to be valued above a true friend's good will.' **1160** He also says that 'a faithful friend is a strong defense; he who has found him has found a great treasure.' You shall then consider if your true friends are discreet and wise. For the book says, 'Always ask counsel of a wise man.' By this same reasoning you should call to your counsel those friends who are old enough to have seen and become expert in many affairs and have been proven in counseling. For the book says that 'in the ancient is wisdom, and in length of days prudence.' And Tullius says that 'great things are not accomplished by strength or dexterity but by good counsel, authority, and knowledge, three things that are not enfeebled by age but grow stronger and increase day by day.' **1165**

"Then you shall keep this for a general rule: call first to your counsel a few friends who are esteemed; for Solomon says, 'May you have many friends, but let one out of a thousand be your counselor.' Although at first you tell your decision to only a few, you may tell more people afterward if needed. But make sure that your counselors have those three qualities of which I have spoken, namely, that they be true, wise, and mature in experience. And don't always act in every case by one counselor alone; sometimes it's necessary to be counseled by many. **1170** For Solomon says, 'There is safety where there is much counsel.'

"Now that I've told you by which people you should be counseled, I will teach you next whose counsel you ought to avoid. First you should avoid the counsel of fools; for Solomon says, 'Take no advice from a fool, for he can only advise according to his own pleasure and inclination.' 'The distinctive quality of a fool,' says the book, 'is that he's quick to see evil in everyone else and all goodness in himself.'

"Also avoid the counsel of flatterers, who try to praise you by flattery rather than tell you the truth. **1175** Thus Tullius says, 'The greatest of all curses in friendship is flattery.' So you need to stay away from flatterers more than any other people. 'You should sooner dread and flee from the sweet words of flattering praisers,' says the book, 'than from the sharp words of your friend who tells you the truth.' 'The words of a flatterer,' says Solomon, 'are a snare to catch the innocent.' He also says that 'he who speaks sweet and pleasant words to his friend sets before his feet a net to catch him.' Therefore Tullius says, 'Incline not your ears to flatterers, nor take counsel in flattering words.' **1180** And Cato says, 'Consider well and avoid sweet and pleasant words.'

"You should also avoid the counsel of your old enemies who are reconciled. The book says that 'no person returns safely into the grace of his old enemy.' And Aesop says, 'Do not trust him whom you've made war upon or held in enmity, nor tell him your counsel.' And Seneca says why: 'Don't suppose that where a great fire has burned there remains no trace of warmth.' **1185** Therefore Solomon says, 'Never trust an old foe.' Though your enemy is reconciled, assumes a humble expression, and bows his head to you, never trust him at all. His feigned humility is surely more for his own profit than for any love of you, for he thinks that by such a feigned appearance he'll have victory over you that he may not have by strife or war. And Peter Alphonsus says, 'Have no fellowship with your old enemies, for if you do good to them they'll pervert it to wickedness.' You must also avoid the counsel of your servants who bear you great reverence, for perhaps they say things more for dread than for love. **1190** As a philosopher says, 'No person is perfectly true to him whom he fears too greatly.' And Tullius says, 'There is no secret where drunkenness reigns.' You should also be suspicious of those who advise you one thing privately and the opposite publicly. **1195** For 'it is a kind of hindering trick,' says Cassiodorus, 'when a man seems to do one thing publicly and works the opposite privately.' You should also be suspicious of the counsel of wicked people. For the book says, 'Blessed is the man who has not walked in the counsel of scoundrels.' You shall also avoid the counsel of young people, for their counsel is not mature.

"Since I've shown you, sir, from which people you should take your counsel and whose counsel you should follow, **1200** I will now teach you how you should examine your counsel according to Tullius. In examining your counselor you should consider many things.

"First you shall see that the truth be stated and preserved concerning the purpose and point upon which you'd be counseled. In other words, state your case truthfully. For he who speaks falsely may not be well counseled in the matter in which he lies. You should then consider the matters that reasonably agree with what you purpose to do by your counselors, **1205** and whether your might may achieve it, and whether the greater and better part of your counselors are in accord. Then you shall consider what things may follow from that counsel, such as hate, peace, war, grace, profit, damage, and many other things. In all these affairs you should choose the best and reject all else. You shall then consider from what root the substance of your counsel is produced and what fruit it may conceive and generate. You should also consider all the causes from which these affairs originated. **1210**

"When you have examined your counsel as I've said, and considered which course is the better and more profitable, and have had it approved by many wise and mature people, you shall then consider whether you can perform it and bring it to a good conclusion. For surely it is not reasonable for any man to begin a matter unless he can carry it out as he ought, nor should anyone take upon himself so heavy a burden that he might not bear it. For the proverb says, 'He who tries to embrace too much retains very little.' **1215** And Cato says, 'Attempt only those things you can do, lest the burden so oppress you that you are forced to abandon what you started.' If you are in doubt whether you may carry something out, choose to wait patiently rather than begin it. And Peter Alphonsus says, 'If you have the power to do anything of which you might repent, it's better to think "no" than "yes." ' It's better, that is, for you to bite your tongue than speak. Then you may understand by stronger reasons why it's better to wait patiently than begin a work within your power that you shall repent. **1220** They say well that one should be forbidden to attempt anything if he has doubts about carrying it out. After you've examined your decision, as I've said before, and know well that you may carry out your plan, pursue it steadfastly to its conclusion.

"It's time now and reasonable to show you when and why you may change your counselors without reproach. Certainly a man may change his purpose and decision if the cause ceases to exist, or when a new situation occurs. For the law says that 'for things that newly occur, new counsel is needed.' **1225** And Seneca says, 'If your decision has come to the ears of your enemy, change your decision.' You may also change your decision if you find that evil or damage may occur through error or any other cause. Also, if your decision is dishonest, or comes from a dishonest cause, change your decision. For the law says that 'all promises that are dishonest are of no value,' as are those that are impossible to keep or can hardly be performed. **1230**

"Take this for a general rule: every decision that is established so strongly that it may not be changed under any possible circumstance, that decision, I say, is wicked."

Melibeus, when he had heard his wife's instructions, said, "Dame, now you have taught me well and suitably in general how I should govern myself in choosing and retaining my counselors. But now I'd be pleased if you would descend to particulars and tell me what you think of the counselors we've chosen in our present need." **1235**

"My lord," she said, "I beseech you in all humility that you not object to my remarks nor disturb your heart though I say things that displease you. For I intend, God knows, to speak for your good, for your honor, and for your profit as well. Truly I hope that in your benignity you will take it with patience. Trust me well that your decision in this matter should properly be called not a counsel but a foolish motion or movement, in which counsel you have erred in many a sundry way. **1240**

"Above all you have erred in the assembling of your counselors. You should have first called a few people to your counsel; you might have shown it to more afterward if there had been need. But for sure you called suddenly a great multitude, very burdensome, annoying to hear. You erred also by not calling to your counsel only your true, old, and wise friends; you have called strangers, young people, flatterers, reconciled enemies, and people who reverence you without love. **1245** You have erred also by bringing with you to your counsel anger, covetousness, and rashness, three things contrary to every honest and profitable counsel, three things you have not done away with either in yourself or in your counselors as you should. You have erred also by showing to your counselors your desire and inclination to make war right away and take vengeance. They have seen which way you lean by your words, **1250** and have therefore advised you rather for your desire than your profit. You have erred as well in that it seems enough to you to be advised by these counselors only, with little consultation, whereas more counselors and deliberation were needed for so great and grave an enterprise. You have erred as well by not examining your decision in the way I have said, nor in due measure, as the case requires. You have erred also by making no distinction between your counselors, that is, between your true friends and false counselors; **1255** nor have you known the will of your true, old, and wise friends. You have cast all their words in a hodgepodge and, inclining your heart to the majority, have agreed with the greater number. Since you well know that a greater number of fools can always be found than of wise men, and since these are the counsels in congregations and multitudes where men have more regard for the number than the wisdom of persons, you see well that in such counsels fools have the mastery." **1260**

Melibeus again answered, "I grant well that I have erred; but just as you've told me that he's not to blame who changes his counselors in certain situations and for just causes, I'm ready to change my counselors as you would advise. 'To sin is human,' so the proverb says, 'but to keep at it is the work of the devil.' "

Dame Prudence, in reply to this axiom, said, **1265** "Examine your counsel, let us see which of them have spoken most reasonably and counseled you best. And since examination is necessary, let's begin with the surgeons and physicians who spoke first. I tell you that the surgeons and physicians have spoken to you discreetly as they should, stating very wisely that a proper part of their duty is to do what is honorable and beneficial to all, to offend no one, and to use their skill diligently in the treatment of those in their care. **1270** And, sir, I advise that they be liberally and royally rewarded for their noble words wise and discreet, the more attentively to devote themselves to curing your dear daughter. Although they are your friends, you shouldn't allow them to serve you for nothing, you should show them your generosity and reward them. **1275** As for the proposition that the physicians promoted, namely that in maladies one contrary cures another, I'm eager to know your opinion, how you interpret that text."

"Certainly," said Melibeus, "here's how I understand it: just as they've done me a bad turn, I should do them another. **1280** As they avenged themselves on me and did me wrong, so shall I avenge myself on them and do them wrong; then have I cured one contrary by another."

"See," said Prudence, "how readily every man is inclined to his own desire and pleasure! Certainly the physicians' words should not be understood this way. To be sure, wickedness is not contrary to wickedness, nor vengeance to vengeance, nor wrong to wrong, rather they are similar. **1285** So one vengeance is not cured by another, nor one wrong by another, rather each one increases and aggravates the other. Here's how the physicians' words should certainly be understood: goodness and wickedness are two contraries, as are peace and war, vengeance and forbearance, discord and accord, and many other things. Surely wickedness shall be cured by goodness, discord by accord, war by peace, and so forth. **1290** With this Saint Paul the Apostle agrees in many places. 'Do not render evil for evil,' he says, 'nor wicked speech for wicked speech, but do good to them who do you evil and bless those who speak evil to you.' And in many other places he admonishes peace and accord.

"But now I will speak of the counsel given to you by the lawyers and the wise, **1295** who all agreed, as you have heard, that above all else you should diligently protect yourself and fortify your house; they also said that in this situation you should work prudently and with great deliberation.

"And, sir, as to the first point, concerning your protection, you should understand that he who is at war should continually pray meekly and devoutly, above all else, **1300** that Jesus Christ in his mercy will protect him and be his sovereign help in his need. For surely no one in this world may be counseled nor protected sufficiently without the protection of our Lord Jesus Christ. With this opinion the prophet David agrees, saying, 'If God doesn't keep the city, he watches in vain who keeps it.' Now your personal safety, sir, you should commit to your true friends, proven and known; **1305** you should ask them for help in safeguarding yourself. 'If you need help,' says Cato, 'ask a true friend, for there is no better physician.' Next you should keep away from all strangers and liars; be always suspicious of their fellowship. For Peter Alphonsus says, 'Don't keep company with a stranger along the road until you have known him a while. If he falls into your company by accident, without your consent, **1310** ask as subtly as you may about his life and livelihood. And conceal your route, say you're going where you aren't. And if he carries a spear, keep on his right side, on his left if he carries a sword.' Next you should wisely avoid all such people and their counsel as I have said before. Then you should be careful not to so despise your adversary, nor to consider his strength so little, that through any presumption of your own strength you neglect your self-defense; **1315** for every wise man dreads his enemy. 'Happy is he,' says Solomon, 'who has no dread at all, for surely evil shall befall him who through his own hearty rashness presumes too much.' Then you should continually watch out for ambushes and all manner of spies. For Seneca says that 'the wise man who dreads evils avoids evils, **1320** nor does he fall into perils who avoids perils.' Though it may seem you are in a safe place, always endeavor to protect yourself not only from your greatest enemies but from your least. 'A man who is prudent,' says Seneca, 'dreads his least enemy.' Ovid says that 'the little weasel will slay the great bull and wild hart.' **1325** And 'a little thorn,' says the book, 'may sorely prick a king, and a hound will hold the wild boar.' Now I don't say you should be so cowardly that you fear where there is no danger. The book says that 'some people greatly desire to deceive, but fear to be deceived.' Yet you shall fear being poisoned, and keep yourself from the company of scorners. 'Have no fellowship with scorners,' the book says, 'but flee their words as venom.' **1330**

"Now as to the second point, your wise counselors advising you to fortify your house with great diligence, I'd like to know your opinion, how you interpret those words."

"Certainly," Melibeus answered, "here's how I understand it: I should fortify my house with towers like a castle and with other kinds of structures, and with ballistic engines and other military equipment; then I and my house shall be so defended that my enemies shall not approach out of fear."

"Fortifying by great towers," Prudence answered at once, "and by other great structures is sometimes related to pride. **1335** Men also build, with much expense and labor, high towers and other great structures that are not worth a straw unless defended by true friends who are mature and wise. And understand well that the best protection that a rich man may have for himself and his goods is that he be loved by his subjects and neighbors. As Tullius says, 'There is a kind of protection no man may vanquish or overcome, and that's for a lord to be loved by his citizens and people.' **1340**

"Now, sir, as to the third point, your old and wise counselors saying you ought not suddenly nor hastily to proceed in this manner but rather should prepare with great diligence and deliberation, I believe they spoke wisely and truly. For Tullius says, 'Before beginning any endeavor, prepare yourself with great diligence.' So I counsel that before you begin to take vengeance in war, in battle, in fortification, **1345** you prepare with great deliberation. 'Long preparation before battle,' says Tullius, 'leads to quick victory.' And Cassiodorus says, 'The protection is stronger when long considered.'

"But now let's speak of the decision agreed to by your neighbors who show you honor without love, your old enemies reconciled, your flatterers **1350** who counseled you certain things privately and the opposite publicly, and the young people who advised you to avenge yourself and make war right away. And certainly, sir, as I've said, you greatly erred in calling such people to your counsel, counselors sufficiently reproached by the reasons mentioned.

"But nevertheless let's descend to the particular. You should first proceed according to the precepts of Tullius. **1355** It's certainly not necessary to inquire into the truth of the case, for it's well known who they are who have done you this trespass and injury, how many trespassers there are, and in what way they have done you all this wrong.

"You should then examine the second condition that Tullius adds. He calls it 'consistency,' meaning **1360** who are they, how many and what sort, who agreed with your decision to take rash vengeance. Let's also consider who they are and how many who were in accord with your adversaries. As to the first point, certainly it is well known who the people are who were in accord with your rash impetuosity; for truly all those who counseled you to make sudden war are not your friends. Let's consider now what they are like whom you cherish as your personal friends. **1365** For though you are mighty and rich, you are nevertheless alone. Certainly you have no child but a daughter, no brothers nor first cousins, nor any other close relatives, to keep your enemies fearful of disputing with you or destroying you. You know also that your riches must be variously divided, **1370** and when each person has his part they would give little regard to avenging your death. But your enemies are three, and they have many children, brothers, cousins, and other close relatives. Even if you were to slay two or three, enough would live to avenge their death and slay you. And though your relatives are more dependable and steadfast than those of your adversaries, your relatives are but distantly related; they are not blood relatives, **1375** while your enemies' relatives are close. In that, their situation is certainly better than yours.

"Then let's consider also whether the counsel of those who advised you to take sudden vengeance is in accord with reason. And you surely know well that it isn't. For by right and reason no vengeance may be taken on anyone except by the judge who has jurisdiction, when it's granted that he take whatever vengeance, violent or restrained, that the law requires. **1380**

"Moreover, regarding what Tullius calls 'consistency,' you should consider whether your might and power are sufficient and consistent with your impetuosity and counselors. And certainly you may well say that it isn't. For properly speaking, we surely may do only that which may be done justly. And certainly you may not justly take any vengeance by your own authority. **1385** Then you may see that your power is not consistent nor accordant with your impetuosity.

"Let's examine the third point, which Tullius calls 'consequence.' You should understand that the vengeance you intend to take is the consequence, and from that follows additional vengeance, peril, war, and other damages without number of which we are not yet aware.

"As for the fourth point, which Tullius calls 'engendering,' **1390** you should consider that this wrong done to you was engendered by your enemies' hate, and that avenging it would engender further vengeance, and much sorrow and wasting of riches, as I've said.

"Now, sir, as for what Tullius calls 'causes,' which is the last point, you should understand that the wrong you have received has certain causes, which clerks call *Oriens* and *Efficiens,* and *Causa longinqua* and *Causa propinqua*, meaning the ultimate cause and the immediate cause. **1395** The ultimate cause is almighty God who is the cause of all things. The immediate cause is your three enemies. The accidental cause was hate. The material cause is your daughters' five wounds. The formal cause was their manner of action, bringing ladders and climbing in at the windows. **1400** The final cause was to slay your daughter. They succeeded as far as they were able. But to speak of the ultimate cause, as to what end they should attain or what shall finally become of them in this situation, I cannot judge but by conjecture and supposition. We should suppose they shall come to a wicked end, because the Book of Decrees says, 'Seldom, or with great pain, are causes brought to a good end when they have been badly begun.'

"Now, sir, if men ask me why God allowed this injury to be done to you, I of course cannot give a good answer with certainty. **1405** For the Apostle says that 'the knowledge and judgments of our Lord God Almighty are very deep, where no man may comprehend or examine them sufficiently.' But by certain presumptions and conjectures I hold and believe that God, who is full of justice and righteousness, has allowed this to happen for just and reasonable cause.

"Your name is Melibeus, meaning 'a man who drinks honey.' **1410** You have drunk so much honey of sweet temporal riches, and delights and honors of this world, that you are drunk and have forgotten Jesus Christ your creator. You have not paid him such honor and reverence as you owe, nor have you heeded well the words of Ovid: 'Under the honey of bodily goods is hid the venom that slays the soul.' **1415** And

Solomon says, 'If you find honey, eat only a sufficient amount, for if you eat too much you will vomit' and be needy and poor. Perhaps Christ holds you in contempt, turning his face and ears of mercy away from you, and has allowed you to be punished in the manner in which you've trespassed. You have sinned against our Lord Christ, **1420** for certainly the three enemies of mankind, being the flesh, the devil, and the world, you have allowed to enter your heart willfully by the windows of the body, and you have not defended yourself sufficiently against their assaults and temptations, so that they have wounded your soul in five places. The deadly sins have entered your heart by your five senses. In the same way our Lord Christ has willed and permitted that your three enemies enter your house by the windows, **1425** and they wounded your daughter in the aforesaid manner."

"I see well," said Melibeus, "that you endeavor by many words to overcome me, so that I won't avenge myself against my enemies; you show me the perils and evils that might result from such vengeance. But anyone who considered all the perils and evils that might result would never take vengeance, and that would be a pity, **1430** for by taking vengeance are good men divided from the wicked, and they who have a will to do wickedness restrain their wicked purpose when they see trespassers chastised and punished."

"Certainly I grant you," said dame Prudence, "that from vengeance comes much good as well as evil; but vengeance belongs only to judges and those who have jurisdiction over evildoers. I say, moreover, that just as a private citizen sins in taking vengeance on another man, **1435** so a judge sins if he does not take vengeance on them who deserve it. For as Seneca says, 'That master is good who tries scoundrels.' And 'a man fears to act outrageously,' says Cassiodorus, 'when he knows it will displease the judges and sovereigns.' Another says, 'The judge who is afraid to do what is right turns men into scoundrels.' And Saint Paul the Apostle, in his Epistle to the Romans, says, 'Judges do not bear the spear without cause; **1440** they bear it to punish scoundrels and evildoers and to defend good men.' If you would take vengeance on your enemies, you should turn to the judge who has jurisdiction, and he shall punish them as the law asks and requires."

"Ah!" said Melibeus, "that kind of vengeance doesn't please me in the least. I am mindful of how Fortune has cherished me from my childhood and helped me through many a critical situation. **1445** I call upon her now, believing, with God's help, that she will help me avenge my shame."

"If you worked by my counsel," said Prudence, "you certainly wouldn't call upon Fortune in any way nor bend or bow to her. For 'things foolishly done with trust in Fortune,' says Seneca, 'shall never come to a good end.' He says also that 'the brighter and more shining Fortune is, the more brittle and sooner broken she is.' **1450** Don't trust in her, she's neither steadfast nor stable; when you trust her to be certain help, she will fail you and deceive you. And as Fortune, you say, has cherished you from childhood, I say that all the less you should trust in her and her wisdom. For Seneca says, 'Fortune makes a great fool of whomever she has cherished.' **1455**

"Now since you desire and ask vengeance, and that taken by law before the judge doesn't please you, and that taken with hope in Fortune is perilous and uncertain, you have no other remedy but to turn to the sovereign Judge who avenges all injuries and wrongs. And he shall avenge you as he himself witnesses, where he says, 'Leave vengeance to me and I shall inflict it.' " **1460**

Melibeus said, "If I don't avenge myself of the injuries men have done to me, I invite them and all others to injure me again. For it's written: 'If you take no vengeance for an old injury, you summon your adversaries to inflict a new one upon you.' For my sufferance men would inflict me with so many injuries that I might not endure it; I'd be brought low and held in contempt. **1465** For men say, 'In much suffering shall many things befall you that you won't be able to suffer.' "

"I grant you," said Prudence, "that much suffering is certainly not good. But it still doesn't follow that everyone injured by men should take vengeance; that should be left to the judges who alone shall avenge shameful actions and injuries. So the two authorities you quote are to be understood only with reference to judges. **1470** For when they are tolerant of wrongs and injuries, inflicted without punishment, they not only invite a man to do new wrongs but command it. A wise man says also that 'the judge who doesn't correct the sinner commands and bids him to sin.' Judges and sovereigns in their lands might so tolerate scoundrels and evildoers that in time they would grow powerful enough to throw out the judges and sovereigns, **1475** depriving them in the end of their lordships.

"But let's now suppose you were allowed to avenge yourself. I say you are not powerful enough to avenge yourself now; if you would compare your might with that of your adversaries, you would find that in many ways, as I've shown you, their condition is better than yours. So I say that it's good that you submit and be patient for now. **1480**

"Furthermore, you know well the common saying that it's madness for a man to contend with someone stronger than he is; to strive with a man of equal strength is perilous; and to contend with a weaker man is folly. So a man should avoid contending as much as possible. For as Solomon says, 'It is a great honor for a man to keep himself from contention and strife.' **1485** If a man mightier than you does you injury, study how to allay the injury, and get busy with that rather than with avenging yourself. For 'he subjects himself to great peril,' says Seneca, 'who contends with a man greater than he is.' And Cato says, 'If a man of higher estate or degree or mightier than you causes you any trouble or injury, endure it; for he who has once injured you may at another time help you.' **1490**

"Again, suppose you have both the might and permission to avenge yourself. There are many things, I say, that should restrain you from taking vengeance and incline you to be patient and endure the wrongs done to you.

"First and foremost, if you please, consider your defects, for which God, as I've told you, has allowed you to have this tribulation. **1495** For the poet says that 'we ought to take patiently the tribulations that come to us when we consider how we deserve them.' And Saint Gregory says that 'when a man considers well the number of his defects and sins, the pains and tribulations that he suffers will seem less to him; and the heavier and more grievous he considers his sins, the lighter and easier will seem his pains.' **1500** You should also incline your heart to adopt the patience of our Lord Jesus Christ, as Saint Peter says in his Epistles. 'Jesus Christ,' he says, 'has suffered for us and given an example for every man to follow in imitation; for he never sinned, nor did a villainous word ever isue from his mouth. He did not curse men who cursed him, nor did he threaten those who beat him.' Likewise the great patience that the saints in Paradise had, suffering tribulations though guiltless, **1505** should greatly inspire you to patience. You should also endeavor to be patient considering that the tribulations of this world last but a little while, they are soon past and gone, while the joy that a man seeks to gain by patience in tribulations is everlasting, according to what the Apostle says in his Epistle. 'The joy of God,' he says, 'is eternal,' that is, everlasting. **1510** Also trust and believe steadfastly that he is not well brought up, not well taught, who cannot be patient. For Solomon says that 'a man's learning and wisdom is seen in his patience.' And in another place he says that 'he who is patient governs himself by great prudence.' And again, 'An angry man causes brawls, the patient man quiets others.' He says as well, 'It is more valuable to be patient than to have great strength, 1515 and he who has lordship over his own heart is more praiseworthy than he who by force or strength takes great cities.' And therefore Saint James says in his Epistle that 'patience is a great virtue of perfection.' "

"I certainly grant you, dame Prudence," said Melibeus, "that patience is a great virtue of perfection: but every man may not have the perfection that you seek, nor am I of that number of truly perfect men, 1520 for my heart may never be at peace until the time it is avenged. Though my enemies faced a great peril in injuring me, taking vengeance upon me, they took no heed of the peril but fulfilled their wicked desire. So I think men shouldn't reproach me though I face a little peril to avenge myself and though I go to great excess by avenging one outrage by another." 1525

"Ah," said Prudence, "you state your will as you like, but there's not a case in the world in which a man should use violence or perform an outrageous act to avenge himself. As Cassiodorus says, 'He who avenges himself by violence does as much evil as he who did the violent deed.' You should therefore avenge yourself according to justice, that is, by the law, not by outrageous acts and violent deeds. Also, if you take vengeance for your enemies' violence in a way other than that commanded by justice, you sin. 1530 Therefore Seneca says that 'a man shall never avenge evil by evil.' If you say that justice requires a man to protect himself against violence with violence, and against fighting with fighting, you are certainly right when such defense is immediate—no interval, tarrying, or delay—to protect, not avenge, oneself. It's proper that one be moderate enough in such defense 1535 that other men have no cause or reason to reproach him for defending himself against violence and outrageous acts, for otherwise it would be unreasonable. You know perfectly well that the defense you now make is to avenge, not protect, yourself, so it follows that you have no desire to perform the deed moderately. I therefore think patience is good, for Solomon says that 'he who is impatient shall have great injury.' "

"I certainly grant," said Melibeus, "that when a man is impatient and angry in a matter that doesn't concern him, it's no wonder when it harms him. **1540** For 'he is guilty,' says the law, 'who interferes or meddles in things that don't concern him.' And Solomon says that 'he who interferes with another man's quarrel or strife is like him who takes a dog by the ears.' For just as he who takes a strange dog by the ears is sometimes bitten, it's reasonable that he should be injured who through impatience meddles in another man's affairs that don't concern him. But you well know that this deed—my injury and my misfortune—involves me very closely. **1545** So although I am angry and impatient, it's no wonder. And, saving your grace, I can't see that it might greatly harm me if I should take vengeance. For I'm richer and more powerful than my enemies; and you know well that all this world's affairs are governed by money and great possessions. As Solomon says, 'All things money obey.' "**1550**

Prudence, when she had heard her husband boast of his wealth and disparage his adversaries' power, said, "Certainly, dear sir, I grant that you're rich and mighty, and that riches are good for those who have properly acquired them and can use them well. For just as a man's body may not live without his soul, it may not live without temporal goods either. And by riches a man may acquire great friends. **1555** Therefore Pamphilus says, 'If a cowherd's daughter be rich, she may choose from a thousand men which one she would take for her husband; for of a thousand men, not one would forsake or refuse her.' And Pamphilus says as well, 'If you are very happy—that is, very rich—you shall find a great number of comrades and friends. And if your fortune change so that you become poor, farewell friendship and fellowship, for you shall be alone, except for the company of poor people.' **1560** Pamphilus says, moreover, that 'they who are enslaved and in bondage by birth shall be made worthy and noble by riches.'

"And just as by riches there come many goods, so by poverty come many harms and evils. For great poverty forces a man to do many evil things. Thus Cassiodorus calls poverty the mother of ruin, that is, the mother of destruction and misfortune. **1565** And Peter Alphonsus says, 'One of the greatest adversities of this world is when a man, free by nature or gentle birth, is forced by poverty to live on the charity of his enemy.' And Innocent III says the same in one of his books. He says that 'sorrowful and unhappy is a poor beggar's condition; if he does not beg for food, he dies of hunger; and if he begs, he dies of shame. In any case necessity forces him to beg.' **1570** And Solomon says that 'it is better to die than to have such poverty.' And so 'it is better,' he says, 'to die a bitter death than to live in want.' For the reasons I've told you and many others I could say, I grant you that riches are good for those who have properly acquired them and for those who use them well. I will therefore show you how you should conduct yourself in the gathering of riches, and in what manner you should use them. **1575**

"First, you should acquire them without great desire, with full deliberation, gradually and not too quickly. For a man who is too desirous abandons himself first to theft and to all other evils; thus Solomon says, 'He who hastens too intently to become rich shall not be innocent.' He says as well that 'the riches that quickly come to a man soon and easily go, but the riches that come little by little keep increasing.' **1580**

"And, sir, you should acquire riches by your intelligence and labor for your profit, without doing wrong or harm to any other person. For the law says that 'no man makes himself rich who harms another person.' This is to say that nature forbids by right that any man make himself rich at the expense of another person. As Tullius says, 'No sorrow nor dread of death nor anything else that may befall a man **1585** is so much againt nature as a man's increasing his own profit at the expense of another.

" 'And though the great and mighty men acquire riches more easily than you, you shouldn't be idle or slothful in pursuit of profit, for you should in every way flee idleness.' For Solomon says that 'idleness teaches a man much evil.' And Solomon says as well that 'he who labors and busies himself to till his land shall eat bread, **1590** but he who is idle and devotes himself to no business or occupation shall fall into poverty and die of hunger.' And he who is idle and slothful can never find a suitable time to make his profit. For there is a poet who says that 'the idle man excuses himself in winter on account of the great cold, and in summer by reason of the great heat.' For these reasons Cato says, 'Stay awake and don't be too disposed to sleep, for too much rest nourishes and causes many vices.' And Saint Jerome says, 'Do some good deeds, that the devil who is your enemy should not find you unoccupied.' **1595** For the devil doesn't easily take into his service those he finds occupied in good works.

"In acquiring riches, then, you must flee idleness. Afterward, you should use the riches you have acquired by your intelligence and labor in such a way that men won't consider you too stingy or sparing or too wasteful, that is, too liberal in spending. For just as an avaricious man is blamed for being stingy and miserly, **1600** so he is blamed who spends too liberally. Thus Cato says, 'Use the riches that you have acquired in such a way that men won't have reason to call you a niggard or miser; for it's a great shame to have a paltry heart and rich purse.' He also says, 'The goods that you have acquired, use in moderation.' **1605** For they who foolishly waste and squander their goods dispose themselves to another man's goods when they have no more of their own.

"I say then that you should flee avarice, using your riches in such a way that men won't say your riches are buried but that you have them in your power. **1610** For a wise man reproves the avaricious one, and says thus in two verses: 'Wherefore and why would a man bury his goods through his great avarice when he knows well that he must die? For death is the end of every man in this present life.' And for what cause or reason does he join or knit himself so securely to his goods that all his wits may not separate or part them, **1615** when he well knows, or ought to know, that when he's dead he shall take nothing with him out of this world? Therefore Saint Augustine says that 'the avaricious man is likened to hell, for the more it swallows, the more desire it has to swallow and devour.' And just as you would avoid being called an avaricious man or miser, take care and so govern yourself that men won't call you foolishly wasteful. **1620** 'The goods of your house,' as Tullius says, 'should not be hidden or guarded so closely that they may not be opened by pity and mercy,' that is, shared with those who have great need; 'nor should your goods be so open as to be every man's goods.'

"In acquiring your goods and using them, you should always have three things in your heart: our Lord God, your conscience, and a good name. **1625**

"First, you should have God in your heart, and for riches do nothing that may displease God, who is your creator and maker, in any way. For according to the word of Solomon, 'It is better to have a few goods with the love of God than to have many goods and treasures and lose the Lord God's love.' And the prophet says that 'it is better to be a good man and have few friends and treasures **1630** than to be considered a scoundrel and have great riches.'

"And yet I say you should always make an effort to acquire riches, so long as you acquire them with a good conscience. 'There is nothing in this world,' the Apostle says, 'of which we should have so great a joy as when our conscience bears us good witness.' And the wise man says, 'The wealth of a man is good when sin is not on his conscience.' **1635**

"Next, in acquiring your riches and using them, you must very earnestly and diligently see that your good name be always kept and preserved. For Solomon says that 'it is better and more helpful for a man to have a good name than to have great riches.' Thus he says in another place: 'Make a great effort to keep your friend and your good name; for it shall abide with you longer than any treasure, be it ever so precious.' 1640 And certainly he shouldn't be called a gentleman who isn't diligent and earnest, in accord with God and good conscience, all else put aside, to keep his good name. 'It is the sign of a gentle heart,' says Cassiodorus, 'when a man loves and desires to have a good name.' And Saint Augustine says that 'there are two things that are necessary, a good conscience and a good reputation; that's to say, a good conscience for your inner self, and among your neighbors a good reputation.' 1645 And he who trusts so much in his good conscience that he offends and reckons as nothing his good name or reputation, and doesn't care if he keeps his good name, is nothing but an unfeeling churl.

"Sir, now I have shown you how you should acquire riches and use them, and I see well that for the trust you have in your riches you would stir up war and battle. I counsel you to begin no war because of faith in your riches, for they are not sufficient to maintain wars. 1650 Thus says a philosopher: 'That man who desires and would under all circumstances have war shall never have sufficient wealth; for the richer he is, the greater expenditure must he make if he would have honor and victory.' And Solomon says that 'the greater the riches a man has, the more wasters he has.'

"And, dear sir, though because of your riches you may have many people, it still isn't proper or good to start war when you may in other ways have peace for your honor and profit. 1655 For the victory in battles in this world lies not in great multitudes nor in the virtue of man, but in the will and the hand of our Lord God Almighty. Thus Judas Maccabeus, who was God's knight, when he should fight against his adversaries who had a larger and stronger multitude of people than did the Maccabees, inspired his small company with fresh courage in this way: 1660 'As easily,' said he, 'may our Lord God Almighty give victory to a few as to many; for victory in battle comes not from the great number of people but from our Lord God in heaven.'

"And, dear sir, inasmuch as no man is certain of being so worthy that God should give him victory, any more than he is certain whether he's worthy of God's love or not, every man, according to what Solomon says, should greatly dread starting wars. 1665 And because many perils occur in battle, and sometimes the great man is slain as soon as the little man, it is written in the Book of Kings: 'The outcomes of battles are governed by chance and are uncertain, for as readily is one hurt with a spear as another'; and because there is great peril in war, a man should flee and avoid war as much as he possibly can. **1670** For Solomon says, 'He who loves danger shall perish in it.' "

Then Melibeus replied, "I see well, dame Prudence, by your fair words and the reasons you have shown me, that war doesn't please you; but I haven't yet heard your counsel on how I should act in this case."

"I certainly counsel you," she said, "to settle with your adversaries and make peace with them. **1675** For Saint James says in the Epistle that 'by concord and peace small riches grow great, and by strife and discord great riches decrease.' And you know well that one of the greatest and most sovereign things in this world is unity and peace. Thus our Lord Jesus Christ said to his apostles: 'Happy and blessed are they who love and bring about peace, for they shall be called children of God.' " **1680**

"Ah," said Melibeus, "now I well see that you don't love my honor and my renown. You know well that my adversaries began this debate and contention by their violence, and you see as well that they don't request or pray for peace, nor do they ask to be reconciled. Would you then have me go and humble myself and obey them and ask them for mercy? That would truly not be to my honor. **1685** For just as men say that 'familiarity breeds contempt,' so it goes with too great a humility or meekness."

Dame Prudence made a pretense of anger. "Certainly, sir, saving your grace," she said, "I love your profit as I do my own, and have always done so; neither you nor anyone else ever saw the contrary. Yet if I said that you should bring about the peace and reconciliation, I wouldn't have done wrong or spoken amiss. **1690** For the wise man says, 'Dissension begins with another man; reconciliation begins with yourself.' And the prophet says, 'Turn away from evil and do good; seek after peace and pursue it, as much as you can.' Yet I don't say you should sooner sue to your adversaries for peace than they should to you. For I know well that you're so hard-hearted that you would do nothing for me. **1695** And Solomon says, 'He who has too hard a heart shall have mishap and misfortune at the last.' "

Melibeus, when he had heard her make pretense of anger, said, "Dame, don't be displeased, I pray, by the things I say, for you well know that I'm wrathful, and that is no wonder; and they who are angry don't know what they do or say. **1700** Thus the prophet says that 'troubled eyes have no clear sight.' But speak to me, counsel me as you please, for I'm ready to do just as you desire; and if you reprove me for my folly, I'm the more bound to love you and praise you. For Solomon says that 'he who reproves him who does folly shall find greater favor than he who deceives him by sweet words.' " **1705**

"I make no pretense of anger," then said dame Prudence, "except for your greater profit. For Solomon says, 'He is worth more who reproves or chides a fool in his folly showing him a pretense of wrath, than he who supports him and praises him in his misdeeds and laughs at his folly.' And Solomon says, too, that 'by the sadness of a man's countenance,' that is, by his sorrowful, heavy expression, 'the fool corrects and amends himself.' " **1710**

Then Melibeus said, "I don't know how to answer so many fair reasons as you put to me and show me. Tell me briefly your will and your counsel, I am ready to fulfill and perform it."

Then dame Prudence revealed all her will to him. "I counsel you," she said, "above all things to make peace between God and yourself, reconciling yourself to him and his grace. **1715** For as I've already told you, God will send your enemies to you and make them fall at your feet, ready to do your will and commandments. For Solomon says, 'When the ways of a man are pleasant and pleasing to God, he converts the hearts of the man's enemies and constrains them to beseech him for peace and favor.' **1720** Let me speak with your enemies, I pray, in a private place, so they won't know it's with your will or assent. And then, when I know their will and intent, I may counsel you more surely."

"Dame," said Melibeus, "do your will and your pleasure, for I put myself wholly in your rule and control." **1725**

Then dame Prudence, on seeing her husband's good will, deliberated within her own mind how she might bring this difficult situation to a good conclusion. When she saw her time, she sent for these enemies to come to her in a private place, and wisely demonstrated to them the great benefits that come from peace, and the great evils and perils found in war. **1730** She told them in a kindly way how they ought to have great repentance for the injury and wrong they had done to Melibeus their lord, and to her and her daughter.

On hearing dame Prudence's gracious words, they were so surprised and delighted, she gave them such great joy, that it was a wonder. "Ah, lady," they said, "you have shown us the blessings of sweetness, according to the saying of David the prophet; **1735** for the reconciliation that we are not worthy to have in any way, unless we request it with great contrition and humility, you have presented to us through your great goodness. Now we see well that the wisdom and knowledge of Solomon is very true. For he says that 'sweet words multiply and increase friends, and make scoundrels merciful and meek.' 1740

"Certainly," they said, "we commit our conduct and cause in this affair wholly to your good will and are ready to obey the word and commandment of our lord Melibeus. We therefore pray, dear and benign lady, as meekly as we can, that it please your great goodness to carry out in deed your gracious words. For we feel and acknowledge that we have immoderately offended and grieved our lord Melibeus, 1745 to such an extent that we cannot make amends to him. We therefore oblige and bind ourselves and our friends to his will and commandment. But he may have so much rancor and anger toward us, because of our offenses, that he would impose such a penalty that we may neither bear nor sustain it. Therefore, noble lady, we beseech your womanly pity 1750 to give such thought to this matter that neither we nor our friends be dispossessed or destroyed through our folly."

"Certainly," said Prudence, "it is a hard and perilous thing for a man to put himself utterly under the arbitration and judgment, as well as the power and might, of his enemies. For Solomon says, 'Believe me, and give credence to what I shall say: you people, followers and governors of Holy Church, never give to your son, wife, friend, or brother 1755 any mastery over your body while you live.' Now since he forbids any man to give over his body to his brother or friend, by strong reason he forbids a man to give himself to his enemy. I nevertheless counsel you not to distrust my lord, for I'm well aware that he truly is merciful, meek, generous, courteous, 1760 and doesn't desire or covet goods or riches. For there is nothing in this world he desires except reputation and honor. Moreover, I know well and am sure he'll do nothing in this situation without my counsel; and I shall so work in this matter that, by the grace of our Lord God, you shall be reconciled to us."

"Honored lady," they then said with one voice, "we submit our goods to your will and discretion, 1765 and are ready to come whatever day it pleases your honor to appoint for us to make our obligation and bond as strong as it pleases your goodness, that we may fulfill your will and that of our lord Melibeus."

On hearing the answers of these men, Prudence bade them go again privately, then returned to her lord Melibeus and told him how she found his enemies fully repentant, **1770** acknowledging humbly their sins and trespasses, and how they were ready to suffer any penalty, beseeching his mercy and pity.

Then Melibeus said, "He is truly worthy to be pardoned and forgiven for his sin who makes no excuses for his sin but acknowledges it and repents, asking indulgence. For Seneca says, 'There is pardon and forgiveness where there is confession,' **1775** for confession is neighbor to innocence. And he says in another place that 'he who has shame for his sin and acknowledges it is worthy of remission.' So I assent and resolve to have peace; but it's good that we not have it without the assent and will of our friends."

Prudence was truly glad and joyful. "Certainly, sir," she said, "you have answered well and sensibly; **1780** for just as by the counsel, assent, and help of your friends you have moved to avenge yourself and make war, so without their counsel you should not be reconciled nor make peace with your enemies. For the law says, 'There is nothing as naturally good as something unbound by whom it was bound.'"

Dame Prudence then sent immediately for her relatives and old friends who were true and wise, and told them in order, in Melibeus's presence, the circumstances as stated above, **1785** and prayed them to give their advice as to what would be best to do in this case.

When Melibeus's friends had deliberated, examining the matter with great care and diligence, they consented fully to have peace and tranquillity, and that Melibeus should receive his enemies with heartfelt forgiveness and mercy. **1790**

When dame Prudence had heard her lord Melibeus's assent and his friends' counsel in accord with her will and intention, in her heart she felt wonderfully glad. "There's an old proverb," she said, "that says, 'Do today the good that you may do, don't wait until tomorrow.' **1795** So I counsel you to send messengers such as are discreet and wise to your enemies, telling them on your behalf that if they're for peace and accord they prepare at once to come to us." And this in fact was done. **1800**

When these trespassers repenting their folly, that is, Melibeus's enemies, heard what the messengers said, they were very glad and joyful; they answered very meekly and benignly, thanking their lord Melibeus and all his company, and prepared at once to go with the messengers and obey Melibeus's commandment. **1805**

They went immediately to the court of Melibeus, bringing with them some of their true friends to serve as their pledges and surety. When they came into his presence, Melibeus told them, "It's a known fact **1810** that without need, cause, or reason you have done great injuries and wrongs to me and my wife Prudence, and to my daughter as well. You entered my house by violence and have done such outrageous acts that all men well know that you deserve death. So I want to know if you would submit the punishment and avenging of this outrage to the will of my wife Prudence and me." **1815**

The wisest of the three said, "Sir, we know well that we are unworthy to come into the court of a lord so great and worthy as you. For we have greatly trespassed, and are so guilty of offense against your lordship that we truly deserve death. Yet, for the goodness and mercy that all the world witnesses in you, **1820** we submit to the excellence and benignity of your gracious lordship and are ready to obey all your commandments, beseeching you to consider in your merciful pity our great repentance and humble submission, and to grant us forgiveness for our outrageous trespasses and offenses. For we know well that your liberal grace and mercy reach farther into goodness than do our outrageous sins and trespasses into wickedness, **1825** though we are cursedly and damnably guilty against your high lordship."

Melibeus very kindly took them up from the ground, received their obligations and promises by their oaths on their pledges and sureties, and assigned them a certain day to return to his court and receive the sentence and judgment that he would command for the aforesaid reasons. **1830** When matters were arranged, each man returned to his house.

Dame Prudence, when she saw opportunity, asked her lord Melibeus what vengeance he intended to take.

"Certainly," Melibeus replied, "I firmly intend to dispossess them of all they ever had, and to send them into exile forever." **1835**

"That would certainly be a cruel and unreasonable sentence," said Prudence. "For you are rich enough and have no need of other men's goods; you might easily get a reputation for covetousness this way, which is a vicious thing and ought to be avoided by every good man. For according to the saying in the Apostle's message, 'Covetousness is the root of all evils.' **1840** It would therefore be better for you to lose that many goods of your own than to take their goods in this way; for it's better to lose goods with honor than to win goods with dishonor and shame. Each man should exert every effort to obtain a good name. He should not only stay busy keeping that good name but always try to add to it. **1845** For it's written that 'the good reputation or good name of a man soon disappears when it is not renewed.'

"I think it's excessive and unreasonable for you to say that you will exile your enemies, considering the power they have given you over themselves. For it's written that 'he is worthy to lose his privilege who misuses the power given to him.' **1850** And suppose you might impose that penalty on them by right and by law, which I trust you may not; I say you might not be able to carry it out, and that would mean a return to war as before. So if you want men to do you homage, you must judge more mercifully, **1855** that is, you must give lighter sentences and judgments. For it's written that 'men most obey him who most mercifully commands.' So I pray that you decide in this case to overcome your heart. For Seneca says that 'he who overcomes his heart conquers twice.' And Tullius says, 'There is nothing so commendable in a great lord **1860** as when he is merciful and meek and grows readily calm.'

"I pray you'll now forbear taking vengeance, that your good name be kept and preserved, that men may have cause and reason to praise you for your pity and mercy, and that you may have no cause to repent anything you have done. **1865** For Seneca says, 'He conquers in an evil manner who repents his victory.' So let mercy, I pray, be in your heart, to the end and with the intent that God Almighty have mercy on you in his last judgment. For Saint James says in his Epistle, 'Judgment without mercy shall be given to him who has no mercy on another person.' "

When Melibeus had heard dame Prudence's great arguments and reasons, all her wise instructions and teachings, **1870** his heart began to favor the will of his wife, considering her true intent, and he agreed then completely to act according to her counsel; and he thanked God, from whom proceeds all virtues and all goodness, for having sent him a wife of such great discretion.

When the day came for his enemies to appear in his presence, Melibeus spoke to them with kindness. **1875** "Although in your pride, great presumption, and folly," he said, "and out of your negligence and ignorance, you have misbehaved and trespassed against me, inasmuch as I see your great humility and know that you are sorry and repent your sins, I am constrained to grant you grace and mercy. **1880** I therefore receive you in my grace, and forgive you utterly for all the offenses, injuries, and wrongs that you have done against me and my family, to this effect and to this end: that God in his endless mercy will at the time of our dying forgive us our sins that we have committed against him in this wretched world. For undoubtedly if we are sorry and repent the sins and offenses that we have committed in the sight of our Lord God, **1885** he is so generous and merciful that he will forgive us our sins and bring us to the bliss that never ends. Amen."

The Monk's Tale

PROLOGUE

Merry Words of the Host to the Monk

When ended was my tale of Melibee,
Of Prudence and of her benignity,   1890
Our Host said, "As I am a faithful man,
And by that precious *corpus Madrian*,
Rather than have a barrelful of ale
I would my own good wife had heard this tale!
Of patience not the slightest bit has she   1895
Like that of Prudence, wife of Melibee.
By God's bones, when I have to beat my knaves
She goes and fetches great club-headed staves
To me, and cries out, 'Slay the dogs! Lay on
And break them up, their backs and every bone!'   1900
    "And if somebody from my neighborhood
Won't bow to her in church, or if he should
Toward her be too bold or out of place,
When she comes home she gets right in my face:
'False coward,' she will cry, 'avenge your wife!   1905
By *corpus* bones, now I will have your knife,
My distaff you can have to go and spin!'
From day to night that's just how she'll begin.
'Alas,' she'll say, 'that I was in such shape
I wed a milksop, such a coward-ape   1910
Neath everybody's domineering hand!
For your own wife you don't dare take a stand!'
    "Such is my life unless I will to fight;
Right out the door must be my rapid flight
Or else I am but lost—unless I be   1915
Like some wild lion, act foolhardily.
I know full well someday she'll make me slay
A neighbor, then I'll have to run away;

414

For I'm a dangerous man with knife in hand,
Though I admit that I don't dare to stand   1920
Up to her, for she's big in either arm,
As, by my faith, he'll find who does her harm.
Let's leave this matter now and forge ahead.
    "Be of good cheer, my lord the Monk," he said,
"For you shall tell a tale, I truly say.   1925
Look, there stands Rochester close by the way!
Ride forth, my lord, and don't break up our game.
But by my oath, I do not know your name,
If it's Don John that you should be addressed,
Don Thomas or Don Alban—which is best?   1930
You're of which order, by your father's kin?
I swear to God, you're very fair of skin;
The pasture must be fertile you frequent,
You don't look like some ghost or penitent.
You are, upon my faith, some officer,   1935
Some worthy sacristan or cellarer,
For, by my father's soul, I would surmise
At home you are a master. In no wise
Are you a novice or poor cloisterer,
Instead a wise and wily governor,   1940
One big-boned, too, and brawny. I would say
You're quite a handsome fellow all the way.
God give to him confusion, utter strife,
Who brought you first to the religious life!
A treading rooster you'd have been, all right;   1945
Had you the liberty as you have might
To satisfy desire in such a way,
Then many a creature you'd have sired today.
Alas, why do you wear so wide a cope?
God give me sorrow but, if I were pope,   1950
Not only you but every man of strength—
His head shorn to however short a length—
Would have a wife. The loss is to all earth,
Religion's taken all the corn of worth
From treading, we're but shrimps, we laity.   1955
A wretched root comes from a feeble tree;
Our heirs will be so feeble, weak, and tender

They may not have the strength well to engender.
And that is why our wives are known to try
Out you religious folk: you satisfy   1960
The debts of Venus better than we may.
By God, it's not with counterfeit you pay!
Please don't be angered by my playful word,
For often, sir, in game a truth is heard."

   This worthy Monk took all of this in patience,   1965
Then said, "I'll try with all my diligence—
Keeping within the realm of probity—
To tell for you a tale, or two or three.
If you would like to listen, I've some words
I could impart about a life, Saint Edward's;   1970
Or else, to start with, tragedies I'll tell,
Of which I have a hundred in my cell—
Tragedy is to say a certain story,
As old books bring to mind, about the glory
Of one who stood in great prosperity,   1975
But who then tumbled from his high degree
To wretched end, woe that was never worse.
These commonly have been set down in verse,
In six feet that men call hexameter.
In prose as well, though, many others were,   1980
In meter too—all manner of device.
That ought to be enough words to suffice.
   "Now pay attention if you'd like to hear.
But first I ask, to make this matter clear,
If out of order I should tell these things   1985
(Be they of popes or emperors or kings)
As ages go (as written you will find),
And tell a few before and some behind
As they may come back now to my remembrance,
That you'll excuse me for my ignorance."   1990

THE MONK'S TALE

De Casibus Virorum Illustrium

I shall bewail in form that's tragical
The harm of them who stood in high degree
And fell, who had no remedy at all
To bring them out of their adversity.
For surely when Fortune may choose to flee,   1995
There is no man who may her course withhold.
Let no man trust in blind prosperity;
Beware by these examples true and old.

LUCIFER

With Lucifer, though of the angelic band,
Not of the human race, I will begin.   2000
Though Fortune cannot harm or have a hand
With angels, from on high he for his sin
Fell into hell, and he is yet therein.
O Lucifer, angel brightest of all,
Now you are Satan, who may never win   2005
From misery, to which has been your fall.

ADAM

Lo, Adam in the field of Damascene:
By God's own finger created was he
And not conceived by sperm of man unclean.
He ruled all Paradise, except one tree.   2010
No man on earth has held such high degree
Since Adam, who, for his misgovernance,
Was driven from his high prosperity
To labor and to hell and to mischance.

SAMSON

Behold Samson, who was annunciated   2015
By the angel long ere his nativity,
And was to God Almighty consecrated,
And stood in honor while he still could see.
There never was another such as he,
To speak of strength and, with it, hardiness;   2020
But to his wives he broke his secrecy,
And slew himself thereby in wretchedness.

This noble, mighty champion without
A weapon save his bare hands still could slay
The lion, which he tore, ripped inside out,   2025
While to his wedding he was on his way.
His false wife could so please him, so could pray,
She learnt from him his secret; she, untrue,
Went to his foes, his secret to betray,
And then forsook him, taking someone new.   2030

Three hundred foxes Samson took in ire
And bound their tails together; once in hand,
All of the foxes' tails he set afire
(On every fox's tail he tied a brand);
They burnt up all the crops grown in the land,   2035
The olive trees and vines, as they would pass.
He also slew a thousand men by hand,
No weapon save the jawbone of an ass.

When they were slain, he thirsted so that he
Was all but lost; he prayed that God on high   2040
Might on his pain look with some clemency
And send him drink or else he'd have to die;
Then in that ass's jawbone, which was dry,
Out of a molar sprang at once a well
From which, in short, he drank. None can deny   2045
God was his help, as *Judicum* can tell.

One night in Gaza by his proven might,
In spite of all the Philistines so nigh,
The city gates he plucked up, set them right
Upon his back, and carried them up high   2050
Onto a hill for everyone to spy.
O noble, mighty Samson, loved and dear,
Had you not let your secret be known by
Your women, you'd have been without a peer!

This Samson never touched strong drink or wine.   2055
No razor ever touched his head, no shear,
By precept of the messenger divine,
For all his strength was in his hair. And year
By year, for twenty winters, Samson's sphere
Was that of judge in Israel's governance.   2060
But soon he shall be weeping many a tear,
For women shall bring Samson to mischance!

Delilah was his lover whom he told
That in his hair was where his strength all lay,
And Samson to his enemies she sold;   2065
While he was sleeping in her lap one day,
She had his hair all clipped and shorn away,
And let his foes observe, come for their prize;
For when they had him in this weakened way,
They bound him tightly, then put out his eyes.   2070

Before his hair had thus been clipped away,
Men simply had no bond, this man to bind;
Now he's imprisoned in a cave where they
Have bound him to the handmill, there to grind.
O noble Samson, strongest of mankind,   2075
Once judge with glory, wealth, and blessedness!
Well you may weep with eyes that now are blind,
To fall from where you were to wretchedness.

This captive's end was as I now shall state.
His foemen held a certain feast one day   2080
In their great temple, splendid and ornate;

And there the fool for them they had him play.
But at the last he brought them disarray;
He shook two temple pillars till they fell—
Down came the temple, all, and there it lay,   2085
He slew himself and slew his foes as well;

For each and every prince who there had gone,
And some three thousand others, too, were slain
When that great temple fell with all its stone.
From speaking more of Samson I'll refrain.   2090
Be warned by this example old and plain:
Men shouldn't be confiding to their wives
Something that should in secrecy remain
If it might touch upon their limbs or lives.

HERCULES

Of Hercules, the sovereign conqueror,   2095
His deeds sing praise, the strong, renowned and bold,
The flower of his time, none mightier.
He slew and skinned the lion; it is told
How centaurs he brought low; in days of old
He slew the harpies, cruel birds and fell;   2100
He took from the dragon apples of gold;
He drew out Cerberus, the hound of hell;

He slew Busiris, tyrant cruel and vile,
And had his horse consume him, flesh and bone;
He slew the fiery serpent full of bile;   2105
He broke one horn that Achelous had grown,
And Cacus he slew in a cave of stone;
He slew the giant, Antaeus the strong;
The grisly boor he slew with ease, and on
His mighty shoulders bore the heavens long.   2110

No other being since the world began
Brought down so many monsters as did he.
This whole wide world his fame was quick to span,

His strength and worth of such immensity,
And every realm on earth he went to see.   2115
He was too strong for any man to hold.
At earth's each end, instead of boundary
He set a pillar (so has Trophee told).

This noble champion had a lover
Whose name was Dejanira, fresh as May;   2120
As from these learned men you may discover,
She sent to him a shirt, bright fresh array.
Alas, that shirt, alas and wellaway!
So poison-soaked it was, he put it on
And, when he'd worn it less than half a day,   2125
It caused his flesh to fall right off the bone.

But still some learned men will her excuse
And say that one called Nessus was to blame;
Be as it may, I will not her accuse,
On his bare back he wore it just the same.   2130
His flesh the venom blackened, overcame;
And when he saw no other remedy,
He raked hot coals about himself: by flame,
Not poison, he preferred his death to be.

So died this worthy, mighty Hercules.   2135
Who may in Fortune trust a single throw?
Who travels through this dangerous world with ease?
Ere one's aware he's laid so often low.
The wisest man is he who comes to know
Himself; be wary, for when Fortune goes   2140
To flatter, it's so she may overthrow
In such a way as man may least suppose.

NEBUCHADNEZZAR

The great and mighty throne, the precious treasure,
The glorious scepter, royal majesty
Belonging to the king Nebuchadnezzar,   2145
The tongue can scarcely utter. Twice did he

Against Jerusalem win victory
And vessels of the temple bear away.
In Babylon, seat of his sovereignty,
In glory and delight he held his sway.   2150

The fairest children of the royalty
Of Israel he had gelded, quickly done,
And took each of them into slavery.
Now Daniel of these Israelites was one;
The wisest child of all, he had begun   2155
To serve as dream-interpreter of the king.
(Among Chaldean sages there was none
Who from his dreams could prophecy a thing.)

This proud king had a statue made of gold,
Sixty by seven cubits; he decreed   2160
This golden image by both young and old
Be feared and worshipped. Those who wouldn't heed
To red flames of a furnace he would feed,
He'd order burnt all those who disobeyed.
Daniel would not assent to such a deed,   2165
Nor would his two young comrades so be swayed.

This king of kings was arrogant and vain;
He thought that God who sits in majesty
Would never take from him his great domain.
But he lost that dominion suddenly,   2170
And after like a beast he came to be:
He ate hay like an ox and lay about
Right in the rain, wild beasts his company,
Until a certain time had run its route;

Like eagle feathers grew his hair; as well,   2175
His nails grew out, like bird claws to appear;
Then God relieved him for a few years' spell
And gave him sense. With that and many a tear
He thanked God and was evermore in fear
Of doing wrong or being out of place,   2180
And till the time that he lay on his bier

He knew that God was full of might and grace.

BELSHAZZAR

His son and heir—Belshazzar was his name—
Held power after Nebuchadnezzar's day
But took no warning from his father's shame;   2185
He was so proud of heart and in array,
And lived in so idolatrous a way,
And on his high estate himself so prided,
That Fortune cast him down and there he lay
And suddenly his kingdom was divided.   2190

For all his lords he gave a feast one day
And bade them be as merry as could be;
And then he called his officers to say,
"Go now and bring the vessels all to me,
The ones my father in prosperity   2195
Took from the temple of Jerusalem;
For prizes left us by our elders, we
Give thanks to our high gods and honor them."

His wife, his lords, and all his concubines
Then drank, as long as appetite would last,   2200
Out of these noble vessels sundry wines;
Then on a wall his eyes Belshazzar cast
And saw an armless hand inscribing fast,
Which made him quake in fear. Upon the wall
This hand, which had Belshazzar so aghast,   2205
Wrote *Mane, techel, phares,* that was all.

There wasn't one magician in the land
Who could interpret what this writing meant,
But Daniel then at once explained the hand.
He said, "My king, God to your father lent   2210
Glory and honor, kingdom opulent;
But he was proud, of God he showed no dread,
And therefore God great woe upon him sent

And took from him the kingdom he had led.

"Then he was banished from man's company,   2215
With asses dwelt, ate hay as his reward,
Just like a beast, though wet or dry it be,
Till grace and reason would to him afford
The knowledge that dominion's of the Lord
Over every kingdom and creature;   2220
Then God had pity on him and restored
To him his kingdom and his human feature.

"And you, who are his son, are proud also,
And know all these things as a verity;
A rebel to the Lord, you are his foe   2225
And from his vessels drink so brazenly;
Your wife, your wenches too drink sinfully
Mixed wine from those same vessels, while you pray
To your false gods in curst idolatry.
For such, your retribution's on the way.   2230

"This hand was sent from God that on the wall
Wrote *Mane, techel, phares*, trust in me;
Your reign is done, you count for naught at all;
Your kingdom is divided, it shall be
Given to Medes and Persians," augured he.   2235
This king was slain upon that very night;
Darius then replaced him in degree
Although he had no lawful means or right.

My lords, examples hereby you may take:
Security is not a lord's to know;   2240
Whenever Fortune chooses to forsake,
She takes away one's reign, one's wealth also,
And friends as well, though they be high or low.
If it's to Fortune that friendships are due,
Mishap, I guess, will turn a friend to foe;   2245
This is a common proverb and it's true.

ZENOBIA

Zenobia, once of Palmyra queen,
As Persians wrote of her nobility,
So worthy was in armaments, so keen,
For hardiness she had no rivalry,   2250
For lineage, for all gentility;
From royal Persian blood she was descended.
I won't say none was lovelier than she,
Yet her looks had no need to be amended.

I find that from her childhood on she fled   2255
The role of women; to the woods she went,
Where blood of many wild harts she would shed
With arrows broad, which to the mark she sent
To quickly land her game. And by her bent
She later on in life would would also kill   2260
Lions, leopards, bears, all torn and rent,
In her strong arms she had them at her will.

She dared to seek the wild beast in its den
And run along the mountains all the night
And sleep beneath a bush; and she would win   2265
In wrestling, by her very force and might,
From any youth though strong he be to fight;
Against her not a thing could hold its ground.
She kept her maidenhood with all her might,
For to no man would she deign to be bound.   2270

Some friends of hers at last, though, got her married
To Odenathus, prince of that same land,
Though she had long resisted them and tarried.
And he, my lords, as you should understand,
Felt much the same as she. But when her hand   2275
He'd taken, very close the couple grew;
They lived in joy, their life together grand,
They held each other dear, their love was true.

Except one thing: she never would assent
In any way that he should by her lie   2280
More than one time; it was her sole intent
To have a child, the world to multiply.
But just as soon as she might then espy
That by the deed she'd still failed to conceive,
At once she'd let him give it one more try—   2285
But only once, that much you can believe.

And if she bore a child from that event,
She wouldn't let him have back at the game
Till after forty full weeks came and went,
Then once more she would tolerate the same.   2290
Though he go wild or manage to be tame,
He'd get no more from her; she said to him
That wives thought it but lechery and shame
If otherwise their husbands play with them.

Two sons by Odenathus she would bear   2295
And rear to virtue and good education.
But let's get back now to our tale. I swear,
She was so worthy of one's admiration,
So wise, so giving with due moderation,
In war untiring, and so courteous too,   2300
None had in war a greater dedication
To work, though men may search this whole world through.

Her wealth of goods was more than can be told,
In vessels as well as in what she wore
(For she would dress in precious stones and gold).   2305
And when not on the hunt, she'd not ignore
Her study of foreign tongues; she'd master more
When she had leisure time, for her intent
Was to be educated in all lore
So that her life in virtue might be spent.   2310

But that we might deal briefly with the story,
So doughty was her husband as was she
That they had conquered many a realm of glory

Within the East, fair towns that formerly
Had been possessions of the majesty   2315
Of Rome. In their strong grip they held them fast,
As there was not one foe could make them flee
As long as Odenathus was to last.

Whoso would read of battles that she fought
Against Shapur the king and others too,   2320
And how all of her works came to be wrought
And why she won, what titles then her due,
And after, all the woes she suffered through,
How she would be besieged and hauled away—
Let him go to my master Petrarch, who   2325
Wrote quite enough about it, I daresay.

When Odenathus died, she mightily
Held to the realms, for with her own strong hand
She fought against her foes so brutally
That not one king or prince in all the land   2330
Was less than glad when brought to understand
That she, through grace, his realm would not invade.
They made with her peace treaties long to stand,
And let her be where she rode forth and played.

Not Claudius, the Roman emperor,   2335
Nor Gallienus, Rome's prior sovereign,
Was brave enough to make a single stir;
Not one Egyptian or Armenian,
No Syrian, not one Arabian,
Upon a field of battle dared to fight,   2340
Lest by her hand they wind up carrion
Or by her many warriors put to flight.

In kingly habit too her sons would go,
Heirs to their father's kingdoms one and all;
Their names were Thymalao and Hermanno   2345
(The forms, at least, by which the Persians call
The two). But Fortune puts in honey gall,
Not long endures this mighty governess;

Out of her queendom Fortune made her fall
To misadventure and to wretchedness.   2350

Aurelianus, when administration
Of Rome fell to his hands, without delay
Made plans against her for retaliation;
With all his legions he marched on his way
Against Zenobia. Let's briefly say   2355
He made her flee and finally captured her;
He fettered her, with her two sons, that day
And won the land, and went home conqueror.

Her chariot of priceless gems and gold,
Among the things taken in victory   2360
By this Aurelianus great and bold,
He had them haul in front for all to see;
But walking first in that parade was she,
With gilded chains hung from her neck, upon
Her head a crown, befitting her degree,   2365
Her clothing all decked out with precious stone.

Alas, Fortune! she who put fear into
Kings, emperors, and other worldly powers,
Is gaped at by the crowd, alas! She who
Once donned a helmet through war's darkest hours,   2370
And won by force the strongest towns and towers,
Now bears upon her head a crown so cheap;
Now she who bore the scepter decked with flowers
Shall work with a distaff to earn her keep.

PETER, KING OF SPAIN

O Peter, noble, worthy pride of Spain,   2375
Whom Fortune held so high in majesty,
Well should men of your piteous death complain!
Out of your land your brother made you flee,
And after, at a siege, by treachery
You were betrayed; he led you to his tent   2380

And by his own hand slew you, so that he
Might then usurp your powers of government.

A shield of snow, eagle of black therein
(Crossed by a lime-rod emberlike, aglow)
This cursedness concocted, all this sin;   2385
A wicked nest brought violence and woe—
Not Charlemagne's Oliver (one, we know,
Of truth and honor), but from Brittany
A "Ganelon," by bribe corrupted so
He brought this worthy king to treachery.   2390

PETER, KING OF CYPRUS

O worthy Peter, Cypriot king who fought
At Alexandria masterfully
And captured it, who many a heathen brought
To woe! Your lieges in their jealousy,
For naught but envy of your chivalry,   2395
Have slain you in your sleep before the morrow.
So Fortune's wheel can govern what shall be
And out of gladness bring mankind to sorrow.

BARNABO OF LOMBARDY

O Barnabo Visconti, Milan's great
God of delight, scourge of Lombardy, why   2400
Should not all your misfortunes I relate
Once you had climbed to an estate so high?
Your brother's son, in double sense ally
(Your nephew and your son-in-law as well),
Put you inside his prison, there to die,   2405
Though why or how I do not know to tell.

COUNT UGOLINO OF PISA

Now of Count Ugolino's darkest hour
No tongue can tell without great sympathy.
Not far outside of Pisa stands a tower
In which he was imprisoned—not just he   2410
But with him there his little children three,
The eldest being just five years of age.
Alas, O Fortune, what great cruelty,
Such birds as these put into such a cage!

The reason that he'd been condemned to die   2415
Was the bishop of Pisa (in that day
Ruggieri), who had told of him a lie;
The people then rose up against his sway
And had him put in prison, in the way
That you have heard. The food and drink he had   2420
Was not at all sufficient, safe to say;
What little bit he had was poor and bad.

It happened that one day upon the hour
When food to him had usually been brought,
The jailer locked all doors about the tower.   2425
He heard it well although he uttered naught,
Till soon there fell upon his heart the thought
That by starvation they planned his demise.
"Alas that I was born!" he cried, distraught,
Then tears began to flow from both his eyes.   2430

His youngest son, whose age was only three,
Then asked him, "Father, why is it you weep?
When will the jailer bring our food? Have we
No single crumb of bread that you could keep?
I am so hungry I can't even sleep.   2435
Would God that I might always sleep, instead
Of feeling in me hunger's gnawing creep!
There's nothing I would rather have than bread."

So day by day this child began to cry,
Till in his father's lap he finally lay   2440
And said, "Farewell, my father, I must die!"
He kissed his father, died that very day.
And when his father saw he'd passed away,
His grief was such he bit his own two arms
And cried, "Alas, O Fortune! Well I may   2445
On your false wheel lay blame for all my harms!"

It was for hunger, so his sons believed,
That he had gnawed his arms and not for woe.
"No, Father, don't do that," they said, aggrieved,
"But eat our flesh instead. Not long ago   2450
Our flesh you gave us; take it back just so,
And eat enough." That's what they had to say,
And in a day or two both were to go
Lay in their father's lap and pass away.

And he, too, in despair died of starvation,   2455
This Count of Pisa. Such was his demise,
Cut down by Fortune from so high a station.
No more on this tragedy I'll advise;
If you would hear it in more lengthy wise,
Then read in that great poet of Italy   2460
Called Dante, for so well he does devise
It word for word and tells it totally.

NERO

Though Nero was as vile and villainous
As any fiend that ever lay in hell,
This whole wide world (as writes Suetonius)   2465
Both east and west, from north to south as well,
Was subject to his rule, albeit fell.
With rubies, sapphires, pearls of purest white
Were all his clothes embroidered; one could tell
In precious stones he took a great delight.   2470

More pompous, proud, fastidious in array
No other Roman emperor was than he;
Whichever robe he'd choose to wear one day
No day thereafter he desired to see.
Gold-threaded nets were brought in quantity   2475
When he desired to fish a Tiber bend.
His every wish acquired legality,
For Fortune would obey him like a friend.

He had Rome burnt for his delight, a whim,
And senators he ordered slain one day   2480
That he might hear the cries that came from them.
He slew his brother, by his sister lay,
And mangled his own mother—that's to say,
He slit his mother's womb that he might see
Where he had been conceived. O wellaway   2485
That he held her no worthier to be!

Not one tear from his eye fell at the sight,
He simply said, "A woman fair was she."
The wonder is how Nero could or might
Be any judge of her late beauty. He   2490
Then ordered wine be brought, which instantly
He drank—he gave no other sign of woe.
When power has been joined to cruelty,
Alas, how deeply will the venom flow!

This Nero had a master in his youth   2495
To teach to him the arts and courtesy,
This master being the flower of moral truth
In his own time, if books speak truthfully;
And while this master held authority,
So wise he made him in both word and thought   2500
That it would be much time ere tyranny
Or any vice against him would be brought.

This master Seneca of whom I've spoken
To Nero had become a cause of dread,
Chastising him for every good rule broken,   2505

By word, not deed. As he discreetly said,
"An emperor, sir, must always be well bred,
Of virtue, hating tyranny." Defied,
He wound up in a bath where he was bled
From both his arms, and that's the way he died.   2510

This Nero as a youth was also taught
Before his master always to arise,
Which afterwards was great insult, he thought,
For which he had him sent to such demise.
But nonetheless this Seneca the wise   2515
Chose in a bath to die in just that way
Rather than in some torture they'd devise.
So his dear master Nero chose to slay.

Now it befell that Fortune wished no longer
To suffer Nero's pride, such haughtiness;   2520
For although he was strong, she was the stronger.
She thought, "By God! I am a fool, no less,
To set a man so full of wickedness
In high degree, an emperor to call.
By God, I'll pluck him from his loftiness;   2525
When he may least expect, soon he shall fall."

The people rose against him then one night
For his misdeeds; and when he so espied,
He sneaked outside as quickly as he might
And went to where he thought he'd be allied.   2530
But as he knocked, and all the more he cried,
The faster would the doors shut one and all;
Himself, he knew, he'd thus come to misguide.
He went his way, no longer dared he call.

The people shouted, rumbling to and fro,   2535
With his own ears he heard the cry they made:
"Where is this traitorous tyrant, this Nero?"
He went half crazy, he was so afraid,
As to his gods then pitifully he prayed
For help, though none would come. So terrified   2540

That he felt on his bier already laid,
He ran into a garden, there to hide.

And in this garden he two fellows found
Who sat beside a bonfire great and red;
These churls he begged, he asked that they be bound   2545
To slay him, that they then chop off his head,
That with his body, after he was dead,
Spite not be made because of his ill fame.
But Nero had to slay himself instead,
Upon which Fortune laughed as if in game.   2550

HOLOFERNES

There was no other captain of a king
Who brought more kingdoms under subjugation,
None stronger in the field in everything
In his own time, of greater reputation,
Not one more arrogant in his high station,   2555
Than Holofernes. Fortune kissed him to it
With wantonness, led him through every nation,
Until he lost his head before he knew it.

Not only did this world stand thus in awe
For fear of losing goods and liberty,   2560
But he made every man renounce his law;
"Nebuchadnezzar is our god," said he,
"No other god on earth shall worshipped be."
Against him only one town made a case:
Bethulia, a strong community,   2565
Eliachim the high priest of the place.

Take notice of how Holofernes died:
Amid his soldiers he lay drunk one night
Within his barnlike tent so large and wide;
And yet for all his pomp and all his might,   2570
Judith, a woman (as he lay upright,
Asleep), cut off his head. Then from his tent

She stole, evading every soldier's sight,
And with his head back to her town she went.

KING ANTIOCHUS THE ILLUSTRIOUS

What need to tell of King Antiochus,   2575
Of all his high and royal majesty,
His lofty pride, his works so venomous?
Another such a one was not to be.
Go read of who he was in *Maccabee,*
Read there the words he spoke so full of pride,   2580
And why he fell from high prosperity,
And on a hill how wretchedly he died.

Fortune had so ensconced him in his pride
That truly he believed he might attain
The very stars that shone on every side,   2585
Weigh in the scales each mountain of the chain,
And every flood tide of the sea constrain.
God's people he especially would hate,
Brought death to them in torment and in pain,
Believing God might not his pride abate.   2590

When Nicanor and Timotheus too
Had by the Jews been vanquished totally,
He had so great a hatred for the Jew
That he ordered his chariot to be
Prepared at once, and swore avengingly   2595
That right away upon Jerusalem
He'd wreak his ire with utmost cruelty;
But his objective soon eluded him.

God for his threat so sorely had him smitten
With an internal wound that had no cure,   2600
Inside his gut he felt so cut and bitten
That it was pain he hardly could endure.
This vengeance was a just one, to be sure,
For many a fellow's gut had felt his blow;
But still, his evil purpose to secure,   2605

He wouldn't be deterred despite his woe,

He ordered armed immediately his host.
But then, before he knew it, God once more
Had moved against his pride and haughty boast:
He fell out of his chariot as it bore.   2610
His skin and limbs the tumble scraped and tore
Till he could neither walk nor mount to ride;
Upon a chair men carried off the floor
He had to sit, bruised over back and side.

The wrath of God had smitten him so cruelly   2615
That evil worms all through his body crept,
By cause of which he stank so horribly
That none within the household where he kept,
Whether he be awake or when he slept,
Could long endure his smell. In this abhorred   2620
Condition, this mischance, he wailed and wept,
And knew of every creature God is Lord.

To all his host and to himself also
The way his carcass stank would sicken till
No one could even bear him to and fro.   2625
And in this stink, this horrid painful ill,
He died a wretched death upon a hill.
And so this evil thief and homicide
Who caused so many others tears to spill
Has the reward that goes to those of pride.   2630

ALEXANDER

The story of Alexander is so well known
That part if not the tale's entirety
Has been heard once by everyone who's grown.
This whole wide world, to speak with brevity,
He won by strength (or by celebrity,   2635
As for him towns in peace would gladly send).
The pride of man and beast wherever he

Would go he toppled, to this world's far end.

There's no comparison that one can make,
Above all other conquerors he'd tower;   2640
For all this world in dread of him would quake,
Of knighthood, of nobility the flower,
As Fortune made him heir to fame and power.
Save wine and women, nothing might arrest
His zeal, in arms and labor, to devour;   2645
The courage of a lion filled his breast.

Would it add to his glory if I told
Of Darius and a hundred thousand more—
The kings, the princes, dukes and earls bold
Whom he fought and brought under heel in war?   2650
As far as man had ever gone before
The world was his. What more need I recall?
Were I to write or tell you evermore
Of his knighthood, I couldn't tell it all.

Twelve years, says *Maccabees,* he reigned, this son   2655
Of Phillip of the Macedonian race,
As king of Greece, its first and greatest one.
O worthy Alexander, of noble grace,
Alas, such sad events as in your case!
By your own men poisoned, the six you threw   2660
Has Fortune turned instead into an ace.
And yet she hasn't shed one tear for you.

Who'll give me tears sufficient to complain
Of nobleness's death, of the demise
Of one who held the world as his domain   2665
Yet thought it still not large enough in size,
His heart always so full of enterprise?
Alas! who now shall help me as I name
False Fortune and that poison I despise
As two things that for all this woe I blame?   2670

JULIUS CAESAR

Through wisdom, manhood, and great labor's throes,
From humble bed to royal majesty
This Julius as a conqueror arose.
For he won all the West by land and sea,
By strength of hand and by diplomacy,   2675
And made each realm to Rome a tributary;
And then of Rome the emperor was he,
Till Fortune would become his adversary.

O mighty Caesar, who in Thessaly
Faced Pompey, your own father-in-law, who drew   2680
About him in the East all chivalry
As far as where each day dawn breaks anew,
Through your knighthood that host you took and slew
(Except the few who then with Pompey fled),
The East thereby put in such awe of you.   2685
Thank Fortune that so well you marched ahead!

Here I'll bewail a little, if I might,
Pompey the Great, this noble governor
Of Rome who from the fray had taken flight.
One of his men, a false and traitorous cur,   2690
Beheaded him that he might win the favor
Of Julius, who received the severed head.
Alas, Pompey the Eastern conqueror,
That to such end by Fortune you were led!

To Rome again repaired this Julius,   2695
With laurel crowned, upon his victory.
Then came the time when Brutus Cassius,
Who envied Caesar's high prosperity,
Began conspiring in full secrecy
Against his life. With subtlety he chose   2700
The place of death, and planned that it should be
By way of daggers as I shall disclose.

This Julius to the Capitol one day
Had made his way, as frequently he chose;
There fell upon him then without delay 2705
This traitor Brutus and his other foes,
Who with their daggers gave him several blows
And left him there to die when they were through.
He groaned at but one stroke for all his throes,
Or else at two, if all his tale is true. 2710

This Julius Caesar was so manly-hearted
And had such love for stately probity
That, even as his wounds so sorely smarted,
He drew his mantle over hip and knee,
So that his private parts no one could see; 2715
As he lay in a daze, the deathly kind,
And knew that he was wounded mortally,
Thoughts of decorum still were in his mind.

Lucan, you're one authority I'll note,
Suetonius, Valerius also, 2720
The story's fully there in what you wrote
Of these two conquerors; to them we know
That Fortune first was friend and later foe.
No man can put trust in her favor long,
We must keep both eyes on her as we go; 2725
These conquerors bear witness who were strong.

CROESUS

This wealthy Croesus, once the Lydian king
Whom even Persia's Cyrus held in dread,
Was caught in pride until men said to bring
Him to the fire, and that's where he was led. 2730
But such a rain the clouds above then shed,
The fire was quenched and he was to escape.
This was a lesson, though, he left unread,
Till Fortune on the gallows made him gape.

When he escaped, the urge he couldn't stem   2735
To go and start a whole new war again.
And well he might, as Fortune sent to him
Such good luck that he'd made off through the rain
Before he by his foes could there be slain.
There also was a dream he dreamt one night   2740
That made him feel so eager, proud, and vain,
On vengeance he set all his heart and might.

He was upon a tree, in dream he thought,
Where Jupiter bathed him down every side,
And Phoebus a fair towel to him brought   2745
To dry himself. This added to his pride,
And of his daughter standing there beside
Him—she in whom, he knew, was to be found
Great insight—he asked what it signified,
And she at once his dream set to expound: 2750

"The tree," she said, "the gallows signifies,
And Jupiter betokens snow and rain,
And Phoebus, with his towel so clean, implies
Beams of the sun, as best I can explain.
By hanging, Father, surely you'll be slain;   2755
Washed by the rain, by sun you shall be dried."
Such was the warning given, short and plain,
By Phania, his daughter at his side.

And hanged indeed was Croesus, that proud king,
His royal throne to him was no avail.   2760
No tragedies may signify a thing,
There's naught in song to cry out and bewail,
Except that Fortune always will assail
With sudden stroke the kingdom of the proud;
For when men trust her, that's when she will fail   2765
And cover her bright visage with a cloud.

Here the Knight stops the Monk in his tale

The Nun's Priest's Tale

PROLOGUE

"Whoa!" said the Knight, "good sir, that's quite enough!
You've said what there's to say about such stuff
And even more—a little of distress
Is quite enough for most folks, I would guess.   2770
As for myself, it's worse than a disease
To speak of those who had great wealth and ease,
Then hear about their sudden fall and grief.
The opposite is joy and great relief,
As when a man who is in poorest state   2775
Climbs upward, Fortune lessening the weight,
Till he's abiding in prosperity—
A thing for gladness, so it seems to me,
And of such things it would be good to tell."
        "Aye," said our Host, "by Saint Paul and his bell,   2780
You speak the truth. This Monk, he chatters loud.
He tells how Fortune covered with a cloud
I know not what, and, too, of tragedy,
As you have heard. It is no remedy
For one to be bewailing, to complain   2785
That such-and-such is done. It's all a pain,
Just as you say, to hear of such distress.
        "Sir Monk, no more of this, God may you bless;
Your tale's a nuisance, you annoy us by
Such talk, it isn't worth a butterfly,   2790
For in it we can find no sport or game.
And so, Sir Monk—or Sir Piers by your name—
I pray that something else you might expound.
But for your bells with all their clanging sound
(Those bells hung on your bridle), I confide,   2795
By heaven's King who for all of us died,
I would have fallen long ago asleep
Although the mire might be so ever deep;

441

Then would your tale have all been told in vain.
For certainly, as clerks can well explain,   2800
If there's a man who has no audience,
It doesn't help if he makes any sense—
Yet I know well there's sense enough in me
If anything's reported sensibly.
Say something of your hunting, sir, I pray."   2805
    "No," said the Monk, "I've no desire to play.
Let's have another tale, as I have told."
Then spoke our Host, his speech both rude and bold,
Without delay to the Nun's Priest. He said,
"Come forth, you priest—Sir John, now come ahead!   2810
Tell something that will gladden us inside,
Be blissful, though a nag you have to ride.
So what if you've a horse both foul and lean?
If he will serve you, should you care a bean?
Be merry in your heart and always so."   2815
    "Yes, sir," said he, "yes, Host, so may I go,
If I'm not merry I know I'll be blamed."
To tell his tale at once the fellow aimed,
And here is what he said as he went on,
This gentle priest, this kindly man Sir John.   2820

THE NUN'S PRIEST'S TALE

    A widow who was rather old and poor
In a small cottage dwelt in days of yore,
Beside a grove that stood within a dale.
This widow whom I tell of in my tale
Had from the day that she was last a wife   2825
In patience led a very simple life,
So little were her gain and property.
With what God gave her, though, she thriftily
Cared for her daughters and herself. Three cows
She had, no more, along with three big sows,   2830
And but one sheep named Molly—that was all.
And sooty were the bedroom and the hall
In which she'd eaten many a scanty meal.

With pungent sauce she never had to deal.
No dainty morsel passed her throat, it's not   2835
A fancy diet found in such a cot,
So overeating never caused her qualm.
A temperate diet was her only balm,
With exercise and a contented heart;
The gout did not stop dancing on her part,   2840
And apoplexy never hurt her head.
She had no wine to drink, nor white nor red,
Her board was mostly served with white and black
(Milk and brown bread, of which she found no lack),
Broiled bacon, and sometimes an egg or two.   2845
Her work was much like dairywomen do.
    She had a yard that was enclosed about
By paling and a dried-up ditch without,
In which she had a cock named Chanticleer,
In all the realm of crowing without peer.   2850
His voice was merrier than the play
Of the church's organ each holy day.
And surer was his crowing than a clock
(Even that of the abbey), for this cock
By instinct knew each move of the equator   2855
As it progressed, that none too soon nor later
But on the dot, fifteen degrees ascended,
He crowed the hour no clock so well attended.
His comb was finest coral-red and tall,
And battlemented like a castle wall.   2860
His bill was black and like the jet it glowed,
His legs and toes like azure when he strode.
His nails were whiter than the lilies bloom,
Like burnished gold the color of his plume.
This gentle cock commanded at his leisure   2865
A flock of seven hens to do his pleasure,
His paramours and sisters, each of whom
Like him had wondrous coloring in her plume.
But she with fairest coloring on her throat
Was that one called fair damsel Pertelote;   2870
Discreet and gentle, showing courtesy,
She was so gracious, such nice company,

Right from the day she was seven nights old,
That she had Chanticleer's heart in her hold
Completely, as if under lock and key.   2875
He loved her, that was his felicity.
And such a joy it was to hear them sing,
At morning when the sun would brightly spring,
In sweet accord, "My Love's Gone Far Away."
(For in those days, so I have heard men say,   2880
The beasts and birds alike could speak and sing.)
    It so befell, as day began to spring,
That Chanticleer was on his perch, with all
His seven wives there with him in the hall,
Beside him being fairest Pertelote,   2885
When he began to groan down in his throat
As men in troubled dreams have done before.
And when fair Pertelote thus heard him roar,
She was aghast and said to him, "Dear heart,
What's ailing you that makes this groaning start?   2890
For shame, so sound a sleeper to complain!"
    "My lady," Chanticleer sought to explain,
"I pray, don't take me wrong in my distress.
By God, I dreamt I was in such a mess
That even now my heart is full of fright.   2895
May God," he said, "help me divine it right
Lest into foul captivity I go.
I dreamt that I was roaming to and fro
Here in our yard when I espied a beast
Much like a hound, who would have at the least   2900
Laid hold of me and left me cold and dead.
His color was betwixt yellow and red;
His tail as well as both his ears had hair
With tips of black, unlike his coat elsewhere.
His snout was small, a glow was in each eye.   2905
Still of that look I fear that I could die,
And this has caused my groaning, there's no doubt."
    "Oh fie," she said, "faint-hearted you've turned out!
Alas," said she, "for by the Lord above,
Now you have lost my heart and all my love.   2910
I cannot love a coward, there's no way!

For certainly, whatever women say,
We all desire, if heaven let it be,
Wise, hardy men of generosity,
Husbands discreet—not niggards, fools aghast,   2915
Afraid of every weapon that comes past,
Nor haughty boasters. By that God above,
How dare you say, for shame, to your true love
That anything can make you so afeard!
Have you no manly heart to match your beard?   2920
Alas! can you be so afraid of dreams?
Illusion's all it is, not what it seems.
Such dreams from overeating come to pass,
Or else from humors (if not simply gas)
When they get too abundant as they might.   2925
For sure this dream that you have had tonight
Resulted from there being great excess
In your red bile—the very thing, God bless,
That makes folks when they're dreaming have such dread
Of arrows or of fire that's flaming red,   2930
Of red beasts that pursue to bite and maul,
Of strife and of fierce dogs both great and small;
Like melancholy's humor comes about
To make so many sleeping men cry out
For fear of big black bears, and bulls to boot,   2935
Or else black devils that are in pursuit.
Of other humors I could tell also
That torture many a sleeping man with woe,
But I will pass as lightly as I can.
    "Look at Cato, who was so wise a man: 2940
Did he not say to 'pay no mind to dreams'?
Now, sire," she said, "when we fly from the beams,
For love of God please take a laxative.
On peril of my soul, as I may live,
This counsel is the best, I will not lie: 2945
Of choler and of melancholy hie
To purge yourself. And there's no need to tarry
Though in this town there's no apothecary,
For I myself will teach you of the herbs
That aid your health when choler so disturbs;   2950

And in our yard these very herbs I'll find,
And these will by their property and kind
Purge you beneath as well as purge above.
For this do not forget, for God's own love:
You have a very choleric temperament.   2955
Beware unless the sun in its ascent
Should find you with hot humors so intense;
For if it does, then I would bet a fourpence
You'll have a tertian fever or an ague,
And either one could be a bane to you.   2960
A day or two you'll have some worm digestives,
Then after that you'll take your laxatives—
Some laurel, fumitory, centaury,
Or hellebore, that grows here as you see;
Or else the caper and the dogwood berry,   2965
Or ivy growing in our yard so merry.
Go pick them where they grow and take them in.
Be merry, husband, by your father's kin,
And do not dread a dream. I say no more."
    "Madam," said he, "I thank you for your lore.   2970
But nonetheless, concerning Master Cato
(So much renowned for all his wisdom, though
He said that dreams are not a thing to dread),
By God, in many old books it is read
That many a man of more authority   2975
Than ever Cato was—or woe is me—
Says the exact reverse of Cato's sentence,
And has discovered by experience
That dreams have often been significations
Of joy as well as tribulations   2980
That folks endure as this life may present.
Of this there is no need for argument,
Experience is proof enough indeed.
    "One of the greatest authors men may read
Says once upon a time two fellows went   2985
Upon a pilgrimage with good intent,
And came upon a town wherein they found
Such people congregated all around
That there was lack of lodging. Up and down

They couldn't find one cottage in the town   2990
In which they both might be accommodated.
And so it was, as circumstance dictated,
That for the night they parted company
And each of them sought his own hostelry
And took his lodging as it might befall.   2995
So one of them was lodged inside a stall
In a barnyard with oxen of the plow;
The other one lodged well enough somehow,
Whether it was by fate or by the fortune
That governs each of us in equal portion.   3000
   "It so befell that long before the day,
This man dreamt in his bed there as he lay
That he could hear his friend begin to call,
Saying, 'Alas! for in an ox's stall
Tonight I will be murdered where I lie.   3005
Dear brother, come and help me or I die.
Come here,' said he, 'as quickly as you can!'
Out of his sleep with fright uprose the man;
But once awake, he was not overwrought
And lay back down without a further thought—   3010
He felt such dreams were only fantasy.
Twice in his sleep this vision came to be,
And then he thought his friend had come again
For yet a third time, saying, 'I am slain!
Behold my bloody wounds so wide and deep!   3015
Rise early in the morning from your sleep
And at the west gate of the town,' said he,
'A cart that's full of dung there you shall see,
In which my hidden body is contained.
Now boldly see that this cart be detained.   3020
They murdered me, in truth, to get my gold.'
Then each detail of how he died he told
With such a piteous face, so pale of hue.
And you can trust he found the dream was true;
For in the morning, at the break of day,   3025
To his friend's lodging place he took his way;
And when he came upon the ox's stall
For his companion he began to call.

"Here's what at once he heard the hosteler
Reply: 'Your friend is gone. The fellow, sir,   3030
Went out of town as soon as it was day.'
The man became suspicious right away,
Recalling what he dreamt. He didn't wait
A minute more, but to the western gate
Out of the town he went, and saw at hand   3035
A dung cart headed out to dung some land
(At least it so appeared), and its array
Was just as you have heard the dead man say.
Then he began to cry out heartily
For justice to avenge this felony: 3040
'My friend last night was murdered, here to lie
Flat on his back inside this cart! I cry
Out to you ministries, all you,' said he,
'Who in this town are in authority,
For help! Alas, my friend is lying slain!'   3045
What more about the tale need I explain?
The people cast the cart then to the ground,
And in the midst of all the dung they found
The dead man who so lately had been slain.
    "O blessed God, so just and true, again   3050
As always murder is revealed by thee!
Murder will out, as day by day we see;
It's loathsome and abominable to God,
Who, just and reasonable, spares not the rod,
Will not allow that murder hidden be.   3055
Though it abide a year, or two or three,
Murder will out, that's all I have to say.
The officials of the town without delay
Commanded that the carter then be racked;
The hosteler was tortured, too, in fact,   3060
And soon they both confessed to their misdeed,
And hanging by the neck was then decreed.
    "Here men may see that dreams are things to dread.
And truthfully in that same book I read,
In the very next chapter after this   3065
(I speak the truth, or banish me from bliss),
Of two who would have sailed the ocean for

A certain cause upon some foreign shore,
Had not the wind developed so contrary
That in a city they were forced to tarry—   3070
A merry city on the harborside.
But then one day, when it was eventide,
The wind began to change to suit them best;
Jolly and glad the two went to their rest,
That early they might sail when day began.   3075
But then great marvel fell upon one man;
It happened as he slept, for as he lay
He dreamt a wondrous thing toward the day.
He thought a man was standing at his side,
One who commanded that he should abide.   3080
'Tomorrow if you sail as you intend,
You shall be drowned. My tale is at an end.'
He woke and told his friend the dream and prayed
That he'd agree his voyage be delayed.
One day, at least, he begged him to abide.   3085
His friend, though, from his bed nearby his side
Began to laugh, and scorn upon him cast.
'No dream,' said he, 'makes my heart so aghast
That I'll delay to do as best it seems.
I do not give a straw for all your dreams.   3090
For dreams are just illusions, only japes.
Men always dream of owls or else of apes,
Of things amazing to absurd degree,
Things that have not, and will not, come to be.
But as I see that here you will abide,   3095
Thereby forsaking willfully the tide,
God knows I'm sorry and I say "Good day." '
And so he took his leave and went his way.
But half his course the fellow hadn't sailed
When—I don't know by what mischance it failed—   3100
Quite suddenly the vessel's bottom rent
And ship and man beneath the waters went,
In sight of other ships that were beside,
That sailed with him upon that very tide.
And so, my dear and fairest Pertelote,   3105
Of old examples such as this take note.

No man should act so carelessly about
His dreams. I say to you without a doubt
That many a dream is one to sorely dread.
    "Look, in the life of Saint Kenelm I've read   3110
(His father was Kenulphus, noble king
Of Mercia) how he dreamt a dreadful thing
A little before his death. Upon that day
He dreamt about his murder. Right away
His nurse explained it in detail, and she   3115
Then bade him guard himself from treachery.
But as he was but seven years of age,
He put too little stock in dreams to gauge
One of them right, so holy was his heart.
By God, I'd give my shirt if, for your part,   3120
You would have read this legend as have I!
    "Dame Pertelote, I'm telling you no lie.
Macrobius says a dream came long ago
In Africa to worthy Scipio
That was affirmed, and says that dreams can mean   3125
A warning of things men have later seen.
And furthermore, I pray you take a look
In the Old Testament. Look in the Book
Of Daniel—were his dreams all vanity?
Or read of Joseph and there you will see   3130
That dreams are sometimes (I don't say they're all)
A warning of things that later befall.
Look at the king of Egypt, mighty Pharoah,
His baker and his butler—did they know
Nothing of dreams' effects? Whoever traces   3135
Through history the events of sundry places
May read of visions many a wondrous thing.
Did Croesus, when he was the Lydian king,
Not dream that he was sitting on a tree,
Which signified that hanged he was to be?   3140
Look at Andromache, young Hector's wife:
The day that Hector was to lose his life,
She had a dream that day before the dawn
Of how his life was to be lost if on
That morning he should go into the fray.   3145

She warned him but to no avail; that day
He still went forth to fight the foe again,
And promptly by Achilles he was slain.
But that's a story much too long to tell;
It's almost day, on such I cannot dwell.   3150
For my conclusion I will simply say
That from this vision I shall have someway
Adversity. And I say furthermore
That in these laxatives I put no store—
They're venomous, I'm well aware of it.   3155
Fie on them, for I like them not a bit!
    "Now let us speak of mirth, no more of this.
Dame Pertelote, if ever I have bliss,
One thing God's given me with special grace;
For when I see the beauty of your face,   3160
The scarlet red you have about your eyes,
It makes my dread all wither and it dies,
As certainly as *In principio,*
Mulier est hominis confusio—
Madam, the meaning of this Latin is   3165
'A woman is man's joy and all his bliss.'
For when I feel at nighttime your soft side
(Although, alas, upon you I can't ride,
Because our perch is built so narrowly),
Such joy and comfort swell inside of me   3170
That I defy nightmare as well as dream."
And with that word he flew down from the beam,
For it was day. His hens flew to the ground,
And with a "chuck" he called them, for he found
That in the yard a bit of kernel lay.   3175
Royal he was, his fear had gone away.
Dame Pertelote was feathered by this cock
And trodden twenty times ere nine o'clock.
Then, with a grim look like a lion's frown,
Upon his toes he wandered up and down,   3180
Not deigning to set foot upon the ground.
He chucked each time another corn he found,
And all his wives came running to his call.
Thus royal as a prince within his hall

I leave this Chanticleer there in his yard.   3185
To his adventure next I'll give regard.
   Now when the month in which the world began
(The month of March, when God created man)
Was over and indeed had been exceeded
(The days were thirty-two that were completed),   3190
It happened that this cock in all his pride,
His seven wives all walking by his side,
Cast eyes up to the brightly shining sun
That in the sign of Taurus then had run
Some twenty-one degrees and even more.   3195
He knew by nature and no other lore
That it was nine, and blissfully he crew.
"The sun," he said, "has climbed the heavens through
More than forty and one degrees, no less.
Now Madam Pertelote, my happiness   3200
On earth, hear how these blissful birds all sing,
And see the newborn flowers, how they spring;
My heart is full of solace, revelry!"
But sad fate then befell him suddenly;
The latter end of joy is always woe.   3205
God knows how worldly joy will quickly go;
A rhetorician who can well indite
Might safely in his chronicle so write,
For it's a royal notability.
Let every wise man listen now to me—   3210
This story is as true, I undertake,
As the book of Lancelot of the Lake
That women hold so much in great esteem.
And so I'll turn again now to my theme.
   A black-marked fox, iniquitous and sly,   3215
Who'd lived for three years in the grove nearby
(By heaven's high design right from the first),
That very night had through the hedges burst
Into the yard where Chanticleer the Fair
And all his wives were accustomed to repair.   3220
There in a bed of cabbages he lay
Completely still till well into the day,
Waiting his time on Chanticleer to fall,

As gladly do homicides one and all
Who wait to ambush and to murder men.   3225
O false murderer, lurking in your den!
O new Iscariot, new Ganelon!
O false dissembler, like the Greek Sinon
Who brought the Trojans sorrow so severe!
A curse upon that day, O Chanticleer,   3230
When to that yard you flew down from the beams!
Full warning you were given by your dreams,
That very day would bring adversity.
But that which God foreknows is what must be,
Or so, at least, some learned men contest.   3235
As any worthy scholar will attest,
In schools there is a lot of altercation
About the matter, mighty disputation
(A hundred thousand men are in the rift).
In this the grain from chaff I cannot sift   3240
As can the holy doctor Augustine,
Boethius, or Bishop Bradwardine,
Whether God's knowing what our futures bring
Constrains me so that I must do a thing
(By which I mean simple necessity),   3245
Or whether there's free choice granted me
To do the thing or not (though there is naught
That God does not foreknow before it's wrought),
Or if his knowing constrains not one degree
Beyond conditional necessity.   3250
But I will have no part of such debate;
My tale is of a cock, as I'll relate,
Who took his wife's advice, to his dismay,
And walked within the yard that very day
Despite what he had dreamt, as I have told.   3255
How often women's counsels prove so cold;
A woman's counsel brought us first to woe,
From Paradise poor Adam had to go,
From where he'd been so merry and at ease.
But as I don't know whom it might displease   3260
If I should give to women's counsel blame,
Please let it pass, I'm only making game.

Read authors where such stuff is their concern,
And what they say of women you may learn.
These words have been a cock's, they are not mine;   3265
No harm in any woman I divine.
    Sunbathing in the sand, fair Pertelote
Lay blithely by her sisters, while the throat
Of Chanticleer made song as merrily
As that of any mermaid in the sea.   3270
(The *Physiologus,* with truth to tell,
Says mermaids sing both merrily and well.)
It so befell that as he cast his eye
On the cabbage bed, to catch a butterfly,
He caught sight of the fox there lying low.   3275
He didn't have the least desire to crow—
He cried at once "Cock, cock!" with quite a start,
As any man fear-stricken in his heart.
By instinct every beast desires to flee
When he has seen his natural enemy,   3280
Though never laying eyes on him before.
    This Chanticleer would not have tarried more
Once he espied the fox, had not the latter
Said, "Gentle sir, alas! what is the matter?
I am your friend—are you afraid of me?   3285
I'd be worse than a fiend, most certainly,
To do you harm. And please don't think that I
Come here upon your privacy to spy;
The reason that I've come is not a thing
Except that I might listen to you sing.   3290
For truly you've a voice as merry, sire,
As any angel's up in heaven's choir.
Because of this, in music you've more feeling
Than had Boethius, or all who sing.
My lord, your father (his soul blessed be)   3295
And mother (she of such gentility)
Have both been in my house, to my great pleasure.
To have you, sir, I'd love in equal measure.
For when men speak of singing, I must say—
As may my eyes see well the light of day—   3300
Till you, I never heard a mortal sing

As did your father when the day would spring.
And all he sang was surely from the heart;
That more strength to his voice he might impart,
He used to strain himself until his eyes   3305
He'd have to blink, so loud were all his cries;
And he would have to stand up straight on tiptoe
And stretch his neck as far as it would go.
And he was one of such discretion, sire,
No man was to be found in any shire   3310
Who could in song and wisdom him surpass.
I've read the story *Sir Burnel the Ass,*
Wherein it's said that there was once a cock
Who from a priest's son suffered quite a knock
Upon his leg (a foolish lad's caprice),   3315
For which he made him lose his benefice.
But there is no comparing to be based
Upon your father's wisdom, his good taste,
And a wounded cock's avenging subtlety.
Now, sir, please sing, for holy charity;   3320
Let's see how well your father you repeat."
Then Chanticleer his wings began to beat,
As one who'd been betrayed but couldn't see,
So ravished was he by such flattery.

    Alas! my lords, there are within your courts   3325
False flatterers and other lying sorts
Who please you, by my faith, more than the man
Who speaks to you the truth as best he can.
In *Ecclesiastes* read of flattery;
Beware, my lords, of all their treachery.   3330

    This Chanticleer stood high upon his toes;
Stretching his neck, he let his two eyes close
And loudly he began to crow. Apace
The fox Sir Russell sprang out from his place
And by the throat grabbed Chanticleer. He bore   3335
Him on his back toward the woodland, for
The fox as yet by no one was pursued.

    O Destiny, you cannot be eschewed!
Alas, that Chanticleer flew from the beams!
Alas, his wife did not believe in dreams!   3340

And on a Friday fell all this distress.

 O Venus, goddess of all pleasantness,
Since servant you have had in Chanticleer,
Who used his powers in your service here
More for delight than world to multiply,   3345
Why would you suffer him this day to die?

 O Geoffrey, sovereign master, when was shot
And slain your worthy Richard, did you not
Complain so sorely of his death? O would
I had your gift and lore, so that I could   3350
Chide Friday as you did! (For it was on
A Friday Richard died, as is well known.)
Then I would show you how I could complain
For Chanticleer, for all his fear and pain.

 Surely not such a cry or lamentation   3355
Did ladies make at Troy's devastation—
When Pyrrhus seized King Priam by the beard
And with his straight, unsparing sword then speared
And slew him (so relates the *Aeneid*'s bard)—
As made all of the hens there in the yard   3360
When they had seen the plight of Chanticleer.
Shrieked Pertelote so loudly all could hear,
More loudly than did King Hasdrubal's wife
When her husband at Carthage lost his life
And Romans made the town a conflagration.   3365
(So filled with torment and with indignation,
The queen jumped willfully into the fire
And burnt to death, as death was her desire.)
O woeful hens, your crying is the same
As when by Nero Rome was set aflame   3370
And tears were shed by senators' wives
Because their husbands all then lost their lives.
(They had no guilt but Nero had them slain.)
Now to my tale I will return again.

 This simple widow and her daughters heard 3375
The woeful crying of the hens. They stirred
Themselves at once, leapt up and ran outside;
The fox toward the grove they then espied,
Bearing away the cock upon his back.

They cried out "Help!" and "Mercy!" and "Alack!   3380
Hey, hey, the fox!" And after him they ran,
And joining in with staves came many a man,
And our dog Collie, Talbot too, and Garland,
And Malkin with a distaff in her hand.
Ran cow and calf and even all the hogs,   3385
So frightened by the barking of the dogs
And shouting of each woman, every man.
They thought their hearts would burst, so hard they ran.
They yelled like fiends in hell, such was the cry;
The ducks all quacked as if about to die;   3390
The geese in fear flew up above the trees;
Out of the hive there came a swarm of bees.
God knows, the noise was hideous and loud!
I'm certain that Jack Straw and all his crowd
Did not produce a shouting half as shrill   3395
(When they had found a Fleming they could kill)
As all the noise directed at the fox.
They brought out trumpets made of brass and box,
Of horns and bone, on which they blew and tooted;
They also shrieked, they whooped as well as hooted,   3400
Until it seemed that heaven itself would fall.
    Good men, I pray, please listen one and all,
For see how Fortune upsets suddenly
The hope and pride now of her enemy!
This cock, who on the fox's back still lay,   3405
Despite his fear said to the fox, "I say,
What I would do, my lord, if I were you,
So help me God, is tell those who pursue,
'Turn back, you fools, you haughty churls all,
And may a pestilence upon you fall!   3410
For now that I have reached the woodland's side,
In spite of you this cock shall here abide—
I'll eat him up right now in front of you!'"
    The fox replied, "In faith, that's what I'll do."
But as he spoke those words, without a pause   3415
The cock broke nimbly from the fox's jaws
And immediately flew high up in a tree.
And when the fox had seen his captive flee,

"Alas," he said, "O Chanticleer, alas!
Against you I am guilty of trespass.   3420
I made you fear what it was all about,
To grab you in the yard and bring you out.
But, sir, I did it with no ill intent.
Come down, and I will tell you what I meant—
The truth, so help me God! You have my oath."   3425
    "Nay," said the cock, "a curse upon us both.
And first I curse myself, by blood and bone,
If more than once I let you lead me on.
You shall no more, with words so flattering,
Inveigle me to close my eyes and sing.   3430
For him who wills to blink when he should see,
God never let there be prosperity!"
    "No," said the fox, "but God bring to defeat
One whose demeanor is so indiscreet
That when he ought to hold his peace he chatters."   3435
    Lo, such it is to trust in one who flatters,
Be negligent, and act so carelessly.
    But you who judge this tale frivolity
(As it's about a fox, or cock and hen),
Take seriously the moral, gentlemen.   3440
For all that has been written, says Saint Paul,
Is written so that we might learn it all.
So take the fruit and let the chaff be still.
    Now, gracious God, if it should be thy will,
As says my lord, make all of us good men   3445
And bring us to high heaven's bliss! Amen.

EPILOGUE

    "Sir Nun's Priest," our Host said immediately,
"Your balls and your behind now blessed be!
Of Chanticleer that was a merry tale.
I swear, were you a layman, without fail   3450
A real hen-treader you'd have been, all right.
Had you the will as much as you've the might,
The hens that you'd need in your flock, I hold,

Would number seventeen some sevenfold.
What muscles by this gentle priest possessed,   3455
So thick a neck, and see how large a breast!
He's like a sparrowhawk, so sharp his eye,
His color not in need of any dye
From Portugal or such to make it redder.
Good luck, sir, for your tale, among the better!"   3460
    And after that, our Host with merry cheer
Spoke to another pilgrim as you'll hear.

The Second Nun's Tale

PROLOGUE

That minister and nurse to every vice,
Known in the English tongue as Idleness,
That portress of the gate where sins entice,
We should by her own opposite suppress—
That is to say, by righteous busyness, 5
For thereto our full effort should be brought
Lest by the fiend through Idleness we're caught.

For he who with his thousand-corded net
Is always waiting for his net to snap
On any idle man whom he can get, 10
Can, having seen, so easily entrap
That till one's caught right by the coat or flap
He doesn't know he's in the devil's hand.
Well should we work and Idleness withstand.

And even if men didn't fear to die, 15
All men of reason well could see, no doubt,
That Idleness is rotten sloth whereby
No good or gain can ever come about;
For Idleness, held in sloth's leash, is out
To sleep and eat and drink and nothing more, 20
Out to consume what others labor for.

And to remove us from such idleness,
The cause by which disorder is so great,
I've done my duty, that with busyness
Your saintly legend I may now translate, 25
Your glorious life and passion to relate,

460

You with your garland rose- and lily-laden:
I mean you, Saint Cecilia, martyred maiden.

Invocacio ad Mariam

To thee, of all virginity the flower,
About whom Saint Bernard so loved to write,   30
I pray here at the start. Grant me the power,
O comfort of us wretches, to indite
Thy maiden's death, and how she won the fight
Against the fiend, by merit won her glory,
Eternal life, as men read in her story.   35

O maiden Mother, daughter of thy Son,
O mercy's well, of sinful souls the cure,
In whom God chose to dwell that good be done;
So meek, so high above all creatures, pure,
Ennobling our nature to ensure   40
That no disdain the Maker had to bind
His Son in flesh and blood, clothed as our kind.

Within the blissful cloister of thy womb
Eternal love and peace took shape of man,
Of all this world the Lord and Shepherd, whom   45
Earth, sea, and sky still praise as they began.
And thou, O spotless Virgin, true to plan,
Bore by thy body, still in purest state,
The One who every creature did create.

Within thee is combined magnificence   50
With mercy, goodness, and such sympathy
That thou, who art the sun of excellence,
Will help not only those who pray to thee
But oftentimes, through thy benignity,
Thou freely helpest ere men make petition;   55
Thou goest before them as their lives' physician.

Help me, O blissful maiden fair and meek,
This banished wretch, in desert full of gall;
Think of that Canaanite, she dared to speak
About how even dogs might eat of all   60
The crumbs that from their master's table fall;
And although I, unworthy son of Eve,
Be sinful, yet accept that I believe.

And since one's faith is dead without good works,
To labor now give me the wit and space,   65
Released from where the dark that's deepest lurks!
O maiden, thou so fair and full of grace,
Be thou my advocate in that high place
Where without end they sing the song "Hosanna,"
Mother of Christ, O daughter dear of Anna!   70

And with thy light my soul imprisoned light
That's so disturbed by this contamination
That is my flesh; disturbed, too, by the blight
Of earthly lust, of falsehood, affectation.
O haven of our refuge, O salvation   75
Of those who are in sorrow and distress,
Now help me in this work I'm to address.

I pray that you who read now what I write
Forgive me if I show no diligence
To tell with craft or skill what I indite;   80
I use the words and gist in truest sense
Of him who for this saint in reverence
The story wrote; I only follow it.
Amend my work, I pray, where you see fit.

Interpretacio nominis Cecilie quam ponit
Frater Jacobus Januensis in Legenda

   Of Saint Cecilia's name first I will tell;   85
Its meaning men may in her story see.
In English, "heaven's lily" says it well,

For purity, for her virginity;
Or for the whiteness of her honesty,
Her conscience green, or yet for her good fame,   90
No sweeter savor: "lily" was her name.

It also means "a pathway for the blind,"
Such fine examples her good teaching set;
Or else Cecilia, in one book I find,
Can be a compound, two words having met,   95
"Heaven" and "Leah"—here, then, we may get
The "heaven" from the thought of holiness,
The "Leah" her untiring busyness.

Cecilia can be also said to mean
"One without blindness," what with her great light   100
Of wisdom and her virtues clearly seen;
Or else, as well, this maiden's name so bright
Is "heaven" matched with "leos," for by right
Men well might her the "people's heaven" call,
Example of fine works to one and all.   105

For "leos" we in English "people" say,
And just as men may in the heavens see
The sun and moon and stars, the whole array,
So in this maiden's generosity
The people saw faith's magnanimity,   110
The wholeness, too, of clearest sapience,
And many shining works of excellence.

And just as these philosophers declare
That heaven's swift and round and full of fire,
So Saint Cecilia, she so white and fair,   115
Was swift and busy, good works to inspire,
And round and whole in that she'd never tire,
Her charity burnt ever like a flame.
I now have told you all about her name.

THE SECOND NUN'S TALE

This bright Cecilia, as her story's told,   120
Was born in Rome from blood of noble kind
And, from the cradle up, raised in the fold
Of Christ, and bore his gospel in her mind.
She never ceased, as in the book I find,
To say her prayers and God to love and dread,   125
Beseeching that he guard her maidenhead.

And when this maiden to a certain man
Had come to be betrothed—he was a lad
Quite young in years, his name Valerian—
So humble and devout a heart she had   130
That on the day of marriage she was clad
(Beneath her golden robe so lovely) in
A shirt of haircloth right next to her skin.

And while the organs played, her heart inside
To God above was singing silently: 135
"Lord, to my soul and body too be guide,
Keep me unstained, lest I confounded be."
For love of him who died upon a tree,
Each second day and third she spent in fast,
Each day in fervent prayer from first to last.   140

Then came the wedding night, when to the bed
With her new husband she would have to go;
And privately at once to him she said,
"Sweet husband whom I love, and dearly so,
There is a secret I would have you know,   145
And gladly I will tell you here and now
If you will not betray it, by your vow."

Valerian at once began to swear
That in no case, no matter what it be,
Would he betray what secret she'd declare;   150
And then she told her husband finally,

"I have an angel watching over me
With such great love that, though I sleep or wake,
My body he protects, will not forsake.

"And if he senses, out of doubt or dread,   155
You'd touch me or would love in carnal ways,
At once he'll leave you numbered with the dead,
He'll slay you while still in your youthful days.
If in pure love you lead me, though, with praise
He'll love you, too, for your clean righteousness,   160
And with his joy and brightness he will bless."

Forewarned as God desired, Valerian
Said, "If I'm to believe you, let me see
With my own eyes this angel if I can;
And if true angel he turns out to be,   165
Then I will do as you have asked of me;
But if you love another, by my oath
This sword of mine I'll take and slay you both."

Cecilia then immediately advised,
"If you desire, this angel you will see,   170
That you'll believe in Christ and be baptized.
Go to the Appian Way, which is," said she,
"Not far from town, in miles it numbers three;
And to the poor folks who are dwelling there
You'll speak directly as I'll now declare.   175

"Tell them that by Cecilia you are sent
To see good Urban, who's now very old,
In private need and with the best intent.
And when this good Saint Urban you behold,
Tell him the words that by me you'll be told;   180
And when from sin he's purged you in your heart,
This angel you will see ere you depart."

Valerian went straight out to the place
And, just as he'd been told, he met inside
The catacombs Saint Urban face-to-face,   185

Among the tombs where Urban had to hide.
Valerian at once set to confide
His message; and when finished, in reply
For joy Saint Urban raised his hands up high.

As Urban from his eyes the tears let fall,   190
"Almighty God, O Jesus Christ," said he,
"Who sows chaste counsel, Shepherd of us all,
The fruit of that same seed of chastity
That thou hast sown in her, take unto thee!
Lo, busy as a bee, without a guile,   195
Thy sweet handmaiden serves thee all the while.

"To thee this very spouse she newly took,
One fierce as any lion, she sends here
As meek as any lamb could ever look!"
And with that word there started to appear   200
An aged man, in white clothes bright and clear,
Who with a book gold-lettered in his hand
Came there before Valerian to stand.

Valerian fell down then as if dead,
So fearful at the sight; but by the hand   205
He helped him up, then in his book he read:
"One Lord, one faith, one God, no others stand,
One Christendom, one Father in command,
None else above, he governs everywhere."
And all in gold these words were written there.   210

And when he'd read, then said this aged man,
"Do you believe or not? Say yea or nay."
"All I believe," replied Valerian,
"For nothing truer under heaven's sway
Might anyone believe, I dare to say."   215
The old man disappeared, he knew not where,
And then Pope Urban christened him right there.

When he went home, he found inside her room
An angel standing at Cecilia's side.

Of roses and of lilies in their bloom 220
This angel held two chaplets sanctified;
The angel gave the first crown to the bride,
Then, as I find this legend to relate,
He gave the second chaplet to her mate.

"With body clean and with unblemished thought 225
Keep always these two chaplets," then said he.
"For to you I from paradise have brought
Them, they shall never withered be
Nor lose their lovely fragrance, trust in me;
And on them not one person will lay eyes 230
Unless he's chaste, hates wickedness and lies.

"And you, Valerian, who have so soon
Accepted righteous counsel, now you can
Ask what you wish and you will have your boon."
"I have a brother," said Valerian, 235
"One whom I cherish as no other man.
I pray you'll to my brother grant the grace
To know the truth, as I do in this place."

The angel said, "God's pleased with your request;
You both, bearing the palm of martyrdom, 240
Shall come into his feast among the blest."
With that his brother Tiburce there had come,
And when he caught the savor, all and some,
The scent of rose and lily in the air,
Amazement filled his heart right then and there. 245

"From where, I wonder, at this time of year
Could there be coming such sweet scent," said he,
"Of rose and lily that I'm smelling here.
Though in my own two hands they were to be,
The scent could not go deeper into me; 250
The sweet perfume that in my heart I find
Has changed me all into some other kind."

Valerian replied, "Two crowns have we,

Snow white and rosy red, both shining clear,
Although these crowns your eyes have yet to see.   255
And now as through my prayers you've smelt them here,
You also shall behold them, brother dear,
If only you will now without ado
Believe aright and know the good and true."

Tiburce replied, "You're saying this to me   260
In truth, or in a dream I'm hearing this?"
Valerian then answered, "Certainly
We've dreamt till now, my brother; now we've bliss,
For finally in truth our dwelling is."
"You know this to be true?" asked Tiburce. "How?"   265
Valerian replied, "I'll tell you now.

"The angel of the Lord this truth has taught
To me, which you will see if from the spell
Of idols you'll be cleansed, or else see naught."
The miracle of these two crowns as well   270
Saint Ambrose in his preface likes to tell;
This dear and noble doctor solemnly
Commends it, as he speaks accordingly:

"That martyr's palm by her might thus be gained,
Had Saint Cecilia, by God's gift so blest,   275
From world as well as marriage-bed abstained;
Valerian and Tiburce then confessed
Their sins, upon which God, by kind behest,
Two crowns of flowers, sweet as flowers grow,
Sent by his angel to them there below.   280

"This maiden brought these men to highest bliss;
The world now knows it's worthy to refrain,
Devoted to chaste love, be sure of this."
And then Cecilia showed him, made it plain
To Tiburce, that all idols are in vain   285
(They cannot speak, nor can they hear a sound),
And from his idols bade him turn around.

"Whoever won't believe it," he confessed,
"Is but a beast and that is not a lie."
And when she heard these words, she kissed his breast,   290
So glad that he the truth could well espy.
"This day I take you as my own ally,"
Then said this blessed maiden, fair and dear;
And after that she spoke as you will hear:

"Behold, just as the love of Christ," said she,   295
"Made me your brother's wife, in such a way
I take you now as an ally to me,
Since you despise your idols as you say.
Go with your brother, be baptized today
And so be cleansed, that you may then behold   300
The angel's face of which your brother told."

Then Tiburce answered, saying, "Brother dear,
Tell me where I'm to go, and to what man."
"To whom?" said he. "Now come, be of good cheer,
I'll lead you to Pope Urban as I can."   305
"To Urban?" Tiburce asked. "Valerian,
My brother, that's to whom now you would lead?
I think I'll have to wonder at the deed.

"That Urban," then said Tiburce, "can you mean
Who's been condemned to be among the dead,   310
Who walks about in hiding, can't be seen,
Into the daylight dares not stick his head?
They'd burn him in a fire, one flaming red,
If he were found, if seen where he may hide;
They'd burn us, too, if found there by his side.   315

"And while we seek that same eternal state
That's hidden up in heaven secretly,
They'll burn us up down here at any rate!"
To this Cecilia said courageously,
"It's well and good that men might fearfully   320
Lose this their earthly life, my own dear brother,
If this were all of life, there were no other.

"But there's a better life some other place
That never shall be lost—no doubt be brought—
Of which God's Son has told us through his grace.   325
It's through the Father's Son that all is wrought,
And all the creatures blest with gift of thought
The Holy Ghost, which from the Father springs,
Endows with souls. There's no doubt of these things.

"By miracle and word the Father's Son,   330
When he was in the world, informed us here
That there's another life that's to be won."
And Tiburce then replied, "O sister dear,
Did you not just advise and make it clear
That there is but one God, and truthfully?   335
How, then, can you bear witness now to three?"

"That I shall tell," said she, "before I go.
The mind of man is threefold: memory,
Imagination, intellect. Just so,
Within one Being of divinity   340
Three personages very well may be."
And of Christ's birth she then began to preach
To him with vigor, all his pains to teach,

With much about his passion; how God's Son
Was in this world below, in flesh's hold,   345
To grant full pardon for what man had done
While bound in sin and care so dark and cold;
These are the things that she to Tiburce told.
And Tiburce, after this, in good intent
With his dear brother to Pope Urban went,   350

Who, thanking God and with heart glad and light,
Then baptized him and made him in that place
One perfect in his learning, heaven's knight.
And Tiburce after this was blest with grace
Till every day he saw in time and space   355
The angel of the Lord; and every boon
He asked of God was granted to him soon.

It would be very hard here to explain
How many wonders Jesus for them wrought;
But finally, to tell it short and plain,   360
By officers of Rome they soon were caught
And to the prefect Almachius brought,
Who questioned them and, knowing their intent,
Before the Jovian image had them sent.

"Chop off the heads of those," was his command,   365
"Who will not sacrifice to Jupiter."
At once these martyrs then were in the hand
Of Maximus, the prefect's officer;
But when these saints to whom I here refer
Were being led away in summary fashion,   370
This Maximus shed tears in his compassion.

When he had heard what these saints had to say,
He asked the executioners for leave
To take them to his home by straightest way;
And there with preaching, before it was eve,   375
They made the executioners believe;
And Maximus and his whole family, too,
From false faith turned to that one God who's true.

Cecilia came, when it was fall of night,
With priests, and all were baptized without fear;   380
And afterward, when broke the morning light,
Cecilia said with her unfailing cheer,
"You now are knights of Christ, you're loved and dear;
Cast off the works of darkness, all their harm,
In armor of God's brightness now to arm.   385

"The good fight you have fought, your race is through,
And truthfully your faith you have preserved.
So claim the crown of life laid up for you;
The Judge of righteousness whom you have served
Will give it as reward, as you've deserved."   390
And when these words as I relate were said,
Toward the shrine these two by men were led.

But when they had been brought before the thing,
To tell you briefly how it all turned out,
They burnt no incense, made no offering,   395
But down upon their knees they knelt about
With humble hearts, each to the last devout,
For which they were beheaded in that place.
Their souls departed to the King of grace.

This Maximus, when he had witnessed this,   400
At once with tears described what had occurred:
He'd seen their souls ascend to heaven's bliss,
With angels full of clearest light. So heard,
He soon converted many with his word,
For which the prefect then by thongs with lead   405
Had him so whipped that soon the man was dead.

Cecilia took his corpse and, quickly gone,
By Tiburce and Valerian would she
Inter him gently underneath the stone.
Then Almachius ordered hastily   410
His officers to go fetch openly
Cecilia, that he then might witness her
Make proper sacrifice to Jupiter.

But they, too, were converted by her lore
And sorely wept, for they with faithfulness   415
Believed her word, and cried out all the more,
"Christ Jesus, Son of God, is nothing less
Than truly God—and that's what we profess—
And has so good a servant, one to cherish.
We say this in one voice, though we perish!"   420

The prefect heard of this, and to his hall
Bade she be brought, this creature he would see;
And here is what he asked her first of all:
"What kind of woman are you?" To which she
Then answered, "One born of nobility."   425
"I ask," said he, "though it cause you to grieve,
What is your faith and what do you believe?"

"You have begun your questions foolishly,"
She said, "for you expect two answers by
One question asked; you question stupidly."   430
To such a comment he responded, "Why,
From where could come so churlish a reply?"
"From where?" she answered, and then she explained,
"From conscience and good faith that is unfeigned."

"You pay no heed," then Almachius said,   435
"To all my might?" She answered in this way:
"Your power's such a little thing to dread.
For every mortal's power, all his sway,
Is like a wind-filled bladder, safe to say.
For all its pride, when it's blown up and thick,   440
Can be laid low with just a needle's prick."

"How wrongfully have you begun," said he,
"And still persist in wrong, will not refrain.
Our mighty princes, have they generously
By order and by law not made it plain   445
That every Christian shall be brought to pain
Who won't renounce his Christian faith, but he,
If only he'll repent, may then go free?"

"Your princes err just as your nobles do,"
She said, "for by some crazy ordinance   450
You make us guilty when it isn't true.
For even though you know our innocence,
Because we Christians offer reverence
To Christ, and as we bear the Christian name,
Of crime we are accused, we get the blame.   455

"But as we know that name so virtuous,
That we should then renounce it cannot be."
"Choose one of two," the prefect said, "show us
A sacrifice or spurn Christianity,
For that way you'll escape and now be free."   460
This holy blessed maiden laughed instead,
And to this prefect here is what she said:

"O judge confused in folly, you would now
Have me renounce, deny my innocence,
And make myself a sinner? Look, see how   465
This man dissembles while in audience!
He stares and rages, hardly making sense."
Then Almachius said, "Unhappy wretch,
Do you not know how far my might can stretch?

"Did not our mighty princes to me give   470
The power, yea, and the authority
To say which folk shall die and which shall live?
Why do you speak so proudly, then, to me?"
"I only spoke steadfastly," answered she,
"Not proudly, for, in speaking for my side,   475
We Christians hate that deadly sin of pride.

"And if to hear the truth you do not fear,
By right I'll show now in an open way
How great a lie it is you've uttered here.
Your princes gave to you the might to slay   480
Or give a person life, that's what you say;
But you can only take life and destroy,
You have no other power to enjoy.

"Though you indeed may say your princes made
You minister of death (that's not a lie),   485
Your lack of other power bare is laid."
"Now quit your brazenness," was his reply,
"To our gods sacrifice before you die!
Insult me, I don't care what you infer,
That I can bear like a philsopher;   490

"But those same insults I will not abide
Against our gods, you've spoken blasphemy."
"You foolish thing!" Cecilia then replied,
"So far you haven't said one word to me
That hasn't shown me your stupidity   495
And that in every way you are and were
A worthless judge, an ignorant officer.

"You're blind to everything that meets your eye;
For something that is seen here by us all
To be a stone—as men may well espy—   500
That very stone a god you choose to call.
I tell you, let your hand upon it fall
And test it well and stone is what you'll find,
Since you can't see it with your eyes so blind.

"The people will so scorn you, what a shame,   505
They'll laugh at all your folly, for well nigh
Among all men the knowledge is the same,
That mighty God is in his heavens high;
These images, as you should well espy,
Can't help you or themselves, however slight,   510
For in effect they are not worth a mite."

Those words she said, and more of like degree,
And he, enraged, then ordered men to lead
Her to her house, and "Burn her there," said he,
"Inside a flaming bath." As he decreed,   515
So right away these men performed the deed;
They put her in a bath and shut it tight,
And built great fire beneath it day and night.

But all that night, and through the day that sprang,
For all the fire, the heat that was so rife,   520
She coolly sat and never felt a pang
Nor shed one drop of sweat, had not a strife.
But in that bath she was to lose her life,
For Almachius, wicked his intent,
To slay her in the bath his lackey sent.   525

Three strokes into her neck he was to hew,
This executioner, but in no way
Did he succeed in chopping it in two;
And as there was a law back in that day
That no one such a penalty should pay   530
As to receive a fourth blow, hard or light,
He didn't dare another blow to smite.

And so half dead he left her lying there,
Her neck cut open; on his way he went.
The Christians there around her then took care   535
To stop her bleeding using sheets. She spent
Her final three days then in much torment,
But never ceased the Christian faith to teach
To those she had converted; she would preach,

And gave them all her goods, each little thing,   540
To take to Urban, with this word also:
"This one request I made of heaven's King,
That I might have three days, no more, just so
To recommend to you, before I go,
These souls, and that my house I might commence   545
To build into a church of permanence."

Saint Urban with his deacons secretly
The body fetched, and buried it by night
Among his other saints, and fittingly.
As Saint Cecilia's Church her house by right   550
Is known (Saint Urban blest it, well he might),
In which today men give in noblest ways
To Jesus and his saints their servants' praise.

The Canon's Yeoman's Tale

PROLOGUE

When Saint Cecilia's life was finished, we
Had ridden less than five miles—we would be   555
At Boughton under Blean—when from the back
A fellow overtook us clothed in black,
Though white his surplice underneath. He rode
A hackney, dappled gray, with such a load
Of sweat it was astonishing to see;   560
He must have ridden hard, two miles or three.
His Yeoman's horse as well was sweating so
It looked like it could scarcely even go.
The harness round its breast was soaking wet;
A magpie it appeared, such spots of sweat.   565
One doubled bag upon its crupper lay,
So he'd brought little clothing, safe to say.
This worthy man, dressed light for summer's start,
Made me begin to wonder in my heart
What he might be, until I understood   570
The way in which his cloak was sewn to hood,
And thinking on it finally came to see
That some sort of a Canon he must be.
His hat hung at his back, kept by a knot,
For he had ridden more than at a trot—   575
He'd spurred, in fact, as if a fellow mad.
A burdock leaf beneath his hood he had
To fight the sweat and cool his head. And yet
It was a joy to see the fellow sweat!
His forehead dripped just like a still will do,   580
One filled with plantain, pellitory too.
When he'd caught up with us, then bellowed he,
"May God preserve this jolly company!
I've ridden hard and for no other sake
Than that you people I might overtake,   585

477

To ride with such a merry company."
His Yeoman, too, was full of courtesy,
And said, "I saw you, sirs, at early day
As from your hostelry you rode away.
I warned my lord and master here, as he   590
Would eagerly enjoy your company
While riding, for he likes to joke and play."
    "God bless you, friend, for warning him that way!"
Then said our Host. "For surely I surmise,
As far as I can judge, your lord is wise.   595
He's jolly, too, I'd wager that it's true!
Can he relate a merry tale or two
To gladden all this company as well?"
    "Who, sirs? My lord? Indeed, no lie I tell,
Of merriment and all such jollity   600
He knows more than enough. And, trust in me,
If you knew him as well as I do now,
You'd marvel at his cunning, wonder how
His work in many ways can be so clever.
He's undertaken many a great endeavor   605
That any here would find too hard for them
To bring about, unless they learnt from him.
As humbly as he rides here, if you got
To know him it would profit you a lot;
Then his acquaintance you'd not trade away   610
For quite a tidy sum—on that I'd lay
My money down, all that's in my possession.
I warn you, he's a man of high discretion,
One as surpassing as has ever been."
    "Well," said our Host, "I pray you'll tell us, then,   615
Is he a cleric? Say what he may be."
    "Nay, greater than a cleric, certainly,"
This Yeoman said. "In words, Host, that are few
I'll tell you something of what he can do.
    "I say, he knows such arts of subtlety—   620
But you won't learn of all his craft from me,
Though in his work I sometimes help him still—
That all this ground on which we ride, until
We've gone from here to Canterbury town,

My lord could turn completely upside down   625
And pave it all with silver and with gold."
    And when this Yeoman had this story told,
Our Host responded, "*Benedicite!*
This thing's a marvel—what more can I say?—
To see the way your lord, so wise and clever   630
That all men should respect him, should, however,
Pay little mind to his own dignity.
The coat he's wearing isn't worth a flea
And shouldn't be by such a fellow worn.
As I may walk, it's filthy and it's torn!   635
Pray tell me why so sloppily he goes.
Can't he afford to buy some better clothes
If his deeds match your words? Now tell me more,
Explain this matter to me, I implore."
    "Why?" said the Yeoman. "Why ask that of me?   640
God help me, he'll find no prosperity!
(I wouldn't want to swear to what I say,
So keep it as a secret, sir, I pray.)
I think that he's too wise for his own good;
What's overdone won't turn out as it should,   645
For it is then a vice, clerks rightly say.
I think he's dumb and foolish in that way.
For when a fellow has too great a wit,
It often happens he misuses it;
So does my lord, for which my grief is sore.   650
May God amend it! I can't tell you more."
    "No matter, my good Yeoman," said our Host.
"But since about his art you know the most,
Tell how he does it, I sincerely pray,
Since he's as sly and crafty as you say.   655
Where do you dwell, if that you may confide?"
    "In the outskirts of a city," he replied.
"In corners and blind alleyways we lurk
Where all your thieves by nature do their work,
Reside in secrecy and fear, from where   660
They dare not show their faces. So we fare,
If I should speak the truth, my lord and I."
    "Now," said our Host, "permit me asking why

You've such discoloration in your face."
   "Saint Peter," he replied, "it's a disgrace!   ·   665
I'm so accustomed on the fire to blow
I think my whole complexion's changed, although
I don't go looking into mirrors—I
Stay hard at work, to learn to multiply.
We blunder right along, stare in the fire,   670
And for all that we fail in our desire,
We never have results when we conclude.
A lot of folks, however, we delude
And borrow gold—be it a pound or so,
Or ten or twelve, as high as we can go—   675
And make them think, at least, that we can take
A pound of gold and two pounds from it make.
It's false, but still we always have good hope
It can be done, and after it we grope.
But it's a science that's so far ahead   680
That though we vow, no matter what is said,
It can't be caught, it slips away so fast,
And it will make us beggars at the last."
   Now while this Yeoman said this, there drew near
His lord the Canon, close enough to hear   685
All that was said. For always when he'd see
Men talking, he'd react suspiciously;
As Cato says, "The guilty without doubt
Will alway think he's being talked about."
That's why he drew so near him, that he may   690
Hear everything the Yeoman had to say.
Here's what he told his Yeoman when he'd heard:
"Now hold your tongue, don't speak another word,
For if you do you'll dearly pay! For me
You slander here before this company,   695
And tell things, too, that you should keep concealed."
   "Tell," said our Host, "no matter what's revealed!
His threats aren't worth a mite, don't give 'em store."
   "In faith," said he, "I don't much anymore."
   And when this Canon saw no other way—   700
His Yeoman would his secrets give away—
He turned and fled in sorrow and in shame.

"Ah," said the Yeoman, "now for fun and game!
All that I know I'll tell you on the level.
He's gone, and may he run into the devil!   705
For henceforth I will never meet him now,
For penny or for pound, and that's a vow.
Before he dies may he be brought to shame
And grief for dragging me into his game!
For by my faith, it's been hard work and tough;   710
Say what you will, I feel it well enough,
And yet for all my pain and all my grief,
My woe and labor, trial without relief,
To leave it I could never find a way.
I wish to God I'd wits enough today   715
To tell you all that figures in that art!
But nonetheless at least I'll tell you part.
And since my lord is gone, I'll nothing spare;
Such things as those I know I will declare."

THE CANON'S YEOMAN'S TALE

PART I

Though with this Canon I've dwelt seven years,   720
For all his science I'm still in arrears;
For everything I had I've lost thereby,
And, God knows, so have many more than I.
Though fresh and bright I once was wont to be
In clothing and in other finery,   725
Now I must wear a stocking on my head.
And though my color once was healthy red,
It now is wan and has a leaden hue—
Whoever tries this art will sorely rue!—
My eyes so bleared they still can hardly see.   730
Lo, what advantage lies in alchemy!
That slippery science has so stripped me bare
That I have nothing, here or anywhere;
And I'm still so indebted by the gold

That I have borrowed—let the truth be told—   735
That while I live I can't repay it ever.
Let every man be warned by me forever!
Whoso takes up this science, for my part,
If he persists, is done in from the start.
So help me God, there's nothing he can gain   740
Except an empty purse and addled brain.
And when he by his crazy foolishness
Has lost his goods through all this risky mess,
He then entices others with their pelf
To lose it all as he has done himself.   745
For rascals find their comfort and delight
In seeing fellow men in pain and blight—
Or so a scholar taught me once. But out
With that, for it's our work I'll tell about.
        When in the place where we're to exercise   750
Our elvish craft, we seem to be so wise,
The terms we use so technical and quaint.
I blow the fire until my heart is faint.
Why should I tell you the exact proportions
Of things we work with, measured out in portions—   755
Five ounces, maybe six (all which would be
Of silver), or some other quantity?
And why should all the names be duly stated
Of arsenic, burnt bones, iron fragmentated
And ground to finest powder? Why recall   760
How in an earthen pot we put it all,
How we put salt into it, paper too,
Before the powders as I've said to you,
How with a plate of glass the pot is covered,
With other things such as may be discovered?   765
Why tell how we will seal both pot and glass
So that no bit of air might ever pass,
And of the fires—some warm and others hot—
And of the care and woe that is our lot
In trying as we do to sublimate,   770
Which is to calcine or amalgamate
Quicksilver (also called crude mercury)?
Results from all these tricks we never see.

Our arsenic, our mercury sublimate,
Lead oxide ground on porphyry (the weight   775
Of each of these to certain ounces brought)—
None of it helps, our labor is for naught.
Nor rising gases that evaporate
Nor all the matter left in solid state
Can in our work be of the least avail;   780
We've wasted all our labor and travail,
And all that we've spent on it, for our cost,
By twenty devils, is all money lost.
    Now there are many other things as well
Pertaining to our craft that I can tell.   785
I can't say in what order they should fall,
For I am not a learned man at all,
But I'll relate them as they come to mind,
Though not arranged according to their kind:
Armenian clay, borax and verdigris,   790
And vessels made of glass and earth; with these,
Our urinals, retorts for distillation,
Assaying vessels, flasks for sublimation,
Our vials and our alembics—all such stuff
As that, all of it costing quite enough.   795
There is no need for me to list them all—
Like waters used for reddening, bull's gall,
Arsenic, brimstone, sal ammoniac;
Of herbs, too, I could tell without a slack,
Herbs like valerian or like moonwort   800
Or agrimony. I could long report
On how our lamps keep burning day and night,
Our purpose to accomplish, if we might;
Or of our furnaces for calcining,
Of water that we use for whitening;   805
Chalk, unslaked lime, egg-white, a whole array
Of powders, ashes, droppings, piss, and clay,
Wax-coated bags, saltpeter, vitriol,
And various kinds of fires from wood and coal;
Some salt of tartar, table salt, potash,   810
Stuff burnt, congealed; of clay made with a dash
Of horse's hair (or else the human sort);

Rock alum, yeast, some tartar oil and wort,
Ratsbane and argol; other things we use
That will absorb, and things that interfuse;   815
Our work with silver, too, its citronation,
And our cementing and our fermentation;
Our ingots, crucibles, and so much more.
    I'll teach you now, as I've been taught before,
The seven bodies and four spirits, all   820
In order as I've often heard him call.
For the first spirit, quicksilver's the word;
The second, arsenic; of course, the third
Is sal ammoniac; the fourth, brimstone.
The seven bodies? Listen how they're known: 825
Gold's Sol and silver's Luna, so say we,
And iron is Mars, quicksilver Mercury,
While lead is Saturn, Jupiter is tin,
And Venus copper, by my father's kin!
    But by this cursed craft no man alive   830
Can gain enough out of it to survive;
For all he spends to bring such things about
Is money lost, of that I've not a doubt.
Come forth, if it's a fool you'd like to be,
And learn about the art of alchemy;   835
If you have money, then step forward, sir,
And you too can become philosopher.
You think it's knowledge easy to acquire?
Nay, nay, God knows! Be he a monk or friar,
A canon, priest, or any we might say,   840
Though he sit at his books both night and day
To learn this elvish and this foolish lore,
It's all in vain—God knows, it's even more!
To teach an ignorant man this subtlety—
O fie! don't speak of such, it cannot be!   845
For whether he's a learned man or not,
Both kinds will find they share a common lot;
For both will in the end, by my salvation,
Find in this art of multiplication
The very same result for their travail;   850
That is, in what they try they both will fail.

Yet I forgot to mention these to you:
Corrosive waters, metal filings too,
The softening of substances, as well
As how to make them hard; I didn't tell   855
Of oils, ablutions, metals we can fuse—
It's more than any book you can peruse,
No matter where. And so it's for the best
That I don't bother naming all the rest.
I think already I've told you enough   860
To raise a devil looking mighty rough.

    Aye, let it be! The philosophers' stone,
Elixir called, we search for on and on,
For if we had it we'd be safe and sound.
I swear to God who's up in heaven found,   865
For all our craft and all our tricky gear,
When we are finished, it still won't appear.
It's made us spend much money, which is sad—
Indeed for sorrow we've gone nearly mad.
But that good hope still creeps into our heart;   870
We keep supposing, though we ache and smart,
That in the end we'll find it, have relief.
But that's a nagging hope, a hard belief;
I warn you well, the search is never-ending.
That hoped-for time has led men into spending,   875
Who trusted in it, all they ever had.
And yet it's never made them really sad,
For it's an art that's to them bittersweet,
Or so it seems—if they had but a sheet
With which they could enwrap themselves at night, 880
One ragged coat to walk in by daylight,
They'd sell them, that in this they might persist;
Till everything is gone they can't desist.
And they are marked wherever they have gone,
For by the smell of brimstone they are known.   885
They stink, for all the world, just like a goat;
It's such a strong and rammish smell to note
That though a fellow be a mile away
He'll be infected by it, safe to say.
So if you wish, by smell and threadbare clothes   890

An alchemist you'll know each place he goes.
And if someone should ask him privately
The reason why he's clothed so raggedly,
At once he'll whisper in the fellow's ear,
"If they knew who I am, these people here,   895
To slay me for my science they'd assent."
See how these folks take in the innocent!
    But let's pass on now to the tale I've got.
Before upon the fire we put the pot,
My lord will add thereto a certain weight   900
Of metals—he and no one else (I'll state
This openly, now that the fellow's gone)—
For as a crafty man he's surely known.
I know at least that he's had such a name,
Yet he can seldom live up to his fame.   905
Do you know why? In frequent episodes
It bids us all goodbye, the pot explodes!
These metals have such volatility
That our walls are not strong enough to be
Resistant unless made of lime or stone;   910
These metals pierce, right through the walls they hone
Or some go plunging right into the ground
(That way we've often lost more than a pound),
Across the floor some others scatter out,
Some shoot right through the roof. Without a doubt,   915
Although the devil never shows his face,
He must be right there with us in the place!
In hell itself where he is lord and sire
There couldn't be more turbulence and ire.
For when our pot explodes, as I have told,   920
Each man in his chagrin will start to scold.
    One blames it on the way the fire was built,
A second claims the blower bears the guilt—
Since I'm the blower, I get scared at once.
"Straw!" says the third, "you're everyone a dunce.   925
The whole thing wasn't mixed right anyhow."
"Nay," says the fourth, "shut up and listen now.
We didn't burn beech wood and that's the story,
No other cause, if I may go to glory!"

For me, I can't say why it went so wrong,   930
But well I know we argue hard and long.
    "Well," says my lord, "it can't be helped for now;
Next time I'll be more wary. Anyhow
I'm sure the pot was cracked. Be as it may,
Don't take it all in so confused a way.   935
Get busy and as usual sweep the floor;
Take heart, be glad and cheerful as before."
    The rubbish then is swept into a mound,
Then canvas on the floor is spread around,
And as this trash is thrown into a sieve   940
We sift and poke with all we have to give.
    "By God," says one, "there's still some metal here,
Though we don't have it all. It would appear
That even though this went awry somehow,
The next time may go better. We must now   945
Invest our goods in this. Upon my creed,
There's never been a merchant guaranteed
Success in every venture, trust in me.
Sometimes his goods are lost upon the sea,
And sometimes they're transported safe to land."   950
    "Peace!" says my lord. "Next time I'll have in hand
The way to bring our craft more to its aim,
And if I don't, sirs, give me all the blame.
There was a fault somewhere, that much is known."
    Another says the fire too hot had grown;   955
But be it hot or cold, I dare to say
That in our quest we never find the way.
We always fail to reach our aspiration
And madly rage in our exasperation.
And when we're there together, everyone   960
Among us seems to be a Solomon.
But everything that glitters is not gold,
As often I have heard the saying told;
Not every apple pleasing to the eye
Is good, though men may praise it to the sky.   965
That's how it is with me, right by the rule:
Who seems the wisest is the biggest fool,
By Jesus! When it comes time for belief,

Who seems the truest is the biggest thief.
That much you'll know before I part from you;   970
You'll know it by the time my tale is through.

PART II

Among us a religious canon goes
Who could infect a whole town if he chose
Though great as Rome and Troy and Nineveh,
Another three plus Alexandria.   975
His tricks and his deceit so limitless
No man could put in writing, I would guess,
Though he should live to see a thousand years.
In all this world for lies he has no peers;
For he gets so wound up in what he'll say   980
And speaks his words all in so sly a way
Whenever he converses with someone,
He'll make the man a fool before he's done—
Unless, like him, the man's a devil too.
He's hoodwinked many a man and isn't through,   985
Long as he lives he'll do it all the while.
And yet men ride and walk mile after mile
To seek him, make acquaintance, none of them
Aware of the deceit that governs him.
And if it's your desire to hear me out,   990
Right here and now that's what I'll tell about.
But you religious canons, honors due,
Please do not think that I would slander you
Though I tell of a canon. There's no doubt
That every order has some rogue about,   995
And God forbid a whole group be maligned
Because of one man's folly. I've no mind
To slander you at all; it's to amend
A certain wrong, that's all that I intend.
It's not for only you this tale is told   1000
But others too. You well know how of old
Among Christ's twelve apostles there were none
But Judas who betrayed, the only one.

So why should all the rest be given blame
When guiltless? As for you I say the same,   1005
Except for this—pay heed to what I say:
If there's one Judas in your house today,
Then throw him out at once, that's my advice,
If you fear any taint of shame or vice.
And do not be displeased by this, I pray,   1010
But in this matter hear what I've to say.
    In London was a priest who sang the mass
For those deceased; and years had come to pass
In which such pleasant service he'd afforded
To his landlady where he roomed and boarded   1015
That she'd not suffer him to pay a thing
For board or clothes though he dress like a king,
And he had lots of silver in his purse.
But that's for neither better nor for worse,
I'll go on with my tale to its conclusion   1020
On how a canon brought him to confusion.
    This canon so deceitful came one day
To see this priest where in his room he lay
And asked him for a loan, a quantity
Of gold, for which he'd pay him back. "Lend me   1025
A mark," he said, "till just three days are through
And at that time I'll bring it back to you.
And if you find I'm telling you a lie,
Have me hung by the neck next time I'm by."
    This priest gave him a mark right on the spot,   1030
For which this canon thanked the priest a lot
And took his leave, went right off on his way.
He brought the money back right to the day
And gave it to the priest, all he had lent,
Which made the priest delighted and content.   1035
    "For sure," he said, "it doesn't bother me
To lend a man a noble, two or three,
Or anything I have in my possession,
Whenever he is of such true discretion
He keeps the time appointed to repay;   1040
And such a man I cannot turn away."
    "What!" said the canon, "I would be untrue?

For me that would be really something new.
My word's a thing that always I will keep
Until that very day when I shall creep   1045
Into my grave, so help me God. Indeed
Of that you can be sure as of your creed.
Thank God, and in good time may it be said,
There's never been a man who's been misled
For having gold or silver to me lent;   1050
No falsehood in my heart I've ever meant.
And, sir, since you have been so good to me
In showing me such generosity,
For being kind I'll tell you in return
About my secret. If you wish to learn,   1055
I'll teach you plainly how," as he went on,
"My works I have performed, as yet unknown,
What I've accomplished in philosophy.
Watch closely and with your own eyes you'll see
A master stroke by me before I've ceased."   1060
    "Yes, will you, sire? Saint Mary!" said the priest.
"Then so perform, I humbly beg of you."
    "As you command, sir, faithfully I'll do,"
The canon said, "or God bring me to grief."
    See how he offered services, this thief!   1065
Such proffered service stinks, old wise men say,
And certainly it's true, as right away
I'll by this canon verify. For he,
Being the very root of treachery,
Takes great delight in seeing for his part—   1070
Such fiendish thoughts are gathered in his heart—
How many Christians he can bring to grief.
From his dissembling ways God grant relief!
    This priest had no idea with whom he dealt,
Of his impending harm he nothing felt.   1075
O simple priest! O foolish innocent,
Soon hoodwinked by your greed! Unlucky gent,
In judgment you're so blind you cannot see,
You've no awareness of the treachery
This fox has shaped for you! From all his tricks   1080
You cannot flee, you'll soon be in a fix.

And so that I might draw to the conclusion
That deals, unhappy man, with your confusion,
I'll hasten now to tell immediately
About your folly, your stupidity,   1085
And the deceit, too, of that other wretch,
As far as I can get my wits to stretch.
    You think, Sir Host, this canon was my lord?
By faith and heaven's queen whom I've adored,
It was another canon and not he,   1090
One with a hundred times more subtlety.
He's brought folks to betrayal every time;
Of his deceit it numbs my wit to rhyme.
Whenever of his falsehood I may speak,
The shame makes me turn red from cheek to cheek.   1095
At any rate my cheeks begin to glow,
For my face has no color, well I know;
From various kinds of metals many a fume,
As you have heard, has acted to consume
And waste away my face's ruddiness.   1100
Now hear about this canon's cursedness!
    "Sir," said he to the priest, "let your man go
For quicksilver and bring it, promptly so—
More than an ounce, have him bring two or three;
And when he comes, without delay you'll see   1105
A wondrous thing like none you've ever spied."
    "It surely shall be done," the priest replied.
He bade his servant fetch it right away;
The servant, always ready to obey,
Went out at once and soon came back again   1110
With this quicksilver (briefly to explain),
Three ounces, which he gave the canon there.
The canon laid them down with gentle care,
And then he bade the servant coals to bring,
That he might get to work, no tarrying.   1115
    The coals were fetched at once on his request,
And then this canon took out of his vest
A crucible, and to the priest said he,
"Take in your hand this instrument you see,
And then as soon as you have put therein   1120

An ounce of this quicksilver, you'll begin,
In Christ's name, to become philosopher.
There are but few to whom I'd offer, sir,
To show my science to such a degree;
Here by your own experience you'll see   1125
How this quicksilver I'll transmogrify
Right here before your eyes, without a lie,
And turn it into silver, just as fine
And good as any in your purse or mine
Or any other place. And I will make   1130
It malleable—if not, call me a fake,
One who's unfit in public to appear.
I have a powder—one that cost me dear—
To make it work, the source of all my skill,
Which I'm about to show you. If you will,   1135
Now send away your man; let him stay out,
And shut the door, while we two are about
Our secret science, no one then to see
While we're at work in this philosophy."
    With all that he was told the priest complied;   1140
The servant as commanded went outside,
His master shut the door without delay,
And they began their labor right away.
    Bade by this canon reprehensible,
The priest set on the fire this crucible,   1145
Then busily into the fire he blew.
Into the crucible this canon threw
A powder—I don't know what it contained,
If made of chalk or glass, but though obtained
Whatever way it wasn't worth a fly   1150
Except as means to fool the priest. Then high
He bade him pile the coals till spread above
The crucible. "As token of my love,"
The canon said, "the hands shall be your own
That bring this work to pass here, yours alone."   1155
    "O thank you!" said the priest with happy smile,
And as the canon asked he made the pile.
And while he toiled, this fiendish, lying wretch,
This canon—may the devil come and fetch

Him!—from his coat an imitation coal 1160
Took, made of beech, in which was drilled a hole;
Some silver filings in this hole were packed,
An ounce of them, and to conceal the fact
Were tightly sealed with wax. Now be aware
That this device was not made then and there, 1165
The canon had prepared it long before
Just like some other things—I'll tell you more
About them later—that this canon brought.
He'd come to cheat the priest, that was his thought,
And by the time they'd part indeed he would; 1170
He couldn't quit till he had skinned him good.
Just speaking of him so depresses me!
I'd have my vengeance on his falsity
If I knew how, but he flits here and there,
Too shifty to abide long anywhere. 1175
    But, sires, now pay attention, for God's love!
He took this coal that I was speaking of
And in his hand he held it secretly.
And while the priest was working busily
To bed the coals as you have heard me say, 1180
This canon said, "No, friend, that's not the way,
The coals are not arranged as they should be.
But I shall soon take care of that," said he.
"Now let me meddle for a while, for by
Saint Giles, I have compassion for you. Why, 1185
I see that you're so hot you're soaking wet.
Now here's a kerchief, wipe away the sweat."
And while the priest stepped back to wipe his face,
This canon took his coal—such a disgrace!—
And centered it on top so that it sat 1190
Above the crucible; he blew, with that,
Until the coals burned at a rapid rate.
    "Now let us have a drink," he said, "and wait,
For all will soon be well, as I contend.
Let's sit a while and make us merry, friend." 1195
And when this canon's imitation coal
Had burnt, all of the filings from the hole
Fell right into the crucible below—

They naturally could not help doing so
Since they were placed so evenly above it.   1200
But still, alas! this priest knew nothing of it,
For all the coals he deemed to be the same
And had no inkling of this canon's game.
And when his time this alchemist espied,
"Rise up, Sir Priest," said he, "step to my side.   1205
Now since I know that you've no mold around,
Go out, bring any chalkstone to be found—
If I have any luck, I'll shape the thing
Exactly like a mold. And also bring
A bowl or pan as filled as it can be   1210
With water. After that you'll surely see
Our labor thrive and brought to full fruition.
And yet that you may harbor no suspicion
While you're away, may not distrust or doubt,
I will not leave your presence, I'll go out   1215
With you and come right back with you again."
The chamber door—to keep it short and plain—
They opened and then shut, then took the key
And went forth on their way in company,
Then both came back again without delay.   1220
Why should I tarry all the livelong day?
He took the chalkstone and then like a mold
He gave it shape the way you'll now be told.
    I say, this canon took out of his sleeve
A bar of silver—evil make him grieve!—   1225
That weighed an ounce. And listen now to me
While I recount his cursed trickery!
    In length and width he used this bar to form
His mold, and yet so slyly did perform
That you can bet the priest did not perceive;   1230
And then again he hid it up his sleeve.
From the fire the material he took
And poured it in the mold with merry look;
And then when he was set, he threw it in
The water pan, and told the priest right then,   1235
"Now see what's there, reach in and grope around.
I'm hoping there's some silver to be found.

Why, what the devil else could be in there?
A silver shaving's silver, God's aware!"
He found a bar, when he went reaching in,   1240
Of finest silver. Filled with joy then
This priest became on seeing it was true.
"God's blessings on you and his Mother's too
And all the saints', Sir Canon!" said the priest.
"And may I have their curses at the least   1245
If I—when you've agreed to teach to me
This noble craft of yours, this subtlety—
Do not then serve you every way I may."
    The canon said, "Yet first I will assay
A second time while you pay closest heed,   1250
An expert to become, that in your need
You may perform yourself some other day
This crafty science when I'm gone away.
Another ounce of quicksilver now bring,"
The canon said, "don't say another thing   1255
But do with it just as you've done so far,
As with the first that's now a silver bar."
    The priest went right to work, he forged ahead
To do all that this cursed canon said,
And blew hard on the fire, that hopefully   1260
The effect that he desired would come to be.
The canon was preparing all the while
Again this foolish cleric to beguile;
For show, the canon now was holding there
A hollow stick—now listen and beware!—   1265
The end of which contained an ounce, no more,
Of silver filings (as he'd put before
Inside his coal); and it was tightly sealed
With wax, that not one filing be revealed.
And while this priest was busy, with his stick   1270
This canon stepped beside him and was quick
To throw once more some of his powder in.
May the devil beat him out of his skin
For all of his deceit, to God I plead!
For he was false in every thought and deed.   1275
And with this stick, contrived as you have heard,

The coals above the crucible he stirred
Until the fire with all its heat began
To melt the seal of wax—as every man
Who's not a fool well knows would come about.   1280
The filings in the stick went pouring out,
And right into the crucible they fell.
    What more, good sirs, would you want me to tell?
When he had been beguiled again, this priest,
Supposing all was true, to say the least   1285
Was so delighted I cannot express
In any way his mirth and happiness.
He offered to the canon as before
His goods and services. "Yes, though I'm poor,"
The canon said, "you'll find that I have skill.   1290
And let me warn you, there's more to it still.
Is any copper hereabout?" said he.
    "Yes, sire," replied the priest, "there's bound to be."
    "If not, go buy us some, the quickest found.
Good sir, be on your way, don't stand around."   1295
    He went his way, and with the copper came,
And in his hand this canon took the same,
And measured just an ounce, no more, in weight.
    My tongue is much too simple to relate—
I've not the wits—this canon's treachery;   1300
He was the root of all iniquity.
To those who didn't know he seemed a friend,
Though all his works were fiendish to the end.
To tell of all his lying wears me out,
But nonetheless that's what I'll tell about,   1305
That other men be made aware thereby
And for no other cause, that's not a lie.
    The crucible he put the copper in
And set it on the fire, and powder then
He threw in, too, and bade the priest to blow,   1310
For which the priest must then stoop down as low
As he had done before. All was a jape—
As he desired, the priest he made his ape!
After he cast this copper in the mold,
He put it in the water pan I told   1315

About before, then stuck in his own hand.
Now up his sleeve (as you well understand)
He had that silver bar that he could fetch.
He slyly took it out, this cursed wretch—
The priest did not suspect this crafty man—   1320
And left it at the bottom of the pan,
Then felt down in the water to and fro,
Removing while he did, and deftly so,
The copper bar—the priest would never note—
And hid it, grabbed the priest then by the coat,   1325
And said to him, in furtherance of his game,
"Stoop down, by God, or else you are to blame!
As I helped you before, help me in kind,
Reach in your hand and see what you can find."

 The priest brought up the silver bar, and then   1330
Said to the canon, "Let's go take them in
To a goldsmith, these bars we've made, and see
What they are worth. For by the Trinity,
I wouldn't use them—I will pledge my hood—
Unless they're really silver, fine and good.   1335
Let's put them to the proof without delay."

 And so with these three bars they took their way
To a goldsmith, who put them to the test
With fire and hammer. No man could contest,
Not one could say they weren't what they should be.   1340

 This foolish priest, who's gladder now than he?
There hasn't been one bird at sight of day,
No nightingale in all the month of May,
Who's ever sung to such delighted measure;
No lady's ever been as full of pleasure   1345
While singing songs of love and womanhood,
No hardy knight as joyous as he stood
In his dear lady's grace, as for his part
This cleric was, to learn this sorry art.
He spoke then to the canon, saying thus: 1350
"For love of God who died for all of us,
If I deserve to know, what price, pray tell,
Would you require, this formula to sell?"

 "By Our Lady," he said, "the price is high,

For in all England just one friar and I   1355
And no one else alive such bars can make."
    "No matter, sire," the priest said, "for God's sake,
What shall I pay you? Tell me now, I pray."
    "It's really quite expensive, as I say,"
The canon said. "So help me God, if you   1360
Desire it, sir, then in a word or two
It's forty pounds. It surely would be more
But for the friendship you showed me before."
    The priest at once this sum in nobles found
And took it to the canon, every pound,   1365
This formula to have as a receipt.
The canon's work was fraudulent deceit.
    "Sir Priest," he said, "I do not look for fame
In what I do, instead I hide the same;
And if you love me, keep my secrecy.   1370
For if men knew of all my subtlety,
By God, they'd be so envious in view
Of what in this philosophy I do,
They'd kill me, it would end no other way."
    The priest said, "God forbid! what's that you say?   1375
I'd rather spend all that belongs to me—
Or else may I go crazy—than to see
You come to such an end, have such ill fortune."
    "For your good will may good luck be your portion,"
The canon said. "I thank you, sir. Good day!"   1380
And never once, when he had gone his way,
This priest saw him again. And when he had
A chance to try this formula, too bad!
He couldn't make it work. Well you can see
How hoodwinked and beguiled he'd come to be.   1385
So that is how he makes his infiltration,
That he might bring such folk to ruination.
    Consider, sirs, how in each rank is found
A strife twixt men and gold that's so profound
What gold there's left to win is all but none.   1390
This alchemy has blinded many a one
Till in good faith I think that it must be
The greatest reason for such scarcity.

Philosophers so vaguely speak about
Their craft, it's something folks can't figure out   1395
For all the wit that folks have nowadays.
But let them chatter on just like the jays
And set their hearts on terminology;
What they attempt will never come to be.
With ease a man can learn to multiply   1400
And turn what wealth he has to naught thereby!
   See, there's such profit in this lusty game
That it will turn one's mirth to grief and shame,
Will empty out the heaviest of purses,
And afterwards lead folks to purchase curses   1405
On those to whom they lent what they had earned.
O fie, for shame! Those who have once been burned,
Can they not flee the fiery heat? I say
To those who use this craft, refrain today
Before you're ruined. Better late than never,   1410
To live unprosperously would seem forever.
Prowl all you will, your goal you'll never find;
You're just as bold as Bayard who, though blind,
Still blunders forth as if no danger's known;
He's just as apt to run into a stone   1415
As go around it while he's on his way.
That's how you multipliers fare, I say.
And if your own two eyes can't see aright,
See that your mind at least still has its sight.
Look far and wide, what alchemy will bring   1420
Is nothing, it won't gain for you a thing;
You'll waste all you have managed to acquire.
Before it burns too fast, put out the fire;
Don't meddle further in that art, I say,
Or else your thrift will all be swept away.   1425
Right here and now to you I will impart
What philosophers have said about this art.
   Now listen, here's what Arnold of New Town
In his *Rosarium* has written down—
Here's what he says, and this is not a lie: 1430
"No man can mercury transmogrify
Without its brother knowing." He refers

To Hermes, father of philosophers,
As who first said it. He informs us, too,
The dragon doesn't die—no doubt it's true—   1435
Unless it's by his brother he is slain.
And what's meant by the dragon (to explain
What he has said) is mercury, none other,
And brimstone's what is meant by saying brother,
For out of Sol and Luna come these two.   1440
"Therefore," he said—hear what I'm telling you—
"Let no man stir himself, this art to learn,
Unless he understands and can discern
The meanings of what say philosophers.
He's still a foolish man if he so stirs;   1445
This cunning science," so his writing goes,
"Is secret of all secrets, heaven knows."
        A disciple of Plato had occasion
To speak with him about this situation
(His book called *Senior* tells us that it's so),   1450
And here is what this fellow asked to know:
"What is the name of that most secret stone?"
        And Plato said, "As Titan it is known."
        He said, "What's that? Has it another name?"
        And Plato said, "Magnesia is the same."   1455
        The fellow said, "Sir, is it to be thus?
This is *ignotum per ignocius.*
Good sir, what does Magnesia mean, I pray?"
        "It is a water that is made, I say,
Of the four elements." He asked him then,   1460
"Tell me the most essential part that's in
That water, sir, if you are willing to."
        "Nay," Plato said, "that surely I'll not do.
Philosophers have sworn from first to last
That to no one the secret would be passed,   1465
And not in any book does it appear.
To Christ our Lord it is so very dear
He won't allow that it revealed should be
Except where it may please his deity
So to inspire mankind, and to withhold   1470
From whom he will. There's no more to be told."

And so I will conclude: since God up there
Wills not that the philosophers declare
How one may find the philosophers' stone,
It's my advice that best it's left alone.   1475
For whoso would make God his adversary
By doing work that's to his will contrary
Is one who certainly will never thrive,
Though multiplying long as he's alive.
Here's where I stop, for ended is my tale.   1480
May God help every true man in travail!

The Manciple's Tale

PROLOGUE

Do you know where there stands a little town
That they call by the name Bob-up-and-down
That's under Blean, down Canterbury way?
That's where our Host began to joke and play,
Declaring, "What, sirs! Dun is in the mire!   5
Is there no man for charity or hire
Who will awake our friend who lags behind?
With ease a thief might rob and bind him. Mind
The way he naps! For cock's bones, look at how
He's almost falling off his horse right now!   10
Is that a London cook, bad luck be sent?
Have him come forth, he knows his punishment;
For, by my faith, he'll tell for us a tale,
Be it not worth in hay enough to bale.
Wake up, you Cook! May woe come straight from God,"   15
He said. "What's ailing you, all day to nod?
Did you have fleas all night, or are you boozy?
Or did you labor all night with a floozy
And that's why now you can't hold up your head?"

This Cook, completely pale, no trace of red,   20
Said to our Host, "God bless my soul, I don't
Know why I feel so heavy, but I want
To go to sleep more than I'd want as mine
A gallon drawn from Cheapside's finest wine."

"Well," said the Manciple, "if it will ease   25
You some, Sir Cook, and no one else displease
Who rides along here in this company—
And if our Host should, by his courtesy,
Desire it—I'll excuse you from your tale.

For in good faith, you're looking very pale;   30
Your eyes have got a dazed look, too, I think,
And well I know your breath's a sour stink.
You've shown quite well you're in an unfit way;
You'll get no praise from me, that's safe to say.
See how he's yawning, look, this drunken soul,   35
As though at once he'd swallow us in whole.
Keep shut your mouth, man, by your father's kin!
The devil of hell stick his foot therein!
Your curst breath will infect us one and all.
Fie, stinking swine! May evil you befall!   40
Consider, sirs, this lusty man before us:
Now, sweet sir, would you do some jousting for us?
For that, I think, the shape you're in is fine!
You've drunk what I believe they call ape-wine,
That's when a man starts playing with a straw."   45
This made the Cook so angry that we saw
Him nodding at the Manciple his head
For lack of speech. His horse then threw him, spread
Him out; they had to lift him off the grass.
A fine cook's show of horsemanship! Alas,   50
He should have stuck to ladling! Before
They got this Cook upon his horse once more,
They had to do much shoving to and fro
To lift him, which entailed much care and woe,
So heavy was this sorry, pallid ghost.   55
And to the Manciple then spoke our Host:
    "Because this man is under domination
Of that which he has drunk, by my salvation
I know that he would lewdly tell his tale.
For be it wine or old or newborn ale   60
That he has drunk, he's speaking nasally,
He's wheezing too, and has a cold. And he
Will also have more than enough to do
To keep him and his nag out of the slough;
If yet again he tumbles off, adrift,   65
Then we'll all have enough to do to lift
His heavy, drunken carcass to the mount.
So tell your tale, for he's of no account.

"Yet, Manciple, in faith, it's bad advice
So freely to reproach him for his vice.   70
Another day may come along for sure
When he will get you back as with a lure;
He'll speak, I mean, of what seem little things
Like finding errors in your reckonings,
Which wouldn't look good if it came to light."   75
    "No, that could cause real trouble! Well he might,"
Said the Manciple, "bring me to the snare.
I'd rather wind up paying for the mare
On which he rides than have him with me strive.
No, I'll not make him mad, as I may thrive!   80
I only spoke in jest. Do you know what?
It happens that here in this gourd I've got
A draught of wine, indeed of ripest grape.
Now right away you'll see a clever jape,
I'll have this Cook drink of it if I may.   85
On pain of death he will not tell me nay."
    And certainly, to tell what came to pass,
The Cook drank deeply from this gourd, alas!
Why did he need it, having drunk enough?
And when into this gourd he'd blown a puff,   90
He passed the gourd back to the Manciple.
With that the Cook was happy, fanciful,
And thanked him as much as his wits allowed.
    Our Host broke out in laughter great and loud,
And said, "I well can see it's necessary,   95
Wherever we may go, good drink to carry,
For it will turn both rancor and distress
To peace and love, and many a wrong redress.
    "O Bacchus, now may blessed be your name
That you can turn the serious into game!   100
Worship and thanks be to your deity!
Enough on that, no more to hear from me;
Tell us your tale now, Manciple, I pray."
    "Well, sir," said he, "pay heed to what I say."

THE MANCIPLE'S TALE

When Phoebus dwelt here on the earth below   105
As mentioned in old books of long ago,
No other youth as lusty as was he
Was in this world, none matched his archery.
He slew the serpent Python on a day
When sleeping in the sun he saw it lay;   110
And many another noble, worthy deed
He with his bow performed as men may read.
    All instruments of music he could play,
And sing in so melodious a way,
His voice so clear, the sound of it enthralled.   115
Not Amphion, the king of Thebes, who walled
That entire city with his singing, could
Sing half as well as this young Phoebus would.
He also was the most attractive man
There's ever been since this world first began.   120
To talk about his looks what need is there?
In all this world none living was as fair.
His life was thus fulfilled with nobleness
And honor, one of perfect worthiness.
    This Phoebus was of young manhood the flower   125
In charity as well as knightly power,
And for his pleasure (and as sign of glory
Of triumph over Python, goes the story)
He always carried in his hand a bow.
    Now in his house this Phoebus had a crow   130
That in a cage he'd fostered many a day
And taught to speak as men may teach a jay.
As white as is a snow-white swan, this crow
Could imitate the speech, exactly so,
Of any man when he would tell a tale.   135
And in this world there was no nightingale
To any hundred-thousandth of degree
Could sing a song so well and merrily.
    Now in his house this Phoebus had a wife

For whom he had more love than for his life,   140
And whom both night and day with diligence
He sought to please and show due reverence,
Except (to tell the truth) that he was zealous
To keep her under watch, for he was jealous.
A fellow tricked he didn't want to be,   145
As any man would feel of his degree;
But it's in vain, such effort is for naught.
A good wife who is clean in deed and thought
Should surely not be watched continually;
The labor is in vain, it's plain to see,   150
To guard a shrew, it never will succeed.
I hold that it's sheer folly, there's no need,
It's labor wasted, keeping watch of wives;
Old learneds have so written in their lives.

    Now to the purpose as I started out: 155
This worthy Phoebus ever went about
To please her, trying hard to keep her favor
With all his manhood and his good behavior,
That no man might supplant him in her grace.

    But God knows well, there's no man may embrace,   160
As to constrain, a certain thing or feature
That nature by design sets in a creature.

    Take any bird and put it in a cage,
And all your good intentions then engage
To raise it tenderly with meat and drink,   165
With all the dainties of which you can think,
And keep it as unspotted as you might;
Although his golden cage be ever bright,
This bird would rather twenty-thousandfold
Be in a forest that is rude and cold,   170
Be eating worms and live in wretchedness.
This bird will always try for nothing less
Than his escape, if any way there be;
This bird will always want his liberty.

    Let's take a cat and raise him well with milk   175
And tender meat, and make his couch of silk,
Then let him see a mouse go by the wall—
At once he'll leave the milk and meat and all,

And every dainty that is in the house,
Such appetite he has to eat a mouse.   180
Here you may see his lust has domination,
And appetite will rout discrimination.
 A she-wolf's nature, too, is villein's kind.
The basest wolf that ever she can find,
The one that has the least of reputations,   185
She'll take when she desires to have relations.
 By these examples, that which I've in mind
Are men who've been untrue, not womankind.
For men are prone to lecherous appetite,
Indulge with lower creatures their delight   190
Rather than with their wives, fair though they be,
So ever true, with all gentility.
Flesh lusts for novelty to such a measure
(A curse upon it!) we can take no pleasure
In virtuous pursuits more than a while.   195
 This Phoebus, who had not one thought of guile,
Was soon deceived for all his charm. For she
Another fellow had also, and he
Was unacclaimed, unworthy all around
To be compared with Phoebus. To compound   200
This evil, which would bring much harm and woe,
Their sin was to recur, and often so.
 It so befell, with Phoebus gone one day,
His wife sent for her lover right away—
Her lover? Surely this is knavish speech!   205
Forgive me for it, that I do beseech.
But Plato, wise, has said, as you may read,
The word must be accordant with the deed.
If men would speak of something properly,
The word must to the deed then cousin be.   210
Now I'm a plain man, and there is, I say,
No difference, to speak in truthful way,
Between a wife who is of high degree,
If with her body she immoral be,
And some poor wench, unless it should be this   215
(Assuming that they both have gone amiss):
The genteel one, as her estate's above,

Shall be known as his lady, as in love;
Whereas the other, poor upon her bench,
Will be known as his lover or his wench.   220
But still, as God knows well, my own dear brother,
Men lay the one as low as lies the other.
     Just so, between some tyrant or usurper
And some outlaw, some thief out for his supper,
I say the same, there is no difference.   225
To Alexander someone said, with sense,
That as a tyrant is of greater might
By force of arms to go and slay outright
And burn down house and home right to the ground,
Behold, he's called a captain. Turn around,   230
And as the outlaw has the lesser arms
And may not do as much by way of harms
Nor bring a country to so great a grief,
He's called by men an outlaw and a thief.
But as I'm not a learned man of writ,   235
I will not talk of texts a single bit;
I'll to my tale where I was at before.
Phoebus's wife sent for her paramour,
At once in wanton lust they did engage.
     The white crow, there inside his hanging cage,   240
Beheld their work but didn't say a word.
When Phoebus, though, his lord, came home, the bird
Began to sing "Cuckoo! cuckoo! cuckoo!"
     "What, bird?" said Phoebus. "What's that song from you?
Were you not wont so merrily to sing   245
That to my heart it brought rejoicing
To hear your voice? Alas! what song is this?"
     "By God," said he, "I'm singing not amiss!
Phoebus," he said, "for all your worthiness,
For all your charm, good looks, and nobleness,   250
For all your song and all your minstrelsy,
For all your watch, hoodwinked you've come to be,
By one of little reputation who
Does not possess, when he's compared to you,
The value of a gnat, upon my life!   255
For on your bed I saw him screw your wife."

Would you hear more? This white crow right away
Then boldly offered proof, began to say
Just how his wife performed her lechery,
To his great shame and hurt, and told how he   260
Had seen with his own eyes what had occurred.
    This Phoebus turned away when he had heard
And thought his grieving heart would break in two.
His bow he bent, an arrow set thereto,
And in his ire his wife he soon had slain.   265
That's how it was, there's no more to explain.
His instruments he broke then mournfully,
His harp and lute, guitar and psaltery;
He broke as well his arrows and his bow,
And after that he said this to the crow: 270
    "You traitor with scorpion's tongue," said he,
"You've brought me to my ruin and misery!
Alas, that I was born! Why have I life?
O gem of my delight, my dearest wife!
To me you were so constant and so true,   275
Now you lie dead with face so pale of hue,
And guiltless, that's for sure, I dare to swear!
O rash hand, that so foully you should err!
O troubled mind, O ire so wildly spent,
So recklessly to smite the innocent!   280
Distrust, so full of false suspicion, where
Were your discretion and your wits? Beware
Of being reckless, everyone! Without
Strong witness, don't believe, there's room for doubt.
Don't strike too soon, before you think it through,   285
Be soberly advised on what to do
Before you act, before you give effect
To anger caused by what you may suspect.
Alas, a thousand people reckless ire
Has wholly ruined, brought them to the mire!   290
Alas, that I shall slay myself for grief!"
And to the crow he said, "You lying thief!
I'll pay you back right now for your false tale.
For you once sang just like a nightingale,
But now, false thief, that song you'll do without,   295

And your white feathers, too, shall all come out,
And all your life you nevermore shall speak.
Thus vengeance on a traitor men shall wreak.
Henceforth you shall be black, and your offspring,
And no sweet noise you'll ever make or sing   300
But ever cry against the storm and rain,
As token that through you my wife is slain."
He sprang upon the crow without delay
And all of his white feathers plucked away;
He turned him black, bereft him evermore   305
Of song and speech, and slung him out the door
To the devil (who needn't give him back).
And it's because of this all crows are black.
   By this example, lords, you will, I pray,
Beware and take much care in what you say: 310
Don't ever tell a man in all your life
Another man has bedded with his wife;
He'll surely hate you in a mortal way.
Lord Solomon, as learned students say,
Taught man to watch his tongue. But as I said,   315
I'm not a learned man, I'm not well-read.
Here's what my mother taught me all the same:
"My son, think of the crow, in our Lord's name!
Keep well your tongue and keep your friend. My son,
A wicked tongue's worse than a fiend, for one   320
Can cross himself from fiends and so be blest.
My son, God in his goodness saw it best
To wall the tongue with teeth and lips and cheeks,
For man should always think before he speaks.
My son, so often it's for too much speech   325
That many a man is wrecked, as scholars teach;
But speaking little and at proper place
Will generally bring no one to disgrace.
My son, your tongue you always should restrain
Except for times when taking special pain   330
To speak of God in honor and in prayer.
The first virtue, if you would learn, is care
In speech, my son, restraining well the tongue;
This children learn when they are very young.

My son, from too much speech with ill advice,   335
Where less had been enough speech to suffice,
Has come much harm; so I was told and taught.
Wherever words abound, sin wants for naught.
A rash tongue serves what purpose, do you know?
For as a sword, my son, with cutting blow   340
Can cleave an arm in half, it's also true
A tongue can cut a friendship right in two.
A loudmouth is to God abominable.
Read Solomon, so wise and honorable;
Read David's psalms, let Seneca be read.   345
Don't speak, my son, but only nod your head.
Pretend that you are deaf when hearing chatter
A jangler makes about some dangerous matter.
The Flemings say, and learn it if you please,
'The less the jangle, how much more the ease.'   350
My son, if nothing wicked you have said,
You need not of betrayal have a dread;
But he who speaks amiss, I dare to say,
May not call back his words in any way.
A thing that's said is said, forth it will go   355
Though he repent and wish it wasn't so.
He is his thrall to whom a fellow's told
A tale that he'd much rather now withhold.
My son, be careful, of all tidings do
Not be the author, be they false or true.   360
Where you may go, among the high or low,
Hold well your tongue and think about the crow."

The Parson's Tale

PROLOGUE

When his tale the Manciple had ended,
The sun from the south line had descended
So low that it was by my calculation
Not twenty-nine degrees in elevation.
The time was four o'clock then, as I guess,   5
For eleven feet (a little more or less)
My shadow was at that time and location
(Such feet as if my height in correlation
Into six equal segments would be hewn).
By then the exaltation of the moon   10
(That's Libra) started steadily to ascend,
As we were entering a village end.
At this our Host, as he was wont to be
The leader of our jolly company,
Declared, "Lords one and all, as I see now   15
We're lacking no more tales but one, and how
My judgment and decree have come to pass,
We've heard, I think, from every rank and class;
With all that I've ordained we're nearly done.
I pray God give good fortune to the one   20
Who tells this tale, that it may be inspired.
    "Sir Priest, are you a vicar," he inquired,
"Or parson? By my faith, give true retort,
Be what you will but don't break up our sport,
For every man but you his tale has told.   25
Undo your bag, let's see what it may hold;
For by your bearing I would think, by glory,
You ought to knit up for us quite a story.
Tell us a fable, for cock's bones, right now!"

The Parson answered right away, here's how: 30
"You won't get any fable told by me;
For Saint Paul, as he writes to Timothy,
Reproves those who abandon truthfulness
For fable-telling and such wretchedness.
Why should I sow by hand chaff to the breeze   35
When wheat I could be sowing if I please?
I say therefore that if you wish to hear
Virtuous matters, morals that are clear,
And if you'll give me proper audience,
I'll gladly, doing Christ all reverence,   40
Give you some righteous pleasure as I can.
But trust me well, I am a Southern man:
Romances I can't tell, no 'rum, ram, ruff,'
And rhyme, I hold, is hardly better stuff.
So if you please—I won't gloss words, God knows—   45
I'll tell for you a merry tale in prose
To knit up this whole fest, make end of it.
And Jesus, by his grace, send me the wit
To show you, while on this trip we engage,
The way of that most glorious pilgrimage   50
Called heavenly Jerusalem. And so,
If you will grant as much, at once I'll go
Ahead now with my tale, for which I pray
For your assent. No better can I say.

   "But nonetheless I put this meditation   55
Before all students for their emendation,
For I am not a learned man. I take
The meaning only, trust me well. I make
Therefore the statement first that my selection
I willingly submit to their correction."   60

   To this word we agreed without ado,
For, as it seemed, it was the thing to do
To end with something in a virtuous sense
And therefore gave him space and audience,
We bade our Host say to him that each one   65
Among us wished the tale might be begun.

   And so our Host with that spoke for us all:
"Sir Priest," said he, "good fortune you befall!

Tell us your meditation, but with haste,
The sun is going down, no time to waste;   70
Speak fruitfully, and that in little space,
And to do well may God send you his grace!
We'll gladly hear now what you wish to say."
With that he spoke, proceeding in this way.

THE PARSON'S TALE

*Jer. 6. State super vias, et videte, et interrogate de viis antiquis, que
sit via bona, et ambulate in ea; et invenietis refrigerium animabus vestris,
etc.*

Our sweet Lord God of heaven who wishes no man to perish but
wishes that we all come to the knowledge of him and to the blissful life
that is everlasting, **75** admonishes us by the prophet Jeremiah, saying,
"Stand upon the ways and look, ask about the old paths (that is, the old
opinions) where the good way is, and walk in that way, and you shall find
refreshment for your souls, etc."

Many are the spiritual ways that lead people to our Lord Jesus Christ
and to the kingdom of glory. Of these ways, there is one most noble and
appropriate that cannot fail any man or woman who through sin has
gone astray from the direct way to the heavenly Jerusalem. **80** This way
is called Penitence, about which man should gladly hear and inquire with
all his heart—to know what Penitence is, why it is called Penitence, how
many ways are the actions and workings of Penitence, how many kinds
of Penitence there are, and which things belong and are necessary to
Penitence and which things hinder it.

Saint Ambrose says that Penitence is the lament of man for the sins
he has committed, and to do nothing more for which he should lament.
And some Church Father says, "Penitence is the lamenting of man who
sorrows for his sin and torments himself because he's done evil." **85**

Penitence under certain circumstances is true repentance of a man
who holds himself in sorrow and other pain because of his sins. To be
truly penitent, he must first bewail the sins he has committed, and
steadfastly purpose in his heart to confess and make satisfaction and
never do anything more for which he should bewail or complain, and to
continue in good works, for otherwise his repentance is of no use. For

as Saint Isidore says, "He is a trickster and mocker and no true repentant who soon after does anything for which he ought to repent." Weeping and not to cease sinning is of no use. **90** Men nonetheless hope that every time a man falls, be it ever so often, he may arise through Penitence if he only has grace. But let me tell you, that's in very great doubt. For as Saint Gregory says, "He scarcely can rise out of his sin who is under the burden of evil habit." So repentant people who stop their sinning, renouncing it before sin leaves them helpless, Holy Church considers sure of salvation. As for him who sins and truly repents in his last moments, Holy Church still hopes for his salvation, by the great mercy of our Lord Jesus Christ, because of his repentance. But take the surer way.

Now that I've told you what Penitence is, you should understand that there are three functions of Penitence. **95** The first is that if a man is baptized after he has sinned, Saint Augustine says "he cannot begin a new pure life unless he's repentant for his old sinful life." For surely if he is baptized without penitence for his old sins, he receives the mark of baptism but not the grace nor the remission of his sins until he has true repentance. Another need for repentance is when men commit mortal sin after they have received baptism. The third is when men after their baptism fall from day to day into venial sins. **100** Of this, Saint Augustine says, "The penitence of good, humble people is the penitence of every day."

There are three kinds of Penitence. One is solemn, another public, the third private. Solemn penance is in two ways. One way is to be put out of Holy Church during Lent, for such things as slaughtering children. The other is when a man has sinned openly, the sin being reported and discussed in the region, and then Holy Church by judgment constrains him to do open penance. Public penance is when priests enjoin men together in certain cases, perhaps to go on pilgrimages in only an undergarment or barefoot. **105** Private penance is that which men do time and again for secret sins, for which we shrive ourselves privately and receive private penance.

Now you shall understand what is suitable and necessary for true, perfect Penitence. This depends on three things: Contrition of Heart, Confession of Mouth, and Satisfaction. On this Saint John Chrysostom says, "Penitence constrains a man to accept patiently every punishment imposed, with contrition of heart, shrift of mouth, satisfaction, and exercise of all manner of humility." This is fruitful penitence against three things by which we anger our Lord Jesus Christ: **110** delight in what we think, carelessness in what we say, and deeds that are wicked and sinful. Over against these wicked sins is Penitence, which may be likened to a tree.

The root of this tree is Contrition, which hides itself in the heart of him who is truly repentant, as the root of a tree hides itself in the earth. From the root of Contrition springs a trunk that bears branches and leaves of Confession and fruit of Satisfaction. As Christ says in his gospel, "Produce worthy fruit of Penitence"; for men will know this tree by its fruit, not by the root hidden in the heart of man or by the branches or leaves of Confession. **115** As our Lord Jesus Christ says also, "By their fruit you shall know them." From this root springs also a seed of grace, which seed is the mother of security and is tart and tastes hot. The grace of this seed springs from God, through calling to mind judgment day and the pains of hell. "In fear of God," as Solomon says, "man renounces his sin." The heat of this seed is the love of God and the desire for everlasting joy. **120** This heat draws the heart of man to God and causes him to hate his sin. For truly there is nothing that a child savors so well as the milk of his nurse, and nothing is more abominable to him than that same milk mixed with other food. In the same way sin seems the sweetest thing of all to the sinful man who loves it, but from the time he steadfastly loves our Lord Jesus Christ and desires life everlasting, there is nothing more abominable to him. For truly the law of God is the love of God; as the prophet David says, "I have loved your law and hated wickedness and hatred." He who loves God keeps his law and his word. **125** The prophet Daniel saw this tree in spirit, so to speak, right after the vision of King Nebuchadnezzar, whom he counseled to be penitent. Penance is the tree of life to those who receive it, and he who remains in true penitence is blessed; such is the opinion of Solomon.

In this Penitence of Contrition man should understand four things: what Contrition is, what moves a man to Contrition, how he should be contrite, and what Contrition's benefit is to the soul. Thus it is: Contrition is the true sorrow a man feels in his heart for his sins, with firm purpose to shrive himself, do penance, and sin no more. According to Saint Bernard, this sorrow shall be "heavy and grievous, very sharp and poignant in the heart." **130** First because man has offended his Lord and Creator; sharper and more poignant because he has sinned against his heavenly Father; and sharper and more poignant still because he has angered and sinned against him who redeemed him, who with his precious blood delivered us from the bonds of sin, from the cruelty of the devil, and from the pains of hell.

Six motives ought to bring man to Contrition. First, a man should remember his sins, and take care that that remembrance be in no way a source of delight; he should have great shame and sorrow for his sins. For as Job says, "Sinful men do deeds worthy of damnation." And as Hezekiah says, "I'll remember all the years of my life, in bitterness of heart." 135 And God says in the Apocalypse, "Remember from whence you have fallen"; for before the time of your sin, you were children of God and members of the kingdom of God; but because of your sin you have become enslaved and vile, agents of the fiend, the hate of angels, the disgrace of Holy Church, food for the false serpent, and perpetual material for the fire of hell. And yet more foul and abominable because you trespass as often as does the hound who returns to eat his vomit. And fouler yet for your long continuance in sin and your sinful habits, for which you're as rotten as a beast in his dung. Such thoughts make a man feel shame, not delight, for his sin, as God says by the prophet Ezekiel: 140 "You shall remember your ways, and they shall displease you." Sins are truly the ways that lead men to hell.

The second motive that ought to make one loathe sin is this: "Whoever commits sin," as Saint Peter says, "is a slave of sin"; sin puts a man in great servitude. That's why the prophet Ezekiel says, "I went sorrowfully in loathing of myself." Certainly a man should have loathing for sin and withdraw from that servitude and bondage. Look, what does Seneca say on the matter? "Even if I knew that neither God nor man would ever know, I would not stoop to sin." And the same Seneca says, "I am born to greater things than to be enslaved by my body, or to make my body a slave." 145 No man or woman can make a fouler slave of the body than to give that body to sin. Albeit the foulest churl or foulest woman living, and least of all in value, yet fouler would that body be, more in servitude. The farther a man falls, the more he is enslaved, the viler and more abominable to God and to the world. O gracious God, well should man loathe sin! Once free, through sin he's now enslaved. Thus Saint Augustine says, "If you loathe your servant because he has transgressed or sinned, then loathe yourself when you have sinned." 150 Regard your own value, don't be vile to yourself. Alas! well should people loathe being servants and slaves to sin and be sorely ashamed of themselves, since God in his endless goodness has set them in high estate, or given them intelligence, strength of body, health, beauty, prosperity, and redeemed them from death with his heart's blood, and they in return for his noble goodness requite him so unnaturally, so evilly, to the destruction of their souls. O God of goodness, you women of such great beauty, remember the proverb of Solomon: 155 "A fair woman who's unchaste with her body is like a gold ring in a sow's snout." For just as a sow roots in any filth, she roots her beauty in the stinking filth of sin.

The third motive that should bring a man to Contrition is fear of judgment day and of the horrible torments of hell. For as Saint Jerome says, "Each time I think of judgment day, I tremble, for whenever I eat or drink or whatever else I do, the trumpet seems ever to sound in my ear: 160 'Rise up, you who are dead, and come to the judgment.' " O good God, a man ought greatly to fear such a judgment, "where we all shall be," as Saint Paul says, "before the throne of our Lord Jesus Christ," where he shall require an assembly in which none may be absent. Surely there will be no excuse for non-appearance in court, no defense will avail. And not only will our sins be judged, but also our works will be openly known. 165 And as Saint Bernard says, "No pleading shall avail, no trickery. We shall account for every frivolous word." We shall have a judge who cannot be deceived or corrupted. And why? Surely all our thoughts are disclosed to him; neither prayer nor bribery shall corrupt him. Thus Solomon says, "The wrath of God will spare no one for prayer or for gift." So at judgment day there's no hope for escape. That's why Saint Anselm says, "The anxiety of sinners will be great at that time. There the stern and wrathful judge shall sit above, and below the horrible pit of hell will be open to destroy him who must acknowledge his sins, shown openly before God and every creature. 170 There will be on the left side more devils than the heart can imagine, to drag and draw the sinful souls to the torments of hell. And within the hearts of men shall be the biting conscience, and everywhere outside shall be the world afire. Where then shall the sinner flee to hide? Certainly he may not hide, he must come forth and show himself." For surely as Saint Jerome says, "The earth shall cast him out, and the sea also, and the air, which shall be full of thunder and lightning." Now truly, whoever remembers these things, I guess, will not be turned by his sin to delight but to great sorrow for fear of the torments of hell. 175 Thus Job says to God: "Suffer, Lord, that I may wail and weep awhile before I go, without return, to the dark land covered with the darkness of death, to the land of misery and of darkness where there is the shadow of death, where there is no kind of order, only grisly dread that shall last forever."

Look, here you may see that Job prayed for some respite, to weep, bewailing his trespasses, for truly one day of respite is better than all the world's treasure. And inasmuch as a man may acquit himself before God by penitence in this world, not by treasure, he should pray to God to give him some respite, to weep and bewail his trespasses. For certainly all the sorrow that a man might have from the beginning of the world is little compared to the sorrow of hell. **180**

That's why Job calls hell "the land of darkness"; he calls it "land" or earth, understand, because it's stable and shall never come to an end, and "dark" because he who is in hell is deprived of physical light. For surely the dark light from the ever-burning fire shall for him turn everything in hell to pain, for it shows him to the devils that torment him. "Covered with the darkness of death"—that is, he who is in hell shall lack the sight of God, for surely the sight of God is life everlasting. "The darkness of death" is the sins that the wretched man has committed that prevent him from seeing the face of God, just like a dark cloud between us and the sun. **185** "Land of misery," because there are three kinds of wants, in contrast to three things in this world that living folks have: honors, pleasures, and riches. Instead of honor, in hell they'll have shame and disgrace. For you well know that men call "honor" the reverence that man shows to man, but in hell is neither honor nor reverence. For certainly no more reverence shall be shown to a king than to a knave. That's why God says by the prophet Jeremiah, "The same people who despise me shall be despised." Great lordship is also called "honor"; there no man shall serve another but with torment and harm. Great dignity and high social station are also called "honor," but in hell they shall all be trampled upon by devils. **190** "The horrible devils," God says, "shall come and go upon the heads of the damned." And this is because the higher they were in this present life, the more they shall be degraded and trampled upon in hell.

Instead of the riches of this world they shall have the misery of poverty. And this poverty shall be fourfold. First, lack of treasures, of which David says, "The rich who with all their hearts embrace worldly treasure shall sleep in the slumber of death; nothing of all their treasure shall they find in their hands." The misery of hell, moreover, shall be in lack of food and drink. For as God says by Moses, "They shall be wasted with hunger, and the birds of hell shall devour them with bitter death;

the gall of the dragon shall be their drink, the venom of the dragon their morsels." **195** Their misery shall furthermore be in lack of clothing; they'll be naked in body except for the fire in which they burn and other foul treatment, and naked in soul with respect to all virtue, the soul's clothing. Where then are the bright robes, soft sheets, and fine undergarments? Look what God says of them by the prophet Isaiah: "Under them shall be strewn moths, and their coverlets shall be worms of hell." Furthermore, their misery shall be in lack of friends. For he is not poor who has good friends, but there is no friend in hell; neither God nor any creature shall befriend them, and each shall hate every other with mortal hate. **200** "The sons and daughters shall rebel against father and mother, and kindred against kindred, and they shall chide and despise each other," both day and night, as God says by the prophet Micah. And the loving children, who formerly loved each other so carnally, would eat each other if they could. For how shall they love each other in the torments of hell, when they hated each other in the prosperity of life? Trust well, their carnal love was mortal hate; as says the prophet David, "Whoever loves wickedness hates his soul." And whoever hates his own soul can certainly love no other person in any way. **205** So in hell is neither solace nor friendship, and the more carnal the kinships are in hell, the more cursing, the more chiding, and the more mortal hate among them.

Furthermore they shall lack all sensual pleasures. For certainly these follow from the appetite of the five senses, which are sight, hearing, smell, taste, and touch. But in hell their sight shall be full of darkness and smoke, and thus full of tears, and their hearing full of lamentation and gnashing of teeth, as says Jesus Christ. Their nostrils shall be full of awful stench, and, as says Isaiah the prophet, "Their taste shall be full of bitter gall." As for touch, their bodies shall be covered with "fire that shall never be quenched and worms that shall never die," as God says by the mouth of Isaiah. **210**

And lest they expect not to die from pain, fleeing it by their death, they shall understand the words of Job: "There is the shadow of death." Certainly a shadow has the likeness of that of which it is shadow, but it is not the same thing. Such is the pain of hell, it's like death in its horrible anguish. How so? It constantly pains them as though they should die at once, but they certainly shall not die. For as Saint Gregory says, "For such wretched, miserable persons shall be death without death, end without end, lack without lack. For their death shall live forever, their end shall be always beginning, and their lack shall not fail." 215 And thus says Saint John the Evangelist: "They shall seek death and not find it, they shall desire to die and death shall flee them."

Job also said that in hell is no ruling order. For though God has created all things in right order, there being nothing without order or unnumbered, they who are damned are not at all in order and maintain no order, for the earth shall bear them no fruit. As the prophet David says, "God shall destroy the fruit of the earth to deprive them," neither shall water give them moisture, nor the air refreshment, nor fire light. 220 For as Saint Basil says, "God shall give the burning fire of this world to the damned in hell, but the light clear and bright he shall give to his children in heaven," just as the good man gives meat to his children and bones to his hounds. Because there is no hope of escape, Saint Job finally says, "horror and awful dread shall dwell in hell without end."

Horror is always fear of harm to come, and this dread shall dwell in the hearts of those who are damned. They have therefore lost all their hope for seven reasons. First, God who is their judge shall show no mercy toward them; they may not please him or any of his saints; nor may they give anything to be ransomed; 225 nor may they have voice to speak to him; nor may they flee from torment; nor may they have within them, to deliver them from that torment, any goodness to show. Thus Solomon says, "The wicked man dies, and when he is dead he shall have no hope of escaping from torment." Whoso would then well understand these torments, and carefully consider how he deserves these very torments for his sins, should certainly be more inclined to sigh and weep than to sing and play. For as Solomon says, "Whoever had knowledge of the torments established and decreed for sin would lament." "That same knowledge," as Saint Augustine says, "makes a man lament in his heart." 230

The fourth point that should move a man to Contrition is the sorrowful awareness of the good he has omitted to do here on earth, and also the good he has lost. Truly his good works are lost whether he did them before falling into mortal sin or while he lay in it. Surely the good works he did before falling into sin have all been rendered null and void by his frequent sinning, and the good works he did while he lay in sin are utterly dead with respect to eternal life in heaven.

The good works, then, that have been nullified by frequent sinning, the ones that he did while loved by God, shall never be recovered without true penitence. 235 Thus God says by the mouth of Ezekiel that "if the righteous man turns from his righteousness and works wickedness, shall he live?" No, all the good works he has done shall never be remembered, for he shall die in his sin. Here's what Saint Gregory says on the subject: "We should understand this above all, that when we commit deadly sin, it is useless to recall and recite the good works we have done before." Truly the effect of deadly sin is such that we can't depend on any good deed done before to gain eternal life in heaven. 240 But good works nonetheless revive, they come again, helping to gain eternal life in heaven, when we have contrition. Truly, though, the good works that men do while in mortal sin, inasmuch as they were done in mortal sin, shall never return to life. For surely that which never had life can never regain it. Still, though they in no way assist in obtaining eternal life, they do help to reduce the severity of hell's torments, or to get temporal riches, or to have God sooner enlighten and kindle the heart of the sinner that he might repent. They also help accustom a man to do good works, so that over his soul the fiend may have less power. 245 So the merciful Lord Jesus Christ wills that no good work be lost, for it shall be of at least some use. But inasmuch as good works done by men while living good lives have all been nullified by later sin, and all good works men do while in mortal sin are utterly dead with respect to everlasting life, well may the man who has done no good sing that new French song, *"Jay tout perdu mon temps et mon labour."*

For certainly sin deprives a man of both good nature and the goodness of grace. The grace of the Holy Spirit truly acts like a fire that cannot be idle; for fire ceases to exist as soon as it ceases its function, and just so grace ceases to exist as soon as it ceases its function. 250 Then the sinful man loses the goodness of glory, promised only to good men who labor and work. Well may he be sorry, then, who owes his whole life to God from beginning to end and has no goodness with which to pay God his debt for his life. Trust well, "He shall have to account," as Saint Bernard says, "for all the goods given to him in this present life, and for how he has spent them; not so much as a hair of his head shall perish, nor one moment lapse of his time, that he shall not have to account for."

The fifth thing that should move a man to Contrition is remembrance of the passion suffered by our Lord Jesus Christ for our sins. 255 For as Saint Bernard says, "While I live I'll remember the hardships that our Lord Christ suffered in preaching, his weariness in toiling, his temptation when he fasted, his long vigils when he prayed, his tears shed in pity for good people, the woe and the shame and the filth that men said to him, the foul spittle that men spat in his face, the filthy scowls and the buffets men gave him, the insults he received, the nails with which he was nailed to the cross, and all the rest of the passion he suffered for my sins and not at all for any guilt of his own."

And you should understand that in man's sin is every manner of order or orderly arrangement turned upside down. **260** For it's true that God, reason, sensuality, and the body are ordered so that each of these four things should have lordship over the others. That is, God should have lordship over reason, and reason over sensuality, and sensuality over the body. But truly when man sins, this whole orderly arrangement is turned upside down. So when the reason of man will not be subject or obedient to God who is his lord by right, it loses the lordship it should have over sensuality and also over the body. Why? Because sensuality then rebels against reason, and that's how reason loses lordship over sensuality and the body. **265** Just as reason is rebel to God, sensuality is rebel to both reason and the body.

And certainly this disorder and rebellion our Lord Jesus Christ redeemed with his dear precious body, and hear in what way. Inasmuch as reason is rebel to God, man deserves to have sorrow and die. Our Lord Jesus Christ suffered this for man, after being betrayed by his disciple and arrested and bound, so that his blood burst out at each nail in his hands, as says Saint Augustine. Inasmuch as man's reason, moreover, won't subdue sensuality when it may, man deserves to have shame. And for man our Lord Jesus Christ suffered this, when they spat in his face. **270** Furthermore, inasmuch as man's wretched body is rebel to both reason and sensuality, it deserves to die. And this our Lord Jesus Christ suffered for man on the cross, no part of his body free from great pain and bitter passion. And Jesus Christ suffered all this who never sinned. It may therefore be reasonably said of Jesus: "I am too much afflicted for the things for which I never deserved punishment, and too much defiled by disgrace that man deserves to have." So the sinful man may well say, as says Saint Bernard, "Curst be the bitterness of my sin, for which so much bitterness must be suffered." For it was certainly because of the diverse disorders of our wickedness that the passion of Jesus Christ was ordained, in accordance with diverse things. **275** Man's sinful soul, in coveting temporal prosperity, is certainly deceived by the devil, and in choosing carnal pleasures is scorned by deceit; it's tormented by impatience with adversity, spat upon by servitude and sin's subjection, and at last is finally slain. For this disorder of sinful man was Jesus Christ first betrayed; he was bound who came to unbind us from sin and punishment. He was then scoffed at who should only have been honored in all things. Then his face, which all mankind should desire to see—the face in which angels long to look—was evilly spat upon. Then he was scourged who had no guilt at all. Then finally he was crucified and slain. **280** Thus accomplished was the word of Isaiah: "He was wounded for our misdeeds and defiled for our felonies." Now since Jesus Christ took upon himself the pain of all our wickedness, sinful man should much weep and bewail that for his sins God's Son of heaven should endure all this pain.

The sixth thing that should move a man to Contrition is the hope of three things: forgiveness of sin, the gift of grace to do well, and the glory of heaven with which God shall reward a man for good deeds. And inasmuch as Jesus Christ gives us these gifts through his generosity and noble goodness, he is called *Iesus Nazarenus rex Iudeorum. Iesus* means "savior" or "salvation," through whom men should hope to have forgiveness of sins, which is properly salvation from sins. **285** That's why the angel said to Joseph, "You shall call his name Jesus, who shall save his people from their sins." And on this point Saint Peter says, "There is no other name under heaven that is given to any man by which he can be saved, but only Jesus." *Nazarenus* is the same as "flourishing," by which a man should hope that he who gives him remission of sins shall also give him grace to do well. For in the flower is the hope of fruit in time to come, and in the forgiveness of sins is the hope of grace to do well. "I was at your heart's door," says Jesus, "and called that I might enter. He who opens to me shall have forgiveness of sin. I will enter into him by my grace and sup with him" for the good works he shall do, which works are the food of God, "and he shall sup with me," through the great joy that I shall give him. **290** Thus shall man hope, on account of his works of penance, that God shall give him his kingdom, as he promises in the gospel.

Now a man should understand how his contrition should be. I say that it shall be universal and total; that is, a man shall be truly repentant for all the sins he's committed in the pleasure of his thoughts, for pleasure is perilous indeed. There are two kinds of consent. One is called consent of feeling, when a man is moved to sin and takes long pleasure in thinking about that sin; his reason well perceives it's a sin against God's law, yet his reason doesn't restrain his sinful pleasure or appetite, though he sees perfectly well its irreverence. Though his reason doesn't actually consent to committing the sin, some authorities say that such long-dwelling pleasure is most perilous, be it ever so little. **295** A man should also sorrow, especially for all he has ever desired, with full consent of his reason, against the law of God, for then without doubt there is mortal sin in consent. For surely there's no mortal sin that isn't first in man's thought, afterwards in his pleasure, and then in consent and deed. So I say that many men never repent or confess such thoughts and pleasures but only great sins outwardly committed. Wherefore such wicked thoughts and pleasures, I say, are subtle beguilers of those who shall be damned.

Man ought to sorrow, moreover, for his wicked words as well as for his wicked deeds, for surely to repent one sin and not all, or to repent all sins except one, is useless. **300** For certainly God Almighty is wholly good, and he therefore forgives all or nothing. That's why Saint Augustine says, "I certainly know that God is enemy to every sin." So shall he who persists in one sin have all his other sins forgiven? No.

Contrition, furthermore, should have extraordinary sorrow and anxiety. Then God shall show complete mercy. Therefore when my soul was anxious within me, I remembered God, that my prayer might go to him.

And contrition must be continuous, one must intend steadfastly to confess and to amend his life. **305** For truly as long as contrition lasts, a man may hope for forgiveness; from this comes hatred of sin by which he destroys sin, as much as he can, in both himself and others. Thus says David: "You who love God hate wickedness." For trust well, to love God is to love what he loves and hate what he hates.

The last thing that men should understand about contrition is this: in what way is contrition of use? I say that it sometimes delivers a man from sin; thus "I said," says David (that is, "I faithfully resolved"), "that I would confess, and you, Lord, remitted my sin." And just so, contrition is useless without a firm purpose to confess if one has opportunity, just as confession or satisfaction without contrition is of little worth. **310** Contrition, moreover, destroys the prison of hell, makes weak all the strengths of the devils, and restores the gifts of the Holy Spirit and of all good virtues. And it cleanses the soul of sin, delivering the soul from the pain of hell, from the company of the devil, and from sin's servitude, and restoring it to all spiritual blessings and to the company and communion of Holy Church. Furthermore, it makes him who was a son of wrath into a son of grace. And all these things have been proved by holy writ. So he who would pay attention to these things would surely be wise; truly he should never in his life desire to sin but should give his body and all his heart to the service of Jesus Christ and thereby do him homage. For truly our sweet Lord Jesus Christ has spared us so mercifully in our sins that if he didn't have pity on man's soul, a sorry song we all might sing. **315**

*Explicit prima pars Penitencia et sequitur
secunda pars eiusdem*

The second part of Penitence is Confession, which is a sign of contrition. Now you shall understand what Confession is, whether or not it should be done, and which things are appropriate to true Confession.

First you should understand that Confession is true showing of sins to the priest. "True" means that one must confess all the circumstances that he can relating to his sin. All must be said, nothing excused, hidden, or covered up, and don't boast of your good works. **320**

It's necessary, moreover, to understand where sins come from, how they increase, and what they are.

Saint Paul says this about the origin of sins: "Just as by man sin first entered the world, and through that sin death, so death entered all men who sinned." And this man was Adam by whom death entered the world, when he broke God's commandments. Thus he who was first so mighty that he shouldn't have died became one who had to die whether he wished to or not, like all his progeny in this world, who sinned in that same man. Consider, when Adam and Eve, in the state of innocence, were naked without shame in Paradise, **325** how the serpent, wiliest of the beasts that God had created, said to the woman: "Why did God command you not to eat of every tree in Paradise?" The woman answered, "We eat of the fruit of the trees of Paradise, but truly of the fruit of the tree in the middle of Paradise God forbade us to eat, we are not to touch it, lest perchance we die." The serpent said to the woman, "No, no, you shall not die, truly! God knows that on that day when you eat thereof, your eyes shall open and you shall be as gods, knowing good and evil." The woman then saw that the tree was good for eating and fair to see, a pleasure to the eyes. She took the tree's fruit and ate it, and gave some to her husband and he ate, and at once the eyes of both were opened. And when they knew they were naked, they sewed a kind of breechcloth from fig leaves to hide their sexual organs. **330** There you may see that deadly sin is first suggested by the devil, manifested here by the serpent; afterward comes delight of the flesh, shown here by Eve; and then the consent of reason, shown here by Adam. For trust well, though the fiend tempted Eve or the flesh, and the flesh took delight in the beauty of the forbidden fruit, certainly until Adam or reason consented to the eating of the fruit he still remained in the state of innocence. We took from Adam the same original sin: for we are all physically descended from him and engendered by vile and corrupt material. When the soul is put in our body, original sin is incurred right then, and what was first only affliction of concupiscence is afterward both affliction and sin. Therefore we are all born sons of wrath and everlasting damnation were it not the baptism we receive that takes away our guilt. But truly the affliction dwells with us with respect to temptation, and that affliction is called concupiscence. **335** When wrongfully disposed or ordered in man, this concupiscence makes him sinfully covet, by covetousness of the flesh, through eyesight with regard to earthly things, and by covetousness of high places through pride of heart.

Now speaking of the first kind of covetousness, that is, concupiscence, according to the law of our sexual organs, made lawfully by God in his righteous judgment, I say that inasmuch as man disobeys God who is his Lord, the flesh disobeys him through concupiscence, called also nourishment of sin and cause of sin. So all the while that a man has the affliction of concupiscence within him, he cannot help but be sometimes tempted and moved in the flesh to sin. This will not fail as long as he lives. It may well grow feeble and fail by virtue of baptism and by the grace of God through penitence, **340** but it shall never be so fully quenched that he won't be sometimes inwardly moved, unless chilled by sickness, the evil enchantment of sorcery, or cold drinks. For behold what Saint Paul says: "The flesh strives eagerly against the spirit, and the spirit is against the flesh; they are so contrary and so strive that a man may not always do as he would." This same Saint Paul, after his great penance in water and on land (in water night and day in great peril and pain, on land in famine, thirst, and cold, without adequate clothing, and once almost stoned to death), yet said: "Alas, I, miserable man! who shall deliver me from the prison of my miserable body?" And Saint Jerome, when he had long lived in the desert with no company but wild beasts, with no food but herbs and water to drink, and no bed but the naked earth, so that his flesh was as black as an Ethiopian's because of the heat and almost destroyed by the cold, **345** said that lechery burned and boiled throughout his body. Therefore I know very well that they are deceived who say that they are not tempted carnally. Witness Saint James the Apostle, who says everyone is tempted through his own concupiscence, that is, each of us has reason and cause to be tempted by the nourishment of sin that is in the body. Thus says Saint John the Evangelist: "If we say that we are without sin, we deceive ourselves and truth is not in us."

Now you shall understand how sin grows or increases in man. First there's the nourishment of sin that I spoke of before, that same fleshly concupiscence. **350** After that comes the suggestion of the devil, that is, the devil's bellows, with which he blows in man the fire of fleshly concupiscence. After that, a man considers whether or not to do as he is tempted. If he withstands and turns aside the first enticing of his flesh and the devil, it's not sin. If it so happens he doesn't do this, he immediately feels a flame of delight. Then it's good to beware and keep well on one's guard or he'll fall right away into yielding to sin; then he'll sin if he has time and place. Here's what Moses said on this matter and the devil: "The fiend says, 'I will keep after the man by wicked suggestion, and I will ensnare him by the stirring of sin. And I will choose my quarry or prey by deliberation, and accomplish my desire with delight. I will draw my sword in the consenting.' **355** For as surely as a sword separates something in two, consent separates God from man. 'Then I will slay him with my hand in his sinful deed,' says the fiend." For certainly man is then utterly dead in his soul. Thus is sin accomplished by temptation, delight, and consent, and then the sin is called actual.

In truth there are two kinds of sin: either venial or mortal. When man loves any creature more than Jesus Christ our Creator, truly it is mortal sin. Venial sin is when man loves Jesus Christ less than he should. The commission of this venial sin is truly quite perilous, for it diminishes more and more the love men should have for God. So if a man burdens himself with many such venial sins, though he sometimes unloads them with confession, gradually they will certainly diminish all the love that he has for Jesus Christ. **360** In this way venial passes directly into mortal sin. For surely the more a man burdens himself with venial sins, the more he is inclined to fall into mortal sin. So let's not neglect to discharge ourselves of venial sins. As the proverb says, "Many small make a great."

And heed this example. A great wave of the sea sometimes comes with such violence that it sinks a ship. The same harm is sometimes done by the small drops of water that enter through a little crack in the bilge and into the bottom of the ship, if men are so negligent that they don't bail in time. So although there's a difference between the two kinds of sinkings, the ship is still sunk. So it sometimes goes with mortal sin, and harmful venial sins when they multiply so greatly in a man that the same worldly things that he loves and through which he venially sins are as great in his heart as the love of God, or greater. 365 So the love of anything that is not set in God or done principally for God's sake, though a man love it less than God, is a venial sin. And it's mortal sin when the love of anything weighs as much or more in the heart of man as the love of God. "Deadly sin," says Saint Augustine, "is when a man turns his heart from God, the supreme goodness that may not change, and gives his heart to something that may change and vary." And surely that means everything save God in heaven. For truly if a man gives to a creature the love that he owes to God with all his heart, as much of his love as he gives to that creature he steals from God; and therefore he sins. He is a debtor to God but doesn't pay all his debt, which is all the love of his heart. 370

Now since man understands generally what venial sin is, it's appropriate to tell specially of sins that many a man perhaps doesn't consider to be sins and thus doesn't confess, though they truly are sins, as these clerks have written. Every time a man eats or drinks more than is sufficient to sustain his body, he is certainly sinning. It's also a sin when he speaks more than needed. Also when he doesn't hear graciously the complaint of the poor. Also when he's in good health and, without reasonable cause, won't fast when he should. And when he sleeps more than needed, or for the same reason is late for church or other charitable acts. Also when he uses his wife without the principal desire of engendering to the honor of God, or with the intent of paying to his wife the debt of his body. 375 Also when he won't visit the sick and the prisoner if he may. Also if he loves his wife or child or some other worldly thing more than reason requires. Also if he flatters or blandishes more than he should for any necessity. Also if he reduces or withholds his alms to the poor. Also if he prepares his food more sumptuously than needed or eats too hastily because of fondness for delicious food. Also if he tells idle tales at church or at God's service, or if he speaks idle words of folly or wickedness, for he shall account for it at the day of judgment. Also when he promises or gives a pledge that he will do things that he may not perform. Also when he thoughtlessly or in folly slanders or derides his neighbor. Also when he wickedly suspects something that he knows isn't true. **380** These things and more without number are sins, as Saint Augustine says.

Men should now understand that although no earthly man may avoid all venial sins, one may curb himself by the burning love that he has for our Lord Jesus Christ, and by prayers and confession and other good works, so that it only disturbs a little. As Saint Augustine says, "If a man loves God in such a way that everything he does is truly in and for the love of God, because he burns with the love of God, a venial sin will annoy a man who is perfect in the love of Christ as much as a drop of water will annoy or hurt a furnace full of fire." Men may also curb venial sin by receiving devoutly the precious body of Christ, **385** also by receiving holy water, by almsgiving, by general confession or *Confiteor* at mass and at compline, and by blessing of bishops and of priests and other good works.

Explicit secunda pars Penitentie

*Sequitur de Septem Peccatis Mortalibus et
dependenciis circumstanciis et speciebus*

Now it is necessary to tell of the Seven Deadly Sins, that is, the capital sins. They all run on one leash but in different ways. They are called capital because they are the chief ones, the sources of all other sins. The root of these seven sins is Pride, the general root of all sins, for from this root spring certain branches, as Wrath, Envy, Accidie or Sloth, Avarice or (to common understanding) Covetousness, Gluttony, and Lechery. And each of these capital sins has its branches and twigs, as shall be told in the following sections.

De Superbia

Though no man can fully count the number of twigs and sins that come from Pride, I'll show part of them as you will see. **390** There is

Disobedience, Boasting, Hypocrisy, Disdain, Arrogance, Impudence, Haughtiness, Insolence, Contemptuousness, Impatience, Strife, Contumacy, Presumption, Irreverence, Perverse Obstinancy, Vainglory, and many another twig I cannot set down. Disobedient is he who disobeys the commandments of God, his sovereigns, and his spiritual father. A boaster is he who boasts of the evil or the good he has done. Hypocrite is he who doesn't show himself as he is and shows what he is not. Disdainful is he who disdains his neighbor, that is, his fellow Christian, or who disdains to do what he should. 395 Arrogant is he who thinks that he has the good things in him that he doesn't, or believes that he deserves to have them, or who judges himself to be what he isn't. Impudent is he who for pride has no shame for his sins. Haughtiness is when a man rejoices in evil he has done. Insolent is he who despises all others in comparison with his own worth and his knowledge, speech, and bearing. Contemptuousness is when he may suffer neither master nor equal. 400 Impatient is he who will not be taught by or reproved for his vice, and who by strife knowingly makes war upon truth and defends his folly. *Contumax* is he who through his indignation is against every authority or power of those who are his rulers. Presumption is when a man undertakes an enterprise that he should not or may not do, and this is called audacity. Irreverence is when men do not honor those whom they should, but in turn wait with expectant desire to be reverenced. Perverse obstinancy is when a man defends his folly and trusts too much in his own intellect. Vainglory is to have pomp and delight in his temporal rank and to glorify himself in this worldly estate. 405 Jangling is when a man speaks too much before people, when he clatters like a mill and pays no attention to what he's saying.

Yet there is a private sort of Pride that expects to be greeted first before greeting another though the latter may be worthier. He also expects or desires to sit in a higher place at table, to precede another in walking, kissing pax after mass, or being censed, or to precede his neighbor to the offering, or to do similar things contrary to propriety, all because he aims in the proud desire of his heart to be magnified and honored before the people.

Now there are two kinds of Pride, one within man's heart and the other without. All that I've said and more belong to the Pride in man's heart; the other kinds of Pride are without. 410 Yet one kind of Pride is a sign to the other, just as a tavern's pleasant leafy arbor is a sign of the wine in the cellar. And this is noted in many things such as speech, bearing, and outrageous states of dress. If there had been no sin in clothing, Christ certainly would not so soon have noted and talked about the clothing of that rich man in the gospel. And Saint Gregory says that "precious clothing is blameworthy because of its costliness, softness, and newfangledness, and for its excess or inordinate scantiness." Alas! can men today not see the sinful, costly states of dress, particularly the excess or immoderate scantiness? **415**

As for the first sin, that of excessive clothing, it is expensive to the detriment of the people, not only in the costly embroidery, the ostentatious notched ornamentation, the undulating vertical strips, the coiling decorative borders, and such waste of cloth in vanity, but also in the costly fur in their gowns, so much punching with blades to make holes, and so much slitting with shears. Furthermore, the excessive length of these gowns, trailing in the dung and the mire, on horse as well as on foot, both of men and of women, is such that all that trailing cloth is in effect wasted, consumed, threadbare, and rotten with dung, rather than given to the poor, to their great loss. And that is in various ways; that's to say, the more the cloth is wasted, the more it must cost the people for its scarcity. **420** And furthermore, if they were to give such punched and slit clothing to poor people, it would not be suitable to wear because of their estate, nor sufficient to relieve them from inclement weather.

On the other hand, to speak of the horribly immoderate scantiness of clothing, there are these short-cut coats or short jackets that for their brevity, and with wicked intent, don't cover men's shameful members. Alas! some in their tight pants show their protruding shape, their horrible swollen members, till you'd think they had a hernia. And their buttocks look like the hind end of a she-ape at full moon. Moreover, the wretched swollen members that they show through newfangled clothing, in dividing their hose into white and red, make it look like half their shameful private parts were flayed. **425** And if they divide their hose into other colors, such as white and black, or white and blue, or black and red and so forth, then it seems by the variance of colors that half their private parts might be corrupted by Saint Anthony's fire, or by cancer, or by some other mischance. The hindmost part of their buttocks is a real horror to see. For certainly that foul part of their bodies where they purge their stinking ordure they show people proudly in contempt of decency, the sort of decency that Jesus Christ and his friends took care to show during their lives. Now as to the outrageous dress of women, God knows that though the faces of some of them seem chaste and gracious enough, they indicate lechery and pride in their arrangement of apparel. **430** I don't say that style in the clothing of a man or a woman is unsuitable, but certainly excessive or immoderately scanty clothing is blameworthy.

The sin of adornment or ornamentation may also be found in riding, as in too many elegant horses, fair, fat, and costly, being kept for pleasure. And many a base rogue is kept because of them; there's also overly sumptuous harness such as saddlebags, cruppers, poitrels, and bridles covered with precious cloth and rich bars and plates of gold and silver. Thus God says through the prophet Zechariah: "I will confound the riders of such horses." These people take little note of the riding and harness of God's Son of heaven, when he rode upon the ass with no other trappings but the poor clothes of his disciples. Nor do we read that he ever rode on any other beast. **435** I say this with regard to the sin of excess and not to sensible style. Pride, moreover, is notably found in maintaining a great retinue when of little or no profit, especially when that retinue, in the insolence of their high or official position, are cruel and abusive to the people. Certainly such lords sell their authority to the devil in hell when they support the wickedness of their retinue, as do people of low degree such as those who keep hostelries and support theft by their servants in many kinds of deceits. **440** Those kinds of people are the flies that seek honey or the hounds that seek carrion. Such people strangle their authority, and the prophet David says this about them: "Let death come upon their authority and let them go down alive into hell, for in their houses are iniquities and wickedness and not the God of heaven." Certainly they may make amends, but just as God gave his blessing to Laban by the service of Jacob and to Pharoah by the service of Joseph, God will give his curse to authorities who support their servants' wickedness unless they come to amendment.

Pride in one's table appears very frequently, for certainly rich men are invited to feasts and poor people are turned away with rebuke. The excess appears in the different kinds of food and drink, particularly those foods baked in pastry shells and serving dishes, with flames of burning spirits and painted and castellated with paper, all such waste that it's an outrage to imagine. **445** Also in utensils so precious and music so elaborate that a man is stirred all the more to pleasures of lust. If he thereby sets his heart less upon our Lord Jesus Christ, it is surely a sin, and certainly the pleasures might be so great in this case that through them a man might easily fall into sin that is mortal. Truly the kinds that arise from Pride, when they arise from premeditated evil, considered and planned, or from habit, are without doubt mortal sins. When they arise from unpremeditated weakness, and as suddenly disappear, I guess they're not mortal although they're grave sins.

Now men might ask where Pride comes from. I'd say that sometimes it springs from the good things bestowed by nature, sometimes from the benefits bestowed by fortune, and sometimes from the blessings bestowed by God's grace. 450 To be sure, the good things bestowed by nature consist either in goods of the body or goods of the soul. The goods of the body are health, strength, agility, beauty, nobility of birth, and freedom. The goods of the soul are good intellect, acute understanding, subtle ingenuity, native ability, and good memory. Benefits bestowed by fortune are riches, high degrees of lordships, and people's praise. The blessings bestowed by God's grace are such things as personal knowledge, power to endure spiritual suffering, benignity, virtuous contemplation, and withstanding temptation. 455 For a man to pride himself in any of these goods is great folly. Considering the good things bestowed by nature, God knows that sometimes we have by nature as much harm as profit. Bodily health, for example, departs very quickly and is often the cause of the sickness of our souls. The flesh, God knows, is a great enemy to the soul, so the more healthy the body the more we're in danger of falling. To take pride in the strength of one's body is foolish as well. For the flesh strives eagerly against the spirit, and the stronger the flesh the sorrier will the soul be. And on top of all this, bodily strength and worldly rashness drive a man very often to peril and disaster. 460 To take pride in one's nobility also is folly. Often the nobility of the body destroys that of the soul; we are in any case all from one father and one mother, we are all of one nature, rotten and corrupt, both the rich and the poor. Truly only one kind of nobility is praiseworthy, that which adorns a man's spirit with virtues and moral qualities and makes him a good Christian. Trust well, whichever man sin has mastery of is a perfect slave to sin.

Now there are general signs of nobility such as avoiding vice, debauchery, and servitude to sin in word, work, and manner; practicing virtue, courtesy, and purity; and being liberal, that is, generous in moderation, for that which surpasses moderation is folly and sin. 465 Another is to remember kindnesses one has received from other people. Another is to be benign to one's good subordinates; as Seneca says, "There is nothing more appropriate to a man of high estate than graciousness and pity. When these flying insects that men call bees make their king, they choose one that has no prick to sting with." Another is for a man to have a noble and diligent heart to accomplish highly virtuous deeds.

Now certainly for a man to pride himself in the blessings of God's grace is also outrageous folly, for the gift of grace that should have directed him to goodness and remedy directs him to poison and ruin, as says Saint Gregory. **470** Surely also a man who prides himself in the benefits bestowed by fortune is a very great fool. For sometimes he who was a great lord in the morning is a miserable wretch before nightfall. And sometimes a man's riches are the cause of his death; his sensual pleasures are sometimes the cause of the grave malady from which he dies. Indeed, popular approbation is sometimes too false and fickle to trust—today they praise, tomorrow they blame. The desire to have the people's approbation has caused the death, God knows, of many an eager man.

Remedium contra peccatum Superbie

Since you understand what Pride is, what its parts are, and where it comes from, **475** you shall now understand Pride's remedy, which is humility and meekness. That is the virtue through which a man has true self-knowledge, not esteeming nor respecting himself with regard to his just deserts but being always aware of his moral weakness. Now there are three kinds of humility: of heart, of mouth, and of deed. Humility of heart is of four types. One is when a man considers himself worth nothing before God of heaven. Another is when he despises no other man. The third is when he doesn't care if men think him worthless. The fourth is when he isn't sorry for his humility. **480** Humility of mouth is also fourfold: moderate speech, humility of speech, confession with one's own mouth that he's just as he thinks he is in his heart, and praise for rather than belittling of another man's goodness. Humility in deeds is of four kinds as well. The first is when one puts other men before himself. The second is to choose the lowest place in every way. The third is to assent gladly to good counsel. The fourth is to accept gladly the decision of one's sovereign or whoever is in higher degree. Certainly this is a great act of humility.

Sequitur de Invidia

After Pride I will speak of the foul sin of Envy, which according to the philosopher is "sorrow over another man's prosperity"; and Saint Augustine says it is "sorrow over other men's good fortune and joy over other men's misfortune." This foul sin is directly against the Holy Ghost. Although every sin is against the Holy Ghost, goodness belongs naturally to the Holy Ghost, so Envy, coming naturally from malice, is naturally against that goodness. **485** Now malice has two species: one is hardness of heart in wickedness, or such blindness of the flesh that man isn't aware or doesn't think he's in sin, which is the hardness of the devil. The other species of malice is when a man wars against truth when he knows it's the truth, and when he wars against the grace that God has given his neighbor. And all this concerns Envy. Certainly, then, Envy is the worst sin that can be. Any other sin is only opposed to one special virtue, but Envy is against all virtues and all goodness. For it is sorry for all the goodness of one's neighbor, making it different from all other sins. There is scarcely any sin that doesn't have within it some delight, but Envy has within it only anguish and sorrow. **490**

The kinds of Envy are three. The first is sorrow over another man's goodness and prosperity, and since prosperity is naturally a matter of joy, Envy is a sin against nature. The second kind of Envy is joy over another man's misfortune, and that's naturally like the devil who always rejoices in man's suffering. From these two kinds comes backbiting, and this sin of backbiting or detraction has certain parts as follows. Sometimes a man praises his neighbor with wicked intent, for at the end he always makes a wicked point, makes a "but," more deserving of blame than the rest is worthy of praise. The second kind is when the backbiter with wicked intent turns upside down all the goodness of a man's action or words. **495** The third is to belittle the goodness of his neighbor. The fourth kind of backbiting happens after men speak well of someone; the backbiter, despising him whom they praise, will say, "By my faith, there's another man better than he." The fifth kind is gladly to consent and listen to the evil that men speak of other people. This is a great sin that constantly increases in proportion to the backbiter's wicked intent.

After backbiting comes grumbling or complaining; sometimes it springs from impatience with God and sometimes with man. It's with God when a man grumbles against the pain of hell, poverty, loss of property, or rain or storm; he grumbles either that scoundrels have prosperity or that good men have adversity. **500** All these things a man should suffer patiently, for they come from the just judgment and ordering of God. Sometimes grumbling comes from avarice, as when Judas grumbled against Mary Magdalene when she anointed the head of our Lord Jesus Christ with her precious ointment. This kind of muttered complaint is like a man grumbling about the goodness that he himself does or what other people do with their property. Sometimes complaining comes from Pride, as when Simon the Pharisee grumbled against Mary Magdalene when she approached Jesus Christ and wept at his feet for her sins. And sometimes grumbling arises from Envy, as when one discloses a man's private misfortune or accuses him falsely of something. **505** Servants often complain, grumbling when their lord bids them do lawful things. As they dare not openly refuse to obey their lord's commandments, for sheer spite they will speak ill and grumble, complaining in private. Men call these words the devil's *Pater noster;* though the devil never had any *Pater noster*, the ignorant folk give it such a name. Sometimes it comes from Anger or private hate, which nourishes rancor in the heart as I shall refer to hereafter. Then comes bitterness of heart, through which every good deed of one's neighbor seems bitter or displeasing. **510** Then comes discord that dissolves all sorts of friendships. Then comes scorn of one's neighbor although he does ever so well. Then comes accusation, when a man seeks a pretext to annoy his neighbor, which is like the craft of the devil who waits night and day to accuse us all. Then comes malignity through which a man annoys his neighbor privately if he can; if he can't, nevertheless his wicked will shall not fail to burn his house secretly, or poison or slay his beasts, and such things as that.

Remedium contra peccatum Invidie

I will now speak of the remedy for this foul sin of Envy. First and foremost is the love of God, and loving one neighbor's as oneself, for truly the one may not exist without the other. **515**

And trust well that in the name of your neighbor you shall understand the name of your brother, for we all have physically one father and one mother, that is, Adam and Eve, and one spiritual father, God of heaven. You are obliged to love your neighbor and desire for him all goodness. Thus God says, "Love your neighbor as yourself," for salvation both of life and of soul. Moreover, you shall love him in word, including kindly admonition and chastisement, and comfort him in afflictions, and pray for him with all your heart. And in deeds you shall so love him as to do to him in charity as you would have it done to you. Therefore you shall do him no damage with wicked word, nor do harm to his body, property, or soul through enticement by wicked example. **520** You shall not desire his wife nor any of his things. Understand also that included in the name of neighbor is a man's enemy. Certainly a man shall love his enemy by the commandment of God, and truly your friend you should love in God. You should love your enemy, I say, for God's sake by his commandment. For if it were reasonable to hate one's enemy, truly we who are God's enemies would not be received by God to his love.

A man shall do three things in return for three kinds of wrongs that his enemy does to him. In return for hate and rancor he shall love him in heart. For chiding and wicked words he shall pray for his enemy. For his enemy's wicked deeds, he shall do him a good deed. **525** For Christ says, "Love your enemies and pray for them who speak ill of you, also them who harass and persecute you, and do good to them who hate you." This is how our Lord Jesus Christ commands us to act toward our enemies. Truly nature compels us to love our friends, and indeed our enemies have more need of love than our friends, and certainly to those with more need should men do good. In that deed, moreover, we have the example of the love of Jesus Christ who died for his enemies. And as that love is the more difficult to achieve, so much greater is the merit; thus loving our enemies confounds the venom of the devil. Just as the devil is defeated by humility, so is he mortally wounded by our love of our enemy. **530** So love is the medicine that casts out the poison of Envy from man's heart. The kinds of love in this section will be explained more fully in the sections that follow.

Sequitur de Ira

After Envy I will describe the sin of Anger. Truly whoever is envious of his neighbor will commonly find a source of wrath in word or in deed against him whom he envies. Anger comes from Pride as well as from Envy, for he who is proud is envious and is easily angered.

This sin of Anger as described by Saint Augustine is the wicked desire to be avenged by word or deed. **535** According to the philosopher, Anger is a man's hot blood stirred in his heart through which he desires harm to him whom he hates. Truly a man's heart, by the heating and stirring of his blood, becomes so turbulent that he is beyond all rational judgment.

But you should understand that Anger is of two kinds, one good, the other wicked. Good Anger is zeal for goodness through which a man is angry at wickedness and against it. Thus a wise man says that Anger is better than jesting. This Anger is accompanied by kindness and is Anger without bitterness, Anger not against the man but against his misdeeds, as the prophet David says: *"Irascimini et nolite peccare."* **540** Now understand that there are two kinds of wicked Anger. One is sudden or unexpected Anger with no consideration or consent of reason. This means that man's reason does not consent to sudden Anger and it is therefore venial. Another very wicked Anger comes from evil intent, premeditated in the heart, with wicked will to do vengeance; to this his reason consents and it is therefore a mortal sin. This Anger is so offensive to God that it troubles the soul, from which it chases the Holy Ghost and wastes and destroys the likeness of God, that is, the virtue that is in man's soul. It puts into him the likeness of the devil and takes man away from God who is his rightful lord. **545** This Anger is a great pleasure to the devil, for it's the devil's forge that is heated with the fire of hell. Just as fire is mightier than any other element to destroy earthly things, so Anger is mighty to destroy all spiritual things.

Just as the fire of small coals, almost dead under ashes, will kindle again when touched with brimstone, so Anger will always kindle again when touched by the pride that is hidden in man's heart. Certainly fire may not come out of anything if it wasn't first naturally there, such as fire drawn out of flints with steel. And just as pride is often a matter of Anger, so rancor is the nurse and keeper of Anger. **550** There is a kind of tree, as Saint Isidore says, that will burn a whole year or more when men make a fire from it and cover the coals with ashes. It happens the same way with rancor; once it's conceived in the hearts of some men, it will last perhaps from one Easter to the next and longer. But such a man is a long way from the mercy of God the whole time.

In this devil's forge three scoundrels are busily at work: Pride, that always blows and increases the fire by chiding and wicked words; Envy, holding the hot iron to man's heart with a pair of long tongs of prolonged rancor; **555** and last stands the sin of Contumely, or strife and quarreling, which hammers and forges by evil reproaches. Certainly this cursed sin injures both a man and his neighbor. Almost all the evil that any man does to his neighbor comes from wrath. Certainly outrageous wrath does all that the devil ever commands him to do, for he spares neither Christ nor his sweet Mother. And in his outrageous anger and ire, alas! many a man then feels totally wicked in his heart toward both Christ and all his saints. Is this not a cursed vice? Yes, it certainly is. Alas! it takes away a man's wit and reason and all the gracious spiritual life that should keep his soul. **560** It takes away God's due lordship over man's soul and the love of his neighbor. It wages war against the truth. It robs man of the quiet of his heart and subverts his soul.

From Anger come these stinking offspring: first, hate, which is deep-rooted wrath; discord, through which one forsakes his old friend long beloved; and then war and every kind of harm done by man to his neighbor's body or property. From this cursed sin of Anger comes manslaughter also. And understand well that homicide, which is manslaughter, occurs in several ways. Some kinds of homicide are spiritual and some bodily. Spiritual homicide is by way of six things: first, hate, as Saint John says: "Whoever hates his brother is a murderer." **565** Homicide is also by backbiting. "They have two swords," says Solomon, "with which they slay their neighbors." For truly it is as wicked to take away a man's good name as his life. Homicide is also in giving wicked counsel by fraud, as in counseling to impose wrongful tributes and taxes. "Like a roaring lion and a hungry bear," as Solomon says, "is a cruel lord" who withholds or reduces the hire or wages of servants, or commits usury or withholds his alms for the poor. Of this the wise man says, "Feed him who is almost dead from hunger"; for truly if you don't feed him, you kill him. And all these are mortal sins.

Manslaughter in deed is when you slay indirectly with your tongue, as by commanding or counseling someone to slay another. **570** One is by law, as when a judge condemns someone who deserves to die. But let the judge be careful to do it justly, not for the delight of splling blood but for the preservation of righteousness. Another homicide is that done out of necessity, as when one man slays another in self-defense, there being no other way to escape with his life. Certainly, though, if he may escape without slaughtering his adversary but slays him, he sins and must suffer penance for mortal sin. **575** Also when a man prevents the conception of a child, and either makes a woman barren by her drinking venomous herbs through which she may not conceive, or else slays a child by potions that produce abortion or by putting certain things in her private places. Also men or women sin unnaturally if they emit their orgastic fluids in a manner or place where no child may be conceived. And if a woman has conceived and hurts herself and slays the child, it is still a homicide. What can we say about women who murder their children for fear of worldly shame? Certainly it's a horrible homicide. It is also homicide if a man approaches a pregnant woman and through his lust the child is killed, or if one deliberately strikes a woman and she loses her child. All these are homicides and horrible mortal sins.

From Anger come many more sins in word, thought, and deed, as when one places the blame upon God, perhaps for something of which he himself is guilty, or when he despises God and all his saints, as do these cursed gamblers in different countries. **580** They commit this cursed sin when their hearts fill with wickedness toward God and his saints. And when they treat irreverently the sacrament of the altar, that sin is so great that it may hardly be remitted except that the mercy of God surpasses all their works, he is so great and benign. Next from Anger comes venomous wrath. When a man is sharply admonished in his confession to renounce his sin, he becomes angry, answers with wrathful scorn, and finds excuse for his sin in the frailty of his flesh. He did it to keep company with his friends, he says, or else the devil enticed him, or he did it because of his youth or a temperament so lacivious that he may not forbear, or else, he says, it is his destiny till a certain age, or he got it from his ancestors, and other such things. **585** These kinds of people are so wrapped up in their sins they don't want to free themselves. For truly no person who perversely excuses himself for his sin may be delivered from his sin until he meekly acknowledges it.

After this comes swearing, which is directly opposed to God's commandment and often occurs because of wrath and Anger. God says, "You shall not take the name of the Lord your God in vain." And our Lord Jesus Christ, according to Matthew, says, "Do not swear at all, neither by heaven, for that is the throne of God, nor by the earth, for that is his footstool, nor by Jerusalem, for that is the city of the great king, nor by your head, for you cannot make one hair white or black. But let your speech be 'Yes, yes' or 'No, no,' what's over and above that comes from evil"—thus says Christ. **590** For Christ's sake, do not swear so sinfully, dismembering Christ by soul, heart, bones, and body. You seem to think the cursed Jews had not dismembered Christ's precious body enough, that you should dismember him more. If the law compels you to swear, be ruled in your swearing by the law of God, as says Jeremiah, chapter four: "You shall keep three conditions: swear in truth, in judgment, and in justice." In other words, swear truthfully, every lie is against Christ, for Christ is the real truth. And consider well that in the case of every frequent swearer not compelled by law to swear, the plague shall not depart from his house while he practices such illicit swearing. You must take an oath in court, however, when you're required by the judge to witness the truth. Also, you shall not swear on account of envy, favor, or bribery, but on account of justice and its declaration to the glory of God and to help your fellow Christian. **595** So every man who takes God's name in vain, or falsely swears, or takes on himself the name of Christ to be called a Christian man yet lives contrary to Christ's way of life and his teaching, indeed takes God's name in vain. Consider also what Saint Peter says in the fourth chapter of Acts: *Non est aliud nomen sub celo, etc.,* "There is no other name under heaven given to man whereby we must be saved"; only the name, that is, of Jesus Christ. Note, too, how precious is the name of Christ as Saint Paul says in the second chapter of Philippians: *In nomine Jesu, etc.,* "In the name of Jesus every knee should bow, of those in heaven, on earth, and under the earth"; for it is so high and so worshipful that the fiend in hell should tremble to hear it mentioned. It seems, then, that men who swear so horribly by his blessed name revile it more blasphemously than did the cursed Jews or the devil who trembles when he hears that name.

Now since swearing, unless done lawfully, is so strictly forbidden, it is even worse to swear falsely and needlessly. **600**

What should we say about those who delight in swearing and consider it a noble act or a manly deed to swear great oaths? And what about those who out of sheer habit will not stop swearing great oaths, though the cause is not worth a straw? Certainly this is a horrible sin. Swearing suddenly without thinking is also a sin. But let's go now to that horrible swearing of exorcism and magic spells, as these false enchanters or necromancers do over basins full of water, or over a bright sword, or in a circle, or on a fire, or over the shoulder bone of a sheep. I can only say that they act cursedly and damnably against Christ and all the faith of Holy Church.

What shall we say of those who believe in divination by the flight or noise of birds or beasts, or by lots, necromancy, dreams, creaking of doors, cracking of houses, gnawing of rats, and such contemptible things as that? **605** Certainly all these things are forbidden by God and Holy Church. They are cursed who set their belief on such filth until they are converted to Christian living. If charms for wounds or maladies of either man or beast have any effect, perhaps it is because God allows it, that people might have more faith and more reverence for his name.

I will now speak of lying, which generally is a word falsely meant with the intention of deceiving one's fellow Christian. In some lies there is no advantage to anybody, and in others benefit and profit result for one man and distress and damage for another. One kind of lying is to save one's life or property. Another kind comes from delight in forging a long tale, painted in full detail, with a wholly false basis. **610** Some lies happen because a man would support his word, and others come from carelessness without forethought and such.

Let us now touch on the vice of flattery, which usually occurs only because of fear or covetousness. Flattery is generally wrongful praise. Flatterers are the devil's nurses who nurse his children with the milk of deceit. Solomon says truly that "flattery is worse than detraction." For sometimes detraction makes a haughty man more humble, as he dreads such detraction, but flattery makes a man more arrogant in his heart and countenance. Flatterers are the devil's enchanters, for they make a man think that he is like what he isn't. **615** They're like Judas, they betray a man to sell him to his enemy, the devil. Flatterers are the devil's chaplains, always singing *Placebo*. I count flattery among the vices of Anger, for often if a man is angry with another he will flatter somebody to get him to support his quarrel.

Now we speak of such cursing as comes from an angry heart. Malediction in general may be said to engender every kind of harm. Such cursing removes a man from the reign of God, as Saint Paul says. And such cursing often turns back upon him who curses, as a bird returns to its nest. **620** Above all things, men ought to avoid cursing their own children, consigning their offspring to the devil, as far as possible. Certainly it is a great peril and a great sin.

Let us speak then of chiding and reproach, which greatly wound a man's heart, for they unsew the seams of friendship within it. Not easily may a man become fully reconciled with him who has openly reviled, reproached, and slandered him. This is a horrible sin as Christ says in the gospel. Now note that he who reproaches his neighbor does so either for some painful physical affliction ("leper," "crippled scoundrel") or for committing some sin. If he reproaches him for a painful affliction, the reproach turns to Jesus Christ, for pain is righteously sent from God and by his permission, whether leprosy, mutilation, or malady. **625** If he reproaches him uncharitably for sin—"you lecher," "you drunken scoundrel," and so forth—then the devil, always joyful when men sin, rejoices. Chiding certainly comes only from a wicked heart. For the mouth often speaks the full heart. Understand, in any case, that when a man chastises another, he should beware lest he chide or reproach him. Truly, unless he be wary, he may very easily kindle the fire of anger and wrath, which he should quench; he may even slay him whom he should chastise with graciousness. For as Solomon says, "The pleasing tongue is the tree of life," that is, of spiritual life, and truly an unrestrained tongue slays the spirit of both the reproacher and the reproached. Look what Saint Augustine says: "There is nothing so like the devil's child as he who often chides." Saint Paul says as well, "The servant of God ought not to chide." **630** While chiding is an evil thing between all kinds of people, it's even more inappropriate between a man and his wife, for then there is never a rest. That's why Solomon says, "A house that is uncovered and leaking and a chiding wife are alike." If a house has many leaks, when a man avoids one leak he gets hit by another. So it goes with a chiding wife; if she doesn't chide him in one place, she chides him in another. Therefore, "a morsel of bread with joy," says Solomon, "is better than a house full of fine foods with chiding." Saint Paul, in chapter three of Colossians, says, "Wives, be subject to your husbands, as is proper before God, and you husbands love your wives."

Next we speak of scorn, a wicked sin, especially when one scorns a man for good works. **635** Certainly such scorners behave like the foul toad that can't stand to smell the sweet savor of the vine when it flourishes. These scorners are partners with the devil, for they have joy when the devil wins and sorrow when he loses. They are adversaries of Jesus Christ, for they hate what he loves, that is, salvation of the soul.

Now we will speak of wicked counsel, for he who gives wicked counsel is a traitor. He deceives him who trusts in him, as Achitophel deceived Absolon. Nevertheless, his wicked counsel is first against himself. For as the wise man says, "Every evil living person has this trait: he who would injure another, first injures himself." **640** And men should understand that one ought not receive his counsel from people who are false, angry, or hostile, or who love their own profit too much, or from people too worldly, particularly in counseling souls.

Next comes the sin of those who sow and plant discord among people, a sin that Christ utterly hates. And no wonder, for he died to make concord. They do more shame to Christ than those who crucified him; for God loved friendship among people more than he loved his own body, which he gave up for unity. Therefore they are comparable to the devil always busy making discord.

Then there is the sin of the double tongue, such as speaking pleasantly before people and wickedly behind their backs, or speaking with pretense of good intention or playful manner but with wicked intent.

Now comes betrayal of secrets through which a man is defamed; certainly he may not easily repair the damage. **645**

Then comes threatening, which is an open folly; for he who often threatens, threatens often more than he may perform.

Next come foolish words, of no profit to him who speaks them or to him who listens. Foolish also are words that are needless or with no ordinary profit intended. Although foolish words are sometimes venial sins, men should fear them nonetheless, for we shall give reckoning for them before God.

Now comes chattering, which may not be without sin. And as Solomon says, "It is a sign of open folly." That's why a philosopher, when asked how to please people, said, "Do many good works and speak few idle words." **650**

After this comes the sin of jesters, who are the devil's apes, for they make people laugh at their jesting speech as people do at the pranks of an ape. Saint Paul forbids such jests. Just as virtuous and holy words comfort those who work in the service of Christ, so the evil words and tricks of jesters comfort those who work in the service of the devil. These are the sins that come from the tongue, from Anger and from other sins as well.

Sequitur remedium contra peccatum Ire

The remedy for Anger is a virtue that men call Meekness, that is, Humility, and also another virtue that men call Patience or Long-Suffering.

Humility restrains and represses the stirrings of what is in a man's heart so that it does not leap out by way of anger or wrath. **655** Long-suffering endures sweetly all the annoyances and the wrongs that men do. Saint Jerome says of humility, "It neither speaks nor does harm to any person, nor becomes inflamed against reason for any harm that men do or say." This virtue sometimes comes naturally, as the philosopher says: "Man is a perceptive being, by nature humble and amenable to goodness; but when humility is perfected by grace, it is worth all the more."

Patience, another remedy for Anger, is a virtue that kindly permits every man's goodness, and by which a man is not angry for any harm done to him. The philosopher says patience is that virtue that endures humbly all the outrages of adversity and every wicked word. 660 This virtue makes a man like God and makes him a good Christian, as Christ says. This virtue vanquishes your enemy. As the wise man says, "If you would vanquish your enemy, learn to endure." And you should understand that man suffers four kinds of bodily or personal grievances for which he must have four kinds of patience.

The first grievance is wicked words. Jesus Christ suffered this so patiently without complaint, when the Jews reviled and reproached him so often. Therefore suffer patiently, for the wise man says, "If you strive with a fool, though the fool may be laughing or angry, you shall have no rest." The second grievance is damage to your property. Christ suffered very patiently when despoiled of all that he had in this life, which was nothing but his clothes. 665 The third grievance is bodily suffering, such as Christ suffered so patiently in his passion. The fourth grievance is to be overworked. It's a great sin, I say, when people work their servants too hard or outside of the proper times, as on holy days. Here again Christ suffered very patiently, teaching us patience, when he bore upon his blessed shoulder the cross upon which he would suffer cruel death.

Here may men learn to be patient; not only should Christians be patient for the love of Jesus Christ and for the reward of blissful eternal life, but even the old pagans, who never were Christian, commended and practiced the virtue of patience.

Once upon a time a philosopher was provoked by his pupil's great trespass, and brought a stick to beat the child. 670 When this child saw the stick, he asked, "What do you plan to do?" "I'm going to beat you," said the master, "for your correction." "In truth," said the child, "you should straighten yourself out first, for you have lost all your patience over a child's offense." "Indeed," said the master, now weeping, "you speak truly. Take the stick, my dear son, and correct me for my impatience."

From patience comes obedience, through which a man is obedient to Christ and to all those to whom he ought to be obedient in Christ. And understand well that obedience is perfect when a man willingly and eagerly, with an entirely good heart, does all that he should do. **675** Obedience generally is to perform the precepts of God and of one's sovereign, to whom one should be obedient in all justice.

Sequitur de Accidia

After the sin of Envy and Anger, I will now speak of the sin of Sloth. For Envy blinds the heart of a man, and Anger troubles him, and Sloth makes him sluggish, moody, and peevish. Envy and Anger make the heart become bitter, which is the mother of Sloth and takes away one's love of all goodness. So Sloth is the anxiety of a troubled heart; as Saint Augustine says, "It is affliction of goodness and joy at others' ill fortune." Certainly this is a damnable sin, for it wrongs Jesus Christ by taking away the service that men owe to Christ with all diligence, as Solomon says. But Sloth is not diligent. It does everything with displeasure and perverseness, slackness and apology, idleness and disinclination. Therefore the book says, "Cursed is he who does the Lord's work negligently." **680** So Sloth is enemy to every period or state of man's existence, for the state of man is in three modes. There is the period of innocence, like the state of Adam before he fell into sin, which constrained him to work for the worship and adoration of God. Another period is the state of sinful man, in which condition men are bound to labor, praying to God for correction of their sins and that he grant they may rise above them. A third period is the state of grace, in which one is bound to works of penitence. Certainly to all these things Sloth is an enemy and contrary, for it loves no activity at all. Now this foul sin Sloth is also a very great enemy to the livelihood of the body, for it makes no provision regarding temporal necessity but idles away and sluggishly wastes all temporal goods by its carelessness. **685**

The fourth thing is that Sloth is like those who are in the pain of hell because of their sloth and their indolence. The damned are so bound that they may neither do well nor think well. Sloth makes one feel weary and hindered from doing any good, so that God abominates Sloth, as

Saint John says. Now comes Sloth that will suffer no hardship or penance. For truly Sloth is so tender and sensitive, as Solomon says, that he would suffer neither hardship nor penance and thus ruins all that he does.

Against this rotten-hearted sin of Sloth, men should strive to do good works, and manfully and virtuously have the courage to do well, calling to mind that our Lord Jesus Christ rewards every good deed, be it ever so little. Great is the habit of labor, as Saint Bernard says, for it gives the laborer strong arms and hard sinews, while sloth makes him feeble and tender. **690**

Then comes the dread to begin any good works. For he who is inclined to sin thinks it is too great an enterprise to undertake works of goodness; he considers in his heart that the circumstances of goodness are such a grievous burden to bear that he dare not start any good works, as Saint Gregory says.

Now comes hopelessness, the despair of God's mercy that comes sometimes from too great a sorrow or from too great a fear, as one imagines he has committed such great sins that it would not avail him to repent them. Through this despair or fear he abandons himself whole-heartedly to every kind of sin, as Saint Augustine says. This damnable sin, if it continues until death, is called sinning against the Holy Ghost. **695** This horrible sin is so perilous that when one is in despair there is no felony or sin that he is afraid to commit, as was shown by Judas. So above all others this sin is most offensive and hostile to Christ. Truly he who despairs is like the cowardly champion who needlessly says "I surrender." Alas! he is needlessly defeated and in needless despair. Certainly the mercy of God is ever ready for the penitent and is above all his works. Alas! can't one recall Saint Luke's gospel, chapter fifteen, where Christ says that "there will be more joy in heaven over one sinner who does penance than over ninety-nine just who need no penance?" **700** Consider, too, in that same gospel the joy and the feast of the good man who had lost his son, when the son had returned with repentance to his father. Can't they also remember (Saint Luke, chapter twenty-three) what the thief who was hanged beside Jesus said? "Lord, remember me when you come into your kingdom." "Truly I say to you," said Christ, "this day you shall be with me in paradise." Certainly there is no sin of man so horrible that it may not be destroyed in his life by penitence through virtue of Christ's passion and death. Alas! why should man then despair, since his mercy is so ready and generous? Ask and receive. **705**

Then comes somnolence, being sluggish slumbering, which makes a man indolent and dull in body and soul; and this sin comes from Sloth. Certainly the time when a man shouldn't sleep is the morning, unless there is reasonable cause. For truly morning is most suitable for saying one's prayers, for honoring and thinking of God, and for giving alms to the poor who first come in Christ's name. Consider what Solomon says: "Whoever would awake early in the morning and seek me shall find me."

Then comes negligence or carelessness, caring for nothing. If ignorance is the mother of all evil, negligence is surely the nurse. 710 Negligence has no regard for when or how well he may get something done.

The remedy for these two sins, as the wise man says, is that "he who fears God neglects nothing that he ought to do." And he who loves God will make an effort to please God by his works and devote himself fully in all that he does.

Then comes idleness, the gate of all sins. An idle man is like a place without walls; the devil may enter on every side and shoot at him with temptations while he's unprotected. This idleness is the bilge of all wicked and evil thoughts, all chatter, trifles, and filth. 715 Heaven is surely the reward for those who labor, not for those who are idle. And David says that "those who do not take part in the labor of men shall not be scourged by men"—that is to say, in purgatory. So it certainly seems they'll be tormented by the devil in hell unless they do penance.

Then comes the sin that men called *tarditas,* as when a man is too tardy or delays in turning to God. And that is a great folly. He is like one who falls in a ditch and won't rise. And this vice comes from a false hope. He thinks he shall live a long time, but that hope very often fails.

Then comes laziness. One begins a good work, then neglects it and stops, like those in governance who neglect someone they govern when they encounter hostility or annoyance. 720 These are the modern shepherds who deliberately allow their sheep to run to the wolf in the briers, or take no heed of their own guardianship. From this comes poverty and destruction, both spiritual and temporal. Then comes a kind of coldness that freezes a man's heart. Then comes lack of devotion, through which a man is so blinded, as Saint Bernard says, and has such languor in his soul that he may neither read or sing in church nor hear or think of any devotion, nor may he labor with his hands in any good work without it becoming unpleasant and distasteful to him. He waxes sluggish and slumbrous, and will soon be wrathful, inclined to hatred and envy.

Then comes the sin of worldly sorrow, called *tristicia,* that slays a man, as Saint Paul says. **725** For such sorrow contributes to the death of the soul and the body as well. A man becomes weary of his own life. Such sorrow, then, often shortens a man's life before his time comes naturally.

Remedium contra Peccatum Accidie

Against this horrible sin of Sloth and its branches is a virtue called *fortitudo* or strength, a disposition through which a man despises harmful things. This virtue is so mighty and vigorous that it dares to oppose mightily and guard itself from perils that are wicked, and to wrestle against the assaults of the devil. It uplifts and strengthens the soul, just as Sloth casts it down and enfeebles it. For this *fortitudo* endures by long-suffering the hardships that befit it. **730**

This virtue has many species, the first called magnanimity, or great courage. For great courage is needed against Sloth lest it swallow the soul by the sin of sorrow or destroy it by despair. This virtue makes people undertake difficult things, wisely and reasonably, by their own free will. And as the devil fights against man more by cunning and trickery than by strength, men should oppose him by intelligence, reason, and discretion. Then there are the virtues of faith and hope in God and his saints to accomplish the good works in which one firmly proposes to continue. Then comes confidence or a sense of security, when a man fears no hardship in the good works he's begun. **735** Then comes great achievement, the performance of great works of goodness, which is why men should perform them, for in the accomplishment of great good works lies the great reward. Then there is constancy, that is, stability of spirit, which should be in the heart by steadfast faith, and in the mouth and bearing, as well as in feeling and deed. There are still other special remedies for Sloth in different works, in consideration of the pains of hell and the joys of heaven, and in trust of the grace of the Holy Ghost, who will give one the might to perform his good intentions.

Sequitur de Avaricia

After Sloth I will speak of Avarice and Covetousness, of which sin Saint Paul, in I Timothy, chapter six, says, "The root of all evils is Covetousness." Truly when a man's heart is encumbered and troubled, and his soul has lost the comfort of God, he seeks the empty solace of worldly things. **740**

Saint Augustine describes Avarice as a keen eagerness in the heart to have earthly things. Some others say that Avarice is to acquire many earthly things and to give nothing to those who have need. And understand that Avarice consists not only of land and goods, but sometimes of knowledge and glory. In every kind of excessive thing is Avarice and Covetousness. And the difference between Avarice and Covetousness is this: Covetousness covets what you don't have; Avarice withholds and keeps what you do have, without rightful need. Truly Avarice is a damnable sin, for holy scripture speaks against it and curses it, for it wrongs Jesus Christ. **745** It takes from him the love that men owe him, turns it backward against all the reason, and makes the avaricious man have more hope in his goods than in Jesus Christ, to whose service he pays less attention than to keeping his treasure. That's why Saint Paul, in Ephesians, chapter five, says that an avaricious man is in bondage to idolatry.

What is the difference between a worshipper of idols and an avaricious man, except that an idolator perhaps has only one or two idols while the avaricious man has many? For every florin in his coffer is his idol. Certainly the sin of idolatry is the first thing that God prohibited in the ten commandments, as Exodus, chapter twenty, bears witness: **750** "You shall not have strange gods before me, nor shall you make for yourself a graven thing." Thus an avaricious man who loves his treasure before God is a worshipper of idols.

From Covetousness come these severe lordships through which men are oppressed by taxes, customs duties, and tolls, more than their reasonable obligation. They also take from their tenants arbitrary fines, which might more reasonably be called extortions. Some lords' stewards say these arbitrary fines and oppressive exactions are just, as a serf has nothing temporal, they say, that is not his lord's. But these lordships do wrong who seize from their tenants things that they never gave them, as Augustine says in *De Civitas Dei,* book nineteen.

It is true that the condition of slavery and its first cause is sin, as recorded in Genesis, chapter nine. **755** Thus you may see that sin, not nature, deserves slavery. So these lords should not glory in their lordships, since by natural condition they are not lords over slaves, rather slavery comes first by reason of sin. Furthermore, the law that says the temporal goods of serfs are the goods of their lords should be understood to mean the emperor's goods to defend them in their rights, not to rob or despoil them. Thus Seneca says, "It is prudent to live kindly with your slaves." Those whom you call your serfs are God's people, for humble people are Christ's friends; they are intimate with the Lord. **760**

Consider well that serfs originate from the same kind of seed as lords do. The serf may be saved as easily as the lord. The same kind of death that carries off the serf sweeps away the lord. So I counsel you, do right by your serf as you would that your lord did by you if you were in his shoes. Every sinful man is a slave to sin. I counsel each of you lords to work in such a way with your serfs that they love you rather than dread you. I know well that there are degrees above degrees, as is reasonable, and it's right that men do their duty when it's due, but certainly extortions and contempt for your underlings are damnable.

Furthermore, you know well that these conquerors or tyrants very often make slaves of those who are born of blood as royal as their own. **765** Slavery was unknown until Noah said that his son Canaan should be a slave to his brothers for his sin. What should we say, then, of those who rob and extort Holy Church? Certainly the sword first given to the newly dubbed knight signifies that he should defend Holy Church, not rob or pillage it; whoever does so is a traitor to Christ. And as Saint Augustine says, "They are the devil's wolves that harry the sheep of Jesus Christ." They do worse than wolves, for when the wolf has his belly full he ceases to harry sheep. But not so the pillagers and destroyers of the goods of Holy Church, for they never cease to rob.

Now as I have said, since sin was the first cause of slavery, and this world was all the time in sin, the whole world was in slavery and subjugation. **770** But since the coming of grace, God ordained that some people be higher in estate and degree and some lower, with each served according to his rank and degree. So in some countries where slaves are bought, when slaves are converted to the faith they are freed from slavery. And certainly the lord owes to his man what the man owes to his lord. The Pope calls himself the servant of the servants of God; but the estate of Holy Church might not have been established, nor the common profit preserved, nor peace and rest on earth, if God had not ordained that some men have higher degrees and some lower. So authority was established that lords might keep, maintain, and defend their subjects and underlings according to reason and as far as it lies in their power, not that they might destroy or harass them. So I say that those lords who like wolves wrongfully devour the possessions or goods of the poor, without mercy or moderation and without making amends, 775 shall receive the mercy of Jesus Christ only in the same measure they have meted it out to the poor.

Now comes deceit between merchant and merchant. You should understand that there are many kinds of buying and selling; one is material, the other spiritual; one is honest and lawful, the other dishonest and unlawful. The merchandising of material is lawful and honest when a kingdom or country, ordained self-sufficient by God, out of its abundance helps another country in need. Then must merchants bring their goods from one country to the other. That other merchandising that men practice with fraud, treachery, and deceit, with lies and false oaths, is cursed and damnable. 780

Spiritual buying and selling is properly simony, that is, the eager desire to buy spiritual things, things that pertain to God's sanctuary and to those responsible for spiritual welfare. This desire if pursued by a man to the fullest, even though it prove fruitless, is a deadly sin; if he is in holy orders, he is disqualified from practicing them. Certainly simony is named after Simon Magus, who would have bought with temporal goods the gift of the Holy Ghost that God had given to Saint Peter and the apostles. Understand therefore that both he who sells and he who buys spiritual things—whether by goods, contrivance, or worldly entreaty of worldly or spiritual friends or kindred—are called simoniacs. If entreaty is made for one who is not worthy and able, it is true simony if he takes the benefice; if he is worthy and able, it is not. 785 The other kind is when people entreat for a person to be preferred to a benefice only for the wicked worldly regard that they have for that person, and that is foul simony. But in service for which men give spiritual things to their servants, the service must be righteous and not otherwise, without fraudulent dealings, and when the person is worthy. As Saint Damasus says, "All the sins of the world compared to this sin are as nothing." For it is the greatest sin there may be after the sin of Lucifer and the Antichrist. By this sin God loses completely the church and the soul that he redeemed with his precious blood to those who give churches to them who are unworthy. For they put in thieves who steal the souls belonging to Jesus Christ and destroy his patrimony. 790 Through such unworthy priests and curates ignorant men have less reverence for the sacraments of Holy Church; and such givers of churches put out the children of Christ and put into the church the devil's own son. Those who ought to protect lambs sell the souls to the wolf that harries them.

Therefore they shall never have a share of the lambs' pasture, which is heaven's bliss.

Now comes gambling with its appurtenances, such as backgammon and raffles, from which come deceit, false oaths, quarrels, all robberies, blaspheming, renouncing of God, hate of one's neighbors, waste of goods, misspending of time, and sometimes even manslaughter. Certainly gamblers may not be without sin while they practice that craft.

From Avarice as well come lies, theft, false witness, and false oaths. And understand that these are great sins and directly against the commandments of God, as I have said. **795**

False witness is in word and in deed. It's in word when for anger, bribery, or envy you take away by false swearing your neighbor's good name, his goods, or his heritage. You bear false witness when you wrongly accuse him or excuse either him or yourself. Beware you inquests and notaries! Susannah, for false witness against her, was subjected to great sorrow and pain, and many another like her.

The sin of theft is directly opposed to God's commandment both materially and spiritually. Material theft is taking your neighbor's goods against his will whether by force, trickery, or false measure, coming stealthily with false indictments against him, borrowing goods with no intention of returning them, and such things as that. **800** Spiritual theft is sacrilege, that is, damaging holy things or things sacred to Christ, in two ways: every wicked sin or violence that men do in holy places such as churches or churchyards may be called sacrilege; and they are guilty of sacrilege as well who falsely withhold the prerogatives that belong to Holy Church. Plainly and generally, sacrilege is to rob things, whether holy or unconsecrated, from a holy place, or holy things from an unconsecrated place.

Relevacio contra peccatum Avaricie

Now you shall understand that the alleviation of Avarice is generous mercy and pity. Men might ask why this is so. It's because the avaricious man shows no pity or mercy to a man in need; he delights in keeping his treasure, not in rescuing or alleviating his fellow Christian. Therefore I will speak first of mercy. **805**

Mercy, as the philosopher says, is a virtue by which a man's courage is stirred by the misery of anyone in distress. After this comes pity in performing charitable works of mercy. To be sure, these things move a man to the compassion of Jesus Christ who gave himself for our sins and suffered death for mercy's sake. He forgave our original sin and thereby released us from the pains of hell, reduced the pains of purgatory by penitence, and gave us the grace to do well and attain the bliss of heaven. The kinds of mercy are to lend and to give, to forgive and to release from obligation, to have heartfelt pity and compassion for the distress of one's fellow Christian, and also to chastise where needed. **810**

Another kind of remedy for avarice is reasonable generosity. But truly one must consider here the grace bestowed upon us by Jesus Christ in both temporal and eternal goods. One must also remember the death that he shall receive—he knows not when, where, nor how—and that he shall forego all that he has, save only what he has distributed in charity to the poor.

But as some people are immoderate, men ought to avoid that foolish generosity called waste. He who is prodigal does not give his goods, he loses them. Truly whatever he gives to minstrels and such, for vainglory, for worldly renown, is a sin and no work of charity. He sinfully loses his goods who seeks with the gift of them nothing but sin. **815** He's like a horse that seeks to drink stirred-up or muddy water rather than clear water from a well. And as they give where they shouldn't, to them belongs that curse that Christ shall give at the day of judgment to those who shall be damned.

Sequitur de Gula

After Avarice comes Gluttony, which is directly opposed to the commandment of God. Gluttony is immoderate desire to eat or drink, or to do enough to satisfy this inordinate craving. This sin has corrupted the whole world, as shown well in the sin of Adam and Eve. Consider, too, what Saint Paul says of Gluttony: "Many so walk of whom I've often told you—and now I tell it weeping—that they are enemies of the cross of Christ; their end is death, their god is their belly, and their glory is in the shame that they so relish earthly things." **820** He who is addicted to this sin of gluttony may not withstand sin. He must be in servitude to all vices, for it's the devil's hiding and resting place.

This sin has many species. The first is drunkenness, the horrible burial of man's reason. When a man is drunk he has lost his reason, and this is a mortal sin. On the other hand, when a man's not accustomed to strong drink and perhaps doesn't know its strength, or has a weakness in his head or has labored so that he drinks all the more, even if he's drunk it is no mortal sin but venial. The second kind of gluttony is when a man's spirit becomes confused, for drunkenness robs him of the discretion of his wits. The third kind of gluttony is when a man devours his food and has no good manners. **825** The fourth is when, through the great abundance of his food, the humors in his body are distempered. The fifth is forgetfulness from too much drinking, as when a man sometimes forgets before morning what he did in the evening or the night before.

The species of Gluttony are distinguished in other ways according to Saint Gregory. The first is to eat before it's time. The second is when a man procures food or drink that's too rich. The third is when men partake beyond moderation. The fourth is fastidiousness, great attention to preparing and garnishing one's food. The fifth is to eat too greedily. These are the five fingers of the devil's hand by which he draws people to sin. **830**

Remedium contra peccatum Gule

Against Gluttony is the remedy of abstinence, as Galen says, but I don't consider that meritorious if done only for the health of the body. Saint Augustine recommends that abstinence be practiced for virtue and with patience: "Abstinence is worth little unless it is willingly done, is strengthened by patience and charity, and is practiced for God's sake and in hope of the bliss of heaven."

The companions of abstinence are moderation, holding to the "golden mean" in all things; shame, which avoids all dishonor; contentment, which seeks no rich foods or drinks and has no regard for extravagant preparation of food; measure, which reasonably constrains the unbridled appetite for eating; soberness, which restrains excessive drinking; and frugality, which restrains the voluptuous pleasure of sitting long and luxuriously at one's food, so that some people, to have less leisure, willingly stand to eat. **835**

Sequitur de Luxuria

After Gluttony comes Lechery, for these two sins are cousins so closely related that often they will not part company. This sin is of course very displeasing to God, for he himself said, "You shall not commit adultery." So against this sin he levies great punishments in the old law. If a bondwoman were taken in this sin, she should be beaten to death with staves; if a gentlewoman, she should be slain with stones; and if a bishop's daughter, she should be burned by God's commandment. Furthermore, because of the sin of lechery God inundated the whole world with Noah's flood. And after that he burned five cities with lightning and sank them into hell.

Let us speak then of that stinking sin of Lechery that men call adultery among wedded folk, that is, when either one or both of them be wed. **840** Saint John says that adulterers shall be in hell in a pool of burning fire and brimstone—in fire for their lechery, brimstone for the stink of their filth. The breaking of this sacrament is without doubt a horrible thing. It was made by God himself in paradise and confirmed by Jesus Christ, as Saint Matthew witnesses in the gospel: "A man shall leave his father and mother and cleave to his wife and they shall be two in one flesh." This sacrament signifies the joining together of Christ and Holy Church. And not only did God forbid adultery in deed, he commanded that you should not lust after your neighbor's wife. "In this commandment," says Saint Augustine, "is forbidden all kinds of lecherous craving." Look what Saint Matthew says in the gospel, that "whosoever shall look on a woman to lust after her has already committed adultery with her in his heart." **845** Here you may see that not only is the deed of this sin forbidden but also the desire to do that sin.

This cursed sin grievously harms those who practice it. First in their soul, for they constrain it to sin and punishment of death that is everlasting. It grievously harms the body, too, for it dries it up, wastes it and ruins it, and of his blood one makes a sacrifice to the fiend of hell. It also wastes his property and substance. And certainly if it is a foul thing for a man to waste his property on women, it is a fouler thing yet when women for such filth spend their property and substance on men. This sin, as the prophet says, takes away from men and women their good fame and all their honor. It's very pleasing to the devil, for by it he wins the greatest part of this world. **850** And just as a merchant delights most in the trade that's most profitable, so the fiend delights most in this filth.

This is the other hand of the devil with five fingers to catch people and bring about their bondage. The first finger is the lascivious gaze between men and women; it slays just as the basilisk slays people by the poison of its glance, for craving eyes follow craving of the heart. The second finger is evil touching in a wicked manner. Just as touching warm pitch defiles one's fingers, "whoever touches and handles a woman," says Solomon, "fares like one who handles a scorpion that stings and suddenly slays through poisoning." The third is foul words that like fire immediately burn the heart. **855** The fourth finger is kissing, for truly one would be a great fool to kiss the mouth of a burning oven or furnace. Those who kiss in wickedness—that mouth is the mouth of hell—are greater fools yet, especially these old, senile lechers who would kiss though they can't do more and defile themselves. They are surely like hounds, for when a hound comes by the rose bush or such, though he can't piss he'll heave up a leg and make a pretense of pissing. And many a man thinks he may not sin in any lechery with his wife, but that opinion is false. God knows, a man may slay himself with his own knife, and from his own cask make himself drunk. Whether it's his wife, child, or any worldly thing that he loves more than God, it's his idol and he is an idolator. **860** A man should love his wife in moderation, patiently and temperately; then she's as if she were his sister. The fifth finger of the devil's hand is the stinking deed of Lechery. Certainly the fiend puts the five fingers of Gluttony into a man's belly, and with his five fingers of Lechery grips him by the loins to throw him into the furnace of hell, where men shall have the fire and worms that last forever, the weeping and wailing, the sharp hunger and thirst, and the horror of devils that shall trample them forever without respite.

From Lechery, as I said, arise diverse species, such as fornication, which is between a man and a woman who are not married; this is a mortal sin against nature. **865** Everything that is an enemy and destroyer of nature is against nature. Indeed a man's reason clearly tells him it's a mortal sin, inasmuch as God forbade lechery. And Saint Paul gives him the just deserts due only to one who commits mortal sin. Another sin of Lechery is to rob a maiden of her maidenhood, for whoever does so casts a maiden out of the highest degree of honor in this present life; he robs her of that precious fruit that the book calls a hundredfold. I can say it in no other way in English, but in Latin it's called *Centesimus* *fructus.* To be sure, whoever does this is the cause of many damages and shameful injuries—more than any man can reckon—just as he is sometimes the cause of damages done by his beasts in a field when they break through hedge or fence and destroy that which cannot be restored. **870** For maidenhood may not be restored any more than an arm cut off from the body may return again to grow. She may have mercy, I'm well aware, if she's penitent, but she shall never again be undefiled.

Although I've spoken somewhat of adultery, it's good to consider still more of its perils to avoid that foul sin. Adultery in Latin means to approach another man's bed; thus those who were formerly one flesh surrender their bodies to others. From this sin, as the wise man says, result many evils. First there's breaking of faith, and faith is the key of Christian doctrine. **875** When that faith is broken and lost, truly Christianity is without fruit and useless. This sin is also a theft, for theft generally is to seize a man's possessions against his will. Certainly the foulest theft ever is when a woman steals her body from her husband and gives it to her lecher to defile; and she steals her soul from Christ and gives it to the devil. This is a fouler theft than to break into a church and steal the chalice, for these adulterers break spiritually into the temple of God and steal the vessel of grace, that is, the body and the soul, for which Christ shall destroy them, as Saint Paul says. Truly Joseph had great fear of this theft when his lord's wife entreated him to do a villainous evil. "Behold, my lady," he said, "how my master has placed in my guardianship all that he has in this world, leaving nothing that is not in my power except you who are his wife. **880** How then can I do this wicked thing and sin so horribly against God and my lord? God forbid it!" Alas! all too little is such truthfulness found nowadays. The third evil is the filth through which they break God's commandment and defile the founder of matrimony, that is, Christ. As the sacrament of marriage is so noble and worthy, so much the greater is the sin of breaking it; for God made marriage in paradise, in the state of innocence for mankind to multiply in God's service. To break it is therefore more grievous, for often from such breaks come false heirs who wrongfully occupy other people's inheritances. So Christ will put them out of the kingdom of heaven, the inheritance of good people. From this breakage people often unknowingly wed or sin with their own relatives. And in particular these male lechers frequent these lascivious women in their brothels, which may be likened to a common privy where men purge their excrement. **885** What shall we say as well about pimps who live off the horrible sin of prostitution, making women pay them a certain amount from the selling of their bodies, sometimes even that of a pimp's own wife or child? Clearly these are cursed sins. Understand as well that Adultery is aptly set in the ten commandments between theft and manslaughter, for it's the greatest theft that may be, the theft of body and soul. It's also like homicide, for it cuts in two, breaks in two, those first made of one flesh. By the old law they should therefore be slain. But by the new law, that is, the law of mercy, Jesus Christ said to the woman who was found in adultery and should have been stoned according to the law and desire of the Jews: "Go, and have no more will to sin," or "will no more to commit sin." Truly the vengeance for Adultery is under the jurisdiction of the punishments of hell unless prevented by penitence. **890**

There are yet more species of this cursed sin, as when one or both of the parties may belong to a religious order, or if one has entered into holy orders, as subdeacons, deacons, priests, or knights hospitalers. And the higher one is in orders, the greater is the sin, greatly aggravated by the breaking of the vow of chastity when the order was received. For it's true that holy orders are chief among all the treasures of God, his special sign and mark of chastity, to show that they are joined in chastity, the most precious life there is. These people in orders are specially dedicated to God, are of the special household of God, so when they commit mortal sin they are the special traitors of God and his people. For they live off the people, to pray for the people, but while they're such traitors their prayer does not benefit the people. Priests are angels by the high spiritual worth of their ministry, but in truth Saint Paul says that Satan transforms himself into an angel of light. **895** Truly the priest who practices mortal sin may be likened to the angel of darkness transformed into the angel of light. He seems like an angel of light but in truth is an angel of darkness. Such priests are the sons of Eli, shown in the Book of Kings to be the sons of Belial, that is, the devil. Belial means "without judge," and so they fare; they think they're as free, without judge, as a bull in the field that takes whatever cow he likes. So they fare among women, for just as a free bull is enough for a whole farm, a wicked priest's corruption is enough for a whole parish or district. These priests of Eli, as the Bible says, did not serve the people through their priesthood nor did they serve God. As the Bible says, they weren't satisfied with the boiled meat they were offered but took even the raw meat by force. **900** Just so, these scoundrels are not satisfied with meat roasted and boiled, with which the people feed them in great reverence; they would have the raw meat of men's wives and their daughters. And these women who consent to their sexual immorality do great wrong to Christ, to Holy Church, to all saints and all souls. For they rob them of those who should worship Christ and Holy Church and pray for Christian souls. Therefore such priests, and their concubines who also consent to their lechery, shall have the malediction of the whole ecclesiastical court until they are converted to Christian living.

The third kind of adultery is sometimes between a man and his wife. That's when they regard sexual union as just for their fleshly delight, as Saint Jerome says, and care for nothing but their coupling; because they are married, they think everything's all right. **905** But in such people the devil has power, as the angel Raphael said to Tobias, for in their coupling they put Jesus Christ out of their hearts and give themselves over to filth.

The fourth kind is sexual union with blood relatives, with those who are related by marriage, or with those whom their fathers or blood relatives had intercourse with in the sin of lechery. This sin makes them like hounds that don't worry about kinship. And certainly kinship is of two kinds, either spiritual or physical. The spiritual is to couple with one's relatives by baptism. For just as he who engenders a child is his physical father, so his godfather is his spiritual father. In this regard as well a woman may couple with her relative by baptism with no less sin than with her own physical brother.

The fifth kind is that abominable sin of which scarcely any man ought to speak or write. Nevertheless it's openly mentioned in holy scripture. **910** This cursedness men and women do with different intentions and in different ways; although holy scripture speaks of this horrible sin, certainly holy scripture may not be defiled, no more than the sun that shines on the dunghill.

Another sin pertaining to lechery comes during sleep, and as often to virgins as to those who are defiled. This sin, which men call pollution, occurs in four ways. Sometimes it's from faintness due to an overabundance of humors in one's body; sometimes it's from infirmity, enfeebling the ability to retain the physical secretions, as medical science mentions; sometimes it's from excessive food and drink; and sometimes it's from sinful thoughts stored up in one's mind when he goes to sleep and which may not be without sin. Because of these occurrences men must look after themselves wisely, or else they may grievously sin.

Remedium contra peccatum luxurie

Now comes the remedy for Lechery, and that's generally chastity and continence, which restrains all the inordinate impulses that come from lascivious passions. **915** And ever greater the merit he shall have who most restrains this sin's wicked inflaming with passion. And there are two kinds of chastity, specifically in marriage and in widowhood.

Now you should understand that matrimony is the lawful union of a man and woman by virtue of the sacramental bond through which they may not be separated as long as both of them live. This, as the book says, is a great sacrament. God made it, as I've said, in paradise, and would have himself born in marriage. And to hallow marriage he was at a wedding where he turned water into wine. This was the first miracle that he worked before his disciples. A true consummation of marriage cleanses fornication and replenishes Holy Church with good lineage, for that is the end of marriage. And it changes mortal sin into venial sin between those who are wedded, and unites the hearts of the wedded as well as their bodies. **920**

This is true marriage that was established by God before sin began, when in paradise natural law was in its proper stage of development. It was ordained, as Saint Augustine says, that one man should have but one woman, and one woman but one man, for many reasons.

First, because marriage is figuratively expressed between Christ and Holy Church. And the other is because a man is head of a woman; at least by God's ordinance it should be so. For if a woman had more than one man, she'd have more heads than one, and that would be a horrible thing before God. Also, a woman might not please too many men at once. There would never be peace nor quiet among them, for everyone would demand what concerned him. Furthermore, no man would know his own offspring nor who should have his heritage, and the woman would be less beloved from the time that she was joined in marriage with many men.

Next comes how a man should behave toward his wife, and that's namely with patient endurance and reverence, as Christ showed when he first made woman. **925** He did not make her from Adam's head, so she shouldn't claim too great a lordship. For where the woman has the mastery she causes too much confusion. There needn't be any examples of this, daily experience should suffice. Also God certainly did not make woman from Adam's foot, so she shouldn't be held too low, for she cannot suffer patiently. But God made woman from Adam's rib, because a woman should be a companion to man. A man should behave toward his wife in faith, truth, and love, as Saint Paul says, and love her as Christ loved Holy Church, so well that he died for it. So should a man die for his wife if need be.

Now Saint Peter relates how a woman should be subject to her husband. First there's obedience. **930** Also as canon law says, a woman, as long as she's a wife, has no authority to swear or bear witness without permission of her husband, who's her lord or at least should be by reason. She should also serve him with most proper behavior and be modest in dress. I know well they should give heed to pleasing their husbands, but not by their elegant clothes. Saint Jerome says that "wives who are dressed in silk and in precious purple may not clothe themselves in Jesus Christ." What does Saint John say in this matter? And Saint Gregory says that "no person seeks precious clothing except for vainglory, to be honored the more before the people." It's a great folly for a woman to have fair clothing outwardly and be inwardly foul. **935** A wife should also be modest in appearance, behavior, and laughter, and discreet in all her words and deeds. And above all worldly things, she should love her husband with her whole heart and be true to him with her body. So also should a husband be to his wife. Since her body is her husband's, so should her heart be, or else between them there is no perfect marriage.

Then shall men understand that for three reasons a man and his wife may have intercourse. The first is the intent to beget children in the service of God, for that is the ultimate purpose of matrimony. Another motive is to pay each other the debt of their bodies, for neither of them has power over his or her own body. The third is to avoid lechery and dishonor. The fourth in truth is a mortal sin. **940** As for the first, it is meritorious; the second as well, for as canon law says, she has the merit of chastity who pays to her husband the debt of her body even though it's against her pleasure and her heart's desire. The third kind is venial sin, and truly there may scarcely be any of these without venial sin because of the corruption and delight. The fourth kind is when they couple for none of the aforesaid causes but only for erotic love, to achieve their burning delight and not caring how often they do it. Truly it's a mortal sin and yet, I'm sorry to say, some people will exert themselves more in doing it than is needed to satisfy their sexual craving.

The second kind of chastity is to be a clean widow, avoiding the embraces of men and desiring the embraces of Jesus Christ. These are wives who have lost their husbands, also women who have practiced lechery and are relieved of guilt through penitence. **945** And if a wife should keep herself completely chaste with her husband's permission, never giving him occasion to sin, it would be for her a great merit. This kind of woman who observes chastity must be clean in heart as well as in body and thought, modest in clothing and in countenance, and abstinent in eating and drinking, in speaking and doing. Such women are the vessel or box of the blessed Magdalene, filling Holy Church with good fragrance.

The third kind of chastity is virginity; it is necessary that one be holy in heart and clean of body. Then is she the spouse of Jesus Christ and the beloved of angels. She is worthy of the praise of this world, and is like the martyrs in equanimity; she has in her that which tongue may not tell nor heart think. Virginity bore our Lord Jesus Christ, and he himself was a virgin. **950**

Another remedy for Lechery is to refrain especially from such things as give occasion to that dishonor, such as sensual gratification, eating, and drinking. Surely when the pot boils over, the best remedy is to remove it from the fire. Sleeping long in great quiet is also a great nurse to Lechery.

Another remedy for Lechery is to avoid the company of those by whom one fears to be tempted; although the deed is resisted, there is great temptation. Truly a white wall, although not consumed by the fire of a candle placed next to it, is blackened from the flame. Very often I read that no man should trust in his own perfection unless he is stronger than Samson, holier than David, and wiser than Solomon. **955**

Now having told you as I'm able about the Seven Deadly Sins, and some of their branches and their remedies, I would tell you of the ten commandments if I could. But so lofty a doctrine I leave to theologians. Nevertheless I trust they have all been touched on in this treatise, singly and together.

Sequitur secunda pars Penitencie

Now inasmuch as the second part of Penitence, as I began in the first chapter, consists of oral Confession, I say with Saint Augustine:

"Sin is every word and every deed, and all that men desire sinfully, against the law of Jesus Christ; and this is to sin in thought, word, and deed by your five senses, which are seeing, hearing, smelling, tasting, and feeling."

The purpose now is to understand the circumstances that make each sin worse. **960** You should consider what you are that commits that sin, whether you are male or female, young or old, nobly born or in bondage, free or in servitude, sound or sick, wedded or single, in orders or lay, wise or foolish, cleric or secular; if she's your relative, bodily or spiritually, or not; if any of your relatives have sinned with her; and many more things.

Another circumstance is whether it's done in fornication or in adultery or not; in incest or not; as a virgin or not; by means of homicide or not; as horrible great sins or small; and how long you have continued to sin.

The third circumstance is the place where you've committed the sin, whether in another man's house or your own; in a field or a church or a churchyard; in a church consecrated or not. For if a man or woman through sin or wicked temptation spills orgastic fluid in a consecrated church, it is cut off from religious privilege until purified by the bishop. **965** And the priest who did such a dishonor should be interdicted; for the rest of his life he should never again sing mass, for every time he did so he would commit a mortal sin.

The fourth circumstance is the use of go-betweens or messengers, for enticement or consent to get together for revelry. For such companionship many a wretch would go to the devil in hell. So they who incite or connive in the sin are partners in the sin and the sinner's damnation.

The fifth circumstance is how many times one has sinned, if he can remember, and how often he has fallen. For he who often falls in sin despises the mercy of God, increases his sin, and is ungrateful to Christ. He becomes less able to withstand sin and sins more easily; **970** he arises more slowly and is more reluctant to confess, particularly to his own confessor. So when people fall again into their old follies, they either forsake completely their old confessors or divide their confessions in different places; but truly such divided confessions do not deserve God's mercy for their sins.

The sixth circumstance is why a man sins, as by which temptation, and if he himself brings that temptation or is incited by other people. It matters if he sins with a woman by force or by her own assent, and whether or not the woman, in spite of all she could do, has been violated. She shall tell in confession whether or not it was for covetousness or poverty, and if by her own contriving, and other such details.

The seventh circumstance is in what manner one has committed his sin; or how a woman has allowed what men have done to her. **975** The man shall tell this in fullest detail, including whether he has sinned with common brothel women, committed his sin on holy days, on fasting days, or before or after his last confession—perhaps breaking the penance imposed—and by whose help and whose counsel, if by sorcery or trickery; all must be told.

All these things, depending on how great or small, oppress a man's conscience. And the priest, who is your judge, by considering your contrition may better decide on your penance. For understand well that if a man, having defiled his baptism by sin, would come to salvation, there is no other way but by contrition, confession, and satisfaction for sin; **980** and especially by the first two, if there's a confessor to whom he may confess, and by the third if he lives to perform it.

Now if a man would make a true and profitable confession, there must be four conditions. First, it must be in sorrowful bitterness of heart, as King Hezekiah said to God: "I will recount all my years in the bitterness of my soul." This condition of bitterness has five signs. The first is that confession be shamefaced, not covering or hiding one's sin, for he has sinned against God and defiled his soul. Thus Saint Augustine says, "The heart labors for shame of his sin"; and because he feels great shame, he deserves to have great mercy from God. **985** Such was the confession of the publican who would not lift up his eyes to heaven, for he had offended God of heaven. For such feeling of shame he had at once God's mercy. So Saint Augustine says that such shamefaced people are nearest to forgiveness and remission. Another sign is humility in confession; of this Saint Peter says, "Be you humbled under the mighty hand of God." The hand of God is mighty in confession, for thereby God forgives your sins, he alone having the power. And this humility shall be in the heart and in outward sign; for just as he has humility before God in his heart, he should outwardly humble his body to the priest who sits in God's place. Since Christ is sovereign, and the priest is intermediary and mediator between Christ and the sinner, the sinner, being lowest by way of reason, **990** should not sit as high as his confessor but kneel before him or at his feet, unless some malady prevents it. For the priest won't remember who sits there but in what place he sits. If a man who has trespassed against a lord and who comes to ask for mercy and makes his accord, sits down right by the lord, men would consider him outrageous, not worthy anytime soon of forgiveness or mercy. The third sign is that your confession should be tearful; if a man can't weep with his eyes, let him weep in his heart. Such was the confession of Saint Peter, for after forsaking Jesus Christ he went out and wept very bitterly. The fourth sign is that one should not be too ashamed to confess. **995** Such was the confession of Mary Magdalene, who spared nothing for shame but before those at the feast went to our Lord Jesus Christ and confessed to him her sin. The fifth sign is that people obediently receive the penance that is enjoined for their sins, for truly Jesus Christ, for the sins of one man, was obedient unto death.

The second condition of true confession is that it be done soon. For truly if a man had a deadly wound, the longer he tarried to cure it the harder the healing, indeed the more it would putrefy and hasten his death. And so it is with sin that is a long time unconfessed. Certainly a man ought to confess his sins soon for many reasons: for fear of death, which often comes suddenly, man knows not what time nor what place; one continuing sin leads to another; **1000** and the longer a man tarries, the farther he is from Christ. And if he delays until his last day, scarcely may he confess or remember his sins or repent them because he is so grievously ill. And as he has never in his life listened to Jesus Christ when he has spoken, he shall cry to Jesus Christ on his last day and scarcely will Christ listen to him.

And understand that this condition must have four essentials. Your confession must be prearranged and with forethought, for wicked haste is unprofitable; a man must confess his sins, whether of pride, envy, or whatever, according to species and circumstances; he must comprehend in his mind the number and greatness of his sins and how long he has lain in sin; he must be contrite for his sins and steadfastly purpose, by the grace of God, never to fall into sin again; and he must dread and watch himself, to flee the occasions of sins to which he is inclined. **1005**

Also you should confess all your sins to one man, not a part to one man and a part to another with the intent, for shame or dread, to divide your confession, for that does nothing but strangle your soul. For surely Jesus Christ is entirely good, in him is no imperfection, so he forgives all perfectly or else not at all. I don't say that if you're referred to a confessor who assigns penance for a certain sin, you are bound to show him the remainder of your sins that you've confessed to your curate, unless you wish to for humility, for that's not dividing your confession. Nor do I say when I speak of division of confession that if you have your curate's permission to confess wherever you like to a discreet and honest priest, you can't confess to him all your sins. But let no blot be neglected, let no sin be untold, as far as you can remember. 1010 And when you confess to your curate, tell him all your sins since you last confessed; that's not a wicked intent to divide confession.

Also true shrift requires certain conditions. First that you confess not under constraint but of your own free will, and not to shame anyone nor for malady nor other such things. For it's reasonable that he who trespassed by free will should by free will confess it; that no one but himself tell his sin; and that he not disclaim or deny his sin nor be angry with the priest for his admonition to leave sin. The second condition is that your confession be lawful, that is, that you who confess, and the priest who hears your confession, be truly in the faith of Holy Church, and that a man not lack hope as did Cain or Judas in the mercy of Jesus Christ. 1015 And a man must accuse himself, not another, of his own trespass; he shall blame and impute guilt to himself and his own malice for his sin. But if another man is the cause or instigator of his sin, or a person's estate is such as to aggravate his sin, or if he can't fully confess without naming the person with whom he has sinned, he may tell as long as his intention is not to backbite the person but only to declare his confession. Nor shall you lie in your confession, saying perhaps for humility that you have committed a sin of which you were never guilty. For Saint Augustine says, "If for humility you lie about yourself, then if you were not in sin before you are now for your lying." 1020 You must also declare your sin by your own mouth and not by any writing, unless you have become unable to speak, for you have committed the sin and you should bear the shame. Nor shall you color your confession by fair, subtle words to cover your sin, for then you deceive yourself, not the priest. You must tell it plainly, be it ever so foul or horrible. You shall confess to a priest who is discreet to counsel you; and you shall not confess for vainglory, hypocrisy, or any cause except the fear of Jesus Christ and the healing of your soul. Nor shall you run to the priest suddenly to tell him carelessly your sin, as if to tell a joke or a tale, but go with forethought and great devotion.

And generally, confess often. If you fall often, you may arise often by confession. 1025 And if you confess a sin that you've already confessed before, the greater is the merit. As Saint Augustine says, you shall the more easily have remission and grace from God, both for sin and for pain. To be sure, once a year at least it is lawful to receive Communion, for once a year all things are renewed.

Now I have told you about true Confession, which is the second part of Penitence.

Explicit secunda pars Penitencie,
et sequitur tercia pars eiusdem

The third part of Penitence is Satisfaction by temporal punishment for sin, and that most generally consists of charitable works and bodily pain. Now there are three kinds of charity: contrition of heart, where a man offers himself to God; mercy for the sinfulness of one's neighbor; and giving good counsel and comfort, physically and spiritually, wherever men have need, particularly for food for their sustenance. **1030** And note the things a man generally needs: food, clothing, and shelter; charitable counsel and visits in prison and when sick; and burial of his body in death. If you can't visit the needy in person, visit them by your messengers and by your gifts. These are general alms or works of charity of those who have temporal riches or sound judgment in counseling. You shall hear about these works at the day of judgment.

These works of charity you shall accomplish by your own means, promptly and secretly if you may. But if you can't do it privately, don't fail to work charitably although men see it, so long as it's done not for thanks of this world but only for the favor of Jesus Christ. **1035** For as Saint Matthew witnesses, chapter five, "A city cannot be hidden that is seated on a mountain. Neither do men light a candle and put it under a bushel but rather on a candlestick, that it may give light to all who are in the house. So let your light shine before men that they may see your good works, and glorify your father who is in heaven."

Now to speak of bodily pain, it consists of prayers, vigils, fasting, and the virtuous teaching of prayers. And you shall understand that prayers signify a merciful desire of the heart that addresses itself to God and expresses itself by word outwardly to remove evils and to have spiritual and durable things and sometimes temporal things. In the prayer *Pater noster* Jesus Christ has included most other prayers. Certainly it is invested with three things that make it worthier than any other prayer. Jesus Christ composed it himself. **1040** It is short, the easier to learn and retain in the heart and to be more often a help. A man shouldn't weary of saying it or excuse himself from learning it, it's so short and easy. And it contains in itself all good prayers. The explanation of this holy prayer so excellent and worthy I entrust to the masters of theology, but this much I will say: when you pray that God should forgive your trespasses as you forgive those who trespassed against you, be sure that you don't lack charity. This holy prayer also diminishes venial sin, and therefore belongs especially to penitence.

This prayer must be truly said in good faith so that men pray to God properly, discreetly, and devoutly; and a man shall always submit his will to the will of God. **1045** This prayer must also be said with great humility, very purely and reverently, without annoying anyone else. It must also be accompanied by works of charity. It is effective also against the vices of the soul; for as Saint Jerome says, "The vices of the flesh are avoided by fasting, and by prayer the vices of the soul."

After this you should understand that bodily pain consists of keeping vigil, for Jesus Christ says, "Watch and pray that you don't enter into wicked temptation." You should understand also that fasting consists of three things: abstinence from food and drink, abstinence from worldly pleasure, and abstinence from mortal sin, that is, a man must keep himself from mortal sin with all his might.

You should understand that God ordained fasting, to which four things belong: **1050** generosity to poor people; spiritual gladness of heart, without anger, annoyance, or complaint about fasting; reasonable hours for eating; and eating in moderation. That is, a man shall not eat at unsuitable times, nor sit the longer at his table to eat because he fasts.

Then shall you understand that bodily pain consists of discipline or teaching, by word, writing, or example, and in wearing next to the skin hair shirts, garments of coarse worsted or of mail, for penance for the sake of Jesus Christ. But take good care that such kinds of penance on your flesh do not make you angry or bitter in heart or annoyed with yourself; for it is better to cast away your hair shirt than the sweetness of Jesus Christ. Thus Saint Paul says, "Clothe yourself as they who are God's chosen, with a merciful heart, kindness, long-suffering, and such kinds of clothing." With these Jesus Christ is more pleased than with hair shirts or shirts made of mail.

Next is discipline by breast-beating, scourging with rods, kneelings, and tribulations; **1055** by suffering patiently wrongs that are done to you;

and by patient endurance of maladies or loss of worldly goods, whether of wife or child or friend.

Then you shall understand which things hinder penance, and these are four in kind: dread, shame, hope, and despair. To speak first of dread, in which one believes that he may not endure penance, its remedy is to consider that bodily penance is not much to dread compared to the pain of hell so cruel and so long that it lasts without end.

Now against the shame that one feels about confession, especially these hypocrites who would be held so perfect that they have no need to confess, **1060** a man should reason that if he wasn't ashamed to do foul things, he certainly shouldn't be ashamed to do fair things like confession. A man should also bear in mind that God sees and knows all his thoughts and deeds, to him nothing may be hidden or covered. Men should also remember the shame that is to come at the day of judgment of those who are not penitent and confessed in this present life. For all creatures in heaven, on earth, and in hell shall see openly all that they hid in this world.

Now to speak of the hope of those who are negligent and sluggish in confessing, it consists of two things. **1065** First, a man hopes to live long and to acquire many riches for his delight; he'll confess afterward, and that, so he says, seems early enough. Another is the overconfidence that he has in Christ's mercy. Against the first vice, he should consider that our life has no certainty, and that all the riches in this world are in jeopardy and pass as a shadow on the wall. As Saint Gregory says, it is appropriate to God's great righteousness that the pain never cease for those who would never withdraw from sin but continue in sin of their own free will; for that perpetual will to commit sin they shall have perpetual pain.

Despair is of two kinds: despair of Christ's mercy, and the thought that one might not persevere long in goodness. **1070** The first despair comes from one's thinking that he has sinned so greatly and so often, and has so long lain in sin, that he shall not be saved. Certainly against that cursed despair he should consider that the passion of Jesus Christ is stronger to unbind than sin is to bind. Against the second despair he shall call to mind that as often as he falls he may arise again by penitence. And though he has lain in sin ever so long, the mercy of God is always ready to receive him. Against the despair of thinking that he should not long persevere in goodness, he shall remember that the feebleness of the devil may accomplish nothing unless men would allow it. And he shall also have the strength of God's help, and Holy Church, and the protection of angels if he desires. **1075**

Then men shall understand what is the fruit of penance. According to the word of Jesus Christ, it is the endless bliss of heaven, where joy exists without opposites such as woe or grievance; there all evils of this present life are past; there is security from the pains of hell; there is the blissful company that evermore rejoices each in the other's joy; there the body of man that used to be so foul and dark is brighter than the sun; there the body that used to be sick, frail, feeble, and mortal, is immortal and so strong and sound that nothing may harm it; there is neither hunger, thirst, nor cold, but every soul filled with the sight of the perfect knowledge of God. This blissful reign men may gain through spiritual poverty, the glory through humility, the fullness of joy through hunger and thirst, and the rest through labor, and the life through death and mortification of sin. **1080**

Chaucer's Retraction

Here the maker of this book takes his leave

Now I pray to all who hear or read this little treatise, that if there is anything in it that they like, they thank our Lord Jesus Christ for it, from whom proceeds all wisdom and goodness. And if there is anything that displeases them, I pray also that they ascribe it to the fault of my ignorance and not to my will, which would readily have spoken better if I had the knowledge. For our book says, "All that is written is written for our doctrine," and that is my intention. Therefore I beseech you, for the mercy of God, that you pray for me that Christ have mercy on me and forgive my sins, especially my translations and compositions of worldly vanities, which I revoke in my retractions: **1085** such as the book of *Troilus and Criseyde,* and the book of *The House of Fame*, the book of *The Legend of Good Women, The Book of the Duchess,* the book of Saint Valentine's day of *The Parliament of Fowls, The Canterbury Tales* (those that tend toward sin), the book of the Lion, and many another book, if they were in my remembrance, and many a song and many a lecherous lay; that Christ for his great mercy forgive my sins. But for the translation of Boethius's *Consolation of Philosophy* and other books of saints' legends, homilies, moralities, and devotions, I thank our Lord Jesus Christ and his blessed Mother, and all the saints of heaven, beseeching them that they from henceforth unto my life's end send me grace to lament my sins, and to meditate upon the salvation of my soul, and grant me the grace of true contrition, confession, and satisfaction for sins in this present life, **1090** through the benign grace of him who is king of kings and priest over all priests, who bought us with the precious blood of his heart; so that I may be one of those at the day of judgment that shall be saved. *Qui cum Patre et Spiritu Sancto vivit et regnat Deus per omnia secula. Amen.*

Here ends the book of *The Canterbury Tales*,
compiled by Geoffrey Chaucer,
on whose soul may Jesus Christ have mercy.
Amen.

Glossary

alchemy A pseudoscience concerned with the transmutation of base metals into gold (477-501).

Alma redemptoris mater An anthem ("Gracious Mother of the Redeemer") used especially during Advent and Christmas season liturgy (370).

Almagest An astronomical treatise by *Ptolemy* (85, 159, 162).

Amor vincit omnia "Love conquers all" (5).

Angelus ad virginem A hymn on the Annunciation (86).

Apollo Greek god of light, music, archery, and prophecy (301, 311). Also called *Phoebus*.

Apostle, The Saint Paul (156, 158, 341, 401, 411).

Argus A hundred-eyed giant in Greek mythology (37, 163, 275).

Austin See *Saint Augustine*.

Bacchus The Greek god of wine (265, 328, 504).

bachelor A young knight or aspirant to knighthood (3, 82, 177, 285); an unmarried man (253).

Bath An English city nearby which was the parish of Saint Michael, a cloth-producing center (12).

Bayard A name for a horse (109, 499).

bel ami "Fine friend" (336).

belle chose "Beautiful thing" (165, 166).

benedicite "Bless you" (passim).

benefice Payment for performing the duties of an ecclesiastical office (passim).

blissful martyr Saint Thomas à Becket (1118?-1170), the murdered Archbishop of *Canterbury*, enshrined at Canterbury Cathedral (1, 22).

Boethius A Roman statesman and philosopher (c. 475-c. 525), author of a treatise on music, and whose major work *The Consolation of Philosophy* was translated from Latin by *Chaucer* (184, 285, 453, 454, 573).

Boughton under Blean The town of Boughton in the Blean forest, five miles from *Canterbury* (477).

Breton A native or inhabitant of Brittany on the coast of France (303).

Bruges See *Flanders*.

canon A priest who either lived in a community of priests (canons regular) or had institutional permission to live alone (canons secular) (477, 488).

Canterbury A city, about 55 miles southeast of London, where the shrine of Saint Thomas à Becket in Canterbury Cathedral was an object of pilgrimage (1, 20, 21, 478, 502).

Cassiodorus A Roman statesman and writer (c. 485-c. 585) (391, 399, 402, 403, 406).

Cato Dionysius Cato (third century A.D.), author of a collection of moral apothegms (passim).

Chaucer The English poet (1340?- 1400) portrays himself in the *Tales* as a corpulent pilgrim disparaged for his "wretched rhyming" (specifically *Sir Topaz*, a parody of metrical romances) (1, 120, 373, 381, 573).

Cheapside A main shopping section of medieval London (20, 117, 342, 502).

Chichevache "Lean cow," being a fabled cow who fed only on patient wives (250).

chough A bird believed to be a tattler (160).

Christopher A medal representing Saint Christopher, patron saint of travelers and foresters (5).

Cicero Marcus Tullius Cicero (106- 43 B.C.), Roman orator and philosopher (303).

clerk A clergyman (88, 172, 338); a student, being ostensibly an aspirant to the clergy (86, 88, 108, 113, 167); any man of learning (13, 184, 272).

colors Figures of speech (215, 285, 303).

Cor meum eructavit "My heart has uttered" (from Psalm 45) (205).

corpus bones "God's bones" (335, 414).

corpus dominus Properly corpus domini, "the Lord's body" (364).

corpus Madrian "Body of Madrian" (an unidentified saint) (414).

Cytherea Aphrodite, Greek goddess of love (Roman *Venus*), born near the island of Cythera (51, 59).

depardieux "In the name of God" (passim).

Deus hic "God be here" (200).

Diana Roman goddess of the forest and of childbirth (45, 51, 54-55, 60- 62, 320).

Dun is in the mire A game involving the moving of a heavy log (500).

Dunmow bacon A side of bacon traditionally awarded to any couple who had gone for a year without quarreling (159).

Ecclesiasticus See *Jesus son of Sirach*.

Flanders A leading medieval cloth-producing country (now part of Belgium and France), including the cities of Bruges, Ghent, and Ypres (3, 12, 339, 354, 358, 359, 360, 374).

Fleming A person from *Flanders* (117, 457, 511).

franklin A landowner of free but not noble birth (9, 302).

friar A member of a mendicant order (Dominicans, Franciscans, Carmelites, Augustinians) (6, 97, 175, 176, 187, 198, 199, 204, 215).

Fury An avenging Greek goddess (71, 309).

Geoffrey Geoffrey de Vinsauf, author of a treatise on the writing of poetry that included a lament for the death of Richard the Lion-Hearted (456).

Ghent See *Flanders.*

Great Sea The Mediterranean (2).

humors Four bodily fluids (blood, phlegm, red or yellow bile, and black bile) believed to produce the sanguinary, phlegmatic, choleric, and melancholic temperaments (12, 37, 293, 305, 445-446, 561).

Ignotum per ignocius "Explaining the unknown by the unknown" (500).

In manus tuas "Into thy hands (I commend my spirit)" (from Luke 23:46) (114).

In principio "In the beginning" (opening words of the Gospel of John in Latin) (7, 451).

incubus An evil spirit that impregnates sleeping women (177).

Inn of Court A law school (15).

Irascimini et nolite peccare "Be angry and do not sin" (Psalm 4:5 in the Latin Vulgate) (539).

Jack of Dover Probably a pie or fish (116).

jane A Genoese coin worth half-a penny (244, 374).

Janus The two-headed Roman god of beginnings, after whom the month of January is named (317).

Jay tout perdu mon temps et mon labour "I have wasted all my time and effort" (522).

Je vous dis sans doute "Truly I say to you" (202).

Jesus son of Sirach The Jewish scribe (second century B.C.) who wrote Ecclesiasticus (171, properly the Book of Sirach) in the Catholic Bible (278, 383, 385, 386, 389).

Juno The wife of *Jupiter* (36, 41, 42).

Jupiter The supreme Roman god (64, 73, 74, 80-81, 278, 440, 484, 509, 510).

Knight of the Shire A member of Parliament (10).

limiter A *friar* begging in an assigned area or limit (7, 176, 187).

lists An arena for tournaments (49, 50, 63, 68, 301).

Lollard A follower of John Wycliffe (1320?-1384), who led a heretical movement called Lollardry (153).

manciple The purchasing agent of a college, monastery, etc. (15, 106, 500).

Mars The Roman god of war (27, 42, 45, 51-54, 59, 63-65, passim).

marshal The master of ceremonies at a feast (20, 270).

Mercury The Roman god of commerce and messenger of the gods (37, 172, 265, 301, 484).

Mulier est hominis confusio "Woman is man's ruin" (451).

multiplication Transmutation of base metals (484, 499, 501). See *alchemy.*

Newgate A London prison (118).

Ovid A Roman poet (43 B.C.-A.D. 18) noted for his love poetry and the *Metamorphoses,* a collection of myths and legends (passim).

palmers Pilgrims who returned from the Holy Land with palm branches as emblems (1).

pardie "By God" (passim).

pardoner A seller of indulgences, which relieved those who bought them of penances imposed for sin (18, 158, 159, 336-339, 351-352).

Paternoster The Lord's Prayer (from the opening words *Pater noster*) or one of various formulaic prayers (such as the White Paternoster) used as charms (92, 96, 537, 569).

Petrarch Francesco Petrarca (1304-1374), the Italian poet whose translation into Latin of the story of Griselda from Boccaccio's *Decame-*

ron was Chaucer's source for *The Student's Tale* (216, 249).

philosopher/philosophy An alchemist/*alchemy* (in addition to the terms' regular meanings) (8, 325, 484, 485, 490, 492, 499-501).

Phoebus *Apollo* (40, 119, 278, 285, 291, 311-312, 317, 328, 505-510).

Placebo "I will please" (from Psalm 114:9 in the Vulgate) (208, 543).

Pluto Greek god of the underworld (55, 61, 71, 312); depicted also in *The Merchant's Tale* as the king of Fairyland (273, 278).

prioress A nun equivalent in rank to the prior of a monastery (4, 22, 364).

psaltery A stringed instrument similar to the harp (8, 86, 88).

Ptolemy Alexandrian astronomer (second century A.D.) whose earth-centered system was the cosmology of the Middle Ages (159, 162, 214).

Questio quid juris "The question is, what point of law?" (17).

Qui cum patre "Who with the Father" (200, 573).

Radix malorum est Cupiditas "Cupidity (greed) is the root of all evil" (1 Timothy 6:10) (336, 338).

Ram The sign of Aries in the zodiac (1, 294).

reeve The manager or foreman of a manor (16, 84, 85, 117).

Rouncivalle A hospital at Charing Cross (near London) that was a cell of the Spanish convent of Our Lady of Rouncivalle (18).

Saint Augustine Christian philosopher (354-430 B.C.) quoted often in *The Parson's Tale* (see also 405-406, 453); also referred to as Austin (5-6, 359, 364).

Saint Denis A French town near Paris (353).

Saint Julian Julian the Hospitaler, a patron saint of innkeepers and travelers (9).

Saint Loy Saint Eligius of France, a patron saint of carters (4, 194).

Saint Paul's porch The portico of Saint Paul's Cathedral, where clients would consult with lawyers (9).

Saint Ronyan Perhaps a corruption of Ronan (a Scottish saint), a pun on the French word rognon (kidney), or both (335, 336).

Saturn Roman god of agriculture and the father of *Jupiter* (30, 36, 64-65, 70, 71, 484).

Seneca Roman philosopher and dramatist (3 B.C.-A.D. 65), known particularly for his moral philosophy (passim).

Sergeant of the Law A member of an elite order of lawyers (9).

Southwark A London borough (1, 19, 84).

squire A knight's attendant (3, 38, 39, 46, 66, 213, 266, 270, 284, 302, 308, 323, 324).

Straw, Jack A leader of the Peasants' Revolt of 1381 (457).

summoner An official who served summonses for an ecclesiastical court (17, 175, 187, 188, 196, 197).

Tabard An inn, its sign shaped like a tabard or smock (1, 19).

Te Deum laudamus A hymn ("We praise thee, O God") sung often at matins (203).

trental An office of thirty masses sung for a soul in purgatory (199).

Tullius *Cicero* (passim in *The Tale of Melibee*).

vavasor A landholder ranking below a baron (10).

Venus Roman goddess of love (30, 36, 41, 51, 52, 59-60, 64-65, passim).

veronica A medal representing Saint Veronica's veil, which according to tradition bore a miraculous image of Christ (18).

yeoman A freeman (105); an assistant or subordinate (190, 478); an attendant in a noble household (3, 66, 72).

Ypres See *Flanders*.

Zephyrus Greek god of the west wind (1).